SelectEditions

SELECTED AND EDITED

SelectEditions

BY READER'S DIGEST

THE READER'S DIGEST ASSOCIATION, INC.
MONTREAL • PLEASANTVILLE, NEW YORK

READER'S DIGEST SELECT EDITIONS

Vice President, Books & Home Entertainment: Deirdre Gilbert

CONTENTS

Richard North Patterson

NO SAFE PLACE

As a presidential hopeful, Kerry Kilcannon has enough courage and charisma to go all the way to the White House. The only thing that could stop him is a scandalous secret from his past. Or a desperate man bent on vengeance.

Bad news for Kilcannon— they're both out there.

"A top-ranking thriller."
—*Publishing News*

THE CAMPAIGN
April, the year 2000

AT EIGHT in the morning of his last day in Boston, Sean Burke paced the corner of Kenmore Square, waiting for the abortionist, a 9-mm handgun in the pocket of his jacket.

Sean knew his enemy from the demonstrations—a slight man with hollow cheekbones and gray soulless eyes that ignored the pickets even when they cried out, "Don't kill me, Mommy," in the imagined voice of a fetus. Part of Sean prayed for him to come; another part, frightened and irresolute, hoped he would not. He encouraged himself by imagining the faces of the children he would save.

He passed forty minutes this way. And then the man was there, emerging from the subway.

Sean swallowed. His throat was dry, his mouth sour. Clumsily he reached a gloved hand into his left pocket and popped the last antacid pill into his mouth, teeth grinding it to chalk.

Dr. Bowe disappeared inside the building. It was an old brownstone hotel, converted to offices. Sean knew only that the clinic was on the first floor. A court order required pickets to stay outside and keep the walkway clear. The red carpet, the Operation Life activists had named it. But all their protests had not stopped the flow of blood.

The chalk in Sean's mouth tasted bitter. If he acted, he would have to leave all he knew behind—the church where he served as caretaker, his room above the parish offices, Father Brian, who worried, in his soft-voiced way, about Sean's "intensity." In the streets of Charlestown they would call Sean a murderer.

Let God be his judge, then. God and the children.

But Sean stood frozen, a slender man with lank black hair and pale blue eyes. Alone, as he had felt almost all his life, he watched the pageant of the city pass him by—workers rushing from the subway, students heading for Boston University. They did not notice him and would not have understood had they known.

Then he saw her—a young woman in a wool coat, knit cap pulled tight over her curly red hair, her face more Irish than Sean's own. Pausing on the sidewalk, she gazed at the glass doors beneath the letters that spelled Kenmore Building.

She was there for the abortionist, he was certain. If she did not enter, perhaps he would grant the clinic a reprieve. Just for today.

"Please," he murmured, "save your baby."

With a shrug so small that Sean perhaps imagined it, the young woman walked toward the door. He felt the anger come. As he touched the gun in his pocket, his hand shook.

He was five feet from the door, then four feet. Damp with sweat, Sean paused in front of the door, taking a last deep breath.

He walked into the dim hallway, looking to both sides. He saw a travel agency, an accountant's office. And then he found it. A green door with metal letters: THE BOSTON WOMEN'S CLINIC.

Sean took the wool cap from his inside pocket and pulled it over his head. He murmured a final prayer and opened the door.

The red-haired girl was there. She gazed up at him from behind her magazine, as if surprised.

"Yes?" the receptionist asked.

Sean turned to her. Softly he said, "I'm here for Dr. Bowe."

Her skin was as pale as parchment. She stared up at him from her swivel chair, still but for her left hand. There was a panic button beneath her desk, someone had told him; the day the others had occupied the waiting room, she had used it to call security.

"Don't." Sean's voice was harsh now. The red-haired girl dropped her magazine.

The receptionist's throat moved in a convulsive swallow, choking her words. "What do you want?"

Sean took out his gun. "To stop you," he answered, and pulled the trigger.

There was a soft concussive sound, almost lost in the red-haired girl's cry. Sean watched in stupefaction as the woman died in front of him, blood trickling from her forehead. Only when she hit the carpet did Sean turn to the girl.

"Don't move." His voice came out panicky, too high. He stumbled down the hallway.

The abortionist was in the room where he did his work, bent over a file cabinet in the corner. He barely had time to peer sideways before Sean shot at his temple. He fell to his knees, pitching forward.

Sean heard a gasp behind him.

A nurse stood in the door, her mouth forming words that would not come. Sean did not want to kill her. She was a tool, like the receptionist. But he had no choice.

"I'm sorry," he murmured, and shot her in the chest. He stepped across her crumpled body and walked down the hallway in a trance. The young woman shivered on the couch, too frightened to move. Tears streamed down her face.

Sean knelt in front of her, giving comfort, seeking it. "I had to stop him. Your sympathy should be with your baby, the life I came to save."

Comprehension filled her eyes. "I'm not pregnant," she stammered. "I only came here for an IUD."

Sean felt the blood rush to his face. He stood. Humiliated and confused, he dropped his gun and ran from the building.

The feeling came to him. He was a small and lonely boy, terrified of his father, despairing of his mother's blank indifference. There was no safe place for him.

Two hours later a plane lifted into the air, and Sean Burke left Boston forever.

RAISING THE MAUSER, THE gunman stepped from backstage, bracing his wrist with his left hand. His target turned to smile at the woman beside him, sharing his applause with her.

"Kil-can-non," the crowd chanted, and then Senator James Kilcannon saw the assassin. His mouth fell open.

The gunman took one last step forward and fired. Jamie Kilcannon crumpled, falling onto his side, then his back. There was a pool of blood beneath his head.

"Kerry . . ."

Kerry Kilcannon snapped awake, staring at Clayton Slade.

The hotel bedroom was dark around them. "Kerry," Clayton repeated. His voice was quiet, but his full black face was intent. "What is it?"

Kerry realized he had bolted upright, gripped by fear. But Clayton was more than his campaign manager; he was Kerry's closest friend. There were no lies between them.

"My brother," Kerry answered. "It's the same, always."

Clayton exhaled softly. Amidst the deep disorientation of his dream Kerry could hear voices from the television in the other room. They were in a hotel suite in Portland, he remembered— another room in a four-month trail of hotels and motels.

Clayton braced Kerry's shoulders. "You've won, Kerry. We think Mason's conceding any minute."

Kerry gave himself a moment to recover. Rising, he walked into the sitting room in boxer shorts.

There were two others in the room, gazing at the television: Kit Pace, Kerry's press secretary, who in her intelligence and directness was an ideal reflection of his campaign, and Frank Wells, the graying, elegant professional who was his media adviser. Turning, Kit gave Kerry's lean frame a sardonic once-over. "Not bad for forty-two," she said. "Heading for California, Dick Mason retains the lead in body fat."

Kerry raised both hands in a mock gesture of triumph.

On the television a pert newswoman stood in a ballroom filled with Kerry's supporters, trying to speak over the cheers. "Twelve years after the assassination of James Kilcannon on the eve of the California primary," the woman began, "only that same primary would seem to stand between Senator Kerry Kilcannon and his late brother's goal—the Democratic nomination for President."

Frank Wells turned. "Congratulations, Kerry."

Kerry shook his head. "Seven days yet," he murmured.

"A few weeks ago," the newswoman was saying, "the conventional wisdom was that Kerry Kilcannon could not overtake a sitting Vice President. But Kilcannon has managed to persuade more and more voters to hold Dick Mason responsible for the President's recent misfortunes—a near recession, the collapse of welfare reform, and a series of revelations arising from apparently illegal campaign contributions."

Kerry heard a new voice, the anchorman's: "What can we expect in California, Kate?"

"Seven more days with no holds barred," the newswoman answered. "So far the base that Kilcannon has assembled has elements of the party's old coalition—particularly minorities—as well as women attracted by his proposals on education, day care, job training, and crime."

BUT it was far more than that, Clayton thought. Standing to Kerry's right, he watched him in the dim light of the television. After their fifteen years of friendship Kerry's profile was as familiar to Clayton as the profiles of his wife and daughters, as the painful memory of the son Clayton and Carlie had lost. Kerry's thin Irish face, at once boyish and angular, reminded Clayton of the impulsive lawyer he had first met in Newark. The wavy ginger hair was much the same, and, as always, Kerry's blue-green eyes reflected his quicksilver moods—sometimes cold, at other times deeply empathic or crinkled in amusement. But the man who had emerged from the cross-country gauntlet of primaries was changed.

The key was that Kerry had learned to touch people in ways Clayton had never seen from anyone before this. It had first struck him at the end of a long day in New Hampshire.

Kerry, speaking to a small gathering at a senior center, had asked for questions from his audience. An old woman stood, so thin that Clayton found it painful to look at her. She was poor, she said, her voice quavering with shame. At the end of every month she had to choose between food and medicine.

Then her voice broke, and the only sound in the deadly silence was her sobbing, muffled by the hands over her face. Kerry had stepped from behind the podium. He put his arms around the woman, seemingly oblivious to those around them, whispering words no one could hear.

Afterward Kerry had declined to repeat what he had said to her. It was the old woman who had told CBS. "I won't let that happen to you," Kerry had murmured. "I promise."

It was instinct, Clayton was sure—somehow Kerry could feel what it was to be someone else. The clip of him comforting the old woman ran on all three networks.

"Kilcannon's message," Clayton heard the CNN reporter summarize, "is that Dick Mason is too weak, too compromised, too mortgaged to special interests. Not even yesterday's slip of the tongue, in which Kilcannon opined that an unborn fetus was a life, seems to have affected his support among Oregon women."

KERRY leaned back in his chair, closing his eyes.

He had been tired yesterday. Cornered by a pro-life activist in a local TV audience, he had told the truth. As a matter of policy he was pro-choice, but it was his personal belief, as a Roman Catholic, that a fetus was the beginning of life. To claim that life did not exist until three months, or six months, was splitting moral hairs.

Watching the television, Frank Wells murmured, "You just can't say that. Women are too frightened."

Kerry opened his eyes. "I was tired," he said mildly. "Telling the truth is my own funny way of diverting Dick's attention."

Kit Pace leaned forward, her stocky frame radiating the intensity of her concern. "Kerry, please, eliminate the word life from your vocabulary. The idea that women are taking a life will inflame the pro-choicers. Especially with that Boston thing this morning."

Slowly Kerry nodded. "Insane," he murmured. "Three dead people, their families. Who would do that?"

"God knows." Kit paused, and then Dick Mason appeared on the screen.

The Vice President was flanked by Jeannie Mason and their three children—a girl and two boys, their faces as clean and unthreatening as their father's. He was everyone's favorite neighbor—friendly, a little overweight, always pleased to help. Mason's smile for the crowd was broad, his chin tilted at a Rooseveltian angle of confidence and challenge.

Imagining the emptiness in Dick Mason's stomach, the almost inconceivable prospect that a lifetime of striving might come to nothing, Kerry saw in his opponent's smile an act of will. He wondered if what helped sustain Dick Mason was lingering disbelief.

"YOU can't win," the President had said to Kerry.

It had been five months ago, in the Oval Office. Above his thin smile the President's eyes were keen. "You've got the virus. You looked around and decided you were better than anyone in sight. Including Dick and me."

Kerry shrugged and smiled, waiting him out. As a child, he had learned the gift of watchful silence.

"That's only the first step," the President said at length. "The easiest and the most deluded. Later you find out that the demands of a presidential campaign are much greater than you imagined." He paused, then finished softly. "It's not enough that Jamie wanted it, Kerry. It all has to come from you."

Kerry felt himself flush with anger. The President raised a hand. "That wasn't meant as an insult. What I'm saying is that you've yet to face the realities of starting a campaign from scratch. Dick Mason understands because he's been Vice President for eight years. And Dick's the only one of you that's been through the moral X ray our media friends reserve for someone on the national ticket, and survived it. You join this club at your peril, Kerry."

On the eve of the New Hampshire primary the President had endorsed Dick Mason. It had cost Kerry the primary. But Kerry and Clayton would not give up. And then the surprises started—a breakthrough in Florida, a split in Illinois and Ohio, an outpouring of small contributions. Then came wins in Michigan, Pennsylvania, Nebraska, and now Oregon. They had fought the opposition—a sitting Vice President—to a draw.

California, their final stop, would decide things. In the latest poll Dick Mason led by three percent.

But there was one historic fact that Dick could not avoid and no one else would ever forget: Kerry's brother had died there. Kerry was certain that James Kilcannon would have savored this irony.

BUTTONING his shirt, Kerry watched Dick Mason quiet his supporters.

On the television screen Dick's face was solemn now. "Before I congratulate Senator Kilcannon"—there were boos, and Dick raised a placatory hand—"I'd like to request a moment of silence for the three victims of the brutal act of terrorism committed this morning at the Boston Women's Clinic."

The Vice President bowed his head, and silence fell. When Dick looked up again, his mouth was a thin line of determination.

"I want to assure the victims' families that the perpetrator of this cowardly act will be brought to justice. And I want to assure everyone that we are unequivocal in our defense of every woman's right to choose, unmolested and unafraid."

Kerry stopped knotting his tie. "These Boston murders were made for him."

On the screen Mason raised his head, his hair a shiny silver-blond beneath the television lights. "To Senator Kilcannon," he continued, "I say two things. First, Kerry, congratulations on a hard-won victory. Second, I challenge you to a final debate in California about the future of our party and our nation—anytime, anywhere." Mason grinned, and then he shouted above the cheers of his supporters, "You may be running, Kerry, but you can't hide."

"What *is* this?" Kit Pace asked. "You won the only debate he'd sit still for, and he's ducked you ever since."

But Kerry was watching Dick and Jeannie and the kids wave to the crowd. Jeannie Mason was terrific.

It was far more than that she was pretty—though Jeannie was surely that. It was her humor, a recognition that much of the political pageant was really quite absurd. Even her attempt at a political spouse's robotic gaze of admiration was leavened with amusement. Jeannie tended the home front with brisk efficiency and campaigned for her husband tirelessly.

Kerry had met her at the dinner party of a doyenne of Washington politics, the widow of a wealthy former statesman. Patricia Hartman's invitation had signaled Kerry's arrival in Washington, but the fact that her interest derived from his brother's murder would have discomfited him even had he not seldom seen such opulence.

"That's a Matisse," Hartman had noted as Kerry stopped to study an oil painting, her voice suggesting that he required an explanation. Kerry simply nodded. He was already bedeviled by the thought that at dinner he might pick up the wrong fork.

"Will your wife be moving here soon?" his hostess asked. "I'm so anxious to meet her."

This was a probe, Kerry knew. But to dissemble would have made him feel awkward. "Not soon," he said. "Maybe not at all."

The bluntness of his response seemed to surprise her. "Oh," she told him firmly, "she *must*. A serious career in politics demands a total commitment." Turning to the dinner table, Hartman said, "Well, I've seated you next to Jeannie Mason. Ask her for advice—she's such a help to Dick, you know."

With the joy of a death row inmate Kerry shuffled to the table.

Seated next to him, the fresh-faced blonde introduced herself. With quiet humor Jeannie added, "I saw Patricia walking you through orientation. Have you memorized the rules yet?"

Her irony surprised him. "Just one," he answered. "That Meg should quit her job and move here. Patricia says I should ask you for advice."

The smile flickered. "I just hope she didn't call me an asset. It makes our marriage sound like my husband's balance sheet."

"I think that's what Meg's afraid of," Kerry ventured.

Jeannie gave him a reflective glance. "She's right to be. Sometimes it's not easy." She smiled again. "Patricia will manage to forgive your wife. She always needs an extra man at dinner."

Kerry felt himself relax. There was something inherently kind about her, and honest. Perhaps for that reason he did not feel the need for self-protection. On the evidence of his wife, Kerry had reflected, Dick Mason must surely be worth knowing.

Twelve years later Jeannie still made him consider that there might be more to Dick than he had come to believe. And, Kerry had to concede, he felt something else: envy. Even before their divorce Meg had considered Kerry's first run for the Senate a betrayal tantamount to adultery. She would not have come here happily.

Abruptly Clayton stood. "Let's go," he said. "It's showtime."

THE ballroom was jammed. Glancing about, Clayton saw that everything was in order. The signs were painted on both sides, the better to be seen on television. There were young people rather than local officeholders on the platform to underscore Kerry's outsider status. Two members of the Secret Service detail stood at the base of the platform. Noticing the Service was a habit Clayton had formed weeks earlier. "Somewhere there's some nut out there," he had said to Peter Lake, the special agent in charge, "oiling up his gun so he can go for the doubleheader."

Kerry walked to the podium. *"Kerry,"* the crowd began chanting. Kerry smiled. "That's me."

There were laughter and cheers, and then Kerry held up a hand. "There's still a lot to do," he said, "and, together, we will do it. We will train mothers and fathers for meaningful work, help educate their children. We will protect our right to choose in the deepest and broadest sense. For it is not just *women* who deserve a choice; it is everyone who chooses to work for a brighter future."

The crowd erupted.

Minutes later Kerry was able to finish with his signature line: "Give me your help and your vote, and together we'll build a new democracy."

Clayton watched from one side of the platform. Don't do it, he silently instructed Kerry. But of course, Kerry did. Stepping from behind the podium, he went down the steps and plunged into the crowd. Damn, Clayton thought as Kerry took each hand, each face, a moment at a time, looking into the eyes of the person in front of him. "Thank you," he kept repeating. "Thank you. We'll make it, I think." Next to him, the Secret Service and the camera people jockeyed for position.

"Senator," a young NBC correspondent called out, pushing a microphone between two well-wishers. "Will Dick Mason's new emphasis on abortion rights cause trouble for you in California?"

Intent on his supporters, Kerry ignored him.

"*Senator.*" The newsman twisted his body to thrust the microphone at Kerry and then, quite suddenly, fell.

Kerry felt an involuntary rush of fear. The crowd rippled with confusion. An agent pulled Kerry away, shielding his body.

"It's Mike Devore from NBC," Kerry managed to say. "I think something's wrong with him." Kerry could see the newsman on the floor, his face contorted in pain, a swarm of agents around him. Some pushed onlookers aside; others bent over the fallen man.

"Looks like he tripped," one of them said. "He may have broken his ankle." He pulled out his cell phone to call 911.

The paramedics were there in ten minutes, carrying a stretcher. They took the reporter away. Kerry resumed shaking hands, suddenly feeling tired and mechanical.

Clayton Slade appeared behind him. "Ready to roll," he said crisply, and the Service convoyed them to Kerry's limousine. Clayton did not mention the incident.

LIGHTS flashing in the darkness, the motorcade of black Lincolns rolled toward the airport. Kerry's car was flanked by cops on motorcycles. There were two Secret Service agents in the front seat;

Clayton and Kerry sat in back, staring into the formless night of a city that could have been anywhere.

Once more Kerry marveled at the vortex he had created, of which the motorcade had become a symbol, a force that swept up thousands of people. Kerry had stepped into the crowd out of more than the need to prove to himself what he could never prove—that he was not afraid. He also needed to meet people one at a time.

He turned from the window and slumped in his seat. It was nearly midnight. The flight to San Diego would take three hours. He hoped he could sleep.

IN THE lead press bus of the Kilcannon motorcade, Nate Cutler allowed himself to wonder what he was doing with his life.

He had been with the Kilcannon campaign since January. Three months on the road. He was headed for California now, but he still had his wardrobe from Iowa and New Hampshire. He hadn't had a haircut for six weeks and was down to his last set of clean underwear.

Nate looked around the bus. At thirty-nine he was small, dark, wiry, and resilient, and this last was a good thing. His peer group in the press was an energetic bunch, predominantly female and sometimes a decade younger. They were usually joking or exchanging gibes. Now, at the end of a long day, they looked like rows of ghostly heads. Some talked; others tried to sleep.

"Kilcannon was *on* tonight," someone said behind him—Ann Rush of the *Times*, Nate was pretty sure.

"He always is when he believes it." The voice belonged to Greg Asher of the *Globe*. "I think Kilcannon cares."

That was what Nate was doing with his life, he admitted to himself—chronicling the only interesting politician in the race.

For Nate, Kerry Kilcannon was a relief. The last years of the '90s had not been a heroic time. The politics were small-bore, petty men taking small chances for selfish reasons, trying to manipulate enough of a cynical public to keep themselves in office. The politicians seemed smaller than their ambitions, except, perhaps, for Kerry Kilcannon.

Nate viewed Kilcannon with a mixture of journalistic detachment and personal regard. In his dealings with the press Kilcannon was honest, accessible, and often humorous. And Nate credited him with the sincerity of his beliefs.

Nate started. There was a vibration from the pager in the pocket of his sport coat. He took out his cell phone and called the sky-page center. The message was terse: Call Katherine Jones ASAP at a San Diego number.

Nate sat back, curious. The only Katherine Jones he knew of was the executive director of Anthony's Legions, a group named after Susan B. Anthony and devoted to raising money for pro-choice women candidates. Nate had never met her.

Glancing around at his colleagues, he decided not to return the call until they reached the landing strip.

Kilcannon's chartered plane was on the runway, a shadowy silver and black. A Secret Service agent stood by, ready to inspect the ID tags the press wore. Nate walked out onto the darkened tarmac so that no one could hear him and dialed the number.

It was the Meridian Hotel in La Jolla. He asked for Katherine Jones. After a moment a brusque woman's voice answered.

"This is Nate Cutler," he told her.

"Good. I want to meet with you tomorrow. In confidence."

Her peremptory manner annoyed him. "On what subject?"

There was the briefest hesitation, and then the woman answered, "Kerry Kilcannon."

KERRY Kilcannon's voice rose. "It is everyone who chooses to work for a brighter future."

Rising from the edge of the bed, Sean Burke turned up the volume. Now Kilcannon seemed to look straight at Sean. "It is every mother, father, son, or daughter who refuses to lose one more person they love to a coward with a gun."

Sean's hands began to shake. He was not violent by nature, he told himself. He had only killed so that the innocent might live.

The motel room seemed to close in on him, making him feel

trapped and smothered, the two sensations he feared most. He got up and turned on both bedside lamps. His stomach hurt.

When he turned back to the television, he flinched. Paramedics were hauling a body on a stretcher through the same glass doors Sean had entered that morning, now three thousand miles away. A newswoman was speaking. "The sole witness, a twenty-two-year-old woman, told police that the unidentified assailant was slender, about six feet tall, with dark hair and blue eyes."

Sean went to the bathroom and swallowed two antacid pills. The television, he realized, was eroding his resolve, making him weak. He forced himself to turn it off.

Sitting on the bed, Sean began listening for sounds. He had done this when he was a small boy, covers pulled over his head, waiting for the echoes of his father's rage—an angry voice, a slammed door, his mother's cries. Now the only sounds he could hear were the hum of car tires, the unearthly whir of air-conditioning in a cheap motel room—strange noises in an alien city. Sean felt scared and angry.

He had never been to San Francisco. And seven days was not much time.

AT FOUR in the morning, when the Washington bureau chief called, Lara Costello had been awake for the last five hours.

She had returned from Africa three weeks earlier, after two years in the Middle East, Bosnia, Rwanda—anywhere there was an election, a famine, a war. Three weeks was plenty of time to readjust sleeping patterns, Lara told herself, but she was having trouble making the transition.

She had walked to the bedroom window of her rented town house and gazed out at the quiet Georgetown street, imagining her neighbors resting up for tomorrow's bureaucratic wars on the Hill. This would become her reality, she knew. It would just take time.

Overseas she had force-fed herself new cultures, made new friends, developed new skills—in short, learned how to survive. Perhaps it was melodramatic, but even the worst things were part of her—mutilated bodies, dying children, tortured prisoners. And,

Lara thought, her broadcasts had sometimes helped, by pressuring her own government to try to relieve hunger or stop the systematic slaughter. It was difficult to have worked so hard, cared so deeply, and then to leave.

But Lara's work had made her a public figure, and the network wanted her home. The image of a young woman broadcasting from harsh conditions was compelling. Besides, the president of the news division had observed with irony, Lara had a quality as important as her gender. She had black hair, intense dark eyes, a sculptured face, and pale flawless skin. She was a pretty woman. In television that counted, especially if one's next assignment was on the star track—anchorwoman for a prime-time weekly news show.

Lara had turned from the window and looked around her bedroom. She would rebuild her life in the city she once had wanted desperately to leave. Then, she told herself sardonically, somehow she could bear the burdens of celebrity and a job most of her colleagues would kill for. She did not expect sympathy. The only people who would understand her restiveness were overseas: journalists in sub-Saharan Africa, AID workers, human rights activists.

He would have gotten it, she suddenly knew. At times she had believed that he could grasp what it was like. But the thought of him deepened her sense of solitude.

That was what she was thinking when the telephone rang.

The bureau chief, Hal Leavitt, did not apologize for the lateness of the hour. "We've got a problem," he said without preface. "Mike Devore's broken his ankle. There's no one to cover Kilcannon in California."

Lara felt stunned. She sat on the edge of the bed, trying to collect herself.

"Look," Hal said, "I know you've got another week's vacation, but I thought of you right away. You're from California, and you know Kilcannon from covering the Hill."

Lara drew a breath. "And I've been overseas for two years, haven't followed the primaries, don't know the issues." She paused. "Hal, it's the worst idea I've ever heard."

"It's only seven days, Lara. We'll have a clippings file ready. You can read it on the plane. When you land in Los Angeles, call Mike Devore. He'll get you up to speed." Hal's voice became crisp. "The car's coming at nine."

Desperate, Lara searched for excuses. "There's something else." She paused again, choosing her words with care. "When I first came to the Hill, Kerry Kilcannon helped me get oriented and gave me a little credibility. I liked him, and I *don't* admire Dick Mason. I worry about my own professionalism here."

There was silence, and then Hal responded in a voice of strained patience. "*All* reporters have personal feelings, Lara."

Lara felt sick at heart. What could she say? Only the truth would get her off this assignment. And the truth could destroy not just her career but his.

"Seven days," she said at length. Mechanically she walked to her desk and picked up a pen. "Give me some names—campaign manager, press secretary."

He did that. Lara found herself staring at the name Clayton Slade.

"Do you have their schedule tomorrow?"

"Sure. I'll fax it to you."

Lara thanked him and got off. She was still sitting at her desk, hands over her face, when the fax came through.

The Kilcannon campaign was overnighting at the Hyatt in downtown San Diego. With the three-hour time difference, it was roughly one thirty. Lara waited until eight forty-five, just before the limousine came, to place the call.

AT SIX o'clock, when the Secret Service escorted Kerry back from the hotel gym to his room, Clayton was waiting. He had already brewed the pot of coffee provided by the hotel.

Kerry wiped the sweat off his forehead. "Good workout?" Clayton asked.

Kerry stopped to look at him. Clayton looked narrow-eyed and pained. His bulky form slumped in the chair.

"What is it?" Kerry asked.

Clayton sat back. "Lara Costello just called me. She's replacing Mike Devore." His voice was quiet, unhappy. "She clearly doesn't know if *I* know, but she figures I probably do, and she wants you to be prepared."

Kerry stood, arms crossed, head down.

"I'm sorry," Clayton said. "It's bad timing."

Kerry rubbed the bridge of his nose. After a time he murmured, "I'll be all right."

"You'll have to be." Clayton rose from his chair. "There's a speech that goes with this, pal, and it's my bad luck to have to give it. You're a candidate for President. The reporters who follow you around are trained observers, at the top of their game. Start giving Lara Costello meaningful glances across the tarmac, and somebody will wonder why."

Kerry gave him a resentful stare. "I'm not stupid, Clayton, and she's not interested."

Clayton's eyes were steady. "A lot of people have a lot invested in this, Kerry. It's a choice between Lara and your candidacy. If you choose the presidency, don't go near her."

Kerry gazed around the sterile room. "No one knows."

Clayton frowned. "At least *three* people know—her, you, and me, because you told me."

"I was a mess." Kerry shook his head. "At the end, she wouldn't see me."

He felt Clayton's hand on his shoulder. "I'm sorry, pal. I know how you feel." He waited a moment. "But I also know *you,* and you're the best candidate in the race. Don't let yourself lose."

Turning from Clayton, Kerry walked to the window. For some moments he stared out at San Diego harbor, watching the first shimmer of sunshine turn the water light gray.

How did I get here? he wondered. Forty-two years of living—thirty before Jamie's death, and then the twelve very different years of which Lara had become a part. But the skein of circumstances was so long, so tangled, that there was no simple answer.

KERRY Kilcannon's clearest memory of early childhood was of his father sitting on the edge of his bed.

It began as many other nights had begun—with the sound of Michael Kilcannon coming home drunk. He would teeter up the stairs, talking to himself, pausing to take deep wheezing breaths. Kerry would lie very still. Michael would stumble past Kerry's and Jamie's rooms to the bedroom at the end of the hall, and the beatings would begin. Through his tears Kerry would imagine his mother's face at breakfast—a bruised eye, a swollen lip. No one spoke of it.

But on this night it was Kerry's door that flew open.

Michael Kilcannon flicked on the wall light. The six-year-old Kerry blinked at the sudden brightness, afraid to move.

His father was a strapping man in his red-haired, florid way and, when sober, a dad Kerry was desperately proud of—a policeman, a hero, possessed of a ready laugh and a reputation for reckless courage. But that night Michael Kilcannon had been to Lynch's Ark Bar, a neighborhood mainstay, and his fleshy face was suffused with drink and anger.

Michael staggered toward Kerry and sat on the edge of the bed, breathing hard. "Bastards." His voice was hostile, threatening.

Kerry's heart pounded. Maybe if he said something . . .

"What is it, Da?"

His father shook his head, as if to himself. "Mulroy. I'm as good a man—better. But *he* makes sergeant, not me."

Mary Kilcannon appeared in the doorway. Her long black hair was disarranged, her skin pale in the light. Entering, she placed a tentative hand on her husband's shoulder. Softly she said, "Michael, leave the boy alone." Her words had an edge her son had never heard before.

Michael Kilcannon shrugged his heavy shoulders and rose. With a slap so lazy yet so powerful it reminded Kerry of a big cat, he struck Mary Kilcannon across the mouth.

She reeled backward, blood trickling from her lip. Tears stung Kerry's eyes. He was sickened by his own fear and helplessness.

"We were *talking*." Michael's voice suggested the patience of a reasonable man stretched to the breaking point. "Go to bed." He turned from her and sat on the bed. He did not seem to notice that Kerry was crying.

After this, Kerry never knew when it would happen. On some nights his father would come home and beat his mother. On others he would open Kerry's door and pour out his wounds and anger. Kerry learned to fight sleep or any sign of inattention that might set his father off. Michael never touched him.

As long as Kerry listened, he knew that his father would not beat Mary Kilcannon.

As DEEPLY as Michael Kilcannon terrified him, so Kerry loved his mother.

Like his father, she had emigrated from County Roscommon. At twenty-one she gave birth to James Joseph. Kerry Francis had not been born until she was thirty-three. Between, there was a string of miscarriages. Mary retained a faded prettiness, like a rose preserved in the pages of a book. What Kerry adored was her laughing green eyes. The mere sight of Kerry seemed to make her smile.

They lived in the Vailsburg section of Newark, populated by Irish and a scattering of Italians. The streets were treelined and quiet, with neat two-story wooden houses inhabited by the families of policemen and firemen, civil servants, and small-business men. There were playgrounds with basketball hoops, and in the winter the fire department flooded a section of Ivy Hill Park and turned it into a skating rink.

Mary Kilcannon taught Kerry to skate there, laughing as he

flailed his arms, clapping with pleasure as his efforts became surer. She made him forget what was already clear—that he would never be as tall as Jamie or as agile at sports. She was the one person on earth Kerry was certain loved him as he was.

But outside their home, Kerry knew, Mary Kilcannon would always be known as James's mother.

It began with how much Jamie favored her, so closely that only his maleness made him handsome instead of beautiful. By seventeen Jamie was six feet one, with an easy grace and hazel eyes. He was student-body president of Seton Hall Prep, captain of its football team, second in his class. Girls adored him.

Because of Jamie's size and his attainments, Michael Kilcannon came to observe a sort of resentful truce with his older son. But Jamie did not raise his hand, or his voice, to help his mother. He seemed driven by a silent contempt for both parents.

Then Jamie left for Princeton on a full scholarship. He did well at college, played defensive halfback on the football team, became involved in campus politics. Kerry would sometimes hear his brother, through the thin wall between their bedrooms, practicing his speeches, testing phrases, pauses.

Years later, on the night James Kilcannon won election to the New Jersey state senate, he barely acknowledged either parent. It was in keeping with how he had gotten there—going away to Princeton, becoming a leader of anti-Vietnam demonstrations, casting his lot with the reform wing of the Democratic Party. To his supporters he was attractive, articulate, the antithesis of machine politics. They did not know or care about his family.

Kerry never forgot the Christmas vacation of Jamie's second year away.

Jamie, home for the week, was running for something. He practiced a speech late into the night. Sleepless, Kerry listened to his brother's muffled voice in the next room.

Michael Kilcannon came home. Hearing his footsteps, Kerry sat up in bed, expectant. A moment later Mary Kilcannon cried out in pain.

The only sign that Jamie had heard was silence on the other side of the wall. Tears ran down Kerry's face.

No, Kerry would never be his brother James.

HE DID not have to worry. At Sacred Heart School no one mistook him for Jamie.

Kerry was short, slight, and a recalcitrant student. He fought often, though never against anyone weaker than he was. His rage seemed close to suicidal—he challenged only boys who were bigger, older. More often than not he would absorb a beating that did not end until someone stopped it. By the time he was twelve, his fist-fights were so frequent, so violent, that he hovered on the edge of expulsion.

Michael Kilcannon took a rough pride in his son's combativeness; Kerry had distinguished himself at little else. In desperation Mary turned to Kerry's godfather. And when the principal called Kerry to his office, Liam Dunn was there.

Kerry was surprised. Though Liam always asked after him and never forgot his birthday or his name day, his selection as Kerry's godfather had been more for the prestige it conferred. Liam had long ceased to be his father's partner on patrol. He was councilman for the West Ward, into which Vailsburg fell.

"Hello, Kerry," said Liam. Gently he touched the boy's elbow and steered him from the room.

For block after block of Vailsburg they simply walked, occasionally making small talk. They stopped at Ivy Hill Park.

"Why don't we sit awhile," Liam said.

They found a green wooden bench. For a time Liam was quiet, content to watch the park. Kerry studied him. He was in his mid-forties, like his father, and big. His short hair was quite red, his seamed face soft only in the chin. His eyelids were so heavy that they seemed half closed. But when he turned to Kerry, his eyes were clear, penetrating.

"I hear you fight."

Kerry could only nod.

"It seems not well enough," Liam said. "Tell me, do you know why you fight?"

"I hate bullies."

Something seemed to move in Liam's eyes. "Your mother is afraid for you. Do you want that?"

Kerry could not look at him. He felt Liam's large hand on his shoulder. "If you want to fight, Kerry, you need to learn how. There's a place for that, a man who can teach you boxing. Until you learn, there'll be no fighting. For your mother's sake." Liam smiled now. "Not to mention your own."

As Kerry gazed at him, Liam stuck out his hand. Kerry took it. "Good," Liam said. "We've made an arrangement."

They walked in silence to the school, Liam seemingly preoccupied. He stopped at the edge of the playground. "I've been thinking," he said. "There's a favor you can do for me."

Kerry was surprised. "What?"

"On Sundays, after Mass, I visit the bars to chat a little, see people. Some Sundays I may need you to help me remember things."

"What about my father?" Kerry asked.

Liam's eyes grew hooded. "It'll be fine with Michael."

On Tuesday and Friday afternoons Kerry Kilcannon would go to the CYO gym to box. It was a half-lit rabbit warren of rooms with pictures of Golden Glovers on the walls. Kerry felt small and out of place. When his coach, Jack Burns, asked him to hit the heavy bag, Kerry uncorked a series of angry left-hand haymakers. At length, he missed entirely, and the swinging bag knocked the ninety-five-pound twelve-year-old to the floor.

"I guess you're left-handed," Jack said.

Jack was large, gray-haired, and patient. For the first three weeks he tried to teach Kerry to fight as left-handers did—using the weaker arm, his right, to lead with a jab, then following with the left. But all Kerry wanted to do was throw a wild left hook and try to decimate whatever stood in his way.

Finally Jack took Kerry aside. "You'd do much better using your brain," he said.

This stung Kerry. "I want to be better."

Jack nodded. "Then there's a way. If you've the patience."

He began teaching Kerry to box like a right-hander—to use the left hand not as a power punch, but as a jab. Hour after hour Jack stood Kerry in front of the heavy bag. *Whack, whack, whack.* Kerry felt his anger surge through each punch. The rage he did not understand became his friend, his servant.

This routine went on for months. One day Kerry realized that he loved the smell, the feeling, of his own sweat, fighting through fatigue. Outside the gym he kept his word to Liam Dunn.

HIS other new activity was with Liam himself—going to the bars on Sundays.

To Kerry, bars were a dark mystery—the place where his moody father became the devil who seemed more furious every night. "The Irish disease," Liam said of drunkenness. "But there's more to the bars than that."

There was. After Mass on Sunday the taverns served as community center, employment service, political intelligence system, and meeting place. A politician who didn't know the bars, Liam said, was a fool waiting to discover himself.

So they would go to the bars, Liam and Kerry, up and down the main drag of Vailsburg, to Higgins's Tavern, Lenihan & O'Grady's, Cryan's Tavern, Malloy's, Lynch's Ark Bar. In six months Kerry came to know thirty Irish tavern owners.

He came to like the bars, too, for their gregariousness, their Celtic memorabilia, their dark wood, the sound of men and women laughing. He listened, and he learned.

Liam Dunn would join the crowd, let people have a word about their problems, the hope of a job for a cousin on the way from Ireland, the need of money for a promising boy at Seton Hall. He said he'd do what he could, then usually did more than he implied was possible. Liam, Kerry decided, truly cared what became of people who needed help.

He could never imagine Liam Dunn practicing his speeches like

Jamie, though Liam could, when he wished to, capture a room for himself. Once, when Kerry asked why Jamie was not here learning politics, Liam said only, "He's a gifted boy, doing it his own way, running for state senate. He may go far, that one."

"But shouldn't he be working with you?" Kerry asked.

This made Liam smile. "Last thing Jamie needs or wants, Kerry. This is a bit *small* for the lad, and more power to him. Perhaps he can build us a highway or two."

At the end of one Sunday, Liam took Kerry to the same bench in Ivy Hill Park.

"I hear the boxing goes better," Liam said. "School, too—no more D's, and not a fight to your name." He patted Kerry roughly on the shoulder. "All that, and you begin to understand politics. No telling how well you can do."

Thinking of Jamie, Kerry clenched his fists. "I'll never run for anything."

"No need to," Liam answered. "You'll find the thing that's best for you." He paused for a moment. "Do the right thing, Kerry, and things tend to come out right in the end. But the first is the only part you control. And sometimes going to bed square with yourself is a day-to-day kind of thing."

At SIXTEEN Kerry Kilcannon fought in the Golden Gloves. He had fought in exhibitions, trained tirelessly. This was the only way he could know how good he was.

His father and mother came to Kerry's first match, part of a crowd numbering a few hundred, Michael somewhat contemptuous of his son's chances, Kerry's mother unsure if she could watch. Perhaps, Kerry thought bleakly, it reminded her of home.

His opponent was a barrel-chested Italian boy, Joey Giusti. The bell rang, and Joey almost ran across the ring. Kerry could read the contempt in his eyes, the eagerness of a bully.

As Joey uncorked his first left hook, Kerry ducked. The hand sailed over his head; then Kerry hit the boy with a left jab to the nose.

Whack.

Joey blinked, stunned, and Kerry hit him with three more.

Whack, whack, whack.

When Joey covered his face with his gloves, Kerry started on his ribs. Left, right, left, as he drove punch after punch into Joey's midsection. The boy gulped, swallowing hard, and suddenly the referee was between them.

The pride Kerry felt was new, and he carried it quietly. Not so his father. "You're finally good for something," Michael said with heavy-handed jocularity.

At seventeen Kerry was as big as he would ever get: five feet ten, a full three inches shorter than his brother, the state senator, and his father, the policeman. His senior-year B's and C's captured him a slot at Seton Hall University, a few blocks from his home. For the longer range, Michael suggested that Kerry go into the police department. "It's enough for a lot of us," he said, "and no point worrying about why you're not your brother. After all, who is?"

Kerry did not respond. His father's failure was etched in the deepening creases of his face and in his bleary eyes. The only relief he found beyond drink was abusing his wife and belittling his son.

One night Mary Kilcannon needed stitches on her upper lip. Kerry drove her to the hospital, despair in his heart. When she came out of the emergency room, Kerry held her, cradling her face against his shoulder. "Leave him, Mom," he murmured. "Please. It can't be God's will that you should stay."

"It's only the drink." Mary closed her eyes. "Divorce is a sin, Kerry. And what would I do?" The look on her once pretty face, now pale and thin, pierced him.

Kerry wondered how it would feel to kill his father.

The next Saturday, after midnight, Kerry heard Michael's feet on the stairs, the ponderous breathing as his father reached the top. Kerry's mouth was dry. He lay on his bed, listening, feeling so much hatred that he barely registered his mother's scream. He stood without thinking and went to his parents' room.

His mother lay in a corner, dressing gown ripped. Blood came from her broken nose. Her husband stood over her, staring down as if stunned, for once, by what he had done.

The look on her face made Michael turn, startled. "You," he said in surprise.

Kerry hit him with a left jab.

Blood spurted from his father's nose. Kerry hit him three more times, and Michael's nose was as broken as his wife's. He let out a moan of agony, his eyes glazing over. Kerry moved forward.

His mother stood, coming between them. "No!" she screamed.

Kerry pushed her to the bed with fearful gentleness. "Stay," he commanded. "Let *me* finish this."

She did not move again.

In the dim bedroom Michael struggled to raise his fists. Kerry hit him in the stomach. His father reeled back and fell in a heap.

Kerry stood over him, sick with rage. "Touch her again, Da, and I'll kill you. Unless you kill me in my sleep." He paused for breath. "And I wouldn't count on doing that. I'm too used to waiting up for you."

After that night Michael Kilcannon never hit his wife again. His younger son never hit anyone.

The next year, at the age of thirty, Kerry's brother, James, was elected a United States Senator.

THE CAMPAIGN
Day One

SITTING alone on the patio of the San Diego Meridian, *Newsworld*'s Nate Cutler took in the palm trees, the soft ocean breeze, and the curious subtropical light he associated with California.

For the last few minutes Nate had been holding the Democratic nomination in his hands. When he first read the document, he had been stunned. "How did you get this?" he had asked.

Katherine Jones lit a cigarette. "All that matters," she said, "is whether this document is authentic. And whether the counselor's story checks out."

Nate appraised her. Katherine Jones reminded him of a Buddha figure without the compassion—gimlet-eyed, heavy-lipped, self-satisfied.

"Not quite all, Katherine. You came to *me.*"

Jones drew on her cigarette. "Based on what Kilcannon's said, he is *not* a reliable friend to pro-choice women. This document exposes him as an adulterer and a hypocrite."

"Perhaps."

"Just say you're uncomfortable," she said abruptly, "and we can go to the *Times.*"

"If my editors decide it's news," Nate answered in an even tone, "we'll print it. But they'll ask me how my source got a confidential counseling document."

Jones responded with weary patience. "The person I got it from has never met or spoken to the woman who wrote this memorandum. *I've* never spoken to her."

"And this lady won't talk on the record, correct?"

Jones shrugged. "Maybe you can persuade her to go public. As it was explained to me, she's come to doubt the morality of her work." She pointed at the document. "You *knew* her patient, right? When you worked at the *Times?*"

Nate's smile turned sour. "As an old editor of mine used to say, 'We're equal-opportunity destroyers.' "

"You *could* be. Because if you run this story, it will bury both Kerry Kilcannon and Costello."

That was true, Nate guessed. Looking at Jones, he felt very tough and very cold.

After she left, Nate reread the counselor's notes. He could not easily imagine ending someone's chance to be President, let alone that of a man he believed essentially decent. Far less had Nate conceived of destroying a friend for something that was at its heart as private as it was shattering. But what unsettled Nate most was his rush of excitement at what could be the political story of any journalist's career.

It was seven o'clock. He had roughly an hour to catch Kerry Kilcannon's motorcade. Then he would call his editor.

CLAYTON Slade sat with Kerry at the long wooden table of a meeting room in the San Diego Hyatt, preparing to preside at the morning strategy meeting. With seven days to go, he appeared calm.

"Let's get rolling," Clayton said, and looked around the table. The California working group had been picked by both Kerry and himself. They had chosen Kit Pace, the quick-tongued press secretary, in part because a visible woman aide would help a candidate who had no wife; Frank Wells, the gifted media consultant; the campaign pollster Jack Sleeper, young and bearded and cocky; and Nat Schlesinger, a wealthy public relations executive whose experience in presidential politics had begun with James Kilcannon.

"Let's start with Kerry's schedule," Clayton said to Wells.

"Okay." Wells dived in. "First, we all know that California's a media state. This isn't New Hampshire—no way Kerry shakes hands with twenty-five million people. Instead Kerry will have events in at least three of the five big TV markets every day. That's Los Angeles, San Diego, Orange County, the San Francisco Bay Area, and Sacramento and the Central Valley. Roughly ninety percent of the votes."

Wells looked around the table. "He'll have a new emphasis each day, driving home his positions on a major issue. Today is women's day. We start with school loans in San Diego, day care in Sacramento, and, in Los Angeles, visit a battered-women's shelter." He turned to Jack Sleeper. "Every poll Jack takes says that combating domestic violence resonates with women across economic lines. And psychologically it feeds on the shooting in Boston."

Jack Sleeper nodded. "In our tracking poll last night, Kerry, abortion rights was the number one concern of nine percent of females most likely to vote. That's a five percent jump, and we think it's mostly a reaction to the killings."

"Be sure to mention the shooting at your event in San Diego," Kit Pace said to Kerry. "Don't let Mason stay in front."

As was his custom, she noted, Kerry had let others speak before he did. "And tomorrow?" he asked Wells with an edge of irony. "Once I've gotten over the shock of Boston?"

"You don't get over it. Tomorrow you highlight your anticrime positions. The major event is a speech to victims' families about gun control." He paused and then finished, "There's no way Dick Mason trumps that one, Kerry."

Kerry stared at him. For a moment the room was silent. Tomorrow was the twelfth anniversary of James's assassination. "I'll want to see that speech," Kerry said softly. "In advance."

Clayton made a note. In a bland voice he said, "Let's move on."

Wells fidgeted with his glasses. "As of now, Friday's urban day. An event on job creation. Encouraging the high-tech industry. A brief meeting with black and Hispanic leaders—"

"Brief?" Kerry asked. "Haven't any of them been shot?"

Wells seemed to wince. Kerry said in an even tone, "I understand you're being practical, Frank, but I won't treat minorities like a dirty secret. On Friday I'm going to the Latino section of San Francisco and then to South Central Los Angeles. Period."

There was another brief silence; then Wells spread his hands in an expression of despair, half serious and half joking. Because Kerry resisted following his advisers' blueprint by rote, he drew their admiration and frustration in roughly equal measure.

"What about the economy?" Kerry asked. "I need to emphasize job security."

"The economy is critical," Wells answered. "You should hit that closer to election day, like Saturday and Sunday. And Clayton says you may need to squeeze in a debate."

Kerry nodded. "So Dick Mason told all America last night. I don't think I could duck it if I wanted to."

Wells paused for a moment. "That brings up one more problem, Kerry. Abortion. Mason means to stick it to you."

Kerry raised his eyebrows. Softly he said, "I know that. But he's wasting his time. Even with all that's happened, abortion's about the fourteenth issue most people care about. No one ever won just by being pro-choice." His voice was patient. "Anyhow, what I said the other day about 'life' isn't all that new—people are just listening closer."

Jack Sleeper frowned. "Kerry, my tracking poll last night has Dick Mason winning by two percent. Your base in California is women—fifty percent. All Dick has to do is steal enough of that base to win. *Don't* let yourself get drawn into a debate about abortion." He shook his head as though in wonderment that he needed to explain this.

The telephone rang. Clayton rose to answer, listened for a moment, and then signaled to Kerry.

"Dick Mason just landed in Boston. He's speaking in front of the abortion clinic in an hour."

We should have guessed, Kerry thought. "New federal legislation," he said at once. "Unleash the resources of the FBI. Anything this President can do for him."

Kit Pace looked up. "Maybe you should go to the funerals."

"No," Clayton said crisply. "Kerry will call the families, but he won't follow Dick Mason around like a dog, trying to be like him. This campaign will be won in California, and we've got a plan."

Clayton thought he had made himself sound confident, but the pensive look on Kerry's face mirrored his own questions.

AT EIGHT o'clock, when Nate Cutler returned to the Hyatt, the press assembly area buzzed with nervous activity. Some of his colleagues were leaving their suitcases on the stretch of sidewalk designated by the Secret Service. Cops with a metal detector and a dog trained to sniff out explosives were going through their luggage, which the Service would not return until they reached that night's hotel. No one complained about the security. Everyone knew that John Hinckley had shot Ronald Reagan while standing amidst the press corps, and James Kilcannon's assassin had insinuated himself among the stage crew. Nate put his ID tag around his neck and went quickly inside to call where no one could overhear.

On the phone, Nate's editor, Jane Booth, spoke as loudly as she could. Her office door was shut, she had assured him, and no one else would hear.

"It's a killer story," she said, "with two big questions: Can we source it? and if we can, Will we decide to print it?"

Nate could already imagine agonized editorial meetings—the political editor, the managing editor, the executive editor, and the publisher would have to approve the decision as to whether *Newsworld* should change the course of this campaign.

"What do you think?" Nate asked. "Will we print it?"

"We damned well *should*." Jane's tone was combative. Nate could imagine her, gaunt and intense, pacing as she spoke. "This story sheds real light on who Kilcannon is. People should know what drives him."

Nate glanced around him. "The idea that we're *explaining* him ignores the fact that we'd be *eliminating* him."

"There's a serious question of judgment here," Jane snapped. "Kilcannon was sleeping with a reporter who covered him."

"So pull up what she wrote about him," Nate replied. "Maybe she gave him a break, maybe she didn't."

"Do you think *we* should give *her* a break, Nate?"

"No," he said in a lower voice. "But I've got a confidential counseling document that describes a woman in emotional extremity, talking to a stranger who was ethically bound to protect her secrets."

Jane cut in. "The real problem is sourcing it. Our rule is two sources, even now, and you say this counselor doesn't want to speak on the record."

"The *real* problem," Nate answered, "is proving it. Any nut with a political axe to grind could put any fiction in a document and swear it's true." He checked his watch. "Look, Jane, only two people in the world know the truth. At some point we're going to have to ask them. I need to know how to approach Kilcannon."

There was a thoughtful pause. "Wait on that, okay? Costello's here in Washington. I'll ask someone to invite her out to lunch."

Imagining Lara's feelings, Nate became queasy at the thought of such an ambush. He knew the pressures *Newsworld* could put on her, the implicit threats to check with neighbors or ex-colleagues should she deny an affair.

Already, Nate thought, Lara Costello was beginning to seem like the victim of a drive-by shooting. "Well," he said, "I'd better run. Leave a message on voice mail to let me know what's happening."

"Will do."

Nate got to the press buses with about a minute to go. There were a couple of seats left in the third bus. He walked to the back and found himself sitting next to a cameraman from NBC.

"So," Nate asked, "who's replacing Mike Devore?"

The man shrugged. "With all respect to Mike, we've gotten an upgrade. It's Lara Costello."

Nate sat back. "Lara," he said. "It'll be nice to see her."

SEAN Burke stood alone on the corner. Van Ness Avenue was slick with rain. A moment before, a bus had splashed through a puddle and soaked the bottom of Sean's jeans. Chilled, he gazed at the abandoned auto showroom across the street, papered with signs that read KILCANNON FOR PRESIDENT.

Sean felt disoriented. It was nine in the morning. By this time yesterday he had killed the abortionist, three time zones away. All that seemed real was the woman he had spared.

Sean could see her frightened green eyes, could imagine her describing the killer to the police artist. Soon they would show the sketch to members of Operation Life.

Who would be the one to give him up? he wondered. Who would say, "It's a little like Sean Burke"? And then the police would go to Father Brian and find that Sean had vanished.

His hope was that he had vanished in the maze of a new city, under a new name, long enough to do what must be done.

Seven days. Hands in his pockets, Sean felt the cool drizzle on his face. The lining of his stomach felt raw. His pocket seemed empty without a gun.

When the light changed, Sean crossed the street and forced himself to enter Kilcannon headquarters.

The building felt as vast as a church. Voices issued from behind cheap partitions and echoed from tile floors to fifty-foot ceilings. A receptionist sat at a cafeteria table. Her black eyes were as opaque as obsidian. Remembering the eyes of another receptionist, Sean looked away.

"I'm here for Senator Kilcannon," he said.

"All right. Please have a seat and fill out a volunteer form."

Sean wrote the name "John Kelly." The form asked for his activity preference. The list of tasks meant nothing to him. All Sean cared about was that Kilcannon would come to San Francisco, that headquarters must know his schedule. He put a check mark near any job that might keep him in this building.

The last question was "Best times to volunteer."

Carefully he wrote "Every day until next Tuesday" and gave the form to the receptionist. She picked up the telephone.

The man who emerged from behind the partitions had curly hair and a pleasant, easy smile. In T-shirt and blue jeans, he could not have been much older than Sean. He glanced at the form and then gave Sean a firm handshake.

"Rick Ginsberg," he said. "It's great you're giving us so much time."

Sean stared at the tiles. "I'm kind of on vacation."

"You're not from here, I guess."

Sean shook his head. "New York City."

Ginsberg smiled again, then touched Sean on the shoulder. "Come on," he said. "Let's find you something to do."

AS THE plane took off from San Diego, Kerry was tired yet fully awake, like someone on a coffee jag. He had already done *Good Morning San Diego* and given his first speech. Ahead for the day were stops in Sacramento, then Los Angeles.

Tomorrow morning, Kerry realized, Lara would be in the rear of the plane. Somehow he would make himself meander through the press section, chatting, until he reached where she was sitting and, as twenty reporters listened, say how nice it was to see her. The moment would feel like death—pretending that he had never looked into her face and wished their lives were different.

He stared out the window.

He did not know how much time had passed before the wheels touched down, bounced once, and settled onto the runway. The motorcade was waiting.

IT WAS not until Kerry Kilcannon finished his speech calling for expanded day care that Nate was able to phone his editor again.

He stood outside the filing center, a tent by the landing strip at Sacramento's Mather Field, speaking into his cellular as softly as he could. "Lara Costello's coming here," he said. "The regular NBC guy broke his ankle."

For a moment Jane Booth was silent. "I can't believe her arrogance, Nate. Or her lack of integrity. You're not doubting it's a story *now,* are you?"

The question did not require an answer. "Have you gotten to her counselor?" Nate asked.

"We did." Jane sounded wired. "Her name is Nancy Philips. She confirmed that Costello was a patient, that Costello met with her in confidence, that she talked about the affair with Kerry Kilcannon. According to Philips, Costello was devastated."

"Yeah," Nate said. "That's pretty clear from the notes."

"The problem is that Philips won't talk on the record. She feels almost as guilty about what she's doing now as about what she *used* to do."

"Why shouldn't she?" Nate asked. "I mean, ruining Lara's life should give this lady at least a little pause."

Jane was briefly silent. "You still don't like this, do you?"

"I never said my feelings were important, Jane. Just that I have them."

Jane's tone became clipped, businesslike. "We need another source, Nate. We don't have a story yet."

Nate hesitated. "And you want me to do what?"

"Confront Lara Costello when she gets there. Ask her about Kilcannon. She may tell the truth or, far more likely, get caught in an obvious lie."

"Or she may tell Kilcannon."

"She may." Jane spoke more quietly now. "And if Kilcannon begins avoiding the press, that's interesting, too."

SEAN stood with Rick Ginsberg in a vast open area where volunteers sat at long tables, with telephones in front of them.

"Our job," Ginsberg explained, "is to identify the Kilcannon voters and get them to the polls. This is where we need you."

Sean was silent. That the volunteers were as young as he was made him feel apprehensive. It was like the first-day-of-school feeling when he was eleven—wondering what the others knew about him, or thought they knew. The loneliness had never left him.

But Ginsberg did not seem to notice. "Anyhow," he went on, "it's pretty simple. Each volunteer is given a list of voters, coded by precinct, neighborhood, party registration, and, if possible, ethnicity. All you need is to follow the script we give you. I'll start you out."

Walking across the room, Rick found him a seat at the end of a table, next to a slender strawberry blonde with a ponytail and a sweatshirt with USF in red letters. In profile her face was delicate, like china. Her eyes were cornflower blue. Hanging up the telephone, she made an entry in her log.

"Okay, John," Rick said, pointing to Sean's place. "By every telephone is a computer list of names. Just place the call, follow the instructions, and record what happened—contact, no contact, who each contact's voting for." Ginsberg patted Sean on the back and left. Motionless, Sean read the script in front of him: "Hello. My name is [volunteer name] from the Kilcannon for President campaign. I'm calling to see whether you intend to support Kerry Kilcannon."

Next to him, the blond woman placed another call. "Hello," she said brightly. "I'm Kate Feeney . . ."

Sean picked up the telephone, stabbing out the first number on his list. The phone screeched, the sound of a misdialed call. He slammed down the telephone. His face was red, his anger like a pulse.

Kate Feeney seemed to hesitate, then turned. In a pleasant voice she said, "I guess Rick forgot to tell you about the phone system. You dial 9 first."

Caught in his frustration, Sean did not know what to say.

Smiling, Kate reached over, hit 9, and listened for a dial tone. "Here," she said. "It works."

Sean took the phone from her hand. Her skin, grazing his, was cool. "Thanks," he managed to say.

Reluctantly Sean dialed again.

"Hello?" a man answered.

Sean swallowed. "This is John Kelly. I'm calling to see if you're supporting Kerry Kilcannon for President."

"Oh, yes," the man said. "He reminds me of his brother."

All at once Sean felt relieved. Suddenly he was connected to this person. He took the man through the questions and, thanking him, hung up.

Kate Feeney looked up from her computer log. "A Kilcannon voter on your first hit," she said. "Not bad."

Sean paused for a moment. Picking up the telephone again, he felt more confident.

WHEN they landed in Los Angeles, Nate Cutler saw a black stretch limousine waiting near the press buses. He paused, letting his colleagues pass him. Debarking from the plane, they straggled toward the buses. The Senator was a distant figure, shepherding a local politician to a black Lincoln.

As Nate watched, the rear door of the stretch limousine opened. Stepping onto the tarmac, the slender dark-haired woman watched the candidate. She stayed quite still until Kilcannon disappeared inside the Lincoln.

Nate walked across the airstrip and boarded the last press bus.

He felt tense, detached from the others. He leaned back in the seat and closed his eyes, listening to the desultory chatter around him—Mason's speech, Kilcannon's day. And then suddenly the bus became quieter. He opened his eyes.

Lara Costello stood at the front of the bus looking for a seat. She proceeded down the aisle. Now and then she stopped to say hello, but many of the faces she did not know. Nate thought that it must be strange to vanish, spend two years abroad amidst great suffering and privation, and then return suddenly famous, with a salary ten times that of everyone else here.

Then Lara saw him.

"Nate," she called. Her pleasure seemed genuine. When he stood, she hugged him fiercely, then leaned back to study his face.

"You look good," she said. Gazing back at her, Nate felt that combination of deep liking and sheer male desire that, two years before, had made him feel uneasy in her company. But nowhere as guilty as he felt now.

He said, "You look good, too." But not the same, he thought. Lara appeared leaner, her eyes older, more watchful. She seemed confident, quite self-possessed, and maybe a little haunted.

She smiled again. Nate paused, trying to conceal his discomfort. "Can I buy you a drink later on?" he asked.

She touched him on the wrist. "I'd really like that, Nate."

He could hardly look at her.

CLAYTON Slade stood next to Peter Lake, the special agent in charge, waiting for Kerry's last speech of the day.

They were on the campus of a junior college in Los Angeles, selected because of its outreach program for battered women. It was five o'clock. The sky was a cloud-streaked blue, and the palm trees were deep green in the fading sun. The plaza where Kerry was to speak was set amidst a spacious lawn; the knoll where Clayton and Peter were standing offered the best view.

To Clayton everything appeared in order—the Service people siphoning the crowd through magnetometers; the volunteers gathered in front of the platform, holding signs; the press bleachers on the other side of the plaza. There was only one three-story building overlooking the plaza. Clayton knew that the Service had secured the rooms facing the speakers platform and placed sharpshooters on the rooftop. A young Latina county commissioner had just assured the crowd that "the next President of the United States will be here in ten minutes." With luck, Kerry's speech would make both the early and the late evening newscasts.

"Seems like good advance work," Peter Lake observed.

"At least so far." Clayton noted that Peter never stopped watching his agents. Kerry Kilcannon was what the Service called a high-risk protectee, and Clayton felt fortunate that Peter Lake was running the detail.

At fifty-three Peter had the stocky frame of the linebacker he had been in college. He had first been drawn to the Service when, at thirteen, his father had taken him to see John F. Kennedy speak. His father had adored Kennedy, but what fascinated Peter was the Secret Service detail. "I guess I missed the point," he'd remarked dryly to Clayton, but Clayton had come to know better. The desire to protect was the deepest part of Peter's nature.

Sometimes this had led to conflict. It was in *Kerry's* nature to be a Secret Service nightmare. What Kerry feared most was to look fearful. This drove him to plunge into crowds, to change his schedule on impulse, to refuse to wear a Kevlar vest despite several requests from Peter Lake. At length, Kerry Kilcannon's Secret Service detail became as large as the President's own. Peter had fifty agents running in three eight-hour shifts, with teams leapfrogging California to cover each event.

All at once Clayton thought how drained Peter and his agents must feel—they were as taut as the assassin they were watching for. He placed a hand on Peter's shoulder. "Six more days," he said.

Over on the press platform, Lara Costello scanned the crowd, distracting herself by noting details she might use: that the crowd was young and multiracial; that, knowing they had an attractive candidate, they had used Kerry's picture on their signs.

"Kerry, Kerry, Kerry," the crowd began chanting.

Suddenly he was on the platform, a slim figure in shirtsleeves. Lara felt the briefest pulse, the tightness of a caught breath. She could not see his face well from a hundred feet away. Perhaps she only imagined that Kerry saw her or that this moment—Kerry suddenly quite still—lasted more than a few seconds. But in that brief time she experienced two years' worth of regret, loss, the guilt that never quite left her. Then she shut it down, like a curtain drawing closed, and Kerry began to speak.

A FEW minutes into his speech Kerry noticed them—a handful of women scattered among the cheering volunteers. Their faces were tense, and they did not join in the applause.

Now, as he spoke, they edged closer to one another.

"It is not just battered women who suffer." Kerry scanned the faces before him. "The children who witness the brutality of a father to a mother are scarred by that experience forever, by helplessness, by anger, by the prospect—borne out by bitter experience—that many of them will practice abuse as adults."

That group of women still watched him intently, seeming detached from the excitement surrounding them. Suddenly forming a line, they held a banner aloft for the TV cameras.

ABORTION IS A RIGHT, the banner read, NOT A FAVOR.

The women began a chant. *"We will not apologize,"* they called out. *"We will not apologize."*

Watching from the bleachers, Nate Cutler felt the pieces fall into place: the memo in his pocket, Mason's speech in Boston, the demonstrators now.

Next to him, Lara Costello seemed taut. "Who *are* they?" she asked.

"Anthony's Legions, I expect—militant pro-choicers."

When he turned to her, Lara was quite pale.

"WE WANT to be heard," a trim woman with glasses and long gray hair called out. "And we want answers. You've said a fetus is a life. Do your personal and religious beliefs mean that a woman who has an abortion is a murderer? You also say that you're pro-choice. Does that mean a woman has an absolute right to choose?"

For a moment Lara shut her eyes.

The crowd was silent, waiting.

"First," Kerry said crisply, "I support the right to choose. My personal and religious beliefs are just that—I don't propose to force them on anyone. Only a woman can make this difficult judgment based on her *own* life and her *own* beliefs."

Kerry turned to the woman. "Those positions are as clear as I can make them. They're the same as Dick Mason's, or any of the politicians in this country who call themselves pro-choice.

"And," he added softly, "they are absolutely devoid of moral content or *any* thought too complicated to fit onto a bumper sticker."

"Uh-oh," Nate said. "He was almost out of this." But those listening seemed rapt. Lara felt herself stand straighter.

Kerry faced the crowd again. "Having an abortion is the most wrenching decision some women will ever have to make. No 'position' *I* take will ever change that. An abortion is not just another operation, and the words we use to avoid that truth—like procedure and choice—beg the difficult questions each woman must face alone."

Once more he turned to the trim woman with glasses. "Your rights are safe with me. You needn't apologize for anything. But *I* refuse to apologize for believing what I believe."

For a long moment there was silence, and then the applause started—a solemn sound, different from cheers. To Lara it was the sound of respect.

Beside her, Nate was quiet.

SEAN Burke looked at his watch. Eight fifty-five. In twelve hours he had dialed one hundred and ninety-seven telephone numbers. There had been no time to find a gun.

Next to him, Kate Feeney talked on the phone, her face intent. As the day wore on, Sean had felt a tenuous connection grow. Kate would offer a word of encouragement or a smile. At midafternoon she had shared her turkey sandwich.

Kate was saying in a cheery voice, "I'm calling to see if you're supporting Senator Kilcannon for President."

Her words shook Sean from his reverie. When he stopped to think, his fears overtook him. Sean hit 9 and made his last call, hoping to get an answering machine.

"Hello?" the woman responded.

Sean could feel the dampness on his forehead. "My name is John Kelly, from the Kilcannon campaign. Is this Louise Degnan?"

"It is." Her voice was polite but reserved. "I haven't decided, if that's why you're calling. I doubt I'll decide before Tuesday."

It was his mission, Sean thought, to make sure the Tuesday election never came. In a hollow voice he asked, "Do you know about the Senator's stands on women's issues? Like protecting battered women and children . . ."

The woman paused. "I'm not sure I do, actually."

"Well, he's always been like that." The pit of Sean's stomach felt empty. "I mean, his first job was prosecuting men who beat up women. He even saved a kid's life." Abruptly his voice fell off. "Maybe we can send you some pamphlets."

"That would be fine, Mr. Kelly."

Sean closed his eyes. "Thank you," he said.

When he hung up, his fingers felt clumsy, the telephone heavy. He would not look at Kate.

"That was good," he heard her say. "What you told her."

When he turned to her, Kate's eyes seemed guileless. Wisps of blond hair fell across her pale brow. Sean felt his face redden.

"You were nice and sincere. People feel that." Kate was smiling a little, but Sean could not tell whether it was pity or deception. He realized that with girls there was something he did not quite comprehend.

Looking into Kate Feeney's face, Sean felt a hand on his shoulder. He flinched, startled. Kate's eyes widened at his reaction. Quickly he turned to see who had found him.

Rick Ginsberg smiled down at him. "You did a great job, John. Thanks."

Staring at the coordinator's pleasant face, Sean felt surprise, then relief. Rick squeezed his shoulder and hurried on. All around, women in suits or men with loosened ties had begun to chat among themselves, freed from the telephones. A T-shirted student put a stack of pizza boxes on one table.

"Can you stay?" Sean heard Kate ask. "This is where you get to meet people."

Once more the fear of being known struck Sean like a blow to the chest. "No," he mumbled, "I can't."

TEN minutes before she was to meet Nate Cutler at the hotel bar, Lara heard a knock on the door of her room.

It was Nate. "Can I come in?" he asked.

Lara felt surprise war with apprehension. "Is something wrong?" she asked.

Nate closed the door behind him. "It's about Kerry Kilcannon." His voice erased whatever ambiguity the words might have had. "We know you had an affair with him, Lara. It ended two years ago, when he was still married. Just before he decided to run for President."

She turned away. She was overwhelmed by the swiftness of this. Walking to the window, she gazed out at Los Angeles, its lights flickering in the night. Her voice was soft, clear. "If you know all that, why come to me?"

"You know why. We're asking for comment."

She turned on him, and then anger at the devastating betrayal of their friendship overtook her. "You're asking me for *help*. It's the reporter's oldest trick: Say whatever *might* have happened as if it's true, then hope your victim confirms it."

Nate watched her eyes. "This is hard for me," he said at last. "It's also my job. You'd do it to me if you had to."

She had put him on the defensive, Lara saw. It gave her more time to consider who could know about Kerry. "You won't do anything to me, Nate. Because you don't have anything, and you *can't* have anything. I won't dignify this, on *or* off the record. You float some innuendo that could ruin two lives, and you want an *answer?*"

Nate was silent. Then he said, "You'd better sit down, Lara."

The words held a compassion that unnerved her more than what had come before. Slowly she crossed the room and sat on the edge of the bed. He took some papers from his pocket—two pages—and placed them in her hands.

Lara read the first words. Shock came, then nausea. A film of tears kept her from reading more. "Leave," she said. "Please."

Nate folded his arms as if to stop himself from reaching for her. "You know I can't. Not yet."

Lara turned from him and waited until she could read again.

The counselor's notes were scattered, digressive. But Lara saw herself as she was then, helplessly sobbing in the counselor's office. All that she had wanted was for Kerry to be with her.

Softly Lara asked, "Why do you assume this is authentic?"

"Come off it, Lara—"

She spun on him. "*You* come off it. Any sick or malicious person can make a lie look more authentic by writing it down."

Nate rested one finger on the memo. "This is *you* talking, Lara. I can hear your voice." His own voice was quiet. "I remember how quickly you left the *Times.* This is why, isn't it?"

Lara remembered it all—the fierce desire to get away, to bury herself in something so new, so completely divorced from the past, that it would block out all thought of Kerry Kilcannon. She stood, the papers clutched in her hand.

"If this is true," she said, "someone has violated my privacy in a terrible way. Shouldn't that bother you just a little?"

Nate found his bearings now. "Personally, yes. Professionally, it can't. This story's too important. It *is* true, isn't it?"

Lara made herself detach, think like a reporter. *Newsworld* was aggressive but not unethical. They needed more than they had.

"Well?" Nate asked.

Lara remembered Kerry's agonized voice on the telephone. She could at least protect his privacy, the freedom to pursue his ambitions. In her heart she owed him that.

"It's not true, Nate." Her mouth felt dry. "Off the record, yes, I had an affair. But not with Kerry Kilcannon." She paused, searching for words that might protect them both. "We were friends, in a way. But that's all it ever was."

"You weren't lovers?"

Lara drew a breath. "We weren't lovers."

"He never came to your apartment?"

Lara stood straighter. "No more questions, Nate." She walked to the door. Just before she opened it, she turned to him. "But it's been wonderful to see you."

Inwardly Nate winced. He made himself walk to the door and then, quite gently, took the memo from her hands. "You're sure about this, Lara."

"Wouldn't you be?"

Leaving, Nate heard the door close with a muffled click.

INSIDE, Lara leaned her face against the door.

What had happened with Kerry could get out now. Even if *Newsworld* never printed it, their reporters would interrogate her neighbors and Kerry's, spreading rumors as they went. Soon the affair might be gossip at cocktail parties, then a story in the tabloids. The question was whether to warn Kerry. She was not sure what good it would do to burden him. She had already given him what he needed most. A lie.

The telephone rang. Lara hesitated. When she lifted the receiver and answered, she sounded as ill and wary as she felt.

"This is Clayton Slade." His voice was deep, polite. "If you have time, I need to see you."

Lara closed her eyes. "Why not," she said at last. "I wasn't sleeping, anyway."

CLAYTON sat in a chair, gazing at Lara with frank curiosity.

She sat down on the bed. "You know," she said. "Everything."

Slowly Clayton nodded. "Yes. I came to ask you to be careful—for *both* your sakes."

Lara gave him a sardonic smile. "Maybe I can help here, Clayton. You want me to stay away from him. You expect me to adhere to the highest standard of journalistic ethics. And if I don't, you'll personally make sure that I wind up in Des Moines, covering the sewage commission."

Clayton's own smile flashed. "My speech was more polite. You've got the substance, though." Abruptly his face became serious. "There's something I need to ask you. Who else knows about this? Besides the person who *had* to know?"

Lara stood, arms folded. Her choice was between the last betrayal of her principles and yet another lie, this time to Kerry Kilcannon. His best friend watched her, waiting.

"*Newsworld* knows," she said simply.

FOR twenty minutes Clayton listened. When she was finished, Lara's face was ashen.

Out of kindness he tried to conceal how appalled he was—for Kerry, for her, even for himself. His first words were practical and direct. "You believe it's this counselor?"

"Or someone with access to her files." Lara looked down, her expression pensive, haunted. "Ever since Nate left, I've been trying to remember her. I was such a wreck, she could have been anyone, as long as what I told her never left that room. I can hardly see her face now." She looked at him. "Whoever it is, we're never talking about this again. You're on your own."

In the last few hours her world had collapsed, her past had returned to haunt her, and she had compromised everything that was important to her as a journalist.

Clayton drew a breath. "Do you want me to tell Kerry anything?"

Her eyes met his, and then she looked away. "No. Nothing."

Clayton hesitated. "Well," he said finally, "I've got a job to do."

Lara stood with him, hands in the pockets of her robe. "Good luck."

Clayton was quiet for a moment; there was nothing left to say. "You, too," he answered, and left.

WHEN Sean turned on the news, the picture seemed blurred. It was the bedside lamps, he realized. Too bright, they cast reflections. Moving closer to the screen, he kept the lights on.

It had happened when Sean was seven, this darkness he could not escape. He still remembered knocking over the wine as he reached across the dinner table, drops spattering across his father's T-shirt, the flash of anger on his face. His father had wrenched Sean from his chair, dragging him across the living-room carpet. In the dim hallway his father opened the closet door.

"Inside," he ordered. His voice was as thick as blood.

Gazing up into his father's eyes, Sean made himself stop crying. He knew his mother would not help him. Slowly the boy walked into the darkness. The door shut behind him; the lock turned.

It was pitch-black. Sean stood there, eyes shut, crying so uncontrollably that his body shook with the effort to make no sound. Finally the spasms stopped.

When Sean opened his eyes, he was blind. The air was hot and close. Panic came, and he groped in the darkness around him. The first thing he touched was thick and rough. He recognized the feel of his mother's wool coat.

Fumbling, the boy pulled the coat from the hanger and spread it on the floor. He lay down, knees curled against his chest. Suddenly he could imagine her on the other side of the closet door, eyes bleak with bitter helplessness.

Last winter, when she was pregnant, the baby had been a small bulge in her stomach. Leaning against her on the park bench, Sean could feel it through the wool coat. In the closet, Sean swallowed, remembering.

Drinking wine, his mother had asked his father if they could find a bigger apartment. Drink made his mother careless. From their arguments Sean sensed that his father resented having another mouth to feed. For several hours he drank and brooded. When his mother asked again, his father rose from his chair in a rage and punched her in the stomach. His mother doubled over in shock and pain. She had gone to the hospital. When she returned, there was no baby.

Even through his mother's coat the closet floor felt hard. Sean shifted, body aching, afraid that he might suffocate. When at last his mother opened the door, his father was gone and it was morning. The boy stumbled from the closet, blinking in the light.

Now Sean gazed blankly at the television.

A woman appeared on the screen. Though her surname was Irish, Sean thought her exotic, almost Latin. "Speaking in Los Angeles," she began, "Kerry Kilcannon capped a day devoted to issues targeting female voters."

On tape Kerry Kilcannon appeared. Sean stiffened with rage. You, he thought. You're Roman Catholic, and you've abandoned your roots and everything you know is right.

Sean stood and began pacing. He had a sudden, visceral memory—his father's eyes, the last time Sean had seen him.

"Lara Costello," the woman finished, "in Los Angeles."

KERRY Kilcannon splashed water on his face.

Exhausted, he had fallen asleep thinking of Lara and then awakened from his dream of Jamie. The face Kerry saw in the bathroom mirror looked haggard. He saw little resemblance to the youthful savior some had imagined.

Kerry Kilcannon, hero. That was what the newscasts had said. In the mirror Kerry studied the scar on his shoulder as if, like the heroism, it belonged to someone else.

For Kerry his own face vanished. In its place was Lara. And then other faces—Meg, Liam Dunn, a small dark-haired boy who had worshipped him, and, as always, Jamie.

His life felt like a series of wrenching accidents, sudden and incalculable, of which Lara was the last. "Life plans are foolish," he had told her once. "It's all so contingent."

At twenty-six he had not known how true that was.

THOUGH he could not have known this, Kerry had foreordained a woman's murder and his own near death the moment he took a job with the Essex County Prosecutor's Office.

When Liam Dunn, who was now chairman of the Essex County Democratic Party, got him the job, he was simply grateful—to Liam for helping him through college and law school at Seton Hall, for the discovery that he had a decent head for law, and for the softness in his mother's eyes at his swearing-in.

Two years before, Mary Kilcannon had found her husband slumped in his living-room chair, dead from a massive heart attack. Michael Kilcannon had been a quiet, brooding figure in his last years, drinking alone, ashamed of what he had become, unable to apologize to his wife or sons. Kerry hardly spoke to him. Then he was gone, and Kerry, to his shock, wept from unresolved anger. He had desperately wanted a father, he realized, but all he had was the terror of his father's moods, the determination never to be like him.

Mary remained in the house where she had raised her sons, and Kerry watched over her. Jamie was now a distant figure, seldom seen in Vailsburg, a handsome Senator whose intellect and eloquence might take him to the presidency at a younger age than Kennedy. Kerry had little interest in Jamie or his world. His ambitions were simpler: to prosecute criminals and warrant his mother's pride.

The Essex County Courthouse, though vast and awe-inspiring in design, had fallen into interior dinginess and disrepair. Kerry shared a ten-by-ten cubicle crammed with a filing cabinet, two metal desks, and rickety wooden chairs. He took little notice of his roommate, Clayton Slade, a heavyset black lawyer with an inclination toward quiet. For the first year he labored doggedly.

Crime by petty crime, Kerry learned to make cops trust him, to deal with witnesses, to weather judges so rude and cynical that their courtrooms were a lawyer's purgatory. By the time the year was over, Kerry had tried more cases than anyone else. He realized he might not be a brilliant lawyer, but he was becoming a decent mechanic.

Then came the Musso case.

BRIDGET Musso was the victim. When the cops arrived, her husband, Anthony, was gone, and she was sprawled on the living-room floor, unconscious. Her face was bruised, and several teeth were broken. But the detail Kerry found most chilling was that her eight-year-old son, John, sat next to her, so uncommunicative that at first they thought he was retarded. His only words to the police were, "I think my mommy's dead."

They rushed Bridget to the hospital and her son to a home for boys. When the police tracked down Anthony Musso in a bar, he claimed that his alcoholic wife had tripped in the bathroom, smashing her face against the sink. He did not ask about his son.

The other problem was Bridget herself. The hospital's admitting report showed a blood-alcohol level well above the legal limit. Kerry knew that a good defense lawyer might impeach Bridget Musso.

Before anything else, he must interview Bridget. Discharged from the hospital, she and her child were living in a city shelter. Kerry reserved a witness room and sent the police to escort her in.

She was red-haired, Irish-looking, and the file said she was thirty-five. But ill health and addiction seemed to have sapped the life from her. There was a slackness to her face, and her pale skin was blotchy. Kerry could smell whiskey on her breath.

"Can you tell me what happened?" he asked.

She touched her face. Beneath her fingers the swollen bruise was fading to green-yellow. When she spoke, Kerry saw her ruined teeth, the stitches on her lip. "Anthony did this," she said dully, and then she shrugged. "Sometimes men get angry."

The words left pinpricks on Kerry's neck. "Your father beat your mother?" he asked gently. "Or you?"

For a time she just looked past him. "Both."

Kerry felt despair, but he stifled the impulse to ask about her past. "That night," he said, "what did your husband do to you?"

For almost an hour, question by question, Kerry negotiated the minefield of her memory—bursts of vivid clarity surrounded by black holes. The memory of a drunk.

SHE was alone in the shabby living room. John was probably in his room. Anthony had not come home for dinner. Waiting, Bridget poured more whiskey into a plastic glass. The music on the rock station seemed to come from far away, a note at a time.

When she awoke, she was on the bathroom floor. The acrid smell of burned pasta sauce reminded her, vaguely, that she had not turned off the kitchen stove. Her husband stood over her, very still, his face in shadows.

"Why do you do this to me, Bridget?" His voice was mournful, a whisper. That was how Bridget knew to fear him. His eyes were dark pools, like her father's.

Bridget began to cry. He jerked her from the floor and slapped her so hard that her head hit the wall.

Dazed, she felt the tears on her face.

He slapped her again. Falling sideways, she clawed at the sink and pulled herself upright to stand. In the cracked mirror her husband's face broke into pieces.

With one powerful hand at the base of Bridget's skull, he smashed her face into the sink.

She cried out in shock and pain. Reeling, she lurched toward the bathroom door.

Her son stood in the doorway, his eyes filled with terror. Bridget stumbled past him into darkness. She remembered nothing more. It was her son who had called 911.

DRAINED, Kerry studied her across the table. The cubicle they sat in was pale green in the fluorescent light.

Kerry kept his voice soft. "I need you to testify."

She shook her head, staring at the battered wooden table. At last she murmured, "If I do, he'll kill me."

Kerry's mouth felt dry. "Bridget, he'll kill you if you don't."

Her greenish eyes, Kerry thought, were close to dead. Only her tears said that she had heard him.

When he returned to his office, Kerry loosened his tie and sat back in his chair, eyes half shut with weariness.

"So," he heard Clayton Slade ask, "how was she?"

Surprised, Kerry turned to him, wondering how much Clayton had divined from Kerry's calls to the shelter, the police. "A mess." Suddenly Kerry realized that it would be a relief to talk like a professional, a lawyer. "Major gaps in memory. Past the legal limit when it happened. Scared to testify."

"What about the injuries?"

"*She* says he slammed her face into the sink. *He* says she fell, drunk."

Frowning, Clayton folded his hands across his stomach. "You're going to need the kid," he said.

Unbidden, the image of his father came to Kerry's mind.

John Musso was eight years old. At eight, Kerry wondered, would he have had the courage to speak for his mother?

THAT evening, self-doubting and far more lonely than he cared to be, Kerry decided to drop by McGovern's for a beer.

To Kerry, McGovern's was the last great Irish bar. Vailsburg had changed, its bars dying off, turned into shops or meeting places. But McGovern's remained as it was in the 1930s, with Irish memorabilia on the walls and fire and police hats suspended from above its oval wooden bar. Its rules were as timeless. Smoking was fine, but a man would be thrown out for cursing in front of a lady. The jukebox featured Irish tunes, and its longtime proprietor, given to dancing the occasional jig, might stand a round or two.

It was a Friday, and McGovern's was filled with smoke, laughter. Kerry took the one empty seat at the bar.

Instantly the proprietor, Bill Carney, appeared with a cool bottle of Kerry's favorite, Killian's Red. "Kerry Kilcannon," he said, smiling, "the fighting prosecutor? So how *are* things on the frontiers of urban justice?"

Kerry grinned and sipped his beer. "Tough cases, long days."

Bill gave him a quick, shrewd look, and his eyes moved to the woman on the next stool. "Do you two know each other?"

Kerry had hardly noticed her. She turned, giving him a quick, mock-critical appraisal. She was pretty—short auburn hair, a snub nose with freckles, large green eyes, and a generous mouth that formed dimples as she smiled. "Should I?" she asked.

Bill gave an elaborate shrug. He turned to another customer, leaving Kerry and the woman to fend for themselves.

Somewhat embarrassed, Kerry said, "Bill's at work again."

Once more the dimples flashed. "My parents met here," she said wryly. "Bill thinks that's a heartwarming link in a great tradition. I've no heart to tell him how miserable they are."

The remark made Kerry laugh. "I'm Kerry Kilcannon," he said, and held out his hand.

Her own hand was cool and dry. "Meg Collins. And I *do* know you. From school at Sacred Heart." She smiled again.

Kerry gave her a puzzled look and then made a connection of his own. "I saw you at a law school party, I think. Aren't you Pat Curran's wife?"

"You did. And I was. We barely outlasted the party."

"I'm sorry," he said, and meant it.

"Oh, it's all right, really." She spoke with brisk good humor, as if to ward off sympathy. She took another sip of beer.

"So what are you doing now?" he asked.

"I'm a legal secretary." Meg made her tone indifferent. "I'd do that till Pat got through law school, the plan was, then finish college. Instead, I'm getting my teacher's certificate at night."

She looked at him, then gazed down at the bar. Around them the talk and laughter afforded a cocoon of privacy. "He was young," she said. "He kept wanting change, excitement, new things. Marriage isn't like that, I discovered."

For a moment Kerry's heart went out to her, but he had no experience to offer, knew too little about Meg's to say. They sat together in silence.

For the next two weeks they met at McGovern's after work, then went to movies or dinner. Though she sometimes seemed drained by the stress of job and school, Meg laughed easily, cheerful in his company. They learned about each other—likes, prejudices, the outlines of their lives. But Kerry found it hard to speak of his work. He wanted Meg to be separate from his concern for the Mussos.

FROM the first moment, sitting with Kerry in the witness room, John Musso could not look at him. He was pale, Kerry saw, with dark hair and the habit of clenching his jaw. His fear showed in a convulsive swallowing.

"My name is Kerry," he said gently.

John would not look up. Only his throat moved.

"I work with the police," Kerry went on. "My job's to help you and your mom."

John was silent. Kerry took a rubber ball from his pocket and placed it on the wooden table, beneath his fingertips.

The boy's eyes moved, surreptitiously, to the ball.

"I'm giving it to you," Kerry said. "Hold out your hand, all right?"

For a moment the boy remained still, blue eyes fixed on the table. His hand slid toward Kerry as if it had a life of its own. When Kerry placed the ball in his palm, John clutched the red sphere so hard that his knuckles turned white.

"Roll the ball to me," Kerry said, "and I'll roll it back. It's a game."

John swallowed again. More from fear than a sense of play, Kerry thought, the boy let the ball slip from his fingers and roll across the table. Kerry took the ball and placed it in John's hand.

"Again?" Kerry asked.

As if in answer, John rolled the ball to Kerry. Silent, they rolled it back and forth. For John Musso the dismal witness room was a refuge, Kerry realized—a few moments with a stranger who, whatever he wanted, did not seem to pose a threat.

"Can I tell you something?" Kerry said at last.

The ball froze in John Musso's hand. "When I was eight," Kerry began, "my dad did things to my mom."

The boy was still.

"He hit her. Like your dad does. I'd lie in bed," Kerry went on, "and wish that someone could help us."

John clutched the rubber ball. For the first time Kerry took it from his grasp, then rolled it back. "I hated what Da did to my mom. I know you hate it, too." Kerry kept his voice soft. "If I can make him stop, maybe your mom will get better. But I'll need your help."

Kerry stopped there, letting hope settle in John's mind. The boy's fingers loosened, and the ball slid from his hand.

Taut, Kerry watched it roll into his own. "You remember that night, John, when the police took your mom to the hospital? How did your dad hurt her?"

There was a long silence, and then John Musso looked up, lips trembling, shutting his eyes just before he whispered, "He smashed her face into the sink."

THREE months later Kerry watched John Musso climb the steps of the Essex County Courthouse, holding his mother's hand. It was remarkable, Kerry thought. He had believed this woman beyond redemption, yet here she was. Though still pallid, Bridget's skin was less blotchy, and her eyes were clear. This was not entirely a mercy, Kerry reflected, for she had nothing to numb her fear.

"I knew you could do this," he told her.

He knelt beside her son. For hours Kerry had worked with him. But the boy's eyes, veiled by dark lashes, were fixed on the stone steps. Gently Kerry said, "I'm glad you're helping your mom."

John did not look up, yet Kerry saw his shoulders square. An attachment, tentative but touching, had grown between son and mother. When they began climbing the last steps, John Musso took both his mother's hand and Kerry's.

A social worker met them at the top of the steps. With a calm he did not feel, Kerry told the boy that she would take him and his mother to a room until their turn came.

For the first time John's fearful eyes met his. In a thin voice he asked Kerry, "You'll be there, right? In court?"

Nodding, Kerry clasped his shoulder. "When you answer the questions, just look at me. Nothing else."

Then he went to the courtroom alone. It was empty. Through the airy ceiling, inlaid with gold, grids of clear glass filtered light onto the judge's marble bench, the jury box. The hand-carved benches were flanked by oil paintings of judges and a fresco of Lady Justice and her suitors. How awesome, he reflected, it would seem to a child.

Sitting at the defense table, Kerry waited for his first glimpse of Anthony Musso, a man who, in three months of jail awaiting trial, had no doubt learned to hate Kerry.

Slowly the courtroom filled—the bailiff; the clerk; the prospective jurors; the public defender, Gary Levin; Judge Frederick Weinstein. Then, at last, Anthony Musso.

He was shorter than Kerry had imagined, barely taller than Kerry himself, though barrel-chested and much stockier. His face was flat, as if hammered on an anvil, and his hair was as black as his eyes. When at last he turned those eyes on Kerry, they were unblinking, implacable, beyond reach.

Staring back, Kerry imagined himself as John Musso, gazing up at his father. The fear he felt was not only of sudden violence but of what lay behind this—a terrible remoteness of feeling, an indifference to the lives he warped.

I'll get you, Kerry promised him across the courtroom, and then the trial began.

The morning went quickly. The jury was impaneled, and Kerry's opening witness, the first cop on the scene, described Bridget's injuries. The emergency-room doctor could not add much. On cross-examination Levin established that Bridget's blood-alcohol content suggested the possibility of motor impairment, which could have caused her to fall.

At two in the afternoon Kerry called Bridget Musso. As a court-room deputy escorted her in, Kerry went to her, touching her elbow, and she took the stand.

Her eyes were fixed, and her face was a frozen mask. Her voice was toneless as, in the presence of the man she feared, Kerry re-created that night.

By the time Gary Levin rose to cross-examine, she appeared drained, bloodless.

"That night," he began crisply, "what were you drinking?"

Bridget looked away. "Whiskey."

"How much?"

Fidgeting, she touched the hem of her skirt. "I don't remember."

"You don't *remember?*" Levin's posture—hands on hips—con-veyed how unimpressed he was. "You were drunk, weren't you? In truth, you were drunk throughout your marriage."

Bridget hesitated. But for three months she had gone to AA meetings, learning to confront her shame. Dully she said, "I'm an alcoholic."

Smoothly Levin said, "You don't remember that night, do you? The night you blame your husband for."

In confusion, Bridget looked to Kerry. "I remember it," she said with belated stubbornness.

"Do you remember when you talked to the police?"

Bridget touched her forehead. "I don't—" she began, then heard herself. "I was afraid."

She stared into some middle distance, unable to look at Kerry, Levin, the jury.

Even before the defense lawyer's eyes flickered to Kerry, Kerry knew that his case rested on the shoulders of an eight-year-old boy.

AS HE took the witness stand the next morning, John Musso's throat twitched. His father stared at him from the defense table. The boy looked pallid, close to nausea, and his face was a yellow-ish hue. His feet did not touch the floor.

Careful to keep his father from the boy's line of sight, Kerry stood close to him. The problem, Kerry knew, was to ensure that his testimony, if John had the courage to give it, did not produce a mistrial. "Kid witnesses are tricky," Clayton had told Kerry. "They don't understand they're only supposed to testify about what the charges are, not everything they ever saw." Before trial, Weinstein had precluded any evidence that Anthony Musso beat his wife beyond the night in question.

Kerry faced the boy, hands in his pockets. "Can you tell Judge Weinstein your name?" he asked.

John swallowed. His voice was slight, reluctant. "John Musso."

"Do you know why you're here?" Kerry asked.

John swallowed again. "I'm here— I'm here to say what happened to my mom."

"Did anyone tell you what to say, John?"

John hesitated, gazing at Kerry. "You did."

Kerry tensed. For the judge or jury to misinterpret John's answer could be fatal. "What exactly did I tell you?"

"To tell the truth." For an instant Kerry experienced relief, and then John added, "If I did that, you said you'd put my dad in jail."

Kerry's nerves jangled. From the bench Weinstein gave him a sharp look, then asked, "John, did Mr. Kilcannon tell you what to say?"

In a slight voice, almost inaudible, he said, "Kerry told me to say what happened."

Turning from Weinstein to the boy, Kerry asked, "You know what happens to people who lie, don't you, John?"

Emphatically John nodded. "Telling lies is a sin against God. Jesus punishes liars."

Kerry raised his eyebrows. Satisfied, the judge said, "Go ahead, Mr. Kilcannon."

The jury, Kerry saw, was watching intently. Kerry asked, "Do you remember the night your mom was hurt?"

For the first time John sneaked a look at his father. Glancing at the defendant, Kerry imagined the fright Anthony could induce in this boy by the simple but inhuman act of never seeming to blink. He waited, wondering if the child would collapse.

"I thought my mommy was dead," he answered, and Kerry heard the fear, the helplessness, that the boy must have felt.

"Do you know *how* your mommy got hurt?"

John's shoulders curled in. "I heard Mommy screaming."

Kerry stood next to John. Softly he asked, "What did you do?"

John folded his arms, seeming to shiver. "I got out of bed."

"Then what happened?"

The boy swallowed again, then started coughing so violently that his body was racked. Kerry went to him, bracing both of his shoulders until the fit subsided. "Are you all right, John?"

John's eyes were pools of fear and, beneath this, pleading. Kerry felt wretched.

"Would you like a recess?" Weinstein asked.

Kerry looked into the boy's face. John Musso wanted to leave, Kerry suddenly knew, but once he did, he might never return. "No," Kerry said coolly. "I have only a few more questions.

"John," he asked, "did you see your mommy?"

John blinked. He murmured, "She and Daddy were in the bathroom. I went there. She was crying." John looked at his mother across the courtroom. Tears welled in her eyes.

"And then what happened?"

In the long pause that followed, the boy closed his eyes. The jury leaned forward. Kerry felt the sweat on his forehead. When at last John spoke, it was in a dull monotone. "My dad grabbed Mommy's hair and smashed her face into the sink."

SLOWLY, deliberately, Gary Levin walked toward John.

"John, your mommy drinks whiskey," he said, "doesn't she?"

John shook his head. In a tone of faint pride he said, "Mommy doesn't drink anymore."

"But she used to."

"Yes."

Levin's voice and manner were kindly. "John," he said, "you like Mr. Kilcannon, don't you?"

Looking at Kerry, the boy nodded. "Yes."

"And Mr. Kilcannon wants you to tell the truth, right? You want him to be proud of you."

The boy nodded again.

"So," Levin said, "isn't it the truth that you met with Mr. Kilcannon and found out it would please him if you said your dad hurt your mom?"

John hesitated and then said, "I wanted to help him."

Levin nodded. "So you did, John. By telling him your dad pushed your mom into the sink. But you don't really *know* what happened, do you?"

John folded his arms again. "I do *too* know." His voice was stubborn, angry.

Almost pityingly Levin said, "Your mommy drinks, doesn't she? And then she hurts herself."

John straightened in his chair, looking at the lawyer with a sudden rage that startled Kerry. "Daddy hurts her. He hurts her all the time." Now he had turned to the jury, his voice piping and insistent. "He punches her in the face and in her stomach."

In the jury box Kerry saw a black woman shudder.

"Your Honor," Levin said at once, "I move for a mistrial."

THEY sat in Weinstein's airy chambers—the judge, Kerry, Levin, and a court reporter.

"The testimony's prejudicial," Levin insisted. "The charge is whether my client is responsible for a single incident—the only one *ever* reported to the police."

Weinstein turned to Kerry. "There's a problem here."

Kerry paused, gathering his thoughts. "Your Honor," he said, "Mr. Levin effectively called this boy a liar. He fought back with the only weapon he had—the truth. The defense got what it deserved." He lowered his voice. "John has suffered enough. To put him through all this again would be an act of cruelty."

Slowly Weinstein nodded and then spoke with what, to Kerry, was surprising compassion. "I agree with Mr. Kilcannon. It's painful to watch this boy. Mr. Levin, I'm instructing the jury to disregard all testimony about any other alleged acts of domestic violence. Motion denied."

Levin frowned. "For the record, Your Honor, if Mr. Musso is found guilty, I'm taking this to the court of appeals."

Weinstein shrugged. "That's what it's there for," he said, and the conference was over.

Back in the courtroom, Judge Weinstein instructed the jury to disregard John Musso's answer. But Kerry knew that they could not; the damage was there. To spare the Mussos further agony, he would have to win twice—here and on appeal.

Resuming his cross-examination, Levin was cautious. "Isn't it the truth, John, that you never told anyone that your dad beat your mom until after you met with Mr. Kilcannon?"

Swallowing, John looked at Kerry. With a small nod Kerry gave his permission.

"Yes," John said.

"And Mr. Kilcannon made a promise, you said? That if you helped him, your dad would go to jail?"

A glance at Kerry, a nervous bob of the head. "He promised."

Levin, Kerry saw, had gained back a little ground. As if sensing this, the lawyer said, "No more questions."

The case for the prosecution was done.

FACING the jury for his closing statement, Kerry tried to be the calm professional, marshaling the evidence: that John Musso's story buttressed Bridget's, that Anthony Musso—as confirmed by the police—had not called 911. The jurors appeared neither antagonistic nor persuaded, as if reserving both their judgment and their emotions.

Gary Levin got up—confident, unapologetic. "All of us," he said, "deplore the acts described by Mr. Kilcannon. But while this is very much Mr. Kilcannon's case, he himself is not a witness. Briefly Levin turned to Kerry. His witnesses are a damaged woman and an eight-year-old boy."

Levin faced the jury. "Bridget Musso," he continued softly, "on the night of her injury, was drunk." He paused, hands in his pockets. "When the police arrived, a young and impressionable boy, John Musso, told them that he thought his mother was dead." The lawyer's eyes swept the jury. "Yet *at no time* did he tell the police how this tragedy occurred."

Levin's voice became sad. "No. He told *Mr. Kilcannon.*"

Looking around him, Kerry saw Bridget Musso, humiliated and clearly frightened, her husband watching her with a soulless, heavy-lidded calm. Then Kerry thought of John Musso waiting in a small room with a stranger and a box of toys, and felt a deep rage at Levin's perversion of a truth he knew in his bones—that the cry for help might take months, or years, or never come at all.

"I do not claim," Levin went on, "that Anthony Musso has been a model husband or father. But he does deserve what the law accords us all—reasonable doubt. You cannot find that the 'truth' presented by Mr. Kilcannon through a troubled child and a woman with no memory is, beyond a reasonable doubt, true."

In the jury's pensive quiet, Levin sat.

Kerry stood, walking toward the jurors. Suddenly he was less aware of the faces in front of him than of his own memory of a small boy. The words came without thought.

"You're eight years old," he said softly. "You're alone in your room. The apartment is dark, and your mother is drinking. Your father is out somewhere—probably in a bar. You've got no one at all.

"Then you hear the front door open and know it's your dad. You hear his voice. And then you hear your mother scream." He paused, scanning the faces before him. "You know who your mother is," he went on. "You know her problems. But, God help you, you need someone in your life to love, and to love you back.

"When your mother cries out, you feel it on your skin, in your stomach. You're afraid to move." Kerry lowered his voice. "But you crawl out of bed and, against your will, start toward the sound of your mother's cries.

"What you see is your father, screaming at your mother while tears run down her face." Kerry's voice became hoarse and slow.

"And then your father takes your mother by the hair and smashes her face into the sink."

The courtroom was hushed. Kerry went on relentlessly. "You shrink back into the darkness. You hide so your father can't see you. Hide, until he leaves.

"Then the only person you've got in the world is lying on the living-room floor, and you're the only one to help her.

"When the police come," he continued, "you tell them you're afraid she's dead. But there's something locked inside you that you're more afraid to say. And someone you're more afraid of than anything in the world."

Kerry stood straighter. "*You* know what happened." He turned to point at Anthony Musso. "*You* know what this man is."

In the silence Musso's unblinking eyes filled with rage, and then Kerry turned to Bridget. "For three months," he said, "Bridget Musso has gone without a drink. She's done her part. You do yours. Tell John Musso that he was right to save his mother."

WHEN the jury instructions were finished and court was adjourned, Kerry said good-bye to Bridget and John and prepared to face a long night of waiting. Then to his surprise he saw Clayton Slade at the back of the courtroom.

"How long were you here?" Kerry asked.

"Some of the mom, most of the kid. All of the closing arguments."

As usual, his face was inscrutable. Kerry could detect no reaction to what Clayton had witnessed. But he was sure that Clayton would be honest and that, for better or worse, his advice would be worthwhile. "Have time for a beer?" Kerry asked.

Clayton nodded. "All right."

Kerry drove them to McGovern's, edgy at Clayton's silence. They sat at a table in the corner and ordered two beers.

"Well?" Kerry asked. "Who wins?"

Behind his glasses Clayton's eyes became bright. "You do."

"Why?"

"Your closing argument." Clayton's face was serious now. "At first I thought you were over the top. Then I realized the problem was *me*—I'd never try to do what you did, and I'd never seen anything like it." He paused, studying Kerry with open curiosity. "You didn't rehearse that, did you?"

Kerry shook his head. "It just happened."

Clayton took another swallow of beer, thoughtful. "So," he asked, "what's domestic violence to you, anyhow?"

The question took Kerry by surprise. He had never talked about this to anyone. Staring at the bottle of beer in front of him, Kerry found himself saying, "My mother."

For a moment Clayton was quiet. "So that's the answer," he said simply.

Kerry looked up. "What do you mean?"

"Find the thing that you can feel. Because if *you* care, you can make a jury care. That's the gift you have."

Kerry felt a great relief that Clayton would not abuse his confidence with intrusive questions. And he realized that beneath Clayton's quiet intelligence was a deep, ineffable kindness.

"Let me buy you dinner," Kerry said.

THE next afternoon the jury found Anthony Musso guilty.

For Kerry the moments following were a blur: the clerk reading the verdict, the polling of the jury, Weinstein setting a date for sentencing. Then two deputies took Musso away, and Kerry went to the witness room.

In the corner John played intently with a Lego set. He did not look up. Bridget's red-rimmed eyes were anxious; her body rigid.

"Guilty," Kerry told her.

Her hand went to her throat. For a moment it seemed that she could not breathe. John became still and gave Kerry a sideways glance, as if hesitant to believe. Kerry went to him, kneeling.

"It's over," Kerry promised. "He can't hurt you now."

John's blue eyes simply stared at him. Then he put his arms around Kerry's neck and, hugging him fiercely, began to cry without making a sound.

WHEN THE MUSSO CASE, SO all-consuming, was over, Kerry Kilcannon found that Meg Collins had waited patiently for him all the while. She had understood his preoccupation with John and Bridget without his needing to explain, and when he was ready, she was there for him. They were married three days before Kerry's twenty-ninth birthday.

In the next year Senator James Kilcannon embarked on a cross-country tour, which culminated in the announcement that he would seek the Democratic Party's nomination for the presidency.

That same year Kerry Kilcannon brought twenty domestic violence cases and won seventeen. He visited women's shelters, worked with the police, lobbied for more progressive legislation. Forcing himself to become a public speaker, he made the rounds of civic groups to call for harsher punishment for abusers. He was relentless in pursuing his cause, and for the first time some of his colleagues labeled him ruthless, too willing to put men in jail to advance his own agenda. Though Kerry found this hurtful, except to Meg and Clayton Slade he never spoke of his own childhood.

As months passed and the time for arguing the Musso appeal drew closer, Kerry kept in touch with Bridget and John. In many ways their lives were difficult. They were poor, and Bridget's health problems and lack of skills made her depend on public assistance. But she stayed sober and was taking courses in bookkeeping, she told Kerry. Kerry believed their lives would be better yet. It was one achievement of which he felt proud.

Another was his friendship with Clayton Slade.

In time Kerry acquired a sense of Clayton's life and came to admire his deep capacity for affection, especially toward his wife, Carlie, and their rambunctious five-year-old twin daughters. The coven was what Clayton called them, in a dry way that confirmed how much they meant to him.

The Slade family lived at the edge of Vailsburg, a few blocks from Mary Kilcannon. One of Kerry's pleasures was going to their home for dinner, and Carlie came to treat Kerry much as she treated Clayton, with a certain wry affection.

Kerry admired both husband and wife. A junior-college teacher, Carlie was smart in her own right, and Clayton was a superior trial lawyer—systematic, thorough, farsighted. Kerry never saw him make an obvious error in judgment. It seemed that Clayton could understand any situation, no matter how complicated or novel. When a large Newark law firm hired Clayton at twice his salary, Kerry was not surprised.

His own marriage was not quite what he had pictured.

Kerry was watchful, attentive to Meg, but often when he reached out to her, she turned her back to him. If he tried to confront a problem openly, Meg would withdraw.

"I'm so sorry," she'd say in a muffled voice. "It's not you, Kerry. Maybe it's Pat. Maybe I'm afraid of being hurt again."

The knowledge of their separateness—her distress—was like a slap in the face.

His spirits leaden, Kerry argued the Musso appeal before a three-judge panel. The court granted Anthony Musso a new trial and ordered his release from prison. When Kerry arrived home, anxious to talk, there was a note on the dinner table. An old girlfriend was in town, Meg had written. She hoped the argument had gone well and couldn't wait to hear about it.

At times Kerry wished that he could talk to Clayton about his marriage. But the two couples were friends, and with the Slades, Meg was different—smiling, vivacious. He felt a bewildering mix of pride, relief that others did not discern his own confusion, a buried resentment that Meg could switch personae so persuasively. Only Kerry suffered her withdrawals, the long, silent weekends that came without warning, when she would stay in bed well into the afternoon. Only Kerry knew what she had told him about children.

They were in the kitchen, making dinner. Kerry had returned from a visit with John and Bridget Musso. Proudly John had shown him a model aircraft carrier he was building and asked Kerry to help him finish it. "Being with a kid is so amazing," he remarked to Meg. "For John the only thing that mattered in the world was finishing that ship together. After a while it was all that mattered to me."

Meg gave him a thoughtful look. "It's nice you can have fun with him. Did you ever think about joining Big Brothers?"

On the surface her comment was benign. That they would have children had always been a given. But by now Kerry was alert to Meg's defenses, her need for indirectness. "Oh," he said with feigned nonchalance, "I've thought more about our own kids. When would you like to fit one in?"

Meg's gaze lowered to the stovetop. "I don't know," she answered. "Not now."

Kerry felt himself tense. "Not now? Or not ever?"

Cornered, Meg looked at him. "You're very traditional," she said. "I'm not sure *what* I am anymore."

THE morning of the second Musso trial was drizzly, bleak.

Kerry brought John and Bridget to court. As they climbed the marble steps to the courthouse, John Musso was quiet and pale. Kerry still remembered the moment he had explained that Anthony was free—the look of fear in this boy's eyes, as eloquent as Bridget's tears. At the door of the courtroom Kerry took John's hand. "One more time," he promised, "and this will be over."

Watching John gaze up at him, his mother brushed back the boy's hair. Kerry looked at them, mother and son. You're so close, Kerry thought. If I can keep you safe this time . . .

He never finished the thought.

Anthony Musso walked toward them down the hallway, right hand in the pocket of his heavy woolen jacket. Only Kerry saw him. Only Kerry had time to register his slow, tight-muscled walk, his heavy-lidded stare at the back of Bridget's head, or to sense that Anthony had not come for a retrial.

No one else was near. From the corner of his eye Kerry saw a sheriff's deputy drinking coffee and chatting with someone in the doorway of an office. Musso stopped. With calm deliberation he drew a black handgun from his pocket.

The next seconds were slow-motion, a series of impressions:

Musso raising the gun, Bridget's lips parting as she saw the look on Kerry's face. A hollow pop sounded, and John's fingers twitched in Kerry's hand. Bridget's head snapped forward. As she stumbled toward Kerry, Anthony Musso aimed at him.

A woman screamed. In a sudden reflex Kerry dived for the door, John's hand still clasped in his. Searing pain shot through his shoulder. His head struck the heavy door with a thud, knocking it open.

Kerry rolled onto his back, John in his arms now, blinding spots before his eyes. Bridget lay beside them. More gunshots echoed. Anthony slumped in the doorway, dead. The last thing Kerry remembered was John Musso lying beside him, shrieking uncontrollably.

KERRY was a hero. The sheriff's deputy had seen him save John Musso's life. That was what Clayton Slade told him when he visited Kerry's bedside.

Kerry lay with his right arm in a sling, his collarbone shattered by Musso's bullet. His thoughts were shamed and solitary.

A woman was dead, a boy orphaned.

"They're looking for the nearest relative," Clayton told him. "There's a great-aunt somewhere—Bridget's mother's sister."

His friend sat beside him in the quiet room. Kerry stared at the ceiling. "God help him," he said at last. "God help me."

Clayton shook his head. "There's nothing you could have done."

Kerry winced from the pain that shot through his shoulder. "I could have saved her," he said. "I saw the gun, and I froze."

Clayton studied his face. "It took two seconds, Kerry. No one could expect that."

"I did, though. From the moment I saw him." Kerry faced the ceiling again. "You know what I think it was? Better her than me. The only accident was saving John."

Clayton rose from his chair, standing over him. "You don't know that, Kerry. You'll never know. It was too fast."

After a time Clayton laid a hand on his arm. "Maybe the deputy made you into someone you're not. But you don't have to do that to yourself."

Kerry looked up at him. "Just live with it, in other words."

Clayton nodded. "You've got a life to live. Enough bad has come out of this already."

FOR two days more Kerry healed, floating in and out of sleep. Mary Kilcannon came once a day. Jamie called from California, where he was campaigning for the Democratic nomination. Reassured that Kerry would recover, he quipped, "I hear you forgot to duck."

"No," Kerry answered. "I remembered. Just not in time."

Jamie laughed. "Next time, Kerry, you'll do better."

When he woke again, he found Meg watching him, wordless. There were tears on her face, Kerry saw. "What's this?" he asked.

She took his hand. "I could have lost you."

Kerry managed to smile. "And then where would you be?"

"Don't joke about it, Kerry. Please."

Her face was shadowed with desperation. She could not seem to stop crying. "That man nearly killed you," she said. "Promise me, please, that you'll get out of domestic violence."

Thinking of Bridget Musso, Kerry flinched inside. "I can't."

"Please." She squeezed his hand tightly.

Kerry closed his eyes. Then he sat up, and his tone became as patient as a parent's to a child. "It was an accident, Meg."

Meg shook her head, and her expression took on the cast of stubbornness. "Promise you'll never take a chance like that again. That's not too much for a wife to ask her husband."

Weary, Kerry lay back on the pillow, still holding her hand. "All right," he answered, and closed his eyes again.

IN THE doorway, Clayton touched the boy's shoulder, then nodded toward Kerry. "You can see now, John. Kerry's fine."

The boy could not keep his eyes off Kerry. What Kerry read there went so far beyond relief that it was painful. Tentative, the boy came to him.

"I'll be down the hall," Clayton told them both, and vanished.

John placed his hand on the sheets, a few inches from Kerry's arm. His eyes were sunken. Since John had stopped crying, the social worker had told Kerry, he had been almost mute.

What to say, Kerry thought, that could make any difference? He clasped John's hand in his own. "Your mom loved you very much, you know. She always will."

The boy swallowed, then looked away. All that Kerry could do was to grasp his hand still tighter. Just as he had done at the moment Bridget died.

Perhaps, Kerry thought, the same memory made the boy's lips tremble, as if to speak.

"What is it?" Kerry asked.

John laid his face on the bed, not daring to look at Kerry. "I want to stay with you," he whispered.

Kerry's throat tightened. *I want to stay with you.*

Did he mean, Kerry wondered, forever? And why not—wasn't this what Kerry owed John Musso?

Gently Kerry touched the dark crown of the boy's head. There was so much to consider—his work, his marriage, his own fitness. He recalled his last impulsive decision, how little he had known about love when he asked Meg Collins to marry him, how dimly he understood it now. Just enough to know that the reasons she could not love him must have begun not with Pat, but in her childhood, planting the seeds of her own subconscious wish—and this Kerry felt more sure of—never to have children. Not their own, and certainly not this child.

He must not temporize, Kerry knew. If he could not take John's life into his hands, nothing was left but truth.

Softly Kerry began to explain about the boy's new home, the great-aunt who was waiting for him. John said nothing more. When Clayton came for him, he did not look back.

IN THE weeks after his release from the hospital Kerry threw himself into his work, unspoken guilt fueling his new intensity. When he called John's great-aunt, the boy would not speak to him.

John was so withdrawn, the woman told Kerry, that she never quite knew what to do. Every week he refused to come to the telephone. Every week her report was the same.

At times Kerry thought of Jamie. He had fought his opponent— a former Vice President—to a virtual draw. Then, to Kerry's astonishment, Jamie made public his involvement with singer Stacey Tarrant. That a potential President was involved with a rock star— however intelligent and socially aware—was deeply controversial. Kerry hoped this candor marked a change in Jamie, a willingness to love at any cost. But all that Jamie told him was, "If you were reckless enough to take a bullet, the least I can do is date in public."

It was the last time they ever spoke.

On a warm April night Kerry worked late. He had called John Musso's great-aunt. John was much the same, she told him. Hanging up, Kerry vainly wished that the damage of childhood were not so hard to heal. These reflections brought him back to Jamie.

The telephone rang.

Meg's voice was stunned, hollow. "Your mother called," she told him. "It's your brother. He's been shot."

Kerry felt numb. It was a moment before he could ask, "How bad is it?"

"They're not sure yet. It just came on the television."

"Go to Mom's," he said. "I'll be right there."

Like an automaton, Kerry walked down the bleak corridors to his boss's office. The television was in a corner, atop an antique hutch. Kerry pushed the button. The picture flickered to life.

Jamie stood on a concert stage, fingers touching Stacey's. The crowd was frenzied; the arena echoed with his name.

"Kil-can-non . . ." With a dazzling smile Stacey turned to him. They stood at the intersection of two spotlights, as if suspended in darkness. Stacey stood aside, giving him the crowd.

From one corner of the stage a slender man stepped forward. The man raised his gun.

As the television cast a glow on the Essex County district attorney's Persian rug, Kerry stood motionless, watching his brother die.

THEY BROUGHT HIM HOME TO Newark. Mary was stoic, tearless, sustained by prayer and Kerry's presence. Jamie's aide, Nat Schlesinger, oversaw the funeral arrangements. Soldiering on through his own grief, Nat treated both Kilcannons with a deep kindness. When Nat asked Kerry if he wished to give the eulogy and Kerry answered, "He deserves someone who knew him," Nat seemed to understand.

They buried Jamie in Princeton. The President was in Europe, but Vice President Bush came, many Congressmen, most Senators. They filed gravely past Kerry and his mother, like emissaries from Jamie's life. Throughout, Liam Dunn was a silent presence, attentive when they needed him but, Kerry sensed, nursing thoughts of his own.

A week later Liam called. Could Kerry come to see him? he wondered. There was a private matter to discuss.

In the spartan office Liam maintained as Essex County chairman, he motioned Kerry to sit.

"How's your mother?" Liam asked.

"Resigned." Kerry tried to find words for what he saw. "It's like she has some immutable core. God, perhaps."

Liam nodded. "And you?"

"I have work."

Liam gave him a long, almost cool appraisal. "I have something to ask you," he said at length. "And it's probably not a fair thing. But then politics, like rust, never sleeps."

"What is it?"

"There'll be a special election this November, Kerry. To fill Jamie's seat." Liam's voice became quieter. "I've talked to the state chairman and most of the committee. We know what we're asking, son. But it's you we're wanting."

Kerry sat back, shaken. "I've never wanted this, even when Jamie was alive. I surely don't want it now, like *this.*" A swirl of emotions brought him to his feet. "All I've got to offer is a dead brother and the name Kilcannon. They'd be voting for a corpse, not for me."

"You've made yourself a fine prosecutor, Kerry, a friend to

women. You're a hero. And yes, you're Jamie's brother. All things to be proud of. Together they can make you a Senator." Liam paused. "If you decide to be one."

Kerry felt the irony crashing down on him. They wanted *Jamie,* not him. What obligation did he have to live his brother's life for him? Kerry could never be James, and the cost would be what he dreaded most—endless comparisons to his brother, the merciless scrutiny of a thousand eyes along a path not of Kerry's choosing, the jeers of those who thought him an opportunist. He slowly shook his head.

Liam's voice was still gentle. "You've your mother to consider, and a wife. You've every right to say no. But before you do, ask yourself how you'll feel if you turn your back on this." Pushing up from the chair, Liam stood. "You understand politics well enough, Kerry. I raised you to. But you've never understood how much you can do."

Kerry looked into his godfather's face.

"Pray on it," Liam said.

WHEN he told his mother of Liam's request, she fell into deep silence. They were sitting in her living room. It was late afternoon, and the room was shadowed.

"What answer have you given him?" she said at last.

"I haven't." He touched her arm.

Tears came to her eyes. "I've always thought there was a reason for things, one that I can't quarrel with." Her hand covered his. "Search your heart, Kerry. Whatever you find there, then that's what you should do. Because I know God loves you even more than I."

HE FOUND Meg in the living room, studying for her last exam. By fall she would be an English teacher. Her job was set.

As calmly as he could, Kerry explained what had happened.

Meg's eyes widened. "You're really thinking about it, aren't you? After all that's happened."

"It deserves at least that much, Meg."

She stood, arms folded. "You've just buried your brother, Kerry. How can you do this?"

"Please, I haven't said I will."

She stared in incomprehension. She then came to him, laying her head against his chest. "Kerry, I nearly lost you." Her voice was muffled by tears. "Please, you promised me."

"I know," he murmured. "But Jamie was alive then."

Kerry felt her stiffen.

She pushed back from him, her face tear-streaked. "I'm sorry. But if you do this, I won't help you. I've got a life here that I've worked hard for." Meg shook her head as if stunned. "I won't stand in your way, Kerry. But if you go to Washington, I won't go with you."

Kerry looked at her. "Well, at least our kids won't miss me."

Tears sprang to Meg's eyes again. Turning, she left the room.

That night Kerry never slept. In the morning he called Clayton Slade. "There's something I need to ask you," he began.

FOUR days later Kerry met with Liam and members of the party's state committee. All of them wanted to keep the seat, and Kerry was the instrument at hand.

It wasn't easy—Kerry's inexperience showed—but at thirty, the same age as his brother, Kerry narrowly won election to the United States Senate.

THE CAMPAIGN
Day Two

TELLING Kerry about Lara—the counselor's notes, Cutler's question, her lie in return—Clayton watched his friend closely.

Kerry's stillness was so complete that he seemed not to breathe. His thoughts could have been anything—a terrible regret, the fear of discovery, the potential destruction of his hopes for the presidency—except for the look in his eyes. So that it did not surprise Clayton that Kerry's first words were, "How is she?"

They sat across from each other in Kerry's suite. It was a little past six. Surrounding them was the hush of a giant hotel in the moments before the clatter of room-service carts began, the muffled sounds of doors opening and closing. They had led this life for so long that Clayton sometimes forgot the utter solitude at its core.

"Devastated," Clayton answered simply. "She didn't lie just for you, Kerry. She did what was best for both of you." He paused, then added quietly, "And Kerry, she doesn't want to see you. For your sake as much as hers."

Kerry looked away.

"So," Clayton said, "*Newsworld* will try to break this before Tuesday. That means Cutler's coming to you next. You have to make a choice."

"*Have* to?" Kerry stood, suddenly angry. "What happened between Lara and me has nothing to do with whether I'm fit to be President. Answering validates his right to ask."

To Clayton the response revealed how shaken Kerry was. Unlike many politicians, Kerry had always been willing to acknowledge whatever difficulties he faced. "A nondenial denial?" Clayton asked. "Everyone knows that means 'I did it.' Without a flat denial he prints it all."

Kerry folded his arms. "So I let Nate Cutler make a liar out of me."

"Or lose the primary."

Once more Kerry was still. Only his questioning look betrayed surprise.

"Lose," Clayton told him, "and the story goes away. But if you win the nomination and *then* the story comes out, you'll be the ruined candidate who dragged his party to disaster."

"And if I lie?"

"No guarantees. But *Newsworld* still has standards. How does it print the story when all it has is innuendo? At least you can hope this gets pushed down to the tabloids, so we can call it sleaze."

"Even though it's true."

"Give them the truth, Kerry, and Lara loses her reputation and her career. So do you." Clayton's voice became slow and emphatic.

"If you don't want to lie, ask yourself this: Are you willing to let down everyone who's worked for you so that whoever is trying to destroy you—Dick Mason or some Republican—can be President?"

Kerry walked to the window, opening the drapes. A sun-streaked smog sat over Los Angeles. He shook his head, his voice a mixture of irony and sadness. "What would my brother have done, do you suppose?"

Twelve years ago today, Clayton reflected, James Kilcannon had been murdered. He waited a moment longer. "What should I tell Kit, Nat, and Frank?"

Kerry did not turn. "Tell them to stall," he said.

AT SEVEN o'clock Clayton Slade did just that. In his hotel suite, face to face with Nat, Kit Pace, Frank Wells, and two pots of coffee, he told the whole story. When he had finished speaking, he watched them sort out the pieces—the counselor's memo, Nate Cutler's visit to Lara Costello, Lara's denial. The gloom was palpable.

Kit's face looked puffy, as if she had been aroused from sleep. Carefully she asked, "If Nate goes to him, what will Kerry say?"

"Right now," Clayton said, "he doesn't see why he should answer at all."

Kit's coffee cup froze halfway to her mouth. "That won't fly," she said bluntly. "One way or another Kerry has to respond."

"What about this woman?" Frank Wells asked. "The counselor who wrote the memo? Can we send someone to talk to her?"

Clayton gave a curt shake of the head. "If *Newsworld* prints this, our visit could become part of the story. And there's no controlling what this counselor might say about it."

There was silence again. "We should sum up what's going *for* us," Kit said at last. "Kerry's divorced now. Adultery's not an ongoing issue. Lara's denied it. That's a huge advantage. Other than Kerry, *she's* the only one who knows for sure. *Newsworld* won't be comfortable with one unnamed source and a memo that could be a political dirty trick. So Nate has to come to us."

She sat back, steepling her fingers. "Until Kerry decides what to do, we can't have him anyplace where Nate can corner him. And one of the things the press likes about Kerry is that he's accessible. Walking through the airplane, saying hello—"

"It's not that bad," Frank Wells interjected. "Our guy's tired, that's all. We've already said that we're saving his time for the California media. For a couple of days, at least, it won't look like we're singling out *Newsworld*."

"That's how it'll have to be," Clayton said to Kit. "We need to buy time."

Nat leaned forward, graying and rumpled, a man who had seen it all and still hoped for the best. "Eventually Kerry will have to deny this, and the denial will have to stick. Otherwise it'll boomerang on us with a vengeance." He drew a breath. "It's the old gotcha game. Once they ask the question and you lie, the press has an absolute obligation to expose you as a liar. I can hear *The New York Times* right now."

Clayton saw his rueful shake of the head.

"A question," Clayton said to him. "Who fed this to Cutler in the first place?"

Nat frowned. "The GOP. It's *their* issue, after all."

Frank Wells shook his head. "Mason. It fits with the past two days." He turned to Clayton. "You know the first rule. If you've got a problem, get it out and live with it. Then hope you can find something about Mason that's even worse. Which gets me to my cynical question: Are our oppo-research people looking for a magic bullet we can use on Dick?"

"That's what they're for. But all we've found are rumors. Although they're bad ones."

Frank raised his eyebrows. "About what?"

"If they're more than that," Clayton said firmly, "I'll let you know. But if they're not, this could backfire."

There was silence, acceptance. "All right," Clayton said. "For now, Kerry avoids Cutler by avoiding the press. If Cutler wants to see him in private, Kit demands to know what it's about."

The others nodded. "I've got one more thing to say," Clayton said. "Your first obligation is to look upbeat, as if nothing has happened. The second is to say nothing about this to anyone."

Clayton let the silence build, and then he looked at all of them. "Now," he said, "we've got work to do. Jack Sleeper's polls say we're still weak on abortion."

BOARDING the bus on Van Ness Avenue, Sean sat alone. His stomach churned. Surreptitiously he took an antacid pill from the pocket of his jacket and slid it into his mouth.

It was ten forty-five. In less than two hours he had placed thirty-eight phone calls. Kate Feeney had worked alongside him. Even as he dialed, he was aware of her face, pale and delicate in profile, the sheen of her blond hair. But girls had never liked Sean. When Kate smiled at him between calls, he hovered between confusion and distrust.

Eyes veiled, he glanced around the bus. The faces seemed alien. The polyglot mix of whites, Asians, Latins, and blacks intensified his sense of being adrift in a strange city. It was like entering the boys home where the social worker had taken him. Alone, he would lie awake in the bunkroom, afraid that they would learn about his father and his mother, about Sean himself. For Sean already knew that the people you wanted love from abused you, or abandoned you, or died.

Even Father Brian, whose faith he had come to share, would betray him if he knew what was in Sean's heart. As he remembered, tears came to Sean's eyes. It was Father Brian who taught him that God loved the weak, the innocent. The unborn child.

It was like a flash of lightning in the brain. When Sean was sixteen, the meaning of his life was suddenly clear. God had blessed him with the gift of anger, to be his soldier.

Shortly before graduation Father Brian had suggested in his gentle way that God might not mean for Sean to be a priest. Alone in the sanctuary, he had prayed for answers. But God had given him no sign. Torn between hope and bitterness, Sean had stepped from the church.

At the bottom of the steps a man waited. He was about thirty, with a gaunt face and black eyes so intense that Sean thought of an archangel. The man came toward him, holding out a piece of paper. "Please," he said, "read this."

Though his voice was soft, it held urgency. As Sean took the leaflet, he felt a current pass from the stranger to him.

"If life is sacred, how can we tolerate murder?" he read. Sean looked up into the stranger's eyes.

"I'm from Operation Life," the man said.

Now the bus sighed to a stop. Startled from thought, Sean saw the street signs and then the storefront he was looking for. The Gun Emporium.

LARA sat in the press section, weary after a sleepless night, edgy from two cups of coffee in a stomach too nauseated for food. Around her the plane buzzed with the crazy energy of fifty up-rooted people, the nomadic press, waiting for takeoff. Moments before, Nate Cutler had taken a seat across the aisle. She had turned to him, coolness in her eyes. Nate had possessed the grace to look away.

The danger, Lara realized, was that others would sense their chill. It was beyond her to feign friendship. Somehow she must blot out Nate's existence, must be a professional until she could get off this plane and return to whatever life was left after *Newsworld* finished scavenging.

The plane began taxiing down the tarmac. Moments later they were in the air.

ALONE in his hotel suite, Clayton Slade stood abruptly. "Can you confirm that?" he said into the telephone.

"We don't know," the head of opposition research answered. "We're trying to get the files. But they're over twenty years old, and it looks like Mason's had them sealed."

Clayton paused. "Other than breaking the law," he directed, "do everything you can."

THE CAVERNOUS STORE WAS empty but for a stocky man with salt-and-pepper hair, polishing a rifle on the counter.

The sound of his own footsteps on the wooden floor made Sean self-conscious. He gazed at the glass cases filled with guns, metallic black or silver beneath the fluorescent lights.

The dealer put down his rifle. "Can I help you?"

"I was thinking about a handgun," Sean murmured.

The man nodded briskly. "What kind?"

"Nine-millimeter, maybe."

Stooping, the man unlocked a gun case, then placed a slender black gun on the counter.

Sean flinched. The gun was so like the one he had used in Boston that he could feel its lightness in his pocket, see the mist of his breath in the chill morning air. For a moment he was certain that the dealer must know who he was.

Mute, he took the weapon in his hand.

"You like this one?" the dealer asked. "Just sign the forms, and in fifteen days it's yours."

Startled, Sean blinked.

The dealer appraised him closely, eyes narrowing. "You know about the waiting period, right?"

Slowly Sean shook his head.

"Fifteen days." The man's tone was flat, disgusted. "State law."

Sean stared at him. "Fifteen days," he murmured. His fingers grazed the trigger. "What if you need it?"

"Ask the politicians." The man paused, and then his voice grew quiet. "You buy one on the street, brother. Whatever piece of garbage you can find, from whatever piece of garbage is selling it. But *we* can't break the law."

Sean put down the gun and walked away.

Outside, he stopped, startled by the brightness of the noonday sun. The block was dingy—sex shops, decaying stores, flophouse hotels. To Sean it seemed like a preview of hell, a parade of human detritus that filled him with loathing—the homeless straggler with rags for shoes, the woman on the stoop jabbering vacantly to no one, the scraggly-haired prostitute, pale and wasted from drugs.

You buy one on the street, brother. Whatever piece of garbage you can find, from whatever piece of garbage is selling it.

Hands shoved in the pockets of his sweatshirt, a young black man leaned against the hotel across the street. Ignoring the jabbering woman, he inspected Sean with contemptuous leisure. In a seeming act of will he stood erect and ambled in Sean's direction. He stopped on the sidewalk three feet away, gazing around him. When he turned to Sean at last, his eyes were as hard as bullets.

"Lookin' for something?" His tone was impatient, as if Sean were occupying someone else's space.

Through his nervousness, Sean felt himself bristle. "Like what?" he asked.

The man gave a fractured shrug. "Maybe a rock?"

"Not drugs." Sean moved closer. "I want a gun."

The man looked around him—quick, darting glances. "A piece?"

Sean nodded. "A hundred dollars."

The man gazed at the sidewalk, lips forming a silent whistle. "Someone find you a piece," he asked, "what kind you want?"

"Handgun. Nine-millimeter. Tomorrow morning." Sean's voice was tight now. "I want it before nine."

The man shrugged. "That's not my office hours."

Sean clutched the front of his sweatshirt. "Nine o'clock."

Deliberately, the man removed Sean's fingers and stared into his face again. "You want a piece that bad, make it four."

Sean felt a helpless anger. "Four," he said. "Right here."

Without another word the man turned and sauntered across the street as if Sean did not exist.

ON THE flight to Elk Grove, Nate Cutler reflected, everyone seemed restless. Other than the pool reporters, no one had seen Kilcannon. He had not visited the press section at all on the flight to Fresno. Now even Kit Pace was more brisk than normal, guiding local reporters to the front. Nate had been trying to accost her all day.

Now she stood at the front of the press section, two rows from him. "This is always a bad day for Kerry," he heard her murmur to the earnest young woman from the Sacramento *Bee*. "Every year. I'm not sure you'll be seeing him back here. But he'll make time for you up front on the flight to Sacramento."

As Nate rose to speak to her, Kit vanished through the curtain. Edgy, he stood in the aisle, looking about him. Around the table where the food was laid out, four reporters were playing a desultory game of hearts. Heading for a sandwich, Nate noticed Rich Powell from Reuters kneeling beside Lara in the aisle, kissing her hand with the obeisance that befit a new princess of the media. "Millions," he said in tones of awe. "*TV Guide* said you're getting millions. Can this be true?"

Lara smiled. "Every word. How are you, Rich?"

"All right. If I had to draw a candidate, I'm glad it's Kilcannon." He paused. "You know him, right?"

Watching her, Nate felt her awareness of him. *"Knew,"* she answered. "I haven't seen or spoken to him since he decided to run."

"Big decision, if you're him." Rich sat in the aisle cross-legged. "See Stacey Tarrant's introducing him in Sacramento? That's kind of amazing. Or maybe just manipulative."

Lara shrugged. "She'll certainly help draw a crowd."

Turning, Nate sat down again, reflective. Lara's tacit message was clear: She had not seen or spoken to Kilcannon. Resuming his silent watch for Kit, he felt an intensity that bordered on obsession.

THE rally at Elk Grove was in a stretch of the American heartland, a patch of dirt near some stables that could have been a fairground. The platform was surrounded by tractors and bales of hay, and in the distance Nate saw silos and wavy fields of wheat. Filling the fifty square yards between the platform and the press bleachers was the kind of eclectic crowd that Kerry seemed to draw: farmers, small-business owners, Asians, high school kids, some Mexican farmworkers.

To rising cheers, Kerry walked to the podium holding a scrap of paper, no doubt with the names of the local worthies he should acknowledge—the mayor, the county commissioners. But when he set down the paper, it blew away in the wind.

Kerry froze, eyes following the paper as it drifted into the crowd, a pantomime of the nonplussed politician. "Oh, no," he said, "there goes my farm program."

There was a chorus of good-natured laughter, from farmers most of all. Flawlessly Kerry acknowledged everyone on the platform before he began to speak.

"The death penalty," he said, "is one of the most painful questions facing a civilized society. Once, several years before I was a Senator, I toured a prison. I saw the faces of men waiting to be executed, and I thought of the sadness, the waste of those lives."

Nate realized he was not speaking from notes. His voice, though quiet, carried easily.

"For a time that was all I could think of. But I since have had occasion to think of all the faces I would never see: those of the men, women, and children these men had killed. For when we give up the notion of private revenge, we do so with the expectation that our laws will pay proper tribute to the value of an innocent life, that, if warranted, the death of the murderer may follow the murder of the innocent."

A few moments before, Nate had noticed Kit standing near the speakers platform. Hands shoved in his pockets, he slowly walked over to confront her. "I need to see the Senator," he said.

Kit frowned. "Not until after Tuesday, Nate. It's not that we don't love you, but most of your readers aren't California voters, and we love *them* best of all."

Nate shook his head. "What I have won't wait that long." He kept his tone patient. "It's about the Senator's personal life."

Kit folded her arms, her eyes less friendly. "Tell me what it is and why it's credible enough to take Kerry's time."

"Quit being the Stepford press secretary, Kit. If this is something Kilcannon can deny, he'll want to do that in private. I'm trying to give him that chance."

"Or?"

"Or we go with the story next Tuesday based on what we have."

Kit studied him. Nate could imagine her calculations: Did *Newsworld* have enough to print?

"I'll think about it," she said finally. Then she walked away.

"Wow," Stacey Tarrant murmured in bemusement. "Jamie would be amazed at all this, don't you think?"

Kerry smiled. "Maybe at me. 'What are you doing?' I can imagine him saying."

They were in the back of Kerry's limousine, cruising toward the skyline of Sacramento. The motorcade had met her plane at a private airstrip so that the two of them would have time to talk. Since Jamie's death they had seen each other rarely, but a certain affinity had developed, a shared understanding. Stacey was a perceptive woman. To a degree that surprised him, Kerry could be direct with her, at ease. It reminded him of Lara.

He turned to the window, watching the towers of the city, light and shadow in the failing sun.

"Do you ever get frightened?" she asked him.

Kerry nodded. "Who's out there? you ask yourself. Someone. But you don't know who, or where."

Stacey tilted her head. "Then why did you decide to run?"

"It's complicated," he said. "If I had a woman I loved, or children, would I have done this, knowing what happened to Jamie? I'm not sure." He paused, trying to explain. "Because I was his brother, some people wanted me to run. Then I looked at the others. The Republicans have all the answers, but too often we disagree. Mason has no answers. What does he believe? What does he *feel*? I've seen him mist up at the funerals of people he despised, show righteous indignation because some pollster told him to. I can't tell which are more promiscuous—Dick's emotions or his beliefs." Kerry shook his head. "I can think of others who might be better than both of us. But here I am, doing the best I can."

Stacey gazed down, her expression pensive. "But you wonder if you're good enough."

"Yes. All the time."

She gave him a long look. "That's something Jamie could never admit."

"Why should he have?"

"Your brother?" Her voice was quiet. "So cool and self-possessed? Because he was afraid of all sorts of things, including being known. I think Jamie was afraid he was this terrible fraud, a self-invented Kennedy, the son of people he could never talk about. But you were probably too young to see that."

The image of a tormented Jamie startled Kerry. "Maybe there were clues," he said at length. "But I could never read them."

Stacey's smile seemed wistful. "I'd have given a lot to hear him say what you just did. Self-knowledge is a gift, Kerry, if you've got the courage for it. It's another reason you should be President."

In the hushed, efficient progress toward their public moment together, Kerry considered her anew. She seemed settled, at peace. Her career was successful, her marriage happy, and she had a daughter, who must now be close to three. For a moment, too private and too sad to speak of, Kerry thought again of Lara. And then he felt the motorcade slow and saw that they had slid into Sacramento.

THE park in Old Town was three blocks square, with a generous lawn. The Secret Service had roped off the borders and was funneling people through magnetometers. Since early morning Kerry's detail had swept the area for bombs, closed the windows of adjoining houses, and secured those homes with a line of fire to the speakers platform.

Clayton stood with Special Agent Peter Lake, watching supporters carrying KILCANNON FOR PRESIDENT signs and, to one side, a section for the curious, the hostile. To Clayton there were far too many men with grim faces and hard eyes, too many signs like the one that read TERMINATE KERRY KILCANNON. The air crackled with tension.

"Stacey Tarrant," Peter murmured. "The anniversary of his brother's death. A speech on gun control. For nuts it's like an alignment of the planets." He nodded toward the crowd. "The Internet was full of stuff like 'Every gun owner should give Kilcannon the reception he deserves.' "

Clayton turned to him. "Did Kerry tell you why he wouldn't wear the vest?"

"All he said was, 'It wouldn't stop a head shot, would it?' It was the nearest he's come to mentioning his brother." Turning to the adjacent houses, he murmured, "He's right, in a way. It could happen. Especially with someone who doesn't care if he lives or dies."

Peter fell quiet. Clayton gazed out at the demonstrators, their numbers swelling.

Especially with someone who doesn't care if he lives or dies.

Now he watched Stacey Tarrant appear on the stage. Slender and erect, she waited out the applause, then let the silence hold for seconds. "Many of you," she told Kerry's supporters, "are survivors of tragedies involving guns, who've had to go on with your lives. No one needs to explain that to Kerry Kilcannon." Turning to Kerry, she finished simply, "The President we deserve—Kerry Kilcannon."

He stepped forward. "You're next," a rough voice called out amidst the cheers. "You're next."

Instinctively Clayton scanned the rooftops, then turned to watch Kerry again.

"Today," Kerry began softly, "is the anniversary of a death."

The crowd was hushed.

"His name was Carlos Miller," Kerry went on, "and he was nine years old. He was murdered in this park, in a drive-by shooting, committed by a racist with an AK-47. He died, as people die every day in this country." Kerry's voice rose. "Last year over forty thousand Americans were killed with firearms. One hundred and ten people *every day*."

He paused, letting the crowd absorb this. "In New Hampshire," he told them, "I promised you a program. Here it is.

"First, everyone who owns a gun should be required to carry a license, conditional on completing a course in firearms use and passing a safety test."

The demonstrators unleashed a wave of jeers and catcalls.

"Second," he continued in a steady voice. "We should ban any weapon whose sole purpose is to kill people—semiautomatic weapons, cheap handguns, cop-killer bullets."

There was a startling riptide of emotion—Kerry's supporters screaming their encouragement, the demonstrators trying to drown them out, faces filled with rage.

Through the public-address system Kerry's voice carried above their taunts. "Every person who owns more than ten weapons should be required to have an arsenal license. And if you sell a gun outside the law, your license goes."

"You go," a demonstrator shouted, and then the cry became a ragged chorus. *"You go, you go."*

Stopping, Kerry stared at his audience. "For all those who have died," he said, "we have work to do."

The applause rose, drowning out the jeers. Suddenly Kerry was in the crowd, shaking hands, stopping to talk to the families of victims, looking into each face as if no one else were there. Guided by agents, Kerry headed toward his limousine. When he slid inside, to find Clayton rather than another politician, Kerry slumped down in the seat, relief washing over him.

After a time they were gliding down the highway toward the airstrip, causing traffic jams on the entry ramps blocked by motorcycle cops. Kerry imagined the frustrated commuters.

"I hope you put those MASON FOR PRESIDENT stickers on our bumpers," he said to Clayton.

Clayton emitted a short laugh, but his tone was without humor. He folded his hands across his stomach. "Cutler cornered Kit today. He wants to discuss a 'personal matter' with you. You've got three days, or they'll go with what they have."

Kerry felt his anger return. "Will they now? Without specifying the question? Tell Kit to wait him out."

"Unless you've decided what to do, time doesn't help."

Kerry gazed at the floor. "Imagine being Lara," he said at last. "Waiting for me to decide. For both of us."

Clayton's eyes were veiled. "There's something else. About Mason.

We have a tip from a cop in Darien, where Mason started out in politics. It's wife beating, Kerry."

Kerry could feel his own astonishment. "Jeannie?"

"She called the police, our man says, then filed a complaint. But Mason had the files sealed."

"This must have been years ago," Kerry murmured.

"Over twenty. We're checking everywhere they've lived since then to see if there's something fresher." Clayton paused a moment. "If Mason's the one who fed the Lara story to *Newsworld,* this should be enough to keep him from giving it to anyone else."

"*If* it was Mason," Kerry retorted. "But we don't know that."

Clayton's voice became emphatic. "If Dick beat Jeannie, does it matter who leaked Lara's story? It won't matter to the press."

Kerry stared at him. "It matters to *me.*"

"But should it? The result's the same—he looks worse than you do." Clayton's tone was soft again. "Kerry, I'm trying to be practical. You don't deserve to lose because of Lara."

Kerry watched the headlights cutting through the darkness, lighting the edge of Mather Field. On the tarmac his plane was waiting to fly them to San Francisco. He thought of Jeannie Mason and her family and then his own family long ago.

"The President was right," he said. "You think you know what it takes to run. But you don't."

Beside him, Clayton stared ahead. "And so?"

"Find out what else is there."

AT TEN forty-five in San Francisco—one forty-five a.m. in Newark—Clayton told Carlie how much he loved her and slowly put down the telephone.

They had a deal: No matter how late, Clayton could call. She missed him, of course, but there was something else neither needed to say—that Clayton did not sleep well without hearing that the twins were fine. Since the death of their son, Ethan, for Clayton not to ask felt like an act of carelessness.

Tonight, as so often, Carlie asked how Kerry was.

This association, too, was something they both understood. When they were at the hospital, waiting for their son to die, Kerry had stayed up with them. Carlie was the one person with whom Clayton had shared the deepest secret of Kerry's life. When Clayton told her Lara was back, Carlie emitted a long sigh. Not for the politics of it, but for Kerry himself.

Go back to Washington, they had told him after Ethan's funeral. *We'll be all right.*

If Kerry had stayed with them, Clayton wondered now, would it ever have happened?

Restless, Clayton turned on the television, the nightly tracking polls next to him on the bed. In five minutes of channel-surfing he saw two "Mason for President" ads stressing the Vice President's "consistent support for every woman's right to choose." The local CBS station featured Mason himself at a breakfast in San Francisco for entrepreneurial women.

The telephone rang.

"Looked at the numbers?" Jack Sleeper asked without preface.

"Oh, yeah," Clayton answered. "Still down three percent state-wide. But Kerry was strong all day."

"Clayton, among pro-choice women the gap's widening." The pollster's voice was firm. "I think we should do a pro-choice event in San Francisco, where the problem's worst."

Tired, Clayton stared at the poll numbers. "I'll talk to Senator Penn," he said. "San Francisco's her base, and we damn sure need her help."

SEAN Burke stared at the television, transfixed.

Kilcannon was in shirtsleeves, standing on a platform before a crowd of farmers, suddenly speaking from Sean's heart. "If warranted," Kerry said, "the death of the murderer may follow the murder of the innocent."

He understands, Sean thought. He knows that I am coming for him, that God's law imposes death on the murderers of children. That his own death is retribution.

Absolved, Sean shivered.

The picture changed. Now Kerry stood in a park, his every word an accusation.

"We should ban any weapon whose sole purpose is to kill people."

Sean felt a sudden wave of nausea. He hurried to the bathroom. When he bent over the sink, spasms racking his body, his spittle was flecked with blood.

Sean dried his face. The lesson life had taught him, he remembered, was to trust no one. Least of all the street kid who had promised him a gun.

Wiping his mouth, Sean swallowed an antacid pill.

ALONE in her room, Lara could not stop crying. It was as if all her strength had been for those who watched her watching Kerry, and when they were gone, she had none.

"I love you," she had imagined telling him. "I want to be with you." Imagined this a thousand times after it was too late. Imagined being selfish no matter what the cost.

Imagined it now. Like a child who did not like the story she had heard and wished to change the ending.

Except that it was *their* story—Kerry's and hers—and she had written the ending herself.

WASHINGTON, D.C.
May 1996–April 1997

THE first time Lara Costello met Kerry Kilcannon left her intrigued and more than a little curious. Though she was new on Capitol Hill, prominent politicians had long since ceased to impress her. She had experienced enough in California to develop an ear for fraud and hollowness, a sense of posturing. On that late spring afternoon she was waiting by the SENATORS ONLY elevator while the Senate debated a proposed constitutional amendment barring desecration of the flag. All she wanted was a quote or two, and her story would be complete.

The door to the Senate swung open, and Ted Kennedy emerged, then Kerry Kilcannon. Which one to approach? Lara wondered, and then Kennedy headed toward the Senate meeting room, Kilcannon toward the elevator.

"Senator?" she said. "Lara Costello, *New York Times.*"

Kilcannon stopped. He was not tall—five ten at most. But what struck her was an incongruous youthfulness—a thatch of tousled hair, the slender build—and then the startling contradiction of his eyes: green-flecked blue irises, giving Lara the unsettling sense of a man who had seen more than someone twice his age.

"I guess you're new," he said, and held out his hand.

His handshake was cool and dry. "Two weeks," Lara answered.

Kilcannon smiled. "Another two, and you'll have had enough." He pushed the button to the elevator. "What can I do for you?"

"I wanted to ask you about the flag amendment."

Kilcannon gave a mock wince. "Isn't it sufficient that I have to *vote* on this thing? Now I have to tell you what I *think?*"

Lara could not tell whether this was teasing or an outright refusal. "I never noticed voting was the same as thinking," she ventured. "It's nice when someone does both."

Kerry cocked his head, appraising her. "Oh, well," he said. "Do you know how many actual cases of flag desecration we've had since 1776?"

"No, I don't."

"Roughly forty. About one every five years. Hardly an epidemic." Kilcannon shrugged. "They trot this out as a distraction. When you've been caught out shilling for the tobacco companies, as several of the sponsors have, it's good to become a patriot."

Surprised by his candor, Lara took out her notepad and began scribbling. "Does that mean you're against?"

Kilcannon did not smile. "A million or so people," he answered, "have died for this flag, not because they liked its colors, but because it stood for something. Like the right to express yourself, even in ways that are outright stupid." Pausing, he added with a trace of humor, "As I'll exemplify tomorrow, when I speak in opposition."

"Do you think you'll win?" she asked.

"Sure. The proponents need a two-thirds vote, and most of my colleagues think it's a bad idea."

The elevator door rumbled open. "Costello is Irish, the last time I noticed," he said.

"So am I, on my father's side. My mother's Mexican." She held out her hand. "Thanks for your time, Senator."

"De nada," he answered. "You may not need this, but if you want to spend a half day with me sometime, watching how this place works, give my office a call." He smiled.

Once more Lara was surprised. "I'd like that."

Kilcannon nodded briskly. "Then I'll be seeing you," he said, and was gone.

And so at nine in the morning roughly two weeks later Lara was settled into a chair in Kerry Kilcannon's office. Glancing around, she studied her surroundings. There were none of the vanity photographs typical of public men. Lara saw only three pictures: a white-haired woman who resembled James Kilcannon, a blunt-faced man with shrewd eyes and red-tinged gray hair, then a black family of five—a stocky father and a slender mother, merry-looking twin girls in their early teens, a sweet-faced boy who could not be over four.

"Are these your parents?" Lara asked.

"My mother." Kilcannon's voice was soft. "The man's my god-father, Liam Dunn."

No pictures of Dad, Lara thought, or brother. Or, for that matter, Meg Kilcannon. "And the family?"

"Friends of mine." He stood, suddenly restless. "Come on," he said. "I'll explain our schedule on the way."

For the next nine hours Kerry Kilcannon was constantly in motion—subcommittee meetings, huddling with aides to make decisions on various bills, a press conference on the lawn in support of school lunch programs, a private visit to the office of the Vice

President to discuss, Lara guessed, Kilcannon's role at the upcoming convention, lunch in the Senate dining room with a group of schoolboys from New Jersey, which Kilcannon seemed to enjoy even though the main topic was why the New Jersey Nets were so lousy.

As hours passed, Lara found herself impressed. Kilcannon's sense of humor remained keen, his attention to each person unflagging. And then he was off again. At six in the evening, leaving her with his office manager, he rushed to the Senate floor.

Two hours later Lara found herself chatting with an aide when Kilcannon reentered his office, suit jacket slung over his shoulder.

He stopped, gazing at her in astonishment. "You're still here?" he asked. "I'd have thought you'd tire of this."

Lara smiled. "The fun never stops."

He glanced at his watch, then seemed to come to a decision. "For me," he answered, "it stops when I'm hungry. The least I can do is buy you dinner."

KINKEAD'S had a light, airy atmosphere. Recognizing Kilcannon, the young woman at the front found them a corner table.

"Power," Lara told him, "is never needing reservations."

Kilcannon smiled. With his public day ended, he seemed at ease. "Now that we've got the table," he answered, "I'm tired of being me. I know all about myself, and if I ever forget something, I can read the *Times*. But all I know about you is that you're curious about what makes people the way they are."

"What should I tell you," she parried, "that I'd ever want you to know?"

He laughed, softening his retort. "Why you're bothering our nation's leaders—questioning our motives, discovering awful truths. Wasn't there a law school back where you come from?"

"That *is* patronizing, Senator. And there was, actually—Stanford. I even thought about it. But it was time to work."

"Why?" he asked. "For someone as bright as you are, I'd have guessed there'd be scholarship money."

Lara nodded. "That wasn't the problem—I'd been on scholarship since second grade. I needed to *make* money, not take more."

The waiter came. They chose their entrées, and Kilcannon ordered chardonnay. "So you were tired of being broke?"

"No," she answered. "I was tired of my *mother* being broke."

Kilcannon tilted his head. "What does she do?"

"Clean other people's houses, watch other people's kids. And raise four more of her own." Even now, Lara realized, she could not speak of her mother's sacrifice without emotion.

"And your dad?"

Was a tall man with eyes like mine, Lara thought, younger in my memory than you are now. "Who knows?" she answered. "When I was ten, he took off with someone else." She gave a dismissive shrug. "I've tried hard to make him irrelevant."

She felt Kilcannon study her. "You never can, I think," he said. "Better to ask what that did to you than pretend it was nothing."

His eyes held no judgment, only interest. Suddenly Lara realized that this was remarkable. No politician had ever asked Lara for a piece of *herself.*

Briefly Kilcannon added, "My father was a difficult man. Still is, in fact."

The delphic remark made Lara smile. "Actually, you've hit a prejudice of mine. The last thing I want is to be my mother, or for my father to be the model for my husband. If I ever have one of those, I'm demanding self-knowledge on arrival."

Kilcannon laughed. "How old are you? Twenty-seven, twenty-eight? You may have to wait awhile."

"Are you speaking from experience?"

"Of course. When I was twenty-eight, I was married and even more clueless than I am now. As Meg could tell you."

It was his first reference to his wife, Lara realized. Though amiable enough, it revealed little. "Does *she* want you to be President?" she asked.

"Meg?" Kilcannon shrugged. "Would you? Like you, Meg has her own life. It's part of what makes politics so hard."

Dinner arrived. As he offered her a portion of his calamari, accepting a little of her tuna in exchange, Kilcannon said, "I still don't know how you became a journalist."

Sitting back, Lara took in the light and shadow of the restaurant, felt the glow of the wine. " 'How I Became a Journalist,' by Lara Costello. 'I became a journalist because . . .' "

"Yes?"

"Because when I was small, I liked to read—everything, even the newspaper. So our parish priest in San Francisco helped me get a scholarship to one of the best schools in the city, Convent of the Sacred Heart. I became the star of the school newspaper."

"So you don't wish you could go back, do something else?"

"No. I like journalism a lot. If I went back anywhere, it might be to where I started."

Kilcannon put down his fork. "Why? What would you do?"

"Maybe something more about people and what they need, not just politicians." Lara finished the glass of wine. "When I first worked for the San Francisco *Chronicle,* I did a series on migrant workers—I speak Spanish, so it helped. I wrote about the conditions in the fields. It got a state journalism award. The only problem is, four years later it's still the work I'm proudest of."

Saying this, Lara realized it was so. She felt Kilcannon watch her across the table.

"If that's true," he said after a time, "you won't want it to be true four years from now. It seems you've done enough for other people."

To her surprise the simple statement touched her. Then came a more unsettling thought: that she had enjoyed Kerry Kilcannon's company more than she had her recent run of young male friends. It was odd that she seemed more comfortable with a well-known Senator, except that he felt more comfortable with himself. When the waiter came with the check, Lara said, "Let me."

Kilcannon shook his head. "It's all covered by campaign funds," he assured her. "From foreign donors."

"A story," Lara answered. "At last."

Leaving the restaurant, they stopped on the curb outside. "Can I give you a ride?" Kilcannon asked.

The thought of asking for anything more set off an internal alarm in Lara, fear that she had lost her distance. "No," she answered. "I can take a cab." She held out her hand. "Thank you, Senator. I enjoyed my orientation. Dinner, too."

Kilcannon gave a mock wince. "Kerry," he said. "And whatever you decide, Lara, good luck."

THE next time Lara talked to him was in August 1996, at the Democratic Convention in San Diego.

Lara had never covered a convention before, and her reaction ranged from amazement to amusement. There was security everywhere—cops on motorcycles, streets blocked off, cars being checked for explosives. Inside, the hall was another world altogether, insulated and surreal: balloons, banks of klieg lights hanging from the rafters, skyboxes for the networks, hospitality suites awash in liquor and canapés, the mass of delegates half listening to empty rhetoric. The purpose was to re-coronate the President and Dick Mason with as little fuss as possible. The problem was Kerry Kilcannon.

She saw him on the convention floor, surrounded by delegates who wanted to shake his hand, to get an autograph. The electricity around him reflected Dick Mason's well-known belief that Kerry was positioning himself to fight him for the presidential nomination in four years' time. The Vice President's minions had already punished the New Jersey delegation for Kerry's anticipated sins in the petty, telling ways through which an incumbent could play hardball: bad hotel rooms well away from the convention hall, limited invitations to parties and outside events, cramped meeting rooms.

But Kerry's immediate sin was his refusal to submit any speech he might give to Mason's handlers for approval. The result was that unless Kerry relented, he was scheduled to speak for no more than ten minutes late Tuesday night, well after the network coverage had stopped. It was, as Nate Cutler quipped, "a special place in media purgatory."

Now Lara darted between two delegates and confronted him, tape recorder in hand.

Kerry gave her a sardonic grin, then gazed up at the skyboxes. "Like a trough for special interests, isn't it? Imagine the migrant workers they could feed."

As was often true with him, Lara thought, beneath the irony lurked a more serious point. "I hear you're staying at a Motel Six, Senator. In Tijuana."

He laughed with what seemed genuine amusement. "Only until they find us something worse."

You don't mind this, Lara thought suddenly. You think Mason looks scared, and you enjoy being an underdog. "Senator, do you think that your problems over speaking time have to do with the year 2000?"

He looked at Lara, then spoke in a serious voice. "The President and Vice President have an election to win. I'm here to support that effort. It's just that sometimes there are differing priorities. I didn't go into politics to secure a place on prime-time television. People expect better."

"Have you said that to the Vice President?"

"Oh, I think he understands." Kilcannon smiled. "But if you really care to know, I'll tell you what I think I'm doing. Off the record."

Lara nodded.

"Mason's a tactical politician," Kerry went on. "He reacts to pressure, not to core beliefs. If I reach people he's not reaching, maybe he'll begin taking reform more seriously, just to head me off. I'll have moved the party without ever having to run."

"Do you think you can?"

"Perhaps." Kerry's gaze fixed on some middle distance. "The problem with confrontation is picking the right issues. Or else I'm just a nasty Irishman who likes a fight. I don't want that."

And then he was off, shaking more hands.

It was nine thirty when Kerry Kilcannon walked to the podium. Back East it was half past midnight, and network television coverage had ceased. Watching from the press section with Nate Cutler, Lara could see that the delegates were tired. But no one knew what Kilcannon would say. By setting himself apart, he symbolized what many delegates were craving—daring, conviction, spontaneity.

"*Ker-ry . . .*" It began as a ragged chant from the New Jersey delegation, slowly spreading.

With a diffident smile Kerry held up his hand, signaling the crowd to stop.

"*Ker-ry, Ker-ry . . .*"

Kerry held up his hand again. "I've got ten minutes," he called out, "so I'll try to be succinct. I'm here to support the President and Vice President. They deserve all the commitment we can offer. And I will do everything in my power to help ensure their reelection."

Waiting, Kerry let the applause build, the sense of reassurance, and then said crisply, "But I also want to talk about the future."

"Well," Lara said, "so much for fervent praise."

Kerry's face was intent now. "There is a terrible disconnect in this country. People don't trust their leaders. More and more, people don't believe we have a program for change. They're no longer sure what we stand for."

Nate whistled softly. The delegates from Connecticut—Mason's people—seemed suddenly restive.

"If this party deserves to lead," Kerry went on, "we must embrace certain truths. That racial discrimination still exists and that we need the courage to challenge it. That too many lives are warped by violence. That too much of our prosperity is built on low wages and shattered dreams. That, in the end, *we* are a family, charged by decency and self-interest to care about every American."

Though he spoke to thousands, Kerry's tone became direct, intimate. "Maybe," he went on, "if we not only say these things but act on them, we will regain the trust we've lost. But we will never be free to act on them unless we face one more fact—that the way we raise campaign money is hopelessly corrupt."

Pausing, Kerry gazed up at the skyboxes and luxury suites, and then his voice cracked like a whip. "How can we inspire trust," he demanded, "when the best we can say for ourselves is that the other party's worse? No wonder people are so fed up."

The audience was silent—startled, Lara thought, by his bluntness, the implicit demand that the President and Mason take the lead.

Kerry stood straighter, scanning the convention floor. "Half of our citizens have already stopped voting." Now his voice became cutting, angry. "What else do they need to tell us? How much more clearly can they spell out their despair? It's about *freedom,* the special interests say. But how many of *you* are 'free' to spend ten thousand dollars to influence a political party? This is the freedom to corrupt, and it is slowly destroying our democracy."

"Well," Nate murmured, "he's off the reservation now."

"Ending it," Kerry went on, "is a moral imperative. I ask all of you to join that effort."

There was a moment's silence, and then the applause began, delegates clapping, stomping their feet, to acclaim a party leader who, for at least this moment, had transformed their convention. After several minutes it showed no sign of ending.

Nate looked at his watch, timing the applause. "He'd better enjoy it now," he remarked. "Mason will cut his throat if he can. And if Kilcannon wants to run, where's the money coming from?"

Another reporter turned to him. "Of course he's running, and he'll find the money somewhere. He's got the name, after all."

It was more than the name, Lara thought. As she remembered him, James Kilcannon had been handsome, elegant, cautious. Kerry was the passionate one, the dangerous one, the Kilcannon who might change the party and challenge the system, perhaps destroying himself in the process. In Washington, Lara felt, there would be no safe place for Kerry Kilcannon.

TWO months later Liam Dunn died, as Kerry's father had, of a sudden massive heart attack.

He had risen early, Kerry's mother told him, for his usual walk around Vailsburg. As on every day the walk had ended at Sacred

Heart, where Liam asked God for the wisdom to be a decent man in a complex world. Then he had driven downtown to party headquarters and died at his desk.

"What better way?" his mother had asked simply.

"No better," Kerry had answered. But when he put down the telephone, he asked that his calls be held, and he sat alone in his office, feeling the hole in his heart.

SACRED Heart was overflowing as it had not been for years. Lara went to the service with the local *Times* reporter. Liam Dunn had been an important man in New Jersey politics and Kerry Kilcannon's mentor. The *Times* believed there was a story in his passing.

The mayor and the governor sat in the first pew, as did several Congressmen. Next to Liam's family was Kerry, with a gaunt, handsome woman Lara recognized as his mother and a pert, pretty one with auburn hair—his wife, Lara assumed. Meg did not seem to speak, nor did she turn to console her husband.

The priest's tribute was warm, as was the eulogy given by Liam's oldest son, who spoke of Liam the husband and father. When Kerry rose, it was to recall the public man.

"Liam Dunn," Kerry said, "left far more than a legacy of kindness—the belief, in spite of all we hear and read, that politics could be an honorable adventure. That in politics, courage and practicality need not be enemies, and that without the other, either one is insufficient."

The church was quiet, mourners nodding. As Kerry's gaze swept over them, he looked incalculably sad. In that moment Lara thought that who he tried to be, what he tried to live up to, involved far more than a murdered brother. And believing that, she felt for Kerry.

After the service the mourners came to the two-story wooden home Liam had lived in most of his life. Reporters were welcome, Liam's son Denis assured her, so Lara found herself there late into the night, talking to neighbors and local politicians.

The house was jammed with people, and the tables were covered with food and drink and photographs of Liam. The mood was as

complex as death itself—brave, nostalgic, sad—and laughter mingled with the voices of recollection. Lara had no chance to talk to
Kerry. He was trapped in his role of public man—shaking hands,
speaking softly, smiling when that was called for.

Meg, Lara found, was an enigma. She seemed quite different
from the subdued woman Lara had noted at the funeral. Here she
was animated, seeking friends out, her warmth and energy offset
only by a somewhat short attention span, a smile that seemed to
flash and vanish. But it was not until Lara returned to the buffet
that she found herself next to Meg.

"Pardon me," Lara said. "You must be Meg Kilcannon. I'm Lara
Costello. I cover Congress for the *Times*."

The warmth in Meg's eyes receded. "That must be interesting,"
Meg said. "What brings you here?"

"Liam Dunn. He and the Senator seemed so close."

Meg nodded. "Kerry really cared about him."

It was a reasonable enough remark, Lara thought, but the distance in Meg's tone puzzled her. She could have been talking about
a rumor she had heard rather than something she felt. Then Meg
was off to seek new company, smiling again.

It was time to go, Lara thought. Glancing around the room, she
went to take leave of Denis Dunn, then stepped into the night.

On the lawn Lara saw a slim figure in shirtsleeves, gazing up at
the moon. She hesitated and then walked toward him. A few feet
away she stopped. There were tears on his face.

Kerry did not turn. "Without Liam, Lara, I don't know what
would have happened to me. When I was twelve—" His voice
broke and then was soft again. "When it comes to death, I'm no
philosopher. It's a weakness, sure."

Lara's fingertips grazed the sleeve of his shirt. "It's not a weakness," she said, and left.

AFTER Liam's death Lara felt a subtle change in her relationship
to Kerry Kilcannon. They entered that ambiguous zone of friendship in which a politician and a reporter use each other for their

own purposes and yet self-interest is tempered by genuine liking. Without saying so, they made up their own rules. Personal conversations were off the record; each would call the other with useful information. Lara was free to drop by his office.

"You've become the Kilcannon expert," Nate told her. "With luck, you'll be White House correspondent."

Even Kerry, who understood her colleagues well, teased her about this. "If I decide I'm never running," he told her, "you can always cultivate Dick Mason."

"Just let me know," she had answered. But Lara found Kerry intriguing for his own sake, a complex mix of toughness and sensitivity, fatalism and calculation.

"Do you ever want kids?" Kerry had asked her one day.

They were sitting on the lawn in front of Capitol Hill, enjoying the first break of spring; Lara had brought sandwiches. The conversation had meandered to Lara's biggest news—for the first time she had become an aunt. His question had followed, asked with the detached curiosity of one friend to another.

"Me?" Lara gazed out at the cherry blossoms, trying to form an honest answer. "I think so. Part of it, I guess, depends on who I'm with. I still haven't figured *that* out."

Kerry was quiet. Never, Lara realized, did he ask about her social life, nor did she ever speak of it. Instinct, perversely, spurred a question she could not resist. "What about you, Kerry? Did you ever want kids?"

Kerry picked a blade of grass. "Yes," he said. "It just never happened. And with politics . . ." He looked up. "At least I get to be godfather," he said, "to Clayton and Carlie's kids." His eyelids lowered, and then he looked at her directly. "The sad thing is that it takes so little. One interested adult can make such a difference, and many kids don't even have that."

There was a flatness in his voice, the tone he sometimes used, Lara had learned, when he was trying to gain distance from his own feelings.

"Ten years ago," he said, "when I was a prosecutor, a young boy got attached to me. I invited him to." His tone became quiet again. "I learned not to create too many expectations, and to know the ones I could keep."

The recollection was hurtful, Lara sensed. In profile, Kerry was still.

"At some point," he said at last, "Meg realized she didn't want a family. Perhaps being Jeannie Mason is not for everyone." He turned to her. "I mean, can *you* imagine being Jeannie?"

"No," she answered. "I can't imagine marrying a politician."

"That's just it. Meg didn't. My career was an accident, one she wanted no part of." He said more softly, "I'll always feel guilty about coming here when our marriage needed my attention most, and I'll always resent Meg for the feeling. I've never known who to blame or whether it would have been different."

And how will it be next year? Lara wondered. Or the year after that. In its second term the administration was foundering, raising anew the potential that Kerry could challenge Mason. "What if you do run?" she asked.

Kerry's expression became almost bleak. "It would make the human cost that much worse—for Meg and for me." Kerry looked into Lara's eyes. "You're part of the cost—the press. If I ran, you'd pick over Meg and our marriage until there was nowhere left to hide."

Lara met his gaze. "Would that really keep you from running?"

"Oh, it should." For a time he was silent. "After Jamie died, I wondered why it had happened that way. Why not me? Every day since then has seemed like a gift. Now the question is, What am I doing to deserve it? And what *should* I do?"

Oh, Kerry, Lara found herself thinking, there should be more to your life than that. Briefly she touched his arm. "Kerry, you deserve a life of your own."

When at first he did not answer, Lara thought she had gone too far. "I have part of a life," he said softly. "I came here as Jamie's brother and somehow turned into me. It's just that a piece is missing sometimes."

Lara felt a strange catch in her throat. Then Kerry glanced at his watch, breaking the moment. "Time to go," he told her.

A FEW days later Lara stopped by Kerry's office. "I came by to ask you out," she told him.

Kerry cocked his head. *"Meet the Press?"*

Lara smiled. "The Congressional Correspondents Dinner. It's six weeks from now, so this will give you plenty of time to rent a tuxedo."

"I *have* a tuxedo," he said with feigned hurt, and then adopted a teasing tone. "But don't you have a boyfriend or something?"

"You mean bring some guy I'm *dating?*" Lara answered in mock horror. "People would think I didn't *know* anyone. Whereas you're at the top of the food chain."

Kerry laughed. "I'd be happy to go."

Leaving, Lara stood on the steps of the Senate's Russell Building, savoring a warm spring day. It would be fun to spend an evening with him, sharing part of a world he knew well. Much much better than a date.

Five days before the dinner Kerry called her at home.

From the first few words Lara knew that something was terribly wrong. "I'm sorry," he said. "There's a problem. I'm in Newark, and I don't know whether I'll be back for the dinner."

Lara felt a stab of disappointment. "Is it Meg?"

"No. Meg's fine." His tone grew weary. "It's Clayton and Carlie's five-year-old, Ethan. He was climbing a tree in the backyard and fell somehow. The fall broke his neck."

"Oh, no," she said, and then asked softly, "Is he alive?"

She heard Kerry draw a breath. "Yes. As of now that's all they're hoping for." There was a long silence, and then Kerry said, "He's paralyzed, Lara."

Inwardly Lara winced. "Oh, Kerry."

"You just can't know—" His voice caught, then went on. "All I can do is be with them, here at the hospital, for as long as they want me."

What to say, Lara wondered, when nothing is adequate? "Don't worry about the dinner," she said at last, and then added quietly, "If you have a chance, call me. I mean, if you want to."

"Yeah." His voice was barely audible. "I'd better go."

When she hung up, Lara closed her eyes.

The next time he called her, Ethan Slade was dead.

It was the morning of the Congressional Correspondents Dinner. At her desk, Lara spoke in an undertone so that Nate and the others would not hear. "How are your friends?"

"As you'd expect. I don't know how anyone gets past this." He sounded utterly dispirited.

"I'm so sorry," she said softly. "For you, too. Where *are* you?"

"Here, in Washington. There were things I had to do, and it's better than doing nothing." Then, as if in an afterthought, he told her, "If you haven't traded me in, I'll come with you tonight."

Lara hesitated. "Are you sure?" she asked.

He said, "It would be better for me, I think."

Lara felt the warmth of being able, perhaps, to help someone she cared for. "We'll make it an early night," she promised.

THE dinner was in the banquet room of the Grand Hyatt—several hundred men in black tie and women in evening dresses, looking about to see who else was there and with whom.

To Lara's now practiced eye Kerry looked drawn, a little tired. He was good company, holding his own in conversation, but his eyes were distant. It was not a night, Lara felt certain, when he had much interest in the rituals of Washington. Leaning over, she whispered, "If you like, feel free to skip the after-dinner party."

As he turned to her, Lara had a sense of intimacy, a private moment amidst a very public event. "Do you need a lift?" he asked.

Lara nodded. "That would be nice."

When the dinner broke up, they left the room, stepping into the cool night. For much of the ride home they were quiet.

Lara lived in a converted brick town house just off Connecticut Avenue. Kerry found a parking place in front. Turning to her, he said, "Thanks, Lara. For asking me, and for leaving."

She hesitated. "Can I give you a cup of coffee?"

Kerry looked down, reflective. Then he glanced up at her again. "Do you have any cognac?" he asked.

LARA'S apartment was on the second floor. Entering with Kerry, she went to the kitchen, poured the cognac into wineglasses. When she returned to the living room, he was sitting on the couch. Lara handed him the glass, taking the chair across from him. "Tell me about the Slades," she said quietly.

Kerry gazed at the glass in his hand. He shook his head. "Clayton and Carlie . . . they were like automatons, both of them." His voice, soft and very sad, made the Slades' grief palpable.

"Did the funeral help at all?" Lara asked. "It does, sometimes."

"Not here. Though I'm not sure what would have helped." Kerry looked up. "The minister tried, but Carlie couldn't stop crying, and Clayton never cried at all. Maybe there's nothing that can explain the death of a five-year-old boy. But for me it was hollow, as so many rituals are." He swirled the brandy in his glass, watching it. "I kept thinking of how I felt when our party chairman put on this memorial dinner to honor Jamie—so meaningless, so full of platitudes."

The sheer pain of what he carried with him left Lara at a loss for words.

In her silence, Kerry seemed ashamed. "*Look* at me," he said with a trace of self-contempt. "Here it's Clayton's son who's dead, and I'm maundering on about Jamie. About myself, really. But I seem to have lost the habit of hiding from you. Or even wanting to."

Suddenly Lara felt conscious of everything—the distance between them, the dim light, the slight chill of the room. Their eyes met. Then Kerry stood abruptly, trying to smile. "I'd better go, Lara. Before I tax your patience."

In her confusion, Lara was still. "You don't have to," she said at last. "Not yet. Unless . . ."

Slowly she stood. Her eyes were wide, self-doubting. Kerry could feel the pulse in his own throat.

They were inches apart, not touching. Kerry gazed into her face, stunned and pale and so lovely that it almost hurt to look at her.

"Are you sure?" he asked. Then his fingers grazed the nape of her neck, and her eyes shut in answer.

Her mouth was soft, warm. Nothing mattered now—not Meg, not his career. Only her.

THE CAMPAIGN
Day Three

JUST before dawn Lara awoke.

In the dimness of her room, the confusion of past and present, Kerry was still with her. She could feel the turmoil of his emotions, the touch of his fingers, the soft timbre of his voice.

I want to see you again, he had said.

Rising, she went to the window, opening the blinds.

Not Washington at all. The sprawl of Oakland harbor, green water, the distant towers of San Francisco appearing in the dawn, silver fingers in the wisps of morning fog. A city she had always loved.

Turning from the window, she went to her suitcase for a fresh set of clothes.

NATE tossed clothes into the suitcase as he spoke into the phone. "What about his wife?"

"Ex-wife," Jane Booth corrected. "And probably a good thing, given her reaction. We knocked on her door and asked if she knew about Lara Costello. She looked blank. We spelled it out—right down to the date of the counselor's notes. Meg got very quiet and then said, 'That explains it, doesn't it.' "

Nate could not help but feel squeamish. He could imagine Meg Kilcannon's feeling of betrayal. "Meaning?" he asked.

"The divorce. Kilcannon asked her one week later. It was a surprise, Meg said." Jane's voice became dry. "It sounds as if she's bitter."

"Well," Nate said quietly, "I'm sure she is now. Probably enough to go on the record."

"We think so." Jane's tone was willfully oblivious. "But she doesn't know anything except for what we told her. The pressure's still on you, Nate."

"Do you have anything more for me?"

"One thing," Jane Booth reported crisply. "But it's good—from a woman who lived on Lara's floor. She only saw Kilcannon once. He was banging on Costello's door, obviously upset, the woman says. This went on for several minutes, Kilcannon not caring who saw or heard him."

"When was this?" he asked.

"About the time Costello spilled it all to the counselor. Just before Costello left the country for Africa."

What was Kilcannon doing there? Nate wondered. "Interesting," he said. "I'll get to Kit. This morning if possible."

KERRY faced them around the coffee table in Clayton's suite— Jack Sleeper, Frank Wells, Kit Pace, Clayton. It was seven a.m. The subject of Lara Costello hovered, unspoken.

"For two nights running," Clayton said, "the numbers show us soft with pro-choice women. Jack wants us to do an event."

"When?" Frank asked. "And what?"

"The what," Clayton answered, "is a rally in San Francisco featuring Kerry and prominent women who support him. There's a hole in our schedule the Sunday morning after the debate."

Kerry was quiet for a moment and then asked, "What's Mason doing?"

Frank's smile was thin. "New TV spots: Kerry's not a grown-up, Kerry's not pro-choice enough, Kerry's too extreme. The whole pitch is that Dick's calm, he's tested, he's ready."

"On Sunday morning in San Francisco?" Frank shot Kerry a

dubious look. "No one's working, nobody's downtown, and we've only got two days to organize a crowd. Advance will have to do one hell of a job with turnout, or we've got a major embarrassment and the press will be all over it—'Kilcannon Rally Fizzles.' "

Kerry took another hit of coffee. "I'll be over in San Francisco this morning. Any chance I can run by campaign headquarters?"

Clayton frowned. "A spontaneous drop-in? You're flying to L.A. at one, and the speech in South Central is key. Meeting the converted isn't worth a blown schedule."

Kerry nodded. "I understand. These people work hard, though, and I don't often get a chance to say I'm grateful. And if we're asking them to build an event overnight . . ." He sat back. "Tell them I may be dropping in."

FROM the press section Lara watched Nate stalk Kit Pace.

It was nine o'clock, Kerry's first event of the morning. They were in an auditorium at Boalt Hall, the law school at U.C. Berkeley. Kerry was speaking to minority students. Nate was in the pool today, in a cluster of reporters at the side of the stage trying to edge toward Kit. Seemingly unaware of him, Kit busied herself whispering to local reporters, no doubt dispensing favors—a piece of information, a slot to interview Kerry. But what this meant, Lara noted, was that there were always several bodies between her and Nate. Kit's performance was as intricate as dance.

As for Kerry, he was challenging his audience. "As a country," he told them, "we ask very little of our brightest young people. Except, of course, that you repay your student loans."

There was a ripple of laughter. "Isn't that enough?" a young black man called out.

Kerry grinned from the podium. "Too much, for some of you. When John F. Kennedy asked what you could do for your country, he wasn't thinking about compound interest."

The laughter grew. "But that's the point," Kerry went on. "When you graduate from this school, most of you with loans will be able to repay them. The cost of your education will be a down payment on a place among America's elite. Whether you are white or a person of color."

He glanced at his notes and then gazed out again. "What I propose today is a national service requirement. Two years, at any time before you turn thirty, to be spent in any way—the Peace Corps, charitable foundations, the military, or a wide range of public interest work—that you feel embodies your best contribution to our country and to a better society."

Lara watched the students stir in their folding chairs. Next to her, an L.A. *Times* reporter whispered, "There's something absolutely perverse about Kilcannon at times. Shouldn't he be talking about racial justice?"

"I don't think he will," Lara murmured. "They're too comfortable." Quickly she glanced at Nate, and in that moment she saw him catch Kit Pace.

Lara watched them. Forehead next to Kit's, he briefly whispered. Except for a nod, almost imperceptible, Kit was still.

Lara felt a sick feeling—alienation, fear, shame.

SEAN Burke hung up the telephone, and for a moment his thoughts took him back to Boston.

It had been the last call from the leader of Operation Life; the time was ten at night. "Sean," Paul Terris had said simply, "please don't come to meetings anymore."

Sean found that his chest was tight. "Why?"

"You know why. We may agree about goals, but we're far apart on means."

Sean stood. His sparely furnished room—a bed, a desk, the crucifix on the wall—felt shabby and small. "Because we're cowards," he said angrily. "We stand outside these chambers of death while they keep on killing babies."

"So what is 'militant action'? Acts of violence?" Terris's voice was so patient that Sean felt he was being treated like a child. "If we believe abortion is murder, how can we advocate murder?"

But it was clear to Sean. "These murderers violate God's law," he answered. "America executes murderers all the time. Except for the abortionists."

"Sean," Terris said coldly, "if any of us acts on that, decent people will turn their backs. And Operation Life may cease to exist."

Then, in his pain, Sean had seen the truth of his solitude—alone, he was free to act. He would show this club of pacifists the courage they lacked.

FEELING a hand on his shoulder, Sean flinched.

"John," Rick Ginsberg said now, "he's coming."

"Who?" Sean asked, then flushed at Ginsberg's smile.

"The Senator. He'll be here any minute."

Sean swallowed. No gun, he thought, not until four o'clock. That was what the street punk had told him.

Instinctively he patted the inside pocket of his army jacket, feeling for the knife. He had bought it in Boston, unsure of why he needed it, simply because he liked to feel its balance in his hand.

How long would it take, Sean wondered, to pull the knife from his jacket and plunge it into Kilcannon's heart? He clenched his jaw, imagining his hand falling short, the bullet entering his brain.

"Are you all right?" Ginsberg asked him.

All he could do was nod. He was afraid, far more so than when he executed the abortionist. Afraid of the look on Kilcannon's face. Afraid for himself, dying at Kilcannon's feet.

As Rick patted him on the shoulder, Sean turned toward the door. Through the glass he saw people clustered on the sidewalk— the receptionist, volunteers, men in sunglasses who looked like Secret Service agents. Then, as if in a silent film, a black limousine glided to a stop in front of them.

Three feet from the doorway Sean froze. An agent opened the car door. Slowly Kerry Kilcannon got out. Utterly still, Sean watched him through the glass.

Kilcannon waved briefly to the crowd. They moved toward him. As though caught in their vortex, Sean went out the door, eyes locked on Kilcannon's face. Next to Kerry, the agents watched the crowd. He could get to him, Sean suddenly thought, thrust the knife toward Kilcannon's throat before the agents shot him. If only he could see their eyes.

Then, reaching out to shake a hand, Kilcannon saw him. He seemed to hesitate.

Sean flinched, turning away, and scurried down the sidewalk.

Who was he? Kerry thought. Pale, shrinking from contact, with a face unlike the others—hungry, possessed, unsmiling. What was this odd flicker of fear, of recognition?

It was the instinct for danger that made him study faces, looking for the eyes of a man who, like the one who murdered Jamie, wished to take his life. But Kerry had looked into ten thousand faces and had no time to wonder.

He reached out to the blond-haired girl in front of him, smiling. "I'm Kerry Kilcannon," he said. "I wanted to thank you."

She took his hand, grinning like she might never stop. "I'm Kate Feeney," she told him.

Kerry squeezed her hand. "Thanks, Kate. I'll remember you."

SEAN ran. Chest pounding, he fought the sickness rising from his stomach as he dodged pedestrians startled by his panic. Stopping abruptly, he began to gasp. His body shook with coughing, eyes moist with anguish and humiliation.

Coward, he told himself. The frightened child he once had been had returned to claim him.

He reached the Tenderloin district at twenty minutes to four. The street punk was nowhere in sight.

Sean felt wasted, shamed, pathetic. He had run from his moment. Now Kilcannon was safe in his cocoon of security, and Sean had become the walking dead.

Across the street a prostitute with eyes like burn holes loitered on the sidewalk, a figure from hell.

Sean felt hard fingers on his shoulder. Turning, he saw the black street punk. His eyes were glassy, opaque. "I got your piece," he whispered, "in here." He touched the pocket of his pea coat. "But I ain't gonna sell it to you on the street."

Between a liquor store and a tenement hotel they found an alley lined with garbage cans, smelling of rotten food. The man walked a little behind Sean, prodding him deeper into the alley. The dank sunlessness seemed to change the chemistry in Sean's brain, sending a current to his nerve ends.

The man was at his back now. "Turn around," he said.

Even before Sean complied, he could feel the gun against his back.

The soulless eyes stared at him. "Your wallet, man."

Dead, Sean thought. Though his fingers trembled, his mind felt calm, almost peaceful. Slowly he reached for the inside pocket of his jacket. As he found the handle of the knife, he watched the man's eyes. Take your time, Sean told himself. You're already dead. He pulled the knife up to his collar, still hidden.

"Careful, man. Don't make me waste you."

With a flick of his wrist Sean turned the point of the knife to the punk's throat. His eyes shut against the bullet that would rip his stomach apart. "We're both dead," he whispered.

The punk blinked. "Man," he mumbled.

Sean jammed the knife into his throat. The gun clattered on the sidewalk. The punk stared at him, eyes stricken, knees buckling. Sean wrenched the blade out.

The man crumpled, falling onto his side.

Sean stepped back, staring. He wiped the knife on the sole of his boot, put it into his pocket, and reached for the gun.

It was oily, cheap-looking. But when Sean curled his fingers around the trigger, he saw the moment again, transformed: Kerry Kilcannon, eyes widening in fear as Sean aimed.

Slipping the gun into his pocket, he left the alley behind.

KERRY had spent the afternoon in Los Angeles galvanizing minority support. In the Mission District he spoke in shirtsleeves under a bright sun. It was a community under siege, but the crowd had been large and festive, primarily Latin, men and women in jeans and cotton shirts, chatting in Spanish. Later he'd stood on the steps of the Third Baptist Church in South Central and addressed the African Americans.

From his limousine he'd viewed rows of small stucco houses with barred windows, oil-stained asphalt lots, burned-out buildings, men loitering with boom boxes. But here and there were neighborhoods with well-kept lawns and no graffiti, where neighbors organized day care and health centers. This had given him hope.

Now he lay back in the bathtub, achy and exhausted.

Across from him, Clayton closed the lid over the toilet and sat. "Sorry," he said. "But there's no rest for the weary."

Kerry raised his head. "What's this about Dick Mason?"

Clayton clasped his hands in front of him. "We've got the police records," he said. "From Darien. They're from 1978. Jeannie Mason filed a complaint—Dick was drunk, he'd hit her before, and this was one blow too many."

What might have happened, Kerry found himself wondering, if his mother had called the police when he was young—or felt she could have? How might their family be different? "What did they do?" Kerry asked. "The cops."

"Went to the D.A. Who, as it happens, was a friend of Dick's. There was a quiet resolution—charges dismissed."

"Is there anything more recent?" Kerry asked.

"Not yet."

Kerry wiped his face. "Maybe Dick got counseling. If he hadn't, do you honestly think Jeannie would have stuck it out?"

"I don't know." Clayton stood, arms folded. "What I'm pretty sure I *do* know is that Mason's behind this Lara thing. That's why it's coming out now and why he wants the debate. To confront you before Tuesday."

"So plant this, you say. And hope somebody prints it."

Clayton frowned. "There's another problem. Nate Cutler got to Kit today. Unless you give him an interview in forty-eight hours, he says your refusal is a story in itself." Clayton exhaled. "And Kerry, that isn't an arbitrary deadline. It's the last day *Newsworld* can get a story into print."

Kerry turned away. The anger in him felt like a living thing.

"Tell Kit I'll see Cutler on Sunday," he said.

PUTTING down the telephone, Lara closed her eyes. She had called her voice mail at NBC. There was an oblique and carefully phrased message from a former neighbor. A reporter from *Newsworld* had visited, and the woman, disconcerted, had described something that perhaps Lara had never known: a man who resembled a prominent Senator, standing in the hallway, upset, unwilling to leave. He had called Lara's name through the door.

No, Lara thought, she had never known. She was already gone. There was no one on the other side of the door to hear him.

If only she could have seen their end in their beginning.

WASHINGTON, D.C.
April 1997–September 1998

THEY came to need each other's company, each other's thoughts. Sometimes a week or more went by without Lara's seeing him, but every night they would talk on the phone with the frustration of thwarted lovers, the directness of good friends.

By unspoken consent their days together were spent in the present, and in the present there was little they didn't share.

For over a year they had escaped discovery. If anything, Lara Costello's reporting on Kerry Kilcannon was more penetrating, analytical, alert to the prospect that his growing conflict with Mason over Kerry's causes—campaign reform, health insurance for children—might lead him to seek the presidency. Sometimes Kerry would joke about this in passing. But he knew the edge to her coverage, in Lara's mind, preserved her integrity.

"I THINK YOU'RE RIGHT," NATE Cutler told her at lunch one Saturday. "He's going for it. The positions he's taking are like a blueprint for running against Mason."

Lara finished her bite of seared tuna. "Maybe he believes in them. I'm sure he does, actually."

Nate nodded. "Then he's that much more likely to do it and save us all from boredom. Races in both parties—a reporter's dream."

Lara looked down, appetite lost.

He's going for it.

And then it would all close around him: the need for Meg, the Secret Service, the heightened scrutiny of Nate and all their peers. There would be no place left for her.

When she went to Kerry's apartment that evening—fearful, as always, that someone might be following—the conversation was still on her mind. They sat together on the couch, shadows filling the room, and Lara realized that he, like she, must feel time closing in on them.

"Penny for your thoughts," he said.

Lara shook her head. "Give me time," she answered. "I'm trying to sort things out."

Kerry did not press her. He had the grace of silence, Lara thought, a gift she valued.

"Lara," he said at last, "I never thought you wanted more than what we have. But if you ever do . . ."

"I'll tell you. For now, I just need to be quiet." She burrowed against him and after a time fell asleep to the crackle of dying embers in the fireplace.

It was only when he brought her a second cup of coffee the next morning that she said, "There's something I've been meaning to tell you."

He sat beside her on the bed cross-legged. "What is it?"

"I've had a feeler from NBC. Believe it or not, they may want me to do television."

"Oh, I believe it. How do *you* feel?"

"Ambivalent. I did a little of that in college, so it's not completely bizarre." She sipped her coffee. Her tone of reticence, unusual for her, unsettled him.

Lara then turned to him. "They'd send me overseas, Kerry. If that's what I prefer."

It startled him. "Do you?" he asked.

She paused, a troubled look in her eyes. "I would," she said, "except for you. I've been telling myself how stupid that is."

Kerry looked down. Be fair, he admonished himself. Be her friend. He felt her hand gently touching his arm.

"Kerry, I didn't look for this. But we knew that sometime . . ." She shook her head.

Kerry took a deep breath. "I can't tell you what to do, Lara. All I know is how good you'd be. If it's what you want."

Slowly she intertwined her fingers with his, but for the rest of that Sunday they did not talk about it.

At dusk a storm closed in on them. The rain came in sheets, gusts of wind rattling the windows. Lara lit a candle on the coffee table.

From the radio in the background came the first bars of "A Summer Place." "Someone," Lara murmured, "has a sense of humor. Or maybe it's prom night."

Kerry kissed her. "Care to dance?"

The wind became a low insistent moan. In light and shadow the senior Senator from New Jersey and the congressional correspondent for *The New York Times* danced, their bodies lightly touching, confident for once that they could not be seen.

THE morning after Lara's first meeting with the president of NBC News, she knew.

She had been tired for several days—unusual for her. But going to bed early had not helped. This morning she felt nauseated.

Suspended between dread and disbelief, she walked to a pharmacy on Connecticut Avenue and bought a home test kit. Then she called in sick and waited for the kit to confirm what, with uncanny certainty, she already knew.

She was pregnant with Kerry Kilcannon's child.

She sat on the bed, so stunned, so overwhelmed that her emotions seemed to have the gravity of prayer.

There was only one solution. But her thoughts kept slipping to where they should not go—imagining Kerry, laughing and carefree, carrying their baby on his shoulders. Kerry, cast in the role of husband, a picture from an album. The fantasies of a woman who knew the truth, for both of them, even as her heart recoiled.

This was not an abstraction. She had come to love Kerry far more than she thought he knew, and to give him up would be hard enough. To abort their child was more than she should have to bear.

The telephone rang.

"Hi," he said. "Playing hooky?"

"Can I see you?" she heard herself ask.

As LONG as she lived, Lara thought, she would never forget his face at that moment. He gazed at her with such confusion, guilt, and love that no words could have captured it. Silent, she leaned against him.

As he held her, he murmured, "We need to think about this."

Lara closed her eyes. It was painful to feel the consequences hit him, knowing where they led. Leaning back, she took his face in her hands. "There's nothing to decide," she told him.

Gently he removed her hands and went to the window, gazing out at a crisp fall afternoon. He said softly, "There *is* something to decide. I want you to marry me."

Tears of shock came to her eyes. She felt herself caught between irrational hope and the harshness of their reality. "I can't," she managed to say. "You're already married, remember?"

Kerry bowed his head. "I'm well aware of that. But Meg and I should have divorced long ago."

"I think so, too. But you didn't. I don't want you because of a birth-control mistake."

He came to her, grasping her wrists. "But I want *you*. I love you, and I want our child."

"At any price?" Intently Lara looked into his eyes. "Instead of running for President, you'd be a running joke on Letterman. You'd probably lose your Senate seat. How can the ruin of your career be the premise for our marriage?" Lara drew a breath. "I don't want that for you. And I don't want that for me."

"Lara, there's another life involved." Kerry pulled her close. "It's not what we'd have chosen, I know that. But it's here. And if the Senate is the price I pay, I'm willing to pay it."

For the first time Lara felt angry. "Do you think this is easy for me?" she demanded. "You can say anything you like, and *I* still have to decide what's best. And then live with it."

Kerry considered her. Quietly he asked, "What else do you want from me?"

"I want you to *support* me, dammit." Tears sprang to her eyes again. "Please, don't make me do the right thing by myself."

Kerry turned away. "Am I supposed to lie about my feelings," he asked, "because *you're* the one who's pregnant? Doesn't this involve *me,* too?"

The justice of his question undercut her anger, even as she saw, with aching sadness, the chasm opening between them.

He took her hands. "Give us two weeks, all right? We'll both be a long time living with this. Whatever you decide."

Lara felt wrung out. All that was left was to let him hold her, to wish, with bitter longing, that she had never told him.

At four o'clock Kerry had to leave. He had speeches to give in the next few days, Lara remembered—in Philadelphia, Chicago, Denver, San Francisco. The world outside their secret spun on as before.

As he left, he kissed her. "I'll call you," he said. "Every night."

For two years she had counted on it. Now she felt a chill, an instinctive sad finality.

Give us two weeks, he had asked. But every day she felt the life grow inside her.

For three nights he called, not pressing. Every night she asked herself how she would answer if he said, "No matter what you decide, I'm leaving Meg." Every night she wondered why he had not, her decision growing harder, more scarifying.

The day he arrived in San Francisco, she stopped answering the telephone.

Sleepless, he called every hour. He would hear five rings and then the answering machine. "Please, Lara" he implored the spinning tape. "Wait until I get back." Kerry did not say the rest: that whatever she chose, he wished to marry her. That he would say in person.

By the morning he had called twelve times. His hopes for their child had turned to ashes.

IN THE waiting room Lara stared at the forms, her mind echoing with the sound of Kerry's voice. *Please, Lara.*

She had driven to Maryland alone. The clinic had promised privacy; it was small, discreet, anonymous. No one else was waiting.

Lara printed her name.

Please, I love you. I don't want you to face this alone.

Did she want counseling? the form asked.

I want Kerry, her mind answered as her hand scrawled, "No."

A nurse appeared—stout, benign, motherly. Mute, Lara handed her the form.

Looking from the papers to Lara, the nurse touched her gently on the shoulder. "We're ready."

They went to a small room without windows. Lara gazed at the operating table. "I'm sorry," she whispered. "I'm sorry." She did not know to whom.

WHEN it was over, the nurse wiped her forehead with a cool, damp cloth. "It's all right," she murmured. Trembling, Lara felt the nurse's fingers curl around hers. For the first few moments she felt hollow, light-headed.

"Our counselor's here," the nurse said in a tentative voice.

Dazed, Lara said, "I think I need to be with someone. Anyone."

The nurse helped her down a narrow hallway. Inside the last

office a short middle-aged woman with dyed-brown hair sat behind a desk. The counselor gazed at her with deep compassion. "I'm Nancy Philips," she said.

The door shut behind Lara, and she and the woman were alone. Tears ran down Lara's face.

"This can be hard," the woman said. "I know."

Lara told her everything.

When she returned to her apartment hours later, there were three more messages from Kerry. Dully, she listened to them.

From somewhere she summoned the strength to call NBC News and then the *Times.*

Her last call was to Kerry.

KERRY listened to her voice on his answering machine, sickened. She was leaving to go abroad. He should not feel guilty. They had loved each other, and no one had intended this. But now it was done.

"No," he said aloud. *"No."*

"I have to start over," Lara's voice went on. "Please, if you love me, don't make it harder—" Her voice broke. There was the click of the connection breaking.

Kerry hurried to her apartment. Parking by a fire hydrant, he ran to the door, out of breath. Softly he knocked. No answer. He rested his forehead against the door, heard nothing stir inside the room.

In a low insistent voice he began to call her name.

LARA next heard of him on the BBC, alone in a cramped apartment in Sarajevo.

Senator Kerry Kilcannon and his wife, the clipped voice said, were divorcing. Kilcannon had no comment, the report went on, but the divorce was not expected to prevent him from running for President, as was widely anticipated since his party's defeat in the off-year elections.

At least there was that, Lara told herself. If he had not lost everything, then neither had she.

"THIS is Lara Costello, NBC News, with the Kilcannon campaign in Los Angeles."

Kerry Kilcannon bolted upright in his bed. Lara's face vanished from the screen.

Hours before, he had fallen asleep with the television on, two briefing books for the debate beside him. Now dawn was breaking. Kerry struggled to retrieve the pieces of his life, the bricks and mortar of reason.

Lara was an image on the television, out of reach. He was in Los Angeles, on the morning of a debate in which, if Clayton's instincts were right, Dick Mason meant to trap him. It was six o'clock. He had twelve more hours to prepare.

And after that? A confrontation with Nate Cutler. And then a rally in San Francisco, to tame the demons Kerry had unleashed by saying that a fetus was a life.

Take each in turn, Kerry told himself. Until the debate was over, Cutler did not exist. Focus was the candidate's best friend, panic his worst enemy. He supposed this must also be true for Presidents.

CLIPPING articles from the San Francisco *Chronicle,* Sean Burke saw Rick Ginsberg, his hurried footsteps echoing as he went from volunteer to volunteer. "He's coming," he blurted to Sean. "Kerry. How much of the next day and a half can you give me?"

Sean felt Ginsberg's excitement hit him like a current. "All of it," he managed to say.

The volunteer coordinator rested a hand on his shoulder. "In the next twenty-nine hours we'll need bleachers, leaflets and people to pass them out, car pools, a crowd, and all of us to make as many calls as we need to make sure we *have* one. Plus we have to work with the Secret Service."

A second jolt hit Sean—his mission opening up for him.

Rick grinned. "This time, John, you'll meet him for sure."

IN HIS hotel room Nate Cutler sat tethered to his telephone.

Jane Booth's tone was businesslike. "We're trying to get ahold of Kilcannon's phone records, track down every dinner they ever had, every sighting at funny hours. Everything we find, I'll fax you by tomorrow morning at six. So you have it when you meet with him."

"And then?"

"If *she* lies, Nate, that's one thing. But if he lies about stuff like this, it goes to the integrity of a candidate for President."

"What if he refuses to answer?"

"At some point that becomes a story, too. If the details start to pile up, calling us sleazebags isn't going to keep this out of print." She paused a moment. "Tell me," Jane said evenly, "do *you* think Costello warned him?"

Nate considered the evidence. "Yes, probably."

"Then maybe he's seeing her, Nate."

"No way," Nate promptly responded. "Far too big a risk."

There was a long silence. "Start watching her," Jane ordered. "Especially late at night. You can always sleep on the plane."

THE studio was like all TV studios, Clayton decided. Sterile, brightly lit, smaller than it appeared on-screen. The audience— Asian, Latin, white, African American, men and women, young and old—was a carefully selected cross section of Los Angeles. The moderator, a longtime anchorman in the city, was talking with Dick and Jeannie Mason.

To Clayton these moments before a debate were another hollow ritual of politics: the candidates making idle chat, pretending that this was their idea of fun, that they had not come here, figuratively, to cut each other's throats. Clayton headed for Mason's campaign manager, Bill Finnerty, ready to fulfill his role in the charade.

Finnerty stood behind Jeannie Mason. As Clayton approached, he saw Jeannie give Kerry a brief hug and, with a sheepish grin and a roll of her eyes, murmur, "It's all so phony, isn't it?"

With a smile Kerry answered, "It's not too late for the two of us. We can just drop out and leave Dick to his own devices."

Jeannie smiled back. "Tempting, Kerry. But I've sort of gotten used to him." Her expression turned serious. "Good luck, though. As far as I'm concerned, the country could do worse than either one of you. Deep down, Dick thinks so, too."

Was this just a graceful remark, Clayton wondered as he passed them, or a subtle suggestion that Kerry might yet be her husband's choice for Vice President? It could be either. Whatever else Jeannie Mason was, she was a clever woman.

"HELLO, Bill," Clayton said, shaking Finnerty's hand. "How's tricks?"

Above his thin smile, Finnerty gave Clayton a quick, speculative glance. "Just dandy. Your man ready?"

Clayton shook his head. "He's too damned passive. I wouldn't be surprised if he winds up endorsing Dick."

Finnerty stopped smiling. As one professional speaking to another, he said, "It's been a tough race. Things happen, and you just have to go with it." He lowered his voice. "Tell Kerry we're sorry about what we're going to have to do to him tonight. I don't know if he'll ever accept this, but it really isn't personal."

Clayton felt himself freeze, heard his own silence as he stared into Finnerty's ice-blue eyes. Was this affirmation, Clayton thought, or the hoary stunt of spooking the opposing candidate in the last minutes before a debate? Or, worst of all, both.

Calmly Clayton put his hand on Finnerty's shoulder. "Don't worry about Kerry, Bill. But maybe you should apologize to Dick."

Finnerty gave Clayton a look of silent appraisal and then stuck out his hand again. Even before he shook it, Clayton had decided not to tell Kerry. For better or worse, Kerry's mind should be as clear as possible.

Crossing the soundstage, Clayton heard Mason say, "Well, Kerry, this is it." Then, on cue, the stage cleared and the debate began.

FOR the first thirty minutes, Lara thought, Mason dominated the debate.

She was aware of Nate Cutler sitting directly behind her in the press section, watching her. She controlled her nerves by taking copious notes. "American family," she scribbled now and glanced quickly at the stage.

Sitting beside Mason, Kerry listened as the Vice President continued to underscore that he was a parent and Kerry was not.

"Talk is cheap," Mason said dismissively. "But for Jeannie and for me our children have been the focus of our lives. That's why we've taken the lead in fighting for better schools—"

"*Public* schools?" Kerry interrupted. "Because as a parent—as opposed to a politician—you've never seen the inside of one. Like most parents, you don't want your kids going to schools that are overcrowded, underfunded, and unsafe. The question is what happens to other people's kids." Kerry leaned toward Mason. "I support higher standards for teachers. You oppose them. Why? Because the teachers union—one of your biggest contributors—opposes them. Even though many of our best teachers would tell you that *they* deserve better, too."

To Lara's relief, and for the first time, Mason looked momentarily off-balance.

"What this example points to," Kerry concluded, "is the need for comprehensive reform of our system of campaign finance. A fight in which you, Dick, have been conspicuously AWOL."

Mason leaned forward, achieving an expression of sober thoughtfulness. "I don't need any instruction from *you* when it comes to issues. I was leading the fight for our goals when your brother held the seat that you hold now and you were still in law school."

Sitting to the left of the stage, Clayton checked his watch. Mason was angry, Clayton saw, and so—at this condescending reminder of his debt to Jamie—was Kerry. Only ten minutes remained.

Abruptly Mason leaned forward again. "Let's talk about something that's not quite so speculative, Kerry. Let's talk about a woman's right to choose. Now's the time for truth."

Kerry stared at Mason.

"A woman's right to choose," Mason said accusingly, "is newly threatened by the Supreme Court. If you were President, would you appoint justices who share *your* belief that a fetus is a life?"

Kerry willed himself to stay calm. "I'd appoint justices who share my belief in the right to privacy. I'm not interested in personal beliefs but in legal philosophy—"

"What if the choice involved you?"

Stunned, Kerry froze.

Mason seemed to hesitate, as if looking into an abyss. Then the space between them closed, as if the studio, the audience, the press, no longer existed. He pressed on in a tighter voice. "Suppose *your* girlfriend wanted an abortion. Is *she* entitled to choose, Kerry? Or would you insist on your own beliefs?"

In a blinding instant Mason's intentions became clear to Kerry—to shake him so badly that he completely lost his composure. Sickened, he drew a breath. Kerry felt the feral atmosphere. He must stop this now. "Is this the level to which we've sunk?" he asked softly. "Should I ask if you still beat your wife?"

Startled, Mason blinked.

Kerry watched his face. He saw doubt become fear, sapping Mason's energy like a blow to the stomach.

"No answer?" Kerry inquired. "Then let me answer *you*. I support a woman's right to choose, period. But anyone with an ounce of compassion must acknowledge how hard that choice can be. That's what I'd feel—compassion. And, I hope, love."

FOR Lara the last few minutes were a blur. The debate became mechanical, scripted lines delivered to the camera. In the applause that ended it all, Kerry stood first, extending his hand to Mason. With a wan smile Mason took it. What lay between them would be settled elsewhere.

FOR THE CAMERAS, JEANNIE gave Kerry a perfunctory handshake, her blue eyes troubled. "What are you *doing*, Kerry?" she murmured. "Is it what I think?"

Kerry felt tired, drained. Glancing around them, he saw that they had a moment's privacy. "Do you know what Dick's doing?"

She gave a brief shake of the head. "No," she said. "But he's frightened. He never thought you'd come this far."

Kerry exhaled. "And you never thought I'd stoop this low?"

For a moment her eyes shut. Then she opened them, looking into his. "He never did it again, Kerry. You should know that."

Heart heavy, Kerry watched her return to Mason's side, smiling for the cameras.

WATCHING Kilcannon on the screen, Sean felt isolated, as if the enthusiasm of Kate Feeney and the others came from a party he was watching through a window.

When Kate took his hand, he flinched.

"Don't you think Kerry was good?" she asked. "He's so human, and Mason's like this stiff."

Rick Ginsberg emerged from the celebrants, suddenly businesslike. "You two," he said to Sean and Kate. "Stick around—we've got a meeting with the Secret Service to plan tomorrow's rally."

Sean could only nod.

"BASED on a sampling of two hundred Californians," the anchorman said, "forty-five percent of viewers feel that Senator Kilcannon won the debate, thirty-nine percent feel the Vice President did better, and sixteen percent called it a draw."

Kit Pace and Kerry were huddled around the television screen in Kerry's suite.

"You were so good," she murmured.

To Kerry the words seemed retrospective, as if his campaign were already over. He smiled faintly. "It sounds like a eulogy, Kit."

She turned to him, shaking her head, her mouth set in a determined line. "Not to me."

The door opened, and Clayton walked in. He glanced at Kit. "Mind if I take a few minutes with Kerry?"

Kit looked at him a moment, questioning, then congratulated Kerry again and left.

"I've talked to Finnerty," Clayton informed Kerry. "They're laying off you and Lara. They'll return the counselor's notes, with no leaks to anyone else."

"A little late," Kerry said with fresh, cold anger. "The story's pretty close to the surface. And they can't control that counselor."

Clayton frowned. "At least they're motivated. I told Finnerty that if this hits print, we're giving Dick's police files to the tabloids."

Kerry examined the rug. "I don't think I could," he said slowly. "Not for Dick's sake, but for Jeannie's." He looked up again. "How did the counselor's notes get to them, and how did they leak this?"

"They got them from the counselor through the Christian Commitment. Finnerty didn't want their fingerprints on it, so he gave it to the Republicans and to Anthony's Legions."

Kerry felt his stomach clench.

"The Republicans decided they'd rather run against Mason than you."

"Which means that they can use this to cripple me in the general election." Kerry's voice softened. "So it's over. If I manage to win, I find an excuse to withdraw."

Clayton's face took on a stubborn cast. "Let's think about it overnight."

Despite his gloom, Kerry felt empathy for Clayton, and fondness. It was his pragmatic, earthbound friend who, for once, did not want to face reality.

"Somehow we'll go on," Kerry told him. "I've got the Senate, and you've got Carlie, two great daughters, a fat bank account."

The telephone rang. Slowly Clayton rose to answer it. To judge from the clipped dialogue—a series of pointed questions—Clayton managed to sound much like himself.

Hanging up, he turned to Kerry. "The polls have you up three points," he said. "And you're holding among women."

In frustration, Kerry stood, hands jammed in his pockets. "Mason doesn't deserve this nomination. I do."

"Your life just caught up with you, Kerry. The whole thing—your marriage, and Lara."

Kerry turned to him. "I have to see her," he said. "If she's willing."

It was not a question. With a level gaze Clayton answered, "You know what I think."

Kerry folded his arms. "Well, things have changed, haven't they." His voice lowered. "Imagine how she feels tonight. What would you do if you were me?"

Clayton shook his head, still watching him. He said finally, "Peter Lake could probably bring her here. If that's what you're asking."

CLOSE to hyperventilating, Sean could not stop watching the Secret Service agent. His name was Ted Gallagher. White-haired, affable, and alert, he sat next to the advance person, Donna Nicoletti, at the head of three tables usually reserved for phone banks. The others occupied chairs along both sides—three San Francisco cops, two sound-system specialists, several volunteers. Pinned to a sketch board was a diagram of Justin Herman Plaza, with a schedule for the rally. "Eleven forty-five a.m.," it read. "Candidate arrives."

Nicoletti pointed to the diagram. "Here," she said to Gallagher, "is where we want the volunteers with signs. Right behind the press pool so they show up on TV."

From there, Sean thought anxiously, he might get close enough.

Gallagher eyed the diagram. "I want a list," he said to Rick Ginsberg, "for a security check. Names, addresses, Social Security numbers of anyone who'll be near the candidate."

Sean's hands felt clammy. How, he wondered desperately, could he avoid giving his Social Security number?

Gallagher looked around the table. "All of you will be given pins with numbers and color codes, identifying who's permitted within the various perimeters of security. We're rushing magnetometers up here. Plus we have to sweep the area for guns and explosives before *anyone* gets inside."

Sean half listened now. He wondered how close the Boston police had come to him, whether the name Sean Burke was now on a computer or otherwise known to the Service; whether, in the next moment, Gallagher would spot him. To be so close . . .

When he reached for the Diet Coke in front of him, his hand shook. He clutched the aluminum cylinder so hard that he indented its side, causing a metallic click that made him wince.

Standing next to the diagram, Gallagher traced a line from a point marked "end of Sacramento Street" to the speakers platform. "This chute," he said, "is about a hundred feet long. It'll be lined with agents and police. The only people allowed to use it are the volunteers with signs, the press pool, and Senator Kilcannon and his party." His finger jabbed a checkpoint near the platform. "Two agents and your two volunteers will be right here. At eleven o'clock we start checking off the folks with signs. When we're finished, your two people can join the rest. At eleven thirty the press pool arrives."

Gallagher turned to Nicoletti. "At eleven forty-five," she said, "Kilcannon arrives from the airport. He proceeds from Sacramento Street into the chute, shaking hands as he goes. The pool proceeds to the front of the platform. And at twelve o'clock Senator Penn introduces Kilcannon to thunderous applause."

Where, Sean wondered, should he be? The security seemed daunting. It was hard to imagine, especially from a mere diagram, how it would be possible to conceal a gun, let alone assassinate Kilcannon.

The meeting broke into clusters. Sean stayed where he was, irresolute.

As if sensing his isolation, Kate Feeney asked, "What do you want to do tomorrow?"

Sean twitched his shoulders. "I just want to meet the Senator."

She squeezed his arm. "Maybe the two of us can check through the volunteers. That way we'll be close to him."

He turned to her, confused yet touched. Dully, he noticed again the pale skin, the delicate features.

"Let's talk to Rick," she urged him. She clutched his sleeve, standing. Together they walked toward Ginsberg, who was quietly talking to Gallagher. Noticing Kate, Ginsberg turned. "What can I do for you?"

"We'd like to check the people with signs through."

Ginsberg hesitated. "*You* know everyone, right?"

"Right."

"Then sure."

Gallagher looked at Sean, then Kate. The agent asked Ginsberg, pleasantly enough, "You can vouch for these people, right?"

Ginsberg smiled. "Sure. They're superstars."

"Okay." Gallagher headed toward the others, gathering at the center of the room—Nicoletti, the sound people. Sean went to the corner where he had left his jacket folded in an empty desk drawer, in order to conceal the gun.

THERE was a soft tap on the door. Pausing for an instant to prepare himself, Kerry went to answer.

Lara stood in the doorway with Peter Lake at her side, her eyes solemn and unblinking. Kerry made himself look at Peter. "Thanks," he said. "I'll call you."

Lara hesitated, then stepped inside. The door closed behind her.

She stood in the artificial light, dressed in jeans and a sweater, as he was. It had been almost two years, he thought again, since he had seen her. Fresh from the shock of discovering her pregnancy. Lara looked older, more beautiful than ever, but tempered by experience. She seemed determined to wait for him to speak.

For Kerry a slight smile was easier.

She came closer—two steps—and rested her head against his chest. "I'm sorry," she murmured. "For everything."

Gently he clasped her shoulders, his touch light, tentative. "I came back to D.C.," he said softly, "to ask you to marry me no matter what you decided. But you were gone."

When she looked up again, there were tears in her eyes. "Oh, Kerry, it's too late for this. Why hurt each other more?"

Her tone was weary, helpless. She backed away from him, shoving her hands into her pockets. Quietly she said, "Please. Let's talk about something else. We used to be able to talk."

He gestured toward the couch. She sat at one end, facing him. She looked tentative, like a bird about to take flight.

"I'm seeing Cutler tomorrow," he told her. "No choice."

"What are you going to do?"

"About Cutler? Lie, of course."

"I mean about the campaign."

"Withdraw probably. We've found a way to back off Mason, but the Republicans know, too."

Beneath her stillness Kerry sensed a shiver, but her gaze was cool and direct. "Have you ever considered," she said, "that the truth might be an option?"

Briefly the thought made Kerry angry. "Throw you to the wolves, career and all? No way." He softened this with a smile. "Besides, Clayton says it wouldn't work."

He saw the answering trace of humor at the corners of her eyes. Lara tilted her head, as if to readjust her thoughts. "What has it been like, Kerry? Running for President."

She needed to know, Kerry thought. His candidacy was the culmination of her decision. For a moment he looked about the suite—its neutral colors, its look of a way station for a thousand strangers who left no trace.

"The word that comes to me," he said at last, "is more. More pressure—what you say and do affects so many people, and the scrutiny's relentless. Everything and everyone is all about you— the choices are yours, you get all the credit and all the blame—on an epic scale." It was a relief to say what he felt, Kerry realized, in a way he had never done with anyone else. "The President once warned me about the sheer enormity of running, how demanding it was. He was right, but there's something even worse.

"I've come to believe that who I am, and what I believe in, is what the country needs." Pausing, he finished quietly, "It's embarrassing to say it aloud. Even to you."

Her gaze was soft. "Embarrassing? Or painful now?"

She was right, Kerry knew. The thought of giving up ravaged him. "No one could have tried harder, Lara."

Somehow the words seemed to echo with loneliness. Lara looked away.

As if to reach her, Kerry touched her wrist. "I've imagined seeing you again," he said. "A thousand ways. But in my heart it was always as if the last two years had never happened."

IT WAS past midnight when Nate knocked on Lara's door. He did not feel right about this, but his directive was not only to watch Lara but to question her further, the better to prepare himself for tomorrow morning's confrontation with Kilcannon. What Mason had done might make her more susceptible.

No answer.

Puzzled, he leaned his head against the door. He heard nothing stir. He took the elevator from the sixth floor to the lobby and called her from the house phone—twice, for ten rings each.

He put down the phone, reflective. She had to be out. A reporter might not answer the door, but a late-night phone call could be too important to miss. He meandered through the lobby to the bar.

There was the usual collection—bored businesspeople, a handful of his colleagues. But no Lara.

Could they be that foolish? he wondered.

Kilcannon was ten floors above her. There would be agents in front of his suite. Nate collected himself, then walked to the elevator and punched the button for sixteen.

The elevator whistled upward and glided to a stop. There were three agents waiting. To Nate's surprise one was Peter Lake. As agent in charge, Peter did not pull protective duty.

Peter regarded him impassively. "What can I do for you, Nate? This floor's off limits. As you know."

Nate shrugged. "I was going to meet Lara Costello," he said. "Is she already with Kilcannon?"

Nate saw a split-second's hesitance, and then Peter shook his head. "You also know we don't answer questions. But when the pope shows up, I'll ask Kit to phone you."

Nate said good night. Once the elevator door shut, he pushed the button for Lara's floor.

"I LOVE you," Kerry said as they sat on the couch gazing at each other. "Still."

Lara felt her eyes close. How many times had she wished she could have the last days of their affair to live again, to choose some other path. But now she felt diminished, trapped by the reality of decisions she had made. Tears ran down her face.

He took both her hands. "Tell me, Lara."

She looked at him—older now, wearier, but still so much the man she loved. She stood, shaking her head.

"No," she managed.

He rose, his hands on her waist now, his face inches from hers. "Please, *listen* to me."

"You listen to *me.*" She turned on him, caught between anger and despair. "We can't sneak around anymore. It would be all Nate Cutler needs, Kerry. You might as well admit the truth—"

"And if I did?"

"Then whenever you looked at me, you'd see a lost baby and a lost chance. How many months would we last?" She gazed at him steadily. "Kerry, I watched your face tonight. Even after what Mason did, you haven't given up. You're still wondering how to bury this."

He shrugged, silent. At length, he said, "It's hopeless."

"If we go public, it will be. For good."

She watched him, standing in a strange room, so much the captive of his own thoughts and feelings. "Maybe," he said finally, "we could wait. You could go back to your job, I deal with what I have to deal with. Then, after some time has passed . . ."

"We begin dating?"

"Something like that. No one needs to know that I've called you every night." His voice grew soft again. "I've missed that."

"So have I, Kerry. But no matter how long we waited, Nate

would wait us out. And imagine how ripe our story would be if you somehow managed to become President."

"I suppose I'd have to marry you," he answered. "Then the whole country would be stuck."

Suddenly his unwillingness to *see* made Lara angry. "And what a gift I'd be. First Lady of the United States, symbol of heartless abortion. I wouldn't do that to you, me, or other women—never mind that, for myself, I've come to hate what I did. These people play for keeps, Kerry. They'd use me to destroy you."

"Lara—"

"Listen to yourself, Kerry—suddenly we're in the White House. You haven't let it go yet. Maybe you can't."

This left Kerry silent.

"You know I'm right," she told him. "There'd be no safe place for us, ever."

"So I'll withdraw," he answered. "Please, give us a chance."

Heartsick, Lara slowly shook her head. "It's not up to me anymore, Kerry. *They* won't give us a chance. No matter what we do." She looked away. "Let's stop this. Before we do more damage."

Kerry touched her face. "Tell me one thing, then. Do you still love me?"

Despite herself, Lara felt the tears well again. "Oh, Kerry," she murmured, "that's such a sad question."

He took her hands again. "Why?"

Softly she said, "Because the answer doesn't matter."

For a last painful moment she let her hands rest in his. Then she gently disengaged. "It's time to call Peter," she said simply.

NATE sat in the alcove of the sixth floor, reading a *New Yorker.* He could see Lara's door from here.

At one in the morning he had been waiting for forty minutes. What was Lara doing? Nate wondered. He tried to imagine the psychic devastation Dick Mason must have wreaked, and then, in the next pitiless moments, Nate also saw himself, stalking a woman who once had been his friend.

Suddenly there was a soft metallic sound—heavier, somehow, than the opening of the door to a hotel room. Nate rose and quickly turned the corner marked EXIT.

Ten feet away Lara Costello slipped through the door from the stairwell. Turning, she saw him.

His nerve ends jangled. "Hello, Lara."

Her expression was strangely emotionless, unsurprised. She seemed to nod, as though confirming something to herself.

"Where've you been?" he asked.

"Running up and down the fire escape," she answered coolly. "Twenty times, and I'm not even sweating. You should try exercise instead of skulking in hallways."

"Kilcannon," he ventured, and then Lara began walking toward him. "You saw him," Nate said.

With steely deliberation Lara drew one hand back and slapped him hard across the face. Startled, Nate felt pain run through his jaw. He managed to keep looking at her.

She was breathing hard now, and her eyes were molten.

"Don't say his name to me," she told him. "Not you."

He did not answer. She stared at him, her hatred plain. Then she walked past him to her room.

SILENT, Kate Feeney drove Sean to his motel. He, too, was quiet. Surreptitiously he watched her face, lit by the few cars that, at this late hour, sped down the other side of the six-lane avenue.

Just before leaving, Rick Ginsberg had asked for their Social Security numbers. Kate had given hers. Rick scribbled the numbers on a card.

"John?" Ginsberg asked.

Tense, Sean hesitated. "I can't remember," he finally mumbled. "My card's at home—New York."

Rick frowned. "Can you get it from someone? I'll need it first thing tomorrow."

Sean nodded. He had felt chastised, suspect. Perhaps he only imagined Kate studying his face.

"Can you find your number?" she asked now.

He folded his arms, afraid to look at her. "My mother knows," he lied.

Bending forward, he hugged his chest. Sean thought again of his father, a closet door closing between them, and shivered. The acid sourness snaked from his stomach to his throat. "My mother knows," he repeated. "She knows everything."

"John?" Kate's voice had filled with concern. "Are you all *right?* Should we stop?"

Hands covering his face, Sean shook his head. "I feel sick," he murmured.

Kate continued down Lombard Street faster, headed for Sean's motel. He had pills there, Sean thought desperately. He needed to get to them.

Helpless, he sensed, but could not see, Kate turning into the motel parking lot. As the car came to a stop, fear and nausea overcame him. Sean retched miserably into his hands.

He felt Kate gently dabbing at his face with a tissue, then tugging at his jacket. "You need to get this off," she told him.

Docile, Sean let her ease one arm from its sleeve, the left side of his jacket falling free.

The sudden silence in the car felt like a cry suppressed.

Turning, Sean stared at her. Her lips were parted, and she gazed down at the seat. His eyes followed hers.

His gun lay between them, a dull metallic shape.

Kate's eyes moved to his face, appalled. Swallowing, Sean reached for the gun.

I had to stop him, he had said to the red-haired woman. *Your sympathy should be with your baby, the life I came to save.*

"John . . ." Kate's voice was hoarse. "What are you *doing?*"

Hand trembling, Sean raised the gun. There was no one but them—the parking lot was dark, the motel a dim shadow with a flickering fluorescent sign.

"Please," Kate whispered, "I won't tell anyone. Please."

Sean's hand shook more violently. He could feel her breath on his face. Her eyes were beautiful, blue. He could no longer look at them. Closing his eyes, he pulled the trigger.

There was a popping sound, swallowed by the darkness. Sean turned away, sickened. He heard Kate slump against the seat.

You had no choice. You had no choice. The words swirled in his brain—a mantra, a plea for absolution. She would have betrayed the cause in which he was God's soldier.

Her keys were in the ignition. Opening the door, he slid out of the passenger side. He circled the car with jerky steps and flung open the door against which Kate rested. Kneeling, he shoved her into a half-sitting position and then into a fetal ball, curled where he had sat.

Sean slid behind the wheel, slamming the door, and switched on the ignition. Blindly he turned onto Lombard.

He did not know where he was heading. Blocks passed, intervals of dissociation. And then he saw a looming swath of darkness—a grove of trees. He saw markers directing where he should exit: PRESIDIO NATIONAL PARK.

Slowly he entered the park. To his right was the inky blackness of San Francisco Bay. Through towering eucalyptus trees he saw a sliver of a distant glowing span—the Golden Gate Bridge. Sean drove toward it, deeper into the darkness.

He parked in the shadow of the bridge. As he opened the door, a chill wind swept through the pilings. Sean shivered. The only sounds were the cars on the span high above him, the harsh current slamming against rocks.

He lifted Kate from the car, awkwardly cradled in his arms. Feeling sick again, he stopped, panting, at the edge of the rocks.

The water swirled beneath them. At last he loosened his grip. Kate slid from his arms and plummeted twenty feet into the bay.

Tears blurred Sean's vision again. Then he turned away. His mission was before him, paid for with her blood.

He locked the car and walked away into the dark. Half lost, he retraced his route. Several hours later, hungry, sick, exhausted, in the first red streak of dawn, Sean reached the motel.

FACING Nate Cutler, Kerry was gripped by the ironic thought that, six hours earlier, Lara had sat where the reporter sat now.

It was seven a.m. Five hours and four hundred miles away, in San Francisco, he had another speech to give. But that could not matter now.

He let the silence stretch, Nate's question lingering unanswered. With some satisfaction he watched Cutler's own discomfort: the nervous rubbing of the fingers of one hand, a defensive look in the intelligent dark eyes behind the wire-rim glasses.

"Let me understand this," Kerry said at last. "You've got some notes from a psychologist who, by her own admission, has violated confidentiality to advance her political agenda. You've been telling people—though you can't know this—that Lara Costello and I were lovers. And you're doing all this because you're worried about *her* professional ethics?"

Nate seemed to tense. "Are you going to answer the question, Senator? Were you having an affair?"

With exaggerated patience Kerry looked at his watch, then into Nate's face again. "No," he said. "I hope that's not too upsetting."

Nate leaned forward, taut. "How do you explain this memo?"

Kerry fought his anger. "I don't," he answered with a fair show of calm. "I didn't write it."

Nate clasped his hands in front of him. "We have records of long-distance calls from you to her, at all hours of the night."

Kerry fixed him with an unblinking stare. "We were friends," he said. "I liked her very much. You did, too, I thought."

"I'm not a candidate," Nate answered.

Kerry gave him a cold smile. "Well," he said, "that's a relief. As for me, if what you *do* have is news, print away. This race has been focused on the issues for far too long." Kerry stood. "In case you haven't noticed, I'm busy. The question was whether Lara and I were lovers. I've answered it."

His voice flattened. "I have only one more thing to say, Nate." He paused, his words low and emphatic. "I don't expect much for myself. I don't expect my political opponents to be any better than they are. But I expected better from *you* than what you're doing to Lara."

Despite himself, Nate found that the words—delivered with plain anger and contempt—stung him. He stared up at Kilcannon.

The Senator considered him in silence, his wiry frame quite still. He said at last, "It comes down to a matter of conscience, Nate. You can rationalize this as news, just the way you have. But you know that this story, if you print it, stands to benefit your career as surely as it will destroy Lara's. And, perhaps, mine. You know what kind of person she is. And you know, at the least, that I'm not unstable, corrupt, a substance abuser, or any of the other things that would affect what kind of President I'd be. If I were using the power of government to subvert the law, then nothing you did to uncover the truth would be too much. But *this?*" Kilcannon paused again, shrugging. "This isn't just about who I am, Nate. It's about what news should be."

In a quiet voice Nate asked, "Are you telling me it *is* true but that we shouldn't print it in good conscience?"

"What I'm saying," Kerry answered simply, "is that your conscience is your own concern."

Nate watched his face. And then he stood to leave.

Afterward Kerry sat alone, then took some minutes more to focus on the speech in San Francisco.

SEAN found Rick Ginsberg standing outside the barriers on the edge of Justin Herman Plaza.

In the distance, buses full of volunteers had begun to arrive and were waiting in a holding area. Inside the barriers Secret Service agents with dogs or metal detectors walked slowly through the area, eyes downcast. Feverish, Sean felt the weight of the gun inside his jacket.

Ginsberg checked his watch. "Where's Kate?" he asked.

Sean shook his head. Ginsberg stared at him. "She gave you a ride last night, didn't she?"

This time Sean nodded. He did not trust himself to speak.

Ginsberg seemed to scrutinize him further, eyes briefly moving to his jacket, still damp from his frenzied efforts to remove Kate's blood. "Did you get your Social Security number?"

Reaching into his back pocket, Sean withdrew a slip of paper. Ginsberg glanced at it and began to look for Ted Gallagher.

Sean watched helplessly. It was the Social Security number for Sean Burke. He prayed that the name, whatever the Boston police might now suspect, would not yet appear on the Secret Service's computer system.

Before Sean was aware of it, Ginsberg was at his side again. "Damn Kate," he said impatiently.

It was the first time Sean had seen the coordinator fretful, and it increased his own agitation. "What's wrong?" he blurted.

Rick grimaced. "All their magnetometers aren't here yet, and *you* can't check our people through, not by yourself—you don't know enough of them. So I need to vouch for them all."

Sean hung his head, assaulted by confusion: shame at not being valuable to Ginsberg, fear of the computer, shock at his frightening good fortune.

All their magnetometers aren't here.

Turning, Ginsberg put a hand on Sean's shoulder, as if to apologize for his curtness. "Come on," he said. "We'll get these folks checked through. You can hand out the signs."

Sean followed him through the darkened chute where Kerry Kilcannon would enter the plaza. Two agents waited at the rear end of the passageway in front of boxes of signs with KILCANNON printed on both sides.

Ginsberg took a checklist from an agent. "We'll have all the magnetometers here soon," the man told Ginsberg. "But for now, you have to vouch that these people match their names."

A trickle of volunteers started through the chute.

WAITING with Peter Lake on the speakers platform, Clayton was restless. He had preceded Kerry here this morning and still had no account of the meeting with Cutler.

Next to him, Peter kept eyeing the crowd. The plaza was filling with people. A banner floated over them, proclaiming KILCANNON— THE WOMAN'S CHOICE, and volunteers continued to trickle through the chute.

"We just got notification from the FBI," Peter said. "A possible suspect in those Boston shootings apparently flew out to San Francisco right after it happened."

Clayton turned to him. "Do they think he's still around?"

Peter shrugged. "They don't know, but they wanted to alert us. For a right-to-lifer gone insane an event like this could be a lightning rod."

Clayton gazed out at the barriers, the checkpoints, and thought again how dedicated Peter Lake was. "Two more days," he said. "*Then* what will you do?"

Peter rested a comradely hand on his shoulder. "I'm going snorkeling, Clayton, in the British Virgin Islands. With the woman who, as far as I know, is still my wife."

MECHANICALLY Sean handed a sign to a smiling black woman, who thanked him. Next to him, Rick Ginsberg checked her name off on the list. Then the stream of traffic ceased altogether. The last of the volunteers had come through.

"Grab a sign," Rick told Sean.

Sean took a sign, hurrying past Ginsberg and the two agents. He edged through the volunteers, blending among them. The speakers platform was above and to his right, fifteen feet away, the end of the chute to his left. Four Secret Service agents were stationed at the base of the platform.

Sean glanced around him. The others had already started cheering—an Asian woman, a Latin man, a blond lawyer Sean recognized from headquarters. Wordlessly he raised his sign.

LARA and her cameraman stood with their backs to the magnetometers, waiting with the other pool reporters for Kerry to emerge from the line of black Lincolns parked at streetside.

It was like a frieze, she thought—the stillness of the cars, the Secret Service agents beside them. Then an agent took the cell phone from his ear and stepped toward the rear door of a limousine. Briskly he flung it open.

A small woman emerged—Ellen Penn, the junior Senator from California. And behind her, Kerry. More notable women came from the other cars to join them: a local Congresswoman; Dolores Huerta, vice president of the UFW; the female mayor of Sacramento. Kerry greeted each of them, smiling, and the party headed toward the passageway, the pool reporters first backing into the chute, cameras aimed at Kerry. In the semi-chaos Lara suddenly found herself inside the plaza. She became part of a file of pool reporters moving between the platform and Kerry's supporters.

When Kerry emerged into the light, the volunteers erupted in cheers, the sound passing like a contagion to the outer limits of the crowd. As he stopped at the foot of the platform stairs, Kerry noticed Clayton next to him—solid, loyal, watching over him just as he had since the last days of the Musso case. Their eyes met, and despite everything, Kerry smiled.

CATCHING Kerry's eye, Clayton edged toward him. From the platform Ellen Penn introduced the women who had come to vouch for his pro-choice credentials.

Just before Clayton reached him, Kerry saw Lara. He looked into her face and allowed himself the smallest private smile.

"The great leader of the United Farm Workers," Ellen Penn was proclaiming, "Dolores Huerta."

The volunteers erupted in cheers again, waving their signs up and down. Kerry put a hand on Clayton's shoulder. Still watching the crowd, he saw that, behind Lara, a dark-haired volunteer had dropped his sign.

"Peter just told me something," Clayton was saying.

Kerry half listened. The man's expression was different from the others, as unsmiling as the women demonstrators in Los Angeles.

"This nut," Clayton continued, "the one who did the Boston murders. He may be here in San Francisco."

There was something more, Kerry suddenly knew—a rapture in his eyes, then a terrible familiarity.

The man stepped forward. He reached inside his jacket.

Kerry's face froze.

"So," Clayton finished, "no plunging into crowds, okay? Just as a precaution."

The man held a gun now, aimed at them both.

Kerry felt himself turn to lead. With a sudden effort of will he pushed Clayton away from him. "John, no—"

A pop shattered the air, and then Kerry felt a searing pain, a blinding whiteness. He dropped into a sitting position. Shock ripped through his body, numbing his chest. All he could see was that one face, its expression now sickened and appalled.

"John," he whispered.

"Gun!"

As the screaming crowd recoiled, John Musso saw Kerry's lips move. Then Kerry fell back, two agents covering his body. Another two pushed toward John.

Putting the gun to his throat, John thought of Kate Feeney. But the last image in his brain before the bullet tore through it was of Kerry Kilcannon in a witness room, reaching across the table toward an eight-year-old boy.

Lara felt the shriek die in her throat. Dropping her notepad, she rushed forward. She reached the edge of the crush surrounding Kerry, saw agents sealing off the crowd, a photographer beginning to snap pictures. Then she found herself in Peter Lake's strong grip.

"No," he said in a low voice. "You can't."

His face was sickly gray. In near hysteria Lara began to fight him. "Damn you," she spat out, "I have to *be* with him."

"Let her go," someone called to Peter.

It was Clayton, tears streaking his face. "Take her with him," he said thickly. "And get him out of here."

At the end of the chute, paramedics ran forward with a stretcher, convoyed by more agents. Quickly glancing from Clayton to Lara, Peter began to snap out orders. The agents and paramedics started rushing Kerry back through the chute. Lara felt Peter's hand on her arm. She began running with him, heart pounding, leaving behind the chaos, the dead assassin, her work.

The paramedics laid the stretcher in a waiting ambulance, and Lara scrambled in after them. It felt like madness—the sudden acceleration, the nightmare shriek of sirens, the white-coated strangers bent over Kerry's body. Sliding sideways, Lara found a place near his head.

His eyes were open, lifeless. Blood spread from the right side of his chest, a ragged hole in his shirt. One paramedic glanced quickly at his partner. "His lung's collapsing," he said.

Please, God, Lara prayed in silence. Please. She bent her face to Kerry's.

Do you still love me? he had asked her.

Oh, Kerry, she had answered, *that's such a sad question.*

"I still love you," she told him now.

The paramedics did not seem to hear. Intent, they monitored Kerry's pulse, barely seeming to breathe themselves.

Through a film of tears Lara watched Kerry. She felt the ambulance slow, heard the sound of the sirens expiring. The rear doors flew open. Then the stretcher was outside, run by paramedics toward a metal double door. Instinctively Lara hurried after them past a gauntlet of agents and through the door.

It was some moments before she learned that Kerry's life hung in the balance, minutes more until she knew what she must do.

CLAYTON AND KIT PACE COULD only wait. The hospital had given them a cubicle near the emergency room, equipped with a television. Until a doctor came, there was nothing for Kit to tell the reporters waiting outside the hospital. In the agony of helplessness they watched the screen. Now NBC was playing a tape of the shooting—Kerry freezing, then pushing Clayton aside just before the bullet struck him.

A newsman's voice said, "Senator Kilcannon appeared to see his assailant and to push his campaign manager out of harm's way. By one account he called out a name."

"Did Kerry *know* him?" Kit asked with quiet incredulity.

With equal softness, like a story recited to a child that served also to distract a parent from his own heartache, Clayton offered his grim surmise.

"My God," was all that Kit could say.

"He tried to save me," Clayton added at last. "He's seen me through so much. . . ." When his tears began, he did not try to stop them.

LARA stepped inside the phone booth. Dialing, she observed through the glass two nurses gliding by like silent ghosts.

Her bureau chief sounded startled, then angry. "Where *are* you?" Hal Leavitt demanded.

"At the hospital." Lara steeled herself. She told Leavitt what she had seen and that Kerry Kilcannon was still alive.

Leavitt's voice became a newsman's, clipped and focused. "They've sealed off the hospital," he told her. "You're the only one inside. I want you to go live, by telephone."

It was what Lara had anticipated. "I'm ready now," she said.

IN SHARED astonishment Clayton and Kit watched Lara's photograph on the screen, listened to her reporter's voice, cool and factual, tell them what they did not know.

"As of ten minutes ago," Lara said, "Senator Kilcannon was still alive."

Kit gave a small gasp. "My God," she murmured. "How can she do this?"

"When he reached the emergency room," Lara continued, "the Senator had stopped breathing and his blood pressure was zero. The Senator has undergone an emergency procedure to restore his respiratory functions. His vital signs are stable, but he has not regained consciousness and remains in critical condition."

Finishing, Lara told the studio producer, "Give me Hal."

Promptly Leavitt was on the line. "Nice—"

"Hal," she cut in, "get someone else out here."

"Why?"

"Because if he dies," Lara said, "I won't be able to report it."

THE CAMPAIGN
Day Six

KERRY drifted between sleep and waking, dream and thought. The images that came to him were from his deepest past—Vailsburg, his mother, Jamie, Liam Dunn. A small dark-haired boy, an angry man with a gun. He was in Newark, and Anthony Musso had shot him. And then, quite suddenly, he was awake.

There was a tube in his chest, and his throat was raw. He felt feeble, not himself. Gingerly he raised one hand, then the other. Shivering, he inhaled. A searing pain ripped through his chest.

"Everything working all right?" someone asked. "No reason why it shouldn't."

Kerry turned his head slightly. Standing near him was a red-haired man in surgical scrubs. "I'm Dr. Frank O'Malley," he said.

Kerry swallowed once, painfully. "What happened to me?"

O'Malley folded his arms. "You're a tough man, Senator, and a lucky one. The bullet missed your spine, major arteries, and, other than a lung, any vital organs."

Kerry closed his eyes. A fathomless gratitude washed over him, which he lacked the strength to express.

"Barring the unexpected," O'Malley continued, "you'll be fine. In a couple of days you'll be standing. In a couple of months you'll be running. Including for President, if that's what you want. Though I've never understood why anyone would."

Kerry did not answer. He lay there and allowed his soul to catch up with his body. He was alive, and his life belonged to him again, perhaps more profoundly than before.

To Kerry, Clayton seemed sluggish, like a man moving underwater. As he took Kerry's hand in both of his, the sheen in his eyes revealed his emotions.

"You meant to push me out of the way, didn't you?"

Kerry managed to smile. "The plan was to duck behind Ellen Penn," he whispered. "I was using you for leverage."

When Clayton did not smile, Kerry exhaled. "It was a reflex, Clayton. There was no time to *mean* anything."

"Then maybe," his friend answered, "that was what happened before. Your reflex was to protect John Musso."

At once Kerry felt a terrible weight. "It was him, wasn't it?"

Clayton sat next to the bed. "He was the Boston shooter," he said. "They also think he killed a girl who worked for your campaign, the night before. Kate Feeney."

Kerry's stomach tightened. "Kate Feeney," he said. "She was a strawberry blonde, wasn't she? Clayton, *why?*"

"They're not sure. Maybe she found out who he was."

Kerry lay back, the weight becoming despair, the memory of a boy coming to a wounded man in a hospital, much like this one. "What did I do?" he asked. "God help me, what did *I* do?"

"You tried to save him. But he'd seen so much, sustained so much damage . . ." Clayton's tone grew firm. "You were a prosecutor, pal, not an adoption agency. You'd just been shot, your wife didn't want kids, and John had a great-aunt in Boston. She died, unfortunately, a couple of years after he moved."

Kerry turned his head on the pillow. He murmured, "But I was what he needed, and I turned him away."

Clayton looked at him steadily. He seemed to sort through his thoughts. "Do you remember what Liam told you after Jamie died? That politics, like rust, never sleeps?"

Jamie, Kerry thought. There was now another difference between them: Kerry had survived.

"It still doesn't." Clayton's pause signaled his reluctance to go on. "There are hundreds of people standing beneath that window over there. Millions more who are praying for you. You're a hero, a near martyr. All you need to win this primary is to show that you're all right and that you still want it." He let the implicit question linger, then finished quietly, "But you're also a free man."

"How do you mean?"

"You nearly died, Kerry. Recuperation will take time. No one will blame you if you withdraw. If you do that, *Newsworld* probably goes away. Once you're not a candidate, they don't have a story. And in four years, or eight years"—Clayton shrugged—"maybe it's a different world. Right now, *you're* the only story. But if you decide to run, you and Lara are the story again." Clayton looked down.

Kerry felt exhaustion overtake him. "I have to rest," he said at last. "Then I want her here."

Slowly nodding, Clayton left.

LARA stopped a few feet from the bed. There was a nakedness to her expression that Kerry had never seen before. Though she was still, he could sense that every fiber of her being wanted to touch him.

He held out his hand.

So quickly that it startled him, she came to the bed and kissed him gently. He closed his eyes, feeling the warmth of her breathe new life into him.

When their mouths parted, he opened his eyes. "Clayton says you came here with me."

In silent acknowledgment her eyes shut. Kerry could feel his own pulse.

He swallowed, trying to speak again. "Well," he murmured, "I guess we're out of the closet."

She took his hand and, with the smallest shake of her head, pressed it against the side of her face.

"Lara . . ."

A moist film appeared on her eyelashes. Kerry saw her jaw tense, as if she was determined to say what she had come to say. "If I just go away," she began in a near whisper, "Clayton and I think what's happened may help you out of this. Without me you might still be President."

Despite himself, Kerry felt a desperate impatience. "For once, Lara, tell me how you feel."

She looked past him, seeming to slip far away. Then he saw her shoulders square, and she looked at him with new directness.

"I'm in love with you," she said. "So much that it hurts. No matter what, I'll love you for the rest of my life."

He felt his throat constrict.

Gently she brushed the hair back from his forehead. She said, "I need to know something. After all of this, do you still want to be President?"

He hesitated, only for a moment. "Not if it means never seeing you again. Nothing's worth that."

"But suppose you could have us both." Her voice was firm now, insistent. "The presidency and me, free and clear. Isn't *that* what you really want?"

He gazed at the white ceiling. For a time the tragedy of John Musso mingled with the trauma of his own near death, making all ambition seem pointless. But then Kerry found a hard kernel of truth: The man within him had come to believe that he should be President. He owed Lara nothing less than honesty.

He turned to her, saying quietly, "I'd have you both."

She became quite still, lips parted.

"If it takes giving up the race to be with you, Lara, then I'll give it up." He paused, feeling the rawness in his throat. "Or I'll run, and we can take our chances. I think we're strong enough, but that involves some other things I haven't the right to choose for you. So you decide."

Her eyes misted again. "For both of us?"

"As long as, this time, we're together."

She took both his hands in hers, looking intently into his face. At last she said, "Then I guess we're running."

Kerry felt a flood of emotions: wonder, belief in her strength of character, a deeper love than he could express.

Then Lara looked into his face again and kissed his forehead. "I'll go find Clayton," she said.

AT TWO thirty, ample time to make the evening news, Kit Pace appeared in the makeshift pressroom. It was even hotter and more crowded than before, but this time Nate was in the front row.

"He's still in," a reporter predicted. "That's what it's about."

No, Nate thought, he's not. But only I know why.

Looking out over the room, Kit Pace seemed to ignore him. "I have a statement to read," she began, "from Senator Kilcannon: 'I'd like to give my heartfelt thanks for all the prayers and good wishes that have come to me this past day. I can never express how grateful I am to receive them, and to be *able* to receive them.' "

"He's bowing out," someone murmured.

" 'I also want you to know,' " Kit read calmly on, " 'that I'm in this race to the end. My intention, as it always was, is to win the Democratic nomination for President of the United States.' "

"I can't believe it," Nate murmured.

AT FIVE thirty Kerry tried to stand up. His legs felt shaky, uncertain.

Dr. Frank O'Malley grasped one arm, Clayton the other. "You don't have to do this," the doctor told him.

Kerry steadied himself. "I'll manage."

The three men inched toward the third-floor window, the tube in Kerry's chest obscured by his robe. Behind them, a nurse wheeled the pole on which the tube ended with a plastic bag.

"They need to see you," Frank Wells had advised. "To know that you're able to function."

About the window itself, Kerry realized, he had been profoundly incurious. He had no idea how many floors up he was. Though he was touched by the knowledge that countless strangers cared for him, the idea of hundreds keeping vigil below seemed surreal.

They reached the window. There *were* hundreds of them, spread across the lawn—young and old, men and women, of all races. A ragged cheer rose, audible through the glass, and some in the crowd began waving.

Kerry blinked. Suddenly this was not about votes. Raising his arm, he waved back.

BELOW, Nate Cutler watched him. He would be less than human, he told himself, not to feel the elation around him. Or to be haunted by the profile he saw on the roof above—a Secret Service sharpshooter.

It was time, he decided, to return Jane Booth's beeper message. He drifted to the sidewalk. Dialing, he took in the city traffic, the police cars parked in front.

"There's a meeting tomorrow," Jane told him. "In New York. I want you to catch the red-eye. Now that he's in for good, we need to decide what to do."

THE CAMPAIGN
Day Seven

ELECTION day dawned clear and bright. By nine o'clock Clayton arrived with the news that turnout was heavy across the state. Turning to Kerry, Lara said, "That's good for you, I think."

Clayton handed each of them copies of two press releases. Lara read one, smiled, then studied the second more closely. "Mine should be issued through the news division," she said to Clayton.

Clayton raised his eyebrows. "Have you told them yet?"

"Yes." Glancing at Kerry, Lara smiled again. "There was a very long silence."

Clayton shrugged. "At least today it'll be story number two. After all, this election decides the nomination."

Watching her, Kerry wondered again about the wisdom of their decision. She had been a journalist since college, and now, abruptly, might take a path she had never wanted, under a scrutiny so intense that most would find it withering. But with seeming serenity Lara had taken a pencil from her purse and begun to make changes in the margins of the press release.

IT WAS five p.m. in Manhattan—two p.m. in California—when the press releases arrived at the conference room. For the last two hours the conferees—Nate; Jane Booth; Sheila Kahn, the investigative reporter; the managing editor; and Martin Zimmer, *Newsworld*'s owner and publisher—had parsed the facts in painstaking detail. There was much at stake: the character of *Newsworld*, the career of Kerry Kilcannon, the question of what journalism was and should be.

Jane passed out the releases without comment. Nate began reading.

"NBC News," the first began, "announced that reporter Lara Costello had requested and received an indefinite leave of absence.

" 'Between 1996 and 1998,' Ms. Costello said, 'I served as a Capitol Hill correspondent for *The New York Times*. During that period I formed a professional relationship and a personal friendship with Senator Kerry Kilcannon. I deeply valued all of that.

" 'The events of the last few days, and my response to them, have now made it clear to me that my feelings for Kerry Kilcannon go beyond friendship. The Senator has found them enlightening in a similar way. It is plain, therefore, that I cannot continue to report on this campaign or otherwise perform duties which might raise questions regarding my objectivity.

" 'In future weeks I mean to be with Senator Kilcannon as he recovers. I expect that process to be enlightening as well.' "

Smiling quizzically, Nate turned to the second press release.

It quoted Kerry Kilcannon's reaction. " 'If enlightenment takes getting shot,' " it said in its entirety, " 'I'm just glad it worked the first time.' "

Nate reread the sentence and then began to laugh. "Too good—it really is too good."

The managing editor kept staring at the releases. "There goes one leg of the story," he finally said. "The ethically compromised reporter." He turned to Sheila Kahn. "How's Costello's reporting from two years ago?"

She looked dazed. "Bulletproof," she answered. "Costello may have done him favors, but it doesn't show."

"They're lying about an affair," Nate told the group. "Even if we can't prove it. But, to me, this isn't about adultery—there's too much of it around. It's about whether Lara Costello aborted Kerry Kilcannon's child and what role Kilcannon played in that. And now that they're going to be America's sweethearts, the story takes on a certain 'yuck' factor—" Cutting himself off, he gazed at Sheila Kahn across the table. "Do you have any sense this counselor's crazy enough to have made the whole thing up?"

"Crazy? Sure. Who else would do what she's done? But I don't think she made it up."

With a tentative air Martin Zimmer leaned forward. "Isn't this situation," he asked, "the reason you're supposed to need *two* sources? I think we know Costello was at the clinic. But did she tell anyone besides this woman—with ties to the Christian Commitment—that the baby was Kilcannon's?"

Jane Booth frowned. "The circumstances argue for authenticity."

Zimmer turned to Nate. "Mason planted this, right?"

Nate nodded. "The debate made that clear."

Zimmer shifted in his chair. "The question is this: Do we torpedo Kerry Kilcannon on the basis of a single source, provided by Dick Mason?"

Before anyone tried to answer, Jane's secretary arrived with a message. She went to a corner, picked up the telephone, and had a brief conversation. Turning, she explained, "That was a friend at ABC. They've done their first exit polling. It looks like Kilcannon's ahead."

Nate gazed down at the press releases. Alone among the others, he could sense what the laconic words had cost two people and how much their risk might cost them yet. Then Martin Zimmer broke into his thoughts. "I don't like this story," he said simply. "Is there anyone here who does?"

Jane Booth grimaced. "This whole thing smells," she persisted. "Clayton Slade let Costello in the ambulance because he knows the truth. And I don't think anything that's happened—not the shooting, not this meretricious story they've ginned up—cures the ethical problem of a reporter warning a candidate about a story. Especially when *they're* the story." Facing Nate, she demanded, "*You're* satisfied she went to Kilcannon, right?"

Nate nodded. "Or to his people."

"But can you prove it?" Zimmer asked them both.

Jane's eyes narrowed. "No," Nate answered.

"After I asked you to follow her," Jane asked, "did you see anything?"

Nate hesitated. This was her final hope, he knew, of keeping the discussion alive.

"No," he said at last. "But then, who would be that dumb?"

By SEVEN o'clock Jack Sleeper had called Kerry to say that his numbers forecast a substantial victory. "An hour to go," Kerry reminded him. At eight o'clock the polls would close.

When Kerry hung up, Lara asked, "Did you reach Kate Feeney's parents?"

He nodded. "Do you know what her mother told me? That they'd gotten out to vote for me today."

"Then it meant all the more to hear from you." Lara wished there were more comfort she could give him. For the rest of his life, Lara knew, Kerry would be shadowed by the thought that he had abandoned John Musso and thus set Kate's death in motion.

By ten o'clock there were three of them sitting with Kerry—Lara, Clayton, and Mary Kilcannon. Kerry had not wanted his mother to come until now, Lara knew. He had feared that the sight of him badly injured would be a traumatic reminder of Jamie. But Mary's gratitude that he had lived shone from her still handsome face, and she seemed to accept Lara's presence as God's gift to her remaining son.

The returns were sluggish. As always, it seemed, Los Angeles County was slow in reporting. To fill the time, CNN showed a tape of the attempted assassination.

Mary Kilcannon turned away. Lara gripped Kerry's hand. Clayton became quite still.

On the screen, in slow motion, Kerry pushed Clayton aside and reached out to John Musso. The film clip froze on Musso's agonized face.

Silent, Kerry remembered a damaged young boy, then another boy. What, he wondered, had helped *him* rise above his own abusive father? The answer must surely be the concern of a loving mother, the quiet presence of Liam Dunn. And, perhaps, the example of his older brother, so determined to escape Michael Kilcannon that it consumed him.

Suddenly the picture changed. A newswoman spoke from Kerry's Los Angeles headquarters, surrounded by celebrants.

"CNN," she began, "has now projected that Senator Kerry Kilcannon will win the California presidential primary with sixty-two percent of the vote. This gives him a virtual lock on his party's nomination."

"All *right*," Clayton said with quiet elation.

"The Senator's press secretary, Kit Pace, is expected here shortly to read a statement from Senator Kilcannon."

Lara's fingers curled tightly around Kerry's. "You're going to be President, Kerry. I can feel it."

Kerry felt too much to answer. If only Liam Dunn could be here, he thought. And Jamie. He and Jamie would have much to share. His brother had cleared the path that Kerry was meant to follow. Now Kerry had traveled it, and they stood on equal ground.

"Senator Kilcannon's victory," the reporter continued, "follows his acknowledgment of a relationship with NBC correspondent Lara Costello, who, until last month, had been stationed overseas."

"I was planning all along," Lara murmured, "to launder us through Bosnia. I'm just sorry that it took two years."

Turning, Kerry gave her a quiet smile and then became pensive. Soon it would begin again—the travel, the speeches, the crowds, the unceasing calculation, the constant struggle to remain, as Liam had, a decent man in a complex world. He should savor this moment while he could.

He gazed at his mother, who had given him so much; at Clayton, his closest friend; at Lara, to whom, someday, he would be closer yet. Then she smiled at him, and Kerry realized that no matter what came, he was something James Kilcannon had never been: deeply lucky, profoundly blessed. And that their one safe place would be with each other and, in time, their children.

Tomorrow, Kerry knew, he would tell her this. For now, it was enough that she was here.

RICHARD NORTH PATTERSON

For his best-selling legal thrillers—*Degree of Guilt, Eyes of a Child,* and *The Final Judgment*—Richard North Patterson drew on his experiences as an attorney. With *No Safe Place* the author turned to less familiar territory: the high-powered world of presidential politics. Luckily, one of Patterson's early fans, who later became a family friend, was George Herbert Walker Bush. The former President was generous with advice and also gave Patterson introductions to campaign strategists. If you're going to write a book about getting to the White House, it helps to have a friend who's been there.

SOMEBODY'S BABY

ELAINE KAGAN

*S*he was a good girl,
raised to know better.

He came from a world
apart, a tough guy hiding
a heart of gold.

All they did wrong was
fall in love.

Jenny

E HAD a tattoo. Maybe that isn't where to start, but what difference does it make where you start? I was rocked by the tattoo. It wasn't the first boy's chest I had seen, but it was certainly the first tattoo. An eagle, a large majestic blue eagle, his head turned so you could see his kingly splendor in full profile. An eagle in repose, I said. I take that back. I didn't say it; I just thought it. I didn't say anything. There was just the shock of the eagle on the upper left side of his chest, a blue eagle under my fingertips. I didn't find out until much later that he'd had the tattoo done when he was in jail.

Jail.

Not a word in my vocabulary. In my neighborhood in 1959 in Kansas City, nobody knew from jail. They didn't even know from tattoos, much less jail. I had never spoken to anyone like him, not ever in my life. I really didn't have conversations with *those* people, as my mother would have said, with her lips in a thin line and her chin at a particular angle. After all, I was a privileged daughter of the Jewish upper middle class. Jenny Jaffe, the sixteen-year-old only child of Esther and Mose Jaffe, five feet nine inches tall, about a hundred and twenty pounds, skinny and plain, with unruly brown hair pulled high and tight up into a ponytail, pale skin and brown eyes. A midwestern teenage girl, a quiet girl, not particularly popular, not particularly unpopular, just smack-dab in the middle of her senior year of high school. The only thing different about me was that I thought I knew what I wanted. I had a dream. Not anything grand like Martin Luther King's, just a little Jenny Jaffe dream. Not too many people know what they want when they're teenagers, but I was sixteen and I had known what I wanted since I could stand. To be a dancer. Esther and Mose thought that their only child thinking she could be a dancer was a joke.

"Who goes all the way from Kansas City to New York and makes it? Don't be silly. You'll get lost in the shuffle there. You'll go away to college, and you'll learn to be something else."

I hadn't let either of my parents see me dance for years, not since I was a gawky fledgling ballerina in a pink tutu. "My daughter the ugly duckling"—my mother's hiss of a whisper and my father's quiet laugh in the dark recital hall—and from that time on I never let them see me dance. I kept my dream tucked away inside me. Maybe if it hadn't all happened, I never would have gone to New York and become a dancer. I would have scrapped the dream and run away with Will in the blue 1950 Mercury. But then you could also spend the rest of your life having a discussion about what is fate and what you can change. Nothing, if you ask me.

He was pumping gas at the Texaco at Seventy-fifth and Wornall; he actually stared at me while he washed the windshield of my mother's powder-blue Oldsmobile. I turned my eyes and pretended to look for something in my purse. Then he was at Joe's, flipping hamburgers and washing greasy spoons—which was a joke, he added, smiling at my friend Sherry and me as he took the dishes off the table in the next booth. When he smiled, could it be that his eyes got bluer? Was that possible?

I was a senior at Southwest High School. He was an "I don't know what." I didn't know if he'd finished high school. I didn't even know if he'd gone. He was older than me, but I didn't know by how much—maybe just a few years older in numbers but light-years in life. William Cole McDonald. It was later that I learned his full name. At first I only knew "Will" because it was stitched in red over the pocket of his blue Texaco shirt.

"Hi there."

"Oh. Hi," I said.

Riveting beginning. Embarrassing. Trapped in the car, my mother at the wheel, as Will walked around the passenger side to take the gas pump out of the tank. There was something wrong with his right leg; I noticed the limp as he passed my window. A limp and a smile and blue eyes.

"Here you go, ma'am." Now he was at my mother's window with the charge slip.

"Thank you," she said.

"You're welcome and come again, ma'am," he said as my mother signed the ticket and he looked at me. The sun was behind him, and his hair was so blond it was white.

My mother turned the key in the ignition, and we pulled out of the Texaco.

The next time I ran into Will, I thought he just happened to be in the Sealy Drug Store, five blocks from my house. I hadn't seen him for about three weeks. He was standing by the cash register, his head buried in a magazine, one piece of hair falling over his eye.

"Oh, hi," I said when I realized.

"Hi there."

"Is that all you need today, Jenny?" Mr. Sealy said.

"Yeah. Thanks, Mr. Sealy."

Will stood next to me at the counter. "What did you get?"

"Oh. A lipstick."

"Yeah? Let's see."

Mr. Sealy handed me the bag. Will took out the lipstick and looked at it. " 'Pixie Pink,' " he read. "Here, put it on. Let's see."

"Now?"

"Sure."

Mr. Sealy was watching us from behind the counter.

"I don't have a mirror."

"It's okay. I'll be your mirror."

I laughed. I laughed because I thought I might disintegrate. Will was looking at me like I was a movie star. He was looking at me like Mr. Sealy wasn't there.

"Go ahead," Will said.

I put the lipstick on, looking into Will's eyes, while Mr. Sealy watched us, his face scrunched up into a tight frown.

"A little up on the right. Yeah, that's perfect. Boy, Jenny, you sure have a sweet mouth."

"Uh . . ."

"So you want to get a soda or something?"

"Uh . . . sure."

He held the door open for me like I was a grown-up lady, and I was standing with this stranger at Seventy-first and Holmes.

We sat at the counter at Friedson's Pharmacy. I got a Coke; he got a vanilla phosphate.

"So how did you know my name was Jenny?"

"The guy, Mr. Sealy, said it at the cash register. It's kind of romantic. It fits you."

"Oh," I said, laughing. The laugh was strangely high-pitched, somewhere up in the hyena range. "Why? Do I look romantic?"

"Well, you look beautiful, that's for sure."

He looked right at me when he said it. I took a sip of my Coca-Cola. It was a toss-up—I would either choke, and Coke would come shooting out of my nostrils, or I would fall off the stool.

"So I thought maybe we could go out sometime."

My heart did this little zwoop thing up against my rib cage. "Okay," I said. I didn't even think about it. I just said okay. This was not like me. Not at all. "What's your name? I mean besides Will."

"William Cole McDonald, ma'am," he said. "I used to get razzed about it when I was little."

"Why?"

"Well, Cole McDonald . . . as in 'Ol' McDonald,' you know."

"I didn't even think of that."

Before I knew it, it was dark out, and we had been sitting at

Friedson's counter for three hours, and I was late for dinner, and no-body knew where I was. In those lost three hours I had told William Cole McDonald everything there was to know about me. I had no idea why. I could just talk to him—how I really didn't have any close friends, how I really didn't fit in, how I wasn't like the others. And he listened. He sat there on that counter stool with his eyes locked onto mine, and the more he listened, the more I told him. I even told him how much I wanted to be a dancer, how I knew I would get no help from my parents, since they thought the whole thing was a joke.

I told him how I had always been a good girl; he told me how he had always been bad.

"I guess it all started when I was in the first grade."

"Really? What happened?"

"Oh, I told the teacher she had a wart on her nose, and for some reason she didn't like that, so she sent me home."

I choked. Coke sprayed out of me.

He was amazing.

WE WERE together nearly every afternoon after school. I would leave Southwest and take the bus to Miss Lala Palevsky's School of the Dance, and Will would pick me up there afterward and drive me home. At night I was in my room studying, but from five fifteen to six thirty, when my mother thought I was on the bus coming home from dancing school, I was with Will.

He was so different from me. I had been coddled and treasured; Will had been thrown into life like a leaf on the wind. His mother had died when he was only five, and from then on, in many ways, he had been on his own. Will was the only child of his mother and father, but his father had been married a couple of times before Will's mother, and he'd remarried after Will's mother, and there were kids from all those marriages. At one point there were fifteen kids besides him in the house, but Will said that even though there were lots of step and half brothers and sisters, he always felt alone. "We never lived in a house like you, Jenny," he said. "More like shacks or trailers. Once we were even living in some tents strung alongside the road." And they were always moving to places I'd never heard of, places called South Fork and Kernville and Pacoima, which were all somewhere in California. He didn't say any more, and I just studied him—the shadow under his cheekbone, the wave in his hair.

I SQUASHED the forkful of coconut cream pie and pushed it around the plate. "I don't get along with my mother," I told him.

"You mean regular mother-daughter stuff or more?"

"More, I think." How could I explain it? Will had been gypped out of having a mother, and I had a mother who didn't like me. No matter what I did, I couldn't measure up to the fantasy of who Esther had thought she'd have for a daughter, one who looked like her and acted like her. "My mother wants me to be somebody else, someone who doesn't have dreams."

He put his hand on mine. It was the first time he'd ever touched me. It was a Friday afternoon, and we were in a big red booth at Allen's drive-in, having coffee and pie. Will loved pie.

"My mother wants me to be like her, I guess—the kind of person who doesn't want to go anywhere or do anything. She wants me to just stay put and make do."

"Well, she's gonna end up in a world of hurt, then, isn't she?"

I laughed. "Why? Do you think I'll do things out of the ordinary, Will?"

"I think you are a force to be reckoned with, Jenny. I think you're going to do whatever you want to do."

"Oh, Will, you're so crazy. Everybody thinks I'm a nothing."

"Well then, everybody'll be surprised but me."

He took his hand off mine. I stabbed a bite of pie with the fork and ate it. "Yeah," I said, tossing my ponytail. "Maybe they will."

"NO, YOU cannot invite him to eat with us on Rosh Hashanah."

"Why can't I?"

My mother put the lid back on the soup pot and turned to face me. "Because he's not Jewish, because you don't know him, and because I said so."

"*That's* mature."

Her eyebrow went up. "I don't like the way you're talking to me, Jenny. Is that what you're learning from this boy, this Will? How to be rude?"

"I'm not being rude. I'm asking you if I can please invite him to come have lunch with us after services on Rosh Hashanah."

She turned her back to me, took a carrot, and began to chop.

"Mom?"

"Why do you always have to make trouble for me?"

"Does that mean I can't invite him?"

Her shoulders raised. "No, you can't. I said no, didn't I? Why do you make me say it again?"

Not exactly a force to be reckoned with, but at least I asked. I thought of a lot of other things to say, snotty, gutsy things, but I wasn't quite brave enough yet. I was just beginning to be a force, a little bitty force, but I thought I was on my way.

I WAS happy driving downtown with Will in that wonderful old blue Mercury of his. Will loved that car the way I'd never seen anybody love a car. It was a 1950, but you would have thought it was a brand-new Cadillac. He was constantly polishing it; he even called it darlin'. I sat beside him with the radio on my lap—he'd gotten a new radio and hadn't put it in yet—and I was listening to country music. People I'd never heard of, like Kitty Wells and Red Foley, were replacing Johnny Mathis and Dion and the Belmonts in my heart.

"Where are we going?"

"To eat Mexican food."

"Will, I don't think you can get Mexican food in Kansas City."

"Of course you can, Jenny. You just don't know where to go. And after we eat, I'm going to teach you how to play pool."

"Pool?"

"Sure, with those legs of yours, you'll be halfway 'cross the table when you go to make your shot." He laughed and looked at me. "Those legs of yours go all the way to Montana, girl."

There *was* Mexican food in Kansas City. And there were pool halls.

And barbecue places, where there was only beer to drink; and rowdy bars with country bands, where the girls wore too much lipstick, too much Maybelline, and too few clothes. And me, I was the foreigner with the Pixie Pink lipstick and the scrubbed face and the ponytail, the novice who had emigrated from the land of the country clubs.

I turned seventeen between Thanksgiving and Christmas, on December 4. Esther and Mose decided I should have a la-di-da soiree, with the girls in cocktail dresses and the boys in suits and ties. I practically used up all the breath in my body fighting them, but they were determined to have this party.

"I think it would be more exciting if the boys came in cocktail dresses and the girls in suits and ties," Will said.

"It's not a big deal. Just get a suit or a jacket somewhere."

"How 'bout I just don't go? Meet you after the shindig?"

"Why can't you borrow a jacket from somebody?"

"Okay. How 'bout Joe?"

I fell over laughing. Joe owned Joe's, where Will worked on weekends making hash browns and chicken-fried steak and chocolate sundaes. Joe was maybe five feet tall and weighed about two hundred and fifty pounds. Joe's jacket would have been like a postage stamp on Will. Will was six feet two and lean, with muscles in his arms and wide shoulders. He also had the most amazing cheekbones, which was because he was part Shoshone Indian on his mother's side. All together it probably would have been a lot for any girl, even one with more moxie than me, but for me it was everything. I was falling in love for the very first time, and it was with William Cole McDonald, and there was nothing I could do.

"Please, Will, don't make me have a birthday without you."

"You won't like it, Jenny. It'll be trouble."

"Please, Will . . . for me."

"For you . . ." His eyes searched mine. "Okay, I'll be there."

I kissed him. We were standing in the parking lot next to the Jones store. It was about five fifteen and getting dark out, and we had been walking to his car. It was the first kiss we'd ever had. Up until that kiss all our intimacy had been in our talking, our telling each other everything we'd never said out loud before. I kissed him, and he drew his head back and looked at me, and I don't think I breathed. The sky was navy blue behind him, and I felt so small, all five feet nine inches of me, and my heart was beating fast, and Will's arms went around me, and he scooped me up and pressed me into him and kissed me again and again.

I'M SURE the party was beautiful—a cold, clear Saturday night in December, clumps of brilliant stars in a black sky, frost on the windshields, ice and salt crunching under your high heels as you walked up the slick steps of the Oakbrook Country Club, a big fire in the hearth of the foyer, the sound of laughter and music, champagne in stem glasses, a buffet dinner, candlelight, a band, everything my father and the Jaffe, Shafton and Blackman accounting firm could more than pay for. But I saw a pretentious, showy display of affluence, a waste, a sham. I didn't want to be there. I would have been happier eating short ends with Will at Snead's BarBQ.

I wore a red Chantilly lace sheath, silk heels dyed to match, and my grandmother's pearls. I wore my hair down and wild, though my mother had more than suggested it should be in a French twist. They had already started the buffet line, and my mother had asked me twice why I was watching the door. I didn't answer. She didn't know he was coming. I hadn't told anyone.

He wore a black tuxedo and an impeccably tailored white tux shirt and a black silk tux tie and golden studs and black evening shoes. He'd rented the whole thing and hadn't said one word. It was the first time I'd seen Will in anything but his jeans and cowboy boots, and when I saw him in the doorway, I had to hold on to a chair. He walked across the room to me.

"Wow, Jenny, you're beautiful," he said. My mother appeared next to me as if she were attached to my body by boomerang.

"Will, this is my mother. Mom, this is Will McDonald."

"I believe we've seen each other at the Texaco station," she said, her eyes glittering. The only thing missing was a hideous cackle and one of those grotesque flying monkeys the wicked witch had.

"That's right," I said, and took Will's hand. She saw everything, didn't miss a trick.

"What school do you go to, Will? Not Southwest—"

"No, ma'am. I'm all done with school. I'm out in the big world."

"I'm starving," I said. "Let's eat."

"It works for me," Will said, steering me away from the witch. "Evening, ma'am," he said to her over his shoulder.

The fight started after the birthday cake. It seems that David Greenspan had the misfortune of saying something to someone about my breasts. The misfortune was that Will was within hearing distance. Will's fist came crashing out of nowhere, and David's nose was semipermanently crumpled up and inappropriately stuck somewhere to the left of his eyebrow. He was unconscious and spread-eagled across my mother's perfectly planned sweet table, his backside smashing the individual slices of seven-layer chocolate cake and his head bleeding into the silver tureen of whipped cream. I never found out exactly what David Greenspan had said. I only knew it was about my breasts because Sherry's boyfriend heard that much. Will wouldn't tell me anything. All I could get out of him was, "I didn't like the way he looked at you." That was all it took.

And that's all it took for my mother too, and she, of course, convinced my father, who did whatever she told him, and the edict came down loud and clear the very next day: From now on there would be *no more Will*.

But it was too late for me. As far as I was concerned, from then on there was *only Will*.

"JENNY, I love it." It was a soft leather belt with a sterling silver belt buckle on which I'd had his initials engraved. He ran his thumb over the silver, pushed the belt through the loops of his jeans.

"Merry Christmas, Will."

He took a tiny box out his pocket. "Happy Hanukkah, Jenny," he said.

Blue-and-white paper and blue ribbon, and a card with a menorah that said "For Jenny from Will."

"Is it right? I got the paper from the Gregory Drug Store. I asked old Mr. Sealy to help me so I wouldn't get anything wrong."

"Oh, Will." I fumbled with the paper and lifted the lid, and in the center of the cotton was an exquisitely fragile gold ankle bracelet, two delicate chains wound together, so feminine and so beautiful.

"See, it's just like us," he said, cradling the ribbons of gold in his big hand. "You and me." He leaned forward and he kissed me so gently. Then he put the bracelet on my ankle, closed the clasp, and kissed my ankle, and we wound ourselves around each other like the golden chains. It was the first night Will and I made love.

I CAN'T tell you what it was about William Cole McDonald, except everything. What I can tell you is that from the night of my seventeenth birthday until they destroyed us, I spent every waking moment I could with Will. It didn't matter what I had to do or say—I did it or said it, used every trick in the book. My mother caught me repeatedly. She yelled, she screamed, she forbade. It didn't matter. There was no way I was going to give up Will.

But who could know the true power of parents? What they will do when they are faced with defiance. To what depths they will stoop. Who would have thought that despite a love as bright and stunning and meant to be as ours was, they could still win?

Or is that jumping the gun in this saga? It's probably not fair to cheat you out of the details of the breath-stopping, bittersweet romance of me and my William Cole McDonald and his blue tattoo. All the details that would explain to you how he was my passion, my true and consuming and only, only passion in the whole long and lonely fifty-three years of my big-deal, glamorous uptown life. Do you want to hear how Will made me feel pretty? Me, Jenny Jaffe—a plain beige girl, a practically nondescript girl if you saw me then—pretty? But he looked at me and I was pretty. Or do you want to hear how Will thought I was smart? Or how Will thought what I had to say was important? Or how Will turned things around in my head so that I began to believe in myself? Or how Will's loving me changed everything in my life?

"I love you, Jenny. I will always love you. You're my girl."

What I would only give to hear that. . . .

HE HAD a list of names for me: Jen, J, Slim, Punkin, honey, child, kid, squirt, baby, sweetheart. And then he got me my first cowboy boots, and I never wanted to take them off, and he called me Boots.

We were two but one: We never wanted to be with anybody else, and we never wanted to be apart. Sometimes I even went to work with him. I'd sit at the Texaco pretending to read a movie magazine, but I'd really be studying Will's skinny legs and boots coming out from underneath a car. Or I'd sit at Joe's and watch him flip a Denver omelette and catch it in the fry pan behind his back, my heart floating like the puffy yellow egg over his shoulder through the air.

"Did you see that? How was that, huh? You had no idea, did you, that I came from a long line of famous cooks?"

Will smiling, Will laughing. Everything he did was important to me, and everything I did was important to him.

Will watching me from across the room as I danced for him. I actually danced for him. He was the only one. He'd sit on the edge of the bed in his rented room and watch my every move. Then he'd towel the sweat off me and tell me things until I could breathe.

"Someday I'm gonna build you a house, Jen, a big Victorian house with columns and lots of curlicues—"

"And a porch."

"Of course. A porch that goes all the way around, and you can dance on the porch and all through the house—"

"In the middle of our land."

"That's right, in the middle of our land. We're gonna go to New York—I'll take you. We'll go to wherever you need to go, and they'll discover you, and then you'll dance for everybody. You're gonna be a big star, my Jenny."

"I am?" I said, laughing, my breath ragged.

"You am," Will would say to me.

To Will my dream wasn't silly. It was within my reach. He was the only person who believed in me.

IT'S EASY TO SAY THAT I WAS too young, that I was inexperienced. What did I know? It's easy to say it was a first love and first loves never last. They fizzle and burn out and leave you with your guts spewed all over the floor. It's easy to say we never would have made it, that Will was wrong for me, that the sparkle would have dulled and I would have looked at him five or ten years after my seventeenth year and said, Holy cow, Chihuahua, what have I done? Easy to say, but wrong. I have lived a lot of my life now. I am fifty-three years old, I've had most of what there is to have, and I know. It is silly to say who is right for you, because there's no way to figure it. It's the one who takes your heart away. There was never anyone for me but William Cole McDonald, no matter how many years I have spent being married to someone else, trying to love someone else. Will was the one for me. He bent my heartstrings and he stirred my soul.

JANUARY . . .

"But why would you want to rob someone?"

We're in bed. It's very cold in his room and very loud. Three portable gas heaters are blasting at once, but they don't seem to be doing much heating. They're just making a chorus of noise.

Will props his chin up on one hand; his elbow makes a dent in the sheet as he looks at me. "It was never about robbing *someone,* Jenny. It was more about the doing of it because it could be done."

"The danger?"

"Well, maybe"—he shrugs—"but I never thought of that. I guess I never thought of anything. I just did what I did."

"And they caught you." I kiss the blue eagle on his chest.

"Twice," he says, looking at me.

"And what did they do with you?"

"They put me in jail, Boots."

I stare at him. I can hear only the heaters and my heart beating. It's like an ocean inside my head. "Will . . ."

"What?"

"Tell me everything. I want to know everything."

He told me everything. What he stole, how he stole it, how they caught him, and how he felt. Both times he was sent away for armed robbery. For armed robbery they can send you to a prison for five years or for as long as they want.

The first time, he was fifteen years old and it was a liquor store. He stole one hundred and seventeen dollars and fifty-three cents. The second time, he was seventeen years old and it was a grocery store; he stole twelve hundred dollars and change, and he got sent away for "five to life."

He had to serve only three years, but eleven months into those three years they pronounced him incorrigible, and they removed him from the vocational institution where he was serving, and they sent him to a real prison. They deemed him incorrigible because he had nearly killed a man named Newton Breen.

"We were up on this moving pile of dry wood as it made its way to the kiln, and I guess he thought it would be cute to knock me off. He drop-kicked me from behind, and I fell a story and a half, honey, and landed with my leg cracked under me. I spent three months in the hospital, on my back, with my leg in the air. Then they gave me two operations, stuck a handful of pins in me, and wiped their hands, said I'd always limp, that was the best they could do. The day they let me out of the hospital, I went to find Newt."

It seems Will beat Mr. Breen into a coma. It didn't matter that Mr. Breen had tried to kill Will first by throwing him out into the air to plummet over fifteen feet and crash into a cement yard with his leg broken under him; nobody cared. They deemed Will incorrigible and sent him to San Quentin. He served the rest of his three years there and was released on parole.

It was in San Quentin that Will grew up. Whatever Will saw in San Quentin is what made him give up his robbing career.

"I will never be in a jail again, Jenny. I will never do anything that would put me in a situation where I'd have to go."

It had nothing to do with me that Will had determination, that Will had high hopes and believed that he had turned himself around and could do anything. Will had faith in himself because of what had happened to him in his own life. It had nothing to do with me.

FEBRUARY . . .

"But what are you *doing* with him?" Linda said. We were sitting in a booth at Winstead's. "You're certainly not going to marry him. He's not the kind of a person you could be married to." And then she looked at me intensely. "Wait a minute. Have you done it? Is that what this is all about? Have you gone all the way?"

"Linda!" Sherry exclaimed, and then stared at me.

"I'm not a virgin, if that's what you're asking," I said.

"You're kidding!" Sherry gasped.

Linda made three wet rings on the table with her water glass. "You better be careful, Jenny. You certainly don't want to end up with somebody with no future, do you? With somebody who works in a gas station?" She laughed and ran her fingers through her perfect pageboy. "Really, how would you raise your children? And where? In an apartment above the Texaco?"

The waitress stood in front of us, her face flushed. She moved the cheeseburgers off the tray. "Okay, who had the vanilla Coke?"

"Me," Sherry said.

"And one cherry limeade, no ice," she mumbled, "and a frosty malt. Is that it?"

"Yeah, thank you." I busied myself taking the paper off my burger. Maybe they would forget what we'd been talking about.

Linda took a bite of her double. "He's certainly not right for you. He's not exactly somebody who fits in."

"Could we just change the subject?"

"Linda, she doesn't want to talk about it," Sherry said.

"Because you know I'm right, huh?"

I shrugged. "Okay, I give up."

"He doesn't fit in," Linda said.

"To what?"

"To our crowd, with us . . . You *know* what I mean."

"He doesn't?"

Linda raised her eyebrow. "Jenny, you're being *awfully* evasive. You don't want to tell us about him."

"I'm not being evasive."

"Yes, you are. Why are you spending so much time with him? Why are you seeing *only him?* Because you—"

I spoke very clearly when I interrupted. "Because I love him."

Sherry gasped again. "You're kidding. You do?"

"You're making a big mistake," Linda said.

"I can't believe this," Sherry said.

I chewed my burger. I never should have said I loved him. I never should have said anything. I'd forgotten about Linda, how she was like a mosquito bite that wouldn't stop itching. She was never going to let this go. I wiped the corners of my mouth with a napkin and shook a lot of salt on my french fries. I wanted to call Will to come and get me. I wanted to go home and cry.

"Does *he* love *you?*" Sherry asked quietly, her eyes wide.

"I don't know, Sherry. I think he does."

Linda shook her head. "You're being a jerk, Jenny. You're certainly not going to marry him; you're certainly not going to end up with someone like *that.*"

"You don't know anything about him."

"I don't have to. It's clear that he's not right for you."

I laughed. "You sound like your mother."

"You know what I'm saying," Linda said. "Will's beneath you. You honestly think that you can live happily ever after with somebody like that? Will's white trash, Jenny, and you know it. You'll spend the rest of your life living in a trailer park."

It was the first time I ever left Winstead's with half a cheeseburger still on my plate, and it was the first time I took the bus since we all got our driver's licenses, but I refused to get into Linda's car no matter how much Sherry begged me. I held fast to the bus-stop pole in spite of the fact that it was sleeting and freezing, and it was the last time I ever spoke to Linda Lubin in my life. Which, in retrospect, more than made up for leaving half a cheeseburger on my plate.

White trash. The same boy who said that at night we were never really separated, that if I looked at the moon from my bedroom window at the same time he looked at the moon from his, then we were never apart. The same boy who kissed my eyelids, who grinned as soon as he saw me, who was worried whenever I drove anywhere without him, made me call him so he'd know that I got there, who was upset that I'd taken the bus home that day in such bad weather. "I don't want you slidin' around on the ice in some bus, Jenny. You're in trouble, you call me. I'll come get you wherever you are." The same boy who said that sometimes, when he looked at me, he was so happy his heart hurt. White trash.

AND March . . .

"I love you, Jenny," Will said.

The first time. We were outside Jasper's restaurant at five fifteen on the evening of Saint Patrick's Day. All of Kansas City was drinking green beer, and Will held me and leaned against his Mercury and told me he loved me for the first time.

AND April . . .

"Did it snow in any of those places you lived in?" I whisper into the wool collar of Will's coat.

It's too beautiful outside to speak. The hush covers everything, like the twelve inches of new snow. It's too late to be snowing—it's April—but there it is: everything covered in white drifts.

It's a little after six in the morning. My mother thinks I'm fast asleep at a pajama party, but Will picked me up when he got off work at midnight, and I spent the whole night with him. I'd been awake for every second of it. It was the first time I'd ever wangled spending the night. Me in Will's bed for a whole night—I couldn't believe how it felt. Then he said I had to see the dawn break. I protested and refused to open my eyes. He laughed and walked to the window.

"Jenny, it's snowing."

"It can't be snowing. It's spring."

"Spring or no spring, it's snowing. Come and see."

And now I look at him in front of the sunrise, all dressed and standing in the dark and the quiet, and I know we are the only two people alive in the whole world.

Streaks of red inching up into the blackness, where there were still big, chunky white stars, and then yellow, flaming yellow into dark blue, golden yellow lighting up the crystals of frost on every tree limb. It all came alive in front of us, a glistening, dazzling, silent ice show of white, pink, and gold.

"It snowed," Will whispers, "but I don't remember anything quite like this." His arms surround me. "Maybe it's because you weren't there."

"Not anymore," I said, breathing into his neck.

"No, not anymore, not ever. I'll never give you up, Jenny."

My eyes search his. "But why would you have to?"

"I don't know, but I never will."

AND May . . .

"Your mother is worried about you."

"No, she isn't, Daddy. She's mad."

He smiled. "Okay, she's mad. . . . *I'm* worried."

"Why?"

"It's about you and that boy, Jenny. It's no good."

I didn't say anything.

"Of course, pretty soon it'll be over. It's just like I told your mother: It's a passing fancy. How much damage could it do? Come June you'll graduate and then you'll be off to Mizzou."

"Daddy, I'm not going to M.U. I only want to study dance."

"Another passing fancy. It's the same way you felt about being a twirler—remember? And you got over that, didn't you?"

My father adored me, but he didn't know me anymore. He didn't realize I wasn't the same.

AND good old June . . .

I suspect I wasn't the only one who graduated from Southwest High School in a normal cap with a tassel and with a baby inside her, under her gown. Of course, it's only a suspicion.

"It'll be all right, Jenny. Don't worry. I love you. I'm gonna take care of you. It'll be fine. We'll get married; we'll go back to California and have the baby. It's beautiful there, you'll see. You'll love it.

Jenny, this is everything I ever dreamed of—you and a baby. Jenny, I love you so much."

He was intoxicated; he was joyous. My being pregnant wasn't a problem for him. It fit perfectly into his life.

"Everything will be wonderful, you'll see. I can get a good job doing construction there—no, driving a truck. Yeah, I'll drive a truck. Maybe up in the wine country. Would you like that, Punkin, to live in the wine country?"

Wine country? What wine country? Okay, sure.

So I'd marry Will, and I'd live somewhere called the wine country, and I'd have a baby with Will's blue eyes, and he'd drive a truck, and I'd stay home and take care of the baby and wait for him to come home. It sounded good, didn't it? Wait. What home? No, don't worry about it, Jenny. Who cares what kind of home? But could I do it? Could I live in a tent by the side of the road? Is there a bathroom in a tent? Hey, don't get crazy. He said he'd take care of us, didn't he?

"I TOLD you this would happen," she says, looking at my father, and then her eyes move my way. "How could you do this to me?"

I guess I knew my father would tell her, but I was so scared and he was looking at me with such love in his eyes that it slipped out. I told him and he told her, and she went for me in the kitchen while the food stuck to the plates. It's not as if my mother even included my father—not "how could you do this to us," but "how could you do this to me."

"I didn't do this to you."

She pays no attention and looks back to him. "My God, Moe," she says to my father, "we'll have to call Dr. Bart and see if he knows someone. . . . Where will we go?"

"What do you mean? Go to do what?" I say.

"Go to fix this," she says, her voice rising, "to fix this—"

"What do you mean, fix?"

She stops stirring her coffee. The spoon clatters across the kitchen table. She walks to the sink, keeps her back to me.

"Are you talking about an abortion, Mom? Is that what you're talking about? I'm not having an abortion." My heart is slamming against my rib cage. My mother says nothing.

"Daddy?"

My father has turned a sick, bleached yellow. He doesn't look at me, but keeps his eyes focused on his cup.

"I'm going to marry him," I say clearly, my head banging.

"You most certainly are not." My mother spits out the words as if they are individual bullets being propelled from her mouth.

"I'm going to marry Will and have his baby."

"I will not allow you to ruin your life."

I look at my father; he doesn't lift his eyes. I touch his hand.

"I'm not ruining my life," I say to my father's bent balding head. "I'm going to have the baby, Daddy, and marry Will."

"You don't know what you're saying," my mother says.

My father says his words very quietly. "I don't want her to have an abortion, Esther. That's not what I want."

"Oh, really. So tell me, what do you want, Moe?"

"Not an abortion," he says again, and he looks at me for just an instant and then at her. "Maybe she could have the baby."

"Have the baby? Are you crazy? What is she going to do with a baby? Take it with her to college? Leave it here with me? And what are we going to tell everyone? The baby fell out of a tree?"

I can feel myself panicking. I can feel myself about to scream. "Please don't make me have an abortion, Daddy. I'm having the baby. I'm going to marry Will and have the baby. Please."

"And ruin all of our lives. My God, what have you done?" she says, and a sob comes from somewhere deep inside her.

My father stands up from the chair, but he doesn't go to her. He stands motionless like a fence between her and me, and then I'm crying. I want to run from the room, but my mother has crossed the room and planted herself in front of me like a battleship.

"You'll do what I tell you, Jenny," she rages, her flags flying. "You don't know what you want. You're too young to know."

Ah, too young to know. Not too young to get pregnant, not too young to love somebody, just too young to know.

"THEY CAN'T MAKE YOU HAVE an abortion, Jenny. They can't make you. Listen to me."

"I'm listening, Will."

He's pacing at the foot of his bed, where I sit. We've been doing this for three hours. It's hot in the room. Two fans are going, blowing my hair around, and I'm wearing cutoffs and a sleeveless blouse.

"They can't make you do anything. They can't, because they won't be able to." Three long steps and he's in front of me, grasping my hands in his. "We're gonna be outta here. I won't let them do anything to you, Jenny."

"Will . . ."

"We're going to go to Oklahoma and get married."

He grabs me, lifts me up to him until his lips are against mine. "I won't give you up, Jenny. I love you."

The fan makes its half circle and blows hot air across the top of us, chills the sweat on my neck, and I shake.

"Marry me, Jenny," Will says, and I don't even know if I'm happy or sad. I just hold on to him, and I say, "Yes, Will."

WILL would pick me up after he got off work. He'd go to work, get his checks, and at six o'clock he'd be at Lala Palevsky's. I would go there as if I were going to dance class, but I wouldn't go to dance class. I would wait in the parking lot, and at six o'clock he would show up in the big blue Mercury, and we would drive away. My wedding dress was stuffed inside my dance bag—a plain white sheath I'd bought at Harzfeld's—and under the folded dress a pair of cheap white peau de soie heels I'd bought at Chandler's to match the dress. And stockings. And a white garter belt. I'd charged this bounty to my mother. I believed this was not only fair but fitting. If she hadn't been such a maniac about who Will was, she probably would have made my father buy me a wedding bigger than the Missouri State Fair.

I was very excited. I loved him. I loved him so much I had no doubts. We would get married, and then we'd tell them. And if they didn't want to help us, we'd do it on our own. After all, I had a high school diploma. I could work—wait tables, type in an office, sell something in a store. Maybe wine. I could sell wine in the wine country. That was our plan—to go back to California and settle there.

And then comes the unspeakable part: Will didn't show up. I repeat, *Will didn't show up.*

Just picture it: A young girl stands in front of a dancing school on a hot summer evening quietly clutching a canvas bag that holds her neatly folded wedding dress. Hopeful, happy, she waits for a blue Mercury to glide into view, tries not to notice as the light in the sky changes, tries not to panic, tells herself how much he loves her—he loves me, I know he loves me—and finally resorts to those sickening, silent prayers, the ones that if you heard them out loud would cause you to weep: Please, God, let him come and I'll never ask You for anything. Please, God, don't let this be happening. And when the moon is sharp in a black night sky, when the chimes ring clear from the tower of Saint Anthony's twelve times, announcing to her heart that she's been standing there six hours, and her knees buckle, and she lies sprawled and sobbing on the curb, we know then that she will never see the blue Mercury or the blue eyes or the blue tattoo. We know then that a piece of her has been damaged beyond repair.

"I'll pick you up out front, like always, six o'clock, in front of Lala Palevsky's. Six o'clock, my sweetheart. I'll be there."

Why would Will leave me? Why would he run away?

After all, this was *his* plan, running away to Oklahoma, to get married in Oklahoma, of all places. It was what he wanted, so where did he go? I knew in the deepest part of me that Will loved me, so how could he just vanish into thin air?

MY FATHER wasn't in the house. It was just her and me. Four days later, four days of fog and waking and sleeping and not knowing anything around me. In my room, in my bed, not knowing anything except, suddenly, that something must have happened to him. He couldn't have just left me, not without saying something, not without explaining, not Will.

Joe knew nothing.

"Well, I just don't know, Jenny. He finished his shift like he always did, hung up his apron, said so long, and was out that door. I heard the Merc, but I didn't even raise my head."

Mr. Boyer, who owned the Texaco, was full of information.

"Well, let's see now. He picked up his check, all right, but he didn't say nothin' else. Nope. Not as far as I know."

And who else was there? Nobody. No friends, no family, nobody. I had to call the police. A person doesn't just disappear when he loves another person, when they're running away to get married. Something had to have happened to him. I would call the police; they would find Will.

"Put the phone down, Jenny. You're going to make a fool of yourself," the wicked witch said.

"Mom, get out of my room, please."

"There's no reason to call the police."

"Something happened to him."

"Nothing happened to him."

"Leave me alone." I dial. I had a pink Princess telephone; it was quite the thing then.

"Nothing happened to him," she says again.

"You don't know that."

Silence. She stands in front of the window, a dark silhouette surrounded by backlight, my beautiful mother who is supposed to love me. I am her only child.

"Good afternoon," says the male voice on the other end of the telephone. "Officer Stanfill here. How may I help you?"

"Hang up, Jennifer. Nothing happened to him. I *know*."

I look at her. "What do you know?"

"Hello? Hello?" Officer Stanfill says.

"Put the phone down."

"What do you know?"

"I know he wasn't any good for you, that's what I know."

"What did you do?"

"Me? I didn't do anything. It was his choice."

I drop the phone. "What did you do to him?"

"It's not what we did to him. It's what he did to you."

We. She has decided to include my father.

"Tell me, Mother," I say to her, and I get up from my bed with sudden strength, and I think the only reason she answers me is because she's afraid I'm going to cross the room and hurt her. "Tell me," I say again, and she says it right to my face.

"Did you think I would stand still and do nothing while he talked you into running away? Do you think I am stupid, Jennifer? That I would let you ruin your life?" Defiance crosses her face. "We offered him money to leave you," my adoring mother continues. "And he took it and he went away."

MONEY. My beloved parents, Esther and Mose Jaffe, offered my William Cole McDonald money to leave me, and the corker is, he took it and he went. Try to swallow that one.

I never, ever asked how much they gave him. I couldn't ask that. I did the next best thing. I took aspirin. I don't mean "take two and call me in the morning." I mean the bottle. All of them.

It is not easy to kill yourself. It is also not easy to kill a baby floating around inside you. These things I know. The baby part is really only an afterthought, something I tell you in retrospect, because I certainly wasn't thinking about a baby then. It was only me I was trying to get rid of. When the bottle of Bayer failed—after the stomach pumping and the stay in the hospital—I tried starving myself. After they got me home, of course, and after I tried to slit my wrists. Maybe starving would be the easy way out, especially because they were watching me. Since the bad deed with the aspirin, my two adoring parents didn't stop watching me. How could I get my hands on a shotgun when I had two prison guards? Better to try starving.

It's amazing how long you can go without eating. Of course, eventually you pass out, or you have trouble standing, but it's a long time before any of that happens, and a very long time before you starve to death. For me it was only enough time for Esther and Mose to realize that the whole thing was bigger than both of them, that they really didn't know what to do. It had become too late for Esther's abortion plan; she had to come up with something new.

Clever Esther.

I would be sent away. Banished to the Stella Maris Home for You-Know-Whats in Los Angeles. My mother found out about Stella Maris from Father McCaffrey at Our Lady of Lebanon Maronite, who played golf with Rabbi Bierman from Temple Beth-Am.

"You'll stay there until you have the baby, Jenny, and then you'll come home. It's very nice there. Father McCaffrey said so. Just like a hotel. It won't be long, four or five months."

Did she think I would just come back as if nothing had happened?

"Jennifer, are you listening to me?"

Watching me, she and my old father watching me. I shook my head, but I couldn't say anything, which was in accordance with my new plan: I would never say anything to anybody again.

MY ROOMMATE'S name was Rose. She was four months younger than me, two months more pregnant than me, and much more grown up. Her claim to fame was that her baby had been put there by an astronaut. (What an astronaut was doing in her hometown of Fond du Lac, Wisconsin, was beyond me.) He was an astronaut none of us had ever heard of, a backup astronaut for when all the others were busy flying around. Rose had a picture of herself and the understudy astronaut proudly displayed on the little table between our two beds. He had a crew cut, and his arms were around her. The American flag was clearly evident on the pocket of the uniform jumpsuit he wore, proof that he was who she said he was. He also had a wife, three children, and the entire brass of NASA. He wasn't about to have anything to do publicly with a baby he'd made with Rose.

Clumped together by age, we were two to a room, just like in a college dorm. Well, not exactly. We were not supposed to divulge our last names, we were not allowed any phone calls unless specifically arranged with Nurse Rae Lee or Sister Angelica, and we were not permitted to leave. There were twenty-eight of us at all times, because as soon as a girl would have a baby and leave, another would arrive to take her place. Stella Maris was filled to capacity. It was a sprawling whitewashed stucco building, very California, very Spanish, with a red tile roof and cute green trim. On the top floor of the hacienda were the delivery room and the clinic, where we went for our check-ups. This was separate from the church. Church. I had been transplanted into the land of Catholics, about as far from my upbringing as if I had been plunked down in a small village somewhere in Japan.

I had arrived on a Thursday and was picked up at the airport by my social worker, Mrs. Havermeyer of the sad face and thick ankles, and Sister Berl. I said nothing to either of them except yes and no and thank you. Yes, I had a fine flight; no, I didn't want anything to eat; and thank you for showing me to my little room.

Two beds with blue-yellow-and-pink-flowered chenille bed-spreads, a tiny table between the beds, one lamp, one desk, one chair. And a window overlooking a garden Sister Berl called Saint Robert Bellarmine's patio, where we girls could have a picnic if we wanted. Rose was sitting on her bed, her back up against the pillows. We nodded to each other.

Rose had brown eyes and short black curly hair, and she was lost somewhere inside a man's extra-large pink oxford shirt. She didn't appear to be doing anything, just sat there staring. I put my suitcase on the other bed.

Sister Berl gave me an extraordinary smile and glided a step backward; she didn't seem to have feet. "Sometimes the first night is very difficult. It's hard to be away from home."

I didn't say anything. I was overjoyed to be freed from the grasp of the wicked witch and her old-man sidekick. I was thrilled to be away from home.

Sister Berl stood there with her hand on the doorknob; the beautiful smile practically took up her whole face. She moved, and two shiny black leather toe tips poked out from under the hem of her habit. I was relieved to see that she had feet.

"If you want to talk to me, I'm just down the hall," she said.

"Thank you," I replied, looking down at the floor.

"Jennifer," she said, and remained motionless until I looked up at her. "God loves you." Then the black cloth swirled and she was gone.

Rose was watching me as I sat down next to my suitcase. It was devastatingly clear to me that proceeding with my plan was going to be more than difficult. It would be tough to try to kill myself again, tough to remain stalwart anywhere within range of Sister Berl's smile. Neither Rose nor I said a word for five, six minutes. I heard nothing, didn't hear the sound of anyone crying, but I could feel the tears wash down my cheeks. Rose didn't speak until we both heard me breathe. Then she looked at me across the divide that separated our two nunlike narrow beds.

"Welcome to the land of the ghost babies," Rose said.

WE CAME from everywhere, the twenty-eight of us, as far away as Mia, who came from Italy, and as close as Suze, who came from Ojai, which was only an hour and a half away.

I tried valiantly not to let them get close to me, but there were things they knew that I didn't know, and they were persistent, and I was alone. They surrounded me like a flock of birds.

"Jennifer, when Sister Theresa asks you, you don't want to work in the laundry."

Rose put down her fork and chewed on a piece of toast. "Jenny's not going to talk to you, Suze. She doesn't talk to anybody."

I pushed my scrambled egg into my potatoes.

"Well, the laundry's terrible," said Suze.

"You think the kitchen is better?" asked Rose.

"Yeah. You get to eat all that food." Suze looked at me. "Jennifer, you gotta pick someplace or they'll assign you. Everybody's gotta do chores."

Chores went on in the morning after breakfast. If you'd finished high school, you had chores; if you were younger, you had school. I never said anything to Sister Theresa, and I ended up in the laundry. In the months I was there, I must have folded enough miles of clean white sheets to reach Kansas City and return.

When I say there was no school for any of the older girls, I mean that besides no lessons in algebra or English, there were also no lessons on pregnancy. Once a week we went to the clinic and lined up like ducklings to pee in a cup, have our blood pressure measured, and stand on a scale. That was it. No lectures on childbirth, no instructions on breathing, no anything. Twenty-eight girls who were going to be mothers for a day and then give their babies away. So what did *they* need to know? Better to keep them in the dark, better to not even discuss that they were pregnant, much less tell them anything, as in no counseling sessions on what was happening to us psychologically, no therapy sessions about loss or grief or pain, and *no* answer to the most horrifying question that would be thrashing around inside our heads for the rest of our lives: Tell me, Miss Wayward Thing, do you stop being a mother if you give your baby away?

The only schooling we shared was in what labor sounded like. It came from above, and I don't mean heaven. I mean the delivery floor. That's what got me to start speaking—eight hours of lying in the dark listening to Suze give birth.

"Why don't they put her out of her misery?" Rose muttered, turning over yet again as the bed creaked.

I watched the moon through the palm leaves outside the open window. The whole thing started way before midnight, and now it was nearly dawn. I had never heard anyone scream like Suze was screaming. It was too much for me. I broke my vow of silence. "Can't they do something for her?" I said.

Rose flipped over and sat up. "Yeah. They could give her a shot and knock her out, but they won't do that until the end."

Another scream echoed through the garden. Rose got up and walked to the window, lowered her head, and sank to her knees. I watched her fingers move across the tiny crystal rosary beads, heard the whisper of her prayers. I got out of bed and stood next to her. We kept vigil until way after the morning light. Suze stopped screaming a little before eight. That must have been when they knocked her out with the anesthetic.

All babies were born at Stella Maris with the patient unconscious; then, when she woke up, she was told she had had a baby, and she could say whether she wanted to see it or not. Suze chose not. We were not told if the baby was a *he* or a *she,* and if Suze knew, she didn't say anything when she kissed us good-bye. My first good-bye at Stella Maris. I stood at the edge of the room watching tears and kisses, scraps of paper with hastily written addresses shoved into hands. Bonds and friendships made during abnormal captivity are peculiar, powerful ties, but ones that don't go anywhere. What would we have in common after we had served our time? Nothing except a bad memory, because no matter how close we became, each of us left Stella Maris with a sick taste in her mouth. Remember, at the end of your tour you had to give away your *he* or *she*.

IN SEPTEMBER we tried to get over the loss of Suze by having a picnic on Labor Day. Rose was huge. It was clear that Buster—as Rose referred to her baby—was already bigger than she was. Two new things were happening to me: I was talking to people—Suze's labor had had a permanent effect on my reserve—and I began to question whether it would be better to be a Catholic than a Jew.

Looking back, I know it had to do with falling in love with the Stella Maris sanctuary. Just being in there was heady: the hush, the perfume of dead roses and candles and incense, the colors of the stained glass—the red of the blood of Jesus, the gold of the crown, the blue of the sky. I could hide in there forever; sometimes it was the only place where I could breathe. I did not discuss my newfound love of the church with anyone, but Rose saw it. She took it upon herself to give me instruction. She and Mary and Cookie and Mia began my catechism class one day in our room.

"If you aren't baptized, you can't go to heaven. You can't be in the kingdom of God."

"Where do you go, then? Hell?" I asked.

"Limbo," they all answered.

"Limbo?"

"Anyone who hasn't been baptized goes to limbo."

Mary pushed herself up from the chair with both hands behind her. "What is there if you're Jewish?"

"There is no heaven or hell if you're Jewish. You just die and they bury you," I said. "There is no afterplace."

"But what about your soul?" Mary took a cracker out of the package at the foot of my bed, then waddled back to the chair.

"Uh . . ."

Rose sighed. "You don't seem to know very much about being Jewish, Jenny."

"I know. Isn't that strange?"

After several theological discussions, including one where we explored the differences in angels, Mary and I got into a conversation about which angels sing, as in *Angels we have heard on high, sweetly singing o'er the plains.* I said that possibly the lesser angels were more like the chorus, little song-and-dance-man angels, and Mary and Cookie got hysterical laughing. It was decided by Rose that there wasn't enough time to convert me and I should for the time being remain Jewish. It didn't matter so much that I hadn't become Catholic; at least I had laughed. I hadn't laughed for such a long time.

As October approached, Rose tried to push me to talk about what had happened to me, but I couldn't. So instead of talking about me, I listened to endless stories about Rose and the astronaut; Mia and her Salvio, the English teacher; Mary and her mother's dentist; Cookie and the boy next door. There are a million stories in the naked city. These were just twenty-eight of them. Unfortunately, there was a ghost baby in each one.

Cookie had her *he* or *she* in early November, but she refused to say good-bye before she left. Sister Berl said she was feeling too sad.

"Do you think you'll ever see him again?"

"Oh, Rose, I don't know." I looked at her, propped up against the pillows one evening. I'd told her. *Everything.*

She'd finally gotten to me. I'd never divulged any of my story when I had to talk with Mrs. Havermeyer, my social worker. And I'd never said a thing to Sister Berl. Who'd want to undermine that heavenly smile? But Rose had finally gotten to me. Not that she had to really wangle it out of me; she just asked the right things. She asked how I got along with my mother, and the cork came flying out of my mouth.

"I don't believe that's why Will left you," she said.

I traced the chenille flowers across the bedspread with my finger. "Well, that is why he left me," I said.

"You'll see him again," Rose said, and she got off her bed and headed for the shower. At the door she turned and looked at me. "Jenny, you mustn't ever do anything again to hurt yourself."

I didn't say anything.

She opened the door but just stood there. "First of all, I couldn't take it, and second, it would really be stupid."

I smirked.

"Besides everything else," she said, "it's a mortal sin, and you know how I feel about that." She made a funny face at me and walked out of the room. Who would have thought that at such a place as Stella Maris I would find my first true friend?

ROSE went into labor the day before Thanksgiving. I had kept her up practically the whole night talking.

"I don't have anybody I feel close to the way you have the Virgin Mary."

"I know."

"It's not like I don't believe in God, Rose. I do. But you have specific people to pray to, and I just have— I don't know. . . ."

"Jenny," Rose whispered, "you could pray to the Holy Mother if you wanted to. She doesn't ask you if you're Catholic; she listens to whoever needs her, whoever prays."

I smiled in the darkness. "I'll have to think about it," I said.

"Okay."

We didn't drift off until about dawn. And then a couple hours after breakfast she appeared in the laundry room. "Jenny," she said, "I think my water just broke."

They wouldn't let me stay with her; they wouldn't even let me go in and see her during any of it. At Stella Maris you didn't *see* labor until it was happening to you. But I hid on the stairway closest to the delivery room, with my foot wedged in the door so it couldn't close totally. That way I could see a bit of what was going on. When the dreaded doctor arrived, I knew it was the beginning of the end.

SHE REFUSED TO SIGN THE PAPER. She took one look at Buster and all hell broke loose.

"I'm not doing it."

"Rose, you have to."

We were whispering.

"They can't make me."

I was on the floor in the dark of her room. I'd done a pretty good job slithering down the hall when I was sure Sister Angelica was asleep. Have you ever seen a seven-months-pregnant person slither?

"Your parents aren't going to let you keep him."

"Then I'll run away."

Tears from both of us. I squeezed her fingers, stood up, and sat tentatively on the edge of her bed. "Oh, Rose, how will you take care of him? What will you do for money?"

She wiped her nose with the sheet. "I'll get a job. The Holy Mother will help me. I can type, Jenny. I can take shorthand."

"But where will you go?"

"I'll go home. I'll go to Fond du Lac. I have to go home."

"But people will know." I began to sob. "Everyone'll see the baby; they'll know you weren't married and you got pregnant. They'll say terrible things about you."

"I don't care, Jenny. I won't give Buster to anybody."

And she didn't. Her parents arrived. There were lots of pow-wows, but Rose stood her ground. In the end, her parents didn't want to lose their daughter. They agreed to let her bring the baby home. She could live with them until she got a job.

We were allowed to say good-bye to Rose, but we weren't allowed to see the baby. I saw him, though, because I did a little more slithering. I also hid when they went out the gates to get into the taxi-cab. I stood behind the orange trees so I could kiss them good-bye between the bars. Buster had black curls, just like Rose. He was wearing a little blue hat with matching blue bootees. He was five days old and practically as big as Rose.

"You promise to come to Fond du Lac?"

"I promise."

She leaned her head forward, the tip of her nose touching the bars. I was dizzy with the smell of baby powder. "You'll be all right, Jenny. The Virgin Mary will watch over you. I promise."

"Rose," her mother said from the open door of the taxicab.

"I'm coming," she said over her shoulder. "I love you, Jenny."

"I love you too, Rose."

We clutched fingers through the iron bars of Stella Maris. I thought I was going to die. Long after the taxi had gone and it was too cold to stay out in the dark garden anymore, I stood up. My legs were stiff from sitting, and I reached for the statue of Saint Robert Bellarmine to hold on to, but there was something wrapped around my fingers. Rose had wound her tiny crystal rosary beads into my hand. As if they were the only hold I had left on life, I clutched those beads until they made marks on my fingers. I believed Rose and I would see each other again. I didn't know how long it would take, but I truly believed. After all, her baby was named Buster Jaffe Hufstedler. That's what it said on his birth certificate. Hufstedler was Rose's last name; the Jaffe was for me.

The next day I told Mrs. Havermeyer I wanted the adoptive parents to be Catholic.

"But you're Jewish, dear. Don't you want your baby to be raised by a lovely Jewish couple?"

"No, ma'am," I said. "I want the baby to be Catholic." At least the baby would be covered. It would have the Virgin Mary and Jesus and the saints and everybody else I couldn't have.

"Well, if you're sure, dear, I'll call Blessed Children."

I had no idea what she was talking about. As long as the baby was Catholic, I didn't care who she called.

DECEMBER 4, my birthday, was a far cry from the previous year. No fancy shindig at the country club—just a yellow cake with white icing. My birthday present was a new roommate, Sugar Dawes, who "hailed," she said, from Gun Barrel, Texas. She was sweet as sugar, but I didn't care. I didn't want to hear her story. I didn't want to hear anybody's story ever again. I had lost my heart for stories.

After Rose left, I spent most of my time in church, hiding, trying not to be afraid. I spent hours staring at the statue of the Virgin Mary, but she didn't say a word. I had thought she'd send me a sign, some kind of clue. My biggest problem was Buster: I saw him everywhere. When I shut my eyes, I saw him. When I opened my eyes, I saw him. I'd spent eight months pretending that what was inside me was just a sensation, and now, because of Buster, I couldn't do that anymore.

I made it through Christmas, but several days later I went to bed with what I thought was the flu. I woke up with something else.

Pain. Terror. Panic.

More pain. More terror. More panic. More pain. It went on forever, until the doctor came and they hit me with the anesthetic. And then they woke me up. And they told me.

Five pounds, eleven ounces. Eighteen inches. That's what they told me. I could hear the words, but nothing registered. And then they handed me a baby. An incredibly small baby. A *she.*

Sister Angelica put her into my arms. I couldn't speak. I couldn't breathe. I had gotten my sign from Mary.

Ten so tiny fingers and ten so tiny toes and tiny kneecaps and tiny heels and elbows and little shoulders and little ears and one little freckle on the tip of her right earlobe and the sweetest nose with a little dip in it and the sweetest pink mouth and one dimple where the angels had kissed her at the bottom of her left cheek and wisps of blond hair and soft curling brown eyelashes around pale blue almond-shaped eyes. A plastic bracelet strapped to one tiny wrist: FEMALE. JAFFE. DECEMBER 30, 1960. 2:40 P.M.

I couldn't stop looking at her. I couldn't believe that she was real. Quiet, incredibly quiet, looking up at me with Will's eyes. Calm and silent in my arms. I touched her little hand, and she wrapped her tiny fingers around my big finger and held on.

Disbelief.

They would never let me see her alone. One of them always stayed in the room with me, stood near the bed or sat in the chair, and they would only bring her to me at feeding time. The rest of the time she was in the nursery under lock and key. Feeding time was with a bottle, no breast-feeding. I was to stay in the clinic five days, the normal procedure for a normal delivery. The abnormal thing was that after the five days I would go home alone.

How could I leave her? I couldn't. I wouldn't. "Oh, yes, you will," the wicked witch said. There was to be "no discussion" about keeping her. I tried on the telephone as Sister Berl sat holding my hand.

I tried when my mother arrived from Kansas City. Father Vincent at the foot of my bed, his head bowed; Mrs. Havermeyer by the door, her mouth open; and my mother pacing the room in open defiance, her eyes screaming *no.* I remember her elegant gray wool shirtwaist moving about her knees, one strand of pearls swaying over her breasts as gray suede pumps charged back and forth across the floor.

"There is no reason to discuss this. The baby will be put up for adoption, as we agreed when we sent her to you."

"But Mrs. Jaffe—" Father Vincent said.

"There is nothing more to say, Father. I'm furious that you would allow Jennifer to think she could change her mind."

I was sobbing. "I never agreed; I never said anything; I never even thought there would be a baby. Somehow . . . I don't know what I thought." Sister Berl put her hand on my knee.

Father Vincent reached out as if to touch my mother. "Couldn't there possibly be a way that you could help her?"

"I could get a job. Please, Mom, I could get a job."

She whirled so fast the pearls leaped up and made a scallop over her left shoulder.

"Doing what? You never had a job in your life, Jennifer!"

"I could . . . I could work in a dime store."

"Listen to you! Do you know how much it costs to raise a child? Of course not! And you will not live with me, Jennifer, *not with a child.* I won't have everyone talking about us behind our backs, and I won't let you ruin your life."

The words echoed around the room. Nobody said anything.

Father Vincent cleared his throat. "Mrs. Jaffe, if you and your husband decide not to be involved, there are people we can call. The Catholic diocese in Kansas City—"

She cut him off. "She won't be able to do it without me, Father. She isn't capable and she isn't strong."

Father Vincent stood up and locked eyes with the dragon. "If Jennifer is determined, she can do it—with the Lord's help."

She stared at him. "I do not care what Jennifer *thinks* she wants. The baby will be adopted as planned. This is what is best for the baby and for Jennifer. I will not be swayed. With all due respect, Father, I don't need anybody to tell me what to do."

Father Vincent took a step toward her. "Mrs. Jaffe, I—"

"No. There is nothing more to discuss. Jennifer will come home and go to college. She will put all this behind her; she will forget about it in time. I will not let her be burdened with an illegitimate baby and no future at eighteen. I will not let her ruin her life. I will not let my daughter be the talk of the town."

FORGET about it. Put it behind me.

But the "it" was a baby. The "it" was my daughter.

And you'd think that I would have been strong enough to tell the wicked witch Esther to go to hell, but I didn't. I didn't do anything. Mrs. Havermeyer said I didn't have to go back to Kansas City; there were people right there in Los Angeles who could help me find a decent place to live and a job. I remember that word "decent" hitting me in the face. What did that mean—a bathroom down the hall, a hot plate instead of a kitchen, no running water?

Sister Berl tried to talk to me and Father Vincent tried to talk to me about how the church would help, and I listened to them. Oh, how I listened, how I wished, but somewhere in the deepest part of me I knew my mother was right. I couldn't do it without her. Unlike Rose, I would be out there flying solo, just me and my baby without a net, and if I tried to envision the realities of it—me heating a bottle in a little dented pan on a hot plate—all I could see was a curtain of blackness descending over me.

In the end, I proved to be what I always had been, a coward. I let my baby slip through my fingers and fall right out of my life. In the end, God forgive me, I proved my mother was right.

YOU WERE NOT ALLOWED TO sign the paper at Stella Maris. It was against the rules, since they were the middlemen for the adoption, and you could say they coerced you. You had to leave the grounds, so we went by car to Mrs. Havermeyer's office. I don't remember who drove. I don't remember her office, except I threw up in the wastebasket that was by the door. Mrs. Havermeyer held my head, sweet Mrs. Havermeyer of the sad face and the thick ankles, and she introduced me to Mr. Stanley from the Blessed Children's Adoption Agency. He would place my baby with a lovely Catholic couple who would raise her, but first he had to ask me questions before I could sign the paper.

"Has anyone forced you to do this?"

That's what he said. I was holding on to the desktop, and Mr. Stanley was standing on the other side of the desk. Mrs. Havermeyer said, "Are you all right, dear? Are you going to be sick again?" She patted my shoulder.

"Jenny," Mr. Stanley said in a soft voice.

I looked up at Mr. Stanley and I said no, no one had forced me to do this.

That's what I said. Because I hadn't been forced, had I? Let's face it: I was sitting there, nobody had a gun on me, and I'd walked in of my own free will, hadn't I?

I don't remember the rest of the questions. I don't remember signing the paper. I remember blinking, seeing the word "relinquish" swimming around in front of my eyes. "I, Jennifer Jaffe, do hereby relinquish my baby. . . ." Relinquish, as in give up, as in abandon. God forgive me. I gave my baby away. I *relinquished* my baby.

BACK at Stella Maris, Sister Berl waited on the other side of the door. It was the only time they had let me be alone with my baby. It was in a little room on the delivery floor that was saved for these very special occasions. It was the room where you and your baby said good-bye.

My sweet baby.

Her little fingers held my finger; her eyes were open. I rocked her, and I tried to tell her everything. How some wonderful mommy and daddy would take care of her better than I could, how I wasn't a force to be reckoned with, but I knew she would be because she was half her daddy. I told her all about Will, about how I loved him, about how I knew he had loved me. I told her that it didn't matter how we had ended up, that she was a baby who had come from love, and that's what made her special.

And then I told her what it said on her birth certificate—that I had written her daddy's name even though we weren't married and that I had named her Cole Jaffe because I wanted her to be named for both of us. I told her that her other mommy and daddy would probably change her name, but somewhere deep inside she would know who she was. I kissed every part of her, every bit of the silk and down of her, and then I stood up and held her out in front of me and looked into her eyes. I promised her that someday I would see her again, no matter how long it took or how difficult it would be. And then I held her close to me, and I wound Rose's beautiful crystal rosary beads around her tiny wrist. It was the only thing that meant anything to me, the only part of me I could give her to take. I looked at her one more time. In one last look I tried to drink her in and tell her everything I could, and then I opened the door.

Claudia

"READ me, Mommy, one more, one more," Lily said. She slid off Claudia's lap and ran to the basket of books at the end of the small blue sofa. Claudia moved back and forth slowly in the rocker and looked out the open window at the night sky.

For the first time in two months the desert Santa Ana had blown the smog away, and chunky white stars and planets were actually visible over Los Angeles.

"That's a hawk moon, baby," Claudia said to Lily. "See how it's just a skinny little sliver? That's called a hawk moon." Claudia studied her three-year-old daughter, the pudgy little body squatted by the basket, the poof of Lily's last hold-out nighttime diaper clearly visible through the seat of her pink jammies, the wisps of light blond hair curling softly around the child's neck.

"This one," Lily said. She ran back and wiggled up onto her mother. "Read me, Mommy. Do the new baby bird. Grandma Margaret got it for me while you and Daddy were in *the* New York."

"She did, huh? And you like it?"

"Uh-huh."

"Well, okay. *Are You My Mother?* by P. D. Eastman," Claudia read out loud. Then she opened the book and turned to the first page. *"A mother bird sat on her egg,"* Claudia read.

"The egg jumped," Lily said eagerly.

"You know it already, huh, cookie?"

"Mommy, read."

"Sorry . . . *The egg jumped. 'Oh oh!' said the mother bird."*

"My baby will be here!" Lily said emphatically.

" '*My baby will be here!*' " read Claudia. " '*He will want to eat. I must get something for my baby bird to eat!' she said. 'I will be back.' So away she went."*

Lily wiggled in anticipation. "The egg jumped," she said.

Claudia laughed. *"The egg jumped. It jumped, and jumped, and jumped! Out came the baby bird!* Oh, my goodness, he was born, wasn't he? That cute little baby bird was born."

Lily patted her mother's hand.

"Okay, okay, cookie. *'Where is my mother?' he said. He looked for her. He looked up. He did not see her. He looked down. He did not see her. 'I will go and look for her,' he said. So away he went."*

"Down, out of the tree he went," Lily squealed. "Mommy, read."

But Claudia had stopped reading. Her eyes were focused somewhere out the window, somewhere in the black sky to the side of that hawk moon.

Lily went on with emphasis, as if she could read what was on the page in front of her. "Now I will go and find my mother."

"Now I will go and find my mother," Claudia repeated softly. The tears swelled suddenly, surprising her, sliding down her face and into her daughter's hair. *"Now I will go and find my mother. . . ."* Claudia said, but then the words stuck and she could say no more.

SHE stood and looked at her face in the mirror, wiped toothpaste with a wet hand from the sides of her mouth. She'd put Lily to bed right after that book, rocked her a little, and sang to her. Claudia frowned at her reflection. First the dreams again and now this. *"Now I will go and find my mother,"* she mouthed, and she bent her head, splashed water on her face, and reached for a towel. She would go down to the kitchen and get herself a big glass of white wine. First she'd talk to Oliver, and then she'd go.

"Ollie?"

There was no answer from the bedroom, only an announcer on the television screaming out plays from the Knicks game. Claudia moved away from the sink and stood in the doorway watching her husband watch the game. He was perched on the edge of the bed, pitched forward, ready to jump in. Oliver James Morgan, social studies teacher and Saturday morning soccer coach for Canyon High School, now stripped of his chinos and chambray button-down, wearing only striped boxers and white socks.

"Ollie, I've been thinking about something. Something happened while I was putting the baby to bed, and it really threw me, and . . ." She put her hand on the doorframe. "I've been having the *other mother* dreams again, actually for some time now—"

"Come on, Ewing!" Oliver yelled at the television.

"Ollie?"

No answer.

She studied him carefully. He wasn't listening; it was absolutely clear he wasn't listening. "And I think I'm going to go to China," she said.

"Hmm?" he said. He didn't look at her. He just tuned her out.

"Oh, and I think I'm going to look for my parents, the real

ones—" And she stopped. "No, that isn't right, is it? Not the real ones, the *other* ones," she said softly, "not Margaret and John."

"What, babe? You want Chinese?"

There it was, a perfect example of what she used to point out to her patients before she'd left her psychology practice after having Lily: Creative listening—you see, the only thing that got through to him was the word China.

"Come on, Ewing, you moron!"

Oliver shifted his eyes from the TV and looked at his wife poised in the bathroom doorway. Sand-colored, unruly, wavy hair; bright blue eyes; a thin, tall body through a peach nightgown; broad bony shoulders; freckles; tan skinny legs; tan arms. He liked what he saw, and he beamed in appreciation. "What?"

Claudia shook her head. She couldn't tell him; it seemed she'd lost all her energy. "Nothing. I'm going down to the kitchen."

"Okay, babe," Oliver said, looking back at the Knicks game. "You want to order Chinese?"

IT WOULDN'T be difficult. At least that's what they had told her.

"It isn't difficult to find your birth parents, as long as your birth parents are looking for you."

But why would they be looking for her if they gave her up in the first place? More important, why would she be looking for them? That was the real question. It always came back to that.

She stood in front of the cutting board perched over the kitchen sink and stared out at the next morning. She listened for sounds of Lily waking up from her nap. Hearing nothing, she poked a spoon inside the peanut butter jar and then put it in her mouth. Maybe she'd go upstairs and wake Lily. Then she could play with her, and she wouldn't have to think about this stuff anymore. Claudia ran her hand across her face. She was tired from the dreams, that was it.

Outside, a hummingbird poked himself into a pink geranium.

She should just forget about this whole thing. It was ridiculous. It had come out of nowhere, and there was no reason to even consider it. Why look for trouble when your life is working? Isn't that what she would tell a patient? Of course. If your life is perfectly happy, why mess it up with . . . what? Unnecessary parents?

Unnecessary parents. Real parents. *Birth* parents? Yes, that's what the woman had said. She remembered how those words had thrown her. The words had come out of the lady's mouth, the smiling, very fat lady in the very chintzy red dress at EDNA, the search organization where Claudia had gone ten years ago. It was the first time she had ever heard the term birth parents.

Ten years ago she'd gone, right before she'd married Oliver. And it was because of something that had seemed so insignificant really, until you analyzed it.

She'd been sitting in her parents' dining room in the house where she'd grown up—she and her mother, Margaret, sitting next to each other in the beautiful butter-yellow room with the high molded ceilings and the heavy flowered draperies, smiling at each other at the mahogany table as Margaret addressed the thick cream wedding-invitation envelopes with one of her fountain pens with its permanent black ink. And that's when it had gotten to her. She had to figure out later exactly *what* had gotten to her. She had to figure it out for herself, and she had to figure it out for her sessions. She was still interning at the clinic then, so she had to know. "You, as a therapist, you, as a person," Dr. Turner had said, "in order to be a good psychologist, you have to know." Her, as a patient, okay. So what had gotten to her? It was the word *permanent* written on the ink bottle; she wanted to get married for *permanent.* This would be her one and only wedding as far as she was concerned, the only time that she would ever march down that aisle, *permanently* attached to Oliver.

Somehow that was the catalyst, that and the fact that she couldn't address any of the envelopes, because her handwriting looked as if she were a paraplegic, while her mother's looked as if she had taught penmanship at Miss Hickey's Finishing School for Girls. Another way in which she wasn't like Margaret, didn't look like her, and certainly didn't act like her—patient and genuinely kind and soft-spoken. She couldn't even remember hearing her mother really raise her voice. Although Claudia tried to copy Margaret's sweet demeanor, it always felt as if she had been horribly miscast in Olivia de Havilland's role, keeping her teeth clamped together until she thought her eyes would pop. And if she wasn't Miss Mellie, then who was she? Scarlett? All these thoughts collided into a dream-wrenched night for Claudia. Over and over she marched up and down that aisle in her wedding gown, but the mother who was watching her was not Margaret. This *other mother* was not small and dimpled like Margaret; this *other mother* would never wear a moss-green, lacy dress like Margaret; this *other mother,* smiling behind the candles and the white roses, was wearing black. And she looked just like Claudia. She had light brown, wavy hair and was tall and thin, with a smattering of freckles and rotten penmanship. It was hard to know how you could tell about her penmanship from a dream, but it was clear to Claudia that long night that this *other mother* wrote just like her. And looked like her and walked like her. And this *other mother,* this dream mother, Claudia knew, was not a dream.

And shouldn't this *other mother* get to see Claudia become *permanent?*

"WELL, shouldn't she?" Gena had said to Claudia shortly before the wedding. They were having their customary Sunday brunch at Nat 'N' Al's. Best friends since childhood, they'd gone on to Columbia together—Gena in theater arts, Claudia in psych.

Gena pushed at the enormous Reuben sandwich with her finger. "It's not a big deal. After you find her, it could be a very big deal. It could possibly change your whole life, but this part is easy. You just go there, and they put your name on a list, and they see if her name's on the list. They connect you with your real mother, and that's that." She popped a french fry into her mouth.

"That's that, huh? Very funny, ho ho ho." Claudia took a sip of cream soda. "Why do I feel like I want to scream?"

"I don't know. Because you're hungry?" Gena sliced her sandwich into two perfect rectangles and gave Claudia one. "Don't let me eat too many french fries."

"Gena, you don't understand. I haven't thought about this stuff

since I was little. I haven't had these *other mother* dreams for years."
Claudia slumped and put her face in her hands. "This whole thing
is ridiculous. Why don't I just forget about it? Chalk it up to pre-
marriage heebie-jeebies."

"Why shouldn't you want to know who your parents are?"

"Why should I? I have two perfectly wonderful, loving parents.
What do I need more for? Isn't two enough for any girl?"

"What does Dr. Turner say?"

"She says it's up to me."

"Well, that's helpful. What do you say?"

"I say . . . I just don't know. That's what's so awful. I want to
know who they are, but I don't want to know who they are."

"Falling into the don't-make-waves category. What does Ollie
say?"

"He says I should do what makes me feel comfortable." Claudia
laughed. "It's the same thing he says when I ask him what I should
wear."

SOON after that brunch Gena had found this organization called
EDNA that helped people find their parents. "Listen to this," Gena
said, and she read aloud from the pink brochure: " 'EDNA is named
for its founder, Edna Jean Malone, who found the graves of her parents after an exhaustive thirty-three-year search.' Can you imagine?
She finds her parents after all those years, and they're dead?"

Claudia slumped back on Gena's couch. "Wonderful."

"Well, I didn't mean that would happen to you. Yours aren't going to be dead. Don't be ridiculous. I just love the way they put it.
It's so dramatic, don't you think?"

"Gena, I don't know if I really want to do this."

"Oh, come on. Think of it as an adventure. If you don't like it,
you can leave. I'll go with you."

"Oh, that would be good."

"I'll go with you, but you have to stop being such a chicken.
We're not still at Saint Mary Magdalene. Sister Anne isn't going to
catch us and smack us with her ruler across the hands."

Claudia lifted her foot to put it on the coffee table. One long curl fell over her face and moved as she breathed out. "I wish you could go and pretend you're me."

"Ooh, that would be wonderful. Just like in a movie. Can I, Claud? Would you let me? Do you want me to?"

"No." She stood up. "I have to do this. I have to go."

A plain brown door down a hallway, the fake brass letters EDNA, a white, square room in a low stucco building on a side street close to the freeway—it was there that Claudia had a quiet conversation with the very fat lady in the chintzy red dress.

"But what if she *isn't* looking for me?"

"Well then, she won't have put herself on the list saying that she wants to be found, and he won't have either."

"He?"

"Your father," the lady said.

"My father," Claudia repeated, and she had a vision of John, her father—tall, dear, gruff, and conventional, the lawyer-lumberjack, to quote Gena, barred from the forest by a pin-striped suit and a silk tie. Claudia smiled at her father's vision, and the lady smiled back at her. Claudia turned to Gena, but Gena was engrossed in a magazine.

What did Gena care? She knew who her mother and father were; she didn't have a problem with feeling undefined.

"And your name, dear?" Claudia turned her head. The lady's pudgy fingers were poised over the paper, holding her pen.

"Claudia. My name is Claudia."

"Claudia, my sweet angel," she could hear her mother saying to her with that look of pure adoration on her face. Margaret, sitting next to her at Saint Mary Magdalene, her soft fingertips patting one kneecap of Claudia's swinging legs. "Stop kicking the pew in front of you, my sweet angel. You're disturbing Mrs. Vallely."

And now the sweet angel grows up and looks for another mother. Where's your devotion, Claudia? Where's your loyalty?

Claudia had a flash of Margaret sitting at her dressing table, her hands poised over her perfumes and creams as Claudia explained it all over Margaret's shoulder in the mirror: "I just want to see what she looks like, Mommy, that's all." And Margaret's face getting all soft and smudgy but smiling while she nodded her head valiantly. "Of course you do. I understand. I love you. That's all right, dear."

No. She couldn't do that. She couldn't say that to Margaret, that she wanted to find her *other mother*. She would never want Margaret to think that she wasn't mother enough for her.

"Oh, my heart," Claudia said, exactly the way Margaret did, and realized she was clutching her purse to her chest.

"Excuse me?"

Claudia blinked and looked at the fat lady in red. "Excuse *me*. I can't do this," she said, and stood up so fast the chair crashed to the floor. "I'm sorry. Gena, please, we have to get out of here."

So THE *other mother* didn't get to see Claudia become *permanent*. And neither did the *other father*. Just Margaret and John.

"Margaret and John, my *parents,*" Claudia said out loud.

She ate another tablespoon of peanut butter, and then the hummingbird nearly crashed into the window.

Ten years since the pathetic EDNA trip. Ten years since she had walked down that aisle and knelt in front of Father O'Malley and said her vows, and for six years she had been blessed with no more *other mother* dreams and no more *other father* dreams. They came back when she was pregnant. Dreams of floating babies: babies people wanted; blurry women holding blurry babies wrapped in blurry blankets to their chests; and babies people didn't want, graphic images too hard to sleep through.

"You're adopted," they had said to her. Adopted. Who said the word first? Margaret? John? Claudia absolutely did not remember.

Repression. She was a psychologist, after all. She certainly knew about repression. Repression, holding back.

"No, I'm not holding back. I just can't remember."

"And that's what we call repression," Dr. Turner had said.

She had questioned her parents repeatedly, and they had told her the story in detail: how they had sat her down, where they had sat her down. "We were going to tell you in the living room, but Daddy thought your bedroom would be better." Margaret had looked at John with such love in her eyes. Claudia's frilly bedroom with its yellow dotted-swiss ruffles covering everything. She remembered every inch of her bedroom, but couldn't remember how they sat her down.

"On the club chair under the window?"

"No, sweetheart. We all sat on the floor."

She looked at her parents and John laughed. "She doesn't remember, Margaret, that we were once young enough to sit on the floor."

"No, Daddy. It's just that I don't remember."

They were patient; they tried to help her remember. "It was in the afternoon," her mother had said.

"It was on a Saturday," her father had said.

How had she reacted upon hearing the words? "Did I cry?"

"Of course not, sweetheart. Why would you cry when we told you how we had picked you from all the babies?" Margaret said.

Claudia had an image of Margaret and John walking through a huge hall crowded with bassinets, holding up babies one by one.

Do you like this one, dear?

I don't know. Take its bootees off. Let me see its feet.

And the questions that came afterward, all the questions that flooded her, popping up week after week.

"You mean I don't belong to you?"

"Of course you belong to us, Claudia." Margaret smiling at her from across the kitchen table. "You just didn't come out of me; everything else is just the same. I'm your mommy just the same."

"But what happened to the mommy I came out of?"

"What, sweetheart?" John's eyes over the top of his newspaper.

"The mommy I came out of. Not *Mommy*—the *other* one. What happened to her?"

The newspaper descended and he looked at her. "Well, Claudia, I don't exactly know what happened to her, except that she couldn't keep you, and we wanted you so much, and so we got you, you see?"

"Oh."

Quiet. Quiet on the outside but loud on the inside. So many questions battling for position in her little head.

"She didn't want me, Daddy?"

"Oh, no. I'm sure she wanted you very much. There must have been a very good reason why she wasn't able to keep you. There are sometimes reasons in people's lives that prevent them from doing what they want, reasons that—"

Claudia interrupted. "Maybe she wanted a little boy instead."

A faint smile crossed John's lips; he folded his newspaper. "You know, I was thinking maybe we should take a walk around the block. Maybe I'll walk and you can ride your new bike."

"Really?"

So she stopped thinking about who wanted whom while her father encouraged her to pedal her bicycle up and down curbs and fly through the leaves.

"That's it, Claudia. You can do it, right over that curb! That's the way!" John's enthusiasm making her brave on her two-wheeler, the wind pushing her hair back, until she laughed at her old fear of falling off, because her father was cheering her on.

CLAUDIA put away the peanut butter, walked to the wall phone, and dialed. She could picture the phone ringing in Gena's New York apartment. Actually, Gena's phone didn't ring. It made a chirp sound, like a bird.

Gena answered on the third chirp.

Claudia sat down on the kitchen floor, her back up against the refrigerator. "Gena?"

"Yes? Claud?"

"Yeah. Gena, I have to talk to you. I seem to be having a little problem here. Do you remember when we went to EDNA?"

"Who?"

"EDNA, that adoption place. Remember we went right before Ollie and I got married."

"Of course I remember. What about it?"

"Well, I . . ." Claudia took a big breath. "Gena, what I want to know is, do you think you could fly out here and be with me so I could go again?"

AFTER THEY'D TALKED NEARLY past lunchtime, it was clear that Gena couldn't go with her. She was in the middle of rehearsals. "Didn't you remember I was opening in only two months, if you can believe that, and weren't you and Ollie coming in for the opening? You promised, Claudia." So as much as she wanted to, she couldn't leave New York now.

"What happened that you decided to look for them?" Gena went on.

Claudia fingered the phone cord. "I don't know."

"It must have something to do with you having the baby."

"The baby, Ms. Godmother, is already three."

"I know how old the baby is. Maybe you're just a little slow on the realization."

Claudia laughed. "I thought I was the psychologist."

"Well, I'm the actress. I mean, if I was playing you in this particular predicament, suddenly wanting to find your parents after you were so clear all these years about how you *didn't* want to find them, I'd have to know my motivation, my whys. I'd have to know who you are, so I'd know how to play you, so it would be real."

Claudia sighed. "Maybe I don't know who I am."

"Oh, Claud. I wish I could go with you, you know I do."

"Yep, I know."

After they'd hung up, Claudia had fed Lily and played with her until she had this overwhelming urge to call Margaret, to rush over and spill everything. "Oh, nothing. I just have this plan, Mommy, to find my *other mother.* You know, the one that isn't you."

No, she couldn't say that. What could she say?

She'd finally picked up the telephone while Lily colored.

"Oh, nothing, Mom. I just thought I'd come over. . . . Could I come over? Are you doing anything special?"

"Of course not, sweetheart. I'd love for you to come over. I'll make us lunch."

Sweetheart. And will I still be her sweetheart when I tell her what I want to do?

At two o'clock Claudia left the baby with Santos, the maid, and drove to her parents' home. The big pine in the front lawn had just been trimmed; she could see circles of sap where the branches had been sliced, the limbs trying to repair themselves with their own juice. She had looked out on that tree every day as she grew up. My tree, she'd told her parents; it's mine because it's outside my bedroom window. She ran her hand down the bark of the trunk. Would Margaret have enough sap to repair herself after she sliced her with the news?

"Mom?"

"I'm in the kitchen."

The large rooms were hushed and beautiful, and Claudia was flooded with a sense of peace. It was something about the sunlight, the way the gold picked up the thick yellow cream of the stucco and made the living room and dining room quietly shine. Spotless mahogany, oak floors, rich Chinese carpets, Kiwi furniture wax, and pine needles and spice. It was the way she'd felt each time she came home—home from school and home from her first date, home from college and home from grad school, home after she'd married Ollie and after she'd had Lily and now.

"I thought we'd have Two Girls Tuna," Margaret said gaily as Claudia entered the kitchen. "We haven't had it in such a long time."

Two Girls Tuna, a recipe Margaret had retained from her home-ec class some forty years ago: one-half can "fancy" tuna, two celery sticks, finely chopped, one tablespoon mayonnaise, and one dollop of sweet pickle relish.

"Oh, Mom," Claudia said, "Two Girls Tuna." Then she folded her five feet nine inches of bones and angles into Margaret's five feet one inch of soft roundness and was overcome with tears.

"IT'S all right. I've just been waiting," Margaret said, her hand covering her daughter's hand. They sat at the kitchen table in front of Two Girls Tuna atop Boston lettuce, thin slices of tomato, radish roses, and even carrot curls that Margaret had made as if it were still 1957. "I've been preparing for this day for a long time."

"You have?"

"Of course. Since the day we told you that you were adopted, I always knew in my heart that someday you'd want to find them. I was just waiting for you to want to know." Margaret smiled, but the smile seemed breakable. "I'm not afraid, Claudia. I've been a good mother. I know I have."

Claudia leaned forward. "You've been a perfect mother. It has nothing to do with you or Daddy. I just—"

"I'm sure it's perfectly natural for you to want to see them, especially since you've had the baby. You just want to see a little piece of yourself, and you certainly can't see that when you look at me."

She smiled that fragile smile again, and Claudia closed her fingers over the edge of the table. What had possessed her to do this?

Margaret pushed her chair back and stood up. "Come upstairs. I want to show you something."

Claudia followed her mother up the carpeted staircase and into the bedroom, her hand trailing along the banister. Margaret and John's bedroom was still aqua after all these years: the watered-silk bedspread and matching tieback draperies, the brocade sofa, and two small English pull-up chairs, all in different shades of aqua; and the Irish lace sheers behind the draperies were the same soft ivory cream as the walls. No matter how many times Margaret redecorated, the bedroom always turned up aqua and cream. Claudia found this reassuring. She loved being in Margaret and John's bedroom.

Margaret lifted something out from under her lingerie. It was a box, Chinese lacquer, with a flower design in black and white and deep red. Claudia had never seen it before. "This was Great-grandma Nellie's," she said. "She got it at the Panama-Pacific International when her parents took her when she was just a girl— San Francisco in 1915—and she gave it to my mother, and when Grandma Mae died . . ." Her voice trailed off.

Claudia was having trouble breathing. Margaret's mother, Mae, had died a year ago. What did it mean, all this history? Was it right, then, that someday Claudia should get the box?

Margaret walked to the brocade sofa and sat down with the box on her lap; Claudia followed and sat next to her.

Margaret raised the lid and placed it gently on the painted table in front of her. Inside the box were a few folded papers, a small notebook, and then Margaret pulled out something from a creased envelope, something that caught the light coming through the lace sheers. She put whatever it was into her daughter's hands.

"This is what your mother sent with you," Margaret whispered, and Claudia looked down. In her palm lay the rosary beads that Jenny Jaffe had so lovingly wound around her baby's tiny wrist.

This was tangible, these crystal rosary beads. She could feel them, touch them. Claudia's breath caught. The *other mother* had actually existed. She was *real;* she had physically held these beads; she had sent them with her. Claudia looked up at Margaret, but Margaret was sorting through things in the Chinese box.

"Mom . . ."

"Daddy and I named you Claudia, but you see here"—she held out a piece of paper—"that wasn't your real name. They named you Cole. Or she did, because as far as I know, he wasn't with her. But we weren't supposed to know that. It just slipped out. They were very circumspect about what you were allowed to know, and we certainly weren't supposed to know anything except the very peripheral things: if she'd finished high school, if she was a good student, what she looked like, things like that. I wrote it all down. . . . Everything."

Cole? Did she say Cole? The facets of the crystal beads cut into Claudia's palm as she leaned forward to read the words:

> AMENDED BIRTH CERTIFICATE
> Claudia Ellen Magers
> Date of Birth: December 30, 1960
> Time of Birth: 2:40 p.m.
> Original Name: Cole Jaffe

Original name: Cole Jaffe. Cole Jaffe. I am Cole Jaffe, Claudia said to herself in her head.

"But we certainly weren't supposed to know your real name. They were so careful, especially Mr. Stanley, the man who brought you to us from Blessed Children. He was very careful about not slipping any information, especially after he'd let slip that they weren't married."

Margaret's face was pink; she was very excited. Claudia touched her arm. Margaret went on, the words running together. "And then the state just up and sent *this* right along with the adoption decree, and there was your other name, your first one, and I knew we weren't supposed to see it. Some poor clerk must have accidentally mixed it in. I told your father, I was so worried, and he said, 'Well, just put it away, Margaret. It doesn't matter now. It's official. They can't take her away from us. She's ours.'" Margaret lifted her head and looked at Claudia. "And you were, you know. . . . You were ours."

"I still am, Mom."

"Well, I certainly hope so," Margaret mumbled.

"I still am, Mom. I promise," Claudia said, and she wrapped her arms around her mother, one hand squeezing Margaret's shoulder, the other hand closed around Jenny's rosary beads.

"Cole Jaffe." Claudia wrote it across the sheet of paper. What kind of name is Cole? It's a man's name, isn't it? She'd left Margaret after a couple of hours, left her sitting in the aqua bedroom and had driven home in a kind of fog.

She wrote the name again. "Cole Jaffe." She'd never heard of anyone named Cole; it had to be a last name. Maybe it was his name. That's it, it was his last name. Maybe it was *his* last name, and *her* last name was Jaffe. . . . Cole Jaffe.

Claudia looked up from the paper. But Jaffe is Jewish, isn't it? Didn't she know a girl at Columbia named Jaffe?

If Jaffe was her last name, then the *other mother* was Jewish, and if she was Jewish, she wouldn't have sent rosary beads with her baby—

"Mommy!"

Then maybe *he* was Jewish. Maybe his name was Jaffe and her name was Cole.

"Mommy! I can't do this!"

"What, sweetheart?" Claudia turned and there stood Lily, naked except for fuchsia socks. She was holding a pink leotard, and she was hopping around, trying to get one foot through one leg hole.

"SO WHAT HAPPENS NOW?" Ollie said during dinner.

"I don't know."

"We've got the name. We can get a detective if you don't want to go to one of those places like you went to before."

"Don't be silly."

"It's not silly. I bet people do that." He gave her an encouraging look from across the table, laid his silverware on his plate, and put his hand on her arm. "So how are you?"

"I don't know." She sat still for a moment and he waited, his eyes on hers. "It was just this paper with the name on it," Claudia said. "That's what was so unbelievable. All these years she's just had it."

"Hmm. Are you mad?"

"No. I don't think so. I don't know. How could my mother have done this all these years? Kept my name hidden away?"

"Well, you know Margaret. She probably figured she was doing the right thing, until you asked her, I guess."

Silence.

"Cole Jaffe." He reached up and touched the tip of Claudia's nose with his finger. "So you want me to call you Cole?"

"Ollie."

"What?"

"I don't know."

He cupped his palm under her chin. "How 'bout I give Lily a bath and 'read her,' and after she's asleep, I wash the dishes?"

"My goodness."

"In honor of the occasion. And you can just sit in the living room and contemplate your new name."

"Okay, I guess."

"Okay," he said. He stood up and kissed the side of her face. "I love you, whatever your name is."

WHATEVER her name was; whatever she was. Who was she?

Cole Jaffe. Maybe it *was* Jewish. Maybe she was really a Catholic Jew. Wait till she told Gena.

And hadn't it occurred to Margaret that the name might be

Jewish? And why would they give a Jewish baby to a Catholic couple to raise? The thoughts crashed around in her head. All this guessing wasn't getting her anywhere. She had to find out exactly what else Margaret knew. What else was in the little notebook? She said she'd written everything down. What else did she know? Claudia studied the cross, held it between the fingers of her right hand, moved it to her lips and lightly kissed it, touched it to her forehead, her heart, her left shoulder, her right. "In the name of the Father, the Son, and the Holy Ghost," Claudia whispered. And in the quiet of her kitchen Claudia held the rosary beads, and for the first time in a very long time she began the Apostles' Creed.

CLAUDIA got back into bed after she put Lily down for her nap. It had been four days since she'd first learned her real name. Two days ago she had tried to get a copy of her original birth certificate from the hall of records, but she was told those records were sealed.

Claudia hadn't gotten *back* into bed since she was a teenager, except when she had the flu. She didn't fold the spread down, just slipped under it with all her clothes on. That was after she'd thrown the phone book against the wall, and *that* was after she'd ripped out pages 403 and 404. So much for walking through the yellow pages to unseal your life.

DETECTIVES, DETECTIVE AGENCIES . . . Armstrong, Carl . . . Baker and Associates . . . Connor Investigations . . .

If only she could get in touch with Columbo, but he wasn't still on the air, was he? Well, only in reruns, and besides, why should she want to hire someone to find them? *They* weren't the ones who were missing persons; *she* was the one who was missing. Why hadn't they hired Columbo to find her?

Claudia slid down deeper into the bed.

But they hadn't, had they? Nope. They hadn't hired anyone to find her. She hadn't discussed that part of it with Margaret yesterday, after she'd dropped Lily off at nursery school. She'd only discussed what Margaret knew.

"Tell me everything, Mom. I want to know."

"You must look like her, I think, Claudia. Of course, Mr. Stanley didn't say anything about freckles like yours, or if she had a dimple. But she was tall like you, with brown hair—he said that. I wrote down everything he said so I wouldn't forget." She had clasped the small notebook in both hands. "Not that I would have forgotten. Maybe *he* had the dimple like you." She searched her daughter's eyes. "Your . . . uh . . ." Margaret hesitated. "The young man."

Claudia had just gazed at her mother. She would scream if she had to discuss what she was going to call him. "I got the dimple when the angels kissed me, Mom. Don't you remember?"

Margaret had smiled. "Oh, that's what Grandma Mae used to say, didn't she? Goodness."

Claudia stayed where she was now, under the covers; she didn't make a move to answer the ringing phone. She closed her eyes tight and crossed her hands over her chest. Okay, she didn't need Columbo; she'd just go over it again and see what she had.

"Tall," Margaret had said. "You're tall like she was . . . and like him, for that matter. He was six two." Her eyes were brown, not blue like Claudia's. Maybe the blue eyes came from him. Had Margaret told her the color of his eyes? No. What else?

High school, Margaret had said; she'd completed high school, and she was eighteen. Claudia thought about when she was eighteen and a delirious freshman at Columbia, running around inhaling New York, the streets, the noise, the people.

A baby—what would Claudia have done with a baby when she was eighteen? Would she have had it? Left school and had a baby? Left Columbia? And all her dreams? Holy moly.

Well, what were the choices? You either have a baby or—what?—you have an abortion. That's never changed.

And then she remembered. It came to her and she sat up. The last bit of information, the other thing Margaret had said. What was the matter with her? Margaret, sitting at her kitchen table, gripping the cherished notebook. " 'A five-foot-nine-inch eighteen-year-old, brown-haired, brown-eyed Jewish Caucasian girl,' sweetheart—that's what Mr. Stanley said."

Jewish. The *other mother* was Jewish; she had to be the one named Jaffe. Claudia had something. She didn't need Columbo; she had a clue.

THEY met at Marie Callender's. It was Dorothy's choice. "Just call me Dorothy," the woman had said on the phone. She'd wanted to do everything on the phone, but Claudia said please, she'd really rather meet now, and Dorothy had explained how Claudia could just fax her the "nonidentifying" information. That's what Dorothy had called it. Claudia was to contact Blessed Children, say she was the adoptee, give her date of birth, and ask for all the nonidentifying information about her birth parents, and then, when she got that, call Dorothy back. That's when she'd asked Dorothy, please, could they meet.

Dorothy Floye from Tarzana, search consultant *extraordinaire,* looked like someone whose living room smacked of *Good House-keeping* and smelled of cinnamon spice cake. She was round and short, with a big shiny black pocketbook, wearing a sweatshirt in royal blue with rhinestones, Calvin Klein jeans at least one size too small, and white Nike walking shoes. Her hair was copper and teased and sprayed into a feathered helmet; she had gorgeous big green eyes and wore burnt-orange lipstick. They had found Mrs. Floye through someone Oliver knew at school.

"Oh, I don't just do lost birth mothers, honey," she said to Oliver. "I do lost loves, lost relatives of any kind. I'm kind of the queen of the lost."

Ollie laughed, took a swig of his iced tea, and polished off his second piece of cherry pie. Claudia opened a packet of Equal and added it to her coffee. Her hand was shaking.

Dorothy raised her eyes from the papers. "What we have here is an out-of-state search, honey."

"Is that harder?"

"Yeah, but that's okay." She patted Claudia's hand. "We've got some good stuff here. Don't worry, we're on our way."

Claudia had read the nonidentifying papers over and over—in the kitchen, in the bathtub. She could recite them verbatim:

Your birth mother was described by the social worker as being pretty, intelligent, but very independent in her thinking and reluctant to talk. She had decided against relinquishment of the child after its birth but then changed her mind and consented that the child be put up for adoption. She requested that the adoptive parents be Catholic and not of the Jewish faith, as she was. Your birth father was not involved in the planning. Your birth mother declined to speak much about him or their relationship. The attending physician reported that your birth mother was in good health, and there were no complications during the pregnancy or delivery. The birth mother had no siblings and was born in Missouri.

And on and on: the ages of the birth mother's parents, her father's occupation, the physical description of the birth mother, which Claudia partially had from Margaret.

"Jaffe was *her* last name, since it says she was Jewish." Claudia made a desperate effort to smile. "Don't you think?"

"Maybe."

"Do you think his name was Cole?"

"It's hard to know. I try never to second-guess. You never know what went on in their heads, those poor girls. Ostracized, shamed— not like it is now, let me tell you. Nowadays it's perfectly acceptable to have a baby by yourself. La-di-da, you're a *single mother.* In those days, if you tried a stunt like that, you were a disgrace to yourself and your family, and a lot of girls didn't have the courage, or the guts, the money— Oh, don't get me started. I do go on." She took a sip of her coffee, her green eyes shining over the top of the cup.

"Is that what *you* did?" Oliver said.

Claudia couldn't believe what he'd said.

Dorothy laughed. "Yep. I guess I wasn't too circumspect just then, was I? That's how I got into the business. That's how most of us searchers got into the business: We either gave up our babies or faced the music and kept 'em, or we were the ones who were adopted." She took the last bite of her chocolate cream pie. "I didn't put my boy up for adoption. I kept my 'little bastard'—that's what my father called him: 'You want to keep that little bastard, you do it on your own.' " She pursed her lips. "My aunt took me in."

Claudia was speechless.

"You do what you gotta do." She flashed her big green eyes at Ollie. "How old is your baby?"

"She just turned three."

"Oh, I've got a grandson that's three. You got a picture?"

"Sure," Oliver said, reaching into his pocket for his wallet.

Dorothy looked at Claudia. "Sometimes they just made up names and put 'em on the birth certificates, honey. Then it's really hard. We'll just hope she came to Los Angeles, had you, named you with her last name, and went home to Missouri and stayed there."

Oliver held out a color snapshot of Lily, and Dorothy took it. "Oh, a little towhead. What a cutie. Lily, huh?"

"Uh-huh," he said.

"She's a honey." She handed Ollie the photo and picked up the pages Claudia had brought. "You know, you don't really need me."

"Oh, no. I do," Claudia said.

"Don't think for one moment that I don't want to. I just want to make sure you know you can search on your own."

"No." Claudia couldn't find more words; she was terrified. She could see herself walking through the state of Missouri, asking every tall, brunette, Jewish-looking farm woman, "Are you my mother?" Just like the baby bird. Claudia turned to Oliver; she didn't say anything, but just turned.

"We'd like you to do this, Dorothy," Ollie said, rising to the occasion like Sir Lancelot.

"You got me, then," Dorothy Floye said.

"SHE said there were no guarantees, Dad. She said she's had cases where it's taken her two weeks and cases where it's taken two years. Are you sure you don't want wine?" Claudia said, holding the bottle up in front of her open refrigerator.

"No. I'll just have my gin." He studied Dorothy's business card.

Claudia poured herself some white wine and filled a martini glass with Bombay Sapphire gin she kept in the freezer for her father. She carried both glasses to the kitchen table, set the gin in front of him, and sat in the opposite chair.

"What if they're bad people?"

"What?" She didn't think she'd heard him correctly.

"Not everyone's respectable, Claudia. Let's be realistic. Just because it said on a piece of paper that she was a very nice girl in 1960 doesn't mean she's a very nice girl now." He took a sip of gin. "And we don't know a thing about *him,* do we? How do you know one of them won't see the way you were raised, what you and Oliver have here." He extended his hand around her spotless kitchen. "Nice house, nice cars, professional people . . . How do you know that they won't see all of this and want some of it, take you for a ride?"

"I can't believe you're saying this."

"You can't? Well, think about it. I am not all gung ho about this big reunion. I think you should leave well enough alone. Your mother's all upset about this, you know. She won't let on she's upset, but I know better." He put the glass down. "I know what she does in that bathroom when she stays forever and comes out like a little prune. Cries under the sound of the running water."

Claudia looked at him. She had no idea what to say.

"I just don't get it. Didn't we do enough for you, that you have this need?"

"Oh, Daddy. It's not about a need because of something you did or didn't do; it's a need because of me."

"Love you enough, give you enough. Explain it."

"I . . . I can't. I'm sorry, I can't."

"Well, there you have it." He took a swig of the gin. "I say if you can't explain it, you better leave well enough alone. Why open up Pandora's box, Claudie? I think you should let it be."

LATER that evening Claudia sat motionless in the bathtub, lingering while the water turned cool, listening to the sounds of Ollie playing with Lily in the next room. She remembered the nights of her childhood when John would talk her to sleep. She saw him last in the day. It was not her mother who gave her her good-night kiss; it was John. John, who spent most of his life in a crowded court-room, he was the one who claimed the evening's final moments. It was her father's face she saw last before he turned off the light, squeezed into the small yellow chair by her bed. Her big father surrounded by ruffles while he told her stories or they sang.

She reached forward now and lifted the drain lever, releasing the water from the tub. Laughter and shrieking came from the bed-room. Claudia could hear Lily and Oliver from the bathtub. "I'm gonna get you, Daddy," Lily squealed.

She had handed her little Lily to John, her tiny new baby Lily, lost in John's big arms. It was the only time she had seen her father speechless. John, who had something to say about everything, the grand orator stunned and silent, his hands trembling as he held the small pink bundle, saying everything in his silence.

Claudia closed her eyes, leaned her head back against the porce-lain, and listened to the water snorkel its way out of the tub.

"IT's a consent-for-contact form, honey. They didn't send it?"

It was a week later, and the first time Dorothy had called Claudia since they'd met at Marie Callender's.

"I've never heard of it." Claudia moved the phone to her other shoulder. "What is it, Dorothy?"

"You're sure? There was no mention of it existing?"

"No. What is it?"

"You write them, honey, and you ask them if either of your birth parents ever signed a consent-for-contact form."

SHE wrote Blessed Children to see if the *other ones* had signed a consent-for-contact form. And she went to the grocery store, and she drove Lily to and from nursery school. She went to the movies with Ollie; she made veal piccata with rice. She debated cutting her hair short, and she waited, and she walked through her life. All she needed was that consent-for-contact form.

By signing this form, I voluntarily give my consent to the State Department of Social Services or licensed adoption agency to arrange contact with my adult biological child who was placed for adoption.

So simple. As simple as having your name in a box. A box your great-grandmother gets at a world's fair and hands down to your grandmother, who hands it down to your mother, who uses it as a treasure chest hidden under her lingerie.

CLAUDIA stood by the kitchen table and scanned the creased papers she'd pulled from the envelope. Her eyes traveled down the lines of type; she said the quietest "Oh" and sat down, knocking over a bowl of oranges. "Jennifer Jaffe Glass," Claudia read. "Twenty-eight East 82nd Street, New York, N.Y. 10028, (212) 388-0681."

There was nothing else. Nothing from the *other father.* Only this: "Yes, you may let my adult biological daughter contact me, love and kisses, Jennifer Jaffe Glass." Claudia traced her finger around the letters of the black-ink signature. It was messy, loopy and loose, and practically illegible. Claudia brushed the tips of her fingers across her wet cheeks. Nobody could understand this feeling she was feeling, this undeniable euphoria. She knew what this handwriting looked like; it looked like *hers.*

SHE would write, not call, she finally decided.

"Dear Mom"—Claudia stopped writing and looked at the sheet of blue paper. She laughed, pushed the page aside, and put another piece of stationery in front of her.

She put her pen to the paper and scribbled fast:

Dear Whoever-you-are,
Dear You-know-who-you-are-and-I-don't,
Dear To-whom-it-may-concern,

Claudia stopped, her pen poised on the paper.
Okay. Go ahead. You can do this.

Dear Mrs. Glass,

    I guess you're wondering why I'm writing to you after all this time. Well, it's not such a big deal.

    I was just wondering—how come you gave me away?

No.

She ripped the blue paper into halves and quarters and dropped the pieces on the floor.

Dear Mrs. Glass,

    I have brown hair that isn't really curly; it's more wavy, except for this one horrible spot in the back where it frizzes up no matter what I do. Does that happen to you?

Claudia sighed and got up. She walked to the window and stared out at the orange tree, leaned forward until her nose touched the pane. "Dear Mrs. Glass," she whispered. "Remember me?"

Maybe it didn't matter what she wrote. Maybe Jennifer Jaffe Glass wouldn't answer her even if Claudia turned into John Updike and wrote like the wind. Maybe she'd changed her mind and decided, *Who needs a daughter? Not me.*

Maybe Jennifer Jaffe Glass wasn't even in New York anymore. Maybe it was an old address. What if she was dead and he was lost forever? No, even better. . . . What if she answered Claudia's letter and they met, and Jennifer Jaffe Glass took one look at Claudia, threw up her hands, said, *Oh, my goodness, look how you turned out*, and walked away.

Pathetic, she was getting pathetic. Just write the thing, Claudia.

She turned back toward the table, sat down, and picked up the pen. She wrote slowly and as clearly as she could.

Dear Jennifer Jaffe Glass,

    My name is Claudia Morgan and I'm your daughter. I would like to hear from you. Please call me at (213) 322-8217 or write me at 76228 Woodrow Wilson Drive, Los Angeles, California 91684. Thank you.

Claudia studied the sheet of blue paper. She signed the letter, folded it in thirds, inserted it into the already stamped and addressed envelope, hurried out of the kitchen, and opened the front door.

She slid the thin blue envelope halfway into the mail slot, slammed the door shut, turned the lock, and leaned back against the wood. Then she stood there for fourteen minutes, with her hand covering her mouth, until she heard the mailman take the envelope with him as he delivered the mail.

Claudia and Jenny

JENNIFER Jaffe Glass tossed her keys and the mail into the antique blue-and-white platter on the dining-room table, ran her hands through her hair, and stepped out of her high-heeled lizard shoes.

"Ron? Are you home, honey?"

She turned her head to listen. Nope. Of course he's not home; he won't be home until . . . When did he say? She made a face as she pulled off her suit jacket and placed it across the back of a dining chair. She hadn't been listening. She could call the OR and find out. Seven, eight? Darn. She'd have to make dinner.

She walked into the kitchen, filled a big pot with water, a dribble of olive oil, a sprinkle of salt, put it on the stove, and lit the gas.

"Pasta, pasta, pasta," she mumbled, walking out of the room.

She circled the dining-room table, scooped the mail out of the platter, and took it with her as she went up the narrow staircase of the brownstone. Entering the third-floor bedroom, she threw the mail on the bed and undressed. Then she padded barefoot across the thick Aubusson rug and pushed a switch on the wall by the desk. Music came from unseen speakers, country music. She played it only when Ron wasn't home. *"He stopped loving her today,"* George Jones sang over the muffled New York traffic.

She walked back to the bed and picked up the mail. She ought to call Ron and tell him something lovely, perk up his day. She thumbed her way through the bills and the letters, a *Vanity Fair.* What could she tell him—that she was making dinner? That wasn't what he wanted to hear; she knew what he wanted to hear. I love you, come home to me. She couldn't say that.

She slid back across the bedspread and leaned against the big pillows. She put the magazine against her raised knees and opened the front cover, and a blue envelope fell onto her skin. She picked it up and squinted at the handwriting.

"What have we here, Dr. Watson?" she said as she slipped her finger under the envelope flap.

WHEN Ron came home, the house was dark and there was less than an inch of water left boiling in the big pot.

"What is it? My God, Jenny . . ."

He found her upstairs in their bedroom, her body curved into a half circle on the rug, motionless in the dark. He'd thought she'd had a heart attack, his hands on her pulse, her chest, her eyes, the big surgeon brought to his knees in fear.

"Jenny, listen to me. Tell me, where does it hurt?"

She couldn't stop crying, a flood of tears she would have sworn couldn't exist anymore, but there they were. Tears, joyous sobs tearing through her body as if a cork had been pulled out of her, releasing the pain. And poor Ron's face hovering above her as she tried to speak, and he held her, and she clutched the thin piece of crumpled blue paper to her breasts, the letter that had become both a lifeline and the open gate that had released the flood.

"My baby, my baby wants to see me. My baby, Ron. . . ."

WHEN the phone rang, Claudia was holding Lily, washing her face and hands clean from mud from the garden, dipping Lily's little fingers under the running faucet in the kitchen sink.

They'd scooped holes in the mud with their garden spades. Claudia shook the fledgling pansies from their plastic nursery pots, showed Lily how to put in the roots.

"You have to be careful, sweetheart."

"Let me, let me."

"Push the dirt around the roots gently. That's it, gently."

And they'd watered them. "Not too hard, Lily."

"I know, Mommy. Pansy babies," Lily had sung.

And now she'd set Lily down on the sink,—one hand holding on to her, one hand grabbing the phone.

"Hello," Claudia said into the telephone.

At first there was silence, and then a woman's voice said, "Is . . . this . . . Claudia?"

And she knew. "This is Claudia."

"I . . . uh . . ." the woman said, and then, "I'm Jenny. . . . I mean, this is Jenny. Oh, God . . ."

"I . . ." Claudia scooped Lily up off the sink and lowered her to the floor. "This is Claudia," she said again, because she didn't know what to say, and her heart was beating too fast, and she couldn't get her thoughts straight, but the woman didn't say anything. All Claudia could hear now was sobbing on the other end of the phone.

"Hello?" Claudia said into the receiver.

"I'm sorry. I thought I was all cried out." Jenny was sniffling and trying to catch her breath. "This is not happening the way I planned it." She took a breath. "But I don't know what I'm doing anymore. I haven't been the same since yesterday. It's in shreds, your letter. I carry it around with me. I can't put it down. It's crumpled and"—she blew her nose and laughed—"wet. . . ." And then she was quiet.

They were both quiet. Claudia bit her lip.

"I can't think of anything to say except I love you," Jenny said. "Me saying I love you, you probably want to hang up"—she was crying again—"but I just . . . I never stopped loving you, no matter what you think."

Claudia's eyes were focused somewhere over the top of Lily's head, somewhere on the refrigerator, blurry and white.

"I keep seeing your face as if you were still a baby." Jenny sniffed. "I tried to picture all the birthdays—tried to send out messages as if I had powers: 'I love you, baby. Please know I love you, baby, wherever you are.' "

A flood of words, a runaway faucet, fast, breathless. Claudia nodded, her fingers unconsciously moving through Lily's hair.

"Did you have clowns at your birthdays? Balloons? I tried to imagine . . . your face with braids."

Lily looked up at her mother, but Claudia didn't seem to see her. All Claudia could see were her birthday snapshots, Margaret's glowing face above her cake. "Make a wish, sweetheart. Blow out the candles and make a wish."

"Halloween, Christmas, the prom—I tried to imagine you. High school, college . . . You must have pictures." Jenny sniffed. "I'm sorry. I'll shut up, I promise. This isn't like me. I just can't believe you're really there."

Claudia realized Lily was looking up at her. Claudia sat down and smiled to reassure the child, to reassure herself. "I went to Columbia."

"Columbia? You went to school in *New York?* For *four* years?"

"Yes."

A few seconds of silence. "I taught a class there once."

"In what?"

"Dance—dance theory."

"Oh."

Jenny laughed. "I'm about to have a heart attack here. Did you take dance theory?"

"No. Is that what you are, a dancer? Or a teacher?"

"A dancer. Well, I was a dancer. I mean, I still am a dancer—once a hoofer, always a hoofer—but you know, I'm a little long in the tooth now to be dancing where anybody can see me."

"Are you famous?"

Jenny laughed again. "How did we get into this? No, absolutely not. I was just in the chorus. You know, a chorus girl."

A chorus girl. "I never imagined you as a chorus girl."

Hesitation. And then, "*Did* you imagine me?"

"Of course." Claudia could have told her then about all the dreams, about how it always seemed as if everywhere she went she was searching, scanning face after face to find the one that looked like her face. That haunting feeling that something was always missing, but she couldn't remember what it was. But she didn't say any of that. "Were you on Broadway?" was all she said.

"Broadway, sure. Broadway, stock, road companies—whatever there was."

"What if I saw you? I could have seen you. What were you in?"

"Oh, I was probably waaaaay off Broadway long before you got here. I was probably all the way to Indiana before you—"

Claudia laughed.

"Oh, I made you laugh. I will never believe this is happening, never in a billion years."

"It's okay," Claudia said. "Don't cry." Then the tears covered her own face, and Lily said, "What's the matter, Mommy? Don't cry, Mommy." And she climbed up into Claudia's lap and put her arms around her mother's neck.

THEY talked for an hour: important things, stupid things. "A *doctor?* You're a *doctor?*" Jenny said, amazed. "No, just my master's. I never went for my Ph.D." And "*Lucky Lady?* You were in *Lucky Lady?*" Claudia said, amazed. "Yeah, but I was in the back."

"She's funny," Claudia said to Oliver later on.

"Well, you're funny," Ollie said.

She wanted to tell him everything in sequence, but she kept forgetting things, and then she'd remember and she'd run in to tell him. He was sitting in the living room, preparing a social studies test, surrounded by books and papers.

"She likes country music."

"So much for following in her footsteps."

"I know, I know."

And she'd leave and then come back. "Did I tell you she likes her steak really rare, like I do?"

"Yep. How did you get into steak anyway?"

Claudia made a face. "I guess we were talking about food."

Jenny was coming to Los Angeles.

"She said if I wanted her to, if it was okay."

"And you said?"

"I said it was okay."

But would the *other mother*, in reality, look like Claudia's dreams? Would Claudia be like her? What if she hated her? Then what? Go back to New York, you *other mother*, and take that *other father* with you. But Jenny hadn't said a thing about him, as if he didn't exist.

"WHAT did you say?" Gena said over the phone. "When?"

"A week from Thursday."

An intake of breath from Gena. "Have you told Margaret?"

"No, I haven't told her anything."

"Not even that you talked to her?"

"No. I know I have to tell her. I was just kind of waiting—"

"For what? Godot?"

"I don't know. I kind of just wanted to *feel* this without having to deal with Margaret feeling it, you know?"

"Okay, you're right. Did she mention *him?*"

"No."

"Did you?"

"No."

"Is she married?"

"Uh-huh. That's the Glass. Dr. Ron Glass—he's a surgeon."

"Did you ask if she had any other children?"

"No. She brought it up. She said she has two boys, but they are his. They're grown now; they don't live with her."

"Jeez, Claud, she never had any other babies. Just you."

"Yeah. She just had me," Claudia said.

SHE stood in the bedroom discarding outfits, trying on everything she owned. There was no use asking Ollie. If it were up to Ollie, everyone would face life in shorts and a T-shirt, and Gena was too far away from Claudia's closet. She could ask Margaret what she should wear, but then she hadn't even told Margaret yet.

In the end, she wore a skirt. But not before she told Margaret and John.

"She's coming."

"Oh, my goodness." Margaret turned from the sofa. "When?"

"Thursday."

John sat down, put his big hands on the arms of the wing chair. Claudia studied him, tried to read his face.

"Is she coming alone?" he said.

"Yes, I think so."

Nobody spoke. Margaret repositioned herself on the pillows.

"Where's she staying?" John said to Claudia.

"The Beverly Wilshire."

"Well, I guess she has money."

Claudia didn't say anything. Margaret looked down at her hands. "I have to get my hair colored," she said.

Claudia reached across the cushion and touched Margaret's shoulder. "Are you worried? Please don't be worried."

Margaret managed a smile.

"Where are you going to meet her?" John said.

"At the hotel."

"Do you want us to go with you?" Margaret's eyes on her.

"Don't be ridiculous, Maggie," John said.

"I don't think so, Mom. I think I have to go alone."

And they sat there, the three of them.

There were so many things to say, and there was nothing. She had been their baby practically since she was born. She had been their baby and their toddler, their little girl and their big girl, their teenager, their young lady, and now their woman, all grown up. Their daughter. There was no sharing to be done. She'd belonged to them completely—and a week from Thursday all that would be over. A stranger was coming, and as John had said to Margaret as he held her, "You had better prepare yourself, Maggie. The party's over, just like they said in the song."

CLAUDIA, THEY'D NAMED HER Claudia. Jenny picked up her drink. Ron was saying something about a patient. Who was it? When had she stopped listening? Four days ago—no, that was when she'd called her. Five days ago—it was five days since she'd gotten the letter that had fallen into her lap and changed everything. The blue letter that she wouldn't let go of, and Ron thought she'd had a heart attack, so concerned, his face all beaten, cradling her in his arms until she could get up, sitting with her while she babbled into the night as if she'd lost her mind. She smiled now at Ron across the table. She did love him; she knew she did. Make a list. Think of all the good things. His passion for his work, she loved that. His long, gangly arms. She loved how good he was. She took a sip of her martini. The restaurant was crowded, filled with pretty people talking too much, eating pasta primavera, downing espresso.

"You want another drink, Jen?"

"Oh, no, thanks, Ron. I'm fine." Ron: curly gray hair, stubby eyelashes, brown eyes . . . Blue eyes . . . She'd been trying all week not to think about him—his eyes, his hands, his face, his hair. It was more than thirty years ago, forever ago. It was ludicrous that she could still remember it all the way she could.

She'd promised herself that she would never try to find him. She would never see him again. She'd promised herself the day she put the baby in Sister Berl's arms. She would never go back to California, never. And she never did. Big promise for such a chicken to make, for such an ineffectual nothing who couldn't even keep the only baby she would ever have.

Jenny shut her eyes.

"Are you okay?"

"Hmm?"

"You look funny. Are you okay?" Ron asked.

"I'm fine. I was just, you know, off in the stars."

She would never tell her mother about the letter, not that she talked to her anymore, hadn't in years, but oh, wouldn't it have felt good to wallop her with the news? Hi, it's me, your daughter, remember? And remember that thing I was supposed to get over,

Mom? That—what was it? Oh, right, that *baby*. The one I never forgot, no matter what you said. Well, listen to this. . . .

If she longed to tell anybody about the blue letter, it was Rose, and she had been trying her best to tell her. February would be eight months since they'd buried Rose, and every day since the blue letter Jenny'd been camped out, third row on the aisle, in the back of Saint Patrick's, lighting candles at the feet of the Holy Mother, pouring her heart out to the Blessed Virgin and Rose. It was Jenny's place, this place in the church where she had gone for solace since she'd hit New York. It was also the place where she'd sat at each of her baby's birthdays. *I love you, baby. I love you as much as the nice couple. Please remember I love you.* Please let her know, sweet Mary. Please let her know I love her.

Rose and Jenny spoke at least once a week, all the years since Stella Maris, until Rose died.

ALL those years ago Rose had finally moved out of her mother's house, and Jenny finally got an apartment with two dancers who needed a roommate. "It's a fifth-floor walk-up, and I sleep on a ratty wool couch, just me and a few cockroaches."

Rose screaming into the phone from her kitchen in Fond du Lac: "Buster's *standing,* Jenny. He's standing and banging on the table with his pudgy fists. Can you hear him?"

"Are you kidding? They can hear him in Jersey."

And Jenny weeping into a pay phone on Forty-fourth Street. "I got the show, Rose." And Rose is crying right with her, and she says, "Well, all I can say is thank you, Jesus, because if I had lit one more candle for you, Jenny, Saint Agnes would have gone up in smoke."

Sometimes they shared their lives in person: Rose beaming up at Jenny from front-row center; Jenny stretched out on the August grass of Fond du Lac, Buster shrieking with glee as he drenched her with his watering can; Jenny meeting the astronaut, watching his eyes follow Rose around (he never left his wife, and he never left Rose either, and Rose said that was just fine with her); Rose blissfully sniffling into Jenny's shoulder as they clutched hands and watched Buster graduate from junior high and then high school. Jenny and Rose at Saint Patrick's, sitting in Jenny's place together, their heads bowed, that day two years ago when the specialist at Sloan-Kettering said Rose's cancer had spread from her breasts to her bones. If only Rose could have lasted a little longer . . . No, she didn't mean that. How could she have wanted Rose to endure one more second of pain? No, it was all right. Rose surely knew that Jenny had heard from the baby. If there was a way to send a message to the other side, she'd certainly tried.

All this week Jenny kept having the fantasy: She would be driving crosstown in traffic, and the car phone would ring, and it would be Rose. *Oh, Rose, she's alive. My baby's alive, and she wrote me, and I'm going to see her. Oh, Rose.*

Jenny smiled to think of it. Well, if anybody had the power to dial direct from heaven, it would be Rose.

MARGARET stood looking up at the boxes in the closet. They were stacked and on the top shelf, and she would have to stand on a chair if she wanted to reach them. She took the chair from behind Claudia's old desk and dragged it into the closet. She gingerly lifted one leg and then the other until she got up there, rose up on her tiptoes, and got her hand on one box. By the time she came down, she was shaking, but she had jiggled that one box back and forth until it crashed to the floor.

Margaret lifted the box flaps, folds of tissue paper, and then there they were. Tiny white cotton gowns, thin satin ribbon running in and out through the hemlines. Cotton bonnets and knitted bootees and Claudia's first pair of shoes—stiff white leather, the laces tied with bows. Three sweaters with matching hats knitted by Margaret's mother, Mae. She'd tried to give it all to Claudia for Lily.

"Mom, they're too beautiful. I'll wreck them."

"Don't be silly. Let the baby wear them; you wore them."

"Mom, you have to *iron* them. You know I can't iron."

There was no talking to her once Claudia got it set in her head, so Margaret gave up. But she could never bear to pass them on to anyone else, not the things her baby wore.

"We have a baby," Mr. Stanley had said. "Do you think you and Mr. Magers could come by Blessed Children this week and see her?"

She had had a dimple at the bottom of her left cheek, blue eyes like those tiny flowers by the side of the road, and she was sleek and soft and so beautiful. Margaret had prayed long and hard for a baby. She hadn't even asked for one that was beautiful, just a baby, and here was this one with the grave blue eyes and the little fingers curled around Margaret's thumb.

Margaret took the tiny shoes in her hands. She prayed to Jesus that He would let her keep this baby, this baby that was all grown up, this woman who'd been born to a dark-haired mystery girl who now was coming to town. She prayed to Jesus that He would let Claudia keep loving her; she sat on the floor and held the stiff white little shoes in her hands and whispered, "Just let her keep on loving me, Father. Thank You. Amen."

"GOODNIGHT moon and goodnight . . ."

"Where's the little mouse, Mommy?"

"Ahh, let's see. . . . Is he on the cereal bowl? No . . ."

"I know, I know"—Lily was wiggling around in Claudia's lap—"I see him."

"You do? I forget where."

Lily giggling. She loved this game, this ritual, this pretending each night as they turned the page that they wouldn't be able to find the tiny moving mouse.

"Claud, your mother's on the phone."

Oliver moved from the doorway, scooped Lily off Claudia's lap, and took her place in the chair. "Go talk to Margaret. I'll find the little fella. Where is he, Lily? Are you sure he's here?"

"I see him, I see him."

Claudia went into their bedroom, lifted the receiver from the end table. "Hi, Mom."

"Hi, sweetheart. Were you busy?"

"No. Just reading Lily a book."

"So," Margaret said, "how are you doing?"

"You mean about tomorrow?"

"Tomorrow, yes."

"I'm okay, I guess. Maybe . . . I don't know, I feel like I'm going to jump right through my skin."

"Well, I guess so."

Claudia didn't say anything.

"You'll be fine, and she'll be thrilled to see you."

"Oh, Mom."

"I'm so proud of you. She couldn't get a better daughter, Claudia. Nobody could."

Claudia's eyes filled. "Oh, Mommy, thank you."

"Don't be silly."

"I love you so much."

"I love you too, my sweetheart," Margaret said, and paused. "You'll call me?"

"Of course."

"Well, I'll let you go. . . . All right, good luck."

"Thanks."

"Bye, sweetheart," Margaret said, and the line went dead.

Claudia put the phone down and sat motionless on the edge of the bed.

Margaret put the phone down in her house, pushed the desk chair back into place, closed the curtains, and shut the door to her daughter's old room.

JENNY stepped out of the huge marble bathtub in her suite at the Beverly Wilshire, wiggled her toes on the thick white cotton rug, and studied her face in the mirror—shadows under her eyes. She'd hardly slept. She had taken a cab from the airport to the hotel the evening before, checked in, and then gone out for a walk. She'd wandered the streets of Beverly Hills, meandering in and out of the stores, and wound up buying Claudia a very cuddly white stuffed bear. She took him back to the hotel, opened the box, and peeked at him at least three times that evening, and it never occurred to her that she'd bought a stuffed animal for a woman who was thirty-five years old. She had room service bring up her dinner and spent most of the night trying to recall every second she'd ever had with the baby. She had been sure she would never see that baby again, and now she would.

Claudia's letter had been like a white flag, not only a truce but a possible postponement of whatever was going on between her and Ron, and Jenny wasn't even sure what that was. Boredom? Monotony? Tepid, that was the word for their relationship. It would have been easier if they hated each other. Jenny had never had a passion for Ron, and he knew it. She had never pulled any punches; she'd told him straightaway when he'd asked her to marry him.

"I love you. You're a wonderful man and I love you. I love so many things about you—the way you are, the things you do—you know that, but I don't feel the same way as you do about me. Do you want to live with that?"

"You bet."

She'd married him, but maybe she shouldn't have. Thirteen years ago she'd been a forty-year-old first-time bride. Before Ron, she had accepted the fact that she would never marry. She had made it her business to find a reason to walk away from any relationship, but he was so determined that he'd eventually worn her down.

She had walked down the aisle, her hand trembling on Buster's arm, the only child Jenny had ever known—Rose's twenty-two-year-old beaming, hulking boy in a tuxedo. And as he whispered, "I love you, Aunt Jenny," in the blur of Buster's eyes as he leaned in to kiss her, she saw herself standing in front of a dancing school, the dead dream of a wedding in Oklahoma, and Will's face. She stopped short for just an instant, and then Buster lifted her hand from his arm and put it in Ron's hand, and the dream melted away.

Ron had the passion from the very beginning and she didn't, but she told herself she was lucky because, as Rose said, "He adores you, and you've been alone long enough."

He'd asked her if she wanted to have a baby. His two boys were big, fourteen and sixteen, but did she want a baby? *At forty? No, thank you.* He looked at her. She didn't? *No.* Was she sure? He was serious. It wasn't too late. Lots of women were having babies at forty. *No.* She was sure. But why? Well, you see, Ron, *when I was seventeen* . . . And she'd told him, but not quite everything: all about the baby, but not all about Will.

CLAUDIA walked up the three steps from the driveway to the Beverly Wilshire, through the brass doors, and into the lobby.

"May I help you?"

"Oh . . . uh . . . the house phones?"

"Right over there, madam."

"Thank you."

Her hand was sweaty; she nearly dropped the receiver. "Mrs. Glass, please," she said. "Jenny Glass."

"One moment, please," the operator said.

"Hello?" She knew the voice now, low and rich.

"Hi. I'm . . . uh . . . in the lobby."

"Should I come down and meet you?"

"No. I'll come up."

"Good, because I don't know if my legs will work."

Claudia smiled. "Me neither."

"I'm in room nine oh seven."

Claudia watched her face in the mirrors of the sumptuous elevator, tried a few smiles, but she could feel a knot of hysteria about to rise from her throat. As she ran her hand through her hair, the elevator bell went *ting* and the big doors slid open. The door to 907 stood ajar.

Claudia saw Jenny's hand first: pale long fingers, oval short nails with dark red polish, and a wedding band of tiny diamonds. The door moved; the person behind it came into full view.

She was smiling, wearing a simple black sheath that had what Margaret called a bateau neckline. Claudia couldn't believe she could hear Margaret's voice in her head saying "bateau" as she looked at Jenny. Her hair was gray and wavy and chopped off bluntly at her chin. Her face was clean except for mascara and a stain of cherry lipstick, and there was a spray of freckles across her cheeks and her nose. But what somehow mattered more than anything was that Jenny was the very same height as Claudia: They looked directly into each other's eyes.

"You're beautiful," Jenny said, and she put her hand to Claudia's face, and Claudia felt her anxiety melt away just a little. As she looked at her birth mother, she said softly, "I look like you."

LILY loved the white bear; she named him Mash. No one had any idea where that name came from, but Lily was very positive. She looked at him, said his name was Mash, and fell asleep holding him. It never occurred to her that the bear could possibly belong to her mommy. She was sure it was for her.

"Did you want to sleep with Mash?" Ollie whispered in the shadows as they looked at their daughter. "You can tell me. I'm not the jealous type."

Claudia smiled, her face against his bare chest. She turned, and he could feel her lips curve against his skin. He was being very sweet to her, as if she'd just gotten over an illness and it was her first time on her feet. In the light of the reunion no one knew quite how to behave. It could have been taped for *Oprah*—how Jenny's arms just opened and Claudia walked right into them with no hesitation; how they stood there not speaking, two female strangers who were connected by their mere being. If Claudia had had to put a word to it, she felt relieved. It was like a soothing balm, this glimpse of Jenny. The *other mother* dreams could stop now; the vision was real. It was as if the hole in her was patched—not filled, but patched—with this tiny taste of Jenny, and maybe, Claudia thought, as she gazed at her sleeping child from the shelter of her husband's arms, maybe it was more than just relief. Maybe, for the first time, Claudia felt free.

"IT WAS something," Jenny said into the telephone.

"Tell me," Ron said.

"She's lovely. Tall and thin and—"

"Like you."

"Different. Her hair is lighter than mine was, and her . . . Everything is lighter. She's kind of golden," Jenny said, and she laughed, an exquisite, full laugh, and Ron said, "Oh, honey, I'm so happy for you." Then she said, "I can't tell you what I'm feeling. It's all jumbled, but it's good, I know that."

She couldn't tell him, because her mind was moving faster than her lips could. But more than anything, she couldn't tell him because she was flooded with images of Will: Will in the Mercury, Will behind a counter flipping pancakes, Will's face close to hers. Claudia was golden like her father; she had his light. She was a combination of both of them, but she had his stance and his shoulders, and her eyes were Will, startling blue and intense and steady.

The lamps were all on in the room of the Beverly Wilshire when Jenny fell asleep in the chair without supper. She slept slumped in the chair, still wearing her black dress, and she dreamed all the dreams she had long ago buried, all the dreams of Will.

"SO WHAT else?" Gena said. "Tell me. Did you talk about what happened? I mean, how you came to be?"

"No. She didn't seem to want to get into that yet." Claudia cradled the receiver between her chin and her shoulder and pushed the hair back from her face. "She told me about her life in New York, and I told her some stuff about me, but there's no order. It's a skipping, random, stream-of-consciousness conversation." Claudia frowned. "It's catch-up, but you don't know what you're catching up on, so you don't know where to go."

They were quiet for a moment.

"I gave her the rosary beads."

"Oh, Claud, what did she say?"

"She wouldn't take them, said they were mine, and she got really emotional. They were from her friend Rose, who died last year, and they'd been together since Stella Maris."

"Who?"

"The home for unwed mothers where she had me."

"Good grief, is that what it's called?"

"Yeah."

"Is it still there?"

"No."

Neither of them spoke for a few seconds.

"Gena, I couldn't stop looking at her."

"Oh, Claud."

CLAUDIA pulled up the hotel drive, and Jenny stood waiting: a tall, lean woman in sunglasses, a white silk T-shirt, narrow black linen pants, a black cardigan on her arm. Claudia felt the relief slide over her. She wasn't about to tell Jenny the terrifying thought that had hit her: how she would ask for Mrs. Glass in 907, and they would say she had checked out and gone back to New York.

THEY were coming at seven. Margaret was making chicken—what John called her standby chicken. He said she could make it cross-eyed and drunk, she'd made it so many times. Chicken with crumbs and rice with mushrooms, a green salad with cherry tomatoes, and a coconut cake, but first, in the living room, thin slivers of smoked salmon on tiny toasts of pumpernickel, with a mustard-mayonnaise sauce with fresh dill. That's what she was doing when the pain in her arthritic hands nearly toppled her—she was chopping fresh dill. Nausea rising in her throat, she moved to the sink and got a glass of water, drank it, and then had another one. Shaking, she twisted the cap of the Advil with her swollen fingers, hit it against the sink, and twisted it again until it opened. She shook out three caplets, swallowed them, and walked back to the chopping block. She would do this, crippled fingers and all. She would make a lovely dinner, and she would put her best foot forward. After all, she was Claudia's mother; it was her place. Margaret took a breath and steadied herself, and then, with the flourish of a sushi chef, she picked up her knife and attacked the dill.

THE *nice couple* who'd adopted her baby came to life before her. They stepped out of Jenny's dreams alive and kicking, and if they weren't connected by hand to shoulder, they were indeed connected by years of love; it was as plain as the food on their table. John raised his glass to Margaret, and it was as plain as the look on his face. When you signed that paper, you gave your baby to a fantasy *nice couple*, but in reality there were no guarantees. They could turn out to be axe murderers. How would you ever know? And now she knew, and except for an uneasy wash of loneliness, she nearly slid to the floor with relief.

"CAN'T I help you?" Jenny said.

"Oh, my goodness, no," Margaret said. "I've got it." She smiled at Jenny and backed out of the dining room, through the swinging door into the kitchen, the remainder of the coconut cake on the silver tray in her hands. She put the tray on the counter, poked her finger into the white icing, and scooped a fingerful of icing and coconut into her mouth. The woman looked like a French movie star. Angles and bones, and that haircut, stunning. And she'd let it go gray, how brave. Margaret would never dream of giving up her color. She sighed. And charming, she was charming. . . . Or was it disarming? Something underneath the charm: A what? An edge? Well, that probably came with the life. She was sophisticated, worldly, a whole other life from Margaret's. All those stories about all those shows she was in. She hadn't seen John laugh like that in years, especially when she told the one about how she tried out for that show where everyone was Oriental, but she went anyway and danced for them as if she could get into the show, as if they would think she was Chinese. That took spunk, Margaret thought. She couldn't have done that. Of course, how could she pretend she was Chinese? You had to be mysterious and willowy to attempt Chinese, and she'd looked like a hamburger bun from the time she was three. Margaret tugged at her tunic. Well, it was just a whole other way of living—a carefree young dancer on her own in New York while Margaret was in California training to be what? A wife. But she'd never had dreams to be anything else. She couldn't have gone on her own to New York to be a dancer any more than she could fly. Of course, she couldn't have given up a baby either. How in the name of heaven could a woman do that? It was all Margaret could do to remind herself that there were always circumstances. And it was another time, wasn't it? In 1960 no one was raising a baby without a husband—it was a terrible scandal—and if a girl did it, she needed her mother and father to help her, and maybe Jenny's parents couldn't or wouldn't help her. On and on she'd gone, trying to think of all the circumstances that might have made Jenny give her child away, but as much as Margaret tried to think of all those unknown details, as much as she knew that if Jenny hadn't signed the paper, Margaret wouldn't have had Jenny's very own child to love as her own, as much as she didn't want to cast any stones, she knew. Nothing could have made Margaret give a baby away.

"May I come in?"

Margaret turned. It was Jenny.

"Oh, I was just coming out. I'm sorry. . . . Well, if the truth be known, I was picking at this cake, which I certainly don't need."

"It was delicious." Jenny crossed the kitchen and stood next to Margaret. "Everything was so beautiful. You have a lovely home."

"Thank you."

"This was all very kind of you. I couldn't have done it."

"I'm sure you would have done the same if the shoe had been on the other foot."

"But it wasn't, was it?"

"Well, no."

They stood looking at each other. There were a few seconds of silence until Jenny took a sharp breath. "I have to tell you, Margaret. I have to thank you. She's just the way I would have wanted her. Claudia . . ." Jenny stumbled for the words.

"Oh, my dear . . ."

"Mom? Are you washing the dishes? You said you weren't going to do that." Claudia walked into the kitchen, and the two of them turned to her together, and she stopped still in her tracks.

LATER on, the three women sat side by side on the brocade couch, turning page after page of photographs, all the picture albums on the shelves of Margaret's bedroom. Ollie finally left with a sleeping Lily. "You take the baby," Margaret had said. "Claudia can take my car."

Memories, bits and pieces of Claudia's childhood—Jenny was greedy for everything, and Margaret was delighted to tell. No, Claudia didn't break out from strawberries. Do *you* break out? Oh, dear. And no, she never really loved swimming.

"Me neither," Jenny said.

John had fallen asleep on the living-room couch. Claudia covered him with a throw when she went down to get the brandy because Margaret decided the three of them should have a drink.

Jenny had slipped her shoes off. She had one leg tucked under her, and Margaret leaned toward her, her face flushed. A history, Margaret had the history, and here was Jenny, latching onto the details like a fish on a hook. Claudia handed each of them a crystal stem glass of brandy. They were talking about her as if she wasn't in the room.

Yes, she was better in English than in math, and yes, she certainly did have a sweet tooth. Margaret laughed. "It must run in the family," and then she caught herself. "Oh, how silly. It would have to come from you, her sweet tooth, not from me."

"Not from me either," Jenny said, laughing with her. "I'd rather have potato chips."

"Well, maybe her father," chirped Margaret. "Did he like sweets?"

"Pie, he loved pie." And then the smile abruptly faded, and Jenny stood up and the crystal glass of brandy tumbled silently over onto the thick ivory rug.

"Oh, I'm sorry," she said. "What a jerk."

"It's all right; it's nothing. Let me get a towel."

And there was a scramble for towels and soda water and mopping up the amber stain, and the spell was broken. There was no way they would ever get back to that conversation, and Claudia knew she would have to bring it up, to ask Jenny if she wanted to know anything about her father besides his love for pie.

"YOU DON'T NEED HIM," Jenny said the next day as she walked into her suite at the Beverly Wilshire.

Claudia followed. "That's not for you to say."

Jenny began packing her makeup bag. "Oh, yes, it is."

"You're not being fair," Claudia said.

"Life's not fair."

"Don't say that to me."

"I won't help you on this."

"I can't find him without his name. You know that."

"Don't ask me, Claudia." She gathered her clothes and began squeezing them into her suitcase.

"Would you stop what you're doing?"

"No. I don't want to miss my plane."

"What is it? You think you're protecting me?"

"You don't want him in your life."

"Did he rape you? Was he someone you didn't even know?"

"No."

"Did you love him?"

Jenny said nothing. She zipped her suitcase shut.

"I'm a grown-up. Why won't you tell me, damn it!" Claudia's face had turned white. "I found you, Jenny. You didn't find me. It took me years to decide to do this—off again, on again. I nearly made myself crazy, always stopping because of everybody else's feelings. *Why make waves, Claudia? You already have a mother and father. Be a good girl. . . .* But I knew I had to find you even if I made trouble." Her eyes were steady on Jenny's. "And I found you, and I let you into my life."

"I know that."

"And you have no right to stop me from finding him." Jenny shook her head, but Claudia went on. "This secret doesn't belong to you. It isn't just your secret."

Jenny took a breath. "I shouldn't have come here."

"I can't believe you. How can you say that?"

"You should be happy you don't take after me if you don't like what you see." Jenny took a step, but Claudia got in front of her.

"Take after you? I don't even know you."

"I can't help that."

"But you could have, couldn't you?"

The high color drained from Jenny's face. She tried to get around Claudia, but Claudia stopped her. "How could you give me away?"

"I had to."

"Why? Did he make you? Did he want you to?"

Jenny shook her head. Her mouth opened, but nothing came out.

"I'm asking you to tell me his name. It's the only thing I've ever asked of you. You've never given me a damned thing!"

"I can't give you this. Ask me for something else."

"Ask you for something else?" Claudia's shoulders fell; she laughed softly. "And you say you're my mother."

"I *am* your mother."

"No. You haven't earned a right to say that," Claudia said, her face close to Jenny's. "Margaret would give me anything."

The words hung in the air between them.

"I won't tell you."

"You have to." Claudia's eyes met Jenny's. *"You owe me."*

JENNY missed her plane; she missed two planes; she wound up staying another day. *You owe me.* Words that Claudia didn't even know were in her. An umbrella of words that covered: How could you leave me? How could you not know what happened to me and not care? How could you be my mother and never try to find me in all these years?

"I made myself believe I had no right. I don't know how else to explain it to you."

"But how could you live without knowing?"

"I made myself."

"I couldn't live without knowing what happened to Lily."

"Well, I guess I'm different than you."

And they saw each other with their veils down, stepping all over each other's hearts with their words.

Why did you leave me? How could you go?

How did they raise you? What did they say?
Is there a place for me now?
Is there a place for me now?
You owe me.

And Jenny stopped where she was, stared at Claudia, and said the words: "His name was Will." And her eyes filled, and she stumbled backward and fell into a chair. "Will McDonald. William Cole McDonald."

Jenny wouldn't tell Claudia anything more than the bare bones. She loved him; she was supposed to marry him; he left her waiting by the side of the road.

William Cole McDonald, Claudia thought. My *father.*

Will

CLAUDIA left before sunrise. She backed the Volvo down the driveway, holding a hot cup of coffee, some of which splashed over when she shifted from reverse to drive. She didn't care. She wasn't going to stop to mop up the coffee; she wasn't going to stop for anything.

"Do you want me to take you?" Ollie had said.

"No. I want to do it. It's only—what?—three, four hours."

"That's what it looks like on the map."

"Piece of cake."

He laughed and kissed her.

It had taken five months and a million phone calls between Claudia in L.A. and Jenny in New York, but Dorothy Floye had come through.

Claudia looked down at the slip of paper tucked under her leg on the seat: "William Cole McDonald," she read for maybe the hundredth time in Dorothy Floye's slanted scrawl. "General Delivery, Lone Tree, California. Phone unlisted."

By the time she hit the edge of the Mojave, the sky had turned from black to royal blue. The brown dirt spread out from the narrow two-lane highway on both sides of her. California brush and brown dirt and mountains with snow on top—the whole thing looked like a backdrop from MGM.

She had decided not to tell Margaret anything about finding him and not to tell John and not to tell Jenny. Most of all, not to tell Jenny. They spoke nearly once a week. *How are you? Fine. How's Ron? Good, thank you. How's Lily? Oh, she's fine. And Ollie? Great.* That kind of volley, and then the conversations would drift. It wasn't that Claudia didn't enjoy talking to her, but what did they really have to say? What did they really know about each other? Four days of swapped information about what had happened to each of them since Claudia was born. Not a shared history, but individual pasts.

Claudia knew this was her own personal wild-goose chase; she didn't have to tell anybody anything, not yet. And if there was something to tell, she'd tell Jenny face to face in three weeks, when she came back to L.A. to visit.

Three hours out of the city the road did a slow curve and the limit went from 65 to 55 and then to 45, and up ahead the dirt on either side of the road turned from brown to green. WELCOME TO LONE TREE, the sign said, and Claudia laughed out loud, her hands holding tight to the wheel.

"I'VE got a deuce openin' up any minute, honey," the waitress said. Claudia nodded and scanned the crowded restaurant. Maybe everyone in Lone Tree had breakfast at the same time.

"Here we go." The waitress gestured to Claudia with a menu and walked her to a small booth. "Coffee?"

"Yes, please."

She brought coffee in a big mug and cream in a little pitcher, jutted her hip out, and held her pencil poised over her pad.

"Oh," Claudia said, looking up, "I'll have . . . uh . . . eggs, scrambled, and . . . toast. I guess, wheat, and"—Claudia's eyes moved to the four people in the booth across from her, shoveling in large quantities of food, and it occurred to her that she'd never been so hungry—"and bacon."

"You want the Mount Whitney," the waitress said. "Two of everything—two eggs, two pancakes, two strips of bacon."

"Okay," Claudia said. "I'll have the Mount Whitney."

"That's the way."

She stirred Equal into the coffee. What if he was sitting right there in the restaurant? He was blond, Jenny had said, a towhead. She moved her eyes around the room. Well, that guy was blond. No, too young. "Cornflower-blue eyes, Claudia," Jenny'd said softly, "the same as yours." The same eyes and the same name, but she didn't call him Cole, did she? She called him Will.

"Here you go, honey," the waitress said, and Claudia picked up her fork.

THE post office was a block from the restaurant.

"What can I do for you?" the postman asked her.

"I was . . . uh . . . wondering about general delivery."

He squinted. "Yeah?"

"I mean, if you were getting general delivery"—she looked at him—"for instance, like Will McDonald."

"Yeah?"

"He gets general delivery, right?"

"Yeah." He squinted at her again. "Are you one of those postal inspectors?"

"What? Me? Oh, no, really. I'm not a postal inspector, I promise. I'm just a . . . I'm"—she took a breath and looked him right in the eyes—"I'm just looking for Will McDonald, that's all."

He studied her. "You an ex-spouse of Will's or something?"

"No, I'm . . . I'm his daughter," Claudia said.

The postman looked her up and down. "I didn't know Will McDonald had a daughter."

"Well, there's a possibility that he doesn't know either."

"Damn." His eyes lit up. "Talk about a doozy."

Claudia laughed.

"Well, I'll tell you," he said, giving her a wide grin. "He lives right up Owens Road."

IT WAS the road that wound up the mountain to the Sierra Nevada. The postman had told Claudia what to look for, and now Claudia was driving slowly. She didn't want to miss it—a little bend in the road to the right, and then, before the sharp left, there'll be a driveway nearly closed off by trees.

"He's got a lot a vehicles," the postman had said, "but he mostly drives that truck. It's a half-ton, green." Claudia had no idea what a half-ton was, but the truck that was coming up the hill was definitely green. It passed her; she couldn't make out who was driving. Claudia stopped short in the middle of the road, waited a few minutes trying to make her heart slow, and then turned the car around. He was shutting the fence behind his truck when she pulled up. Two rottweilers began barking. He stood with his hand on the latch and eyed her car. Claudia turned off the ignition and got out.

"Enough," he said to the dogs, and they were instantly quiet.

She didn't have to ask anybody; she knew it was him.

Tall, with wide shoulders, a white T-shirt visible at the neck of a stained blue work shirt, the sleeves rolled. His skin was tinted nearly chestnut. He had the beginnings of a gut above long legs in worn blue jeans and big feet in scuffed boots, prominent Indian cheekbones like off the face of a coin, a shock of thick silver hair, a silver mustache, and Claudia's blue eyes.

This must be what it feels like when you're about to pass out, she thought. She kept one hand on the fender; he took his hand off the fence. All her words were lost in facing him. She should have written. What had possessed her to think that she could just walk up to somebody and say what she had to say?

"Beautiful day, isn't it?" he said. His voice had the same timbre as the rottweilers.

He took a couple of steps toward her. There was something wrong with his right leg; he had a limp. "Are you lost?" he said.

"No."

"Well, at least we've got that settled." He smiled. Lots of deep lines around his eyes. Blue eyes, exact shape of hers.

Claudia's eyes filled.

"Are you all right?" he said.

She could feel herself breaking. She shook her head sideways, felt the tears fall, and then shook her head up and down.

"Not sure, huh?" he said softly.

Pieces of the puzzle, all the pieces of the puzzle, the last piece of the puzzle slid into place. A little piece of her that she had seen in Jenny and now a little piece of her that she could see in him.

"I'm Claudia," she said. "My name is Claudia, but that isn't my real name. My real name is Cole." His eyes on hers, a small frown gathering on his forehead. "She named me Cole," Claudia said, as if she'd been holding it in since the onset, behind her rib cage, in front of her heart. She slipped back against the fender. "I'm your daughter," she said to Will.

THE frown had broken into a dazed look of astonishment. She remembered that but not too much after it. There was a creek and an overgrown cabin, more trees than Sherwood Forest, a fleet of trucks, and redwood chairs and a table.

"Did you build these?"

"Afraid so."

He walked her in, gave her water until she got her color back, and then lemonade. He put her in a chair and stood next to her until she got control of the shaking. He didn't say anything. He just stood there, his big hand on her shoulder until she was still. Then he went away and came back with a pitcher of lemonade. He took the chair next to hers. The dogs circled until they saw he was settled, and then they collapsed under the table, as tranquil as lambs.

He took a long drink, then reached up and smoothed his mustache. "Hard to know where to begin," he said.

Claudia put her hands on the chair arms. "You knew about me."

"I knew a baby had been born," he said, and then he nodded, smiling. "I didn't know you were a girl."

· His eyes were bluer than Claudia's, his smile disarming. "How did you know there was a baby?"

"Jenny was pregnant." His face changed. "We were going to get married. Did you know that?"

"Yes." Claudia took a breath. "You didn't know what happened to me?"

"No."

"I was adopted. In Los Angeles. I grew up in Hancock Park."

He leaned forward. "Los Angeles. That's not what I pictured. I thought she kept you," he said. "I thought you grew up with her."

"No. I just found her. This year."

He sat back in the chair. He folded back as if she'd punched him in slow motion. "You just found her," he said.

"Yes."

He didn't move.

"Are you okay?" Claudia said, watching him.

"When?"

"About five months ago. She lives in New York." Claudia shifted in the chair.

"Are *you* okay?" he asked.

"I think so. . . . I don't know what I am."

"You're tellin' me," he said. His face softened. "You look like my mother."

"I do?"

"Your mouth," he said. "What I remember. I don't remember much, but you don't have Jenny's mouth." He lifted his hand, gestured toward the sides of Claudia's lips with his fingers. "My mother," he said. "Definitely . . . here and here." He didn't touch her. His fingers floated about an inch away from her, and she moved her head forward until her cheek collided with those fingers. She couldn't stop herself. She tilted her face and leaned her cheek into his hand. She was flooded with the scent of him, his rough fingers grazing her skin, and they sat there for a full minute, Will cradling Claudia's face in the palm of his hand. Then he dropped his hand, and they sat there, neither of them speaking.

"I went there." He shook his head and gave a quiet laugh. "I went to New York. Looking for her, her and the baby—you. Of course, I didn't know where." He stood up. His eyes had shifted off Claudia; they were focused somewhere beyond the cabin. "Long time ago; it doesn't matter. . . . You want to see the creek?" The dogs moved to his side, and he stood in front of her, extended his hand.

Claudia sat there. "You were *looking* for Jenny?"

"Sweet baby girl," Will said, his voice low, "I've been looking for Jenny all my life."

THEY had dinner that evening at the Lone Tree Café. Claudia had enchiladas rancheras because it was the special. Will ordered the buffet. She had a glass of wine. He said he didn't drink alcohol. He had iced tea, which he didn't have to order, because Stefanie, the waitress, brought it to him as soon as he sat down. Everyone who came into the restaurant acknowledged him.

"Whatcha gonna have tonight?" Stefanie said, giving Claudia the up-and-down.

"This is my daughter, Stefanie," Will said with a sly smile.

She gaped at him. "Well, you old closed-mouth," she said, laughing, and punched Will in the arm.

As they ate, Claudia told him about when she was a little girl, how her yellow room looked with all the ruffles, and how her bed was so high that Margaret had a little stool for her to stand on, and about her rabbit, Captain, and how John taught her to swim and ride her bike.

Will never interrupted, never made a comment. An occasional smile, a nod, a grimace, depending on what she had said, and when she talked about Lily—"she looks like you"—the smile touched his eyes. "She does, huh?"

Later, after dinner, he stood next to her while she registered at the Lone Tree Best Western. He said he'd pick her up in the morning. Eight, was that okay? Didn't want to waste the day away. They'd have breakfast, and then he had some things to show her. Maybe she'd like to go up Mount Whitney. Wait a minute, he didn't mean to be pushy. Could she stay?

Stay? Was he being funny? Of course she could stay.

"What about your family?"

"They'll be fine."

He stood at the motel door and reached his hand out, his fingers grazing her shoulder. "I'm sorry I missed everything when you were little," he said, and took a step backward, hooked his thumb into the top of his jeans pocket. "Good night, baby girl," he said as he shut the door.

Claudia locked the door, and then she stripped off all her clothes and left them in a heap on the floor, pulled back the bedcovers, threw herself across the sheets, and rolled over onto her back. She wasn't going to brush her teeth, she decided. She wasn't going to wash her face. She wasn't going to do anything. Claudia pulled up the covers, reached for the phone, and dialed Ollie. She couldn't stop smiling. She felt six years old.

THE next morning they ate breakfast at the same restaurant where Claudia had eaten the day before. It was just as crowded, and nearly everyone gave a nod or a hello to Will. The same waitress sashayed up to their table, held her pen poised over her pad.

"Whatcha gonna have this morning, honey?" she said to Claudia, and then her eyes shifted. "How ya doin', Will?"

"Fine, Leona."

"Toast or an English?"

"I'll have an English this morning, Leona."

She tilted her head at Claudia.

"French toast," Claudia said, "with syrup."

"Attagirl," Leona said, and walked away.

Claudia put Equal in her coffee. "Everybody knows you."

"Been here a while."

"How long?"

"Sixty-eight."

"You moved here in '68?"

"No. Bought the first piece of the property. Still lived in L.A. Came up bit by bit."

She lowered her coffee cup. "You lived in L.A.?"

He nodded. "Afraid so. Burbank."

"What did you do there?"

"Drove for the movies."

She shook her head. "I can't believe it. We both lived in L.A."

BROWN dirt and blue sky and California shrubs and nothing, miles of nothing—an expanse of flat brown nothing that jammed abruptly into jutting, dark bronze, huge round rocks.

They drove on a rough dirt road winding between the mountains that took them to Darwin, where his mother was from. There they wandered among the leftover shafts of the silver mines, fleeting glints of sparkle nestled in the mountains, and then the boarded-up ghost town where her grandmother had been born.

"It's gorgeous," Claudia said.

"Most wouldn't use that word."

"What would they say?"

"Desolate, I guess. Barren."

"I think it's beautiful," Claudia said.

"That's 'cause you come from a long line of desperadoes. You have a feeling for the land."

"So," Claudia said, laughing, "am I an official desperado now?"

"Yep, just like me."

WHEN they returned to Will's cabin, he fixed her barbecued ribs that he'd left marinating since morning. He cooked while she watched, and there were so many things that she'd planned to ask him, but it was as if the quiet in the cabin was a part of him, and all the questions that Claudia knew she had to ask seemed to dim.

"This is all I've got to show you," Will said as he handed her an envelope.

Her grandmother's hair was dark in the sepia print, and she didn't have their light eyes, but Claudia's mouth was definitely his mother's. He was right. Claudia's mouth and the shape of her face were right there in front of her, frozen by a camera long before she was born.

Claudia lifted her eyes to Will, then lowered them to the photograph. She looked at it for a long time, sat on his sofa, and studied this little lost piece of herself, and he sat across from her and didn't say a word.

"Guess I'll have to come down to L.A. and see that little Lily of yours."

"You certainly will. What about tomorrow?"

"Tomorrow?" Will laughed. "I don't think so."

"Why not?"

He moved his big frame, and the lawn chair creaked. "I don't want to step on anybody's toes, honey."

"Will"—she leaned forward—"I have a place for you in my life."

"Well, that's good. I appreciate it." He turned his face into the shadows. "I'll be down."

"But not tomorrow?"

"Well, maybe I better read up on this grandpa business first." She caught the shine in his eyes. "Now, look, it's best you leave early enough tomorrow to get through Palmdale/Lancaster before their morning traffic. No reason to have to deal with all those people on the road unless you have to."

"Whatever you say," she said.

They sat facing each other in the lawn chairs on the square of grass by the parking lot of the Best Western, only them and the night and the stars.

"I reek of barbecue."

"It's no wonder," Will said. "I thought I was the only man alive who could eat a whole slab of ribs without breathing."

Claudia laughed. She studied the outline of Will's mustache and his jawbone in shadow.

"There are so many things we didn't talk about," she said.

"What?"

"Lots of things. Everything . . ."

"Okay. Go ahead."

She wasn't sure how to ask him, but she knew she had to. "Will, there's something I need to ask you."

"Shoot," he said.

She sat there a moment. "Will, if you loved Jenny so much and you wanted to be with her and the baby"—she took a breath, looked him square in his face—"how could you take the money?"

The creak of the lawn chair as he sat up straight. "What money?"

"The money—the money they gave you to go away."

He stood up fast, his bad leg nearly buckling out from under him. He grabbed for the lawn chair and it keeled over, making a soft plop in the wet grass.

"What?"

"Those bastards."

Claudia's heart was slamming up against her ribs. "What?" She wanted to reach for him, but the look in his eyes stopped her. "You didn't take the money? Will?"

"I'll kill them," he said.

He took off across the grass, and Claudia ran after him, her shoes left lying by the fallen lawn chair.

WILL had planned to pick Jenny up at six in front of the dancing school. He'd already cleared everything out of the apartment. He'd picked up both checks, had worked a double shift at Joe's and asked Joe if he could get his check early. Joe had laughed, asked if he was getting ready for a big night. Then Will had stopped by old man Boyer's and gotten that check too. He was going to go to the bank and be waiting for her right out front in plenty of time. When he drove across Seventy-fifth and Ward Parkway, the clock on the tower read ten to six.

He was going to marry Jenny; everything was okay; his life had changed. And he felt okay about the baby too. It would be hard to have a baby. It wasn't the way he would have planned it, but he would make the best of it, better than the best. He would be a dad and a husband and take care of them. Will's eyes shifted to the rearview mirror and then back to the car in front of him. He'd never felt about anybody the way he felt about Jenny. He moved his fingers lightly around the Mercury's steering wheel and waited for the light to turn green. Ought to take about four hours to get to Pryor, Oklahoma. They'd get a room, be married first thing in the morning. He did a little drumbeat on the wheel. By breakfast they'd be Mr. and Mrs. William McDonald. Will grinned into the air and hit the accelerator as the light turned green.

It was one of the few times in his life he hadn't been paying attention. A brown Dodge with two plainclothesmen, but Will didn't see them. He had Jenny decked out in a wedding dress in front of his eyes. They got him before he made it to the bank's doorway; they cuffed him spread-eagled, facedown across the dirty Dodge fender. The skinny one laughed when he begged them to at least drive by where she was standing so that he could explain. "It's only five minutes from here, just five minutes."

"We ain't got five minutes, buddy, and you're not goin' anywhere except L.A. That'll teach you to violate your parole."

They sat for three hours at the Kansas City airport waiting for the plane to California, and Will never stopped asking them. Finally the skinny one threw up his hands. "Jeez, Pete, I'm gettin' sick of this kid's sob story; let him make the phone call." Pete stayed cuffed to Will as he dropped the money into the pay phone. The phone rang three times, and when she answered, Will said, "Please, Mrs. Jaffe. Please let me talk to her," and Jenny's mother quietly hung up the phone. He knew then that her parents had to have done this. The cops wouldn't tell him anything, but Will knew. Somehow Jenny's parents had found out, because in all the minutes of all the hours, unless somebody tipped them off, how could they know to pick him up just then?

They took him back, threw him in L.A. County for sixty days, and then they moved him to DuVal in Lancaster. Everything was up to the parole board, and the parole board said one year. One year in DuVal if he was a good boy. One year if he minded his manners. But Will didn't need discipline; he didn't need rules. He had one goal and one goal only: Do his time so he could get out and find Jenny and the baby. That was it.

Every letter came back to him—RETURN TO SENDER, ADDRESSEE

UNKNOWN—and the next time he was allowed a phone call, the number had changed. He figured that by the time he got out, they would have probably even moved.

One year. It didn't matter that he hadn't broken any laws in Kansas City; he'd left California without saying "Mother, may I," and that was breaking the rules. He'd left California, he'd found Jenny and loved her, and that love had made a baby. So you're gonna have to pay big-time, boy, because the penalty for wanting love in your life is one year.

He got out of DuVal in August 1961—one year, just like they'd promised. They let him out on a Monday morning at dawn and put him on a bus to meet his parole officer in L.A.

"Once a month, boy. I don't mean phone calls. I want to see your face."

"Okay."

"So you gotta be here. In California. In Los Angeles. And I mean it," D. Francis had said. That's what the cheap sign said on his cheap desk in the parole office in downtown L.A.

Will did not ask him what the D. stood for. He just said "Yes, sir" to the cheap suit and the greasy hair of D. Francis, walked out of his office, and left for Kansas City that afternoon—stood at the interchange, propped his boot on his duffel, and stuck out his thumb. He'd just go there. He had one month to find Jenny and the baby. If there was a baby. If they hadn't made her have an abortion. He'd been worrying about that all year. One month to go to Kansas City and find them and bring them back to California so he could make the meeting with D. Francis, and if his luck held, that would be all the time he would need.

THEY still lived there. Jenny's old man backed the Buick out of the driveway at seven thirty sharp in the morning when he went to play golf. The old lady didn't show her face until around eleven. She backed the powder-blue Olds down the driveway slow as honey, just like always. Will followed her to the Plaza. He ran his hand along the dash of the Merc. Good old Mercury, thanks to Joe, who'd kept it on ice for him the whole time he'd been at DuVal. And here it was, just like he'd left it.

The old lady parked behind one of those fancy department stores, and it took her about ten minutes to get out of the car. She was balancing a purse and gloves and the car keys and trying to put on her jacket, and she had a great big present that was all wrapped up with a pink bow. The card fell away from under the ribbon, and he moved in front of her, scooped it up off the pavement, and extended it in his hand.

"Oh, thank you," she said, taking it, her eyes glued to the card. She tilted her chin up to give him a big thank-you smile, full on.

"Where's Jenny, Mrs. Jaffe?" Will said.

She went white behind her powder and the red on her cheeks and dropped her purse. Will bent down and picked it up, tucked it under his arm.

"Give me my purse."

"Where's Jenny?"

"Give me my purse,"

"Hey, I was only going to help you carry it. You don't seem to be managing so well yourself."

And then he couldn't wait anymore. The questions that plagued him and were the only thing that kept him going—they were about to blow off the top of his head. "Mrs. Jaffe, please, did Jenny have the baby? Is she okay?"

She didn't answer. Her lips were slits, her eyes matching.

"It's my baby, Mrs. Jaffe. I have a right, you know."

"You have no rights," she whispered.

Okay, so it wasn't going to be easy. He had to be careful, figure out his strategy. "It wasn't very nice, your not taking my phone call," he started. Oh, yeah, he started like a real big shot, but then his eyes filled so fast he couldn't stop it, the memories sharp in his heart. "The one from the airport." He choked back the thing in his throat. "What did you tell her, huh? That I just skipped out? Left her standing there like she was nothing? Is that what you said?"

"I'm not afraid of you," Mrs. Jaffe said.

"Yeah? Well, you sure are doin' a good job of looking like it. All I ever did was love her, that's all I ever did. I don't want to do anything to you. Please. I just want to know where Jenny is; then I'll leave you alone."

She leveled her eyes at him. "I'll never tell you where Jenny is," Mrs. Jaffe said. "You'll have to kill me first."

His body froze. He wanted to pitch forward, ram his hand through her face. He staggered. It was just for an instant. "Hey, Mrs. Jaffe," he said, "I'm surprised at you. You, of all people, certainly know I'm not a killer. I'm just a thief."

She inhaled, a sharp sound as if she were choking. Maybe she would just croak right there in the parking lot. He took her purse out from under his arm, placed it delicately on top of the wrapped package with the pink ribbon, and walked away. He drove the Mercury from the Plaza. He would go either to Jenny's friend Sherry or to the dancing school.

He hadn't been sure until he got out of DuVal and wheedled the information out of D. Francis, but in his heart of hearts Will always knew it had to be her folks. Otherwise none of it made any sense. Without somebody meddling, California would have never spent the bucks or the time to go to Kansas City to pick him up and bring him back, not some nobody with a few months left on his parole for a penny-ante robbery.

"Alrighty, let's see here. I don't know why I'm doin' this for you, boy," D. Francis had said, moving his greasy fingers through Will's file, and Will had leaned forward. "Uh . . . Mr. and Mrs. Mose Jaffe, it says here, made the complaint."

Mr. and Mrs. Mose Jaffe. Now he knew for sure. Mr. and Mrs. Mose Jaffe had hired some hot lawyer because he'd gotten their baby pregnant, and all it took was the lawyer running Will's name through the red tape, and there it was. Their big chance to save Jenny, all because he'd violated his parole and left California. With that information they could make more than trouble; they could have him picked up and sent back to California. And they did.

He had no way of knowing what they had said to her. All he

knew was that he'd told her the truth in every letter, in every letter that they had returned.

SHERRY had already left for college. The University of Illinois, her mother said, in Urbana. Was he in her class at Southwest? She didn't remember him; she was so sorry. Had they gone out?

"No. We were just kind of buddies," Will said.

"Oh, now wait a minute," she said, and got all smiley-faced. Maybe she did remember. Was he the William who was on the football team?

Sure, why not? "That's me," Will said, keeping his hand steady on the open screen door.

"You were quite the popular one, weren't you?" Sherry's mother smiled. "You want to come in? Have a Coke?"

"Oh, no, thank you. Uh . . . Mrs. Ronne, you wouldn't know if Sherry's friend Jenny Jaffe left for school already, would you?"

"I don't think so."

"Great. I'll give her a call."

"Oh, no, she's not here. She's somewhere back east, I think. . . ." She kind of trailed off. "But not at school."

"No?"

"Well, I don't know. Sherry and Jenny don't speak anymore, not since the situation."

"Pardon?"

"Well, she went away, and then she came back, and then she went away again." She gave him another knowing look, even raised an eyebrow. "All very hush-hush."

"Oh, right. She was pregnant," he said.

"Uh-huh. I guess all you kids knew Jenny was pregnant."

"I'd heard that," Will said. "So did she have the baby?"

"That's what Sherry heard, but Jenny wouldn't speak to Sherry when she came home—wouldn't speak to anyone, we heard—and then she was gone."

There was a baby! He could have flown. There was a baby and Jenny was okay. The relief swept over him so fast he got dizzy, had to close his eyes. And when he opened them, Sherry's mother was watching him.

"Wow, that's too bad." He furrowed his face in concern. "Did she have the baby with her?"

"Oh, I don't know, William."

He nodded. "Well, thanks so much."

"I'll tell Sherry you were here as soon as I talk to her."

"Yes, ma'am," he said.

She watched him as he got into the Mercury. She kept one hand on the screen door and waved the other hand wildly, as if he were going off to England on a ship or something.

"There's a baby," Will said out loud as he turned the key in the ignition. "I have a baby!" And he let out a yell.

OLD Lala Palevsky was one tough broad, he had to admit it. He found her in the second studio—that's what Jenny had called it. Will had never been in there before. He'd only been in the front. This was a smaller room, the walls all mirrors.

"What do you want?" she said. She sounded like a Russian in a spy movie.

"I'm Will McDonald."

"I know who you are."

"I'm trying to find Jenny."

"Why?"

He kept his gaze steady. "I love her," he said. "Do you know where she is?"

"She is away from here."

"I know that. I need to know where."

"She is a dancer now. Leave her alone."

That was all she said, and she didn't give him time to say anything; she moved past him and left the room. He knew it was useless to try to get anything out of her; he could tell by the way she moved. He got the answer later, when he drove back and broke into the dancing school. Three postcards in her top right-hand desk drawer, no address on any of them, but all three postmarked

NEW YORK CITY. Will ran his thumb over the "Love, Jenny" and put them in the pocket of his shirt.

AS FAR as Will was concerned, New York was too much noise and too many people.

"Why don't ya find anotha place, bud? I taught we went troo dis yestaday."

It was the day doorman at the Imperial; he had a problem with Will hanging by *his* stage door. Will shrugged and took a couple of steps away from the door. He'd already been to the St. James. Now he was at the Imperial, and then he'd go to the Forty-sixth. He'd already had coffee at the Howard Johnson's on Broadway; he was working his way uptown to be at the Vim and Vigor across the street from Carnegie Hall around lunch. That's where they met, swapped information, ate, drank coffee, and smoked lots of cigarettes, in all these places—the dancers, the chorus kids. That's what they called themselves, chorus kids. He'd learned all their haunts and where they went to their dance classes. He hassled every day and night doorman at every theater; he asked every chorus kid who would listen; he pleaded; he described her in meticulous detail. Nobody knew who Jenny was. He'd been there going on three weeks.

He'd been staying in a rathole on Forty-third Street called the Dixon, and he was down to about eight bucks. He had only two days left, two days tops. All he needed was something to go on, just a trace of Jenny, anything. It was at Vim and Vigor that he got his one and only clue. It came from a big blonde who was sitting next to him at the counter eating a tuna sandwich.

"You can always tell the New York girls," she said. "They would never get tuna on white bread."

Will looked at her sandwich. "They wouldn't?"

She shook her head, chewing. "No. Only tuna on rye."

He nodded. "So you're from—"

"Michigan." She smiled at him. "That's how we got to talking. She was the only other one having tuna on white. Jenny Jaffe from Kansas City. I remember. Tall, with big brown eyes."

"Big brown eyes," Will repeated. He couldn't find breath for more words.

"So you two aren't still together?"

"Will be as soon as I find her."

"Pretty sure of yourself, aren't you?"

"I love her."

She chewed a bite of the sandwich. "How do you know she still loves you?"

"I know. So you two had lunch together. Did you see her after that?"

"It wasn't lunch together. We were just both *having lunch*. I never saw her again."

Will frowned. "So you don't know where she lives?"

"Oh, no. It's not like I knew her. Or know her."

Will felt worse than before this girl said she knew Jenny. He had a vision of throwing himself in front of a bus.

She wiped her mouth with the napkin and picked up her check. "Well, I hope you find her."

Will's throat closed. "I'm about running out of ideas here."

She hopped off the stool. "It sounds like you're doing everything." She touched his arm with her fingers. "Maybe she doesn't want you to find her. Did you ever think of that?"

He stared at her. "No."

"Well, maybe you should." She leaned her head toward him. "I hope you find her. I mean it, Will. Good luck," she said, and she was gone.

It took him twenty minutes to get his legs to stop shaking. *Maybe she doesn't want you to find her.* That was his one and only clue. He left New York.

"YOU drove the car all the way back to California, and then you crashed it?" Claudia said, trying to keep her voice calm.

"Yep."

"It reminded you too much of Jenny—the Mercury . . ."

Will didn't say anything. Claudia closed her mouth. It had taken her more than an hour to calm him down, to get him into her motel room, to make him drink some water, to insist he sit down. He had been pacing. Now he was slumped in a chair.

"Then what did you do?"

"Got a job, got married. Went to work for Warner Brothers, driving a truck."

"Will, the married part—"

"What?" He frowned. "I got married, that's all."

"But you still loved Jenny."

He stood up. "You gotta live your life. I been married five times, baby. None of 'em mattered much."

"You never had any other children?"

"No."

"How long were you married?"

"I was never married to any of them for more than two years."

CLAUDIA made great time going back to Los Angeles. She left before dawn, just as Will told her. She was there when Lily got home from nursery school. They ate cheese melted on tortillas and drank lemonade, and she consented to play Lily's favorite, balloon ball. Claudia threw the purple squeaky circle to her daughter, and like background music to Lily's chatter, she ran what Will had told her through her head again and again. How could she tell Jenny? She couldn't tell her on the telephone. Three weeks. She would sit on it for three weeks. She called Will after supper and said she would tell Jenny as soon as she got to L.A.

"I WENT to find Will," Claudia said.

Margaret turned from watching Lily out Claudia's back door. She came over to the table, sat in the chair next to Claudia.

"And?" Margaret said. She held on to the chair, could feel the panic hit her deep in the chest.

"I liked him," Claudia said again.

"Good." Margaret tried to calm herself with a breath.

"You look like I just told you I have cancer."

"My goodness, Claudia, don't talk like that. You know I hate that kind of talk."

"Sorry."

They looked at each other. Claudia smiled at Margaret. "What is it?"

"Oh, it's just"—she sighed—"my uneasiness, that your seeing him will somehow change you and Daddy."

"Did seeing Jenny change you and me?"

"No."

It hadn't, it was true. Margaret and Claudia were the same as they'd always been, and there was also the comfort of the relief. The secret was lifted from her heart when Margaret lifted the lid of Great-grandma Nellie's Chinese box and gave Claudia her real name. All these years of waiting for Claudia to say she wanted to find them, and now she'd found them, and Margaret could breathe. John said it was because the other shoe had finally dropped. Of course, now he would have to face *his* other shoe.

"It didn't, did it? Change between us?"

"No," Margaret said, her face easing into a smile, "it didn't."

Claudia stood up. "I have to tell Daddy."

"You know," Margaret said, "somewhere inside me I knew. I knew you would find him. Isn't that funny?"

"You just know me, Mom," Claudia said.

"MAYBE I'll just sit here," Jenny said to Claudia, and walked out to the patio.

Jenny had arrived the night before, but it had been too late to tell her then. But morning was better, wasn't it? Fresh and new, her head clear, she'd tell her after coffee and . . .

"Jenny?"

"What?"

"I need to talk to you."

She'd whipped her head around. "You found him, didn't you?" The look in her eyes.

She thought it was just about Will.

"You can't rehearse for it," Gena had said. "There's no good way. Just say the words." The words, she had to say the words.

"There was no money, Jenny. They didn't offer him money; they had him arrested. It was all a lie."

Jenny's face as the realization slid over her, the slam of her body into the chair.

"Do you want me to stay with you?"

Jenny didn't answer, didn't look up at her.

"Okay," Claudia said, scraping the metal chair legs across the brick of the patio. "I'll . . . uh . . . be in the house."

JENNY would not fall from the chair, she would not scream, she would not cry, she would not anything, because what difference would it make? What should she do now? What *could* she do now? Fly to Kansas City and shoot her seventy-eight-year-old mother? Take that, Mom. And you thought I was bitter. Hold on to your hat, kid. I'll show you bitter close up.

"When did you get to be so bitter, Jenny?"

Shutting the wrought-iron gate, holding their coats close, their heels poised on the packed snow, Esther's words echoed in the quiet—for the short time that Eighty-second Street could ever be quiet—and that was only when the light had changed and the traffic was stuck on Fifth. But in that wedge of quiet it was suddenly clear to Jenny that she was not going to see Esther anymore. Not see Esther because when she looked at Esther, all she saw was her baby's face. She promised herself, and only when her father died did she forsake her promise. She went to Kansas City, stood next to her mother, threw dirt on the coffin, stayed for three days, and left.

She envisioned Esther now, still elegantly coiffed and beautifully dressed, with a darling red pinhole in the middle of her regal forehead, a pinhole emitting a thin wisp of smoke from the gun that Jenny had shot her with. Take that, Mom. What an idea. Shoot old Esther right between the eyes.

Jenny leaned her head back, closed her eyes. On second thought, why should she dirty her hands? What difference could it make now if the wicked witch was alive or dead? It was all too late, wasn't it? Her father gone, her mother just a dried-up old lady holding on to her meanness with the same voracity with which she held on to her house. She would just let her mother rot there; no need for violence, not now. They'd all lived their lives, hadn't they? You bet. Besides, Esther had probably done her a favor. Look how he'd ended up. Really, what was he? A loner Marlboro man in the middle of nowhere. Jenny put her fingers to her lips. Could she picture herself in the middle of nowhere? She would have had to give up Broadway, the hoopla of her life. The tears raced through her fingers. A trucker, her Will had been a trucker. Just think of it.

I love you, Jenny. You're my girl. She could see him saying it.

Oh, Will.

Jenny ran her hands across her wet cheeks. "Do you want to see him?" Claudia's face swimming in front of her, her hand touching Jenny's.

See him? No. Why? What for?

She shouldn't see him. Why mess up her heart and her head, and what about Ron? Ron, your husband, who loves you and wants to make this work.

Work? Work to love somebody? Don't you either love someone or not? And if you loved somebody and you felt that *something* that touched every part of you, why would it need work?

She was married—that was the reality. There was no reason to see Will. She had spent too many years putting him out of her head. What was the point in seeing him now? Because she knew now he hadn't taken the money? Because there was no money? What difference did it make now? It was too late.

She wiped her face with the bottom of her shirt.

They had nothing in common.

She smiled. They'd never had anything in common, had they?

They never should have been together in the first place; they were a fluke. He was just the only person to ever look at her and listen to her and make her feel real. And special. And pretty. And strong. And everything. She put her face in her hands.

What do you say to someone after thirty-five years? *Hey, Will, whatcha been up to? Did you miss me? Do I look the same?*

What did you do to my life, Mother?

Jenny got up from the chair, wobbled back and forth on the brick patio like a baby taking her first steps. She couldn't stop the sobs— they'd been such a long time in coming—and she didn't really know how she felt, but did it matter? Would there be some peace in labeling this emotion? Happiness? Sadness? Relief? She didn't know; she was too far caught up in it to even care. She knew only one thing. Did she want to see him? Yes.

WILL looked off across the mountains. There was a dry wind coming in off the Sierra, blowing a lot of dust around. He would see Jenny. Claudia had called, and it was for sure, tomorrow. He would leave before the traffic. He tipped back in the porch chair and ran everything through his head again, his eyes on the sky.

LILY stood to her full height, her little hands poised on her hips, and looked up at Ollie. "You made a mess, Daddy."

Ollie turned. "What mess? Where?"

"You're 'posed to put your shoes in the closet. You're not 'posed to leave them where people can fall on them."

"Oh."

She eyed him, his big sneakers shed in the doorway, and then looked to Claudia at her dressing table across the room. "Mommy said so," Lily said with satisfaction.

"Well, Mommy's a little compulsive about such things."

Claudia laughed. "I can't help it. I take after my mother."

"Oh, yeah?" Oliver said, turning to his wife. "Which mother?"

He noted how soft and beautiful her face was as she said it: "Don't be silly, Ollie. Margaret's my mother."

WILL changed shirts three times, and then it occurred to him that what he was doing was silly, since all the shirts were blue.

Jenny circled Claudia's kitchen, looking down at her shoes.

He took 395 onto 14 onto the Golden State heading south.

She brushed her teeth again, fixed her lipstick, wondered why in the world she'd let her hair go gray.

He stayed to the right and moved at a good clip from the Golden State onto 170, passed a woman with a mess of kids in the back seat who should have her license taken away.

She touched Rose's rosary beads on Claudia's dressing table, sent up a small prayer, and wandered from room to room.

He got off at Riverside and went west to Laurel Canyon.

She checked her face again in the hall mirror, went up and down the staircase three times, and then sat on the edge of the top step, her arms hugging her chest.

He took the curves up the canyon, hung a left at Mulholland, caught a glimpse of himself in the rearview mirror, laughed, and then frowned.

She hung her head between her knees, felt the blood rush.

He made a quick right on Woodrow Wilson and found 76228.

She heard the truck pull up.

He parked, got out, slipped an Ace comb out of his back pocket, ran it through the wave in his hair.

She did not look out the window.

He walked up the three front steps, his eyes lowered.

She came down the stairs and stopped, poised at the closed door.

He rang the bell.

She lowered her hand, exhaled, and opened the door.

They looked at each other.

He handed her the rose he'd cut when he left Lone Tree, and she walked into his arms.

ELAINE KAGAN

"I didn't take up novel writing. It took me up," says actress Elaine Kagan, whose movie and TV credits include *Coming to America, Goodfellas, ER,* and *L.A. Law.* She began her writing career almost by accident, while at home raising her daughter, Eve. "I started typing out pieces just to see what would come out," she explains. "One morning I woke up with this story in my head and wrote it down in two days." That became the opening chapter of Kagan's first novel, *The Girls,* which took her five years to complete and which was published in 1994, just as she turned fifty. *Somebody's Baby* is her third novel. Kagan lives in Los Angeles, drives a pickup truck, and describes herself, with a rich, throaty laugh, as "a little irreverent."

Douglas Preston

and Lincoln Child

A buried treasure guarded by an ancient curse? It's hard to believe in this day and age. But something's down there, that much is certain. And once again the Water Pit has lured a band of ambitious adventurers to Ragged Island, a fogbound pile of rocks off the coast of Maine.

Buried treasure? Maybe. But is it worth the risk to find out?

PROLOGUE

ON AN afternoon in June 1790 a Maine cod fisherman named Simon Rutter became caught in a storm and a strong riptide. His dory, overloaded with fish, went badly off course, and he was forced to put in at fogbound Ragged Island, six miles off the coast. While waiting for the heavy weather to pass, the fisherman decided to explore the deserted spot. Inland from the rocky bluffs that gave the islet its name, he found a massive old oak tree with an ancient block and tackle dangling from one limb. Directly underneath it the ground had subsided into a depression. Although the island was known to be uninhabited, Rutter had found clear evidence that someone had visited many years before.

His curiosity aroused, Rutter enlisted the aid of a brother and returned one Sunday several weeks later with picks and shovels. Locating the depression in the ground, the men began to dig. After five feet they hit a platform of oak logs. They pulled up the logs and, with increasing excitement, kept digging. By the end of the day they had dug almost twenty feet, passing through layers of charcoal and clay to another oak platform. The brothers went home, intending to renew their digging after the annual mackerel run. But a week later Rutter's brother drowned when his dory capsized in a freak accident. The pit was temporarily abandoned.

Two years later Rutter and a group of local merchants decided to pool their resources and return to the mysterious spot on Ragged Island. Resuming the dig, they soon reached a number of heavy vertical oak beams and cross joists, which appeared to be the ancient cribbing of a backfilled shaft. At one hundred feet they struck a flat rock with an inscription carved into it:

FIRST WILL YE LIE

CURST SHALL YE CRYE

WORST MUST YE DIE

The rock was dislodged and hoisted to the surface. Moments later, without warning, a flood of seawater burst into the pit. All the diggers escaped—except Simon Rutter. The Water Pit, as the flooded shaft became known, had claimed its first victim.

Many legends grew up about the Water Pit, but the most plausible held that around 1695 the notorious English pirate Edward Ockham buried his vast hoard somewhere along the Maine coast shortly before his mysterious death. The shaft at Ragged Island seemed a likely candidate. After Rutter's death numerous unsuccessful efforts were made to drain the Water Pit. In 1800 two of Rutter's former partners formed a new company and raised money to finance the digging of a second tunnel, twelve feet to the south of the original pit. All went well for the first hundred feet, at which point they attempted to dig a horizontal passage beneath the original Water Pit. Their scheme was to tunnel up from underneath the treasure, but as soon as they angled in toward the original pit, the passage rapidly began filling with water. The men barely escaped with their lives.

For thirty years the pit lay fallow. Then in 1831 the Bath Expeditionary Salvage Company was formed by a mining engineer named Richard Parkhurst. Parkhurst decked over the mouth of the Water Pit and set up a large steam-driven pump. He found it impossible to drain the seawater. Undaunted, he brought in a primitive coal-drilling rig, which he positioned directly over the pit. The drill went well beyond the original depth of the pit, striking planking as deep as a hundred and seventy feet, until the drill was stopped by something impenetrable. When the drilling pipe was removed, bits of iron and scales of rust were found jammed in the torn bit. It also brought up putty, cement, and large quantities of a fiber found to be Manila grass. This plant, which grows only in the tropics, was commonly used as dunnage in ships to keep cargo from shifting. Shortly after this discovery Parkhurst went bankrupt and was forced to leave the island.

In 1840 the Boston Salvage Company was formed and began digging another shaft in the vicinity of the Water Pit. After only sixty-six feet their shaft filled instantly with water, then collapsed.

Undaunted, the entrepreneurs dug yet another, very large, shaft thirty yards away, which became known as the Boston Shaft. Unlike earlier tunnels, the Boston Shaft was not a vertical pit, but was instead cut on a slope. Striking a spur of bedrock at seventy feet, they angled downward for another fifty feet at enormous expense, using augers and gunpowder. Then they drove a horizontal passage beneath the presumed bottom of the original Water Pit, where they found cribbing and the continuation of the original backfilled shaft. Excited, they dug downward, clearing the old shaft.

At a hundred and thirty feet they struck another platform, which they left in place while debating whether to pull it up. But that night a loud rumble awakened the camp. The diggers rushed out of their huts to find that the bottom of the Water Pit had fallen into the new tunnel with such force that mud and water had been ejected thirty feet beyond the mouth of the Boston Shaft. In this mud workmen discovered a crude metal bolt, similar to what might be found on a banded sea chest.

Over the next twenty years a dozen more shafts were dug in an attempt to reach the treasure chamber, all of which flooded or collapsed. Four more treasure companies went bankrupt.

In 1869 a new treasure-hunting company secured the rights to dig on the island. The dig foreman noticed that water rose and fell in the pit in accordance with the tides, and theorized that the pit and its water traps must all be connected to the sea by an artificial flood tunnel. If they could find that tunnel and seal it, the pit could be drained and the treasure removed safely. However, no flood tunnel to the sea was ever found, and the Water Pit remained flooded. The company ran out of money and, like those before, left its machinery behind to rust quietly in the salt air.

By the 1900s the original mouth of the Water Pit was lost among countless flooded side shafts and tunnels that riddled the island. At last the island was abandoned to the chokecherry bushes, its very surface unstable and dangerous, shunned by the mainland townspeople.

It was in 1940 that Alfred Westgate Hatch, Sr., a young, wealthy New York financier, brought his family to Maine for the summer. He learned of the island and, growing intrigued, researched its history. Six years later Hatch purchased the island from a land speculator and moved his family to Stormhaven, the nearest coastal village on the mainland.

As had so many others before him, A. W. Hatch, Sr., became obsessed with the Water Pit and was ruined by it. Within two years the family's finances were drained and Hatch was forced to declare personal bankruptcy. He turned to drink and died soon after, leaving A. W. Hatch, Jr., at nineteen, the sole support for his family.

July 1971

MALIN Hatch was bored with summer. He and his brother, Johnny, had spent the early part of the morning throwing rocks at the hornet's nest in the old well house. That had been fun. But now there was nothing else to do. It was just past eleven, but he'd already eaten the two peanut butter and banana sandwiches his mother had made him for lunch. Now he sat cross-legged on the floating dock in front of their house, looking out to sea, hoping to spot a battleship steaming over the horizon. Even a big oil tanker would do. Maybe it would head for one of the outer islands, run aground, and blow up. Now *that* would be something.

His brother came out of the house and rattled down the wooden ramp to the dock. He was holding a piece of ice to his neck.

"Got you good," Malin said, secretly satisfied that he had escaped stinging and that his older brother had not.

"You just didn't get close enough," Johnny said. "Chicken."

"I got as close as you."

"Yeah, sure. All those bees saw was your skinny backside running away." He snorted and winged the piece of ice into the water.

"No, sir. I was right there."

Johnny plopped down beside him on the dock. "We fixed those bees pretty good though, huh, Mal?" he said, testing the fiery patch on his neck with one finger.

"Sure did."

They fell silent. Malin looked out toward the islands in the bay: Hermit Island, Wreck Island, Old Hump. And, far beyond, the blue outline of Ragged Island, disappearing in the stubborn mist that refused to lift even on this beautiful midsummer day.

Languidly he tossed a rock into the water and watched the spreading ripples without interest. He almost regretted not going into town with his parents. At least it would be something to do.

Malin's eye fell on the small outboard tied at the end of the dock. And he suddenly had an idea—a really good idea.

"Let's take it out," he said, nodding at the skiff.

"You're crazy," Johnny said. "Dad would whip us good."

"Come on," Malin said. "They're having lunch after they finish shopping. They won't be back until three, maybe four. Who's chicken now?"

Johnny's eyes were on the boat. "So where do you want to go that's so great anyway?" he asked.

Malin lowered his voice. "Ragged Island."

Johnny turned toward him. "Dad'd kill us," he whispered.

"He won't kill us if we find the treasure."

"There's no treasure," Johnny said scornfully. "Anyway, it's dangerous out there with all those pits."

Malin knew enough about his brother to recognize the tone in his voice. Johnny was interested. Malin kept quiet, letting the monotonous morning solitude do his persuading for him.

Abruptly Johnny stood up and strode to the end of the dock. When he returned, he was holding two life preservers.

"When we land, we don't go farther than the rocks along the shore, understand?" Johnny's voice was deliberately gruff.

Malin nodded. Neither boy had ever been to Ragged Island. It would make a great story to tell their friends.

"You sit in the bow," Johnny said, "and I'll drive."

Ragged Island was six miles offshore, but Malin figured they could make it in a half hour on such a smooth sea. It was high tide, when the strong currents that swept the island dropped to nothing.

Johnny yanked the starter cord, and the engine sputtered into life. "Cast off!" he shouted. The boat surged from the dock and sent back a creamy wake as it sliced through the ocean. A pair of seagulls rose into the sky, then wheeled past, crying a lost cry.

"This was a great idea," Malin said. "Wasn't it, Johnny?"

"Maybe," Johnny said, "but if we get caught, it was *your* idea."

Even though their father owned Ragged Island, they were forbidden to visit it. Their dad hated the place and never talked about it. Schoolyard legend held that the island was cursed and harbored ghosts. There were so many pits dug over the years that the island's innards were completely rotten, ready to swallow the unwary visitor. He'd even heard about the Curse Stone, found in the pit many years before. Now it was supposedly kept in a special room deep in the church basement.

The island lay dead ahead now, wreathed in mist, like translucent cotton candy. Johnny had tried to explain the local rip currents that caused the fog, but Malin hadn't understood and was pretty sure Johnny didn't either.

The mist approached the boat's prow, and Johnny slowed down. Suddenly they were in a strange twilit world, the motor muffled.

Then they were through the thickest of it, and ahead Malin could see the Ragged Island ledges, covered with seaweed.

They brought the skiff through a low spot in the ledges. Malin could see the greenish tops of the jagged underwater rocks, the kind of rocks so feared by lobstermen at low tide. But now the tide was high, and the little motorboat slid past effortlessly. Malin jumped out and pulled the boat up, feeling the water squish in his sneakers.

Johnny stepped out onto dry land. "Pretty neat," he said non-committally, trying to see over the bluffs into the island.

Just up from the stony beach the saw grass and chokecherry bushes began. The scene was lit by an eerie silver light filtered through the ceiling of mist that still hung above their heads.

"Stay behind me," Johnny said. He walked quickly along the bottom of the bluffs. Malin followed, feeling aggrieved. It was his idea to come out here, but Johnny always took over.

"Hey!" Johnny yelled. "Look!" He bent down, picking up something long and white. "It's a bone. I bet it's the leg bone off somebody who got killed trying to get the treasure."

Curiosity overcame Malin's annoyance. "Let me see," he said.

Johnny handed him the bone. It felt surprisingly heavy and cold, and it smelled bad. "Yuck," Malin said, hastily handing it back.

Johnny motioned for Malin to follow him along the rocks. Excited now by his find, Johnny was bounding ahead, whooping and waving the bone. He moved farther up one bluff, where a bank had recently caved in, spilling dirt and boulders across the shore. He leaped easily over the boulders, then disappeared from view.

There was a sudden sharp cry, and for a terrible moment Malin feared Johnny had hurt himself on the slippery rocks. But then the cry came again—an urgent summons—and Malin scrambled over the rocks and around a bend in the shoreline. Before him, a huge granite boulder lay at a crazy angle, freshly dislodged from the bank by a recent storm. On its far side stood Johnny, pointing, a look of wide-eyed wonderment on his face.

The movement of the boulder had exposed a tunnel at the foot of the bank, with just enough room to squeeze through.

"Cripes," Malin said, running toward the embankment.

"I found it!" Johnny cried, breathless with excitement. "I bet you *anything* the treasure's in there. Take a look, Malin!"

Malin leaned toward the tunnel mouth inquisitively. Deep down, he'd believed his father when he said there never was any treasure on Ragged Island. But now he wasn't so sure.

"I'm going first," Johnny said. "I've got matches. You follow me. And you'd *better* not get lost." Tossing his prize bone away, he dropped to his knees and disappeared through the opening. Malin squirmed after his brother.

There was the snap of a match. They found themselves in a small antechamber, the roof and walls held up by ancient timbers. Ahead, a narrow tunnel led into blackness.

"We'll split the treasure fifty-fifty." Johnny was talking in a very serious voice. "You and me, Mal, equal partners."

The match died as they took another step forward. Malin could see his brother's Red Sox cap in the flickering flame. A sudden stream of dirt and pebbles rattled down through the timbers.

"Don't touch the walls," Johnny whispered, "and don't make any loud noise. You'll cave the whole thing in."

The tunnel took a gentle turn to the left. Suddenly Malin heard a hideous sound, a hollow groan that seemed to erupt from the heart of the island. "Johnny!" he cried, clutching his brother.

Johnny shrugged his arm away. "Malin, it's just the tide."

Malin bit his lip to keep it from trembling.

A few matches later the tunnel turned again and began sloping steeply downward, its walls growing shorter and rougher.

Johnny held his match toward the passage. "This is it," he said. "The treasure chamber would be at the bottom."

"I don't know," Malin said. "Maybe we'd better go get Dad."

"Are you kidding?" Johnny hissed. "Dad *hates* this place. We'll tell Dad *after* we get the treasure."

He lit another match, then ducked into the narrow tunnel. Malin could see that this passage wasn't more than four feet high.

"We're gonna have to crawl," Johnny muttered.

"Dad's gonna kill us!" Malin sobbed loudly. He got onto his hands and knees and followed Johnny down the sloping tunnel. Pebbles and grit from the floor dug into the palms of his hands. Johnny seemed to be lighting a whole lot of matches.

"There's something up ahead," came the whispered voice.

Malin tried to see around his brother. "What is it?"

"It's a door!" Johnny hissed. Malin craned for a view. There it was—a row of thick planks, with two old metal hinges set into the frame of the tunnel. Across the front was an unbroken wax seal.

Malin stared as if in a dream, a dream somehow wonderful and terrifying at the same time. They really had found the treasure.

Johnny handed the matchbox to Malin. "You light the matches while I pull it open. And move back a little, will ya?"

Malin peered into the box. "There's only five left!" he cried.

"Just shut up and do it. We can get out in the dark."

Malin lit a match, and Johnny placed both hands on the ancient iron handle. "Ready?"

Malin opened his mouth to protest, but Johnny was already tugging at the door. It opened abruptly, with a shriek that made Malin jump. A puff of foul air blew out the match. Malin heard Johnny's sharp intake of breath. Then Johnny screamed "Ouch!" Malin heard a thump, and the floor of the tunnel shivered violently. In the close darkness came another noise, low and muffled—a soft, continuous dragging.

"Johnny!" Malin cried. Panic began to overwhelm him. Rising to his knees, choking back sobs, he grabbed a match and scratched it frantically until it flared. In the sudden light he looked around wildly. Johnny was gone. The door was open, but beyond lay nothing except a blank stone wall. Dust hung thickly in the air.

Then wetness touched his legs, and he looked down. In the spot where Johnny had stood there was a large black pool of water. Then he realized the pool was not black, but red. Paralyzed, he watched as the glossy pool spread, surrounding him like a crimson octopus, until the match dropped into it with a sharp hiss and darkness descended once again.

2

THE small laboratory looked out from the Mount Auburn Hospital annex across the leafy tops of maple trees to the slow, sullen waters of the Charles River. A rower in a shell was cutting through the dark water with powerful strokes, peeling back a glittering wake. Malin Hatch watched, entranced by the synchronicity of body, boat, and water.

"Dr. Hatch?" came the voice of Bruce, his lab assistant. "The colonies are ready." He pointed toward a beeping incubator.

Hatch turned from the window, reverie broken. "Let's take out the first tier and have a look at the little buggers," he said.

Bruce opened the incubator and removed a large tray of agar plates, bacterial colonies growing like glossy pennies in their centers. Rows two and three showed good growth, rows one and four were variable, and row five was sterile. In an instant Hatch realized the experiment would be a success. Everything was working out as hypothesized: In a month he'll have published another impressive paper in *The New England Journal of Medicine.* And everyone would be talking yet again about what a rising star he was in the department.

The prospect filled him with a huge feeling of emptiness. Absently he turned toward his desk and began jotting notes into his lab notebook.

The intercom chimed. Bruce jumped up and went out. He returned a moment later. "Visitor," he said.

Probably a researcher from the hospital, Hatch thought. He took a deep breath. "Okay, show him in."

Footsteps sounded in the outer lab. Malin looked up to see a spare figure gazing at him from the doorframe. The setting sun was striking the man full force, modeling the sunburned skin drawn tight across a handsome face, refracting light deep within a pair of gray eyes.

"Gerard Neidelman," the stranger said in a low, gravelly voice.

"Please come in, Dr. Neidelman," Hatch said.

"Captain," the man replied, "not Doctor." Simply by the way he stepped through the door, head bent, hand on the upper frame, it was clear the man had spent time at sea. Hatch guessed he was not old—perhaps forty-five—but he had the narrow eyes and roughened skin of a sailor. And an air of ascetic intensity.

Hatch introduced himself and offered his hand.

"Could we speak in private?" the man asked quietly.

Hatch glanced at his watch and then back into the man's steady gaze. "Bruce, you can head home."

Bruce flashed a brief smile. "Okay, Dr. Hatch. Thanks."

In a moment Bruce was gone, and Hatch turned back to his curious visitor, who had strolled toward the window, shifting a leather portfolio from one hand to the other.

The captain smiled. "You must be wondering why I've barged into your lab. May I ask a few minutes of your indulgence?"

Hatch indicated a vacant chair. "Have a seat. I'm finished for the day, and this experiment is—how shall I put it?—boring."

Neidelman remained standing. He raised an eyebrow. "Not as exciting as fighting an eruption of breakbone fever in the Amazon swamps, I imagine."

"Not quite," Hatch said after a moment.

The man smiled. "I read the article in the *Globe*."

"It wasn't nearly as exciting as the story made it sound."

"Which is why you returned?"

"I got tired of watching my patients die for lack of a fifty-cent shot of amoxicillin." Hatch spread his hands fatalistically.

"The article went on to talk about your travels in Sierra Leone, Madagascar, and the Comoros," Neidelman continued. "But perhaps your life could use some excitement right now?"

"Pay no attention to my grousing," Hatch replied. "A little boredom now and then can be tonic for the soul."

"Perhaps," the captain said. "In any case, it seems you've hit every spot on the globe except Stormhaven, Maine."

Hatch froze. Suddenly it all made sense: the roundabout questions, the seafaring background, the intense look in the man's eyes.

"Let me guess. Does this by any chance have to do with Ragged Island?" A flicker in Neidelman's face showed that he had guessed right. "And you, Captain, are a treasure hunter. Am I right?"

"I prefer the term recovery specialist."

"Everyone has a euphemism these days. And don't tell me: You, and only you, hold the secret to the Water Pit."

Neidelman stood quietly, saying nothing.

"No doubt you also have high-tech gizmos that will show you the location of the treasure?"

"I know you've been approached before," Neidelman said. "I know about the tragedies that befell your family. But there is a vast treasure down there. I know it."

"Of course you do. They all do. Captain Neidelman, faith won't make it true. There is no Ragged Island treasure."

Ignoring this, Neidelman shrugged. "I don't ask you to take it on faith."

There was something so self-confident about the captain's shrug that a flood of anger swept Hatch. "If you had any idea how many times I've heard this same story . . ."

Reaching inside his leather portfolio, Neidelman withdrew a single sheet of paper and wordlessly pushed it across the desk.

The document was a financial report indicating that a company named Thalassa Holdings Ltd. had raised twenty-two million dollars to form the Ragged Island Reclamation Corporation.

Hatch glanced from the paper back to Neidelman, then began to laugh. "You mean you actually had the nerve to raise this money before even asking my permission?"

Neidelman broke into what seemed to be his trademark smile—reserved, self-confident. "Dr. Hatch, I perfectly understand your reaction. But I sense that maybe at last you're ready to learn what really happened to your brother. I understand how your grief has made you hate that island. That is why I come to you with everything prepared. We have equipment at our disposal that your grandfather could only have dreamed of. We have divers, archaeologists, engineers. We'll have an expedition doctor. One word from you, and I promise you that within a month the Water Pit will have yielded up its secrets."

In the ensuing silence the distant bells of Trinity Church tolled. The silence stretched on into a minute, then two, and then five.

At last Neidelman placed the paper back in his portfolio. "Your silence is sufficiently eloquent," he said quietly. "I'll inform our partners that you have declined our offer. Good day, Dr. Hatch." He walked toward the door, then paused. "There *is* something that makes us different. We've uncovered information about the Water Pit that nobody else knows. We know who designed it," the captain said quietly.

Hatch felt his fingers stiffen. "What?" he said.

"Yes. And there's something more. We have the journal kept during its construction."

Hatch shook his head. "That's beautiful," he managed to say. "Just beautiful. I guess I underestimated you. After all these years I have heard something original. You've made my day, Captain."

But Neidelman had gone, and Hatch realized he was talking to an empty room.

It was several minutes before he could bring himself to rise from the desk. As he shoved the last of his papers into his briefcase, he noticed that Neidelman had left his card behind. A telephone number had been scribbled across the top, presumably the hotel he was staying at. Hatch brushed the card into the wastebasket, left the lab, and briskly walked back to his town house through the dusky summer streets.

At two o'clock that morning he found himself back in the lab, pacing before the darkened window, Neidelman's card grasped in one hand. It was three before he finally picked up the phone.

3

HATCH parked in the dirt lot above the pier and stepped slowly from the car. His eyes took in the long, narrow cove dotted with lobster boats and trawlers bathed in a silver light. Even twenty-five years after moving away, Hatch recognized many of the names.

The little town of Stormhaven struggled up the hill, narrow clapboard houses following a zigzag of cobblestone lanes. On the far side of the cove he glimpsed his own boyhood home, its four gables and widow's walk poking above the tree line, the long meadow sloping to the shore and the small dock. Beyond the harbor mouth there was a low fogbank, where the sea merged imperceptibly with sky. It was almost as if the world ended a hundred yards offshore.

Malin headed for the end of the pier, smelling the salt air. The years dropped away, and a powerful bittersweet feeling constricted his chest. Here he was, back in a place he had never expected to see again. It was all he could do to hold back tears.

A car door slammed behind him, and he glanced back to see Gerard Neidelman stride down the pier, erect, brimming with high spirits. Smoke wafted from a briar pipe clamped between his teeth, and his eyes glimmered with unmistakable excitement.

"Good of you to meet me here," he said, grasping Hatch's hand. "I hope this hasn't been too much trouble."

Hatch wondered if the captain had guessed his own reasons for wanting to see the town—and the island—before making any commitment. "No trouble," Hatch replied coolly.

"And where is our good boat?" Neidelman said, squinting out at the harbor, sweeping it appraisingly.

"It's a rental, the *Plain Jane,* over there."

Neidelman looked. "Ah. A stout lobster boat. I don't see a dinghy in tow. How will we land on Ragged Island?"

"The dinghy's at the dock," Hatch said. "But we're not going to land. There's no natural harbor. You'll get a good sense of the place from the water." Besides, he thought, I for one am not ready to set foot on that island.

"Understood," said Neidelman.

A gangplank led down to a floating dock. They motored the dinghy out to the *Plain Jane.* Neidelman boarded while Hatch tied the dinghy to the stern. He clambered aboard, throttled up, and the *Plain Jane* surged forward, slicing through the gentle swell.

"It's going to be chilly out there," Hatch said, glancing at Neidelman's short-sleeved shirt.

Neidelman smiled. "I'm used to it."

"Were you in the navy?" Hatch asked.

"Yes," Neidelman said. "Captain of a minesweeper off the Mekong Delta. After the war I bought a wooden trawler and worked Georges Bank for scallops and flounder. One day the net brought up a huge bolus of encrusted coral. My first mate struck it with a marlin spike, and the thing fell apart like an oyster. Nestled inside was a small seventeenth-century Dutch silver casket. That started my first treasure hunt. I sold the boat, raised capital, and went from there."

As they headed seaward, the last wisps of fog disappeared. Soon Ragged Island would be visible. "I want to hear about the man who designed the Water Pit," Hatch said quietly.

"Have you been to England, Dr. Hatch?" Neidelman asked.

Hatch nodded.

"Lovely country," Neidelman went on. "Have you visited Whitstone Hall in the Pennines?"

"That's the famous one, built like an abbey?" Hatch said.

"Exactly. A delightful example of seventeenth-century ecclesiastical architecture, designed by Sir William Macallan—the man who also designed the Water Pit. Macallan was a great architect, perhaps England's greatest next to Sir Christopher Wren, but a far more interesting man. In addition to his buildings he left behind a monumental text on church architecture. The world lost a true visionary when he disappeared at sea in 1696."

"Lost at sea? The plot thickens."

Neidelman pursed his lips as if finally nettled. "Yes. It was a terrible tragedy. Except"—he turned toward Hatch—"except, of course, he was *not* lost at sea. Last year we uncovered a copy of his treatise. In the margins was what seemed to be a pattern of spottings and discolorations. Our laboratory was able to confirm that the discolorations were actually notes written in invisible ink. Chemical analysis showed the ink to be a compound made from vinegar and onions. Further analysis dated this stain—as invisible inks were then known—to approximately 1700."

"Invisible ink? You've been reading too many Hardy Boys stories."

"Invisible inks were very common in the seventeenth century," Neidelman said calmly. "The colonists referred to it as white ink. Our laboratory was able to recover the rest of the writing, using a chemical wash. It turned out to be a document written in Macallan's own hand in the margins of his book. The document was in code, but a Thalassa specialist decrypted the first half relatively easily. When we read the plaintext, we learned that Sir William Macallan was an even more intriguing architect than the world had previously believed."

"I'm sorry," Hatch said, "but this whole story sounds absurd."

"No, Dr. Hatch, it is not absurd. The coded writing was a secret journal Macallan kept on his last voyage." Neidelman took a moment to draw on his pipe. "The Spanish crown commissioned him to build a cathedral, the greatest in the New World. In 1696 he set sail from Cádiz, bound for Mexico, on a two-masted brig, escorted by a Spanish man-of-war. The ships vanished, and Macallan was never heard from again. It was assumed they were lost at sea. However, this journal tells us what really happened. Their ships were attacked by Edward Ockham. The Spanish captain was tortured into revealing the nature of his mission. Then Ockham put everyone to the sword, sparing only Macallan. The architect was dragged to Ockham in chains. The pirate put a saber to his throat and said—here I quote from the journal—'Lete the king build his owen cursed church, I have ye a newe commission.' "

The captain leaned against the gunwale. "You see, Red Ned Ockham wanted Macallan to design a pit for storing his immense treasure. An *impregnable* pit to which only Ockham would have the secret. They cruised the Maine coast, picked out Ragged Island, the pit was constructed, and the treasure was buried. But shortly thereafter Ockham and his crew perished. And Macallan, no doubt, was murdered as soon as the pit was finished. With them died the secret to the Water Pit."

Neidelman paused, his eyes bright. "Of course that's no longer true. Because the secret did *not* die with Macallan."

"Explain," Hatch said, feeling a strange stir of excitement.

"Midway through his journal Macallan switched codes. We think he did so specifically to record the secret key to the Water Pit. But no seventeenth-century code is a match for our high-speed computers. Our specialists will have it cracked any day now."

"So how much is supposed to be down there?" Hatch asked.

"Good question. The most conservative estimate places the contemporary value of the treasure at"—Neidelman paused, a trace of a smile on his lips—"between one point eight and two billion dollars."

There was a long silence, filled by the throbbing of the engines. Hatch struggled to grasp the enormity of the sum.

Neidelman lowered his voice. "That is, not including the value of St. Michael's Sword, Ockham's greatest prize."

"Come on, Captain," Hatch said with a laugh, "don't tell me you believe such mossy old legends."

"Read Macallan's journal, Dr. Hatch. It is all there."

Hatch stared unseeing at the deck, his mind a turmoil. This is incredible, almost beyond belief. . . .

He glanced up and felt the muscles of his gut tighten involuntarily. There, across the expanse of sea, was the long, low fogbank that concealed Ragged Island.

Neidelman was saying something. Hatch turned. "I'm sorry?"

"I said, I know you have little interest in the money. But in the agreement I've proposed here, you would receive half the treasure. In return for my undertaking all the financial risk, I will receive

St. Michael's Sword. Your share would therefore be in the vicinity of one billion dollars."

Hatch swallowed. "You're right. I couldn't care less."

There was a long pause; then Neidelman raised his binoculars and examined the island of fog. "Why does it remain fogbound?"

"There's a good reason," Hatch said, grateful for the change of topic. "The island's powerful riptide deflects the frigid Labrador Current into the warm Cape Cod Current, and where they mix, you get a large eddy of fog."

"What more could a pirate ask for?" Neidelman murmured.

The patch of fog drew closer. A dark distant outline seemed to appear, only to vanish again. Hatch could now hear the sound of surf and the ringing of the Ragged Island bell buoy, warning mariners away from its reefs.

"Can we get closer?" Neidelman asked.

Hatch steered the boat toward the reefs. Abruptly they broke through the mist, and the island stood revealed in its entirety.

It was little more than a black silhouette, shaped like a peculiar, tilted table, a gradual incline rising from the leeward to sharp bluffs on the seaward coast, punctuated by a hump of land in the center. The surf pounded the bluffs and boiled over the sunken ledges that ringed the island. It was, if anything, even bleaker than Hatch remembered: windswept, barren, a mile long, and eight hundred yards wide. A single deformed spruce stood above the cobbled beach at the lee end of the island, its top exploded by an old lightning strike, its crabbed branches raised like a witch's hand against the sky.

Everywhere, great ruined hulks of machines rose from the waving saw grass and tea roses: ancient steam-driven compressors, winches, chains, boilers. Along the nearest rocks lay the shattered carcasses of several boats, battered by countless storms. Weather-beaten signs, posted every hundred feet above the high-water mark, read:

WARNING!

EXTREME DANGER

NO LANDING

"At last," Neidelman said. Lowering his binoculars, he turned to Hatch. "Doctor?" he inquired.

Hatch was bracing himself on the wheel, riding out the memory. Horror washed over him like seasickness as the bell buoy tolled mournfully in the mist. But mingled with the horror was something new—the realization that there *was* a vast treasure down there, that his grandfather had not been a complete fool who destroyed three generations of his family for nothing. In a moment he knew what his decision had to be—the final answer that was owed to his grandfather, his father, and his brother.

"Dr. Hatch?" Neidelman asked again.

Hatch took a deep breath and relaxed his desperate grip on the wheel. "Circle the island?" he asked, managing to keep his voice even.

Neidelman nodded and raised the binoculars again.

Easing the throttle open, Hatch swung seaward.

"It's a hard-looking place," Neidelman said.

"There's no natural harbor," Hatch replied. "The place is surrounded by reefs, and there's a wicked tide rip. So many tunnels were dug that a good part of the island is unstable."

"What's that wreck?" Neidelman said, pointing at a massive twisted metal structure rearing above the seaweed-slick rocks.

"A barge from my grandfather's effort. Got caught in a northeaster and was thrown on the rocks."

"Did your grandfather leave any records?" Neidelman asked.

"My father destroyed them." Hatch swallowed hard. "My grandfather bankrupted the family with this island, and my father always hated the place. Even before the accident."

"I'm sorry," Neidelman said, his face softening. "I've been so wrapped up in all this that I sometimes forget your personal tragedy. Forgive me if I've asked any insensitive questions."

Hatch continued gazing over the ship's bow. "It's all right."

Neidelman fell silent, for which Hatch was grateful. Nothing was more painful than hearing the usual platitudes from well-meaning people, especially, Don't blame yourself. It wasn't your fault.

A coughing sound suddenly broke from the island. It grew louder, turning into a low rumble and finally breaking into a throaty, heaving groan, like the dying sound of some deep-sea beast. Hatch felt his skin crawl.

"What in blazes is that noise?" Neidelman asked sharply.

"Tide's changing," Hatch replied, shivering slightly in the raw air. "The Water Pit is apparently connected to the sea by a hidden flood tunnel. When the rip current changes and the flow in the tunnel reverses, it makes that noise. At least that's one theory."

The moan slowly subsided before dying away completely.

"You'll hear another theory from the local fishermen," Hatch said. "Notice there aren't any lobster pots around the island? Don't think that's from any lack of lobsters."

"The Ragged Island curse," Neidelman said, nodding, a sardonic look in his eyes. "I've heard of it."

Quite suddenly Hatch realized he could not bear to spend any more time at the island. He nosed the boat westward without explanation, opening the throttle as they once again entered the encircling mist. He did not look back.

"We'll be working closely with a first-rate archaeologist and a historian," Neidelman said at his side. "The knowledge we'll gain about seventeenth-century engineering, high-seas piracy, and naval technology will be of incalculable value. This is as much an archaeological dig as a treasure reclamation."

"I'd want to reserve the right to stop the whole show if I feel conditions are growing too dangerous," Hatch said.

"Perfectly understandable. There are eighteen clauses in our boilerplate land-lease contract. We'll just add a nineteenth."

"And," Hatch said more slowly, "I don't want to be just a silent partner."

"What role do you propose to play?" Neidelman asked.

Hatch shrugged. "You mentioned an expedition doctor."

Neidelman smiled. "You can take leave from the hospital?"

"My research can wait. Besides, we aren't talking about all that long. It's already the end of July. If you're going to do this, it'll have to be over and done within four weeks—for better or worse. The dig can't continue into storm season."

Neidelman leaned over the side of the boat and knocked the dottle from his pipe with a single hard stroke. "In four weeks it *will* be over," he said. "Your struggle, and mine."

HATCH parked his Jaguar in the dirt lot next to Bud's Superette. Bud's looked exactly as he remembered it: the green screen door that didn't shut properly, the ancient Coca-Cola sign, the tilting porch. He stepped inside and began picking up some food for the *Plain Jane,* where he'd decided to stay until the old family house could be readied for him. He pushed his cart toward the front of the store and found himself face to face with Bud Rowell—large, bald, and cheerful—in a crisp butcher's apron. Hatch remembered Bud slipping him and Johnny licorice sticks under the counter many times.

"Afternoon," said Bud, his glance moving over Hatch's face and then drifting to the car parked outside. "Up from Boston?"

Hatch nodded, still uncertain how best to do this. "Yup."

"Vacation?" Bud asked, placing an artichoke into the bag.

"No," said Hatch. "Here on business."

Nobody ever came to Stormhaven on business. And Bud, being a professional gossip, would now have to find out why. "And what kind of business might that be?"

"Business of a delicate nature," Hatch said, lowering his voice.

"I see," Bud said. "Staying in town?"

"Nope," Hatch said. "I'll be staying in the old Hatch place."

At this Bud almost dropped a steak. The house had been shut up for twenty-five years. But Bud had run out of questions.

"Well," said Hatch, "how much do I owe you?"

"Thirty-one twenty-five," Bud said.

Hatch opened the bag and poked his hand in. "Excuse me," he said. "Haven't you left something out?"

"I don't b'lieve so," Bud said stolidly. "It's all there."

"No, it's not." Hatch pointed at a small drawer just below the countertop. "Where's my free licorice stick?"

For the first time, Bud really looked at him.

Suddenly the grocer lumbered around the counter and crushed Hatch's right hand in both of his. "Well I'll be doggoned," he said. "It's Malin Hatch." A huge grin lit up his plump face. "To think you've grown up into such a fine, big young man."

Hatch felt both relieved and embarrassed.

Bud glanced back at the licorice drawer. "You son of a gun," he laughed. "You still eating licorice? Here's one on the house." And he pulled one out and slapped it down on the counter.

They sat in rocking chairs on the porch, drinking birch-beer pop. Under Bud's probing, Hatch related some of his adventures as an epidemiologist in Mexico and South America. But he successfully steered the conversation away from his own reasons for returning. "Tell me what's happened in town since I left," Hatch said.

"Well now," Bud began, "there've been some big changes here." He told how the Thibodeaux house burned to the ground, how Frank Pickett sank his boat after a few too many. "And new houses springing up all over the place. Summer people." Bud clucked disapprovingly. "So you here to sell the house?"

Hatch stiffened slightly. "No. I've come for the summer."

"That right?" Bud said. "Vacation?"

"I already told you," Hatch said. "I'm here on a rather delicate business matter. I promise you, Bud, it won't be a secret long."

Bud sat back, slightly offended. "Maybe it's got to do with those two helicopters I saw hovering over Ragged Island."

Hatch was spared having to reply by the creak of the screen door. He waited while Bud attended to a customer.

"And how's your mother?" Bud asked when he returned.

"She passed away in 1985. Cancer."

"Sorry to hear that. She was a good woman, and she raised some fine . . . a fine son." After a short silence Bud polished off his birch beer. "Seen Claire yet?" he asked nonchalantly.

"She still around?" Hatch replied with equal nonchalance.

"Yup," said Bud. "Been some changes in her life. And how about you? Any family?"

Hatch smiled. "No wife. Not yet, anyway." He put down his empty bottle and stood. "Bud, it's been great visiting with you. I think I'll go and fix myself dinner."

Bud nodded. "One other thing, Malin."

Hatch froze. He knew he'd gotten off too easily. He waited, dreading the question he knew was coming.

"You watch out with that licorice," Bud said with great solemnity. "Those teeth won't last forever, you know."

THE next day Hatch emerged onto the deck of the *Plain Jane,* stretched, then looked around the harbor. The town of Stormhaven was quiet, almost torpid under the heavy summer light. The day before, he'd received a note from Neidelman asking him to rendezvous off Ragged Island at sunset this evening. He checked his watch: almost seven thirty. Time to get started.

Past the harbor the air turned cool. It was somehow cleansing, alone out here. He felt as if the wind might shake loose the accumulated cobwebs and dirt of a quarter century.

Suddenly a dark shadow appeared ahead in the fog surrounding the island. Hatch throttled back and turned to port, preparing to circle. Then, on the lee side of the island, he saw an antique fireboat built of rich brown wood—mahogany and teak. The name *Griffin* was painted across its stern in severe gold letters.

Hatch cut the *Plain Jane*'s engines about a hundred yards off and stared curiously at the boat. If it was Neidelman's command craft, it was an unusual but practical choice. What the thing lacked in speed it made up for in stability. Above the capacious pilothouse and flying bridge, there was a cluster of electronic antennas, loran, and radar, along with a satellite dish. Impressive rig, Hatch thought. He dropped one hand to the instrument panel, ready to give a blast of his air horn.

Then he hesitated. Beyond the mist-shrouded island he could make out a smudge of gray to the south. Slowly it separated into three, then six distinct shapes. He waited in disbelief as a veritable invasion fleet approached the tiny island. A huge sea barge, a tug with a hundred-ton floating crane in tow, and a brace of sleek powerboats bristling with electronics.

Last came an elegant vessel, large and fantastically equipped. The name *Cerberus* was stenciled on its bows. Hatch gazed in awe over the gleaming superstructure, the harpoon gun on the foredeck, the smoked-glass portholes. Fifteen-thousand tonner, he estimated.

The vessels nosed up to the *Griffin*. There was a rattling of chains and singing of hawsers as anchors ran out. Gazing at the boats straddling his port and starboard sides, Hatch could see the occupants staring back. A few smiled and nodded.

The last engine was cut, and a strange, almost spectral, silence fell over the gathering. A minute passed, then two. At last the pilot-house door on the *Griffin* opened and Captain Neidelman emerged. The setting sun gave a burgundy cast to his sunburned face and kindled his fair thinning hair into gold. It was amazing, Hatch thought, how his slender presence projected out over the circle of boats.

Neidelman walked to the edge of the railing and started to speak in a voice that carried easily over the water.

"Today," he said, "Red Ned Ockham's treasure remains at the bottom of the Water Pit, undisturbed for three hundred years. But tomorrow marks the beginning of the end of that long rest."

He surveyed the crowd of vessels. "There is much to do. We must determine the original pit. We must find and seal the underwater channel that allows seawater to enter. We must pump the existing water from the shaft and secure it for the excavation. The challenge is vast. We're dealing with one of history's great unsolved riddles, perhaps the most ingenious creation of the seventeenth-century mind. But the Water Pit is no match for twentieth-century tools. We will make this the greatest—and most famous—salvage in history."

The company erupted into a spontaneous cheer. Hatch realized he was cheering too, as a single tear trickled down his cheek.

A DAY later Hatch stood at the helm of the *Plain Jane* watching the preparations going on around him. At his side two communications monitors emitted occasional chirps and squawks of conversation. The ocean was calm, a perfect day for off-loading, and Captain Neidelman was making the most of it.

Setup had begun at daybreak. The huge sea barge was anchored off the eastern shore, while the hundred-ton floating crane was moored off the western end of the island. Lying in its shadow was the *Griffin*. The large research vessel *Cerberus* remained beyond the circle of mist, silent and still. Its two launches had dropped crews on the island early in the morning. Now the boats were busy offshore.

Crews were already on the move, locating old pits, roping safe trails, tagging ancient junk for removal. Other teams were taking corings from beams in the countless cribbed shafts. These corings would be carbon-14 dated in the *Cerberus* lab in an attempt to pinpoint which shaft was the original Water Pit.

There were perhaps fifty people bustling around the island—all Thalassa employees and all highly paid. Neidelman had told Hatch that the average worker would earn twenty-five thousand dollars.

At the safe northern end of the island—the only area one could walk without fear—a pier and dock had gone up. Beside it, the tug was off-loading a welter of equipment: crated generators, acetylene tanks, compressors, electronic switching equipment. Already onshore were orderly piles of angle iron, corrugated tin, lumber, and plywood. A group of technicians was wiring an island phone system, while another group was erecting Quonset huts. By tomorrow morning one of them would be Hatch's new office. It was amazing how fast things were happening.

Hatch checked his watch. Eleven o'clock: the Maine lunch hour. He went belowdecks, raided the gas-powered refrigerator, and returned with a lobster roll and a bottle of ginger ale. As he ate, a seagull landed on the thrum cap and eyed him quizzically. Hatch flicked a piece of lobster into the air; the gull caught it and then soared off, chased by two other gulls. Soon all three had returned and perched on the taffrail, staring him down with hungry black eyes. Now I've done it, Hatch thought, good-naturedly plucking another piece of lobster from the roll and tossing it toward the birds.

A burst of static on the radio scanner brought Hatch to the railing. There was hysterical shouting on the bands, first from one, then many voices. "Man down!" broke through the riot of sounds.

Suddenly Hatch's private radio burst to life. "Hatch, do you copy?" It was Neidelman. "We've got a man trapped on the island."

"Understood," Hatch said, grabbing his medical bag and leaping into the dinghy. The outboard jumped to life with an angry buzz. Somewhere near the south end there were two narrow gaps in the jagged underwater rocks. Luckily, he remembered where they were. Past the reef, Hatch aimed the boat at a small pebbled area and cut the engine. He felt the shock as the dinghy hit the shore and skidded up across the shingle.

Before the boat came to a halt, Hatch grabbed his kit and was scrambling up the embankment. In a minute he was among a group of white-suited figures clustered around the ragged mouth of a pit. Several ropes were wrapped around a nearby winch.

"I'm Streeter," shouted a lean figure with a marine-style haircut. "Team leader."

Two men began buckling a Swiss Seat harness around Hatch.

Hatch glanced into the pit, and his stomach contracted. Dozens of feet down he could see yellow beams from flashlights and two roped figures frantically working at a thick beam. Beneath the beam Hatch was horrified to see another figure, moving feebly.

"What happened?" Hatch cried.

"He's one of the dating team," Streeter replied. "His name's Ken Field. Triggered some kind of cave-in. His legs are pinned, and the water's rising fast. We've got three minutes, no more. He's all roped, just cut him loose, and we'll haul him up."

Cut him loose? Hatch thought just as he was lowered into the pit. The harness jerked him to a rude halt beside the two rescuers.

The man lay on his back, the massive beam lying diagonally across his left ankle and right knee, pinning him tightly. He opened his mouth, crying out with pain. Beneath him Hatch could see the water, rising at a terrifying rate.

One rescuer was chopping at the beam with a heavy axe. Hatch knew immediately that they could never chop through the beam in time. He mentally reviewed his options, then realized there were none. No time for painkiller, no time for an anesthetic, no time for anything. He began shrugging out of his shirt.

"Take my kit and get yourselves topside!" he shouted to the rescuers. "And stand by to hoist this man up!" He ripped his shirt in half. Twisting one sleeve, he tied it around the trapped man's left leg about five inches below the knee. The other sleeve went around the fat part of the man's right thigh.

"Give me the axe!" he cried to the departing rescuer.

The trapped man's eyes widened. "No!" he screamed.

Hatch positioned himself astride the man, then brought the axe down on the man's left shin with all his might. The man's voice ceased instantly, but his eyes remained open, the cords of his neck standing out. The rising water roiled up around the cut, and it filled with blood. Quickly Malin drove the axe home again, and the other leg came free. The man threw his head back in a soundless scream.

"Pull him up!" Hatch screamed. Immediately the rope went taut and the unconscious man came bursting out, blood and muddy water running from the stumps of his legs. Then a moment later Hatch felt himself hoisted toward the surface. Within seconds he was crouching next to the man in a swale of matted grass. Frantically he felt for the vitals: The man was not breathing, but his heart was still beating, fast and faint.

Hatch immediately began a stabilizing pattern—a ten count of mouth-to-mouth, then a pause to tighten the tourniquet around the left leg; ten more breaths, a pause to tighten the other tourniquet; ten more breaths, then a pulse check.

"Get my bag!" he yelled at the stunned group. "I need a hypo!"

A man grabbed the bag, and Hatch pulled out a syringe and a bottle. Sucking one cc of epinephrine into the hypo, he administered it into the victim's shoulder. Then he returned to mouth-to-mouth. At the five count the man coughed, then drew a ragged breath.

Streeter came forward, a cellular phone in his hand.

"Get the coast guard," Hatch snapped.

Streeter pressed the number, then handed it over wordlessly.

Hatch asked to speak to a paramedic, then quickly described the accident. "We've got a double amputation, one above, one below the knee," he said. "Massive exsanguination, deep shock, pulse is thready at fifty-five, still unconscious. Get a chopper out here with your best pilot. There's no landing spot, and you'll need to drop a basket."

He snapped the phone shut and handed it back to Streeter.

The injured man was beginning to regain consciousness, thrashing feebly and moaning. Hatch sorted through his kit and gave the man five milligrams of morphine. Then he turned to what remained of the legs. Sorting through his kit, he grabbed a needle and thread and began tying off the veins and arteries.

"Dr. Hatch?" Streeter asked.

"What?" Hatch replied, working on a medium-sized vein.

"Captain Neidelman would like to talk to you."

Hatch nodded, tied off the vein, checked the tourniquets, and rinsed the wounds. He picked up the radio. "Yes?"

"How is he?" Neidelman asked.

"He's got a fair chance of survival," Hatch said.

"Thank God."

"You better review some basic safety procedures with your team leader here. This accident was entirely avoidable."

"I understand," said Neidelman.

Hatch switched off the phone and turned to Streeter. "Get this area cleared. We don't want another accident on our hands."

"Right," said Streeter, his lips tightening.

Hatch saw that the man's face was unnaturally dark, blood throbbing angrily in a vein on his forehead.

In a few moments the dull thud of heavy rotors filled the air as a helicopter approached the small group. The door of the cargo bay slid back, and a rescue platform came bobbing down. The injured man was strapped aboard and sent up, and Hatch signaled for the platform to be sent down again for himself. Once he was on board, the chopper dug its nose into the air, heading for the southwest.

An hour later Hatch found himself alone in the silence of an empty operating room. Ken Field, the wounded man, was in the next bay, being cared for by Bangor's best surgeon. The man would live. Hatch's work was over.

He fetched a deep breath, then let it out slowly. This didn't have to happen, a cold voice was whispering inside his head. This was the second time he'd underestimated the power of the island. Never again, he thought, raging. Never again.

Another thought insinuated itself into his mind. Today was the first time he had set foot on Ragged Island since the death of his brother. During the emergency there had been no time to think. Now, alone with his thoughts, it took all the self-control Hatch could muster to control the fit of shaking that threatened to overwhelm him.

DORIS Bowditch, licensed Realtor, strode up the steps of Five Ocean Lane and threw the front door open with a little flourish. Hatch followed her into the cool, dark interior of the house. It hit him immediately, like a blow to the gut: the same smell of old pinewood, mothballs, and pipe smoke.

"Well!" came Doris's bright voice. "What do you think?"

"Fine," said Hatch, taking a tentative step forward. The front parlor was just as he remembered it the day his mother had finally given up and they'd left for Boston: the chintz easy chairs, the old canvas sofa, the Herkeimer upright piano.

"The pump's been primed," Doris continued, oblivious. "The windows washed, electricity turned on, propane tank filled."

"Thank you, Doris," he said, trying to muster a smile. "The house is in wonderful shape."

After she left, Hatch moved to the old piano and ran his hand along the fall board. On the shelf beside the fireplace lay several grimy packs of cards. Hatch felt a fresh stab as he remembered playing poker with Johnny, using wooden matches as chips.

He stepped up to the bow window, letting his gaze fall on the sparkling ocean. Somewhere out on the horizon lay Ragged Island, at rest now after claiming its first casualty in more than a quarter century. In the wake of the accident Neidelman had called a one-day halt to the operation.

Hatch walked slowly into the kitchen. He lingered in the break-fast nook, the scarred table and benches bringing back memories of his father telling sea stories in his slow voice while his dinner went cold. Everywhere he looked the house eagerly offered up memories of a happy childhood. After all, it *had* been happy. It was only the end that was unendurable. If only . . .

THE small group gathered around the antique maple table in the pilothouse of the *Griffin* the following morning looked subdued, even demoralized, after the accident.

As Hatch walked in for the scheduled meeting, he looked around at the nerve center of Neidelman's boat. The pilothouse was con-structed of Brazilian rosewood and brass, with intricate beadboard ceilings and an array of high-tech equipment. The captain himself had not yet emerged from his private quarters below. The only sound in the room was the soft slap of water against the hull.

Taking a seat at the table, Hatch glanced at the people assembled. He had met a few of them informally the first night, but others re-mained strangers. Lyle Streeter, the crew foreman, looked pointedly away from Hatch's smile of greeting.

The captain stooped through the door and walked to the table. When Neidelman's eyes landed on Hatch, he spoke. "How is Ken?"

"Serious, but stable," Hatch replied.

"Thank you, Dr. Hatch, for saving his life."

"I couldn't have done it without Mr. Streeter and his crew."

Neidelman nodded. "The survey crew was taking every precau-tion I deemed necessary. If anyone is to blame for the accident, it is myself. We have overhauled our safety procedures."

He stood up and placed his hands behind his back. "Every day," he said, "we'll be taking risks. All of us. No treasure has ever been buried with such skill and cunning. It will take even more skill and cunning to retrieve it."

Neidelman glanced briefly at each in turn. "As my core team, each person at this table will receive a share in the treasure instead of salary. You know that if we succeed, each of you will become enormously wealthy. That may not seem bad for four weeks' work, until you consider what happened to Ken Field. If any of you are contemplating leaving, now is the time to do it."

The captain lit his pipe with a deliberate slowness while the silence around the table deepened.

At last he spoke through a wreath of smoke. "Very good. Before we get to work, I'd like to introduce you all to the newest member of the expedition." He glanced at Hatch. "As most of you know, this is Dr. Malin Hatch, owner of Ragged Island and partner in this operation. He will be our medical officer."

Neidelman turned. "Dr. Hatch, this is Christopher St. John, the expedition's historian." He was a plump-faced man with a shock of unruly gray hair. His rumpled tweed suit displayed traces of several breakfasts. "You'll find him an expert on Elizabethan and Stuart history, including piracy and the use of codes. And this"—Neidelman indicated a slovenly-looking man in Bermuda shorts, who was picking at his nails with a look of intense boredom—"is Kerry Wopner, our computer expert."

Neidelman continued around the table. "You met our foreman, Lyle Streeter, yesterday. He's been with me ever since our days cruising the Mekong. And here"—he pointed to a small, severe-looking woman—"is Sandra Magnusen, Thalassa's chief engineer. At the end of the table is Roger Rankin, our geologist." He indicated a broad bear of a man. Rankin's blond beard parted in a spontaneous grin.

"Dr. Bonterre," Neidelman continued, "our archaeologist and dive leader, has been delayed and should arrive late this evening." He paused a moment. "Unless there are any questions, that's all. Thank you, and I'll see you all again tomorrow morning."

As the group broke up, Neidelman came around the table to Hatch. "Your medical hut will be stocked and ready by dawn."

"That's a relief," said Hatch.

"You're probably eager for some more background on the project. How about coming by the *Cerberus* around fourteen hundred hours?" A thin smile appeared on his lips. "Starting tomorrow, things are liable to get a little busy around here."

AT TWO P.M. PRECISELY THE *Plain Jane* pulled free of the last ten-drils of mist surrounding Ragged Island. Ahead, Hatch could see the white outlines of the *Cerberus,* riding at anchor. Near the water-line he made out a boarding hatch. The tall, thin shape of the cap-tain was silhouetted within it, awaiting his arrival.

"Quite a little boat you've got here," Hatch called out as he came to a stop opposite the captain.

"Biggest in Thalassa's fleet," Neidelman replied. "She's basically a floating laboratory."

"I was curious about the harpoon gun," Hatch said. "Do you spear whales every now and then?"

Neidelman grinned. "That betrays the ship's origins. It was de-signed as a state-of-the-art whaler by a Norwegian company six years ago. Then the international ban on whaling happened, and the ship became a costly white elephant even before it was fitted out. Thalassa got it for an excellent price." He nodded over his shoul-der. "Come on, let's see what the boys are up to."

Hatch secured the *Plain Jane* to the side of *Cerberus,* then fol-lowed Neidelman through the boarding hatch. The captain led him down a corridor, then stopped at a door marked COMPUTER ROOM.

"We've got more computing power than a small university," Nei-delman said with pride, "including a navigational system and a neural-net autopilot. In emergencies the ship can practically run itself."

The captain walked past a heavy metal door that was partially ajar. Glancing in, Hatch could make out a rack of shotguns and two smaller weapons of shiny metal he couldn't identify.

"What are those?" he asked, pointing to the stubby, fat-bellied devices. "They look like pint-size vacuum cleaners."

Neidelman glanced inside. "Fléchettes," he said. "A kind of nail gun. It shoots tiny finned pieces of tungsten-carbide wire."

"What do you need them for?" Hatch frowned.

"Often we have to work in shark-infested areas," the captain replied. "When you're face to face with a great white, you'll appre-ciate what a fléchette can do."

Neidelman rapped loudly on an unmarked door.

"I'm busy!" came a querulous voice.

Neidelman gave Hatch a knowing smile and eased open the door, revealing a dimly lit stateroom. The walls were entirely covered by banks of electronic equipment: oscilloscopes, CPUs, and countless pieces whose purpose Hatch couldn't begin to guess. The floor was ankle-deep in crumpled papers, dented soda cans, candy wrappers. In the midst of the chaos sat the rumpled-looking figure in flowered shirt and Bermuda shorts, typing feverishly at a keyboard.

"Kerry, can you spare a minute?" Neidelman said.

Wopner turned away from the screen and blinked at Neidelman, then Hatch. "It's your party," he said in a high, irritated voice.

Neidelman smiled indulgently and turned to Hatch. "You'd never know it, but Kerry is one of the most brilliant cryptanalysts outside the NSA."

"Yeah, right," said Wopner, but Hatch could see he was pleased by the compliment.

"Quite a rig you've got here," Hatch said.

Wopner pushed his glasses up his nose. "You think this is something? This is just the backup system. They shipped the main rig off to the island yesterday. Now *that's* something."

"A team's completing the installation of the island network this afternoon," Neidelman said to Hatch. "Like Kerry said, this is the backup system, an exact duplicate of the Ragged Island computer grid. Expensive way of doing things, but a real time-saver. Kerry, show him what I mean."

"Aye, aye, skipper." Wopner tapped a few keys, and a blank screen winked to life overhead. Hatch looked up to see a wire-frame diagram of Ragged Island appear on the screen.

Neidelman gestured at the screen. "Everything on the island— from the pumps to the turbines to the compressors to the derricks— is linked into the network. We'll be able to control anything on the island from the command center."

There was a loud beep; then a column of numbers scrolled up one of the screens.

"That's it," Wopner said, squinting at the data. "We're done."

"Done?" Hatch asked.

"Yeah. Network testing finished."

Neidelman glanced at his watch. "I've got some odds and ends to attend to. Kerry, I know Dr. Hatch would like to hear more about your and Dr. St. John's work on Macallan's codes. Malin, I'll see you topside." Neidelman left the stateroom, closing the door behind him.

Without looking away from the terminal, Wopner picked up a sneaker and hurled it against the far wall. "Hey, Chris!" he yelled. "Time for the dog and pony show!"

Hatch realized that Wopner must have been aiming at a small door set in the far wall of the stateroom. "Allow me," he said.

Opening the door, Hatch saw another stateroom, identical in size but completely different in all other ways. It was well lit, clean, and spare. The Englishman, Christopher St. John, sat at a table pecking away at a Royal typewriter.

"Hello," Hatch said. "Captain Neidelman volunteered your services for a few minutes."

St. John stood and picked up a few old volumes from the desk. "A pleasure to have you with us, Dr. Hatch," he said, shaking his hand, not looking at all pleased with the interruption. He followed Hatch back into Wopner's stateroom.

"Pull up a seat," Wopner said. "I'll explain the real work I've been doing, and Chris can tell you about all those dusty tomes he's been lifting and dropping in the back room."

Hatch pulled a chair up. Wopner typed a few commands, and a picture of Macallan's treatise appeared on the screen.

"Captain Neidelman feels that the second half of the journal contains vital information about the treasure," said Wopner. "So we're taking a two-track approach to break the code. I do the computers. Chris here does the history."

"The captain mentioned a figure of two billion dollars," Hatch said. "How did he arrive at that?"

"Well now," said St. John. "Like most pirate fleets, Ockham's was a ragtag collection of ships he'd captured: a couple of galleons, a few brigantines, a fast sloop, and, I believe, a large East Indiaman.

Nine ships in all. We know they were so heavily laden they were dangerously unmaneuverable. You simply add up their cargo capacities and combine that with the manifests of ships that Ockham looted. We know, for example, that Ockham took fourteen tons of gold from the Spanish plate fleet and ten times that in silver."

"Fourteen *tons?*" Hatch asked dumbfounded.

"Absolutely," said St. John. "And then there's St. Michael's Sword," he added. "An artifact of inestimable value by itself. We're dealing here with the greatest pirate treasure ever assembled. Ockham was brilliant and gifted, which made him all the more dangerous. But his success became a liability. He didn't know *how* to bury such a large treasure. That's where Macallan came in. And, indirectly, that's where *we* come in. Because Macallan kept his secret diary in code."

"Was code writing common in those days?" Hatch asked.

"Common?" St. John laughed. "It was practically universal, one of the essential arts of diplomacy and war. Both the British and Spanish governments had departments that specialized in making and breaking ciphers. Even pirates had crewmen who could crack codes. After all, ship's papers included all kinds of interesting coded documents."

"But coded how?"

"They were usually simple word substitutions. For example, in a message the word 'eagle' might be substituted for 'King George' and 'daffodils' for 'doubloons.' Sometimes they were substitution alphabets, where a letter or number replaced a letter of the alphabet."

"And Macallan's code?"

"The first part of the journal was written with a clever monophonic substitution code. We're still working on the second."

"That's *my* department," said Wopner. He struck a key and a string of gibberish appeared on the screen:

AB3 RQB7 E50LA W IEW D8P OL QS9MN . . .

"Here's the ciphertext of the first code," he said.

"How did you break it?"

"The letters of the alphabet occur in fixed ratios in English: E being the commonest letter, X the rarest. You create what we call a contact chart and bang! The computer does the rest."

St. John waved his hand dismissively. "Kerry is programming the computer attacks against the code, but I am supplying the historical data. Without the old cipher tables, the computer is hopeless. It only knows what's been programmed into it."

Wopner stared at St. John. "Hopeless? Fact is, big mama here would have cracked that code without your precious cipher tables. It just would have taken a little longer, is all."

"No longer than twenty monkeys typing at random might take to write *King Lear,*" said St. John with a bark of laughter.

"Haw haw." Wopner turned back to Hatch. "Well, to make a long story short, here's how it decoded."

There was a flurry of keystrokes, and the screen split, showing the code on one side and the plaintext on the other.

The 2nd of June, Anno D. 1696. The pirate Ockham hath taken our fleet, scuttled the ships, and butcherd every soull. Our captain went to his end scandalously blubbering like a babe. I alone was spared, clapped in chaines and straightaway taken down to Ockham's cabin, where the blackguard drewe a saber against my person and said, "Lete the king build his owen cursed church, I have ye a newe commission."

"Amazing," said Hatch, as he came to the end of the screen. "Can I read more?"

"I'll print out a copy for you," said Wopner, hitting a key. A printer began humming somewhere in the darkened room.

"Basically," said St. John, "the decrypted section of the journal covers Macallan's being taken prisoner, agreeing on pain of death to design the Water Pit, and finding the right island. Unfortunately, Macallan switches to a new code just when they began actual construction. We believe the rest of the journal consists of a description of the design and construction of the pit itself. And, of course, the secret for getting to the treasure chamber."

"Neidelman said the journal mentions St. Michael's Sword."

"You bet it does," Wopner interrupted, hitting the keys. More text popped up:

> Ockham hath unburthened three of his ships in hopes of tak-
> ing a prize along the coast. Today a long leaden coffin trimmed
> in golde came ashore with a dozen casks of jewells. The corsairs
> say the coffin holds St. Michael's Sword, a costly treasure seized
> from a Spanish galleon and highly esteemd by the Captain, who
> swaggerd most shamefully, boasting that it was the greatest
> prize of the Indies. The Captain hath forbidden the opening of
> the casket, and it is guarded by day and night. The men are sus-
> picious of each other and constantly make stryfe. Were it not
> for the cruell discipline of the Captain, I feare every one would
> come to a bad end, and shortly.

"And now here's what the second code looks like." Wopner tapped on the keys and the screen filled again:

$$34834590234582394438923492340923409856 \ldots$$

"The old boy got smart," Wopner said. "No more spaces, so we can't go by word shapes. All numbers too. The computer's work-ing on it as we speak. It's just a matter of time."

"A matter of a waste of time," St. John said. "I'm working up a new set of cipher tables from a Dutch book on cryptography. What's needed here is more historical research, not more computer time. Macallan was a man of his age. He didn't invent this code out of thin air. There must be a historical precedent."

Hatch decided it was time to change the subject. "What exactly is St. Michael's Sword?"

"Well, let's see," said St. John, pursing his lips. "I've always as-sumed it had a jeweled hilt, of course, with chased silver and parcel-gilt, perhaps a multi-fullered blade—that sort of thing."

"But why would it be the greatest prize in the Indies?"

St. John looked a little flummoxed. "I hadn't really thought in those terms. Perhaps it had some spiritual significance."

"But if Ockham had as much treasure as you say, why would he place such an inordinate value on the sword?"

St. John turned a pair of watery eyes on Hatch. "The truth is, Dr. Hatch, nothing in my documentation gives any indication of *what* St. Michael's Sword is. Only that it was carefully guarded and deeply revered. So I'm afraid I can't answer your question."

HATCH sat down in the rocker in his parents' bedroom and picked up a black folder.

First came the printout of the decrypted portion of Macallan's journal. The architect's contempt for the pirate captain came through clearly in every line. This first half of the journal was brief, and Hatch soon laid it aside, now more curious than ever about its encrypted second half. He wondered how soon Wopner would have it cracked.

He returned his attention to a second black folder, which contained the biography of Ockham, and began to read.

Edward Ockham was born in 1662 in Cornwall, England, the son of minor landed nobility. He spent two years at Balliol College, Oxford, before being sent down by the college dons for unspecified infractions.

In 1682 Ockham received his naval commission. Rising quickly, he distinguished himself in several actions against the Spanish. He left the navy to become captain of a privateer.

Early in 1685 he took up slaving, running ships from Africa to Guadeloupe. After two years of profitable voyages Ockham was trapped within a blockaded harbor by two ships of the line. As a diversion, Ockham set his ship afire and got away in a small cutter. The four hundred slaves shackled together in the hold perished in the blaze. Documentary evidence attributes the nickname of "Red Ned" Ockham to this deed.

Over the next ten years Ockham became known as the most ruthless, venal, and ambitious pirate operating in the waters off the New World. Many notorious pirate techniques—such as walking the plank and ransoming of civilian prisoners—can be traced to his innovations.

When attacking towns or ships, he was quick to use torture on any and all in order to ascertain where plunder might be hidden. When laying siege to the heavily fortified Spanish city of Portobelo, he forced the nuns from a nearby abbey to place the ladders against the walls, reasoning that the strong Catholicism of the Spaniards would constrain them from firing.

As his thirst for prizes grew stronger, Ockham turned his attention more and more toward Spanish gold. So adept did he become at anticipating the shipments of gold that some scholars believe he was able to crack the ciphers of Spanish captains and envoys.

Ockham's single greatest accomplishment came in 1695, when his small armada of ships successfully captured, plundered, and sank the Spanish *flota de plata* (silver fleet) bound for Cádiz. The volume of treasure he acquired—in gold bars, silver wedges, pearls, and jewels—has been estimated at over a billion dollars.

Ockham's eventual fate remains a mystery. In 1696 his command ship was found off the Azores, drifting free, all hands dead of an unknown affliction. No treasure was found on board, and scholars of the period agree he had concealed it along the east coast of the New World sometime shortly before his death. Although many legends have arisen, the strongest evidence points to one of three potential sites: Ile à Vache, off Hispaniola; South Carolina's Isle of Palms; or Ragged Island, off the Maine coast.

AT SIX thirty the next morning Hatch throttled down the diesels of the *Plain Jane,* then dropped anchor twenty yards off the lee shore of Ragged Island. He motored the dinghy toward the pier at base camp. Already the day was warm and humid.

Over the last forty-eight hours Ragged Island had grown comfortingly unrecognizable. Yellow crime-scene tape had been strung around the unstable areas of the island, with safe corridors delineated for walking. The meadows above the stony pebbles of the narrow strip of shingle beach had become a miniature city. Trailers and Quonset huts were arranged in a tight circle. Beyond, a brace of massive generators thrummed, wafting diesel fumes into the air. Beside them sat two enormous fuel tanks. In the midst of the chaos stood Island One, the command center, a double-wide trailer festooned with communications gear and transmitters.

Securing the dinghy, Hatch hiked up to base camp and stepped into the Quonset hut marked MEDICAL. His office was spartan but pleasant. He walked around, pleased that Neidelman had purchased the best of everything, from a locked storeroom full of drug cabinets to an EKG machine and a fancy electronic Geiger counter. There was an outer office, an examination room, even a two-bed infirmary.

Stepping outside, Hatch headed for Island One. Inside the command center he found Neidelman, Streeter, and the engineer, Sandra Magnusen, bending over a computer screen. Magnusen seemed all business, and Hatch got the distinct feeling that she didn't like most people, doctors included.

Neidelman looked up and nodded. "Data transfer from *Cerberus* finished several hours ago," he said.

Magnusen's brow furrowed. "This computer's acting flaky."

"Tell me about it," Neidelman said quietly.

"It's sluggish. The island network shows everything normal. But there's a deviation from the simulation that we ran on *Cerberus.*"

Neidelman turned to Streeter. "Where's Wopner?"

"Asleep on the *Cerberus.*"

"Wake him up." Neidelman turned to Hatch and nodded toward the door. They walked out into the hazy sunlight.

"There's something I'd like to show you," the captain said. Without waiting for an answer, he set off at his usual terrific stride. Hatch scrambled to keep up. They followed a roped path, certified safe by Thalassa surveyors, that climbed the incline toward the central hump of land, where most of the old shafts were clustered. A minute later Hatch found himself standing at the edge of a gaping hole. Gingerly he leaned forward. Only blackness showed below.

Neidelman removed a folded computer printout from his pocket and handed it to Hatch. It consisted of a long column of dates. One was highlighted in yellow: 1690±40.

"The carbon-14 tests were completed at the *Cerberus*'s lab early this morning," Neidelman said. "Those are the results."

Hatch took another look. "So what's it mean?"

"This is it," Neidelman said quietly.

"The Water Pit?" Hatch heard the disbelief in his own voice.

Neidelman nodded. "The original. The wood used for the cribbing of this shaft was cut around 1690. All the other shafts date between 1800 and 1930. There can be no question. This is the Water Pit designed by Macallan and built by Ockham's crew." He pointed to another, smaller, hole about thirty yards away. "And that's the Boston Shaft, dug a hundred and fifty years later."

"Why didn't anyone else think of carbon dating?" said Hatch.

"The last person to dig on the island was your grandfather in the late '40s. Carbon dating wasn't invented until the next decade." He waved his hand over the pit. "This afternoon we'll begin construction of a glass-floored observation post. It'll sit atop a large derrick and be fitted with winches and remote sensing gear. We'll be able to look right down the throat of the beast, literally and electronically."

"And what's the hose for?" Hatch asked, nodding toward the enormous metal-jointed tube that snaked out of the pit.

"This morning's dye test." Neidelman glanced at his watch. "When the tide reaches the flood, we'll start pumping a special high-intensity dye into the Water Pit. With the tide ebbing, the dye will travel down into Macallan's hidden flood tunnel and back out to the ocean. All we have to do is find the place where the dye appears offshore, send divers to the spot, and seal the tunnel with explosives. With the seawater blocked, we can pump out the water and drain Macallan's pit. Then we can make the final excavation of the treasure at our leisure."

Hatch opened his mouth, then shut it again with a shake of his head. "Things are moving so fast."

"You said it yourself," Neidelman replied. "We don't have much time." They stood for a moment in silence.

"We'd better get back," the captain said at last. "One of the launches will pick you up. You'll be able to watch the dye test from its deck." The two men turned and headed toward base camp.

Back at base camp, Hatch got his medical kit, then ran to the dock and jumped aboard the powerful launch. Beyond lay its sister launch, waiting to pick up Neidelman and assume its position on the far side of the island.

Hatch was sorry to see Streeter at the helm of his boat. He nodded, getting a curt nod in return. Forward, in the half-cabin, two divers were checking their gear. The geologist, Rankin, was standing beside Streeter. On seeing Hatch, he grinned and strode over.

"Hey, Dr. Hatch!" he said, white teeth flashing through an enormous beard, his long sandy hair plaited behind. "Man, this is one fascinating island you've got. I mean geologically."

"Really? I always thought it was just a big granite rock."

"Granite? It's mica, with a drumlin on top. Wild, man, just wild."

"Drumlin?"

"A really weird kind of glacial hill, pointed at one side and tapered at the other. No one knows how they form, but I'd say—"

"Divers, get ready," came Neidelman's voice over the radio. "Proceed to position."

As Hatch stowed his medical kit, the two divers came out of the cabin, laughing at some private joke. One was a tall man with a black mustache. He wore a wet suit of thin neoprene.

The other, a woman, turned and saw Hatch. A playful smile appeared on her lips. "Ah! You are the mysterious doctor?"

"I didn't know I was mysterious," said Hatch.

"But this is the dreaded Island of Dr. Hatch, *non?*" she said, laughing. "I hope you will not be hurt if I avoid your services."

"I hope you avoid them too," said Hatch, trying to think of something less inane to say. Drops of water glistened on her olive skin, and her hazel eyes sparkled with little flecks of gold. She couldn't be more than twenty-five, Hatch decided. Her accent was exotic—French, with a touch of the islands thrown in.

"I am Isobel Bonterre," she said, holding out her hand.

"The pleasure is mine," Hatch replied.

"And you are the brilliant Harvard doctor that Neidelman has been talking about," she said, gazing into his face. "He likes you very much, you know."

Hatch found himself blushing. "Glad to hear it." He had never really thought about whether Neidelman liked him, but he found himself unaccountably pleased to hear it. He caught, just out of the corner of his eye, a glance of hatred from Streeter.

"Now I must get ready," Bonterre said. She balled up her hair and slid the wet suit hood over it, then donned her mask. The other diver introduced himself as Sergio Scopatti.

Neidelman's voice broke in. "Five minutes to the turn of the tide. Is everyone in position?"

Streeter acknowledged.

"Mr. Wopner, is the program running properly?"

"No problemo," came the nasal voice over the airwaves.

"Understood. Dr. Magnusen?"

"The dye pumps are ready to go, Captain."

"Excellent. Dr. Magnusen, on my signal."

The people on the launch fell silent. On the far side of the island Hatch could make out the other launch riding the even swell just beyond the ledges. The air of excitement increased.

"Start the pumps," Neidelman commanded.

The throb of the pumps came rumbling across the water.

"Pumps at ten," came Magnusen's voice.

"Spotters ready?"

There was a chorus of ayes. Looking toward the island, Hatch could see several teams ranged along the bluffs, with binoculars. All hands peered across the gently undulating surface of the ocean. The water had a dark, almost black color, but there was no wind and only the faintest chop, making conditions ideal. Despite the growing rip current, Streeter kept the boat stationary with an expert handling of the throttles. A minute passed and another.

Bonterre and Scopatti waited, silent and alert. Both had their masks and regulators in place and were already at the gunwales, bolt guns in their hands and buoys at their belts, ready to go over the side.

"Dye at twenty-two degrees," came the voice of one of the spotters.

"Streeter, that's your quadrant," said Neidelman. "Well done!"

Streeter swung the boat around, and in a moment Hatch could see a light spot on the ocean about three hundred yards away.

"Dye at two hundred and ninety-seven degrees," came the voice of another spotter.

"What?" said Neidelman. There was a moment of shocked silence. "Looks like we've got two flood tunnels to seal," he said. "We'll mark the second. Let's go."

Hatch's launch was closing in on the swirl of yellow dye breaking the surface just inside the reefs. Streeter cut the throttle, and the divers went over the side. Hatch turned eagerly to the video screens. At first the image was cloudy; then a large rough crack appeared at the murky bottom of the reef, dye jetting out of it like smoke.

"Le voilà!" came Bonterre's excited voice over the comm channel. The image jiggled as she shot a small explosive bolt into the rock near the crack and attached an inflatable buoy. "Marked!" said Bonterre. "Preparing to set charges."

"Dye at five degrees, ninety feet offshore," came another call.

"Are you certain?" Disbelief mixed with uncertainty in Neidelman's voice. "Okay, we've got a third tunnel. Streeter, it's yours."

"More dye! Three hundred thirty-two degrees."

"We'll take that one," said Neidelman. "How many tunnels did this bloody architect build? Streeter, get your divers up as soon as possible. Just mark the exits for now, and we'll set the explosives later. We've only got five minutes before that dye dissipates."

In another moment Bonterre and Scopatti were up and in the boat, and without a word Streeter took off at a roar. Now Hatch could see another cloud of yellow dye boiling to the surface. The boat circled as Bonterre and Scopatti went over the side. Hatch turned his attention to the video screen.

Scopatti swam ahead, his form transmitted from Bonterre's camera headset, a ghostly figure among the billowing clouds of dye. Suddenly the jagged rocks at the bottom of the reef appeared, along with a square opening, much larger than the others.

"What's this?" Hatch heard Bonterre say in a voice of disbelief.

Just then Wopner's voice crackled over the radio. "Got a problem, Captain. I'm getting error messages, but the system reports normal function."

"Switch to the backup system."

"I'm doing that. Wait, now the hub's getting . . . Oh, no."

Hatch heard the sound of the pumps on the island faltering.

"System crash," said Wopner.

There was an abrupt sharp noise from Bonterre. Hatch glanced toward the video screen and saw it had gone dead. Black.

"What the devil?" Streeter said, frantically punching the comm button. "Bonterre, can you hear me? *Bonterre!*"

Scopatti broke the surface and tore the regulator from his mouth. "Bonterre's been sucked into the tunnel!" he gasped.

"Then go back after her!" Neidelman barked. "Streeter, give him a lifeline! Magnusen, bypass the computers—get the pumps started manually. Losing them must have created some kind of backflow."

"Yes, sir," said Magnusen.

Scopatti clipped a lifeline on and disappeared again over the side.

Hatch stared at the screen with a macabre sense of déjà vu. It was as if she had vanished just as suddenly as . . .

Suddenly the pumps roared into life.

"Line's gone slack," said Streeter.

There was a tense silence, and then Hatch heard gasping over the audio line. With a flood of relief he saw a green square of light growing across the screen: the exit to the flood tunnel.

"Mon Dieu," came Isobel Bonterre's voice as she was ejected from the opening, the view from the camera tumbling wildly.

Moments later Hatch lifted Isobel aboard. Scopatti followed, stripping off her tanks and hood as Hatch laid her down on towels. He opened her wet suit and placed a stethoscope at her chest. She was breathing well, and her heartbeat was fast and strong.

"*Incroyable.*" She coughed, waving a chip of something gray. "Three-hundred-year-old cement! There was a row of stones set into the reef—they looked like the foundation to something. I ended up in a big underwater cavern."

"A cavern?" Neidelman asked over the open channel.

"*Mais oui.* But my radio was dead. Why would that be?"

"I don't have an answer to that," said Neidelman. "Perhaps once we've drained the pit, we'll learn why. Meanwhile, why don't you rest?"

Streeter turned. "Markers set. Returning to base."

The boat rumbled to life and planed across the water. Hatch stowed his gear, listening to the chatter on the radio bands.

"I'm telling you, we've got a cybergeist," Wopner was telling Neidelman. "I just did a ROM dump on the island system and ran it against the ship's. Everything's messed up nine ways to Sunday. But that's burned-in code, Captain. The system's cursed. Not even a hacker could rewrite a CD-ROM—"

"Don't start talking about curses," said Neidelman sharply.

As they approached the dock, Bonterre turned toward Hatch. "Well, Doctor, I did need your services, after all."

"It was nothing," said Hatch, blushing.

"Oh, but it was very nice."

THE stone ruins of Fort Blacklock stood in a meadow overlooking Stormhaven harbor. Across the meadow from the old fort a large yellow-and-white pavilion had been erected, decorated with a banner proclaiming 71ST ANNUAL STORMHAVEN LOBSTER BAKE!

Hatch headed apprehensively up the gentle slope of the grassy hill. Although Thalassa had been in Stormhaven little more than a week, the company's impact had been considerable. Crew members had filled the bed-and-breakfasts. The two restaurants in town were packed every night. The gas station at the wharf had been forced to triple its deliveries. The town was in such a fine mood about the Ragged Island treasure hunt that the mayor had hastily made Thalassa the collective guest of honor at the lobster bake.

Hatch ducked inside the pavilion and went to get some food, stopping along the way to fill a pint cup at an enormous keg. The lobsters and corn had been steamed in piles of seaweed heaped over burning oak. At the front of the line he turned his attention to the nearest cook. The cook flipped over one of the piles of seaweed, exposing a row of lobsters, some ears of corn, and a scattering of eggs. He picked up an egg with a mitted hand and chopped it in half to see if it was hard. That, Hatch remembered, was how they judged when the lobsters were cooked.

"Perfecto!" the cook said. The voice was familiar, and Hatch suddenly recognized his old high school classmate Donny Truitt, below a crop of carrot-colored hair.

"Why, if it ain't Mally Hatch!" said Truitt, recognizing him. "I was wondering when I'd run into you. How the heck are you?"

"Donny," Hatch cried, grasping his hand. "I'm not bad. You?"

"The same. Four kids. Looking for a new job since Martin's Marine went under."

"Four kids?" Hatch whistled. "You've been busy."

"Busier than you think. Divorced twice too. You hitched?"

"Not yet," Hatch said.

Donny smirked. "Seen Claire yet?"

"No," Hatch said, suddenly irritated. "Claire and I were just friends."

"I didn't think *friends* went kissing in Squeaker's Glen."

"That was a long time ago."

Donny chuckled. "She's around here somewhere. Anyway, you'll have to look elsewhere, 'cause she ended up—"

Hatch had heard enough about Claire. "I'm holding up the line," he interrupted.

"You sure are. I'll see you later." Donny waved his fork.

So Donny needs a job, Hatch thought as he headed back toward the table of honor. Wouldn't hurt for Thalassa to hire a few locals.

He found a seat at the table next to Bud Rowell, the storekeeper. Captain Neidelman was two seats down, next to the Congregational minister, Woody Clay. On the far side of Clay sat Lyle Streeter.

Hatch's eyes traveled to Woody Clay. He's obviously an outsider, he thought. Clay had the spare frame of an ascetic, and there was a crabbed, narrow intensity to his gaze. Hatch could see he was ill at ease being part of the table of honor.

Various instruments for lobster dissection lay on the table— hammers, crackers, and wooden mallets—all slick with lobster gore. Two great bowls in the center were heaped with broken shells. Everyone was pounding, cracking, and eating.

Hatch looked across the crowd, scanning for familiar faces. In a flash of recognition he saw the white head and stooped shoulders of Dr. Horn, his old biology teacher. The intimidating yet fiercely supportive Dr. Horn, who more than any other person had fired Hatch's interest in science and medicine.

Hatch turned to Bud, who was sucking lobster meat out of a leg. "Tell me about Woody Clay," Hatch said.

"Reverend Clay? He's the minister. Used to be a hippie, I hear. They say he gave away a big inheritance when he took the cloth."

Hatch glanced over at Clay. As he examined the intense face, the man looked up and met his gaze. Hatch looked away. Out of the corner of his eye he saw the minister rise from the table and approach.

"Malin Hatch?" the man said, extending his hand. "I'm Reverend Clay."

"Nice to meet you, Reverend." Hatch shook the cold hand.

Clay gestured at an empty chair. "May I?"

"I don't mind," Hatch said.

The minister awkwardly eased his angular frame into the small chair and turned a pair of large intense eyes on Hatch.

"I've seen all the activity out at Ragged Island," he began in a low voice. "This operation must be costing a good deal."

"We've got investors," Hatch said.

"Investors," Clay repeated. "My father loved money too. Not that it made him happy. When he died, I inherited his portfolio. When I got to looking into it, I found tobacco companies, mining companies tearing open whole mountains, timber companies that were clear-cutting virgin forests."

"I see," Hatch said.

Clay lowered his voice. "May I ask how much wealth, exactly, you and your investors hope to gain from all this?"

Something in the way the minister said "wealth" made Hatch wary. "Let's just say it's well into seven figures," he replied.

Clay nodded slowly. "I'm a direct man," he began, "and I don't like this treasure hunt."

"I'm sorry to hear that," Hatch replied.

"Money will ruin this town."

Hatch did not reply. On one level he understood what Clay was saying. It would be a tragedy if Stormhaven turned into another overdeveloped, overpriced summer playground. But that didn't seem likely, whether or not Thalassa succeeded.

"This treasure hunt is about greed," Clay said. "Already a man lost his legs. No good will come of this. That island is a bad place, cursed, if you care to call it that. I'm not superstitious, but God does have ways of punishing those with impure motives."

Hatch dissolved in a flood of anger. Impure motives? "If you'd grown up in this town, you'd know why I'm doing this," he snapped. "Don't presume to know what my motives are."

Hatch realized he was shouting. The surrounding tables had fallen silent, the people staring down at their plates. Abruptly he rose, strode past Clay, and made for the fort across the meadow.

THE fort was dark and chill with damp. Hatch entered through the stone archway and took a seat on the stone foundation. Slowly he calmed down, letting the peace of the fort wash away his anger. He felt he could stay there, enjoying the coolness, for hours. But he knew he should return to the festival, putting up a nonchalant front. He stood up and saw with surprise a stooped figure waiting in the archway.

"Professor Horn!" Hatch called.

The man's old face crinkled with delight. "I wondered when you'd notice me," he said, advancing with his cane. He shook Hatch's hand warmly. "That was quite a scene back there."

Hatch shook his head. "I lost my temper, like an idiot."

"Clay is awkward, socially inept, morally rigid. But beneath that bitter exterior there beats a heart as big as the ocean." The professor grasped Hatch's shoulder. "Enough about the reverend. My, Malin, but you're looking well. I'm prodigiously proud of you. Harvard Medical School, research position at Mount Auburn."

"I owe a lot of it to you," Hatch said.

"Nonsense." He shifted his hand to Hatch's arm and held it in a bony clasp. "See me out of the fort, would you? I'm a little shaky on my wheels these days."

They emerged into the sunlight of the meadow.

"So?" Hatch said. "What do you think of this treasure hunt?"

The professor turned toward Malin. "I think you're a fool."

There was a moment of stunned surprise. He'd been prepared for Clay, but not for this. "What makes you say that?"

"You, of all the people on this earth, should know better. Whatever's down there, you won't get it out."

"Look, Dr. Horn, we've got technology those old treasure hunters never even dreamed of."

Dr. Horn shook his head. "Malin, for almost a century I've seen them come and go. And they all ended up the same. Bankruptcy, misery, even death."

"But this *will* be different," Hatch said.

The professor suddenly gripped Hatch's arm again. "I knew your grandfather, Malin. He was a lot like you: young, smart, promising career ahead of him. What you just said is exactly what he said to me fifty years ago." He lowered his voice to a fierce whisper. "Look at the legacy he left your family. You asked my opinion. So here it is: Go back to Boston before history repeats itself."

He turned and hobbled off, his cane flicking irritably through the grass, until he had disappeared over the brow of the hill.

THE NEXT MORNING HATCH closeted himself in the medical hut, taking inventory. There had been a number of injuries over the last several days, but nothing more serious than a few scrapes.

When he finished the inventory, Hatch glanced out the window. He could see Christopher St. John ducking into Kerry Wopner's office. Hatch picked up the two black folders and exited the medical office, following the historian. Maybe there was some progress to report on the code.

Wopner's base camp office was even more messy than his stateroom on the *Cerberus*. Banks of monitoring equipment made it claustrophobic. Wopner occupied the office's lone chair.

"Kerry, do you have a minute?" St. John was saying. "We really need to discuss this problem with the code."

"Do I look like I have a minute?" Wopner leaned away from his terminal with a glare. "I've just now finished an all-island diagnostic. Everything checks out. No problems of any kind."

"That's great," Hatch broke in.

Wopner looked at him incredulously. "Great? It's terrible! We had a system crash, remember? The pumps went south on us. Afterward I compared the island computer system with the one on *Cerberus,* and guess what? The ROMs from here had been altered. Altered!"

"And?"

"And now I run the diagnostics again and everything's fine." Wopner leaned forward. "No deviations. Don't you get it? That's a physical impossibility."

St. John was glancing at the equipment around him, hands behind his back. "Ghost in the machine, Kerry?" he ventured.

Wopner ignored this.

"Things are working now," Hatch said. "So why not move on?"

"And have it happen again? I need to know *why* this failed."

"You can't do anything about it now," St. John said. "Meanwhile, we're falling behind schedule on breaking the final code."

Wopner snapped, "Look, I'm trying to get things moving. Why don't you retire to your library? Come back with some useful ideas."

St. John looked briefly at Wopner. Then he ducked back out into

the gauzy morning light. Hatch followed. A boat horn sounded outside, and he checked his watch. "It's ten," he said. "They'll be sealing the flood tunnels and draining the Water Pit in a few minutes."

LEAVING base camp, Hatch began hiking up the path toward the
observation tower, eager to see the structure that had materialized
over the Water Pit in just forty-eight hours. He could make out the
glassed-in tower, a narrow deck running around its outer edge, and
the massive supports that suspended the derrick almost forty feet
above the sandy ground. Winches and cables dangled from the un-
derside of the tower, reaching down into the darkness of the pit.

Hatch approached the derrick and climbed the external ladder.
The view was magnificent. He could make out the dark purple stripe
of the mainland. The sun glinted off the ocean, turning it the color
of beaten metal. On the far side of the observation deck he could see
Isobel Bonterre, her wet suit shining damply in the sun. She was dry-
ing her hair and talking animatedly to Neidelman.

As Hatch strolled over, she turned to him with a grin. "You will
not believe what I have discovered!"

Hatch glanced at Neidelman, who was nodding, clearly pleased.

"That stone foundation I found on the seabed the other day?" she
continued. "It runs all around the southern end of the island. There
is only one explanation for it: The pirates built a cofferdam along the
southern reefs. They probably sunk wooden pilings, made watertight
with pitch and oakum. Then they pumped out the seawater, exposed
the seafloor around the beach, and excavated the flood tunnels.
When they were done, they simply destroyed the cofferdam and let
the water back in. *Et voilà,* the trap was set!"

"A cofferdam around the entire end of the island?" Hatch said.
"Sounds like a huge task."

"Huge, yes," said Neidelman. "But he had over a thousand
laborers to do it." He checked his watch. "Fifteen minutes until we
blow the explosives and seal those tunnels. Come on inside."

The captain ushered them inside the observation tower. Beneath
the windows that lined the walls, Hatch could see banks of equip-

ment and monitors. Magnusen and Rankin stood at stations in opposite corners of the tower. Against one wall a series of screens showed video feeds from around the island, the command center, and the mouth of the pit itself.

The most remarkable feature of the tower was a massive glass plate that occupied the center of the floor. Hatch stepped forward and gazed down into the maw of the Water Pit.

"Watch this," Neidelman said, flicking a switch on a console.

A powerful mercury arc lamp snapped on, its beam stabbing down into the darkness. Below, the pit was drowned in seawater. Bits of seaweed floated in the water, and brine shrimp, attracted by the light, jerked and played just below the surface. A few feet into the murky water he could make out stumps of old timbers, heavy with barnacles, their ragged lengths disappearing into the depths. The fat pump hose ran along the ground and over the side of the pit, joining half a dozen other, narrower, cables.

"The throat of the beast," Neidelman said with grim satisfaction. He strode toward a bank of controls and snapped the radio to life. "Launches, take your stations. We blow the charges in ten minutes."

Hatch moved to the window. He could see the two launches take up positions offshore. Ringing the southern end of the island, he could make out the electronic buoys that marked the flood-tunnel exits. Each, he knew, had been mined with several pounds of Semtex plastic explosive.

"Island One, report," Neidelman spoke into the radio. "Are the monitoring systems on-line?"

"Wopner here. Everything's hunky-dory."

"Good. Advise me of any changes."

Rankin gestured Hatch over and pointed toward a screen that showed a cross section of the pit, marked in ten-foot intervals down to one hundred feet. Rankin said excitedly, "We'll be able to monitor the water-level drop from here."

"All stations, listen up," Neidelman said. "We'll blow in series. Ten seconds. . . . Fire one."

Hatch looked seaward. For a pregnant moment all seemed still.

Then an enormous geyser ripped out of the ocean, followed by a haze of pulverized rock, mud, and seaweed. A shock wave shivered the windows of the observation deck.

"Fire two," Neidelman said, and a second explosion ripped the underwater reef a hundred yards from the first. One by one he detonated the underwater explosives.

There was a brief pause while dive teams examined the results. After receiving word that all four tunnel entrances were sealed, Neidelman turned to Magnusen. "Let's drain the pit," he said.

There was a roar on the southern shore as the pump engines came to life. Rankin and Bonterre were glued to the depth display, while Magnusen was monitoring the pump subsystem. The tower began to vibrate slightly.

"Water level down ten feet," Magnusen said matter-of-factly.

Neidelman broke into a broad grin. In an instant the observation tower became a place of happy bedlam. Amid the cheering, someone produced a bottle of champagne and some plastic glasses.

"We did it, by heaven," Neidelman said, shaking hands around the room. "We're draining the Water Pit!"

"Water level down fifteen feet," Magnusen said.

Holding his glass of champagne in one hand, Hatch walked toward the center of the room and looked down through the glass floor. As the water was pumped out, it exposed millimeter by millimeter the barnacle-and-kelp-encrusted walls. Perversely, he found himself struggling with a strange feeling of regret. It seemed anticlimactic, almost unfair that they should accomplish in less than two weeks what two centuries of suffering and death had failed to achieve.

"Captain?" Rankin said, staring at his screen. "The water's no longer dropping."

There was a silence as all eyes turned to the glass floor. A faint but continuous hissing began to rise from the pit. The dark surface of the water swirled as bubbles came streaming out of the black depths.

"Increase the pump rate to thirty," Neidelman said.

"Yes, sir," Magnusen said. The roar from the southern end of the island grew stronger.

Without a word Hatch joined Rankin at the geologist's screen.

"The water's back to fifteen feet," Magnusen said.

"How can that be?" Hatch asked.

Neidelman spoke into the radio. "Streeter, what's redline on those pumps?"

"Fifty thousand. But Captain—"

Neidelman turned to Magnusen. "Do it."

Outside, the roar of the pump engines became deafening, and the tower shook violently from their effort. In disbelief Hatch saw the level in the pit begin to rise again.

"We're back at ten feet," Magnusen said implacably.

"Sir!" Streeter crackled over the radio. "The forward seal is beginning to fail! If the hose blows, it could take out the tower!"

Neidelman turned toward Magnusen. "Kill the pumps," he said.

In the descending silence that followed, Hatch could hear the groans and whispers of the Water Pit beneath them.

"Water level returning to normal, sir," Magnusen said.

"This is crazy, man," Rankin muttered. "We sealed all four tunnels. This is a major problem."

Neidelman half turned his head at this, and Hatch could see the hard glitter in the eyes. "It's not a problem," he said. "We'll simply do what Macallan did. We'll cofferdam the shore."

AT QUARTER to ten that evening Hatch left the island, powered up the *Plain Jane,* and pointed the boat into the warm night. The distant lights of the mainland were strung out across the dark. As he looked over the expanse of water, Hatch saw the shadowy form of the *Griffin,* its running lights extinguished. A single point of red glowed out from Neidelman's vessel. Through his binoculars Hatch could see it was the captain, smoking his pipe on the forward deck. On an impulse, Hatch moved slowly toward the *Griffin.*

"Evening," said the captain as he approached.

"To you too," said Hatch, putting the *Plain Jane* into neutral.

"Care to come aboard?" Neidelman asked suddenly.

Hatch tied the *Plain Jane* to the rail, killed the engines, and hopped over, the captain giving him a hand up. "Shall we go below for a glass of port?" Neidelman asked.

"Thanks. I'd love one," Hatch said.

He followed Neidelman down into a large low-ceilinged room and looked around in wonder. The paneling was a rich mahogany, inlaid with mother-of-pearl. Delicate Tiffany stained glass was set into each porthole. At the far end a small fire glowed. Glass-fronted library cabinets flanked either side of the mantelpiece; priceless illuminated manuscripts were arranged face outward. There was also a small shelf devoted to original editions of early pirate texts, including Alexander Esquemelion's *Bucaniers of America.*

Neidelman approached a small felt-covered dry sink, laid with cut-glass ship's decanters and small glasses. Pulling out two tumblers, he poured a few fingers of port into each.

There was a long silence as Hatch sipped his port.

"I meant to ask you," the captain said at last. "What did you think of our reception in town yesterday?"

"By and large everyone seems happy with our presence here. We're certainly a boon to local business."

"What do you mean, by and large?" Neidelman asked.

"Well, not everyone's a merchant. We seem to have aroused the moral indignation of the local minister."

Neidelman smiled wryly. "The minister disapproves, does he?"

"That wasn't the only opposing voice I heard," Hatch continued. "I have an old teacher who thinks we're going to fail."

"And you?" Neidelman asked coolly, not looking at him.

"I wouldn't be in it if I thought we'd fail. But I'd be lying if I said today's setback didn't give me pause."

"Malin," Neidelman said almost gently, "I can't blame you for that. But I see now where we've gone wrong. You see, we've been focusing all our attention on the Water Pit. But I've realized the Water Pit is *not* our adversary. It's Macallan. He's been one step ahead of us all the way. He's *anticipated* our moves."

The captain walked over to the wall and swung open a wood panel, revealing a small safe. He punched several buttons on the adjoining keypad, reached inside, and removed something. It was a leather-bound quarto volume of Macallan's book, *On Sacred Structures*. There in the margins, next to the printed blocks of text, appeared line after line of monotonous characters, broken only by the occasional mechanical drawing of various joints, arches, braces, and cribbing.

Neidelman tapped the page. "Very soon now we'll have the second half of the code deciphered—and with it the key to the treasure."

"How can you be so sure?" Hatch asked.

"Because nothing else makes sense. Why else would he have kept a secret journal? You don't create a bomb without knowing how to disarm it."

Neidelman carefully turned to the title page of the book, then slid it toward Hatch.

The Author respectfully dedicates this humble Work
To Eta Onis

"We haven't been able to determine the identity of this Eta Onis," Neidelman went on. "Was she Macallan's teacher? Confidante? Mistress?" He carefully closed the book.

"I'm embarrassed to say that, until you came along, I'd never even heard of Macallan," Hatch said.

"Most people haven't. But in his day he was a brilliant visionary, a true Renaissance man. He was born in 1657, the illegitimate but favored son of an earl. He read law at Cambridge but turned his attention to the arts, philosophy, and mathematics."

Neidelman returned the volume to the safe.

"How did you come across that volume?" Hatch asked.

Neidelman smiled. "I did some research into Ockham. When his command ship was found floating derelict, it was towed into Plymouth and its contents sold at public auction. We dug up the auctioneer's list at the London Public Record Office, and on it were the contents of a captain's chest full of books. We finally managed to track that volume down in a heap of rotting books in a half-ruined kirk in Scotland."

He stood closer to the fire. "I'll never forget opening that book for the first time and realizing that the ugly soiling in the margins was a white ink. At that moment, I knew—I *knew*—that the Water Pit and its treasure were going to be mine."

THE following afternoon Hatch strode up the narrow yellow-taped path behind the observation tower. He walked around the edge of the southern bluffs until he had a good view of Streeter's crew, wrapping up the day's work on the offshore cofferdam.

Divers had poured an underwater concrete footing directly atop the remains of the foundation of the ancient pirate cofferdam. This was followed by the sinking of steel I beams into the footing. Hatch stared at the enormous beams rising out of the water at ten-foot intervals, forming a narrow arc around the southern end of the island.

There was a flash of red hair. Hatch was pleased to see that one of the crew was Donny Truitt. Neidelman had found him a job, and he seemed to be working efficiently.

A whistle sounded, signaling quitting time. Hatch took a final look around and headed toward the dock. He'd have a simple dinner at home, he decided.

As he started the engines of the *Plain Jane,* he heard a nearby voice cry, "Ahoy, the frigate!" Looking up, he saw Isobel Bonterre coming down the dock toward him, dressed in overalls. Mud was splashed generously across her hands and face. She stopped at the foot of the dock, then stuck out her thumb like a hitchhiker, impishly pulling up one pant leg to expose her tan calf.

"Need a lift?" Hatch asked.

"How did you guess?" Isobel replied, tossing her bag into

the boat and jumping in. "I am already sick of your ugly old island."

Hatch cast off and eased the boat toward the inlet through the reefs. "Making mud pies?" he asked, looking at her dirty clothes.

She laughed. "Of course! It is what archaeologists do best."

"So I see." Hatch brought the boat through the thin circle of mist, and Stormhaven harbor came into view.

"So what is there to do in that one-horse town?" Isobel said, nodding toward the mainland.

"Not much."

"No disco dancing until three? What is a single woman to do?"

"I admit, it's a difficult problem," Hatch replied.

She looked at him, a tiny smile curling the corners of her lips. "Well, I could have dinner with the doctor."

Hatch looked at her. Why not? he thought. "There are only two restaurants in town, you know. Both seafood places, naturally. Although one does a reasonable steak."

"Steak? That is for me. I am a strict carnivore. Vegetables are for monkeys. As for fish—" She made a retching gesture.

"I thought you grew up in the Caribbean," he said, laughing.

"Yes. And my father was a fisherman, and that is all we ate."

They reached the harbor, and Hatch eased the boat up to its mooring. "I must change out of these dirty clothes," Isobel said, leaping into the dinghy, "and of course you must put on something better than that boring old blazer."

"But I like this jacket," Hatch protested.

"You American men do not know how to dress at all. What you need is a good Italian suit. What size are you? Forty-two long?"

"How did you know?"

"I am good at measuring a man."

HATCH picked her up outside her bed-and-breakfast, and they walked down the steep cobbled streets toward The Landing. It was a beautiful cool evening. The clouds had blown away, and a vast bowl of stars hung over the harbor.

They arrived at the restaurant, and the waiter, recognizing Hatch, showed them to a table immediately. Taking his seat, Hatch looked around. Fully a third of the patrons were Thalassa employees.

"*Que de monde!*" Isobel whispered. "One cannot get away from company people."

"It's like that in a small town," Hatch said. "So what was it you were doing today that got you so dirty?"

She leaned across the table. "As it happens, I made a little discovery on your muddy old island." She took a sip from her water glass. "We discovered the pirate encampment."

Hatch looked at her. "You're kidding."

"*Mais non!* Right where the windward bluff is eroding, there was a perfect soil profile—a vertical cut. I was able to locate the remains of an ancient fire. So we ran a metal detector across the site and began finding things. Grapeshot, a musket ball."

They ordered their dinners—steamers and a lobster for Hatch, a bloody top sirloin for Isobel.

"Anyway," she went on, "we dug a test trench just behind the bluffs. Charcoal from a campfire, a circular tent depression. We have gridded the camp and will start excavation tomorrow. My little Christophe is becoming an excellent digger."

"St. John? Digging?"

"But of course. Once he resigned himself to getting his hands dirty, he proved most able. Now he is my prime digger. You wait. When I am through with him, he will be all wire and gristle, like *le petit homme.*"

"Who?"

"You know. The little man—Streeter."

"Ah." The way Isobel said it, Hatch could tell the nickname wasn't meant fondly. "What's his story, anyway?"

Isobel shrugged. "He was under Neidelman in Vietnam. Somebody told me that Neidelman once saved his life during combat. You see how devoted he is to the captain. Like a dog to its master. He is the only one the captain really trusts." She stared at Hatch. "Except for you, of course."

Hatch frowned. "Well, I suppose it's good the captain cares about him. I mean, somebody has to. The guy's not exactly Mr. Personality."

"Whatever. But you are wrong when you say that Captain Neidelman cares about Streeter. There's only one thing he cares about." She gave a nod in the direction of Ragged Island.

As Hatch opened his mouth to change the subject, he sensed someone across the room. When he looked up, there was Claire, coming around the corner. She was just as he'd imagined she would be: tall and willowy, with the same dash of freckles. She saw him and stopped dead.

"Hello, Claire," Hatch said, standing up.

She stepped forward. "Hello," she said, shaking his hand. At the touch of his skin against hers, a pink flush formed on her cheeks. "I heard you were in town." She gave a self-deprecating laugh. "Of course, who hasn't?"

"You look great," Hatch said. And she did: The years had made her slender and turned her dark blue eyes a penetrating gray. She smoothed her pleated skirt unconsciously.

Then, at the restaurant entrance, the minister, Woody Clay, stepped in. As his eyes landed on Hatch, a spasm of displeasure moved across his sallow face. Not here, Hatch thought, bracing himself for another lecture about greed. But sure enough, the minister stopped at their table.

"Woody," said Claire to the minister, "this is Malin Hatch."

"We've met." Clay nodded.

With relief Hatch realized it wasn't likely that Clay would launch into another tirade with the two women looking on. "This is Dr. Isobel Bonterre," he said, recovering his composure. "May I introduce Claire Northcutt and—"

"The Reverend and Mrs. Woodruff Clay," said the minister crisply, extending his hand to Isobel.

Hatch was stunned.

Isobel gave Claire and Woody each a hearty handshake, exposing a row of dazzling teeth. There was an awkward pause, and then Clay ushered his wife away with a curt nod.

Isobel glanced at Hatch. "Old friends?" she asked.

"What?" Hatch murmured. He was staring at Clay's left hand, possessively placed in the small of Claire's back.

An arch smile formed on Isobel's face. "No, I can see I am wrong," she said, leaning over the table. "Old *lovers.* How awkward it is to meet again. And yet how sweet."

"You have a keen eye," mumbled Hatch.

"But you and the husband, you are *not* old friends. In fact, it seemed to me that he does not like you at all."

Their dinners arrived, and Hatch busied himself with his lobster.

"I can see you still carry her torch," Isobel purred. "Someday you must tell me of her. But first, let me hear about *you.*"

ALMOST two hours later Hatch forced himself to his feet and followed Isobel out of the restaurant. He had overindulged ridiculously: dessert, coffee, brandy. Isobel had matched him order for order, yet she did not seem any worse for wear as she breathed in the crisp night breeze.

"How refreshing this air is!" she cried, and looked at him appraisingly. "So what do we do now?"

Hatch hesitated. The archaeologist looked captivatingly beautiful, her tawny skin and almond eyes bewitchingly exotic.

"I think we say good night," he managed to say. "We've got a busy day tomorrow."

"C'est tout?" She pouted. "You Yankees have had all the marrow sucked from your bones." She squinted up at him. "So how exactly *do* people say good night in Stormhaven, Dr. Hatch?"

"Like this." Hatch stepped forward and gave her hand a shake.

"Ah." Isobel nodded. "I see." Then, quickly, she pulled his face toward her, letting her lips graze his caressingly.

"And that is how we say good night in Martinique," she murmured. Then she turned and walked into the night.

THE following afternoon, as Hatch came up the path from the dock, he heard a crash from the direction of Wopner's hut. Hatch sprinted into base camp, fearing the worst. But instead of finding the programmer pinned beneath a rack of equipment, he found him sitting in his chair, a shattered CPU at his feet.

"What happened?" Hatch asked.

"That computer impacted with my foot is what happened. It's all messed up."

"What is?"

"The island computer network. I've been running my program against that blasted second code. Even with increased priority, the routines were sluggish. And I was getting error messages, strange data. So I tried running the same routines remotely, over on the off-shore computer. It ran lickety-split, no errors." He scoffed disgustedly.

"Any idea what the problem is?"

"Yeah. I got a good idea. Some of the ROM microcode was rewritten. Just like when the pumps went haywire."

"I'm not following you."

"Basically, it's *not possible*. Follow that? There's no known process that can rewrite ROM that way. It only happens *here*. Not on the boat, not in Brooklyn. Just here."

"You can't tell me it's not possible. I mean, you saw it happen. You just don't know why yet."

"Oh, I know why—the Ragged Island curse."

Hatch laughed, then saw Wopner was not smiling.

His thoughts were interrupted when St. John appeared in the doorway. "There you are," he said to Hatch. "Isobel sent me to bring you to our dig." St. John turned to Wopner. "Did the program finish executing on the ship's computer?"

Wopner nodded. "No errors. But no luck, either."

"Then, Kerry, there's no choice but to try—"

"I'm not going to rewrite the program. We're running out of time."

"Just a minute," Hatch said, trying to defuse the argument. "We know that Macallan switched to a code containing all numbers. Could there be some pressing reason why Macallan used *only numbers* in the new code?"

The cryptologist and the historian fell into thought.

"Yes!" St. John cried, snapping his fingers. "He used numbers to conceal his code tables! Macallan knew he couldn't leave a lot of alphabet tables lying around where they might be discovered. So he used numbers! He was an architect and an engineer. He was *supposed* to have lots of numbers around. Mathematical tables, blueprints, hydraulic equations—any one of those could have done double duty concealing a code table."

Wopner sat forward. "You might have something there, Chris old boy," he muttered. "If I reprogram the computer to . . . You boys let me be, okay? I'm busy."

Hatch accompanied St. John out of the hut and into the drizzle that cloaked base camp. "Didn't you say that Isobel was looking for me?" he asked.

St. John nodded. "She said to say we've got a patient for you at the far end of the island."

Hatch started. "Patient? Why didn't you tell me first thing?"

"It's not urgent," said St. John with a knowing smile.

They followed a muddy path that wound its way through an area of old shafts. The excavation site itself was spread across a flat meadow lying behind a sharp bluff on the eastern shore. A checkerboard grid had been marked out in white string across an acre of ground. Here and there Hatch could see that some of the meter-square grids had already been opened, exposing rich, iron-stained earth. Isobel Bonterre and several diggers were crowded together on an earthen balk beside one of the squares.

As they walked down to the site, Isobel came over, slipping a hand pick into her belt. Her hair was tied back, and her face and tawny arms were again smeared with dirt.

"Come," she said, grabbing Hatch's hand and pulling him toward the edge of the ditch.

"What's this?" Hatch asked in amazement, gazing down at a dirty brown skull rearing out of the dirt, along with what looked like two feet and a jumble of other ancient bones.

"Pirate grave," she said, triumphantly.

"So this is the patient." Hatch climbed down into the excavated square. He examined the skull for a moment, then turned his attention to the other bones. "Or should I say, patients. Unless this pirate had two right feet, you've got two skeletons."

"Two? *Vachement bien!*" cried Isobel.

The skull was turned to one side, mouth gaping open. There were no obvious pathologies: no musket-ball holes, broken bones. It was clear that the bodies had been buried in haste: The arms lay askew, and the legs were bent. Then Hatch's eyes were suddenly arrested by a golden gleam near one of the feet.

"What's this?" he asked. A compact mass of gold coins and a large gemstone lay embedded in the earth near the lower tibia.

A peal of laughter came from Isobel. "I was wondering when you would see that. I believe the gentleman must have kept a pouch in his boot. A gold mohur from India, two English guineas, and four Portuguese cruzados. All dating prior to 1694. The stone is an emerald, probably Incan, carved into the head of a jaguar."

"The first of Ockham's treasure," said Hatch. "Does the captain know about this?"

"Not yet. Come, there is more."

He climbed out of the excavated square. "You must see the pirate camp itself," Isobel said, "for it is stranger yet."

Hatch followed her to another section of the dig. He could see several blackened areas of charcoal, where fires had been lit.

"Those were probably where the workers who built the Water Pit lived. But look at all the artifacts that were left behind!" She led Hatch to a large tarp. "Two flintlock pistols, three daggers, a cutlass, and a blunderbuss. A cask of grapeshot, musket balls, and several items of silver dinner plate. Never have I found so much so quickly," she said. "And then there's this." She handed a gold coin to Hatch.

It was a massive Spanish doubloon. The gold gleamed brilliantly. The heavy Jerusalem cross was stamped off-center, embracing the lion and castle that symbolized León and Castile.

"Now here is another mystery," said Isobel. "In the seventeenth century sailors never buried people with their clothes on. Clothes were valuable. But if you did bury them clothed, you would at least search them, *non?* That packet of gold in the boot was worth a fortune. And then, why did they leave all these other things behind? Pistols, cutlasses, cannon—these were the heartblood of a pirate. None would leave such things behind willingly."

At that moment St. John came over. "Some more bones are appearing, Isobel," he said, touching her elbow lightly.

"More? In a different grid? Christophe, how exciting!"

Hatch followed them back to the site. As he looked down at the excavation, his excitement gave way to unease. Masses of brown bones were now coming to light, the skeletons stacked three deep in places, sprawled across each other.

A mass grave, Hatch thought. The bodies thrown in willy-nilly.

"What could have happened here?" Isobel asked.

"I don't know," Hatch said, a strange feeling in his stomach.

"There do not appear to be signs of violence on the bones."

"Violence sometimes leaves only subtle traces," Hatch replied. "Or they might have died of disease or starvation. A forensic examination would help."

"Could you do such an examination?" Isobel asked.

Hatch stood at the edge of the grave, not answering at once. It was nearing the close of day, and the light was fading. In the rain, mist, and growing twilight, against the mournful sound of the distant surf, everything seemed to turn gray and lifeless, as if the vitality itself was being sucked out of the landscape.

"Yes," he said after a moment.

"What could have happened here?" Isobel whispered to herself.

AT DAWN the next morning the senior crew gathered in the pilothouse of the *Griffin*. Today there was electricity in the air. Isobel was talking to Streeter, and Wopner was whispering animatedly to St. John. Hatch helped himself to a cup of hot coffee, then settled into a chair next to Rankin.

Neidelman emerged, and he motioned Hatch to the door of the cabin. "I want you to have this, Malin," he said in a low tone, pressing something heavy into Hatch's hand.

With surprise Hatch recognized the gold doubloon Isobel had uncovered the day before. He looked at the captain, mutely questioning.

"It's not much," Neidelman said, "but it's the first fruit of our labors. I wanted you to have it as a token of our thanks."

Hatch mumbled his thanks as he slipped the coin into his pocket, feeling awkward as he took a seat at the table.

Neidelman strode to the head of the table and contemplated his crew. He looked impeccable—showered, shaved, dressed in pressed khakis, the skin tight and clean across his bones.

"I believe there's a lot to report this morning," he said, glancing around the table. "Dr. Magnusen, let's start with you."

"The pumps are primed and ready, Captain," she replied.

Neidelman nodded. "Mr. Streeter?"

"The cofferdam's complete. All tests for stability and structural integrity are positive."

"Excellent." Neidelman looked toward the historian and the programmer. "Gentlemen, I believe you have news."

"We've cracked the second code," Wopner said.

There was an audible intake of breath around the table.

"What does it say?" Isobel blurted out.

Wopner held up his hands. "I said we'd cracked it. I didn't say we'd *deciphered* it. We know what kind of code it is: a polyalphabetic, using somewhere between five and fifteen cipher alphabets. Once we know the exact number, it's just a question of letting the computer do its thing. We should know in a matter of hours."

Neidelman nodded. "Very well." he said. "At ten hundred hours we will start the pumps and begin draining the Water Pit. Mr. Streeter, I want you to keep a close watch on the cofferdam. Mr. Wopner, you'll be monitoring the situation from Island One. Dr. Magnusen will direct the overall pumping process from the observation tower. If all goes according to plan, the pit will be drained by noon tomorrow. Then our crews will insert the ladder array. And the following morning we'll make our first descent."

His voice dropped. "I don't need to remind you that even free of water, the pit will remain a highly dangerous place. Until we've braced it with titanium struts, there could still be cave-ins or collapses. A small team will be inserted to make initial observations and place stress sensors on the critical wooden beams. Once the sensors are in place, Kerry here will calibrate them remotely from Island One. If there is any sudden increase in stress—signaling a possible collapse—these sensors will give us an early warning. Once they're in place, we can insert teams to begin a formal mapping process."

Neidelman placed his hands on the table. "This first team will be Dr. Bonterre, Dr. Hatch, and myself."

He straightened up. "Any questions?"

The pilothouse was still.

The captain nodded. "In that case, let's take care of business."

THE following evening Hatch left the island in high spirits. The pumps had been chugging all the previous day and on into the night. Finally the uptake hoses had struck silt at the bottom of the Water Pit, one hundred and forty feet down. The cofferdam had held. Now a crew was at work with a magnetized grappling hook, clearing out debris that had fallen into the Water Pit over the centuries.

Arriving home, Hatch had dinner, then made a pot of coffee. Most of the dining-room table was covered with a large green canvas. Sipping his coffee, he pulled the canvas away, exposing two of the skeletons that had been uncovered the day before.

Hatch pulled out a small notebook, writing "Blackbeard" on the left side of a page and "Captain Kidd" on the right. Underneath, he began jotting his impressions. Both were male, under forty. They were nearly toothless, a characteristic shared with the other skeletons in the mass grave. The few remaining teeth showed a striking pathology: a separation of the odontoblast layer from the dentin. Hatch wondered whether this was due to disease or simply poor hygiene.

He examined the skull of Blackbeard. Blackbeard's one remaining upper incisor was distinctly shoveled: That implied either East Asian or Amerindian stock. The other pirate, Kidd, had an old wound in the clavicle. There was a deep score in the bone, surrounded by spurs. Cutlass blow? Hatch wondered.

Hatch picked up a femur, which seemed light and insubstantial.

He bent it and to his surprise felt it snap like a dry twig between his fingers. He peered at the ends. Clearly a case of osteoporosis rather than simple graveyard decay.

The pirates were too young for this to be gerontological in origin. Again, it could be either poor diet or disease. But what disease? He turned to his bookshelf and plucked off Harrison's *Principles of Internal Medicine.* He flipped through the index, then turned quickly to the page he was looking for. "Scurvy," it read. "Scorbutus (Vitamin C Deficiency)." Yes, there were the symptoms: loss of teeth, osteoporosis. Mystery solved. He shut the book.

The doorbell rang. Stepping up to the front and glancing out the window, Hatch was surprised to see the stooped form of Professor Orville Horn, leaning on his cane.

"Ah, the abominable Dr. Hatch!" the professor said as the door opened. "I was just passing by and saw the lights burning in this old mausoleum of yours." His gaze landed on the dining-room table. "Hello! What's this?"

"Pirate skeletons," said Hatch with a grin.

The professor's eyes went incandescent with delight. "Marvelous!" he cried. "Where did you get them?"

"Thalassa's archaeologist found a mass grave on Ragged Island," Hatch replied, leading the old man into the dining room. "I thought I'd bring a couple back and try to determine cause of death."

Professor Horn leaned forward with interest, poking an occasional bone with his cane. He picked up the bone Hatch had broken. "Osteoporosis," he said. "All indications point to scurvy."

Hatch felt his face fall. "You figured that out pretty fast."

"Scurvy was endemic on sailing ships in past centuries."

"Maybe it was rather obvious," said Hatch, a little crestfallen. "Come on, let me get you a cup of coffee."

The professor accepted a cup, and they sat drinking in silence.

"Malin," the old man said, "I owe you an apology. I spoke hastily the other day. I still think Stormhaven would be better off without that treasure island, but I have no right to judge your motives. You do what you have to do."

"Thanks."

The professor jerked a thumb in the direction of the dining room. "Now can you explain the circumstances surrounding *that?*"

Stretching out his legs, Hatch related how Isobel found the mass grave, the gold, the astonishing array of artifacts. "What surprises me most," Hatch concluded, "is the sheer body count. The teams had identified eighty individuals by the end of this afternoon, and the site isn't fully excavated yet."

"Indeed." The professor fell into silence, his gaze resting on the middle distance. "Scurvy," he repeated, then roused himself and stood up. "Walk me to the door, will you? I've taken up enough of your time for one evening."

At the door the professor paused. "Tell me, Malin, what are the dominant flora of Ragged Island?"

"Saw grass," said Hatch, "chokecherries, burdock, tea roses."

"Chokecherries and rose hips were a staple part of the diet along this coast in centuries past," the professor said. "Both are extremely high in vitamin C."

"Of course," said Hatch. "I see what you're getting at."

"Seventeenth-century sailors may not have known what caused scurvy, but they *did* know that fresh berries, fruits, roots, or vegetables cured it." The professor looked searchingly at Hatch. "And there's another problem with our hasty diagnosis."

"What's that?"

"It's the *way* those bodies were buried. Scurvy doesn't make you toss fourscore people into a common grave and skedaddle in such a hurry that you leave gold and emeralds behind."

There was a distant flash, then a roll of thunder far to the south. "But what would?" Hatch asked.

Dr. Horn's only answer was an affectionate pat on the shoulder. Then he turned, limped down the steps, and hobbled away.

EARLY the next morning Hatch entered Island One to find it jammed with an unusually large gathering. Isobel Bonterre, Kerry Wopner, and Chris St. John were all talking at once. Only Sandra

Magnusen and Captain Neidelman were silent: Magnusen was quietly running diagnostics, and Neidelman, lighting his pipe, was as calm as the eye of a hurricane.

"Are you nuts or something?" Wopner was saying. "I'm a programmer, not a sewer spelunker."

"There's no other choice," Neidelman said.

"Nothing works right on this blasted island."

"Did I miss something?" Hatch said, coming forward.

"Ah. Good morning, Malin," Neidelman said. "We've had a few problems with the electronics on the ladder array."

"A few," Wopner scoffed.

"The upshot is that we'll have to take Kerry along with us on our exploration of the pit. It's imperative that we get these pressure sensors in place throughout the structure. Once they're linked to the computer network, they'll serve as a warning system in case of structural failure. But Kerry's been unsuccessful at calibrating the sensors remotely from Island One." He glanced at Wopner. "With the network acting flaky, that means he's going to have to come with us and calibrate them manually, using a palmtop computer."

"A major pain," Wopner said petulantly.

Neidelman turned to St. John. "Tell Dr. Hatch about the sentence you just deciphered from the second half of the journal."

St. John cleared his throat self-importantly and read, " 'Ye who luste after the key to the' . . . something . . . 'Pitt shall find . . .' "

Hatch looked amazed. "So there is a key to the pit."

Neidelman smiled. "It's almost eight," he said. "Assemble your gear, and let's get started."

Hatch returned to his office for his medical field kit, then met up with the group as they were trekking toward the observation tower. Bundles of multicolored cable streamed from its dark underbelly down into the maw of the Water Pit. Only it was no longer the Water Pit. Now it was drained and accessible.

Streeter and his crew were standing at the mouth of the pit. Approaching, Hatch saw what looked like the end of a massive ladder peering over the top of the pit. The side rails were made from thick tubes of metal, with rubber-covered rungs in between.

"That's what I call a ladder on steroids," he said, whistling.

"It's more than a ladder," Neidelman replied. "It's a ladder array. Those side rails are made from a titanium alloy. The array will serve as the backbone for the pit's support structure. In time we'll attach a platform lift to the ladder, like an elevator."

He pointed toward the ladder struts. "Each tube is wired with fiber-optic, coax, and electrical cable. Eventually every part of the structure will be computer-controlled. But so far, friend Wopner has not been entirely successful in bringing the installation under re-mote control. Hence his invitation to join us."

Neidelman turned to the group. "Our most important task today is to attach these stress sensors into the beams of the pit." He handed one around. It was a strip of metal, with a computer chip sealed in clear plastic. At each end was a half-inch tack. "Just tap or press it into the wood. Mr. Wopner will calibrate and register it into his palmtop database."

While Neidelman talked, a technician helped Hatch shrug into a harness. Then the man handed him a helmet and showed him how to use the intercom and halogen headlamp. After he arranged his medical kit, he was handed a satchel containing a quantity of the sensors. Neidelman spoke into a mike attached to his helmet. "Mag-nusen, restore power to the array."

A string of lights snapped on along the ladder, illuminating the entire ghastly length of the Water Pit in a brilliant yellow light. De-scending into the earth like some pathway to hell, the pit was a ragged square, ten feet across, cribbed on all four sides with heavy logs. Every ten feet the shaft was crisscrossed by four smaller beams that met in the middle, evidently bracing the sides. The pit was alive, rustling with the sounds of ticking, dripping, and creaking, along with indeterminate whispers and moans.

A distant rumble of thunder rolled over the island; then a hard rain followed. Hatch felt the pit exhale the cold odor of the mud-flat—a powerful smell of salt water mingled with suppuration and decay, the outgassing of dead fish, and rotting seaweed. A sudden thought rushed into his mind: Somewhere in that warren of tunnels is Johnny's body. It was a discovery he both wanted and dreaded with all his soul.

A technician handed Neidelman a small gas-monitoring meter, and he slipped it around his neck. "The only time you are to be unclipped from the ladder array is when it becomes necessary to place a sensor," Neidelman said, glancing at the team. "We'll set them, calibrate them, and get out quickly." He paused, adjusting his helmet. "Okay, clip your lifelines onto your harnesses, and let's go."

By now much of the crew on the island had gathered behind the staging area. A cheer went up. Neidelman took a last look around, waving at the assembled group. Then he stepped to the rim, buckled his line to the ladder array, and began to descend.

Hatch was the last to set foot on the ladder. The others were already stretched out for twenty feet below him. As they went deeper, a curious hush fell over the team. The incessant sounds of the settling pit, the soft creakings and tickings, filled the air like the whispered teeming of invisible sea creatures.

"Everyone all right?" came Neidelman's low voice over the intercom. Positive responses came back, one by one.

"Very well," Neidelman said. "We'll continue descending to the fifty-foot platform, placing sensors as necessary."

As he followed the group, Hatch felt almost as if he were sinking into a deep pool of brackish water. The air was clammy and cold, redolent of decay. Each exhalation condensed into a cloud of vapor.

The ladder array had been deftly threaded through an obstacle course of ancient junk—rotting beams, tangles of metal, discarded pieces of drilling apparatus—although an immense amount had already been removed. The team stopped as Neidelman tapped a sensor into a small opening on one side of the pit.

"Man, it *stinks* down here," said Wopner, bending over his handheld computer to calibrate a sensor.

"Air readings normal," Neidelman said, reading his monitor. "Nothing to worry about. Let's continue. We'll alternate placing the sensors. Since Mr. Wopner must calibrate each one manually, he's going to fall behind. We'll wait for him at the hundred-foot platform."

They began to come across additional openings cut into the cribbed walls, where tunnels branched off the main pit. Neidelman took the first one, placing sensors back twenty feet; Isobel took the next. Then it was Hatch's own turn.

Carefully he stepped back from the ladder into the cross shaft. He felt his foot sink into ooze. The tunnel was narrow and low, stretching off at a sharp upward angle. Stooping, he went twenty feet up the tunnel, then fished a sensor from his satchel and drove it into the calcified earth. He returned to the central pit, placing a small fluorescent flag at the mouth of the shaft to alert Wopner.

As he stepped back onto the array, Hatch heard a loud, agonizing complaint from a nearby timber. He froze, gripping the ladder tightly, holding his breath.

"What was that?" Wopner said a little too loud for that space.

"Just the pit settling," said Neidelman.

As they approached the hundred-foot platform, another sight came into view. Until now the horizontal tunnels opening into the side of the shaft had been crude and ragged. But here they could see a tunnel opening that had been carefully formed.

Isobel shone her light at the square opening. "This is definitely part of the original pit," she said.

"What's its purpose?" asked Neidelman.

She leaned into the tunnel. "I cannot say for sure."

"Mr. Wopner?" Neidelman said, glancing up. "Are you all right?"

"Yes." It was an unusually subdued voice. Looking up, Hatch saw Wopner leaning on the ladder perhaps twenty feet above him, calibrating a sensor and shivering.

Neidelman glanced at Isobel, then at Hatch. "It'll take him some time to calibrate all the sensors we've placed so far," he said. "Why don't we take a closer look at this side tunnel?"

They stepped into a narrow tunnel shored with massive timbers similar to those in the Water Pit itself. They moved forward cautiously for fifty yards. Suddenly the captain gave a low whistle.

Up ahead, Hatch could see a stone chamber perhaps fifteen feet in diameter. It appeared to have eight sides, each ending in an arch that rose to a groined ceiling. In the center of the floor was an iron grating, puffy with rust, covering an unguessably deep hole. They stood in the entrance, each breath adding more mist to the gathering miasma. Hatch found himself becoming slightly light-headed.

Isobel was flashing her light along the ceiling. "*Mon Dieu,*" she breathed, "a classic example of the English baroque style."

Neidelman gazed at the ceiling. "Remarkable," he said.

"But what was it for?" Hatch said.

"If I had to guess," Isobel said, "I would say the room served some kind of hydraulic function, yes?" She blew a long cloud of mist toward the center of the room. It glided toward the grate, then was sucked down into the depths.

"We'll figure it out when we've mapped all this," said Neidelman. "For now, let's set the sensors." He tapped the sensors into joints, then glanced at his gas meter. "Carbon dioxide levels are getting a little high," he said. "We ought to cut this visit short."

They returned to the central shaft to find that Wopner had almost caught up with them. "There are two sensors in a room at the end of this tunnel," Neidelman said to him.

Above, Wopner mumbled something unintelligible, his back to them as he worked with his palmtop computer.

Neidelman turned to Isobel and Hatch. "Let's get to the bottom and tag the rest of the shafts."

Once again they began their descent. As Hatch moved past the hundred-foot platform, he found his legs beginning to shake from weariness and cold. Suddenly he heard Isobel mutter a fervent curse. He looked down, and his heart leaped immediately into his mouth.

Below him, tangled in a massive snarl of junk, lay a skeleton draped in chains and rusting iron. Hatch leaned against the ladder, trembling violently, even as part of his brain realized that the skeleton was far too big to be that of his brother.

"Malin!" Isobel said urgently. "*Malin!* This skeleton is very old. *Comprends?* Two hundred years old, at least."

Hatch waited a long moment, breathing, until he was sure he could answer. "I understand," he said.

Oblivious to Hatch's reaction, the captain aimed his headlamp beneath his feet. Following the beam, Hatch could make out the bottom of the Water Pit itself. A huge snarl of rusting iron gears and rods poked up out of a pool of mud below them.

"Perhaps fifty feet beneath that wreckage," Neidelman said, "lies a two-billion-dollar treasure." Then he began to laugh, a low, soft, curious laugh. "All we have to do now is *dig.*"

Suddenly the radio crackled. "Captain, this is Streeter. We've got a problem here. Recommend you abort your mission at once."

"Why? Is there some problem with the equipment?" Neidelman asked.

"No, nothing like that." Streeter seemed uncertain how to proceed. "Let me patch St. John in to you, he'll explain."

The clipped tones of the historian came across the radio. "Captain, the computer has just cracked several portions of the journal."

"Excellent," the captain said. "But what's the emergency?"

"It's what Macallan wrote. Let me read it to you.

> "I feel it a certainty that Ockham has plans to dispatch me once my usefulness in this vile enterprise has come to an ende. And so, under my direction, Ockham and his bande, unbeknownst, labored to place this treasure in such wise that no man shall ever retrieve it. The Pitt is unconquerable. Ockham believes that he holds the key, and he shall Die for that belief. Ye who decipher these lines, heed my warning: to descend the Pitt means grave danger to lyfe and limbe; to seize the treasure means certayne Death. Ye who luste after the key to the Treasure Pitt shall find instead the key to the next world."

St. John's voice stopped, and the group remained silent. Hatch looked at Neidelman. His eyes were narrow.

"So you see," St. John began again, "it must have been Macallan's ultimate revenge against Ockham—to bury his treasure in such a way that it could never be retrieved."

"The point is," Streeter said, "it's not safe for anyone to remain in the pit until we've deciphered the rest of the code."

"Nonsense," interrupted Neidelman, his face stony. "We're almost done here—just another couple of sensors to set and then we'll come up." He looked upward. "Mr. Wopner?"

The programmer was not on the ladder. "He must be calibrating the sensors we placed inside the vault," Isobel said.

"Then let's call him back." The captain began to ascend the ladder. It trembled slightly under his weight, a slight shudder.

"Dr. Magnusen, what's going on?" Neidelman spoke sharply.

"All normal, Captain. Is there a problem?"

"We're feeling a—" the captain began. Suddenly a violent shudder twisted the ladder, shaking Hatch's hold. Above him Hatch could hear a distant crumbling sound and a low rumble.

"Sir!" came Magnusen's voice. "We're picking up ground displacement somewhere in your vicinity."

"Okay, you win. Let's find Wopner and get out of here."

They scrambled up the ladder to the entrance to the vaulted tunnel. Neidelman peered inside, lancing his beam into the dampness. "Wopner? Get a move on. We're aborting the mission."

Only silence and a faint cold wind emanated from the tunnel. Suddenly, as if galvanized by the same thought, Isobel, Hatch, and Neidelman unclipped from the ladder, stepped inside the shaft, and ran down the tunnel.

When the tunnel opened into the stone chamber, Hatch saw something that sent a chill through his vitals. One of the massive groined stones of the ceiling had swung down against the chamber wall. At floor level, where the fallen ceiling stone pressed against the wall, he could make out the canvas-and-rubber toe of Wopner's sneaker.

"Oh, no," Neidelman said behind him.

Hatch could see Wopner, crushed between the two granite faces. His helmeted head was turned to the side, gazing out sightlessly.

"Hey, Mal!" Hatch heard his brother, Johnny, whisper out of the rushing darkness. "Hey, Mal! Over here!"

Then the darkness closed upon Hatch, and he knew no more.

BY MIDNIGHT THE OCEAN HAD taken on the kind of oily, slow-motion swell that often came after a summer blow. Waiting in his office hut for the coroner to arrive, Hatch stood up from his desk and went to the window, moving carefully through the unlit office. Somehow the dark made it easier to avoid the irregular shape that lay on the gurney, under a white sheet.

There came a soft knock and the turn of a door handle. Captain Neidelman slipped into the hut and disappeared into the dark shape of a chair. The room briefly flared yellow as a pipe was lit.

"No sign of the coroner, then?" Neidelman asked.

Hatch's silence was answer enough.

The captain cleared his throat. "Malin?" he asked softly.

"Yes," Hatch replied, his own voice sounding husky.

"I once led a team working deepwater salvage off Sable Island, graveyard of the Atlantic. We had six divers in a barometric pressure chamber, decompressing after a hundred-meter dive to a Nazi sub loaded with gold. Something went wrong. The seal of the chamber failed. You can imagine what happens—massive embolisms. Blows apart your brain, then stops your heart."

Hatch said nothing.

"One of those divers was my son."

Hatch looked at the dark figure. "I'm very sorry," he said. "I had no idea . . ." He stopped. *I had no idea you were a father.*

"Jeff was our only child. The death was very hard on both of us, and my wife could never quite forgive me." Neidelman shifted in his chair. "These things happen in this business. They're unavoidable."

"Unavoidable," Hatch repeated.

"The point is"—the captain lowered his voice—"we must not let this defeat us."

Hatch sighed deeply. "I suppose I feel the same way. We'll take time to review our safety procedures. Then we can—"

Neidelman sat forward in his chair. "Take time? You misunderstand me, Malin. We must move forward *tomorrow.*"

Hatch frowned. "How can we? Morale is rock-bottom. The workers are saying the whole venture's cursed."

"But that's exactly why we *must* press on," the captain continued, his voice now urgent. "Talk of curses is a seductive, undermining force. And that's really what I'm here to discuss."

He moved his chair closer. "All these equipment troubles we've been having. Everything works just fine until it's installed on the island; then inexplicable problems crop up. It has made for delays. Have you thought about a possible cause?"

"Not really. I don't know much about computers."

Neidelman turned, and even in the dark Malin could feel his stare. "Well, I have been giving it a lot of thought, and I've come to a conclusion. It's not a curse. It's sabotage."

"Sabotage?" Hatch said incredulously. "But who? And why?"

"I don't know. Yet. But it's obviously someone inside, with complete access to the computer system and the equipment. That gives us Rankin, Magnusen, St. John, Bonterre."

"What about Streeter?" Hatch asked.

The captain shook his head. "Streeter and I have been together since Vietnam. When you've been at war—side by side in combat with a man—there can never be a lie between you."

"Very well," Hatch replied. "But I can't think of a reason why anyone would want to sabotage the dig."

"I can think of several," said Neidelman. "Remember, there's a two-billion-dollar fortune to be won here. Plenty of people in this world would shoot a liquor-store clerk for twenty dollars. How many more would commit worse crimes for two billion?"

Neidelman stood up and paced restlessly. "Let us be clear about one thing. A saboteur may well be at work, but it was *Macallan* who murdered Kerry Wopner." He turned suddenly from the window. "Just as he murdered your brother. The man has reached across three centuries to strike at us. Malin, we can't let him defeat us now. We will break his pit and take his gold. *And* the sword."

Hatch sat in the dark, a host of conflicting feelings welling up in him. "I don't know about any saboteur," he said slowly. "But I think you're right about Macallan. Look at what he said in that journal entry. He designed that pit to kill anyone who tries to plunder it.

That's all the more reason to take a breather, study the journal, re-think our approach. We've been moving way too fast."

"This is exactly the kind of pusillanimous attitude Macallan counted on," Neidelman said harshly. "Take your time; don't do any-thing risky; squander your money until nothing's left. No, Malin," the captain said in a level voice, "now's the time to go for Macallan's jugular."

Hatch had never been called pusillanimous before—had never even heard the word used outside of books—and he didn't like it much. He could feel anger rising within him, but he mastered it with an effort. In the tense silence he could make out the faint whine of an outboard engine coming over the water.

"That must be the coroner's launch," Neidelman said. "I think I'll leave this business in your hands." He stepped away and headed toward the door.

"Captain Neidelman?" Hatch asked.

The captain stopped and turned back, hand on the knob.

"That sub full of Nazi gold," Hatch went on. "What did you do? After your son died, I mean."

"We continued the operation, of course," Neidelman answered crisply. "It's what he would have wanted."

Then he was gone, the smell of pipe smoke lingering in the air.

6

As SITE doctor for the Ragged Island venture, Hatch was required to handle the red tape relating to Wopner's death. So, bringing in a nurse from downcoast to watch the medical hut, the following morning he left for Bangor. By the time he returned home to Stormhaven, three working days had passed.

Heading to the island that same afternoon, he soon felt more confident he'd made the right decision in not challenging Neidelman's decision to press on. Though the captain had been driving the crews hard over the last several days, the effort seemed to have dispelled much of the gloom.

Still, the pace was taking its toll: Hatch attended to three cases of illness that afternoon. One man complained of apathy and nausea, while another had developed a bacterial infection Hatch had read about but never seen. Yet another had a viral infection and was running a pretty good fever.

Wandering up the trail to the mouth of the Water Pit the next morning, he could feel that a remarkable amount of work had been accomplished. The ladder array was now fully braced from top to bottom, and a small elevator—the platform lift—had been attached to one side for quick transport to and from the depths.

He stared down into the pit, wondering if his old friend Donny Truitt was on one of the teams working somewhere in the dark spaces beneath his feet. Then he turned and headed back down the path to Island One, where he found Magnusen in front of the computer, her fingers moving rapidly over a keyboard, mouth set in a disapproving line. As usual, she kept working and ignored Hatch.

He looked around. "Excuse me," he said at last. "I wanted to pick up a transcript of Macallan's journal."

"Of course," Magnusen said evenly. She reached into a drawer and filled out a small yellow-colored chit.

"Hand this to the duty guard over in stores," she said.

Hatch placed the chit in his pocket, wondering at Neidelman's choice of guardian. Wasn't she on the shortlist of saboteur suspects?

The door swung open, and St. John entered the command center. "Good morning," he said with a nod.

Hatch nodded back, surprised at the change that had come over the historian since Wopner's death. The plump white cheeks had given way to slack skin and bags beneath reddened eyes.

St. John turned to Magnusen. "Is it ready yet?"

"Just about," she said. "I'm correlating the mapping data."

Hatch looked at the large monitor in front of Magnusen. It was covered with an impossible tangle of interconnected lines in various lengths and colors. St. John stared at the screen wordlessly. "I'd like to work with it for a while," he said at last. "Alone, if you don't mind."

Magnusen nodded, stood up, and left, closing the door to Island One behind her without another word. Hatch turned to leave.

"I didn't mean for you to go," St. John said. "Just her. What a dreadful woman." He shook his head. "Have you seen this yet?"

"No," Hatch said. "What is it?"

"The Water Pit and all its workings."

Hatch leaned closer. What looked like a jumble of lines was, he realized, a three-dimensional wire-frame outline of the pit. St. John pressed a key, and the whole complex began to rotate slowly.

Hatch gasped. "I had no idea it was so complex."

"My job is to examine the pit's architecture for any historical parallels. If I can find similarities to other works of Macallan's, it may help us figure out what booby traps remain."

He struck a few keys. "Let's see if we can clear away everything but the original works." Most of the colored lines disappeared, leaving only red. Now the diagram made more sense to Hatch. He could clearly see the big central shaft plunging into the earth. At the hundred-foot level a tunnel led to the vault where Wopner was killed. Deeper, near the bottom of the pit, five smaller tunnels angled away like the fingers of a hand. There was another, narrow, tunnel angling away from the bottom.

St. John pointed. "Those are the five flood tunnels—the four we found, plus one devilish tunnel that didn't expel any dye during the test. Magnusen said something about a clever hydrological backflow system. I didn't understand half of it." He frowned. "But I'd rather swing from a gibbet than ask that woman for help."

St. John glanced at Hatch, then looked back at the screen. "This tunnel that angles toward the shore isn't part of the central pit. Perhaps it's somehow linked to the booby trap that your brother . . ."

"I understand," Hatch managed to say, his voice sounding dry.

They stared at the screen as St. John began rotating the structure. "You know, until three days ago I admired Macallan enormously.

Now I feel differently. His design was brilliant, and I can't blame him for wanting his revenge on Ockham. But he knew this pit could just as easily kill the innocent as the guilty. The pit was designed to guard the treasure long after Ockham died trying to get it out."

He punched another key, and the diagram began to whirl quickly around the screen.

"Hey, you're going to burn out the video RAM if you twirl that thing any faster!" Rankin, the bearlike geologist, stood in the doorway, wearing a lopsided smile. "Step aside before you break it." Taking St. John's seat, he tapped a couple of keys, and the image obediently stopped spinning. "Anything yet?" he asked the historian.

St. John shook his head. "It's hard to see any obvious patterns."

"Let's turn it around the z-axis at five revolutions per minute." Rankin hit a few keys, and the structure on the screen began rotating again. He glanced at Hatch. "Seems your old architect had some help with his digging, in a manner of speaking."

"What kind of help, exactly?"

"From Mother Nature. The latest tomographic readings show that much of the original pit was already in place when the pirates arrived. A huge naturally formed vertical crack in the bedrock."

"So there were underground cavities all along?"

Rankin nodded. "Lots. Open cracks running every which way. Macallan merely widened and added as needed."

Their talk was interrupted as Neidelman stepped into the hut. He looked at each of them in turn, a smile flicking across his face. "Don't stop on my account."

"I was just helping St. John with the 3-D model," Rankin said.

"I see," Neidelman said. "In that case, I have good news. The final set of measurements has been entered into the network."

"Great," Rankin said, and tapped a few more keys. "Got it."

As Hatch watched the screen, he saw small line segments being added to the diagram with blinding speed. Rankin hit a few keys, and the model began again to spin on its vertical axis.

"Take out all but the very earliest structures," St. John said.

Rankin tapped a few keys, and countless tiny lines vanished. A strangely skeletal image appeared against the blackness of the screen.

"Perhaps this is a pointless exercise," St. John went on. "I mean, what kind of parallels can we really hope to find to Macallan's other structures? What buildings are ten feet across and a hundred forty plus feet tall?"

"The Leaning Tower of Pisa?" Hatch suggested.

"Just a minute!" St. John interrupted sharply. He peered more closely at the screen. "Look at the symmetrical lines on the left, there, and there. Transverse arches." The historian began to trace points of contact across the wire-frame model with his finger. "Yes," he whispered. "That would be the end of a column. And here the base of a buttress."

"Would you mind telling us what you're talking about?" Neidelman said, sharp interest kindling in his eyes.

"It makes perfect sense. Macallan was a religious architect, after all. . . ." St. John's voice trailed off.

"What, man?" Neidelman hissed.

St. John turned to Rankin. "Rotate the y-axis a hundred and eighty degrees."

Rankin obliged, and the diagram on the screen flipped into an upside-down position. Now the outline of the Water Pit stood upright, frozen on the screen, a glowing red skeleton of lines.

Suddenly there was a sharp intake of breath from the captain.

"Unbelievable," he said. "It's a cathedral."

The historian nodded, a triumphant smile on his face. "Macallan designed what he knew best. The Water Pit is nothing but a spire. A bloody upside-down cathedral spire!"

WITH the surveying of the original pit now completed, Neidelman called a half-day halt to activity. Malin took the opportunity to head home for a bit of research. He remembered a large picture book stowed away in the attic, *The Great Cathedrals of Europe*. He wanted a private chance to understand a little better what this discovery of St. John's meant.

In the dim light of the attic he could make out an ancient mahogany wardrobe. And behind the wardrobe were boxes of books. Hatch stepped up to the wardrobe and tried to force it aside. It moved an inch, perhaps a little more. He heaved at it with his shoulders and suddenly the thing went plummeting to the floor with a terrific crash. He bent down curiously, waving away the dust with an impatient hand.

The wooden backing of the wardrobe had broken apart, revealing a narrow recess. Inside, he could make out the faint lines of newspaper clippings and pages covered with loopy, narrow handwriting, their edges thin and brittle.

THE long point of ocher-colored land lay south of town, jutting out into the sea like a giant gnarled finger. On the far side of this promontory the cliff tumbled wooded and wild down to the bay. Countless millions of mussel shells, rubbing against each other in the brittle surf, had given the deserted spot its name, Squeaker's Glen. For students at Stormhaven High School the glen also functioned as the local lovers' lane.

Twenty-odd years before, Malin Hatch had himself been one of those fumbling lovers. Now he found himself strolling the wooded paths again, uncertain what impulse had brought him to this spot. He had recognized the handwriting on the sheets hidden in the wardrobe as his grandfather's. Unable to bring himself to read them right away, he'd left the house, intent on strolling down along the waterfront. But his feet had taken him here.

He looked around the secluded glade as the memories came charging back. Of one May afternoon in particular, full of nervous roving hands and short, tentative gasps. That had been six months before his mother packed them off to Boston. Claire, more than anyone, had accepted his moods; accepted all the baggage that had come with being Malin Hatch, the boy who'd lost the better part of his family.

He sat down on the fragrant grass. A beautiful late summer afternoon, and he had the glen all to himself.

No, not quite to himself. Hatch became aware of a rustling on the path behind him. To his surprise he saw Claire step out into the glade.

She flushed deeply as she saw him. She was wearing a summery, low-cut print dress, and her long golden hair was gathered in a French braid. She hesitated a moment, then stepped forward.

"Hello again," Hatch said, jumping to his feet. "Nice day."

She smiled briefly and nodded.

"How was your dinner?" he asked.

"Fine."

There was an awkward pause.

"I'm sorry," she said. "I must be intruding on your privacy." She turned to go.

"Wait!" he cried, louder than he'd intended. "I mean, you don't have to go. I'd like to catch up." He sat down again and patted the ground next to him.

She came forward and smoothed her dress with a self-conscious gesture he remembered.

"Funny we should meet here, of all places," he said.

She nodded. "What's it been, twenty-five years?"

"Just about." He paused for an awkward moment. "So what have you been doing all this time?"

"You know. Graduated high school. Planned to go to Orono and attend U. Maine, but met Woody instead. Got married. No kids." She shrugged and took a seat.

"No kids?" Hatch asked. Even in high school Claire had talked of her desire for children.

"No," she said matter-of-factly. "Low sperm count."

Hatch—to his own horror—felt a wave of mirth sweep over him at the turn the stumbling conversation had taken. He snorted involuntarily, then burst out laughing. Dimly he realized that Claire was laughing as hard as he was.

"Oh, Lord," she said, wiping her eyes at last, "what a relief it is to just laugh. Especially over this. Malin, you can't imagine what a terribly forbidden subject this is at home."

As the laughter fell away, it seemed as if the years and the awkwardness fell with it. Hatch regaled her with stories of medical school and his adventures in Suriname and Sierra Leone, while she told him the various fates of their common friends.

At last she fell silent. "I have a confession," she said. "This meeting wasn't a complete accident. You see, I saw you walking, and I took a wild guess where you were headed." She looked at him. "I wanted to apologize. I mean, I don't share Woody's feelings about what you're doing here. I know you're not in it for the money, and I hope you succeed."

"No need to apologize." He paused. "Tell me how you ended up marrying him."

She sighed and averted her eyes. "Oh, Malin, I was so . . . There was this part of you I could never reach. It got to me after a while." She shrugged. "Then one day you and your mother were gone."

"Yup. Off to Boston. I guess I was a pretty gloomy kid."

"After you left, I was all set to go to college. And then this young minister came. He seemed so fiery and sincere. He'd inherited millions, and he gave every penny to the poor. He was so different then—full of passion, a man who really believed he could change the world. He was so intense."

"So what happened?"

Claire sighed. "I'm not sure exactly. Small towns can be deadly, Malin, especially for someone like Woody. Nobody cared about politics here. Nobody cared about nuclear proliferation, about starving children in Biafra. I begged Woody for us to leave, but he's so stubborn. He'd come here to change this town, and he wasn't going to leave until he did. Oh, people tolerated him with a kind of amusement. He became more and more . . ." She paused, thinking. "I don't know—he never learned to lighten up." She hesitated. "And now he has something to believe in. With this crusade against your treasure hunt, he has a new cause."

"He'd better start looking for another cause. We're almost done."

"Really? How can you be sure?"

"We made a discovery this morning. Macallan, the guy who built the Water Pit, designed it as a kind of upside-down cathedral spire.

See, Red Ned Ockham wanted this Macallan to build something that would keep his treasure safe until he came back to retrieve it."

"Retrieve it how?"

"Through a secret back door. But Macallan, in revenge for being kidnapped, designed the pit so that *nobody* could get at the treasure. We're using technologies Macallan never dreamed of, and we've been able to figure out exactly what he built. You know how churches have buttressing to keep them from falling down? Well, Macallan just inverted the whole scheme and used it as the supports for his pit during its construction. Then he secretly removed the most important supports as the pit was filled in. If Ockham had ever actually tried to retrieve the treasure, the whole pit would have collapsed on him. That was Macallan's trap. But by re-creating the cathedral braces, we can stabilize the pit and extract the treasure without fear."

"That's incredible," she said.

"Yes, it is."

"Then why aren't you more excited?"

Hatch paused. "Is it that obvious?" He laughed quietly. "I keep telling myself this is all about finding out what happened to Johnny. I'd planned to put my share of the treasure into a foundation in his memory. But every now and then I think about what I could do with all that money."

"That's only natural, Malin."

"Maybe. But that doesn't make me feel any better about it. Your reverend gave all his away, remember?" He sighed. "Maybe he's a little bit right about me, after all. Anyway, he doesn't seem to have caused much damage with his opposition."

"You're wrong about that." Claire looked at him. "His sermons have a huge effect on the fishermen. The haul is down this year, and—in the minds of the fishermen—he's linked that to the dig."

"Claire, the haul is down *every* year. They've been overfishing and overlobstering for half a century."

"You know that, and I know that. But now they've got a scapegoat. He's gotten the fishermen and lobstermen together, and they're planning a big protest."

"Can you find out more?"

Claire fell silent. "I've told you this much," she said after a moment. "Don't ask me to spy on my husband."

"I'm sorry," Hatch said. "I didn't mean that."

Suddenly Claire hid her face in her hands. "Oh, Malin, if only I *could* . . ." Her shoulders sagged as she began to sob.

Gently Malin pulled her head to his shoulder. "I'm sorry," she murmured. "I'm acting like such a child."

"Shhh," Malin whispered quietly, patting her shoulders. As she turned toward him, he pulled his head back just enough to let his lips graze hers. He kissed her tentatively, then a little harder. And suddenly their mouths were locked together. His heart raced as her hands, clutching his shoulder blades, now dug into his shirt.

She pulled away from him. "No, Malin," she said huskily, clambering to her feet and brushing at her dress.

"Claire—" he began, but she had already turned away.

He watched her disappear up the path. An uncomfortable mixture of lust, guilt, and adrenaline coursed through his veins. He'd just done one of the stupidest things he had ever done in his life. Yet as he rose to his feet and moved slowly down a different path, he found his hot imagination turning to what would have happened if she had not pulled herself away.

EARLY the next morning Hatch hiked up the short path toward base camp and opened the door to St. John's office. To his surprise the historian was already there.

"I didn't think I'd find you here so early," Hatch said. "I was planning to leave you a note asking you to stop by the medical office."

The Englishman sat back, rubbing weary eyes with plump fingers. "Actually, I've made an interesting discovery."

"So have I." Wordlessly, Hatch held out a large sheaf of yellowed pages, stuffed into several folders. Making space on his cluttered desk, St. John spread the folders in front of him.

"Where did you get these?" he asked.

"They were hidden in an old wardrobe in my attic. They're records from my grandfather's own research on the treasure. My father burned most of the records, but I guess he missed these."

St. John turned to the parchment. "Extraordinary," he murmured.

"My Spanish is a little rusty, but this is what I found most interesting." Hatch pointed to a folder marked *ARCHIVOS DE LA CIUDAD DE CADIZ*. Inside was a dark blurry photograph of an old manuscript.

"Let's see," St. John began.

> "Records from the Court of Cádiz, 1661 to 1700. Octavo 16. Throughout the reign of the Holy Roman Emperor Charles II, we were sorely troubled by pirates. In 1695 alone, the Royal Silver Fleet was seized by the heathen pirate Edward Ockham at a cost to the crown of ninety million reales. He became our greatest plague, sent by the devil himself. Upon much debate, counselors allowed us to wield St. Michael's Sword, our greatest, most secret, and most terrible treasure. May heaven have mercy on our souls for doing so. *In nomine Patris . . .*"

St. John put the folder down. "What does this mean, 'our greatest, most secret, and most terrible treasure'?"

"No idea," Hatch murmured. "Maybe they thought the sword had some kind of magical power. That it would scare away Ockham."

"Have you shown these to Captain Neidelman yet?"

"No. Actually, I was thinking of E-mailing the transcriptions to an old friend who lives in Cádiz, Marquesa Hermione de Hohenzollern. She's nearly eighty, a bit eccentric, but a top-notch researcher."

"Perhaps you're right to look outside for assistance," St. John said. "The captain's so involved with the Water Pit, I doubt he'd spare the time to look at this."

Hatch gathered the folders to go, then stopped. "You mentioned that you'd made a discovery too."

"That's right. It has to do with Macallan. Take a look at this." St. John took a sheet of paper from his desk and held it out. Hatch examined the single line of letters, which looked like gibberish:

ETAONISRHLDCUFPMWYBGKQXYZ

Then he spelled them out loud. "E-T-A-O . . . Hey, wait a minute. Eta Onis! That's who Macallan dedicated his book to."

"It's the frequency table of the English language," St. John explained. "The order that letters are most likely to be used in sentences. Cryptanalysts use it to decrypt coded messages."

Hatch whistled. "When did you notice this?"

St. John grew self-conscious. "The day after Kerry died. I didn't say anything. I felt so stupid. Here it had been staring us in the face all this time. I realized Macallan had been much more than just an architect. If he knew about the frequency table, he was probably involved with London's intelligence community. So I did some checking. I'm now sure that Macallan worked for the Black Chamber."

"The what?"

"The Black Chamber," St. John continued, "was a secret department of the English post office. Its duty was to intercept sealed communications, transcribe the contents, then reseal them with forged seals. If the documents were in code, they were deciphered and sent on to the king or certain high ministers, depending on the communication."

Hatch shook his head. "I had no idea."

"Not only that. Reading between the lines of some of the old court records, I believe Macallan was most likely a double agent, working for Spain. But he was found out. I think the real reason he left England was to save his life. Perhaps he was being sent to America not only to construct a cathedral for New Spain, but for other, clandestine, reasons."

Hatch nodded. "That would explain why Macallan was so adept at using codes and secret inks in his journal."

"And why his second code was so devilish. Not many people would have the presence of mind to plan a double cross as elaborate as the Water Pit." St. John fell silent a moment. "I mentioned this to Neidelman yesterday."

"And?"

"He told me it was interesting and that we should look into it at some point, but that the priority was stabilizing the pit and retrieving the gold." A pale smile moved quickly across his features. "That's why there's little reason to show him those documents you uncovered. He's simply too involved with the dig to think of anything that isn't directly related."

THE following day was Saturday, but there was little rest on Ragged Island. Heading out through the channel, Hatch frowned at the lead-gray sky. It was already August 28, just days away from his self-imposed deadline; from now on, the weather could only get worse.

The accumulated equipment failures and computer problems had put work seriously behind schedule, and the recent rash of illnesses and accidents among the crew only added to the delays. When Hatch showed up at the medical office around quarter to ten, two people were already waiting to see him. One had developed an unusual bacterial infection of the teeth; the other, alarmingly, had come down with viral pneumonia.

Hatch arranged transportation to a mainland hospital for the second patient and prepared blood work on the first.

It wasn't until almost noon that he had time to access the Internet and E-mail his friend the marquesa, in Cádiz. He attached transcripts of a few of his grandfather's most obscure documents, asking her to search for any additional material on St. Michael's Sword she could find.

He signed off, then turned to the small bundle of mail he'd grabbed from his mailbox that morning. The September issue of the *Journal of the American Medical Association,* a flyer for the firehouse spaghetti dinner, and a cream-colored envelope. He recognized the handwriting instantly.

Dear Malin,

I've decided to leave Clay. I'm going to New York. I'll get a job. It's something I can't avoid any longer. I don't want to stay here, growing more bitter and resentful. It's going to hurt him terribly, but I know it's the right thing to do. I'll tell him after the protest ends.

I also know that you and I are not for each other. I have some wonderful memories, and I hope you do too. But this thing we almost started is a way of clinging to that past. It would end up hurting us both.

Please do not answer this letter or try to change my mind. Let's not spoil the past by doing something stupid in the present.

Love, Claire

The interisland telephone rang. Moving slowly, as if in a dream, Hatch picked up the receiver.

"It's Streeter," came the brusque voice. "The captain wants to see you at the observation tower. Right away."

"Tell him I'll—" Hatch began. But Streeter had hung up.

Hatch stepped along the series of ramps leading to the tower. He grasped the ladder, then climbed to the railing that encircled the control tower.

Neidelman was nowhere to be seen. In fact, the tower was empty of anyone except Magnusen, who was scanning the sensors that monitored the pressure on the timbers in the pit.

That morning Neidelman's crew had been hard at work replacing the missing members of Macallan's original bracing with titanium struts. Hatch learned that they might be ready to begin digging the final fifty feet to the treasure chamber by the end of the day.

Gazing through the floor's glass porthole into the pit below, Hatch saw Neidelman ascending in the lift. Isobel stood beside him, hugging herself, as if chilled.

The captain swung up to the staging platform, then climbed the ladder and went into the tower. Isobel stepped up onto the deck and entered behind him. Both were strangely silent.

Neidelman turned to Magnusen. "Sandra, may we have some privacy for a moment?"

The engineer walked out onto the deck and shut the door.

Neidelman drew a deep breath, his tired gray eyes on Hatch. "Malin, you'd better steady yourself," he said quietly. "We found your brother."

Hatch felt a sudden sense of dislocation, almost as if he were pulling away from the world around him. "Where?" he managed.

"In a deep cavity below the vaulted tunnel. Under the grate."

"You're sure?" Hatch whispered. "No chance of mistake?"

"It is the skeleton of a child," Isobel said. "Twelve years old, perhaps thirteen, blue dungaree shorts, baseball cap—"

"Yes," Hatch whispered, sitting down suddenly. "Yes."

The tower was silent for the space of a minute.

"I need to see for myself," Hatch said at last.

"We know you do," Isobel said, gently helping him to his feet. "Come."

Shrugging into a slicker, stepping onto the small electric lift, descending the ladder array—the next minutes passed in a gray blur. Reaching the hundred-foot level, Neidelman stopped the lift. They crossed a walkway to the mouth of the tunnel.

Hatch stepped into the tunnel, past a large air-filtration unit. Within, the ceiling was now braced by a series of metal plates. A few more nightmare steps and Hatch found himself back in the octagonal stone chamber where Wopner had died. With a tremendous effort Hatch willed his feet forward, past the braced-up stone that had killed Wopner to the well in the center of the room. The iron grating had been removed, and a rope ladder led down into darkness.

"Our mapping team calculated that the shaft beneath the grating intersected the tunnel you discovered as a boy," Neidelman said. "They broke through some kind of watertight seal." He stepped forward. "I'll go first," he said, and disappeared down the ladder.

A few moments later he called up. Hatch bent down and gripped the rails of the narrow ladder.

The well was only four feet in diameter. Hatch climbed down, following the smooth-walled shaft as it curved around a large rock. He was in a small chamber cut into the hard glacial till. Then he noticed that what he thought was a wall, was a massive piece of dressed stone, hewn square.

Hatch took a step forward, then bent down. He unhooked his flashlight from the harness and snapped it on.

Jammed beneath the stone was a skeleton. The Red Sox cap still hung on the skull, trapped behind stone.

The distant part of Hatch could see that Johnny—for this could only be Johnny—had fallen victim to one of Macallan's traps, similar to the one that killed Wopner. Hatch reached out, gently touching the brim of the cap. It was Johnny's favorite. Their father had bought it for him the day the Red Sox won the pennant. It was signed by Jim Lonborg.

Hatch remained motionless, cradling the cold, birdlike bones in his hands, in the sepulchral silence of the hole.

MALIN Hatch swung the *Plain Jane*'s dinghy into the broad, slow reach of the Passabec River, which narrowed and grew calm as he went upstream. Not much farther now. Around the bend and there it was—the shingle beach he remembered so well, its massive banks of oyster shells heaped twenty feet high. It was deserted, as he knew it would be. Most local residents had little interest in prehistoric Indian encampments. Professor Horn had brought him and his brother here the day before Johnny died.

Hatch pulled the dinghy up onto the beach, then retrieved his battered paint box, easel, portfolio, and collapsible chair from the bow. He looked around, deciding on a spot beneath a lone birch tree.

Opening the portfolio, he carefully removed a large sheet of paper. He taped it to the easel, half filled a palette well with water. He then squeezed cerulean-blue paint into the well. Dipping a brush in the well, he laid a flat blue wash over the top two thirds of the sheet.

In the years after Johnny's death he'd never been able to come back to the Indian shell heaps. And yet now Hatch sensed himself turning a corner. Perhaps he could close the chapter and move on.

As he reached for another brush, he heard the sound of an inboard approaching. Looking up, he saw a familiar figure scanning the riverbanks, the tanned skin dark under a large-brimmed straw hat. Isobel caught sight of him and waved, then nosed the Thalassa launch toward the shore and killed the motor.

"Isobel!" he said.

She anchored the boat on the beach, then came toward him, removing her hat and shaking her long hair back. "I have been spying on you. I saw you in your little boat, and I got curious."

So that's how she's going to play it, he thought: business as usual. No dewy-eyed empathy over what happened the day before. He felt vastly relieved.

Her eyes widened. "Look at you! Painting! *Monsieur le docteur,* I never expected such artistic depth."

"You'd better reserve judgment until you see the finished product," he replied, dabbing in the stony pebbles of the beach with short brushstrokes. "Tell me, Isobel, to what do I owe this visit?"

Isobel grinned mischievously. "I wanted to find out why you had not asked me for a second date."

"I figured you thought I was a weak reed. Remember what you said about us northerners—all the marrow sucked from our bones?"

"That is true enough. But I would not call you a weak reed. Perhaps a kitchen match would be a better analogy, *non?* All you need is the right woman to ignite you." She picked up an oyster shell and sent it spinning into the water. "Besides, I was afraid you were seeing the minister's wife. Your old *friend.*"

"That's all she is," Hatch said. "A friend."

Isobel looked at him, a smile slowly forming.

"What are you grinning at?" Hatch said.

Isobel laughed out loud. "I am grinning with relief, monsieur. But you have obviously misunderstood me all along." She slid an index finger along the back of his wrist. "I like to play the game, *comprends?* But only for the right man."

Hatch stared at her for a minute in surprise. Then he lifted the paintbrush again. "I'd have guessed you'd be closeted with Neidelman today, poring over charts and diagrams."

"No," she said, good humor suddenly gone. "The captain no longer has the patience for careful archaeology. He is down in the pit now, preparing to excavate the bottom of the shaft. No screening for artifacts, no stratigraphic analysis. I cannot bear it."

Hatch looked at her in surprise. "He's working today?" Working on Sunday, with the medical office unmanned, was a breach of regulations.

Isobel nodded. "Since the discovery of the spire, he has been a man possessed."

Hatch began cleaning the bristles and replacing the tubes into the paint box. He stood up. "It needs to dry a bit. Why don't we have a climb?"

They scrambled up the side of the tallest shell heap, oysters crunching beneath their feet. From the top Hatch looked past their boats toward the river.

"*Magnifique,*" said Isobel. "What a magical place."

"I used to come here with Johnny," Hatch said.

"Tell me about him," she said simply.

Silently Hatch took a seat, the oysters rustling under his weight. "Well, he loved everything to do with science—even more than me. He had incredible collections of butterflies, rocks, fossils. Johnny would have done amazing things with his life. I think one of the reasons I worked so hard, got through medical school, was to make up for what happened."

"What did you have to make up for?" she asked gently.

"It was my idea to go to Ragged Island that day."

Isobel offered none of the usual platitudes, and again Hatch found himself feeling grateful. He took a deep breath, letting it out slowly.

"After Johnny disappeared in the tunnel," he went on, "it took me a while to find my way out. I don't remember how long. After that, the first thing I remember clearly is arriving at my parents' dock. They raced out to Ragged Island, along with half the town. I'll never forget my father's face when he reappeared at the entrance to the tunnel. He was covered with Johnny's blood. He was yelling out, pounding on the beams, crying."

Isobel remained silent, listening.

"They searched, spent all that night and the next day. When it became clear Johnny couldn't possibly be alive, people began to drop away. The medical team said the amount of blood in the tunnel meant Johnny must be dead, but Dad kept looking. He wandered around, climbed down into the shafts, dug holes. He wouldn't leave the island. Weeks went by. Mom begged him to come home, but he wouldn't. Then one day she came out with food, and he wasn't there. There was another search, and they found Dad floating in one of the shafts. Drowned. Talk turned to suicide."

Hatch had never told anyone this much of the story before, and he never imagined what a relief it was simply to talk.

"We stayed in Stormhaven for another six years. A little town never forgets. Everyone was so . . . *nice*. But the talk never stopped. Finally, when I was sixteen, my mother couldn't stand it any longer. She took me to Boston for the summer. And a year went by, then another. Then I went off to college, and I never came back. Until now."

"And then?"

"Medical school, the Peace Corps, Médecins Sans Frontières, Mount Auburn Hospital. And then one day your captain walked into my office. There you have it." Hatch paused.

"And in a week you retire as one of the richest men in America."

Hatch laughed. "Isobel," he said, "I've decided to put the money into a foundation in my brother's name."

"All of it?"

"Yes." He hesitated. "Well, I'm still thinking about that."

Isobel settled back on the shells, squinted at him skeptically. "I am a good judge of character. You may put most of the money into this foundation. But I will be skinned alive if you do not keep a tidy little sum for yourself. You would not be human otherwise. And I am sure I would not like you so much if you were not human."

Hatch opened his mouth to protest; then he relaxed again.

"Either way, you are a saint," she said. "I have more venal things planned for my share. Like buying a very fast car."

"That's fine," he said. "For you, it's a professional thing. For me, it was personal."

They fell silent, lying on their backs in the late morning sun. Hatch closed his eyes. Vaguely he realized Isobel was saying something, but he was growing too drowsy to listen. And then he drifted off into a peaceful, dreamless sleep.

IN HIS OFFICE THE FOLLOWING afternoon Hatch heard from the marquesa in Cádiz. Reading, then rereading, the E-mail from her, Hatch felt a chill course through him.

There was a knock on the door. "Come in," Hatch said as he sent the marquesa's message to the nearby printer. He glanced up at the workman who stood in the doorway, then froze.

"Oh, my!" he gasped. "What the devil happened to you?"

FIFTY minutes later Hatch was quickly climbing the path toward the Water Pit. The rays of the lowering sun blazed over the water, turning the island's fogbank into a fiery swirl.

The tower was empty save for Magnusen and a technician.

"Where's Neidelman?" Hatch asked.

Magnusen was monitoring a wire-frame grid of the base of the Water Pit. "With the digging team," she replied.

On the wall was a bank of six red phones. Hatch picked up the phone labeled WATER PIT, FORWARD TEAM.

He heard three quick beeps. In a moment Neidelman's voice came over the channel. "Yes?" There was loud hammering in the background.

"I need to speak with you," Hatch said. "It's important. I have some new information about St. Michael's Sword."

"If you must," Neidelman replied. "You'll have to come down here. We're in the midst of setting some braces."

Hatch buckled on a safety helmet and harness. One of the crew members helped him onto the electric lift. He pressed a button, and the small platform lurched and descended. He passed through the gleaming web of titanium struts and cables, marveling despite himself at its complexity. The bottom of the pit came into view. The muck and mire had been removed, and a battery of lights erected.

Stepping off the lift, Hatch went down the ladder into a roar of sound: shovels, hammers, the rush of air-filtration units. Thirty feet below, he reached the actual floor of the excavation. Neidelman stood in one corner, directing the placement of the supports. Streeter hovered nearby, a set of blueprints in his hand.

Neidelman turned his pale eyes toward Hatch. "You know how pressed for time we are," he said. "I hope this is important."

A great change had taken place in the man in the week since Wopner's death. Gone was the look of calm certainty. Now there was a look of haggard, almost wild, determination.

"A couple of days ago," Hatch began, "I came across a stash of my grandfather's papers, documents he'd gathered about Ockham's treasure. Some mentioned St. Michael's Sword, hinting that it was a terrifying weapon. So I contacted a researcher I know in Cádiz and asked her to do some digging into the sword's history."

Neidelman looked toward the muddy ground at their feet. "I'm surprised you took such a step without consulting me."

"She found this." Hatch handed Neidelman a piece of paper.

The captain looked at it briefly. "It's in Old Spanish," he said with a frown. "Summarize it for me."

"It describes the original discovery of St. Michael's Sword. During the Black Plague, a wealthy Spanish merchant set out from Cádiz with his family on a barque. They put ashore along an unpopulated stretch of the Barbary Coast. There they found the remains of an ancient Roman settlement. Some Berber tribesmen warned them not to go near a ruined temple some distance away, saying it was cursed. But after a while the merchant decided to explore the temple. Among the ruins, under a slab of marble behind an altar, he found an ancient metal box that had been sealed shut, with an inscription in Latin. The inscription stated that the box contained a sword that was the deadliest of weapons. He carried the box down to the ship, but the Berbers refused to help him open it. In fact, they drove him from the shore."

Neidelman listened, still looking at the ground.

"A few weeks later, on Michaelmas—St. Michael's Day—the merchant's ship was found drifting in the Mediterranean. The yardarms were covered with vultures. All hands were dead. The box was shut, but the lead seal had been broken. It was brought to a monastery at Cádiz. The monks decided the sword was—and I quote—'a fragment vomited up from hell itself.' They sealed the box again and placed it in the catacombs under the cathedral. The monks who handled the box soon fell ill and died."

Neidelman looked up at Hatch. "Is this supposed to have some kind of bearing on our current effort?"

"Yes," said Hatch steadily. "Very much so. Wherever St. Michael's Sword has been, people have died. Haven't you noticed the rash of illnesses among our crew?"

Neidelman shrugged. "Sickness always occurs in a group of this size. Especially when the work is dangerous."

"This isn't malingering we're talking about. I've done the blood work. In almost every case the white cell counts are extremely low. And just this afternoon, one of your digging team came to me with the most unusual skin disorder I've ever seen. Ugly rashes and swelling across his arms, thighs, and groin."

"What is it?" Neidelman asked.

"I haven't been able to make a specific diagnosis yet."

Neidelman frowned. "Then what are you babbling on about?"

Hatch took a breath, controlling his temper. "You know I don't believe in curses any more than you do. That doesn't mean there isn't some underlying *physical* cause to the legend. The point is, the sword *is* dangerous. We've got to figure out *why* before we plunge ahead and retrieve it."

Hatch paused. "And it isn't just the illnesses. You must know that a big northeaster is brewing. It would be crazy to continue."

"No," said Neidelman, with a tone of finality. "The dig continues."

"Then you leave me no choice. I'm going to have to shut down the dig myself for the season, effective immediately."

"How, exactly?"

"By invoking clause nineteen of our contract."

Nobody spoke.

"My clause, remember?" Hatch went on. "Giving me the right to stop the dig if I felt conditions had become too dangerous."

Slowly Neidelman fished his pipe out of a pocket and loaded it with tobacco. "Funny," he said in a quiet, dead voice, turning to Streeter, "now that we're only thirty hours from the treasure chamber, Dr. Hatch here wants to shut the whole operation down. But of course I see why." Neidelman lowered his voice further. "Now that you've gotten the information you need out of Thalassa, you'd love nothing more than to see us fail. Then next year you could come in, finish the job, and get all the treasure." His eyes glittered with suspicion. "It all makes sense. And to think I came to *you* when I suspected we had a saboteur among us."

"I'm not trying to cheat you out of your treasure. I don't care about your treasure. My only interest is in the safety of the crew."

"The safety of the crew," Neidelman repeated derisively. "I want you to understand something. In thirty hours the treasure will be mine. Now that I know what your game is, Hatch, any effort to stop me will be met with force."

"Force?" Hatch repeated. "Is that a threat?"

"That would be a reasonable interpretation."

Hatch drew himself up. "When the sun rises tomorrow," he said, "if you're not gone from this island, you will be evicted."

Neidelman turned to Hatch. "Your presence is no longer required on Ragged Island. If you leave and allow me to finish as we agreed, you'll still get your share of the treasure. But if you try to stop me . . ." Silently he pulled his slicker aside. Hatch could clearly see the handgun snugged into his belt. "Mr. Streeter, escort Dr. Hatch to the dock."

"Let's go," said Streeter, stepping forward.

"I can find my own way." Hatch climbed out of the excavation to the base of the array, where the lift was already depositing the first diggers of the next shift.

THE rising sun cast a brilliant trail across the ocean, illuminating a crowd of boats packing Stormhaven's small harbor.

Chugging slowly through a gap in the center of the crowd was a small trawler, Woody Clay standing at its wheel. Reaching the harbor entrance, he cut the motor. Raising a battered megaphone, Clay shouted instructions to the protesters, his voice full of conviction. He was answered by a series of roars as numerous engines came to life. The boats cast off their moorings and throttled up, followed by more and more, until the bay filled with the fleet as it headed in the direction of Ragged Island.

THREE hours later and six miles to the southeast, the light struggled down through the damp labyrinth of the Water Pit.

At a hundred and eighty feet, the lowest depths of the pit, neither day nor night had any relevance. Gerard Neidelman stood beside a small staging platform watching the crew dig feverishly beneath him. Neidelman could just make out a clamor of air horns and boat cannon on the surface. He listened for a moment, then reached for his portable telephone.

"Streeter?"

"Here, Captain," Streeter replied from the observation tower.

"Let's have a report."

"About two dozen boats in all, Captain. They've formed a ring around the *Cerberus*. A lot of noise but nothing to worry about."

"Mr. Streeter, I'd like you to meet me at level sixty."

"Aye, aye."

Neidelman took the lift up to the sixty-foot level, arriving just as Streeter completed his descent.

"Only eight more feet to the treasure chamber," Neidelman said to Streeter. "I want all nonessential personnel off the island. We don't want a lot of extra bodies around rubbernecking during the actual extraction. We'll winch the treasure up in the bucket. I'll carry the sword myself."

He fell silent a moment, his eyes far away. "I don't think we're through with Hatch," he began again. "I'm worried we may have been underestimating him all along. We're only hours away from Ockham's treasure, and I don't want any nasty surprises before we get to it. Whatever you do, don't let Hatch set foot on this island again. I leave the matter to your discretion."

Streeter's eyebrows rose momentarily. "Aye, aye, sir."

Neidelman leaned forward. "Keep in touch, Mr. Streeter."

Then he was back on the lift and descending once again.

HATCH stood on the wide old porch of the house on Ocean Lane. To the east a heavy swell was coming in over the sea. The sky was slung with the ugly underbelly of a massive foul-weather front, the clouds churning and coiling as they raced across the water. Down toward the harbor a few vessels from the protest flotilla were already returning.

Closer to home, he turned to see a Federal Express van turning down the old cobblestone lane. It stopped in front of his house, and Hatch came down the steps to sign for the package.

He stepped back into the house, tearing open the box eagerly. Professor Horn and Isobel Bonterre, standing beside one of the pirate skeletons, stopped talking when they saw the package.

"Straight from the Smithsonian's physical anthropology lab," Hatch said. Pulling out a bulky computer printout, he flung himself into a nearby chair and began flipping pages. Soon he sighed, disappointment palpable in the air.

"Not what you were looking for?" the professor asked.

"No," Hatch said, shaking his head, "not at all."

"Malin, you were always too hasty to accept defeat."

Isobel picked up the printout and began flipping through it. "What are all these horrible-sounding diseases?"

Hatch sighed. "A couple of days back I sent off bone sections from these two skeletons and some of the others to the Smithsonian."

"Checking for disease," Professor Horn said.

"Yes." Hatch paused. "Something about Ragged Island—then and now—makes people sick. I figured that somehow the sword was a carrier of disease. Everywhere it went, people died." He looked at the printout. "But according to these tests, no two pirates died of the same illness. They died of a whole suite of diseases, some of them extremely rare."

He grabbed a sheaf of papers from a table. "It's just as mystifying as the test results on the patients I've been seeing the last couple of days. The blood work's always abnormal, but in different ways with each person. The only similarity is the low white blood cells. Lymphocytes, monocytes, basophils—all way down."

He dropped the sheets and sighed bitterly. "This was my last chance to stop Neidelman. If there was an obvious outbreak, maybe I could have persuaded him to quarantine the place."

"What about the legal route?" Isobel asked.

"I spoke to my lawyer. I'd have to get an injunction." Hatch said. "It would take weeks."

"I can understand your concern," the professor said, "but not your conclusion. How could the sword itself be dangerous?"

Hatch looked at him. "Call it a diagnostician's sixth sense. I feel a conviction that this sword is a carrier of some kind."

Hatch walked to the window. Drops of rain had begun to fall, and whitecaps flecked the bay. "I just can't see it. What could streptococcal pneumonia and candidiasis have in common?"

The professor pursed his lips. "Back in 1981 or '82, I remember reading a similar comment made by an epidemiologist at the National Institutes of Health. He asked what Kaposi's sarcoma and Pneumocystis carinii could possibly have in common."

"HIV kills by exhausting the human immune system," Hatch said. "Letting in a host of opportunistic diseases."

"Exactly. So maybe we're looking for something that degrades the human immune system." He stood up. "I wish I could stay, but it's coming on to blow." A heavy boom of thunder echoed across the bay.

As the professor reached for his coat, the door was flung open, and there was Donny Truitt, rain running down his face.

"Donny?" Hatch asked.

Truitt's eyes were puffy, the bags beneath blue-black. He reached down to his damp shirt, tearing it open with both hands. Hatch heard the professor draw in a sharp breath.

Truitt's armpits were spotted with large weeping lesions. He cried out and took a staggering step forward.

Hatch caught Truitt's arm and eased him toward the sofa.

"Help me, Mal," Truitt gasped, grabbing his head with both hands. "I've never been sick a day in my life."

"I'll help," said Hatch. "Lie down and let me examine your chest."

"Forget my chest," Donny gasped. "I'm talking about *this!*"

And as he jerked his head away from his hands with a convulsive movement, Hatch could see with cold horror that each hand now held a mat of thick, carrot-colored hair.

CLAY stood at the stern rail of his single-diesel trawler, the megaphone upended in the fore cabin, drenched and useless, shorted out by the rain. He and the six remaining protesters had taken temporary shelter in the lee of the largest Thalassa ship—a ship they had originally tried to blockade.

Clay was wet to the bone, but a bitter feeling of loss penetrated far deeper than the damp. He looked toward the remnants of his protest flotilla. Six bedraggled boats heaved in the swell. He admitted to himself that the protest, like everything else he had tried to do in Stormhaven, seemed doomed to failure.

The head of the Lobsterman's Co-op, Lemuel Smith, brought his boat alongside Clay's. "It's time to head in, Reverend," the lobsterman shouted. "This is going to be one humdinger of a storm. We can't afford to lose our boats."

Clay was silent. Can't afford to lose a boat. That was it in a nutshell. They didn't see that some things were more important than boats or money. "You go on back, Lem. I'm going to stay."

The lobsterman hesitated. "I'd feel better if you came in now."

Clay waved his hand. "Maybe I'll land on the island, talk to Neidelman myself."

Smith gazed at him for a moment. Clay wasn't much of a seaman. But telling a man what to do with his boat was an unforgivable offense. He slapped the gunwale of Clay's boat. "I guess we'd better shove off, then."

Clay hugged the lee of the *Cerberus,* engine idling, and stared as the remaining boats headed into the heaving sea. Now that it had come to this—now that he was alone, the Almighty his sole companion—he felt an odd sense of comfort. He would wait a little.

He had boat and time enough. All the time in the world.

DONNY Truitt lay on the sofa while Hatch examined him.

"Donny, when did the symptoms begin to show?" Hatch asked.

"About a week ago," Truitt replied miserably. "I started waking up nauseated. Then this rash thing appeared on my chest."

"What did it look like?"

"Red splotches at first. Then it got kind of bumpy. My neck started to hurt too. And I started noticing hair in my comb. First just a little, but then it's like I could pull it all out. There's never been a touch of baldness in my family."

Hatch called an ambulance from the hospital, but it would take at least fifteen minutes. Some of Donny's symptoms were similar to what other crew members had complained of, but, as with the others, there were symptoms he presented that were maddeningly unique.

"Donny," he said, "how are your teeth?"

"Funny you should mention it. Just the other day I noticed one of my back teeth was a bit loose. Getting old, I guess."

Hair loss, tooth loss. Hatch shook his head. Like the professor said, forget the other diseases, subtract them all, and see what's left. Low white blood cell count, nausea, weakness, apathy . . .

Suddenly it became overwhelmingly clear.

Hatch stood up quickly. "Oh, Lord—" he began, horrified at the implications. He looked at his watch: seven o'clock. Just a couple of hours until Neidelman reached the treasure chamber.

Reaching into his medical bag, he pulled out the emergency radio communicator. All Thalassa channels were awash in static.

He stepped into the kitchen, where the professor and Isobel Bonterre had retreated and were talking in hushed tones.

"Isobel," Hatch said, "I have to go to the island. No time to explain. Will you make sure Donny gets on the ambulance?"

"I will come with you. I know the sea, and it will take two to get across in this weather, and you know it."

"Forget it," Hatch said, tugging on boots. "Too dangerous."

He felt a hand laid on his arm. "The lady is right," the professor said. "I don't know what this is all about. But I do know you can't steer, navigate, and land a boat in this weather by yourself. I can get Donny on the ambulance and to the hospital."

Hatch turned to look at Isobel, her determined dark eyes peering out from under the hood of a yellow sou'wester.

"She's as capable as you are," the professor said.

"Why do you need to do this?" Hatch asked quietly.

In answer, Isobel slipped her hand around his elbow. "Because you are special, *monsieur le docteur,* special to *me.*"

They raced out into the driving rain. In the last hour the storm had picked up dramatically, and Hatch could hear the boom of Atlantic rollers pounding the headland.

They dashed through the streaming streets, then made their way along the wharf, carefully stepping down the slick gangplank to the floating dock. All the dinghies had been lashed to the shaking structure. Pulling his knife from a pocket, Hatch cut the *Plain Jane*'s dinghy loose and with Isobel's help slid it into the water.

Not bothering to start the engine, Hatch ran the oars through the oarlocks and rowed out to the *Plain Jane.* The dinghy was flung up and down, slapping the troughs with unwholesome shudders. They clipped the dinghy to a stern bolt on the *Plain Jane* and clambered aboard. Hatch cranked the starter, and the engines sprang to life.

"When we hit the open ocean," he said, "it's going to buck like wild, so keep hold of something. Stay close by in case I need your help with the wheel."

"You are so foolish," said Isobel, nerves turning her good humor testy. "Do you think storms are found only in Maine? What I want to know is what this insane trip is all about."

"I'll tell you," Hatch said. "But you're not going to like it."

CLAY peered through the screaming murk, gripping the wheel with aching arms. The boat struck each towering wave with a crashing blow, foam bursting over the bow.

Earlier, without warning, the *Cerberus* had raised anchor and gotten under way, ignoring Clay's horn, the vast bulk moving inexorably into the black sea. He had followed, fruitlessly hailing, until it disappeared into the darkness.

He looked around the cabin, trying to assess the situation. The ocean was literally boiling. He was trying to steer by the compass, but Clay was no navigator, and with no light he could read the compass only by lightning flashes. There was a flashlight in his pocket, but Clay desperately needed both hands to steer.

Ragged Island was less than a half mile away. Clay knew even a superb mariner would have a difficult job bringing the boat in through the reefs in this weather. But it would be more difficult still to cross the six miles of hell to Stormhaven.

The boat barreled its way into another comber and a sheer wall of water rose off the bows. Clay had just enough time to brace against the wheel and cling with all his might against the blast. As lightning flashed, he pushed the throttle up a tick and listened to the responding rumble of the engine. The boat plowed ahead, surging upward, then plunging again. He realized, dimly, that it might be wise to throttle back, just in case the—

There was a stunning crash as the boat bottomed itself against the reef. Clay was thrown violently forward into the wheel, breaking his nose. Then a wave slammed the boat over on its beam-ends, and he was thrown free of the deck into a perfect chaos of water and wind.

HATCH swung the nose of the *Plain Jane* into the channel. The wind was cold, the sky thick with water. Isobel came up beside him, clinging to the instrument housing with both hands.

"Well?" she screamed in his ear.

"Isobel, I've been a fool," he shouted back. "I've seen those same symptoms a thousand times. Anyone who's undergone radiation treatment for cancer knows them—nausea, loss of energy, hair. White cell counts go through the floor."

Isobel leaned forward, eyes wide despite the blinding surf.

"St. Michael's Sword is *radioactive*. Long-term exposure to radioactivity kills your bone-marrow cells. It cripples the immune system, makes you an easy mark. That's why the Thalassa crew had all those exotic diseases. Severe exposure leads to osteoporosis and loss of teeth. Symptoms similar to scurvy."

"And it might also explain the computer problems," Isobel said. "Radiation causes havoc with microelectronics. But why go out in this murderous storm?"

"The sword's been shut up in a lead box, and yet it's still killed everyone who's come in contact with it for centuries. Who knows what would happen if Neidelman takes it out of the casket! We can't let that happen."

He fell silent abruptly, staring ahead. A white line loomed out of the murk. He realized with horror that it was the breaking top of a wave, towering over the boat. "Help me hold the wheel!" he yelled.

The boat seemed suspended for a moment inside the wave; then it suddenly broke free and tipped over the crest with a violent corkscrew motion.

"How will you convince Neidelman the sword is radioactive?" Isobel hollered.

"When Thalassa set up my office, they included a radiologist's Radmeter—a high-tech Geiger counter. I've never even turned the thing on." Hatch shook his head as they began to climb another wave. "If I had, it would have gone nuts. Neidelman can't argue with that meter."

The wind increased in intensity. Now he could see a massive wave rising up above the *Plain Jane*. Towering far above his head was a smooth Himalayan cliff face of water, growling and hissing like a living thing. Isobel saw it as well. Neither said a word.

The boat rose and kept rising, ascending forever, while the surf gradually filled the air with a waterfall's roar. There was an enormous crash as the comber hit them straight on. Hatch clung desperately as he felt his feet slip from the deck beneath him.

The *Plain Jane* came to rest on its side and began to sink rapidly. Hatch looked rearward. The dinghy had also shipped a quantity of water but was still afloat.

Isobel followed Hatch's eyes and nodded. Clinging to the side, up to their waists in roiling water, they began working their way toward the stern. Fumbling about, Hatch located the dinghy's bow. He scrambled in and looked back for Isobel, pulling her into the dinghy.

Moving aft, Hatch gave the outboard a tug. There was a cough, then a tinny rasp above the scream of the ocean.

"We need to be turned against the sea," said Isobel. "You bail. I will manage the boat."

"But—"

"Do it!" Crawling aft, she jammed the throttle open, swinging the boat broadside to the sea. Just as a great comber bore down, she gave the throttle a sudden twist, lifting it up and over. Immediately she turned the boat again, surfing down the wave's backside, almost parallel to the sea.

This was in direct opposition to everything Hatch had ever learned about boats. "You're going to kill us!" he yelled.

"I surfed the waves as a kid," Isobel shouted. "Keep bailing."

"Not waves like this!"

"Hold on!" Isobel yelled. The little boat became airborne for a sickening moment before skidding sideways over a foaming crest.

"Holy . . . !" Hatch cried, scrabbling at the bow seat.

Suddenly they came into the lee of the island and the wind dropped.

"Turn back!" Hatch cried. "The riptide's going to sweep us past the island!"

Isobel began to reply; then she stopped. "Lights!" she cried.

Emerging from the storm was the *Cerberus,* three hundred yards off, the powerful lights on its forward deck cutting through the dark. Now it was turning toward them. It must have picked up the *Plain Jane* on its scope and was coming to its rescue.

"Over here!" Isobel yelled, waving her arms.

The *Cerberus* slowed, presenting its port side to the dinghy.

"Open the boarding hatch!" Hatch yelled.

The *Cerberus* remained silent and still.

Far above, Hatch thought he could see a single figure looking down at them. Then he noticed the harpoon gun on the forward deck swiveling slowly in their direction. "Turn the boat!" Hatch yelled.

Isobel threw the throttle to starboard, and the little craft spun around. Above, Hatch saw a blue flash. There was a thunderous whump ahead of them, and a tower of water rose twenty feet off their port bow, its base lit an ugly orange.

"Harpoon!" Hatch cried.

Without a word Isobel spun the boat again. As Hatch leaned forward to bail, he saw a strange sight—a narrow line in the water, sputtering and snapping, heading toward them. Then the line reached the bow in front of him, and with a tearing sound the nose of the dinghy vanished in a cloud of sawdust and woodsmoke. Glancing up, Hatch could see Streeter leaning over the *Cerberus*'s rail, a fléchette aimed directly at them.

"Head for the reefs!" Hatch shouted. "If you time the swell, you might be able to ride right over."

Isobel jerked the boat to a new course. The *Cerberus* began to come at them through the storm.

"We'll only get one chance!" Hatch yelled. "Ride the next swell across!"

They bucked along the reef for an agonizingly long instant. Then he yelled, "Now!"

As Isobel turned the ruined dinghy into the roiling water that lay across the reef, there came another huge explosion. Hatch heard a strange crunching noise and felt himself hurtled violently into the air. Then everything around him was churning water, and he felt himself being drawn down. There was only one brief moment of terror before it all began to seem very peaceful indeed.

WOODY Clay lost his footing on a patch of seaweed and banged his shin. The rocks along the shore were slippery and algae-covered. He decided it was safer to crawl.

Every limb of his body ached, his clothes were torn, the pain in his nose was worse than he could have ever imagined, and he was cold to the point of numbness. Yet he felt alive in a way that he had not in many, many years. He had been delivered onto this island. God worked in mysterious ways, but clearly He had brought Clay to Ragged Island for a reason.

Clay scanned the shoreline, gray against a black sky. The surf was battering the cofferdam relentlessly. Every blow of the waves sent massive plumes of spray over the top of the wall.

He began walking along the base of the embankment. He saw nobody and heard nobody. Perhaps the plunderers had evacuated in the face of the storm, scattered like moneylenders from the temple.

As he rounded the point, a strip of yellow police tape caught his eye. Beyond the tape lay a trio of shiny metal braces, and behind them a ragged opening led into the embankment. Clay stepped into the opening, ducking his head under the low roof as he did so.

Inside, it was quiet, snug, and dry. He reached into one pocket and took out his flashlight. He was in some kind of small chamber, which narrowed to a tunnel at the far end. It was very interesting, very gratifying. He had, in a way, been led to this tunnel. Soon—very soon, now—Clay knew that the special task that had been set aside for him would at last be made clear.

ISOBEL Bonterre glanced wildly up and down the rocky shore. Everywhere she looked there were shapes in the sand that could have been the body of Malin Hatch. But when she'd come close enough to investigate, they had all proved to be rocks.

She looked out to sea. She could see Neidelman's boat, the *Griffin,* two anchors securing it close to the reef, doggedly riding out the howling gale. Farther out to sea the *Cerberus* was barely visible, lights ablaze. A few minutes before, she'd seen a small launch put over its side, disappearing around the far end of the island, toward the base camp dock.

Isobel shivered, drawing the waterlogged slicker closer around her. She began heading toward base camp the long way, skirting the black stretch of shoreline. The roar of the surf was so loud that she barely heard the cracks of thunder.

She slowly approached the cluster of huts. The communications tower was dark. One of the island generators had fallen silent, while the other was shaking and howling in protest at the overload. Reaching Island One, she peered in the window. The command center was deserted.

Isobel flitted across the roadway to a window of the medical hut. It, too, looked deserted inside. When she found the door locked, she smashed a window with a rock, reached through the shards of glass, unlocked the window, and swung it open.

She slithered into Hatch's examination room and rummaged through drawers, looking for a gun, a knife, any kind of weapon. She found only a long, heavy flashlight. A door marked MEDICAL SUPPLIES was locked, but two well-placed kicks split it down the middle.

Isobel had no idea what the Geiger counter would look like; she only knew that Hatch had called it a Radmeter. She rummaged through the lower shelves, stopping briefly to slip something into her pocket. She found a small black nylon carrying case with a bold Radmetrics logo on it. Inside was a strange-looking device with foldable handles and a leather strap.

Suddenly she froze. A sharp sound had briefly separated itself from the howl of the storm—a sound like the report of a gun.

She slung the carrying case over her shoulder and headed back to the broken window.

HATCH lay on the rocks, the sea washing around his chest. He was alive, that much he knew; alive with all the pain that came along with it. How long he had lain there he could only guess.

Struggling to a crawl, he managed to make the few feet out of reach of the water. There he rested on a large outcropping of granite, the rock cool and smooth beneath his cheek.

As his head cleared, memories began to return, one by one. He'd fallen out of the dinghy, and the freakish riptide had pulled him to this rocky shore around the end of the island. Ahead he saw the low bluffs that guarded the pirate encampment. Isobel would have landed nearer the beach. If she landed at all.

He staggered partway up the rise, then turned seaward. There was a brief flicker of light, fingering its way along the dark shore. Then it swung upward, the powerful pale light of a halogen beam stabbing into the dark. Instinctively Hatch began backing up the slope.

Then it was flaring in his eyes, blinding him. He dropped and turned, scrabbling up the bluff. He'd been targeted.

The strange stuttering sound he'd heard from the *Cerberus* came again, rattling over the roar of the surf. To his right small puffs of dirt and mud rose madly into the air in a jagged line. Streeter was shooting at him with the fléchette.

Half crawling, half rolling, Hatch crossed the top of the bluff and tumbled down the embankment on the far side, slipping on the wet grass. He saw the glow of the tower lancing through the mists. He oriented himself, then turned down another trail. There it was: a dark hole yawning behind safety tape.

He slipped under the tape and stood at the edge of the Boston Shaft. In the blackness the shaft looked like a vertical drop to him. He hesitated, peering downward. Then there was the sound of footsteps clattering over a metal walkway. He grabbed the slender trunk of a chokecherry bush, swung himself over the edge. But the roots came out with a tearing sound, and Hatch felt himself falling through empty space for a short, terrifying drop.

He hit muddy bottom with a jolt, then scrambled to his feet, shaken but unhurt. There was only the faintest square of sky visible above him, but he saw a shape moving along its edge.

There was a deafening roar, accompanied by a flash of light from an automatic weapon. A second roar followed immediately.

Hatch began running down the tunnel. He knew Streeter had used the muzzle flash from his first shot to aim the second.

Hatch fought to keep from plunging out of control into absolute darkness. After several seconds the incline leveled out enough for him to come to a stop.

Another shot echoed deafeningly within the narrow confines of the tunnel. As Hatch threw himself sideways into the mud, the second shot tore into the cribbing directly behind him.

Pushing himself to his feet, he ran ahead blindly. Another shot came, much closer than he'd expected, and something ripped through his ear with a tearing sting.

He'd been hit. He flattened himself against the wall and waited in the close blackness, muscles tensed. At the next muzzle flash he'd spring back, grab Streeter, and toss him down.

Suddenly there was the flash and roar of a shot. Hatch lunged, trying desperately to beat the second shot, and as he closed on Streeter there was an immense blow to his head. A stunning light filled his eyes, blotting out thought, blotting out everything.

KEEPING as much as possible to the shelter of the rocks and pausing every few moments to listen, Isobel hiked inland from base camp to the narrow marked trail that mounted the rise of the island. She was soaked to the skin. The path climbed, and she topped a rise. The skeletal structure of the observation tower lay several hundred yards ahead, the windows brilliant squares of light etched against the night. From below the tower, as if from a great depth, she could hear the clank of machinery even over the howl of the storm.

Through the glass windows of the tower she could make out a dark shape moving slowly. She saw the broad shoulders of Rankin, the geologist. He appeared to be alone.

She hesitated. It was possible that Rankin might know how to use the Radmeter, but that would mean taking him into her confidence. Streeter was trying to kill them. Were others in on it?

There was a searing bolt of lightning overhead. From the direction of base camp there was a sharp crackle as the last generator failed. The lights atop the tower blinked out for a moment, and then the control tower was bathed in an orange glow as the emergency batteries came on.

Isobel clutched the Radmeter closer. She could wait no longer. Right or wrong, she had to make a choice.

A FACEFUL of mud brought Hatch back to the black reality of the tunnel. His head throbbed from Streeter's blow, and the cold steel of a gun barrel was digging into his torn ear.

"Game's over, Hatch," Streeter whispered. "Understand?"

"Yes," Hatch croaked, choking mud.

"Now get up, nice and smooth. Slip, and you're dead."

Hatch rose to his knees, then to his feet, slowly, carefully, fighting to quell the pounding in his head. He put one foot in front of the other as carefully as he could, trying not to stumble in the darkness. They continued down the shaft, following the wall.

After what seemed an eternity Hatch saw a faint glow ahead, where the tunnel opened onto the main shaft of the Water Pit.

Only the banks of emergency lights running along the ladder array were still lit. Streeter forced him forward onto the metal catwalk that connected the Boston Shaft to the ladder array. Streeter punched a keypad bolted to the side of the lift rail, and in a few moments the lift came into view. Streeter prodded Hatch onto the platform, then took up position behind him.

As they descended to the base of the Water Pit, Hatch saw a freshly dug shaft that led down to the treasure chamber itself. Streeter gestured for him to climb down the ladder.

Then he was at the bottom of the shaft. Streeter dropped to the ground behind him. As he stared, the last ember of hope died away. Gerard Neidelman was kneeling before a massive rusted plate of iron, angling an acetylene torch into a narrow cut about three feet square. In the far corner of the shaft stood Sandra Magnusen, staring at Hatch with cold hatred and contempt.

There was an angry hiss as Neidelman cut the flame on the torch. He raised his visor, staring expressionlessly at Hatch.

"You're a sorry sight," he said simply.

He turned to Streeter. "Where did you find him?"

"He and Bonterre were trying to come back to the island, Captain. I caught up with him in the Boston Shaft."

"And Isobel?"

"Their dinghy was crushed on the reef. There's a chance she survived drowning too, but the odds are against it."

"I see. Pity she had to get involved. Still, you've done well."

Hatch turned to Neidelman. "Gerard, please. Hear me out."

"Hear you out? I've been hearing you out for weeks now, and it's getting rather tedious." He handed the visor and torch to Magnusen. "Sandra, take over, please. We can't waste any time."

"You *have* to listen," Hatch said. "St. Michael's Sword is radioactive. It's suicide to open that casket."

"You never give up, do you? Wasn't a billion dollars enough?"

"Think what's been happening," Hatch went on urgently. "It explains everything. The computer problems. Radiation from the treasure chamber would cause the anomalies Wopner described. And the rash of illnesses we've had. Radiation suppresses the immune system, allows opportunistic diseases to intrude."

The captain stared at him, his gaze unreadable.

"Radiation poisoning causes hair loss, makes your teeth drop out. Just like those pirate skeletons. What else could be the cause of that mass grave? There were no signs of violence. And why do you suppose Ockham's ship was found derelict, the crew all dead?"

Streeter dug the gun barrel cruelly into his ear, and Hatch tried to twist free. "Don't you get it? If you expose that sword, you'll kill not only yourself but who knows how many others. You—"

"I've heard enough," Neidelman said. He looked at Hatch. "Funny. I never thought it would be you. I misjudged you."

There was a final hiss of steel, then Magnusen stood up. "Done, Captain," she said.

The piece of the plate was winched up, and Hatch found his eyes traveling toward the square that had been cut into the iron plate. The opening to the treasure chamber exhaled the faint perfume of frankincense and sandalwood.

"Lower the light," the captain said.

Magnusen swung a basket lamp down into the hole. Then Neidelman dropped to his hands and knees and peered inside.

There was a long silence, punctuated only by the distant sound of thunder. At last the captain rose to his feet, staggering slightly. His damp skin was white. Struggling with suppressed emotion, he mopped his face with a handkerchief and nodded to Magnusen.

Magnusen dropped quickly, pressing her face into the hole.

Hatch could hear her involuntary gasp echo up, strangely hollow, from the chamber beneath. Finally she stood up.

Neidelman turned to Hatch. "Now it's your turn. Surely you want to see what we've worked so hard for."

Hatch took a deep breath. "Captain, there's a Geiger counter in my office. I'm not asking you to believe without seeing—"

Neidelman slapped him across the jaw. The pain to his mouth and ear was so unbearable that Hatch sank to his knees. Then Streeter grabbed him by the hair and twisted his head down into the opening.

Hatch blinked as he struggled to comprehend. The metal chamber was about ten feet square, the iron walls furred with rust. As he stared, Hatch forgot Neidelman, forgot everything.

He could see the treasure had once been carefully wrapped and stored by Ockham and his men. But time had taken its toll. The leather sacks had rotted and split, pouring out streams of gold and silver coins. From the wormy, sprung staves of casks spilled great uncut emeralds, rubies, sapphires, carved amethysts, pearls, and everywhere the rainbows of diamonds. Against one wall lay bundles of elephant tusks, narwhal horns, and boar's ivory.

Along one wall rose a stack of small wooden crates. The sides of the topmost crates had fallen away, and Hatch could see hundreds of rough gold bars stacked back to back. Ranged along the fourth wall were more crates, some of which had broken open, revealing ecclesiastical treasures: gold crosses encrusted with pearls and gemstones, elaborately decorated gold chalices.

Atop the center of this hoard was a long, lead coffin, the golden image of an unsheathed sword etched into its lid. It was strapped with iron bands that anchored it to the vault's floor. A massive brass lock was attached to its top.

Then Hatch was jerked to his feet, and the wondrous, nightmarish sight was gone.

"Get everything ready on the surface," Neidelman was saying. "Sandra will winch the treasure up in the bucket. Two trailers are attached to the ATV, correct? We should be able to get the bulk of the treasure out to the *Griffin* in half a dozen trips."

"And what do I do with him?" Streeter asked.

"Put him where we found his brother," Neidelman said. "And Mr. Streeter—"

Streeter paused in turning Hatch toward the ladder.

"You said there's a chance Isobel Bonterre survived. Eliminate that chance, if you please."

As Isobel clambered cautiously up to the observation post, Rankin turned and saw her.

"Isobel!" he cried, coming forward. "You're soaked. And hey, what's this? Your face is all bloody! What happened?"

"I will explain later," she said, stripping off her wet slicker. "Have you seen Malin?"

"Dr. Hatch?" Rankin asked. "Nope. Things have gotten pretty weird around here. The digging crew reached the iron plate over the treasure chamber around seven. Neidelman sent them home because of the storm. Then he called me up here to relieve Magnusen and monitor the major systems. Only most everything is down. The backup batteries can't support the whole load. Communications have been out since lightning trashed the uplink. They're on their own down there."

Isobel stared down through the glass porthole into the Water Pit. "So who's down there?" she asked.

"Just Neidelman and Magnusen, far as I know."

"How about Streeter?"

"Haven't seen him."

"Has Neidelman broached the chamber?"

"I lost the video feeds. All I got left are the instruments . . ."

His voice died as they became aware of a faint vibration.

"What the devil?" said Rankin, staring at the sonar screen.

"What is it?" Isobel asked.

"How should I know? Probably some tunnel caving in."

"Look, Roger, I need your help." Isobel held the nylon bag up and unzipped it. "Ever seen one of these?"

"A Radmeter?" Rankin said. "Yeah, where'd you get it?"

"You know how to work it?"

"More or less," he said. Clicking it on, he typed a few instructions on the miniature keyboard, and a grid appeared on the small screen. "You aim this detector," he went on, moving a microphonelike device, "and it traces a color-coded map of the radioactive source on the screen. Blues and greens are for the lowest-level radiation, then up through the spectrum. White's the hottest. Hmmm, this thing seems to be on the fritz." The screen was streaked with dashes and spots of blue. "Just like everything else around here."

"The machine is working just fine," said Isobel evenly. "It is picking up radiation from St. Michael's Sword."

Rankin glanced at her, squinting his eyes. "You're jiving me."

"I do not jive. The radioactivity has been the cause of all our problems." She quickly explained.

Rankin nodded suddenly. "I guess it's the only answer that explains everything. I wonder—"

"We do not have time for speculation," interrupted Isobel sharply. "Neidelman cannot be allowed to open the casket."

"Yes," said Rankin slowly, still thinking. "Yes, it would have to be extremely radioactive to be leaking all the way to the surface. It could fry us all."

AT THE base of the Water Pit, Neidelman hooked his lifeline to the ladder and lowered himself through the hole. He landed next to the sword casket, gazing at it almost reverentially, blind to the dazzling wealth that filled the chamber. It was about five feet long and two feet wide, the sides made of engraved lead, the edges decorated with elaborate goldwork.

Neidelman reached out and touched the fine metalwork, surprised to find it almost warm. Over the years no day passed in which he hadn't imagined this moment.

He placed his hands on the iron bands that surrounded the casket. To free the chest, he would have to cut through the bands with the torch. Odd, he thought, that the bands went through slots in the iron floor and seemed to be attached to something below.

The sound of loud breathing disturbed his thoughts. He looked up to see Magnusen peering down through the opening.

"Bring down the torch," he told her.

In less than a minute Magnusen landed heavily beside him. Handing him the acetylene cylinder, she stared at the riches, then picked up a fistful of gold doubloons, letting them slide through her fingers.

As he reached for the acetylene cylinder, Neidelman wrapped his fingers around the thick brass lock that held the box shut. It was an ugly piece of work, heavy-looking and stamped with unbroken ducal seals. So Ockham never opened his greatest treasure, he thought. Strange.

That honor would be reserved for him.

Neidelman twisted the cylinder's stopcock and struck the sparker. There was a small pop, and an intense pinpoint of white appeared at the end of the nozzle.

Carefully he brought the flame to the metal.

HALF conscious, Hatch lay on the bottom of the small stone well of the chamber where Wopner had died. Above, he could hear rattling as Streeter drew the collapsible ladder up the shaft. Then silence fell upon him.

Streeter hadn't even bothered to bind his arms. He knew there was no way to climb thirty feet up the slippery sides of the well back to the vaulted room. Two hours, maybe three, and the treasure would be out of the pit and safely stowed aboard the *Griffin*. Then Neidelman would simply collapse the cofferdam. Water would rush back to flood the pit, the tunnels and chambers . . . the well.

Hatch rolled toward the side of the well, where he could sit up and rest his back against the cold stone. He tried to tell himself that nothing was hopeless. Johnny's bones had ended up in this chamber: That meant the shore tunnel had to be nearby. He would systematically explore the cavity with his hands, every square inch.

He forced himself to his feet. His fingers explored every crevasse, every protuberance. The first quadrant yielded nothing but smooth stones, well mortised. Five minutes went by, then ten, and then he was on his hands and knees, feeling around the floor of the chamber.

Soon he had scanned every reachable spot in the well, and there was nothing, not a thing, that indicated an avenue of escape.

He yelled out for help, first tentatively, then more loudly. As he yelled, some last hidden chink of armor loosened within him. The bad air, the blackness, the peculiar smell of the pit, all conspired to tear away the one remaining veil from that terrible day, thirty-one years before. Suddenly the buried memories burned their way back, and he was once again in that tunnel, match sputtering in his hand, as a strange dragging sound took Johnny away from him forever.

And there, in the thick dark, Hatch's yells turned to screams.

"WHAT is it?" Isobel asked again.

Rankin held up his hand for silence. His head was mere inches from the screen, bathed in an amber glow.

"Jeez," he said quietly. "There it is, all right. Look at that."

Isobel stared at the screen, a snarl of jittery lines underlaid by a large black stripe.

"That black is a void underneath the Water Pit," Rankin said.

"A void?"

"A huge cavern, probably filled with water. I wasn't able to get a clear reading before. But now . . ."

Isobel frowned.

"Don't you understand? It's a *cavern!* We never bothered to look *deeper* than the Water Pit. The treasure chamber, the pit itself—us, too—we're all sitting on top of a piercement dome."

"Is this something else built by Macallan?"

"No, it's natural. Macallan *used* it. A piercement dome is an upfold in the earth's crust." He placed his hands together as if in prayer, then pushed one of them toward the ceiling. "It splits the rock above it, creating a web of fractures and usually a huge cavern that goes deep into the earth. That vibration earlier . . . something was obviously happening in the dome."

Isobel jumped as the Radmeter in her hands suddenly chirped. The shimmering screen turned yellow. Then a message appeared:

DANGEROUS RADIATION LEVELS DETECTED, 240.8 RADS/HOUR
GENERAL RADIATION CONTAMINATION POSSIBLE
RECOMMENDATION: IMMEDIATE EVACUATION

"It's too late. He's opened the casket," said Isobel.

"Let's see if we can get a signature on the source." The geologist began typing again. He was interrupted by a thump on the observation deck. The door flew open, and Streeter stepped in.

"Hey, Lyle," Rankin said before seeing the handgun.

"Come on," Streeter said, motioning the gun toward the door.

"Come on where?" Rankin began. "What's with the gun?"

"We're taking a little trip, just the three of us," Streeter answered. He nodded in the direction of the observation porthole.

Isobel slipped the Radmeter beneath her sweater.

"You mean, into the pit?" Rankin asked. "It's dangerous down there! The whole thing's suspended over—"

Streeter fired the gun at Rankin's right hand.

The sound of the explosion was shockingly loud. "That leaves you one hand to hold on with," Streeter said.

With a gasp of pain Rankin hauled himself to the door.

"Now you," Streeter said, nodding at Isobel. Slowly she began to follow Rankin.

"Be very careful," Streeter said. "It's a long way down."

HATCH leaned against the wall of the chamber, his throat raw from shouting. The air was a suffocating, foul-smelling blanket, and he shook his head, trying to clear the faint but insistent sound of his brother's voice. "Where are you? Where are you?"

He sank to his knees, dragging his cheek along the stone, trying to bring some clarity to his mind. The voice persisted. Hatch drew his face away from the wall, listening now. The voice came again.

"Hello?" he called back tentatively.

"Where are you?" came the muffled cry. "Are you all right?"

The sound seemed to be coming from behind the stone that had pressed his brother's bones into the stone floor.

"No! I'm not all right!" cried Hatch. "I'm trapped!"

"How can I help?" he realized the voice was asking.

Hatch rested, thinking how he should reply.

"Where are you?" he asked at last.

"In a tunnel," the voice said. "It leads in from the shore. My boat was wrecked, but I was saved. Saved by a miracle."

There was only one tunnel he could mean: Johnny's tunnel.

"Wait!" Hatch cried, forcing himself to relive the memory.

There'd been a door with a seal in front of it. Johnny had broken the seal and stepped through. A puff of wind from the tunnel beyond, blowing out the light. . . . Johnny had cried out in surprise and pain. . . . There'd been a dragging sound. . . .

Hatch trembled, overwhelmed by the force of the memories.

By opening the door, Johnny had triggered Macallan's trap. A massive slab of stone moved across the tunnel, crushing Johnny beneath, sealing off the rest of the watertight tunnel.

The tunnel he and Johnny discovered must have been Red Ned Ockham's secret entrance, the one Macallan had constructed for him. But if a treasure hunter were to find the shore tunnel, Macallan needed a way to stop him. The trap that killed Johnny was his answer. A massive dressed stone rolling in from one side, crushing any intruder who did not know how to disarm the trap.

Hatch struggled to keep his mind focused. That meant once the pit was drained, Ockham would have needed a way to reset the trap and continue down the tunnel to reclaim his loot.

So the trap had to work on a simple fulcrum mechanism, the stone delicately poised so that the slightest pressure would cause it to move . . . the pressure of a child's weight.

"Hey!" he cried out. "Do you have a light?"

"A flashlight, yes."

"Look around. Tell me what you see."

There was a pause. "I'm at the end of a tunnel. There's solid stone on all three sides. Big slabs."

"Any chinks or depressions? Anything?"

"No, nothing."

Hatch strained to draw in more air. "What about the floor?"

"It's covered in mud. Can't see it all that well."

"Clear it away."

Hatch waited.

"It's tiled in stone," came the voice.

A glimmer of hope rose within Hatch. "Look closely. Does any piece look different from the rest?"

"No."

Hope slipped away. Hatch held his head in his hands.

"Wait. There is something. There's a stone in the center, here, that's not square. It's tapered slightly, almost like a keyhole. At least I think it is. There's not much of a difference."

Hatch looked up. "Can you lift it away from the others?"

"Let me try." Very faintly Hatch thought he could hear the sound of scratching.

"Okay!" the voice said, a thin tone of excitement carrying through the intervening rock. "I'm lifting it now." A pause. "There's some kind of mechanism in a cavity underneath—a wooden stick, almost like a lever or something."

That must be the fulcrum handle. "Can you pull it up?"

"No," came the voice after a moment. "It's stuck fast."

"Try again!" Hatch called out drowsily.

And then suddenly there was a light and a voice, and Hatch felt himself slip and fall. He breathed in air, faintly perfumed with the smell of the sea. He seemed to have fallen into a larger tunnel as the slab that crushed his brother rolled back. He tried to speak but could only croak. He gazed up into the light, trying to focus his blurry eyes, and saw the Reverend Woody Clay staring back at him.

"You!" said Clay, disappointment huge in his voice. He stepped closer, standing in the low doorway. "What is this place? And what are you doing here?" He peered around, shining the light into the chamber.

"This is the tunnel that killed my brother."

Clay's eyes widened. "Oh," he said. "I'm very sorry."

A series of racking coughs seized Hatch. "Captain Neidelman's in the treasure chamber. We have to stop him. He's about to open the casket that contains St. Michael's Sword."

A look of suspicion darted across the minister's face.

"I've learned the sword is, in fact, deadly. It's radioactive. It could kill us all, and half of Stormhaven, if it ever gets out."

Clay's expression began to brighten, as if his face were suffused with inward light. "I think I'm beginning to understand," he said, almost to himself.

"Neidelman sent a man to kill me," Hatch said. "He's become unhinged."

"Yes," said Clay, suddenly fervent. "Yes, of course he has."

"All we can hope now is that we're not too late," Hatch gasped, staggering to his feet.

"Rest easy, Johnny," he said under his breath. Then he led the way, the Reverend Woody Clay following closely behind.

GERARD Neidelman knelt before the casket for what seemed an infinity. The lock had been broken. The sword was his. He inhaled slowly; then, with reverential slowness, he opened the lid.

The sword lay on perfumed velvet. He placed his hand on the hilt, his fingers sliding smoothly between the beaten-gold basket and grip. The blade itself was sheathed in a gem-encrusted scabbard.

He raised the scabbarded sword—noting its heaviness with astonishment—and brought it carefully into the light.

The scabbard and hilt were of Byzantine workmanship, fashioned of heavy gold, dating to perhaps the eighth or ninth century—an exceedingly rare rapierlike design. The face of the scabbard was thick with cabochon sapphires of a depth, color, and clarity that seemed impossible. The hilt sported four astonishing rubies. Embedded at the bottom of the pommel was a great double-star ruby that had no equal on earth.

Decorating the grip and counterguard was a dazzling array of sapphires in a rainbow of colors—blacks, midnight blues, whites, greens, pinks, and yellows, every one perfect. Such an object had never existed before, nor could it exist again.

Neidelman could see that his vision of the sword had not been misplaced. If anything, he had underestimated it.

Now at last, the moment had come. The blade. Grasping the hilt in his right hand and the scabbard in his left, he began to draw out the sword with exquisite slowness.

The flood of intense pleasure changed first to perplexity, then shock. What emerged from the scabbard was a pitted, deformed piece of metal. It was scaly and mottled, oxidized to a strange, purplish black color. He held it upright, gazing at the misshapen blade—indeed, the word "blade" hardly described it at all.

He reached out and stroked the rough metal, wondering at its curious warmth. Perhaps the sword had been caught in a fire and melted, then refitted with a new hilt. But what kind of fire would do this? And what kind of metal was it? Iron rusted orange, and silver turned black. And it was far too heavy to be tin or any of the baser metals. What metal oxidized purple?

He carefully slid the blade back into its scabbard, glancing over at the casket as he did so. He would bring it to the surface, as well; the casket had its own importance, bound up inseparably with the sword's history. Looking over his shoulder, he was pleased to see that Magnusen had at last lowered the bucket into the chamber and was slowly loading it with sacks of coins.

He returned his attention to the casket and the one iron band that remained, rusted in place around one side. It was a strange way to strap down such a casket. Surely it would have been easier to bolt the straps to the floor of the treasure chamber instead of running them underneath. What were they attached to below?

He backed up and kicked the last iron band, freeing the casket.

The band broke away and shot down through the hole with amazing force, as if it had been attached to a great weight.

Suddenly there was a shudder, and the treasure chamber gave a great lurch. The right end of the floor dropped sickeningly, like an airplane plunging in violent turbulence. Rotten crates and kegs tumbled from the wall, showering gemstones and pearls. Stacks of gold bars toppled in a great crash. Neidelman was thrown against the casket, and he reached out for the hilt of the sword, ears ringing with Magnusen's screams, his eyes wide with astonishment.

THE lift's motor whined as it sank into the pit. Gun in hand, Streeter forced Rankin and Isobel close to the edge.

"Lyle, you *must* listen," Isobel pleaded. "Roger says the pit and the treasure chamber are built on top of—"

"You can tell Hatch about it," said Streeter. "If he's still alive."

"What have you done with him?"

Streeter raised the barrel. "I know what you were planning."

"*Mon Dieu,* you are just as paranoid as Gerard!"

"Shut up. I knew Hatch couldn't be trusted from the moment I set eyes on him. And time proved me right."

"You're insane," Rankin snapped, holding his wounded hand. The great bear of a man, usually affable and easygoing, was enraged. "Don't you get it? That treasure's been soaking up radiation for hundreds of years. It's no good to anyone. The sword's gonna kill us all."

"Poppycock!" Streeter said.

"I saw the readings! The levels of radiation coming from that casket are unbelievable."

"That sword's at least five hundred years old," Streeter said. "Nothing on earth is that naturally radioactive."

"Nothing on earth. Exactly." Rankin leaned forward. "That sword was made from a bloody meteorite."

Streeter barked a laugh, shaking his head.

"The Radmeter picked up the emission signature of iridium-80. Extremely radioactive." Rankin winced with pain as his shattered hand grazed the platform. "Iridium is rare on earth but common in nickel-iron meteorites."

"Streeter, you must let us speak to the captain," Isobel said.

"That's not going to happen. That treasure belongs to the captain, not some hairy gorilla geologist who joined the team three months ago. Or a French whore. It's his, all of it."

Raw anger flared in Rankin's eyes. "You know what?" he said. "The captain doesn't give a damn about you. You're even more dispensable now than you were back in Nam. All he cares about is his precious treasure. You're history."

Streeter whipped the gun to Rankin's face.

"Go ahead," Rankin said. "Do me and get it over with."

Suddenly a rumble roared up from the depths. It was followed by a jarring blow that threw them all down on the platform. The entire structure was shaking violently, titanium struts screeching. Beneath it all was the demonic roar of rushing water.

The lift lurched to a shrieking halt.

"It's begun," Rankin cried hoarsely. "The pit's collapsing into the piercement dome. Perfect timing."

"Shut up and jump down." Streeter waved his gun at the hundred-foot platform, silhouetted a few feet below the lift.

Another jolt shook the lift, canting it crazily.

"Timing?" Isobel shouted. "This is no coincidence. *This* is Macallan's final trap."

"I said, shut up." Streeter shoved her off the lift, and she tumbled, landing hard on the platform. She looked up, shaken but unhurt, to see Streeter kicking Rankin over the edge. He landed heavily beside her. Isobel moved to help, but Streeter was already clambering down to the platform.

"Don't touch him," Streeter said. "We're going in there."

Isobel looked over. The bridge from the ladder array to the Wopner tunnel was trembling. As she stared, the emergency lighting went out and the web of struts plunged into darkness.

Then she saw a faint light descending quickly down the ladder.

"Who's there?" Streeter called up.

The light kept coming.

"You up there!" Streeter called. "Show your face!"

A muffled voice came down, faint and unintelligible. The light came closer. Then it snapped off.

"Whoever it is," Streeter roared, "I'm going to—"

There was a sudden rush from the other side of the platform. Streeter spun around and fired, and in the flare Isobel could see Hatch slamming his fist into Streeter's gut.

Streeter staggered backward on the metal platform, and Hatch came quickly after, punching him twice more, hard, in the face.

Grunting in surprise and pain, Streeter lifted his gun. Hatch froze, his fist hanging in midair, staring at the dim line of the gun barrel. Streeter looked into his eyes and smiled, blood from his nose staining his teeth a dull crimson.

Then he lurched to one side. Rankin had risen up and was butting Streeter toward the edge of the bridge. Streeter regained his balance, turned the gun on Rankin, and fired point-blank.

The geologist jerked back, then slumped to the floor.

Instantly Hatch stepped forward, shoving hard with both hands. The railing gave, and Streeter toppled into space, scrabbling frantically. There was a gasp of surprise or pain; then, more distantly, a smacking sound came from far below.

There was a grunt; the flashlight beam flared wildly; then Woody Clay heaved himself over onto the hundred-foot platform. He had come down slowly from above as a decoy while Hatch had clambered quickly down the backside of the array to surprise Streeter.

Hatch was crushing Isobel to him. "Thank goodness. I thought you were dead."

They were interrupted by a sudden crash. Moments later a large titanium spar came hurtling past them. The entire array quivered along its hundred-and-fifty-foot length. Hatch pushed Isobel and Clay across the shaking metal bridge into the nearby tunnel.

"What's going on?" Hatch panted.

"Gerard has opened the casket," Isobel said. "He must have set off the final trap."

NEIDELMAN WATCHED, paralyzed with shock, as a series of violent tremors shook the treasure chamber. Magnusen, thrown down, now lay partly buried in a great mass of coins, thrashing and clawing.

The shifting of the casket beneath him shook Neidelman from his paralysis. He shoved the sword into his harness and reached for his lifeline just as another terrible lurch came.

Suddenly there was a screech of tearing iron as the seam along the edge of the floor split open. Neidelman watched in horror as the masses of loose gold poured through the opening.

"No, no!" Magnusen cried, grasping the gold to her. A hailstorm of golden ingots buried themselves around her. As the weight of the gold became greater, Magnusen was sucked into the widening crack, her cries of "no, no, no" drowned by the roar of metal.

And then Magnusen disappeared into the shimmering golden stream, down into the void.

Abandoning the lifeline, Neidelman managed to scramble up the pile of gold and grasp the dangling bucket. Hoisting himself inside, he punched a button in the electrical box. The winch whined, and the bucket began to ascend just as a great tremor shook the shaft. Dirt and sand rained down, and the titanium bracings above gave a howl of protest. There was a flicker, and the emergency lights failed. The bucket came to a wrenching stop just below the ladder array.

Making sure the sword was secure, Neidelman lunged upward with desperate strength, grabbing the first rung, then the second, his feet dangling over the ruinous chasm.

As he hung from the array, gasping for air, a black rage crept over his features and his mouth opened, wailing even over the roar of the void beneath him.

"Haaaaatch!"

WHAT are you talking about?" Hatch asked. "What final trap?"

"According to Roger, the Water Pit was built above a formation called a piercement dome," Isobel shouted. "A natural void that goes deep into the earth."

"And we thought bracing the pit would take care of everything." Hatch shook his head. "Macallan was always one step ahead of us."

"These struts are holding the pit together—but not for long."

"In that case, let's get out of here."

Just then a low beeping sounded from beneath Isobel's sweater. She drew out the Radmeter, and handed it to Hatch.

"I got this from your office," she said.

The display was dim—the battery was obviously low—but the message was all too clear:

244.13 RADS/HOUR

GENERAL RADIATION CONTAMINATION PROBABLE

RECOMMENDATION: IMMEDIATE EVACUATION

"Let me see if I can bring the locator up." Hatch began stabbing at the keyboard. "It can't be! Neidelman's on the ladder below us. And he's got the sword." Hatch turned the Radmeter toward Isobel. A ragged patch of white showed on its display. "He must be getting a massive dose from the sword."

"How much of a dose are *we* getting?" she asked.

"We're not in immediate danger. Yet. There's a lot of intervening ground. But the longer we stay, the bigger the dose."

"What are we waiting for?" Isobel hissed. "Let's go!" She began walking toward the array.

Hatch pulled Isobel roughly back into the tunnel.

"We can't go out there," he said. "That sword is so radioactive that even one second's exposure to it gives a lethal dose. Neidelman's out there now, and he's climbing toward us. If we so much as peek out into the main shaft, we're toast."

"Then why is he not dead?"

"He *is* dead. Even massive doses of radiation take time to kill. It's vital that we keep rock and earth between him and us. Let's go back down this tunnel. With luck, he'll climb right past us."

Gesturing for the others to stay back, Hatch crept forward, halting just before the mouth of the shaft. A low-battery alarm began sounding on the Radmeter, and he looked down at the display:

Damn, he thought, it's redlined. They were still within safety limits, shielded by the rock and dirt of the Water Pit. But Neidelman was closer now, and soon—

"Hatch!" came a hoarse voice. "I found Lyle's body."

Hatch said nothing. Could Neidelman know where he was?

"Hatch! I'm coming for you. Do you hear me?"

"Neidelman," he yelled in return. "Stop! That sword is highly radioactive. It's killing you, Captain. Drop the sword!"

"Drop it?" came the answer. "You set this trap. And now you want me to drop the sword? I don't think so."

"What are you talking about?"

"A few well-placed explosives did the trick, right?"

"You're a sick man, Captain," he called out. "You're suffering from cerebral syndrome, the most severe form of radiation poisoning. Feel nauseated? Next will come confusion. Then tremors, loss of coordination, convulsions, death."

There was no answer.

"For God's sake, Neidelman, listen to me!" he cried. "You're going to kill us all with that sword!"

"No," Neidelman said from below. "No, I think I'll use my gun."

Hatch sat up fast. The voice was very close: no more than fifteen feet away. He retreated down the tunnel to the others.

"He'll be here in a few seconds," Hatch told them.

"Is there no way to stop him?" Isobel cried.

Before Hatch could answer, Clay spoke. "Yes, there is," he said. The look on his face was ecstatic, beatific, otherworldly.

"What—?" Hatch began, but Clay had already brushed past him, light in hand. In a flash, Hatch understood.

"Don't do it!" he cried, grabbing for Clay's sleeve.

Clay jerked his arm free and raced to the lip of the tunnel. Then he leaped across the metal bridge to the array and descended quickly out of view.

CLINGING TO THE RUNGS OF the array, Clay climbed down a few feet, then paused to angle his flashlight downward. A great roar was coming from the depths of the pit—the sounds of collapsing caverns and thunderous water, of violent chaos churning in the unguessable depths. The beam settled on the form of Neidelman, perhaps ten feet below.

The captain was toiling painfully up the ladder, his face contorted with effort. Tucked into Neidelman's back harness, Clay saw the flash of a jeweled hilt.

"Well, well," croaked Neidelman. "Why am I not surprised to find the good reverend part of this conspiracy?"

"Toss the sword," Clay said.

Neidelman's answer was to reach into his belt and remove a handgun. Clay ducked as the gun roared.

"Out of my way," Neidelman rasped.

Clay knew he couldn't confront Neidelman on these narrow rungs. A few feet below was a maintenance spar. He put the flashlight into his pocket and used the darkness to descend one rung, then another. The array was trembling more violently now.

He dropped two more rungs in the blackness. A faint flare of reflected lightning showed Neidelman a few feet below him. With a desperate movement Clay dropped another rung and kicked at the captain's hand. There was a clatter as his foot connected and the gun fell away into darkness.

Clay slid onto the spar. Neidelman howled with rage and scrambled up onto the platform. Keeping the frame of the array between them, Clay shone his flashlight at the captain.

Neidelman's face was streaked with sweat and dirt. His skin was frighteningly pallid, eyes sunken. He drew out the sword.

Clay stared at it with a mixture of dread and wonder. The hilt was mesmerizingly beautiful, studded with huge gemstones. But the blade itself was an ugly mottled piece of metal.

"Step aside, Reverend," the captain coughed. "I'm not going to waste my energy with you. I want Hatch."

"Hatch isn't your enemy."

"Did he send you to say that?" Neidelman coughed again, then stared at Clay, eyes glittering.

"You're a dead man," Clay said calmly. "We both are. You can't save your body, but you can save your soul. That sword is a weapon of the devil. Cast it into the depths where it belongs."

"Foolish man," Neidelman hissed, advancing. "Hatch may have cost me the treasure. But I still have *this*."

"It is the instrument of your death," Clay replied evenly.

"No, but it may be the instrument of yours. Now stand aside."

"No," said Clay, clinging to the shaking platform.

"Then die," cried Neidelman, swinging the blade at Clay.

HATCH tossed the now dead Radmeter away and peered out toward the mouth of the tunnel. He waited in an agony of uncertainty, the temptation to creep forward and take a brief look almost overwhelming. But he knew that even an instant's exposure to St. Michael's Sword meant lingering death.

Suddenly the sounds of a struggle erupted. There was a hideous cry followed by a strangled gibbering and the clang of metal. Next came a terrible scream of despair that receded into the roar of the pit.

Hatch crouched, riveted in place by the horrifying sounds. Then a flashlight beam flared upward and stopped, pinpointing the mouth of their tunnel.

Someone was climbing. If Clay had failed, somebody else had to stop Neidelman.

Hatch jumped forward, running toward the mouth of the tunnel. He leaped onto the metal bridge, ready to grab Neidelman.

Three feet down the ladder Clay was struggling upward, his sides heaving, a large gash across one temple. Hatch bent down, hauling him onto the platform as Isobel arrived. Together they helped him into the shelter of the tunnel.

"What happened?" Hatch asked.

"I got the sword," Clay said in a faraway voice. "I threw it into the pit."

"And Neidelman?"

"He . . . he decided to go after it."

There was a silence.

"You saved our lives," Hatch said. "You—" He paused and took a breath. "We'll get you to a hospital—"

"Doctor, don't. Please dignify my death with the truth."

Hatch looked at him a moment. "There's nothing medicine can do except make it less painful."

"I wish there was some way to repay your sacrifice," Isobel said, voice husky.

Clay smiled, a strange smile that seemed partly euphoric. "I knew what I was doing. It wasn't a sacrifice. It was a gift."

He looked at Hatch. "I have one favor to ask you. Can you get me to the mainland in time? I'd like to say good-bye to Claire."

Hatch turned his face away. "I'll do my best," he murmured.

They left the tunnel and crossed the shaking metal catwalk to the array. There was another sickening lurch as they began to climb. The rungs of the ladder grew slick. Nearer the surface the roar of the collapsing pit mingled with the howl of the storm. Rain began to lash their faces, warm after the chill of the tunnel. There was a violent tremor from deep within the pit, and the array gave a shriek as countless supports gave way.

"Go!" Hatch roared, pushing Isobel in front of him. As he turned to follow, he saw with horror the bolts along the central spine of the ladder begin to burst. Another massive tremor and the supports of the observation tower began to buckle above their heads and the ladder array to fold in on itself.

"Look out!" Hatch cried. He reached up, grabbed the bottom of the staging platform, and with Isobel's help managed to haul the minister onto the platform and then to the grassy bank.

Hatch got to his feet. To the south he could see the rising tide pouring through a gap in the cofferdam. A thunderous clang from above spun him around. Freed from its foundations, the observation tower was twisting around and collapsing.

"To the dock!" Hatch shouted.

Supporting Clay between them, Hatch and Isobel ran down the

muddy trail toward Island One. Hatch glanced back to see the observation tower plunging into the pit. Then the crash of a freight train gusted up from below, followed by a roar of water and the snapping of wooden timbers. A cloud of mist shot from the pit and billowed into the night sky.

They moved as quickly as they could to the deserted base camp and the dock beyond. The pier was battered but intact. At its end, the launch from the *Cerberus* bobbed crazily.

In a moment they were aboard. Hatch felt for the key, turned it, and heard himself shout out loud as the engine roared to life.

They cast off and headed out into the storm. "We'll take the *Griffin*," Hatch said, aiming for Neidelman's command boat.

Isobel nodded, hugging her sweater around her.

Alongside the *Griffin*, Hatch secured the launch while Isobel helped Clay on board. As Hatch climbed up behind, lightning tore a jagged path over the island. He watched as an entire section of the cofferdam collapsed. A great wall of water lunged through.

Isobel brought in the anchors as Hatch primed the engines. He glanced toward the rear of the pilothouse. His eyes fell on the large maple table, and he was irresistibly reminded of the last time he'd sat at it. Wopner, Rankin, Magnusen, Streeter, Neidelman . . . now all gone.

His gaze turned to Woody Clay. The minister sat in his chair, gaunt and wraithlike. He returned the gaze, nodding silently.

As Hatch eased the boat out of the lee, a great explosion sounded behind them. Hatch goosed the throttle, moving quickly away from the island.

"*Mon Dieu*," Isobel sighed.

Hatch looked over his shoulder in time to see the second fuel tank explode into a mushroom of fire. Isobel quietly slipped a hand into his.

A third roar came, this time seemingly from the bowels of the island itself. They watched, awestruck, as the entire surface of the island shuddered and liquefied, sending up vast plumes and waterspouts to violate the night.

And then, as quickly as it started, it was over. The island folded in on itself with a wrenching boom as the last section of the coffer-dam gave way. The sea rushed into the open wound and met itself in the middle, rising in a great geyser. In a moment, all that was left was a great boiling patch of sea, worrying a cluster of jagged rocks.

" 'Ye who luste after the key to the Treasure Pitt,' " Isobel murmured, " 'shall find instead the key to the next world.' "

"Yes," Clay said in a weak voice.

"It was a meteorite, you know," she added.

"And the fifth angel sounded," Clay whispered, *"and I saw a star fall from heaven unto the earth: and to him was given the key of the bottomless pit."*

Hatch glanced at the dying minister and was surprised to see him smiling, his sunken eyes luminous. Hatch looked away.

"I forgive you," Clay said. "And I believe I need to ask your forgiveness, as well."

Hatch could only nod.

The minister closed his dark eyes. "I think I'll rest now."

Hatch looked back at the remains of Ragged Island. The fog was rapidly closing in again, enveloping the destruction in a gentle mist. He stared for a long moment.

Then he turned away and aimed the prow of the boat toward Stormhaven harbor.

EPILOGUE

THE North Coast Realty Company had its offices in a small yellow cape on Stormhaven's main square. Hatch sat at a desk in the front window, drinking coffee and staring idly at a bulletin board littered with photographs of properties.

His eyes traveled down the column of photos. MAINE DREAM HOUSE! read one card, burbling with enthusiasm. SUNROOM, BOW

WINDOWS, OCEAN VIEWS, WRAPAROUND TERRACE, WATERFRONT DOCK. $329,000. Underneath was a snapshot of his own house.

"Oh!" Doris Bowditch came bustling up. "There's no reason *that* should still be up there." She plucked the photo from the board and dropped it onto a nearby desk. "I thought you'd made a mistake, not budging from a price as high as all that. But that couple from Manchester didn't bat an eye."

"So you told me," Hatch said, surprised by the regret in his voice. There was no reason for him to stay now, no reason at all. He glanced out the window, past the bay, toward the few jagged upthrusts of rock that marked the remains of Ragged Island. His business—three generations of his family's business—was finished in Stormhaven.

"The closing will be in Manchester," the bright voice of Doris intruded. "Will I see you there?"

Hatch rose, shaking his head. "I think I'll send my lawyer. You'll see that everything's crated and sent to this address?"

Doris peered at the proffered card. "Yes, of course."

Saying good-bye, Hatch stepped outside and walked slowly down the steps to the worn cobbles. He paused a moment, then stepped around his car and pulled open the door.

"Malin!" came a familiar cry.

Turning, Hatch saw St. John lurching toward him at an uneven trot, trying to keep numerous folders beneath his arms.

"Christopher!" he said with pleasure. "I telephoned the inn this morning to say good-bye, but they told me you'd already left."

"I was killing the last few hours at the library," St. John replied. "Thalassa's sending a boat to take the last of us down to Portland. It should be here in the next half hour."

"The Stormhaven library?" Hatch said with a smile. "You have my sympathy."

"Actually, I found the place rather useful. It had just the kind of local history I'll need."

"For what?"

St. John gave his folders a pat. "Why, my monograph on Sir

William Macallan, of course. We've opened up a whole new chapter in Stuart history here."

The basso profundo blast of an air horn shivered the windows of the square, and Hatch looked in time to see a sleek white yacht turn into the channel and approach the pier. "They're early," St. John said, as he held out his hand. "Thank you again, Malin."

"There's nothing to thank me for," Hatch replied, returning the limp shake. "Best of luck to you, Christopher." He watched the historian teeter down the hill toward the dock. Then he stepped into the Jaguar, closed the door, and cranked the motor.

He pulled out into the square and pointed the car's nose south, toward coastal route 1A and Massachusetts. He drove slowly, enjoying the salt air, the play of sun and shade across his face as he passed beneath the ancient oaks that lined the quiet streets.

He approached Isobel Bonterre's bed-and-breakfast and pulled over to the curb. There, balanced on the end post of a white picket fence, sat Isobel. She was wearing a thin leather jacket and a short ivory skirt. A large duffel lay on the sidewalk beside her. She turned toward him, stuck out a thumb, and crossed one leg over the other.

"*Ça va,* sailor?" she called out.

"I'm fine. But I'd watch out if I were you." He nodded toward her tanned thighs. "They still burn scarlet women around here, you know."

She laughed. "Let them try! Your town fathers are fat to the last man. I could outrun them all, even in these heels." She lifted herself from the post, walked over, and knelt by the car, resting her elbows on the passenger window. "What took you so long?"

"Blame Doris the Realtor. She wanted to enjoy every last hard-earned minute of the sale."

"It made no difference." Isobel pretended to pout. "I was busy anyway. Very busy, trying to decide what to do with my share of the treasure."

Hatch smiled. They both knew that nothing had been salvaged from the island, that the treasure could never, ever be reclaimed.

She sighed extravagantly. "Anyway, are you at last ready to drive me out of this *ville horrible?* I am looking forward to noise, dirt, panhandlers, daily newspapers, and Harvard Square."

"Then get in." Hatch reached over and opened the door.

But she remained leaning on the window frame, staring at him quizzically. "You will allow me to buy dinner, yes?"

"Of course."

"And then we shall finally see how you Yankee doctors say good night to young ladies."

Hatch grinned. "I thought we already answered that."

"Ah, but this evening shall be different. This evening will not be spent in Stormhaven. And this evening, I am buying." With a smile, she dug her hand into the pocket of her blouse and pulled out a massive gold doubloon.

Hatch stared in amazement. "Where did you get that?"

Her smile widened. "From your medical hut, *naturellement.* I found it there when I was rooting around for the Radmeter. The first—and last—of the Ragged Island treasure."

"Hand it over."

"Désolée, mon ami." Isobel laughed, holding it away from his reaching fingers. "But finders are keepers. Remember, it was I who dug it up in the first place. Do not worry yourself. It should buy us a great many dinners."

"Get in here," Hatch laughed, dragging her inside the car.

In a moment the Jaguar brought them to the outskirts of town. Hatch had one last glimpse of Stormhaven, a picture postcard of memory caught in his rearview mirror: the harbor, the boats swaying at anchor, the white clapboard houses winking on the hill.

And then, in a flash of reflected sunlight, they were all gone.

DOUGLAS PRESTON AND LINCOLN CHILD

The writing team of Douglas Preston (seated) and Lincoln Child got started one night at the Museum of Natural History in New York City. Preston, a writer at the time for the museum's magazine, was giving an after-hours tour to Child, his nonfiction book editor. Marveling at the dinosaur bones stacked like cordwood, Child said, "You know, this has got to be the scariest building in the world. We should write a novel about it." The result was *The Relic,* which then became a hit movie. *Mount Dragon* and *Reliquary* followed. The team's upcoming novel, *Thunderhead,* will feature archaeologists in the Utah desert. Move over, Indiana Jones.

The Coffin Dancer

Jeffery Deaver

*a*s a master criminalist, Lincoln Rhyme knows what it takes to outsmart a brilliant madman. You put yourself inside the man's head. You think like he thinks, feel what he feels, walk where he walks.

This time, though, Rhyme may have met his match. For when it comes to cunning and deception, the Coffin Dancer is in a league all his own.

Chapter One

WHEN Edward Carney said good-bye to his wife, Percey, he never thought it would be the last time he'd see her.

He climbed into his car, which was parked in a precious space on East Eighty-first Street in Manhattan, and pulled into traffic. Carney, an observant man by nature, noticed a black van parked near their town house. A van with mud-flecked mirrored windows. He glanced at the battered vehicle and recognized the West Virginia plates, realizing he'd seen the van on the street several times in the past few days. But then the traffic in front of him sped up. He caught the end of the yellow light and forgot the van completely. He was soon on the FDR Drive, cruising north.

Twenty minutes later he juggled the car phone and called his wife. He was troubled when she didn't answer. Percey'd been scheduled to make the flight with him—they'd flipped a coin last night for the left-hand seat and she'd won, giving him one of her trademark victory grins. But then she'd wakened at three a.m. with a blinding migraine, the only malady that would ground her. They'd found a substitute copilot, and Percey'd gone back to bed.

Lanky Edward Carney, forty-five years old and still wearing a military hairstyle, cocked his head as he listened to the phone ringing miles away. Their answering machine clicked on, and he returned the phone to the cradle, mildly concerned.

When Ed Carney arrived at the office of Hudson Air Charters, on the grounds of Mamaroneck Regional Airport in Westchester County, a cake awaited to commemorate the company's new contract. As each of the dozen or so employees had a piece, Carney ate a few bites and talked about the flight with Ron Talbot, whose massive belly suggested he loved cake, though he survived mostly on cigarettes and coffee. Wearing the dual hats of operations and business manager, Talbot worried out loud if the shipment would be on time and if they'd priced the job right. Carney handed him the remains of his cake and told him to relax.

He thought again about Percey and stepped away into his office, picking up the phone. Still no answer at their town house. Now concern became worry. People with their own business always pick up a ringing phone. He slapped the receiver down and thought about calling a neighbor to check up on her. But then a large white truck pulled up in front of the hangar next to the office and Tim Randolph, his copilot, arrived. It was six p.m., time to go to work.

Tall, brunette Lauren, Talbot's assistant, had worn her lucky blue dress, whose color matched the Hudson Air logo—a silhouette of a falcon flying over a gridded globe. She leaned close to Carney and whispered, "It'll be okay now, won't it?"

"It'll be fine," he assured her. They embraced for a moment. She offered him some cake for the flight, but he demurred. Ed Carney wanted to be gone. Away from the sentiment, away from the festivities. Away from the ground.

And soon he was. Sailing three miles above the earth, piloting a Lear 35A, the finest private jet ever made, polished silver, sleek as a pike. They flew toward a stunning sunset—a perfect orange disk easing into big, rambunctious clouds, pink and purple, leaking bolts of sunlight.

It was 723 miles to O'Hare Airport, and they covered that distance in less than two hours. O'Hare is the busiest airport in the world, and air-traffic control put them in a holding pattern at eight thousand feet out over the western suburbs of Chicago.

Ten minutes later Carney glanced up at the bright points of constellations in the gunmetal sky and thought, Look, Percey, it's all the stars of evening. And with that, he had what was the only unprofessional urge of perhaps his entire career. His concern for Percey arose like a fever. He needed desperately to speak to her.

"Take the aircraft," he said to Tim.

"Roger," the copilot responded, hands going to the yoke.

Air-traffic control crackled, "Niner Charlie Juliet, descend to four thousand. Maintain heading."

"Roger, Chicago," Tim said. "Out of eight for four."

Carney changed the frequency of his radio to make a unicom call back to company headquarters. When he got Ron Talbot, he asked to be patched through to his home. While he waited, he and Tim went through the pre-landing ritual, checking speed and flaps.

As Tim spoke into his mike—"Chicago, Niner Charlie Juliet, crossing the numbers. Through five for four"—Carney heard the phone start to ring in his home, seven hundred miles away.

Come on, Percey. Pick up. Where are you? Please . . .

Air-traffic control said, "Niner Charlie Juliet, reduce speed to one eight zero. Contact tower. Good evening."

"Roger, Chicago. One eight zero knots. Evening."

Three rings. Where is she? What's wrong?

The knot in his gut grew tighter.

The turbofans sang, a grinding sound. Hydraulics moaned. Static crackled in Carney's headset. And then, at last, a sharp click.

His wife's voice saying, "Hello?"

He laughed out loud in relief. He started to speak, but before he could, the aircraft gave a huge jolt—so vicious that in a fraction of a second the force of the explosion ripped the bulky headset from his ears. Shrapnel and sparks exploded all around.

Stunned, Carney instinctively grabbed the unresponsive yoke with his left hand; he no longer had a right one. He turned toward Tim just as he disappeared out of the gaping hole in the fuselage.

"Oh, please, no, no. . . ."

Then the entire cockpit broke away from the disintegrating plane, leaving the wings and engines behind, engulfed in a ball of gassy fire.

"Oh, Percey," he whispered, "Percey . . ." Though there was no longer a microphone to speak into.

BIG as asteroids, bone-yellow.

The grains of sand glowed on the computer screen. The man was sitting forward, neck aching, eyes in a hard squint.

In the distance, thunder. The early morning sky was yellow and green, and a storm was due. The wettest spring on record.

Grains of sand . . . "Enlarge," he commanded, and dutifully the image on the computer doubled in size.

Strange, he thought. "Cursor down. Stop."

Leaning forward again, straining, studying the screen.

Sand, Lincoln Rhyme reflected, is a criminalist's delight. Bits of rock, it adheres to a perp's clothing like sticky paint and conveniently leaps off at crime scenes to link murderer and murdered. It also can tell a great deal about where a suspect has been. Opaque sand means he's been in the desert. Clear means beaches. Obsidian, Hawaii. Quartz, New England.

But where this particular sand had come from, Rhyme didn't have a clue. Most of the sand in the New York area was quartz and feldspar. Rocky on Long Island Sound, dusty on the Atlantic. But this was white, glistening, ragged, mixed with tiny red spheres and white rings like microscopic slices of calamari. The puzzle had kept Rhyme up till four a.m. He'd just sent a sample to a colleague at the FBI's crime lab in Washington.

Motion at the window. He glanced toward it. His neighbors—two compact peregrine falcons—were about to go hunting in Central Park. Pigeons beware, Rhyme thought, then cocked his head.

Urgent footsteps were on the stairs. Thom had let visitors in, and Rhyme didn't want visitors. He glanced angrily toward the hallway. Two of them—one heavy, one not.

A fast knock on the open door, and they entered. Lon Sellitto was a detective first-grade, NYPD. Beside him was his slimmer, younger partner, Jerry Banks, spiffy in his pork-gray suit of fine plaid, his blond cowlick doused with spray.

The rotund man looked around the second-floor bedroom. "What's different, Linc? About the place?"

"Nothing."

"Oh, hey, I know," Banks said. "It's clean."

"Clean, sure," said Thom, immaculate in ironed tan slacks, white shirt, and the flowery tie that Rhyme thought was pointlessly gaudy, though he himself had bought it, mail order, for the man. The aide had been with Rhyme for several years now, and though he'd been fired by Rhyme twice and quit once, the criminalist had rehired the unflappable nurse-assistant an equal number of times. Thom knew enough about quadriplegia to be a doctor. Rhyme called him, variously, his mother hen or nemesis. Thom maneuvered around the visitors. "He didn't like it, but I hired Molly Maids and got the place scrubbed down. He wouldn't talk to me for a whole day afterward."

"It didn't need to be cleaned. I can't find anything."

"But then he doesn't *have* to find anything, does he?" Thom countered. "That's what *I'm* for."

No mood for banter. "Well?" Rhyme cast his handsome face toward Sellitto. "What?"

"Got a case. Thought you might wanna help."

"I'm busy."

"What's all that?" Banks motioned toward a new computer sitting beside Rhyme's bed.

"Oh," Thom said with infuriating cheer, "he's state-of-the-art now. Show them, Lincoln. Show them."

"I don't *want* to show them."

Thom persisted. "Show them how it works."

"Don't want to," Rhyme snapped.

"He's just embarrassed," the young aide said. "I don't know why he's behaving this way. He seemed very proud of the whole setup the other day."

"Did not." At the moment Lincoln Rhyme was interested only in microscopic rings of sculpted calamari and the sand they nestled in.

Thom continued. "The microphone goes into the computer. Whatever he says, the computer recognizes."

In truth Rhyme was quite pleased with the lightning-fast computer and voice-recognition software. Merely by speaking, he could command the cursor to do whatever a person using a mouse and keyboard could do. He could also turn the heat up or down and the lights on or off, play the stereo or TV, and make phone calls.

"He can even write music," Thom said to the visitors.

"Now that's useful," Rhyme said sourly. "Music."

For a C-4 quad—Rhyme's injury was at the fourth cervical vertebra—nodding was easy. He could also shrug, though not as dismissively as he'd like. His other circus trick was moving his left ring finger a few millimeters in any direction he chose.

"He can play games too," Thom said.

"I hate games. I don't play games."

Sellitto, who reminded Rhyme of a large, unmade bed, gazed at the computer and seemed unimpressed. "Lincoln," he began, "there's a task-forced case. Us 'n' the feds. Ran into a problem."

"Ran into a brick wall," Banks ventured to say.

"We thought you'd want to help us out," said Sellitto.

Want to help them out? "I'm working on something now," Rhyme explained. "For Fred Dellray, in fact." Special Agent Fred Dellray, a longtime veteran with the FBI, was a handler for most of the Manhattan office's undercover agents. Dellray himself had been one of the Bureau's top undercover cops. He'd earned commendations for infiltrating everyplace from Harlem drug lords' headquarters to black militant organizations. "One of Dellray's runners is missing."

"He told us," Banks said. "Pretty weird."

Rhyme rolled his eyes at the unartful phrase, though he couldn't dispute it. Undercover agent Tony Panelli had disappeared from his car across from the Federal Building in downtown Manhattan around nine p.m. a few days earlier. The engine was running, the door open. No blood, no gunshot residue, no witnesses. Pretty weird indeed.

Dellray had a fine crime scene unit at his disposal, including the Bureau's Physical Evidence Response Team. But it had been Rhyme who'd set up PERT, and it was Rhyme whom Dellray had asked to work the scene. The crime scene officer who worked as Rhyme's partner had spent hours at Panelli's car and had come away with no unidentified fingerprints, ten bags of meaningless trace evidence, and—the only possible lead—a few dozen grains of this very odd sand that now glowed on the computer.

Lon Sellitto continued. "They're gonna put other people on the Panelli case, Lincoln. Anyway, I think you'll want this one."

That verb again—want. Rhyme could see that Sellitto was holding back. "Okay, Lon. What is it? Tell me."

Sellitto nodded toward Banks.

"Phillip Hansen," the young detective said significantly.

Rhyme knew the name only from newspaper articles. Hansen— a large, hard-living businessman—owned a wholesale company in Armonk, New York, and he'd become a multimillionaire thanks to it. But the federal government and New York State were expending great energy to shut it down and throw its president in jail, because the product PH Distributors, Inc., sold was not, as he claimed, secondhand military-surplus vehicles but weaponry, often stolen from military bases or imported illegally. Earlier in the year two army privates had been killed when a truckload of small arms was hijacked near the George Washington Bridge on its way to New Jersey. Hansen was behind it—a fact the U.S. Attorney General knew but couldn't prove.

"We're hammering together a case," Sellitto said. "But it's been a bear."

Banks added, "Finally, last week, we got a break. See, Hansen's a pilot. His company's got warehouses at Mamaroneck Airport—that one near White Plains? We checked 'em out. Didn't find anything. But then last week, it's midnight? The airport's closed, but there're some people there working late. Three witnesses see a guy fitting Hansen's description drive out to his private plane, load some big duffel bags, and take off. Unauthorized. No flight plan, just takes off. Comes back forty minutes later, lands, gets back in his car, and burns rubber out of there. No duffel bags."

Rhyme said, "So he knew you were getting close, and he wanted to ditch something linking him to the killings." He was beginning to see why they needed him. "Air-traffic control track him?"

"La Guardia had him for a while. Straight out over Long Island Sound. Then he dropped below radar for ten minutes or so."

"And you drew a line to see how far he could get over the sound. There're divers out?"

"Right. Now, we knew that soon as Hansen heard we had the three witnesses, he was gonna rabbit. So we managed to put him away till Monday. Federal detention."

Rhyme laughed. "What'd Mr. Hansen say to that?"

"Not a word. He knows the drill. Lawyer denies everything and is preparing suit for wrongful arrest, yadda, yadda, yadda. So if we find the bags, we go to the grand jury on Monday and, bang, he's away."

"Provided there's anything incriminating in the bags."

"Oh, there's something incriminating."

"How do you know?"

"Because Hansen's scared. He's hired somebody to kill the witnesses. He's already got one of 'em. Blew up his plane last night outside of Chicago."

And, Rhyme thought, they want me to find the duffel bags. "I'll need maps of the sound," he began. "Drawings of the plane."

"Um, Lincoln, that's not why we're here," Sellitto said.

"Not to find the bags," Banks added.

"No? Then?" Rhyme tossed an irritating tickle of black hair off his forehead and frowned the young man down.

"We want you to help us find the killer. The guy Hansen hired. Stop him before he gets the other two wits."

"And?" Sellitto was still holding something in reserve.

With a glance out the window the detective said, "Looks like it's the Dancer, Lincoln."

"The Coffin Dancer? Are you sure?"

Sellitto nodded. "We heard he'd done a job in D.C. a few weeks ago. Killed a congressional aide mixed up in arms deals. We found calls from a pay phone outside Hansen's house to the hotel where the Dancer was staying. It's gotta be him, Lincoln."

On the screen the grains of sand, big as asteroids, smooth as a woman's shoulders, lost their grip on Rhyme's interest.

"Well," he said softly, "that's a problem now, isn't it?"

Chapter Two

 SHE remembered: Last night, the cricket chirp of the phone intruding on the drizzle outside their bedroom window. She'd looked at it contemptuously, as if Bell Atlantic were responsible for the suffocating pain in her head. Finally she'd rolled to her feet and snagged the receiver on the fourth ring. "Hello?"

Answered by the empty-pipe echo of a unicom radio-to-phone patch. Then a voice, perhaps. A laugh, perhaps.

A huge roar. A click. Silence. No dial tone. Just silence, shrouded by the crashing waves in her ears.

"Hello? Hello?" She'd hung up the phone and fallen asleep again. Until the phone rang a half hour later with the news about Lear Niner Charlie Juliet's going down on approach, carrying her husband and young Tim Randolph to their death.

Now, on this gray morning, Percey Rachael Clay knew that the mysterious phone call had been from her husband. Ron Talbot had explained that he'd patched the call through.

Percey uncorked her silver flask, took a sip. Tears in her eyes.

"Come on, Perce, enough of that, okay?" said the man sitting on the living-room couch. "Please." He pointed to the flask.

"Oh, right," her gravelly voice responded. "Sure." She took another sip. "What the devil was he doing calling me on final approach?"

"Maybe he was worried about your migraine," Brit Hale said.

Like Percey, Hale hadn't slept last night. Talbot had called him too, and Hale had driven down from Bronxville, stayed with her all night, helped her make calls that had to be made. They'd known each other for years. Hale had been one of Hudson Air's first pilots and had worked for free for months until the company turned a profit. Hale resembled a lean, stern schoolteacher, but in reality he was droll and easygoing—the perfect antidote to Percey. He was perhaps her favorite copilot.

"Ah, Brit." She slumped into the couch beside him.

Hale slipped his strong arm around her. She dropped her head to his shoulder. "Be okay, babe," he said. "Promise."

"I've got to call Talbot," she said. "We've got to do something. The company . . ." Ed's death had inflicted a wound in many lives, the airline company's included, and the injury could very well be lethal.

So much to do—but Percey Clay sat paralyzed on the couch. Odd, she thought, as if from a different dimension, I can't move. Oh, Ed.

"You need coffee," Hale announced, heading for the kitchen.

He meant, Lay off the booze. Percey took the hint. She corked the flask and dropped it on the table with a loud clink. "Okay, okay." She rose and paced the living room. She caught sight of herself in the mirror. The pug face. Black hair in tight, stubborn curls. A slight figure and marbles of black eyes that her mother repeatedly said were her finest quality. Meaning her only quality.

A look out the window, past the trees, into the street. She caught sight of the traffic, and something tugged at her mind.

Something unsettling. What? What is it?

The doorbell rang, and the feeling vanished. Percey opened the door and found two burly police officers in the entryway. "NYPD." Showing IDs. "We're here to keep an eye on you until we get to the bottom of what happened to your husband."

"Come in," she said. "Brit Hale's here too."

And it was then that she looked past the cops, into the street, and the elusive thought popped into her mind.

"There's something you should know," she said, and one of the officers took out his notebook. "There was this van, a black van."

"WAIT," Rhyme said.

Lon Sellitto paused in his narration.

Rhyme now heard another set of footsteps approaching. Neither heavy nor light. He knew whose they were. This was not deduction. He'd heard this particular pattern many times.

Amelia Sachs's beautiful face, surrounded by her long red hair, crested the stairs, and Rhyme saw her come into the room. She was in full navy-blue patrol uniform, minus only the cap and tie. She carried a shopping bag.

Jerry Banks flashed her a smile. His crush on her was obvious and only moderately inappropriate—not many officers have a Madison Avenue modeling career behind them, as did tall, striking Amelia Sachs. But the gaze, like the attraction, was not reciprocated.

"Hi, Jerry," she said. To Sellitto she gave a deferential, "Sir."

"You look tired," Sellitto commented.

"Didn't sleep," she said. She pulled a dozen plastic bags out of the shopping bag. "I've been out collecting sand."

"Good," Rhyme said. "But we've been reassigned. Somebody's come to town, and we have to catch him."

"A killer," Sellitto added.

"Pro?" Sachs asked. "OC?"

"Professional, yes," Rhyme said. "No OC connection that we know of." Organized crime was the largest purveyor of for-hire killers in the country. "He's freelance. We call him the Coffin Dancer."

She lifted an eyebrow. "Why?"

"Only one victim's ever got close to him and lived long enough to give us any details. White male, probably in his thirties. He's got a tattoo on his upper arm: the grim reaper dancing with a woman in front of a coffin."

"You traced the tattoo?" Sachs asked.

"Of course," Rhyme said. "To the ends of the earth."

Thom came through the door. "Excuse me, gentlemen and lady," he said. "Work to do." Conversation came to a halt while the young man went through the motions of rotating his boss. This helped clear his lungs. To quadriplegics certain parts of their body become personified; they develop special relationships with them. After his spine was shattered while searching a crime scene some years ago, Rhyme's arms and legs had become his cruelest enemies, and he'd spent desperate energy trying to force them to do what he wanted. But they'd won, no contest, and stayed as still as wood. Then he'd turned to his lungs. Finally, after a year of rehab, he weaned himself off the ventilator. He could breathe on his own. It was his only victory against his body, and he harbored a dark superstition that the lungs were biding their time to get even. He figured he'd die of pneumonia or emphysema in a year or two.

Lincoln Rhyme didn't necessarily mind the idea of dying. But there were too many ways to die; he was determined not to go unpleasantly.

Sachs asked, "Any leads? LKA?"

"Last known address was down in the D.C. area," Sellitto said in his Brooklyn drawl. "That's it. Nothin' else. Oh, we hear about him some. Dellray more'n us, you know. The Dancer—he's like he's ten different people. Ear jobs, facial implants, silicone. Adds scars, removes scars. Gains weight, loses weight. He plans everything. Sets up diversions, then moves in. Real efficient." Sellitto looked strangely uneasy for a man who hunts killers for a living.

Eyes out the window, Rhyme continued. "The Dancer's most recent job in New York was five years ago—Wall Street. Did the hit nice and clean. My crime scene team got to the scene, and one of them lifted a wad of paper out of a trash can. It set off a load of PETN explosive. Both techs were killed; every clue was destroyed."

"I'm sorry," Sachs said. There was an awkward silence between them. She'd been his apprentice and his partner for more than a year and had become his friend too. Had even spent the night here sometimes, sleeping on the couch or even, as chaste as a sibling, in Rhyme's half-ton Clinitron bed. But the talk was forensic. They'd steered clear of personal issues. Now she offered nothing more than, "It must have been hard."

Rhyme deflected the sympathy with a shake of his head. He stared at the empty wall, while within him somewhere deep he felt an empty despair, replaying the horrid crime scene of the explosion.

Sachs asked, "The guy who hired him dimed the Dancer?"

"He was willing to snitch, but there wasn't much he could say." Rhyme inhaled deeply. "He delivered cash with written instructions to a drop box. They never met in person. The worst part was that the banker who paid for the hit changed his mind, but it didn't matter anyway. The Dancer'd told him right up front, 'Recall is not an option.'"

Sellitto briefed Sachs about the case against Phillip Hansen, who'd seen his plane make its run, and about the bomb in the plane.

"Who are the other wits?" she asked.

"Percey Clay, the wife of this pilot killed last night. She's the president of their company, Hudson Air. Her husband was VP. The other wit's Britton Hale, one of their pilots. I sent baby-sitters to keep an eye on them. Fred Dellray's clearing one of the U.S. marshal's witness-protection safe houses for them."

Lincoln Rhyme lost track of what the detective was saying. He was remembering the Dancer's bomb five years ago: The trash can, blown open like a black rose. The choking chemical scent. The seared bodies of his techs.

He was saved from this horrid reverie by the buzz of the fax. Jerry Banks snagged the first sheet. "Crime scene report from the crash."

Rhyme's head snapped toward the machine eagerly. "Time to go to work, boys and girls."

WASH 'em. Wash 'em off.

Soldier, are those hands clean?

Sir, they're getting there, sir.

The solid man, in his mid-thirties, stood in the washroom of a coffee shop on Lexington Avenue, lost in his task.

Scrub, scrub, scrub. Stephen Kall examined his cuticles and big red knuckles. Lookin' clean. No worms. Not a single one.

He'd been feeling fine as he moved the black van off the street and parked it deep in an underground garage. Stephen had taken what tools he needed from the vehicle and climbed the ramp, slipping out onto the busy street. He'd worked in New York before, but he could never get used to all the people.

Makes me feel cringey. Makes me feel *wormy*.

And so he'd stopped here in the men's room for a little scrub.

Soldier, aren't you through with that yet? You've got two targets left to eliminate.

Sir, almost, sir. Have to remove the risk of any trace evidence prior to proceeding with the operation, sir.

The hot water pouring over his hands. Scrubbing with a brush he carried with him in a plastic bag. Squirting the pink soap from the dispenser. And scrubbing some more.

Stephen wore camouflage, though not military. He was in jeans, a work shirt, a gray windbreaker speckled with paint. On his belt were his cell phone and tape measure. He looked like any other Manhattan contractor; no one would think twice about a workman wearing cloth gloves on a spring day.

Walking outside. Still lots of people. But his hands were clean, and he wasn't cringey anymore.

He paused at the corner and looked down the street at the building that had been the Husband and Wife's town house but was the Wife's alone now because the Husband had been neatly blown into a million small pieces over the Land of Lincoln.

So two witnesses were still alive, and they both had to be dead before the grand jury convened on Monday. He glanced at his bulky stainless steel watch. It was nine thirty Saturday morning.

Soldier, is that enough time to get them both?

Sir, I may not get them both now, but I still have nearly forty-eight hours, sir. That is more than sufficient time to locate and neutralize both targets, sir.

There was a squad car in front of the town house, which he'd expected. He started along the sidewalk, his scrubbed hands tingling. The backpack weighed sixty pounds, but he hardly felt it. As he walked, he pictured himself as a local, not as Stephen Kall or any of the dozens of other aliases he'd used over the years.

He turned suddenly and stepped into the doorway of the building opposite the Wife's town house. Stephen pushed open the front door and then looked out at the town house's large front window. He put on a pair of expensive yellow-tinted shooting glasses, and the glare from the window vanished. He could see figures moving around inside.

Stephen bent down and unzipped his backpack.

One cop—no, two cops. A man with his back to the window. Maybe the Friend, the other witness he'd been hired to kill. And yes, there was the Wife. Short. Homely. Boyish. She was wearing a white blouse. It made a good target.

A SITTING transfer into the Storm Arrow wheelchair.

Then Rhyme took over, gripping the plastic straw of the sip-and-puff controller in his mouth. He drove into the tiny elevator, formerly a closet, that carried him down to the first floor of his town house, where Thom and Amelia Sachs were waiting.

In the 1890s, when the place had been built, the room into which he now wheeled had been a parlor off the dining room with fleur-de-lis crown molding and solid oak floors. The combined rooms were now a messy space filled with density-gradient tubes, a gas chromatograph–mass spectrometer, a very expensive electron microscope hooked to an X-ray unit. Here too were the mundane tools of the criminalist's trade: goggles, latex and cut-resistant gloves, beakers, tongs, scalpels, jars, plastic bags, examining trays. A dozen pairs of chopsticks (Rhyme ordered his assistants to lift evidence the way they picked up dim sum at Ming Wa's).

Rhyme steered the sleek candy apple–red Storm Arrow into position beside the worktable. Thom placed the microphone over his head and booted up the computer.

A moment later Sellitto and Banks appeared in the doorway, joined by Fred Dellray, who'd just arrived. He was tall and rangy, with skin dark as tires. He was wearing a green suit and an unearthly yellow shirt.

"Hello, Fred."

"Lincoln. Amelia."

"Hey." Sachs nodded as she entered the room.

Dellray loped across the room, stationed himself beside the window, crossed his lanky arms. No one—Rhyme included—could peg the agent exactly. He lived alone in a small apartment, loved to read literature and philosophy, and loved even more to play pool in tawdry bars. Once the jewel in the crown of the FBI's undercover agents, Fred Dellray had over a thousand arrests to his credit. It was only a matter of time before he'd be recognized by some dealer or warlord and killed. So now he reluctantly ran other undercover agents and CIs—confidential informants.

"So, mah boys tell me we got us the Dancer hisself," the agent muttered, the patois pure Dellray. "The Dancer . . . shoot. Better nail him this time."

"Any details about the hit last night?" Sachs asked.

Sellitto read through the wad of faxes and notes. "Ed Carney took off at six eighteen. Hudson Air had just gotten a new contract to fly—get this—body parts for transplants to hospitals around the Midwest. Hear it's a real competitive business nowadays."

"Cutthroat." Banks smiled at his own joke.

Sellitto continued. "The client was U.S. Medical and Healthcare. Carney had a real tight schedule. Chicago, St. Louis, Memphis, Cleveland, layover in Erie, and back this morning."

"Any passengers?" Rhyme asked.

"Just the cargo," Sellitto muttered. "Everything's routine about the flight. Then about ten minutes out of O'Hare a bomb goes off."

"There an NTSB report?" Rhyme asked.

"Report won't be ready for two, three days."

"Well, we can't wait two or three days," Rhyme griped loudly. A pink scar from the ventilator hose was visible on his throat, but Lincoln Rhyme could shout like a sailor.

"I'll call a buddy in the Windy City," Dellray said. "He owes me. Have 'im ship us whatever they got pronto."

Rhyme nodded. "I want every single bit. We have to have it."

"Well, Linc," Sellitto said, "the plane was a mile up when it blew. The wreckage's scattered over a whole subdivision."

"I don't care," Rhyme said. "Are they still searching?"

Dellray placed a call to the FBI special agent at the site.

"Tell him we need every piece of wreckage that tests positive for explosive. I'm talking nanograms. I want that bomb," Rhyme said.

Dellray relayed this; then he looked up, shook his head. "Scene's released."

"What?" Rhyme snapped. "After twelve hours? Inexcusable."

"They had to get the streets open. He said—"

"Fire trucks!" Rhyme called.

"What?"

"Every fire truck, ambulance, police car responding to the crash. I want all their tires scraped and the trace sent here."

Dellray managed to get a promise from Chicago that the tires of as many emergency vehicles as possible would be scraped.

"Not 'as many as,' " Rhyme called. "All of them."

Dellray rolled his eyes, relayed that information, and hung up.

Suddenly Rhyme cried, "Thom! Thom, where are you?"

The beleaguered aide appeared at the door a moment later. "In the laundry room, that's where."

"Forget laundry. We need a time chart. Write on that chalkboard right there. The big one." Rhyme looked at Sellitto. "When do the witnesses go before the grand jury?"

"Nine on Monday. The van'll pick 'em up at seven."

Rhyme looked at the wall clock. It was now ten a.m. Saturday. "We've got exactly forty-five hours. Thom, write 'Hour one of forty-five.' " He glanced at the others in the room. He saw their eyes flicker uncertainly. "Think I'm being melodramatic?" he asked. "By seven o'clock on Monday morning either we'll've nailed the Dancer or both our witnesses'll be dead. There're no other options."

Thom hesitated, then picked up the chalk and wrote.

The silence was broken by the chirp of Banks's cell phone. He listened, then looked up. "Here's something," he said.

"What?" Rhyme asked.

"Those uniforms guarding Mrs. Clay and the other witness, Britton Hale? Seems Mrs. Clay told them there was a black van she'd never seen before parked on the block outside her town house for the last couple days. Out-of-state plates."

"She get the tag? Or state?"

"No," Banks responded. "She said it was gone for a while last night after her husband left for the airport."

Rhyme's head eased forward. "And?"

"She said it was back this morning. It's gone now."

"Get on the horn to Central!" the criminalist shouted.

A TAXI pulled up in front of the Wife's town house. An elderly woman got out and walked unsteadily to the door.

Soldier, is this an easy shot?

Sir, every shot requires maximum concentration and effort. But sir, I can make this shot and inflict lethal wounds, sir.

The woman climbed up the stairs and disappeared into the lobby. A moment later Stephen saw her appear in the Wife's living room. There was a flash of white—the Wife's blouse. The two of them hugged. Another figure. A cop? No, the Friend. Both targets thirty yards away.

Stephen's beloved Model 40 was in the van. But he wouldn't need the sniper rifle for this shot, only the long-barreled Beretta. He assessed his target, measuring angles of incidence, the window's potential distortion and deflection. The old woman stood directly in front of the window. He'd hit high, and she'd fall, and the Wife and the Friend would instinctively step toward her, presenting a fair target.

Stephen pulled back the slide to cock the weapon. He pushed the door open and blocked it with his foot, looked up and down the street. No one.

Breathe, soldier. Breathe, breathe, breathe.

He held the gun steady as a rock in his supple hands. He began applying imperceptible pressure to the trigger. He stared at the old woman.

Breathe, breathe.

THE elderly woman wiping tears, the Wife behind her.

They were dead, they were—

Soldier!

Stephen froze, relaxed his trigger finger.

Lights! Flashing silently. The turret lights on a police cruiser. Then two more cars, then a dozen, and an Emergency Services Unit van. Converging from both ends of the street.

Safety your weapon, soldier.

Stephen lowered the gun, stepped back into the dim lobby.

Police ran from the cars like spilled water. They spread out along the sidewalk, gazing up at the rooftops. They flung open the doors to the Wife's town house, shattering the glass. Five ESU officers in full tactical gear deployed along the curb. The Wife and the Friend were flung to the floor. The old lady too.

More cars. Stephen Kall, feeling cringey. Wormy. Sweat dotted his palms, and he flexed his fist so the glove would soak it up.

Evacuate, soldier.

With a screwdriver he pried open the lock to the main door and pushed inside, head down, making for the service entrance that led to the alley. He slipped out. Was soon on Lexington Avenue, walking south through the crowds toward the underground garage where he'd parked his van.

More cops. Sir, trouble here, sir.

They'd closed down Lexington Avenue about three blocks south and were setting up a perimeter around the town house, stopping cars, looking over pedestrians, moving door to door. Stephen saw two cops ask a man to step out of his car while they searched a pile of blankets in the back seat. What troubled Stephen was that the man was white and about Stephen's age.

His skin started to crawl. It felt wormy, moist. He felt sweat prickle on his forehead, under his arms. Thinking, They're everywhere. Looking for him, looking at him. From cars. From the street. From windows.

The memory came back again. The face in the window.

He took a deep breath.

It had happened recently. Stephen'd been hired to kill a congressional aide in Washington, D.C. He had waited for four hours, and when the victim arrived at his house in Alexandria, Virginia, Stephen fired a single shot. Hit him, he believed, but the man had fallen out of sight into a courtyard.

Stephen had climbed over a brick wall to find the aide's body. The shot had been fatal.

But something odd had happened. Maybe it was just a fluke, the way the aide had fallen. But it appeared that someone had carefully pulled up his bloody shirt to see the tiny wound.

Stephen had spun around, looking for whoever had done this. Across the courtyard there was an old carriage house, its windows smeared and dirty. In one of those windows he saw—or imagined he saw—a face looking out at him. He couldn't see the man—or woman—clearly. But whoever it was didn't seem particularly scared. They hadn't ducked or tried to run.

A witness. You left a witness, soldier.

Sir, I will eliminate the possibility of identification immediately, sir.

But when Stephen kicked in the door, the carriage house was empty. He stood there and turned around and around in slow, manic circles. Had it been just his imagination? The way his stepfather used to see snipers in the hawk nests of West Virginia oak trees?

Finally he headed back to his hotel in Washington.

Stephen had been shot at and beaten and stabbed. He'd never once been troubled by the faces of his victims, dead or alive. But the face in the window was like a worm crawling up his leg.

Cringey . . . Which was exactly what he felt now, seeing the black, grimy windows overlooking the street he was walking along. He prayed he wouldn't see a face looking out.

The building where he'd parked the van was within the search perimeter. He couldn't drive out without being stopped. He walked quickly back to the garage and pulled open the van door. He ditched the contractor outfit, dressing in blue jeans, work shoes, a black T-shirt, a dark green windbreaker, and a baseball cap. The backpack contained his laptop, several cellular phones, his small-arms weapons, ammunition, his binoculars, tape recorder, tools, and several packages of explosives.

The Model 40 was in a Fender bass guitar case. He set it with the backpack on the garage floor and considered what to do about the van. It was stolen, and Stephen had never touched the vehicle without wearing gloves. He'd removed the secret vehicle identification number and made the license plates himself. Yet he decided to leave it. He exited the garage through the elevator to the building. Once outside, he slipped away in the crowd headed for the subway.

PERCEY Clay pulled away from the detective who pinned her to the floor. Ed's mother lay a few feet away, face frozen in shock. Brit Hale was against the wall, covered by two strong cops.

"I'm sorry, ma'am, Mrs. Clay," one cop said. "We—"

"What's going on?" Hale seemed mystified.

"We got a call from the task force," the detective explained. "They think the man who killed Mr. Carney is now after you two. Mr. Rhyme thinks the killer was driving that black van you saw."

"Well, we have *those* men to guard us," Percey snapped, tossing her head to the cops who'd arrived earlier.

Hale looked outside. "There must be twenty cops out there."

"Away from the window, please," the detective said firmly.

Percey put her arm around Mrs. Carney. "You all right, Mother?"

"What's going on? What is all this?" she asked, bewildered.

"They might be in danger," the officer said. "Mrs. Clay and Mr. Hale here. Because they're witnesses in that Hansen case. We were told to take them to the command post."

Another officer appeared in the doorway. "Street's secure, sir."

"If you'll come with us, please. Both of you."

"What about Ed's mother?" asked Percey.

"Do you live in the area?" the officer asked.

"No. I'm staying with my sister in Saddle River," she answered.

"We'll drive you back there, have a New Jersey trooper stay outside the house. You're not involved in this, so I'm sure there's nothing to worry about."

"Oh, Percey."

The women hugged. "It'll be okay, Mother." Percey struggled to hold back the tears.

"No, it won't," the frail woman said. "It'll never be okay."

An officer led her off to a squad car.

Percey asked the cop beside her, "Where're we going?"

"To see Lincoln Rhyme. We're going to walk out together, an officer on either side of you. Keep your heads down. We're going to walk fast to that van there. See it? You jump in. Don't look out the windows, and get your belts on. We'll be driving fast. Questions?"

Percey opened the flask and took a sip of bourbon. "Yeah. Who the devil is Lincoln Rhyme?"

THOM appeared in Lincoln Rhyme's doorway and motioned someone inside. A trim, crew-cut man in his fifties, Captain Bo Haumann was head of the NYPD's Emergency Services Unit—the police's SWAT team. Grizzled and tendony, Haumann looked like the drill sergeant he'd been in the service.

"It's really him?" he asked. "The Dancer?"

" 'S what we heard," Sellitto said. Dellray gave a nod.

A slight pause. "I've got a couple of 32-E teams dedicated."

The 32-E officers were mostly ex-military and had been relentlessly instructed in full S&S—search and surveillance—procedures as well as assault, sniping, and hostage rescue.

A moment later a slight, balding man wearing very unstylish glasses entered the room. Mel Cooper was the best lab man in IRD, the department's Investigation and Resources Division, which Rhyme used to head. Cooper had never searched a crime scene, never arrested a perp, had probably forgotten how to fire the slim pistol he grudgingly wore on the back of his old leather belt. Cooper had no desire to be anywhere in the world except sitting on a lab stool peering into a microscope.

"Thought I was going to be looking at sand," Cooper said. "But I hear it's the Dancer." There's only one place the word travels faster than on the street, Rhyme reflected, and that's inside the police department itself. "We'll get him this time, Lincoln. We'll get him."

As Banks briefed the newcomers, Rhyme happened to look up. He saw a woman in the doorway, dark eyes scanning the room, taking it all in. Not cautious, not uneasy.

"Mrs. Clay?" he asked. She nodded. A lean man appeared in the doorway beside her. Britton Hale, Rhyme assumed. "Please come in," the criminalist said.

She glanced at Rhyme, then at the wall of forensic equipment near Mel Cooper. "Percey," she said, turning back to Rhyme. "Call me Percey. You're Lincoln Rhyme?"

"That's right. I'm very sorry about your husband."

She nodded briskly, seemed uncomfortable with the sympathy.

He asked the man, "And you're Mr. Hale?"

The lanky pilot nodded and stepped forward to shake hands, then noticed Rhyme's arms were strapped to the wheelchair. "Oh," he muttered, then blushed. He stepped back.

Rhyme introduced them to the rest of the team, except Amelia Sachs, who at his insistence was changing out of her uniform into jeans and a sweatshirt. He'd explained that the Dancer often killed cops as a diversion; he wanted her to look as civilian as possible.

Betrayed by his own body, Rhyme rarely paid attention to the physical qualities in others. But Percey Clay was hard to ignore. She wasn't much over five feet tall, yet she radiated a distilled intensity. Her eyes, black as midnight, were captivating. Only after you managed to look away from them did you notice her face, which was unpretty—pug and tomboyish.

He realized she was studying him too. Seeing Rhyme for the first time, most people blushed red as fruit and forced themselves to stare fixedly at his forehead so their eyes wouldn't drop accidentally to his damaged body. But Percey looked once at his face—handsome with its trim lips and nose, a face younger than its forty-some years—and once at his motionless limbs and torso, then focused on the crip equipment—the glossy Storm Arrow wheelchair, the sip-and-puff controller, the headset, the computer.

Thom entered the room and walked up to Rhyme to take his blood pressure. "Not now," his boss said. "No."

"Yes, now," Thom said, and took the pressure reading. He pulled off the stethoscope. "Not bad. But you need rest."

"Go away," Rhyme grumbled. He turned back to Percey Clay. Because he was a crip, a quad, because he was merely a portion of a human being, visitors often spoke slowly or even addressed him through Thom. Percey spoke to him conversationally.

"You think we're in danger? Brit and me?"

"Oh, you are. Serious danger."

Sachs walked into the room and glanced at Percey and Hale. Rhyme introduced them.

Hale said to the team, "You're going to have guards for Percey, aren't you? Full-time?"

"Sure, you bet," Dellray said.

"Good," Hale said. "And I think you really ought to have a talk with that guy Phillip Hansen."

"A talk?" Sellitto queried. "But he's stonewalled completely."

"Can't you threaten him or something?"

"Doesn't matter," Rhyme said. "There's nothing he could tell us anyway. The Dancer never meets his clients. Never tells them how he's going to do the job."

"The Dancer?" Percey asked.

"That's the name we have for the killer. The Coffin Dancer."

"Well, that's a little spooky," Hale said dubiously.

Percey looked into Rhyme's eyes, nearly as dark as hers. "So what happened to you? You get shot?"

Sachs stirred at these blunt words, but Rhyme said equably, "I was searching a crime scene at a construction site. A beam collapsed. Broke my neck."

"Like that actor Christopher Reeve."

"Yes."

Hale said, "That was tough. But man, he's brave. I think I would've killed myself if that'd happened to me."

Rhyme glanced at Sachs, who caught his eye. He turned back to Percey. "We need your help. We have to figure out how he got that bomb on board. Do you have any idea?"

"None." Percey looked at Hale, who shook his head.

"Where exactly was the plane before it took off?"

"In our hangar. We were outfitting it for the new charter."

"How easy is it to get inside the hangar?" Sellitto asked.

"The past couple days we've had crews there twenty-four hours."

"You know the crew?" Sellitto asked.

"They're like family," Hale said defensively.

Sellitto rolled his eyes at Banks. "We'll take the names anyway if you don't mind. Check 'em out."

"Our office manager will get you a list."

"You'll have to seal the hangar," Rhyme said. "Keep everybody out. Everybody."

"Whoa," Percey said. She looked at Hale. "Foxtrot Bravo?"

He shrugged. "Ron said it'll take another day at least."

Percey sighed. "The Learjet that Ed was flying was the only one outfitted for the charter. There's another flight scheduled for tomorrow night. We'll have to work nonstop to get Foxtrot Bravo, our other plane, ready. I can't risk losing this contract."

Rhyme said, "I'm sorry. This isn't an option."

Percey blinked. "Who are you to give me options?"

"Hold up," Dellray said. "You're not understandin' this bad guy."

"He killed my husband," she said in a flinty voice. "I understand him perfectly. But I'm not being bullied into losing this job."

Rhyme asked calmly, "Can you give us an hour for the search?"

"An hour?" Percey considered this.

Sachs gave a laugh and turned her surprised eyes on her boss. She asked, "Search a hangar in an hour? Come on, Rhyme."

Rhyme kept his eyes on Percey, who said, "I can live with that."

"Rhyme," Sachs protested, "I'll need more time."

"Ah, but you're the best, Amelia," he joshed, which meant the decision had already been made.

"Who can help us up there?" Rhyme asked Percey.

"Ron Talbot. He's our operations manager."

Sachs jotted the name in her watch book. "Should I go now?"

"No," Rhyme responded. "Wait until we have the bomb from the flight. I need you to help me analyze it." He then asked Fred Dellray, "What about the safe house?"

"Oh, we got a place you'll like," the agent said to Percey. "In midtown Manhattan. U.S. marshals use it for the crème de la crème. Only thing is, we need somebody from NYPD for baby-sitting detail. Somebody who knows and appreciates the Dancer."

Everybody was staring at Jerry Banks. "What?" he asked. *"What?"* And tried in vain to pat down his cowlick.

THREES.

Percey Clay, honors engineering major, certified airframe and power plant mechanic and holder of every license the Federal Aviation Administration could bestow on pilots, had no time for superstition. Yet as she drove in a bulletproof van through Central Park on the way to the federal safe house in midtown, she thought of the old adage: Crashes come in threes.

Tragedies too. First, Ed. Now the second sorrow: what she was hearing over the cell phone from Ron Talbot at Hudson Air.

She was sandwiched between Brit Hale and that young detective Jerry Banks. Hale watched her, and Banks looked vigilantly out the window at traffic, passersby, and trees.

"U.S. Med agreed to give us one more shot." Talbot's breath wheezed in and out alarmingly. One of the best pilots she'd ever known, Talbot had been grounded for years because of his precarious health. "I mean, they can cancel the contract. Bombs don't excuse us from performance."

"But they're letting us make the flight tomorrow."

A pause. "Yeah. They are." She heard him light a cigarette.

"Come on, Ron," she snapped. He was inept with bad news.

"It's Foxtrot Bravo," he said reluctantly.

"What about her?"

N695FB was Percey Clay's Learjet. Everyone at Hudson Air Charters knew that November Six Nine Five Foxtrot Bravo was her pet. It was her child. And on the too many nights Ed was gone, just the thought of the aircraft would take the sting out of the loneliness.

Talbot said, "Getting her outfitted—it's going to be tricky."

"Go on."

"All right," he said finally. "Stu quit." Stu Marquard, their chief mechanic. "He's going over to Sikorsky. He already left."

Percey was stunned. To make the Lear 35A ready for the U.S. Medical run, most of the seats had to be stripped out; refrigerated bays had to be installed. This meant major electrical and airframe work. Without Stu Marquard, Percey didn't know how they could finish in time for tomorrow's flight.

"What is it, Perce?" Hale asked, seeing her grimacing face.

"Stu quit," she whispered. "Left his job to work on choppers."

Hale gazed at her in shock. "Today?"

She nodded. Talbot continued. "He's scared, Perce. They know it was a bomb. The cops aren't saying anything, but everybody's nervous. They're asking if we're closing down until this all blows over."

"No, we're not closing," she said firmly. "It's business as usual."

"Look, about Foxtrot Bravo, I can do most of the work myself," said Talbot, a certified airframe mechanic himself.

"Do what you can. But see if you can find another mechanic," she told him. "We'll talk later." She hung up.

It was mystifying to her that Hudson Air could be so busy yet continue to skirt bankruptcy. Like Ed and Brit Hale and the other staff pilots, Percey was constantly working, so why were they constantly broke? The company had nearly gone under last month, but Ed managed to snare the contract from U.S. Medical. Ed had guaranteed delivery of the cargo on time. If Foxtrot Bravo wasn't ready for tomorrow's flight . . . Percey didn't even want to think about it.

As she rode in the police car through Central Park, Percey Clay looked over the early spring growth. Ed had loved the park. He'd run two laps around the reservoir, then return to find her poring over a navigation log or an advanced turbofan repair manual, drinking a Wild Turkey. Grinning, Ed would poke her in the ribs with a strong finger and ask if she could do anything else unhealthy, and at the same time he'd sneak a couple swigs of the bourbon.

She remembered then how he'd bend down and kiss her shoulder. Ed . . . *All the stars of evening.*

Tears filling her eyes, Percey Clay came to a decision. She unfolded the cell phone again.

Chapter Four
. . . Hour 3 of 45

THE siren wailed. Lincoln Rhyme expected to hear the Doppler effect as the emergency vehicle cruised past. But right outside his front door the siren gave a brief chirrup and went silent. A moment later Thom let a young man into the first-floor lab. The Illinois state trooper's blue uniform was wrinkled and sooty. He was carrying two large canvas satchels and a brown folder.

"The bomb!" Rhyme shouted happily. "Here's the bomb!"

The officer, surprised at the odd collection of law enforcers, must have wondered what hit him as Mel Cooper scooped the bags away and Sellitto scrawled a signature on the receipt and chain-of-custody card and shoved them back into his hand. "Thanks. So long. See ya," the detective exhaled.

Thom smiled politely and let the trooper out of the room.

Rhyme called, "Let's go, Sachs. You're standing around."

She offered a cold smile and walked over to Cooper's table.

What was her problem today? An hour was plenty of time to search a scene, if that's what she was upset about. Well, he liked her feisty. "Okay, Thom, to the blackboard. We need to list the evidence. Make some charts. CS-One, Chicago. The first heading."

"C, um, S?"

"Crime scene," the criminalist snapped. "What else?"

The aide picked up the chalk, brushed some dust from his perfect tie and knife-creased slacks, and wrote.

"What do we have, Mel? Sachs, help him."

They began unloading the plastic bags and plastic jars of ash and bits of metal and fiber and wads of plastic. They assembled contents in porcelain trays. The crash site searchers had used roller-mounted magnets, large vacuum cleaners, and fine mesh screens to locate debris from the blast.

Rhyme was an authority on bombs. After the Dancer left his tiny package in the wastebasket on Wall Street, Rhyme had taken it on himself to learn everything he could about explosives. He'd studied with the FBI's elite Explosives Unit.

Sachs poked over the bags. "Doesn't a bomb destroy itself?"

"Nothing's ever completely destroyed, Sachs. Remember that." Though as he wheeled closer and examined the bags, he admitted, "This was a bad one. See those fragments? That pile of aluminum? The metal's shattered, not bent. That means the device had a high detonation rate. But even so, sixty to ninety percent of a bomb survives the blast. Oh, we've got plenty to work with here."

"Plenty?" Dellray snorted a laugh. "Bad as puttin' Humpty-Dumpty together again."

"Ah, but that's not our job, Fred," Rhyme said briskly. "All we need to do is catch the bastard who pushed him off the wall." He wheeled farther down the table. "What's it look like, Mel? I see battery, I see wire, I see timer. What else? Maybe bits of the container or packing?"

"Nothing near the seat of detonation," Cooper said.

"Interesting," Rhyme mused. "How in the world did he ever get it on board? Lon, read me the report from Chicago."

" 'Difficult to determine exact blast location,' " Sellitto read, " 'because of extensive fire and destruction. Site of device seems to be underneath and behind the cockpit.' "

"I wonder if a cargo bay's there. Maybe . . ." Rhyme fell silent.

His head swiveled as he gazed at the evidence. "Wait, wait!" he shouted. "Mel, the aluminum. Put it under a scope."

Cooper had connected the video output of his compound microscope to Rhyme's computer. What Cooper saw, Rhyme could see. The tech began mounting samples of the minuscule bits of debris on slides and running them under the scope.

A moment later Rhyme ordered, "Cursor down. Double-click." The image on his computer screen magnified. "There, look. The skin of the plane was blown inward."

"Inward?" Sachs asked. "The bomb was on the outside?"

"I think so, yes. What about it, Mel?"

"Those rivet heads are all bent inward. It was outside, definitely. And that explains this." The tech, wearing magnifying goggles, was looking over bits of metal as fast as a cowboy counts heads in a herd. "Fragments of ferrous metal. Magnets. Under the aluminum skin there was steel."

"Any hope of prints? Tell me true, Mel."

Cooper's answer was a faint, skeptical laugh. But he scanned the fragments anyway with the PoliLight wand. Nothing was evident except the blast residue. "Not a thing."

"I want to smell it," Rhyme announced. "We know it's high explosive. I want to know what kind."

Sachs brought a bag to Rhyme's chair and opened it. He inhaled. "RDX," he said, recognizing it immediately.

"You thinking C Three or C Four?" Cooper asked.

"Not C Three," Rhyme said, again smelling the explosive as if it were a vintage bordeaux. "No sweet smell. And strange . . . I smell something else. GC it, Mel."

The tech ran the sample through the gas chromatograph–mass spectrometer, which isolated compounds and identified them. Running the information through a database in many cases could determine brand names.

Cooper examined the results. "You're right, Lincoln. It's RDX. Also oil. And—this is weird—starch."

"Starch!" Rhyme cried. "That's what I smelled—guar flour!"

Cooper laughed as those very words popped up on the computer screen. "How'd you know?"

"Because it's military dynamite. You don't see it often."

"Military, huh?" Sellitto said. "Points to Hansen."

The tech mounted samples on his compound scope's stage. The images appeared simultaneously on Rhyme's computer screen. Bits of fiber, wires, scraps, splinters, dust.

He was reminded of a similar image from years ago, though in very different circumstances. Looking through a brass kaleidoscope he'd bought as a birthday present for a friend. Claire Trilling, beautiful and stylish. The two of them had spent an evening sharing a bottle of merlot and trying to guess what kind of exotic crystals were making the astonishing images in the eyepiece. Finally Claire had unscrewed the bottom of the tube, and they'd laughed. Scraps of metal, wood shavings, a broken paper clip, thumbtacks.

Rhyme pushed those memories aside and concentrated on the screen: a fragment of waxed manila paper—what the military dynamite had been wrapped in. Fibers from the detonating cord. An eraser-size piece of carbon from the battery.

"The timer," Rhyme called. "I want to see the timer."

Cooper lifted up a small plastic bag. Inside was the still, cold heart of the bomb, in nearly perfect shape. Ah, your first slipup, Rhyme thought, speaking silently to the Dancer. He'd accidentally placed the timer behind a thick steel lip in the metal housing that held the bomb, which protected it from the blast.

Rhyme strained forward, looking at the bent clockface. "Run everything through ERC."

The FBI's Explosives Reference Collection was the most extensive database on explosive devices in the world. Cooper typed in the timer's model number and manufacturer. His modem whistled and crackled. A few moments later the results came back.

"Not good," Cooper said, grimacing slightly. "No specific profiles match this particular bomb."

Nearly all bombers fall into a pattern when they make their devices; they learn a technique and stick pretty close to it. Given the nature of their product, it's a good idea not to experiment too much. If the parts of the Dancer's bomb matched an earlier bomb in, say, Florida or California, the team might be able to pick up additional clues from those sites. The Dancer's bomb in Wall Street had been different, but then it served a different purpose. If Rhyme knew anything about the Coffin Dancer, it was that he tailored his tools to the job.

"Gets worse?" Rhyme asked, reading Cooper's face.

"The Daiwana Corporation in Seoul sold a hundred and forty-two thousand of them last year. No coding to track shipping."

"Great. Just great."

"This bomb," Dellray said contemptuously. "What kind of people'd our boy have to rub shoulders with to make this?"

Rhyme shook his head. "It's all off-the-shelf stuff, Fred. Except for the explosives and the detonator cord, the Dancer could've gotten everything he needed at Radio Shack."

"But why plant it outside?" Rhyme pondered. "Percey said there were always people around. And why didn't Ed Carney or his co-pilot see it in their walk-around?"

"Because," Sachs said suddenly, "the Dancer couldn't put the bomb on board until he knew who was in the plane."

Rhyme swiveled around to her. "That's it, Sachs! He was watching. He slipped it on somewhere after Carney got on board. You've got to find out where, Sachs. Better get going."

"Only have an hour—well, less now," said cool-eyed Amelia Sachs as she started toward the door.

"One thing," Rhyme said. "The Dancer's a little different from everybody else you've ever been up against." How could he explain it? "With him, what you see isn't necessarily what is."

She cocked an eyebrow, meaning, Get to the point.

"If you see anyone make a move for you, well . . . shoot first."

"What?" She laughed.

"Amelia, worry about yourself first, the crime scene second."

"I'm just CS," she answered, walking through the door. "He's not going to care about me."

INTO the country.

Amelia Sachs sped through a tunnel of spring trees, rocks on one side, a modest cliff on another. A dusting of green, and everywhere the yellow starbursts of forsythia.

Sachs was a city girl, born in Brooklyn General Hospital, and was a lifetime resident of the borough. Nature for her was Prospect Park on Sundays or, on weekday evenings, Long Island forest preserves, where she'd hide her black sharklike Dodge Charger from the patrol cruisers prowling for her and her fellow racers. Now at the wheel of an Investigation and Resources Division's rapid-response vehicle— the crime scene station wagon—she punched the accelerator, passed a van, and made the turnoff to Westchester County.

She was thinking about bombs, about Percey Clay.

And about Lincoln Rhyme.

Something was different about him today. Something significant. They'd been working together for a year now, and the fact was that she found his brilliance exhilarating and intimidating and—an admission she made to no one—extremely sexy.

Which wasn't to say that she could read him perfectly. What was so special to him about this Coffin Dancer case? And working the scene at the hangar in an *hour?* It seemed to Sachs that Rhyme had agreed to that as a favor for Percey. Which was completely unlike him. Rhyme would keep a scene sealed for days if he thought it was necessary.

These questions nagged, and Amelia Sachs didn't like the unanswered questions.

Though she had no more time for speculation. Sachs spun the wheel of the RRV and turned into a wide entrance to the Mamaroneck Regional Airport. A state trooper waved her through.

SACHS pulled latex gloves onto her hands and wound rubber bands around her shoes to make certain her footprints wouldn't be confused with the perp's. Then she hooked up the Motorola walkie-talkie on her hip to a headset and stalk mike.

"I'm here, Rhyme," she announced.

"And where, Sachs," his voice grumbled through the earphone, "is here?"

"At the intersection of taxiways. Between a row of hangars. At Hudson Air I was told it's where Carney's plane would've stopped."

Sachs glanced uneasily at a line of trees in the distance. She felt exposed. The Dancer might be here now—maybe to destroy evidence he'd left behind, maybe to kill a cop and slow down the investigation. *Shoot first.*

She took the PoliLight box and a large suitcase from the back of the RRV. Inside the suitcase were tools of the trade: friction ridge collection equipment, tweezers, brushes, tongs, scissors, a gunshot residue kit.

One, establish the perimeter.

She ran yellow police-line tape around the entire area.

Two, consider range of media cameras and microphones.

"No media. Not yet. Thank you, Lord."

"What's that, Sachs?" Rhyme asked.

"I'm thanking God there're no reporters."

"A fine prayer. But tell me what you're doing."

"Still securing the scene."

Three, determine the perpetrator's entrance and exit routes.

But she didn't have a clue. He could've come from anywhere, driven here in a luggage cart, a gas truck.

Sachs donned goggles and began sweeping the PoliLight wand over the taxiway. She could see flecks and streaks glowing under the eerie yellow-green light. No footprints.

"Sprayed her down last night," a voice called behind her.

Sachs spun around. Several men in coveralls were standing at the yellow tape. She walked up to them cautiously and checked their picture IDs, then shooed them off.

Great. Every bit of trace, every footprint from the Dancer was gone. Into the microphone she said, "They cleaned the taxiway last night, Rhyme. High-pressure water, looks like."

"Oh, no. Well then, get going, Sachs."

Amelia Sachs spent an hour walking the grid, covering the entire area back and forth in one direction, then turning perpendicular. But she found nothing, and reported this to Rhyme.

"Ah, Sachs, I'll bet there's plenty. Just takes a little bit more effort. The Dancer's not like other perps."

Oh, *that* again.

"Sachs," he whispered, "get into him. You know what I mean."

She knew exactly what he meant. Hated the thought. But oh, yes, Sachs knew. The best criminalists moved through the crime scene not as cops tracking down clues but as the perp himself—feeling his desires, lusts, fears. Rhyme had this talent. And though she tried to deny it, Sachs did too.

"Talk to me," Rhyme said, his voice almost seductive. "You're walking where he's walked. You're thinking what he thinks."

An image in her thoughts: night, the lights of the airfield, the sound of planes, the smell of jet exhaust.

"Come on, Amelia. You know Ed Carney's on the plane. You know you have to get the bomb on board. You'll kill *anyone,* you'll do *anything* to get to your goal. You divert attention, you use people. Your deadliest weapon is deception."

She closed her eyes and felt a dark hope, a vigilance, a hunt lust.

He continued softly. "Where are you hiding?"

Eyes open now. "The whole area's empty. The hangars're all boarded up. There are no trucks. No alleys. No nooks."

"What're you thinking?"

Lights everywhere. Stay hidden. Stay down. Nowhere to hide.

She turned back to the only possible place, the hangar beside the taxiway. It had a broken window, boarded up from inside. She approached it slowly. The ground was gravel; no footprints.

"There's a window. Plywood inside. The glass is broken."

"Is it dirty—the glass that's still in the window?"

"Yes, but the edges are clean. The glass was broken recently."

"Right. Push the board. Hard."

It fell inward and hit the floor with a huge bang.

"What was that?" Rhyme shouted. "Sachs, are you all right?"

"Just the plywood." She was spooked by his uneasiness.

She shone her halogen flashlight through the window. "It's empty. A few dusty boxes. There's gravel on the floor."

"That was him!" Rhyme shouted. "He threw gravel inside so he could stand there and not leave footprints. Okay, now search the window, then climb inside. But look for booby traps first. Remember the trash can a few years ago."

Stop it, Rhyme. Stop it.

"It's clean, Rhyme. No traps. I'm searching the window frame." The PoliLight showed nothing other than a faint mark left by a finger in a cotton glove. "No fiber, just the cotton pattern."

"Good. It's *him*, Sachs. It's not logical for someone to break in wearing cotton gloves when there's nothing to steal."

She ran the Dustbuster and bagged the trace. "Okay, Rhyme. I'll have this and the glass and gravel back to you in forty minutes."

She packed the samples carefully into the RRV and sped to Hudson Air. She hurried into Ron Talbot's office. He was talking to a tall man whose back was to the door. Sachs said, "I found where he was, Mr. Talbot. The scene's released. You can have the tower."

Brit Hale turned around. "Hey, Officer. How you doing?"

She started to nod, then stopped. What was he doing here?

She heard a soft crying and looked into the conference room. There was Percey Clay, sitting next to a pretty brunette. The woman was crying, and Percey, resolute in her own sorrow, was trying to comfort her. Jerry Banks sipped coffee by a window, admiring the Learjet parked in the hangar.

No, no, no. . . .

"Rhyme," Sachs shouted into the microphone, "she's here."

"Who?" he asked acerbically. "And *where* is here?"

"Percey. And Hale too. At Hudson Air."

"No. They're supposed to be at the safe house."

"Well, they're not. They're right here in front of me."

"No, no, no!" Rhyme raged. A moment passed. "Ask Banks if they followed evasive-driving procedures."

Jerry Banks, uncomfortable, responded that they hadn't. "She was real insistent they stop here first to find a mechanic."

"Sachs, the Dancer's there someplace. I know he's there."

"How could he be?" Sachs's eyes strayed to the window.

"Keep 'em down," Rhyme said. "I'll have Dellray get an armored van from the Bureau's White Plains field office."

Sachs said, "Jerry, keep them here." She ran to the door and looked out at the airfield. "How, Rhyme? How'll he come at us?"

"I don't have a clue. How secure is the area?"

"Chain-link fence. Troopers at the entrance, checking IDs."

"But they're not checking IDs of police, right?"

Sachs looked at the uniformed officers, recalling how casually they'd waved her through. "Oh, Rhyme, there're a dozen marked cars here. He could be any one of them."

She called a state trooper up to the door, examined him and his ID closely, and decided he was the real article. The trooper did a fast visual of uniforms and detectives and checked with Central Dispatch. No unknowns and no reports of any officers missing.

"But traffic patrol in White Plains found a body in a Dumpster," the trooper said. "Killed about an hour ago. A real mess."

"Ask him if the hands and face were missing," Rhyme said.

"What?"

"Ask him!"

She did. The trooper blinked in surprise and said, "Yes, ma'am, Officer. Well, the hands at least."

Rhyme blurted, "Where's it now? The body?"

She relayed the question.

"In a coroner's bus. They're taking it to the county morgue."

"No," Rhyme said. "Have them get it to you—fast. It's got the answer to how he's going to come at you."

PEOPLE believe that the rifle is the important tool for a sniper, but that's wrong. It's the telescope.

What do we call it, soldier? Do we call it a telescopic sight? Do we call it a scope?

Sir, we do not. It's a telescope. This one is a Redfield three-by-nine variable. There is none better, sir.

The telescope mounted on the Model 40 was twelve and three-quarter inches long and weighed just over twelve ounces. The parallax had been fixed by the optical engineer in the factory so that the crosshairs resting on a man's heart five hundred yards away would not move perceptibly when the sniper's head eased from left to right.

Hidden in a nest of grass three hundred yards from the Hudson Air hangar and office, Stephen cradled the gun. The Model 40, a 7.62-mm NATO rifle, had a rated effective range of a thousand yards, though he had made kills at more than thirteen hundred. Through the scope he scanned Hudson Air. He couldn't see the Wife, but she'd soon be there. Listening to the tape of his phone tap on the Hudson Air office lines, he'd heard her talk to someone named Ron.

Stephen crawled forward until he was on a slight ridge, still hidden by trees and grass but with a better view of the hangar and the office, separated from him by flat grass fields and two runways. It was a glorious kill zone. Wide. Very little cover.

Two people stood outside the front door. One was a county or state trooper. The other was a woman—red hair dipping beneath a baseball cap. Very pretty. She was a cop, plainclothes. He could see the boxy outline of a Glock high on her hip. He lifted his range finder and put the split image on the woman's red hair. He twisted a ring. Three hundred and sixteen yards.

The grass rustled around him. Worms, he thought.

The face in the window. He put the crosshairs on her chest.

Soldier, what is the sniper's motto?

Sir, it is "One chance, one shot, one kill."

The conditions were excellent. The air was humid, which would buoy the slug. He slid back down the knoll and loaded five rounds into the chamber. Then, lying down in his nest, he planted his left elbow on the ground and spot-welded his cheek and right thumb to the stock above the trigger.

It was hard to see inside the offices, but Stephen thought he caught a glimpse of the Wife. Yes, it was her. She was standing behind a big man holding a cigarette. A young blond man in a suit, a badge on his belt, ushered them back out of sight.

Patience. She'll present again. They don't have a clue you're here. You can wait all day. As long as the worms—

Flashing lights again. Into the parking lot sped a county ambulance. The red-haired cop ran toward the vehicle.

Stephen breathed deeply.

AFTER a quick chat with the medic, Sachs climbed up in the back of the ambulance and unzipped the body bag. As she pulled on latex gloves, she said, "There's no ID, Rhyme. Nobody's got a clue as to who it is. Hands removed with a fine-bladed razor knife."

"Is Percey safe? And Hale?"

"They're in the office. Away from the windows."

"Van should be there in ten minutes. What's he wearing?"

"Just skivvies." Sachs studied the poor man's body.

"Tell me about the corpse, COD."

After a brief search she found the cause of death. "Narrow-bladed knife in the back of the skull. He's overweight, big gut. Tan on his arms. He's got untrimmed toenails and a cheap earring. His briefs are Sears, and they've got holes in them."

"Okay, he's looking blue-collar. Workman, deliveryman. Let's think. Why isn't the Dancer ID-proofing the body? If he'd wanted to, he would've taken the teeth. Is there something else he's trying to hide from us?"

"Something on the vic's hands?" Sachs suggested.

"Maybe. Something he couldn't wash off the corpse easily."

"Oil? Grease?"

"Maybe he was delivering jet fuel," Rhyme said.

Sachs looked around the airport. There were dozens of gasoline deliverymen, ground crews, repairmen, construction workers building a new wing on one of the terminals.

"He's a big guy. He was probably sweating today. Maybe he wiped his head or scratched it. Check his scalp, Sachs."

She did. And there she found it. "I see streaks of color. Blue. Bits of white too. It's paint, Rhyme. He's a painting contractor."

"The ID was probably covered with paint, or the Dancer faked it somehow. He's on the field somewhere, Sachs. Get Percey and Hale down on the floor. Put a guard on 'em and get everybody else out looking for the Dancer. SWAT's on its way."

PROBLEMS.

He was watching the red-haired cop in the back of the ambulance. Through the Redfield telescope he couldn't see clearly what she was doing. But he suddenly felt uneasy.

She jumped out of the ambulance, looking around the field.

Something's happening, soldier.

Sir, I am aware of that, sir.

The redhead began shouting orders to other cops. One ran to his car. Then a second. He saw the redhead's wormy eyes scan the grounds. He rested the reticles on her perfect chin.

She paused, and he saw her talking to herself.

No, not herself. She was talking into a headset. The way she'd listen, then nod, it seemed that she was taking orders from someone. Who? he wondered. Someone who's figured out that I'm here. Someone looking for me. Someone who can watch me through windows and disappear instantly.

A chill down his back—he actually shivered—and the reticles of the telescope danced away. When he reacquired the redhead, she was pointing at the painter's van he'd stolen. It was parked two hundred feet from him, in a lot reserved for construction trucks. Whoever she was talking to had discovered how he'd gotten onto the grounds.

The cringey feeling. Slimy worms crawling up his legs.

What should I do? he wondered. *One chance, one shot . . .*

They're so close, the Wife and the Friend. He could finish everything right now. Five seconds was all it would take.

I need to draw them outside into the kill zone. No time. Think.

If you want a doe, endanger the calf.

Stephen breathed slowly. In, out, in, out. He drew his target. Began applying pressure to the trigger.

The ka-boom rolled over the field, and all the cops hit the ground, drawing their weapons. Another shot, and a second puff of smoke flew from a tail-mounted engine on the jet in the hangar.

The redheaded cop was crouching, scanning for location, pointing a stubby Glock in front of her. Take her out?

Negative, soldier. Stay fixed on your target.

He fired again. Another tiny chunk out of the airplane.

Suddenly there she was—the Wife—forcing her way through the office door, grappling with the young blond cop, who tried to hold her back. No target yet. Keep her coming.

Squeeze. Another shot. A windshield in the cockpit exploded.

The Wife, her face horrified, broke free and ran toward the hangar to close the doors, to protect her child.

Reload. He laid the reticles on her chest. The gun fired just as the blond cop tackled her, and they went down below a slight dip in the earth. A miss. Stay calm, he told himself.

He heard several fast pistol shots. He looked back at the redhead. She was looking for his muzzle flash, squinting as she gazed.

Stephen closed the bolt of the Model 40.

AMELIA Sachs saw a faint glimmer, and she knew where the Coffin Dancer was. His telescopic sight had caught the reflected glint of the pale clouds overhead.

"Over there," she cried, pointing, to two cops huddling in their cruiser. A small grove of trees about three hundred yards away. The troopers took off, skidding behind a nearby hangar to flank him.

"Sachs," Rhyme called through her headset, "what's—"

"Percey. He's shooting to draw her out."

"You stay down, Sachs. Stay down!"

Sachs felt the quiver of panic run down her back. "Percey!" she cried. The woman had broken free from Jerry Banks and rolled to her feet. She was speeding toward the hangar door. "No!"

Sachs's eyes were on the spot where she'd seen the flare of the Dancer's scope. Too far, it's too far, she thought. I can't hit anything at that distance.

If you stay calm, you can. You've got eleven rounds left.

The Dancer fired again. An instant later a bullet passed within inches of her face. She felt the shock wave and heard the snap as the slug burned the air around her.

She uttered a whimper and dropped to her stomach, cowering.

No. You had a chance to shoot before he rechambered. But it's too late now. He's locked and loaded again.

She looked up fast, lifted her gun, then lost her nerve. Head down, she fired five fast shots. But she might as well have been shooting blanks.

Come on, girl. Get up. Aim and shoot. You got six left and two clips on your belt. Do it!

But the thought of the near miss kept her pinned to the ground. All Sachs had the courage for was to raise her head just far enough to see Jerry Banks catch up with Percey and shove her down behind a generator cart. Almost simultaneously there came the sickening crack of the bullet. Banks spun about like a drunk. On his face a look of surprise, then of bewilderment, then of nothing whatsoever.

Chapter Five
. . . Hour 5 of 45

"WELL?" Rhyme asked.

Lon Sellitto folded up his phone. "They still don't know." The detective's doughy, sweat-dotted face was pale. A legendary homicide investigator, Sellitto was usually unflappable. But at the moment his thoughts seemed miles away, with Jerry Banks in surgery—maybe dying—in a Westchester hospital. It was now two on Saturday afternoon, and Banks had been in the operating room for an hour.

Sellitto, Sachs, Rhyme, and Cooper were on the ground floor of Rhyme's town house, in the lab. Dellray had left to make sure the safe house was ready. FBI agents from White Plains had started south from the airport with Percey and Hale, using evasive-driving techniques. Sachs had worked the new crime scenes: the sniper nest, the painter's van, the Dancer's getaway wheels—a catering van. Then she'd sped back to Manhattan with the evidence.

"What've we got?" Rhyme now asked her and Cooper. "Any rifle slugs?"

Worrying a tattered nail, Sachs explained, "They were explosive rounds." She seemed spooked, eyes flitting like birds. "Here's what's left of one." She prodded a plastic bag.

Cooper spilled the contents into a porcelain examining tray. He stirred them. "Ceramic-tipped slugs. Vests're pointless."

There was a bustle of activity at the door, and Thom let two FBI agents into the room. Behind them were Percey Clay and Brit Hale.

Percey asked Sellitto, "How's he doing?" Her dark eyes saw the coolness that greeted her. Didn't seem fazed. "Jerry, I mean."

Sellitto didn't answer. Rhyme said, "Still in surgery."

Her face was fretted. "I hope he'll be all right."

Amelia Sachs turned and said coldly, "You hope?" Towering over Percey, she stepped closer. The squat woman stood her ground as Sachs continued. "Little late for that, isn't it? You got him shot."

"Hey, Officer," Sellitto said.

Composed, Percey said, "I didn't ask him to run after me."

"You'd be dead if it wasn't for him."

"Maybe. We don't know that. I'm sorry he was hurt. I—"

"And how sorry are you? Sorry enough to give blood? To wheel him around if he can't walk? Give his eulogy if he dies?"

Rhyme snapped, "Amelia, take it easy. It's not her fault. The Dancer outthought us."

Sachs gazed down into Percey's dark eyes. "When you ran into the line of fire, what'd you think Jerry was going to do?"

"Well, I didn't think, okay? I just reacted."

"Officer," Hale said, "she did what any pilot would've done."

"Exactly," Rhyme announced. "That's what I'm saying, Sachs. That's the way the Dancer works."

"This's been real pleasant," Percey said dryly, turning toward the door. "But I've got to get back to the airport."

"What?" Sachs almost gasped. "Are you crazy?"

"Impossible," Sellitto said, emerging from his gloom.

"It was bad enough just trying to get my aircraft outfitted. Now we've got damage to repair. And since it looks like every certified mechanic in Westchester's a coward, I'm going to do it."

"Mrs. Clay," Sellitto began, "not a good idea. You'll be okay in the safe house, but there's no way we can guarantee your safety anywhere else. You stay there until Monday, you'll be—"

"Monday," she blurted. "Oh, no. You don't understand. I'm driving that aircraft tomorrow night, a charter for U.S. Medical."

"One question," asked the icy voice of Amelia Sachs. "Could you tell me exactly who else you want to kill?"

Percey stepped forward. She snapped, "I lost my husband last night. I'm not losing my company too. You can't tell me where I'm going or not. Not unless I'm under arrest."

"Okay," Sachs said. And in a flash the cuffs were ratcheted onto the woman's narrow wrists. "You're under arrest."

"Sachs," Rhyme called, enraged, "uncuff her—now."

Sachs fired back, "You're a civilian. You can't order me to do a thing. The charge is reckless endangerment. If Jerry dies, then it'll be criminally negligent homicide or manslaughter."

"Officer," Sellitto said, "you're on real thin ice here."

"Amelia," Rhyme said coldly.

She swung to face him. He called her Sachs most of the time. Using her first name was like a slap in the face.

The chains on Percey's wrists clinked. In a reasonable voice Rhyme said, "Please take the cuffs off and let me have a minute with Percey."

Sachs hesitated. Her face was an expressionless mask.

"Please, Amelia." Without a word she unhooked the cuffs.

OUTSIDE in the hallway Sachs walked to the window and looked at her torn nails. She'd put bandages on the most damaged fingers. Habits, she thought. Bad habits. Why can't I stop?

Sellitto walked up beside her, looked up at the gray sky. More spring storms were promised. "Officer," he said, speaking softly, "she messed up, that lady did, okay. But our mistake was *letting* her mess up. It hurts me to say it, but Jerry blew it."

"No," she said. "You don't understand."

"Whatsat?"

"*I* blew it. It's not Jerry's fault. Or Percey's."

"You? Sachs, you 'n' Rhyme're the ones figured out he was at the airport. He mighta nailed everybody, it wasn't for you."

She was shaking her head. "I saw . . . I saw the Dancer's position before he capped Jerry. I drew a target. I . . . He let off a round at me, and I hit the ground. I'd've had at least three seconds to fire. I knew he was shooting bolt-action."

Sellitto scoffed. "What? You're worried you didn't stand up and give a sniper a nice fat target? Come on, Officer. And three hundred yards with a Glock 9? In your dreams."

"I might not have hit him, but I could've parked enough nearby to keep him pinned down." How could she explain? Shooting— like driving fast—was one of her gifts. She could have saved Jerry. She might even have hit the assassin.

She was furious with herself, furious with Percey for putting her in this position. And furious with Rhyme too.

The door swung open, and Percey asked Hale to join them. He disappeared into the room, and a few minutes later it was Hale who opened the door and said, "He'd like everyone inside."

Sachs found them this way: Percey sitting next to Rhyme in a battered old armchair. Sachs had this ridiculous image of them as a married couple.

"We're compromising," Rhyme announced. "Brit and Percey'll go to Dellray's safe house. Talbot will do the repairs on the plane. Whether we find the Dancer or not, though, I've agreed to let her make the flight tomorrow night."

"And if I just arrest her?" Sachs said heatedly.

"I don't believe it's a good idea," Rhyme said. "There'd be more exposure—court, detention, transport. The Dancer'd have more of a chance to get them."

Amelia Sachs hesitated, then gave in, nodded. He was right; he usually was. But right or not, he'd always have things his way. She was his assistant, nothing more. An employee. That's all she was to him.

Rhyme continued. "Here's what I've got in mind. Percey and Hale'll go to the safe house. But we're going to set a trap. I'll need your help, Lon."

Sellitto leaned forward. "You're sure about this, Lincoln?"

Rhyme's eyes swiveled toward Percey. A look passed between them. Sachs didn't know what it meant, but she didn't like it.

"Yes," Rhyme said, "I'm sure."

"Okay," said Sellitto. "Talk to me."

To Percey Clay the safe house on Thirty-fifth Street didn't appear particularly safe. It was a three-story brownstone structure like many others along this block near the Morgan Library.

They parked in the alley, and she and Hale were hustled through a basement entrance. The steel door slammed shut. They found themselves staring at an affable man in his late thirties, lean and with thinning brown hair. He grinned.

"Howdy," he said, showing his NYPD identification and gold shield. "Roland Bell. From now on you meet anybody, even somebody charming as me, ask 'em for an ID."

Hearing his drawl, Percey asked, "Don't tell me you're a Tarheel?"

"That I am." He laughed. "Hoggston and four years at Chapel Hill. Understand you're a Richmond gal."

"Was. Long time ago."

"And you, Mr. Hale?" Bell asked.

"Michigan," Hale said, shaking the detective's hand.

"Now, I'm a homicide detective, but I keep drawing this witness-protection detail 'cause I have this knack for keeping people alive. So I'll be baby-sitting y'all for a spell. Just remember that everything I tell you t'do's for your own good. All right? Now lemme show you our grade-A accommodations."

As they walked upstairs, Bell said, "Our friends in Justice know what they're doing. Those front windows didn't look too secure when you were driving up, right? Well, here's the front room. Take a peek."

There were no windows. Sheets of steel had been bolted over them. "From the street it looks like dark rooms," Bell explained.

"All the other windows're bulletproof glass. But stay away from 'em all the same, and keep the shades drawn. The fire escape and roof're loaded with sensors, and we've got tons of hidden video cameras. It'd take a ghost with anorexia to get in here." He walked down a hall. "Okay, that's your room there, Mrs. Clay."

"Long as we're living together, you may's well call me Percey."

"Done deal. And you're over here . . ."

"Brit."

The rooms were small and dark and very still. Bell called on his walkie-talkie, and a moment later two uniformed policemen appeared in the corridor. "They'll be out here. Full-time. Now, you need anything, just give a holler."

"As a matter of fact, I do." Percey held up her silver flask.

"Well now," Bell drawled, "you want me to help you empty it, I'm afraid I'm still on duty. But 'preciate the offer. You want me to help you *fill* it, why, that's a done deal."

AFTER talking with Sellitto, Rhyme—along with Sachs and Cooper—worked the evidence from the crime scenes.

"This's from the hangar where he waited for the plane." Sachs held up a bag. She and Cooper brushed the trace onto a large sheet of clean newsprint, then put on magnifying goggles and went over it. Cooper lifted several flecks with a probe and placed them on a slide. "We've got fibers."

A moment later Rhyme was looking at the tiny strands on his computer screen. "What do you think, Mel? Paper, right?"

"Yep."

Speaking into his headset, Rhyme ordered his computer to scroll through the microscopic images. "Looks like two kinds. One's white or buff. The other's got a green tint."

"Green? Money?" Sachs suggested.

"Mel, you have enough to gas a few?" Rhyme asked.

Cooper said they had, and proceeded to test several of them. He read the computer screen. "No cotton and no soda, so it's cheap paper. And the dye's water-soluble, not oil-based."

"So," Rhyme announced, "it's not money." He magnified the screen again. The detail was lost now. Then he saw something. "Those yellow blotches, Mel? Glue?"

The tech looked through the microscope's eyepiece. "Yes. Envelope glue, looks like."

So something—maybe a note—had been delivered to the Dancer in a white envelope. But what did the green fiber signify?

Sachs had made a call. "Ron Talbot at Hudson Air said that Phillip Hansen leases that hangar," she reported. "We're making a good case."

True, Rhyme thought. Though his goal was not to hand the Dancer over to the attorney general with a watertight case. No, he wanted the man's head on a pike.

"Okay, let's move on to the other scenes."

Rhyme wheeled up close to his computer and ordered it to magnify images of the timer found in the plane wreckage. He wondered if it contained a partial fingerprint. Bombers often believe that their prints are destroyed in the detonation and will shun gloves when working with the tinier components of the devices. But the blast itself will not necessarily destroy prints. Rhyme now ordered Cooper to turn the timer in the SuperGlue frame and, when that revealed nothing, to dust it with magnetic powder. Once again he found nothing.

Finally he ordered that the sample be bombarded by a garnet laser, the state of the art in raising otherwise invisible prints, while Rhyme examined it on his screen.

Rhyme gave a short laugh, squinted, then looked again. "Is that— Look. Lower-right-hand corner," he called.

But Cooper and Sachs could see nothing.

Rhyme's computer-enhanced image had found something that Cooper's optical scope had missed. On the lip of metal that had protected the timer from being blown to smithereens was a faint crescent of ridge endings, crossings, and bifurcations. It was no more than a sixteenth of an inch wide and maybe a half inch long.

"It's a print," Rhyme said as Cooper moved to his side.

"Not enough to compare." Cooper gazed at Rhyme's screen.

There are a total of about 150 individual ridge characteristics in a single fingerprint, but an expert can determine a match with only eight to sixteen ridge matches. Unfortunately, this sample didn't provide half that. Still, Rhyme was excited. The criminalist who couldn't twist the focus knob of a compound scope had found something that the others hadn't. Something he probably would have missed if he'd been "normal."

He printed out a hard copy and had Thom put it and the words "green fiber" up on the evidence chart.

"RON, it's Percey. How is everyone?"

"Shook up," he answered. "How're you and Brit?"

"Brit's mad. I'm mad. What a mess this is. Oh, Ron."

"And that detective, the cop who got shot?"

"They don't know yet. How's Foxtrot Bravo?"

"It's not as bad as it could be. I've already replaced the cockpit window. No breaches in the fuselage. We've got to replace a lot of the skin. We're trying to find a new fire extinguisher cartridge. I don't think it'll be a problem."

"But?"

"But the annular has to be replaced."

"The combustor? Replace it? Oh, no."

"I've already called the Garrett distributor in Connecticut. They agreed to deliver one tomorrow, even though it's Sunday. I can have it installed in a couple, three hours."

"I should be there," she muttered. "I told them I'd stay put, but . . ."

"Where are you, Percey?"

And Stephen Kall, listening to their conversation, was ready to write. He pressed the receiver closer to his ear.

But the Wife said only, "In Manhattan. About a thousand cops around us. I feel like the pope or the President."

Ron asked, "Can they stop this guy? Do they have any leads?"

Yes, do they? Stephen wondered.

"I don't know," she said.

As he listened to their conversation, Stephen gazed at the laptop computer in front of him. A message saying "Please wait" kept flashing. The remote tap was connected to a Bell Atlantic relay box near the airport and had been transmitting Hudson Air's conversations to Stephen's tape recorder for the past week. He was surprised the police hadn't found it yet.

"I've been looking for more pilots," Ron said uncomfortably.

"We just need one. Right-hand seat. I'm taking the flight."

A pause. "You? I don't think that's a good idea, Perce. I thought you were hiding out until the grand jury."

"Lincoln agreed to let me take the flight if I stayed here until tomorrow."

"Who's Lincoln?"

Yes, Stephen thought. Who is Lincoln?

"Well, he's this weird man. . . ." The Wife hesitated, as if she wanted to talk about him but wasn't sure what to say. Stephen was disappointed when she said only, "He's working with the police, trying to find the killer."

"Percey, we can delay the flight. I'll talk to U.S. Medical."

"No," she said. "They don't want excuses. If we can't do it, they'll find somebody else. When are they delivering the cargo?"

"Six or seven."

"I'll be there late afternoon. I'll help finish the annular."

"Percey," he wheezed, "everything's going to be fine."

"We get that engine fixed on time, everything'll be *great.*"

"You must be going through hell," Ron said.

"Not really," she said.

Not yet, Stephen corrected silently.

SELLITTO came through the door, and everyone looked at him.

The detective sighed. "He'll live. But he lost his arm. They couldn't save it. Too much damage."

"Oh, no," Rhyme whispered. "Can I talk to him?"

"No," the detective said. "He's asleep."

Rhyme thought of the young man, pictured him poking at his cowlick, rubbing a razor cut on his smooth pink chin. "I'm sorry, Lon."

The detective shook his head the same way Rhyme deflected bouquets of sympathy. "We got other things to worry about."

Yes, they did. Rhyme and Sachs stared at the evidence charts up on the wall. They'd keep going through the motions because it was what you had to do in this business. But Rhyme was very frustrated.

Edmond Locard, the famous French criminalist, said that in every encounter between criminal and victim there is an exchange of evidence. It might be microscopic, but a transfer takes place. Yet it seemed to Rhyme that if anyone could disprove Locard's Principle, it was the ghost they called the Dancer.

He closed his eyes, rested his head on the headrest. A moment later he heard Thom say, "It's nearly eleven. Time for bed."

At times it's easy to neglect the body, to forget we even *have* bodies—times when we have to step out of our physical beings and keep working far beyond our normal limitations. But Lincoln Rhyme had a body that wouldn't tolerate neglect. Bedsores could lead to blood poisoning. Fluid in the lungs, to pneumonia. Exhaustion alone could bring on a stroke.

Too many ways to die.

"You're going to bed," Thom said.

"I have to—"

"Sleep. You have to sleep."

Rhyme acquiesced. The Dancer probably wouldn't make any move before tomorrow morning. Besides, he admitted he was very tired.

"All right, Thom." He wheeled toward the elevator. "One thing." He looked back. "Could you come up in a few minutes, Sachs?"

She nodded, watching the tiny elevator door swing shut.

SACHS gave him ten minutes to take care of bedtime functions. She knew Rhyme talked tough—he had a crip's disregard for modesty. But she knew too that there were certain personal routines he didn't want her to witness. She used the time to take a shower downstairs and change into clean clothes.

She found him in the Clinitron. The lights were dim. Rhyme was rubbing his head against the pillow like a bear scratching his back on a tree. The Clinitron was the most comfortable bed in the world. Weighing a half ton, it was a massive slab containing glass beads through which flowed heated air.

"Ah, Sachs, you did good today."

Except thanks to me Jerry Banks lost his arm. And I let the Dancer get away.

She walked to his bar and poured a glass of Macallan, lifted an eyebrow.

"Sure," he said. "Mother's milk, the dew of nepenthe."

She kicked her issue shoes off and went to the window. There were the peregrines. Beautiful birds. They weren't large—fourteen, sixteen inches. Tiny for a dog. But for a bird, utterly intimidating. Their beaks were like the claws on a creature from one of those *Alien* movies.

"You all right, Sachs? Tell me true?"

"I'm okay."

"You want to stay here tonight?" he asked.

Sachs never slept better than when she slept here. She hadn't enjoyed being close to another man since her most recent boyfriend, Nick. She and Rhyme would lie together and talk. She'd tell him about her pistol matches, about her mother, her goddaughter, about her father's full life and sad, protracted death. She'd ante up far more personal information than he. But that was all right. She loved listening to him say whatever he wanted to. His mind was astonishing.

He'd tell her about old New York, about Mafia hits the rest of the world had never heard about, about crime scenes so clean they seemed hopeless until the searchers found the single bit of dust, the dot of spit, the hair or fiber that revealed who the perp was—well, revealed this to Rhyme, not necessarily anyone else. No, his mind never stopped. She knew that before the injury he'd roam the streets of New York looking for samples of soil or glass or plants or rocks—anything that might help him solve cases. It was as if that restlessness had moved from his useless legs into his mind, which roamed the city—in his imagination—well into the night.

But tonight was different. Rhyme was distracted. She didn't mind him ornery—which was good, because he was ornery a lot. But she didn't like him being elsewhere. She sat on the edge of the bed.

He began to say what he'd apparently asked her here for. "Sachs, Lon told me about what happened at the airport."

She shrugged.

"There's nothing you could've done except get yourself killed. You did the right thing, going for cover. He fired one for range and would've gotten you with the second shot."

"I had two, three seconds. I know I could've hit him."

"Don't be reckless, Sachs—"

The fervent look in her eyes silenced him. "I want to get him, whatever it takes. And I have a feeling you want to get him just as much. You'd take chances too." She added with cryptic significance, "Maybe you *are* taking chances."

This had a greater reaction than she'd expected. He blinked, looked away. But he said nothing else, sipped his Scotch.

On impulse she asked, "Can I ask something? If you don't want me to, you can tell me to clam up."

"Come on, Sachs. Secrets, you and me? I don't think so."

Eyes on the floor, she said, "I remember once I told you about Nick. How I felt, how what happened between us was so hard."

He nodded.

"And I asked if you'd felt that way about anyone, maybe your wife. And you said yes, but not Blaine." She looked up at him.

He recovered fast, though not fast enough. And she realized she'd blown cold air on an exposed nerve.

"I remember," he answered.

"Who was she? Look, if you don't want to talk about it . . ."

"I don't mind. Her name was Claire. Claire Trilling."

"How'd you meet her?"

"Well"—he laughed at his own reluctance to continue—"in the department."

"She was a cop?" Sachs was surprised. "What happened?"

"It was a difficult relationship." Rhyme shook his head. "I was married; she was married. Just not to each other."

"So you broke up?"

"It wouldn't have worked, Sachs. Oh, Blaine and I were destined to get divorced or kill each other. It was only a matter of time. But Claire—she was worried about her daughter, about her husband taking the little girl if she got divorced."

"You ever see her now? Claire?"

"No. That was the past. She's not on the force anymore."

"You broke up after your accident?"

"No, no, before."

"She knows you were hurt, though, right?"

"No," Rhyme said after another hesitation.

"Why didn't you tell her?"

A pause. "There were reasons. Funny you bring her up. Haven't thought about her for years."

He offered a casual smile, and Sachs felt the pain course through her, because what he was saying was a lie. Oh, he'd been thinking about this woman. She knew he had. Sachs didn't believe in woman's intuition. But she did believe in cop's intuition.

Her feelings were ridiculous, of course. She had no patience for jealousy. Hadn't been jealous of Nick's job—he had been under-cover and spent weeks on the street. Hadn't been jealous of the blond hookers he'd drink with on assignments.

And beyond jealousy, what could she possibly hope for with Rhyme? She'd talked about him to her mother many times. And the cagey old woman would usually say something like, "It's good to be nice to a cripple like that." Which just about summed up all that their relationship should be. All that it could be.

It was more than ridiculous, but jealous she was. And it wasn't of Claire, it was of Percey Clay. Percey wasn't an attractive woman, but that meant nothing; Sachs couldn't forget how they'd looked to-gether when she'd seen them sitting next to each other.

More Scotch. Thinking of the nights she and Rhyme had spent here talking about cases, drinking this very good liquor.

Oh, great. Now I'm maudlin. That's a mature feeling.

"You want another hit?" she asked, pouring more liquor.

"No," he said.

Without thinking now, she reclined, laid her head on his pillow. It's funny how we adjust to things, she thought. Rhyme couldn't, of course, pull her to his chest and slip his arm around her. But the comparable gesture was his tilting his head to hers. In this way they'd fallen asleep a number of times.

Tonight, though, she sensed a stiffness, a caution. She felt she was losing him. And all she could think about was trying to be closer. Fragments of his words floated past as he spoke about Claire, then about the Dancer. She tilted her head back and looked at his lips. She kissed him once on the cheek, then the corner of the mouth, then squarely on the mouth.

"Sachs, no. . . . Listen to me. No." But she didn't listen.

She'd never told Rhyme, but some months ago she'd bought a book called *The Disabled Lover.* She was surprised to learn that even quadriplegics can make love and father children. True, he'd have no sensation, but for her part the physical thrill was only a part of the event. It was the closeness that counted. She suspected Rhyme might feel the same way.

She kissed him again. Harder.

After a moment's hesitation he kissed her back. She was not surprised that he was good at it. After his dark eyes his perfect lips were the first thing she'd noticed about him.

Then he pulled his face away. "No, Sachs."

"Shhh, quiet."

"It's just that . . ."

It was what? she wondered. That things might not work out? Things were working out fine. Oh, how she wanted to be here, face to face—as close as they could be. To make him understand that she saw he was her perfect man. He was whole as he was. She unpinned her hair, let it fall over him, kissed him again. He kissed back. They pressed their lips together for what seemed like a full minute. Then suddenly he shook his head violently. "No," he whispered.

She'd expected playful, she'd expected passionate, at worst a flirtatious "Uh-oh, not a good idea." But he sounded weak. The hollow sound of his voice cut into her soul.

Her face burned with shame. All she could think was how many times she'd been out with a man who was a friend and suddenly been horrified to feel him start to grope her like a teenager. Her voice had registered the same dismay that she now heard in Rhyme's. So this was all that she was to him, she understood at last.

A partner. A colleague. A capital F Friend.

"I'm sorry, Sachs. I can't. There're complications."

Complications? None that she could see—except, of course, for the fact that he didn't love her.

"No, I'm sorry," she said brusquely. "Stupid. Too much of that single malt. I never could hold the stuff. You know that." She kept a terse smile on her face as she got up.

"Sachs, let me say something."

"No." She didn't want to hear another word. She wanted to be gone.

"Sachs . . ."

"I have to go. I'll be back early."

Chapter Six
. . . Hour 22 of 45

THE smell of coffee filled the town house.

It was just after dawn, and they were planning strategy for snagging the Dancer.

Would this work? Would the Dancer step into their trap? Rhyme believed so. But there was another question. How bad would springing the trap be? The Dancer was deadly enough on his own territory. What would he be like when he was cornered?

They looked over Dellray's tactical map. "Everybody in place?" Rhyme asked.

Both Haumann's 32-E Emergency Services Unit teams and Dellray's FBI SWAT officers were ready. They'd moved in under cover of night, through sewers and basements and over rooftops in full urban camouflage. Rhyme was convinced that the Dancer was surveilling the safe house.

"You sure he's going in this way, Linc?" Sellitto asked.

Sure? Rhyme thought testily. Who can be sure about anything with the Coffin Dancer? *His deadliest weapon is deception.*

He said wryly, "Ninety-two point seven percent sure."

Sellitto snorted a sour laugh.

It was then that the doorbell rang. A moment later a stocky middle-aged man Rhyme didn't recognize appeared in the doorway. The sigh from Dellray suggested trouble brewing.

The man identified himself as Reginald Eliopolos, assistant U.S. attorney in the Southern District of New York. Rhyme recalled he was the prosecutor handling the Phillip Hansen case.

"You're Lincoln Rhyme? Hear good things about you. Uh-huh. Uh-huh." He started forward. "Fred, good to see you. Hear you've got quite an operation together. Not checking too much with the boys upstairs, but hey, I know about improvising." He walked up to the compound scope, peered through the eyepiece. "Uh-huh," he said, though what he might be seeing was a mystery to Rhyme, since the stage light was off.

"Maybe you could—" Rhyme began.

"Cut to the chase?" Eliopolos swung around. "Sure. Here it is. There's an armored van at the Federal Building downtown. I want the witnesses in the Hansen case in it in one hour. Percey Clay and Brit Hale. They'll go to the Shoreham federal protective reserve on Long Island. They'll be kept there until their testimony. End of chase. How's that?"

"You think that's a wise idea?"

"Uh-huh, we do. We think it's wiser than using them as bait for some kind of personal vendetta by the NYPD."

Sellitto sighed.

Eliopolos's full attention was on Rhyme. "Tell me, did you really think that nobody downtown would remember that this was the perp who killed two of your techs five years ago?"

Well, *uh-huh,* Rhyme *had* hoped that nobody would remember. And now that somebody had, he and the team were swimming in the soup pot.

"But hey, hey, I don't want a turf war. Why would I want that? What I want is Hansen."

As a matter of fact, Rhyme had largely forgotten about Phillip Hansen, and now that he'd been reminded, he understood exactly what Eliopolos was doing. "You've got yourself some good agents out there at Shoreham, do you?" Rhyme asked innocently. "You've briefed them about how dangerous the Dancer is?"

A pause. "I've briefed them."

"And what exactly are their orders?"

"Orders?" Eliopolos asked lamely. He wasn't stupid.

Rhyme laughed. He glanced at Sellitto and Dellray. "See, our attorney friend here has *three* witnesses he hopes can nail Hansen. Percey, Hale, and the Dancer himself. He's using Percey as bait too."

"Only," Dellray chuckled, "he's putting her in a Havahart trap."

"You're thinking," Rhyme said to the attorney, "that your case against Hansen's not so good, whatever Percey and Hale saw."

Eliopolos tried sincerity. "Hey, they didn't even actually *see* him. And A, we might not find the duffel bags. B, the evidence inside them might be damaged."

Sellitto said, "But you get Hansen's hit man alive, he can dime his boss. What would you plead him out to?"

"I don't know. That hasn't been discussed."

"You have paper?" Rhyme said.

"I was hoping you'd be willing to cooperate."

"We aren't."

"Uh-huh. I see. I can get an order to show cause for protective custody in three or four hours."

On Sunday morning? Rhyme thought. *Uh-huh.* "We're not releasing them," he said. "Do what you have to do."

WAKING IN THE GLOOMY SAFE house at dawn, Percey Clay rose from her bed and walked to the window. She drew aside the curtain and looked out at the gray monotonous sky. A slight mist was in the air. Wind 090 at five knots, she estimated. Quarter-mile visibility. She hoped the weather cleared for the flight tonight. Oh, she could fly in any weather, but she liked to see the ground pass by beneath her. The lights at night. The clouds. And above her the stars. *All the stars of evening.*

Percey thought again of Ed and the call she'd made to his mother in New Jersey last night. They'd made plans for his memorial service. She wanted to think more about it, work on the guest list, plan the reception. But she couldn't. Her mind was preoccupied. She rested her head against the glass of the safe house, thinking, There's so much to do. Getting Foxtrot Bravo repaired. Preparing the nav log.

"Hey," a friendly voice drawled.

She turned to see Roland Bell at the door. "Morning," she said.

He walked forward quickly. "You have those curtains open, you better keep low as a bedbaby." He tugged the drapes shut.

"Oh, I heard Detective Rhyme's springing some trap. Guaranteed to catch him."

"Well, word is Lincoln Rhyme is all the time right. But I wouldn't trust this particular killer behind a dime." He peered through the curtains, then turned and said, "Now, how about some coffee?"

HERE were a dozen punchy clouds reflected in the windows of the old town house early this Sunday morning.

Here was a hint of rain.

Here was the Wife standing in a bathrobe at the town house window, her white face surrounded by mussed dark curly hair.

And here was Stephen Kall, one block away from the Justice Department's safe house on Thirty-fifth Street, blending into the shadows beneath a water tower on the top of an old apartment building, watching her through his Leica binoculars, the reflection of the clouds swimming across her thin body. He knew that the glass was bulletproof and would certainly deflect the first shot.

Sir, I will stick to my original plan, sir.

A man appeared beside her, and the curtain fell. Then his face peered through the crack, eyes scanning the rooftops, where a sniper would logically be. He looked efficient and dangerous.

Stephen ducked behind the façade of the building.

After listening to the Wife and Ron over the tapped line, he'd run a renegade software program—a remote star-69—he'd downloaded from the Internet. It returned a 212 phone number. Manhattan. What he'd done next was a long shot.

But how are victories won, soldier?

By considering every possibility, however improbable, sir.

He logged on to the Net and a moment later was typing the phone number into a reverse phone book, which gave you the address and name of the subscriber. It didn't work with unlisted numbers, and Stephen was certain that no one in the government would be so stupid as to use a listed number for a safe house.

He was wrong. "James L. Johnson, 258 East 35th Street" popped onto the screen. He called the Manhattan Federal Building and asked to speak to a Mr. James Johnson, then hung up as the call was being transferred.

And so here Stephen was, within small-arms range of the Wife and the Friend. Thinking of the job, trying not to think about the obvious parallel: the face in the window, looking for him.

Little cringey, not too bad. A little wormy.

The curtain closed. Stephen examined the safe house again.

It was a three-story unattached brownstone, the alley like a dark moat around the structure. The fire escape was real, but if you looked closely, you could see that behind the curtained windows was darkness. Probably sheet steel bolted to the inside frame. He'd found the real fire door—behind a large theatrical poster pasted to the brick in the alley. He could see the glass eyes of security cameras recessed into the walls. Still, there were trash bags and several Dumpsters, and he could climb into the alley from a window in the office building next door and use the Dumpsters for cover to get to the fire door. In fact, there was an open window on the first floor of the office building, a curtain blowing in and out. Whoever was monitoring the security screens would have become used to the motion. Stephen could drop through the window, six feet to the ground, then move behind the Dumpster and crawl to the fire door.

Evaluate, soldier.

Sir, I note the absence of large numbers of tactical personnel, and I have concluded that a single-person assault has a good likelihood of success.

Despite the confidence, though, he felt momentarily cringey, picturing Lincoln the Worm searching for him. A big lumpy thing, a larva, moist with worm moisture, oozing up through cracks.

Crawling up his leg. Chewing on his flesh.

Wash 'em off. Wash them off!

Wash what off, soldier? Are you going soft on me?

Sir, no, sir. I am a knife blade, sir. I am pure death, sir.

Breathe deeply. Slowly calm.

He hid the guitar case containing the Model 40 on the roof, under the water tower. The rest of the equipment he transferred to a large book bag. He pulled on a Columbia University windbreaker and his baseball cap, then climbed down the fire escape.

The office building next to the safe house was empty. Stephen didn't have to kill a soul. The lobby was deserted, and there were no security cameras inside. The main door was wedged open with a rubber doorstop, and he saw furniture dollies stacked beside it. It was tempting, but he didn't want to run into any movers or tenants, so he stepped outside and slipped around the corner. Easing behind a potted pine tree, he broke the narrow window to a darkened office with his elbow and climbed in. He stood still for five minutes, pistol in hand, then eased into the corridor.

Pausing outside the office he believed was the one with the blowing curtain over the alley, Stephen reached for the doorknob. But instinct told him to change his plans. He found the stairs and descended into the musty warren of basement rooms.

Stephen worked his way silently toward the side of the building closest to the safe house. In a dimly lit storage room filled with old appliances, he found a window that opened onto the alley. A tight fit. He'd have to remove the glass and frame. But once he was out, he could slip behind the pile of trash bags.

Stephen thought, I've done it.

Fooled them all. Fooled Lincoln the Worm. This gave him as much pleasure as killing the two victims would.

He took a screwdriver from his book bag and began to work the gray wads of glazier's putty out of the window. He was so absorbed in his task that by the time he dropped the screwdriver and got his hand on the butt of his Beretta, the man was on top of him, shoving a pistol into his neck and telling him in a whisper, "Move an inch and you're dead."

SHORT barrel, probably Colt or Smittie. I smell rust.

And what does a rusty gun tell us, soldier?

Plenty, sir. Stephen Kall lifted his hands.

The high, unsteady voice crackled with desperation. "Drop your gun over there. And your walkie-talkie," he said.

Walkie-talkie? Stephen thought.

"Come on, do it. I'll blow your brains out."

Stephen dropped his gun. "I don't have a radio," he said.

"Turn around. And don't try anything."

Stephen eased around and found himself looking at a skinny man with darting eyes. He was filthy and looked sick. His nose ran, and his eyes were an alarming red. His thick brown hair was matted, and he stank. The battered snub-nosed Colt was thrust forward at Stephen's belly, and the hammer was back. It wouldn't take much for the cams to slip. Stephen smiled a benign smile. "Look, I don't want any trouble."

The man nervously patted Stephen's chest. Stephen could have killed him easily—the man's attention kept wandering. The fingers skittered over his body.

Finally the man stepped back. "Where's your partner?"

"Who?"

"Don't give me any guff. You know."

Suddenly cringey again. Wormy. "I really don't know what you mean."

"The cop was just here."

"Cop?" Stephen whispered. "In *this* building?" He walked to the window and looked out.

"Hold it. I'll shoot."

"Point that someplace else," Stephen commanded. Beginning to see the extent of his mistake, he felt sick to his stomach.

The man's voice cracked as he threatened, "Stop. Right there."

"Are they in the alley too?" Stephen asked.

A moment of confused silence. "You really aren't a cop?"

"Are they in the alley too?" Stephen repeated firmly.

"A bunch of them, while ago. I don't know 'bout now."

Stephen stared into the alley. The trash bags . . . False cover.

"If you signal anybody, I swear—"

"Oh, be quiet." Stephen scanned the alley slowly, patient as a boa, and finally saw a faint shadow on the cobblestones. It moved an inch or two. And on top of a building—on the elevator tower— a ripple of shadow. Somehow Lincoln the Worm had been expecting him here all along, had even figured out that he would try to get through the alley from this building.

The face in the window.

The chocked door, the open window, and the fluttering curtain— a welcome mat. And the alley—a perfect kill zone. The only thing that had saved him was his instinct.

Lincoln the Worm had set him up. Who the devil *is* he?

Rage boiled him. If they were expecting him, they'd be following S&S procedures—search and surveillance. Stephen spun around. "When was the last time the cop checked in here?"

The man's eyes flickered, then blossomed with fear. The black bore of the Colt still pointed at Stephen. "Ten minutes ago."

"What kind of weapon does he have?"

"I don't know. One of those fancy ones. Like a machine gun."

"Who *are* you?" Stephen asked.

"I don't have to answer your questions," the man said defiantly.

He wiped his runny nose on his sleeve with his gun hand. In a flash Stephen lifted his gun away and shoved him to the floor.

"No! Don't hurt me."

"Shut up." Stephen opened the little Colt. There were no rounds in the cylinder. "It's empty?" he asked, incredulous.

The man shrugged. "I— Well . . . see, if they catch you and it's not loaded, they don't put you away for as long."

Stephen thought he might just kill the man for the stupidity of carrying an unloaded gun. "What're you doing here?"

"There're doctors' offices upstairs," the man whimpered. "Nobody's here Sunday, so I hit 'em for samples. Percodan, Fiorinal, diet pills, stuff like that."

"What's your name?" Stephen asked, picking up his Beretta.

"Jodie. Well, Joe D'Oforio. But everybody calls me Jodie."

Stephen stared out the window. Another shadow moved on top of the building. "Okay, Jodie, listen. You want to make some money?"

"WELL?" Rhyme asked impatiently. "What's going on?"

"He's still in the building east of the safe house. He hasn't gone into the alley yet," Sellitto reported. He was with Haumann, Dellray, and Sachs in a fake UPS van parked up the block.

"Why not? He has to. There's no reason for him not to."

"They're checking every floor. He's not in the office."

The one with the open window. Rhyme had debated about letting the curtain blow in and out, tempting him. But it was too obvious. The Dancer'd become suspicious.

"Everybody's locked and loaded?" Rhyme asked.

"Of course. Relax."

But he couldn't relax. Five minutes ago two ESU officers had found a broken window on the first floor. The Dancer'd shunned the open front door but had still moved in for the assault. Then something had spooked him. He was loose in the building, and they had no idea where. A poisonous snake in a dark room. Where was he? What was he planning? Rhyme was growing frantic.

Too many ways to die.

Jodie said, "Who doesn't wanna make money?"

"Then help me get out of here."

"What're you doing here? Are they looking for *you*?"

Stephen looked the sad little man up and down. A loser, but not crazy or stupid. Stephen decided it was best tactically to be honest. Besides, the man'd be dead in a few hours anyway.

He said, "I've come here to kill somebody."

"Whoa. Like, are you in the Mob? Who're you gonna kill?"

"Jodie, be quiet. We're in a tough situation here."

"We? I didn't do anything."

"Except you're at the wrong place at the wrong time," Stephen said. "And that's too bad, because they aren't going to believe you're not with me. Now, you gonna help me?"

Jodie tried not to look scared. "I don't want to get hurt."

"If you're on my side, you'll never get hurt."

The jelly bean eyes were considering. "How much?"

"Five thousand." The little crud was negotiating.

The fear in the eyes was pushed aside by shock. "For real?"

Stephen laughed. "I'm getting paid a lot more than that. Anyway, if we get out of here, I could use your help again."

A sound in the distance. Footsteps coming.

It was the S&S cop, looking for him. Just one, Stephen could tell, listening to the steps. "You going to help me?"

A no-brainer, of course. If Jodie didn't help, he'd be dead in the next sixty seconds. "Okay." He extended his hand.

Stephen ignored it and asked, "How do we get out?"

"See those cinder blocks there? You can pull 'em out. See there? It leads down into an old delivery tunnel."

"Really?" Stephen wished he'd known it before.

"I can get us to the subway. That's where I live. This old subway station." Jodie started toward the concrete blocks.

"No," Stephen whispered. "Here's what I want you to do. Stand there, opposite the doorway."

"But he'll see me. I'll be the first thing he'll see."

"Just stand there and put your hands up."

"He'll shoot me," Jodie whimpered. He wiped his face.

"No, he won't. You've got to trust me."

Jodie sighed. "Okay, okay."

The footsteps were coming closer. Stephen touched his fingers to his lips and went prone, disappearing into the floor.

The footsteps grew soft, then paused. The figure appeared in the doorway. He was in FBI body armor. He pushed into the room, a flashlight attached to the end of his weapon. When the beam caught Jodie's midriff, the cop did something that astonished Stephen. He started to pull the trigger.

It was very subtle. But Stephen had shot so many animals and so many people that he knew the ripple of muscles, the tension of stance just before you fired your weapon. He leaped up, lifting the machine gun away and breaking off the stalk microphone. Driving his k-bar knife up under the triceps, he paralyzed the agent's right arm. The man cried out in pain.

They're green-lighted to kill, Stephen thought. No surrender pitch. They see me, they shoot. Armed or not.

"You stabbed him!" Jodie cried.

"Shut up." Stephen gagged the agent with a rag. "The exit."

"But—" Jodie just stared.

"Now!" Stephen raged. "Wait there."

Jodie ran to the hole in the wall as Stephen pulled the agent to his feet. Green-lighted to kill. Lincoln the Worm had decided he'd die. Stephen was furious.

He plugged the headset back into the man's transceiver and listened. There must have been twelve or fourteen cops calling in as they searched the building.

He didn't have much time. Stephen led the dazed agent out into the yellow hallway and pulled out his knife again.

"DAMN," Rhyme snapped, flecking his chin with spit. Thom stepped up to the chair and wiped it, but Rhyme angrily shook him away. "Bo?" he called into his microphone.

"Go ahead," Haumann said from the command van.

"I think somehow he made us and's going to fight his way out. Tell your agents to form defensive teams."

"Hold on. Hold on. . . . Oh, no."

"Bo? Sachs? Anybody?" But nobody answered.

Rhyme heard shouting voices through the radio. "Assistance. We've got a blood trail . . . basement. Innelman's not reporting in. He was . . . Innelman's here. Hurt bad. Damn, all this blood!"

"RHYME, can you hear me?" Amelia Sachs asked.

"Go ahead."

"I'm in the basement storeroom. It's a mess." She looked around her. The walls were filthy yellow concrete, and blood spatter was everywhere, like a horrific Jackson Pollock painting. Poor Innelman, she thought.

In the hallway two EMS techs and Dellray bent over Innelman, grim-faced. "What'd he do to you, John? Oh, man." The lanky agent stood back while the medics went to work. Innelman's eyes were half open, glazed. "Is he . . . ?" Dellray asked.

"Alive, barely." The medics slapped pads on the stab wounds, put tourniquets on his leg and arm, and ran a plasma line. "We gotta move."

They placed the agent on a gurney and hurried down the corridor, Dellray with him. "Could he talk?" Rhyme asked Sachs.

"No. I don't know if they can save him."

"Don't get rattled, Sachs. We have to find out where the Dancer is, if he's still around. Describe the storeroom."

"Well, there's a window looking out on the alley. Looks like he started to open it, but it's puttied shut. No doors."

"Walk the grid and let's see what we find."

She searched the scene carefully, then vacuumed for trace.

"What do you see? Anything?"

She shone her light around until she found two mismatched blocks. "Got his exit route, Rhyme. Some loose concrete blocks."

"Don't open it. Get SWAT there."

She called several agents down, and they pulled the blocks out, sweeping the inner chamber with flashlights mounted on their H&K submachine guns. "Clear," one agent called.

Sachs drew her weapon and slipped into the cool, dank space. It was a narrow, declining ramp leading through a hole in the foundation. She waved the PoliLight wand over the places where the Dancer would logically have gripped with his hands. "Whoa, Rhyme. Fresh fingerprints . . . Wait. But here're the glove prints too. I don't get it. Maybe he thought he was safe and took the gloves off." Then she shone the eerie yellow-green glow at her feet. "Oh, they're not his prints. He's with somebody else. Rhyme, he's got a partner."

"WHAT'VE you got?" Rhyme asked.

Sachs had returned to his town house, and she and Mel Cooper were looking over the evidence collected at the scene. Sachs and SWAT had followed the footsteps into a Con Ed access tunnel, where they lost track of both the Dancer and his companion.

She gave Cooper the fingerprint she'd found. He scanned it into the computer and sent it off for an AFIS search. The automated fingerprint identification system linked digitized criminal, military, and civil service fingerprint databases around the country. Then she held up two transparent electrostatic prints for Rhyme to examine. "These're the footprints in the tunnel. The Dancer's matches a print in the office he broke into."

"Wearing average ordinary factory shoes," Rhyme said. "Hold the other one closer, Sachs."

The smaller shoes were very worn at the heel. There was a large hole in the right shoe; through it you could see a lattice of wrinkles.

"Looks like his friend's homeless," Rhyme said. "And leaving fingerprints at the scene? This guy's no pro. He must have something the Dancer needs."

"A way out of the building, for one thing," Sachs suggested.

Turning to the trace evidence, Cooper mounted samples onto a slide and slipped it under the compound scope. He patched the image through to Rhyme's computer.

"Command mode, cursor left," Rhyme ordered. "Stop. Double-click." He examined the monitor. "More mortar from the cinder block. Dirt and dust. Where'd you get this, Sachs?"

"I scraped it from around the cinder blocks and vacuumed the floor of the tunnel. I also found a nest behind some boxes where it looked like somebody'd been hiding."

"Good. Okay, Mel, gas it. There's stuff I don't recognize."

The chromatograph rumbled, separating the compounds for identification. Cooper examined the screen, then exhaled a surprised breath. "He's a drugstore, Lincoln. We've got secobarbital, phenobarbital, Dexedrine, amobarbital."

"Damn," Sellitto muttered. "Reds, dexies, blue devils. So the Dancer's got a cluckhead for a sidekick. Go figure."

Sachs said, "All those doctors' offices there. This guy must've been boosting pills."

"Got an E-mail," Cooper said. "The AFIS report on the fingerprints. Whoever the guy is, he has no record anywhere."

"Why!" Rhyme snapped. He felt cursed. Couldn't it be just a little easier? He muttered, "What's in that bag, Sachs?"

A square of paper towel smeared with a faint brown stain. "I found that on the cinder block he moved. I think it was on his hands."

"Why do you think that?"

"Because I rubbed my hand in some dirt and pushed on another cinder block. The mark was the same."

That's my Amelia, he thought. For an instant his thoughts returned to last night—the two of them lying in bed together. He pushed the thought away. "What is it, Mel?"

"Looks like it's grease. Impregnated with dust, dirt, bits of wood, organic material. Animal flesh, I think. All very old. And look there."

Rhyme examined some silvery flecks on his computer screen. "Metal. Ground or shaved off something. Gas it."

Cooper did. "Petrochemical. Crudely refined, no additives. Iron with traces of manganese, silicon, and carbon."

"Wait." Rhyme gazed at the ceiling. "Old steel, made from pig iron in a Bessemer furnace."

"And here's something else. Coal tar."

"Creosote!" Rhyme cried. "I've got it. The Dancer's first big mistake. His partner's a walking road map."

"To where?" Sachs asked.

"To the subway. That grease is old; the steel's from old fixtures and tie spikes. The creosote's from the ties. That's what the Dancer wanted him for. A place to hide out. The Dancer's friend's probably a homeless druggie living in some abandoned tunnel or station."

Rhyme realized that everyone was looking at a man's shadow in the doorway. He stopped speaking.

"Dellray?" Sellitto said uncertainly. "What is it?"

"Innelman. Lost too much blood. He just died."

"I'm sorry," Sachs said.

Rhyme thought of Dellray's runner, Tony Panelli—probably dead by now, the only clue to his whereabouts the grains of curious sand. And now another friend gone.

Dellray looked at Rhyme with frightening eyes. "You know why he got cut? A diversion. To keep us off the scent. You got any leads?"

"Not much." He explained about the Dancer's homeless friend, the drugs, the hidey-hole somewhere in the subway. "But we still have more evidence to look at."

"Evidence," Dellray whispered contemptuously. "A diversion. That's no damn reason for a good man to die. No reason at all."

"Fred, wait. We need you."

But the agent didn't hear. He stalked out of the room.

Chapter Seven
. . . Hour 24 of 45

"Home, sweet home," Jodie said.

A mattress, old clothes, canned food. A book or two. This fetid subway station where Jodie lived, somewhere downtown, had been closed decades before. A good place for worms, Stephen thought grimly.

They'd made their way two or three miles from the safe house, completely underground, moving through the basements of buildings, tunnels, huge sewer pipes. Finally they'd entered the subway tunnel and made good time, though Jodie, pathetically out of shape, gasped for breath trying to keep up with Stephen.

There was a door leading out to the street, barred from the inside. Slanting lines of dusty light fell through the board slats. Stephen peered outside into the grim spring overcast. Derelicts sat on street corners; bottles of Thunderbird were strewn on the sidewalk, and crack vial caps were everywhere.

Stephen heard a clatter behind him and turned to see Jodie dropping stolen pills into coffee cans, organizing them. He opened his book bag, counted out five thousand dollars. "Here's the money."

Jodie's eyes flipped back and forth between the bills and Stephen's face. The thin hand reached out and took the five thousand.

Stephen said, "Help me again, I'll pay you another ten."

The man's red, puffy face broke into a cautious smile. He poked through his coffee cans, swallowed a pill. "It's a blue devil. Makes you feel nice, all comfy. Want one?"

"Um . . . no," Stephen said.

Jodie closed his eyes and lay back. "Ten thousand." After a moment he asked, "You killed him, didn't you?"

"Who?" Stephen asked.

"Back there, that cop?"

"Maybe I killed him. I don't know. That wasn't the point."

"You were in the army, right? I knew it."

Stephen was about to lie. Changed his mind suddenly. He said, "No. I was almost in the army. Well, the marines. My stepfather was a marine. I tried to enlist, but they wouldn't let me in."

"That's stupid. Wouldn't let you? You'd make a great soldier." Jodie was looking Stephen up and down, nodding. "You're strong. Great muscles. I"—he laughed—"I don't hardly get any exercise, 'cept running from kids want to mug me. You're handsome too. Like the soldiers in the movies."

Stephen started blushing. "Well, I don't know about that."

"Come on. Your girlfriend thinks you're handsome, bet."

A little cringey. Worms starting to move. "You got water?"

Jodie pointed to a box of Poland Spring. "Stole a case." Stephen opened two bottles and began washing his hands.

"No girlfriend, huh?" The drugs made Jodie's voice slurred.

"Not right now," Stephen explained carefully. "It's not like I'm a fairy or anything, if you were wondering."

"I wasn't," Jodie said from his hazy plateau. "I don't have one either. How could I? I'm not good-looking like you."

Stephen felt his face burn hot, and he scrubbed harder. His hands tingled. He suddenly felt swollen with an odd feeling—of talking to someone who might just understand him. "See, I don't kill people just to kill them. Killing's a business. Look at Kent State. I was just a kid then, but my stepfather told me about it. You know those students got shot by the National Guard?"

"Sure, I know."

"Now, to me it was stupid shooting them. Because what purpose did it serve? You should've targeted the leaders and taken them out. Infiltrate, evaluate, delegate, isolate, eliminate."

"That's how you kill people?"

"You infiltrate the area. Evaluate the difficulty of the kill. You delegate the job of diverting everyone's attention from the victim—make it look like you're coming at them from one way, but it turns out that it's just a delivery boy or something and meanwhile you've come up behind the victim. Then you isolate him and eliminate him."

"You know," Jodie said, "you'd think professional killers'd be crazy. But you don't seem crazy."

"I don't think I'm crazy," Stephen said matter-of-factly.

"The people you kill, are they bad? Like Mafia people?"

"Well, they do bad things to people who pay me to kill them."

Jodie laughed dopily, eyelids half closed. "Well, some people'd say that's not exactly how you figure out what's good or bad."

"Okay, what *is* good and bad?" Stephen responded. "Some professional killers call their victims subjects. One guy I heard about calls them corpses. Even before he kills them. It's easier for him to think of them that way, I guess. Me, I don't care. I call 'em what they are. Who I'm after now are the Wife and the Friend. They're people I kill, is all. No big deal."

Jodie considered what he'd heard and said, "You know something? I don't think you're evil. Evil looks innocent but turns out to be bad. You're exactly what you are. I think that's good."

Stephen blushed again. Finally he asked, "I scare you, don't I?"

"No," Jodie said. "I wouldn't want to have you against me. No, sir. But I feel like we're friends. I don't think you'd hurt me."

"No," Stephen said. "We're partners."

"You talked about your stepfather. He still alive?"

"No, he died." Stephen watched Jodie hide the cash in a slit in his filthy mattress. "What're you going to do with the money?"

Jodie sat up and looked at him with dumb but earnest eyes. "Can I show you something?" He lifted a book out of his pocket. The title was *Dependent No More.* "I stole it from this bookstore on St. Marks Place. It's for people who don't want to be, you know, alcoholics or drug addicts anymore. It's pretty good. It mentions these clinics you can go to. I found this place in New Jersey. You spend a month, but you come out, you're clean."

"That'd be good for you," Stephen said. "I approve of that."

"Yeah." Jodie curled up his face. "It costs fourteen thousand."

"Somebody's making some bucks there." Stephen made a hundred and fifty thousand dollars for a hit, but he didn't share this information with Jodie, his newfound friend and partner.

Jodie sighed, wiped his eyes. The drugs made him weepy. Like Stephen's stepfather when he drank. "My whole life's been so messed up," he said. "I went to college. Oh, yeah. Worked for a company. Then I lost my job. I'd always had a pill problem. Oh, well."

Stephen sat down next to him. "You'll get your money and go into that clinic there. Get your life turned around."

Jodie smiled blearily at him. "My father had this thing he said, you know? When there was something you had to do that was hard. He'd say, 'It's not a problem; it's just a factor.'"

"Not a problem, just a factor," Stephen said. "I like that." And he put his hand on Jodie's leg to prove that he did.

A LABYRINTH.

The New York City subway system extends for over 250 miles and incorporates more than a dozen separate tunnels that crisscross four boroughs. A satellite could find a sailboat adrift in the North Atlantic quicker than Lincoln Rhyme's team could locate two men hiding in the New York subway.

The criminalist, Sellitto, Sachs, and Cooper were poring over a subway map taped inelegantly to Lincoln Rhyme's wall. Rhyme ordered his computer to dial a number and in a few moments was connected with Sam Hoddleston, chief of the Transit Authority Police. Rhyme briefed him about the Dancer and his partner. "We think he's in an abandoned area," he said. "We're guessing Manhattan. We've got a map here, and we're going to need your help in narrowing it down."

"Whatever I can do," the chief said.

Rhyme now considered the rest of the evidence left by the Dancer's partner. "The dirt's loaded with feldspar and quartz sand. Very little rock and none of it blasted or chipped, no limestone or Manhattan mica schist. So we're looking at downtown, where the subway's built on soupy ground, not bedrock. Maybe somewhere close to Canal Street."

Hoddleston wasn't optimistic. There were dozens of connecting tunnels, platforms, and portions of stations that had been closed off over the years. But he agreed to fax over a list of the most likely ones.

Five minutes later the fax machine buzzed and Thom set the list in front of Rhyme. "Okay, Sachs, get going." She nodded as Sellitto picked up the phone to call Haumann and Dellray to have the S&S teams get started. Rhyme added emphatically, "Amelia, you stay in the rear now, okay? You're crime scene, remember? Only crime scene."

ON A curb sat Leon the Shill. Beside him was the Bear Man—so named because he wheeled around a shopping cart filled with stuffed animals, supposedly for sale, though only a psychotic parent would buy one of the tattered lice-ridden little toys for their child. The two shared an alley near Chinatown, surviving on bottle deposits, handouts, and a little harmless petty larceny.

Leon and the Bear Man were looking across the street. There lay another homeless man, black and sick-looking, with a twitchy and mean—though presently unconscious—face.

"He's dying, man," Leon said. "Oughta call somebody."

"Le's take a look," the Bear Man responded.

They crossed the street, skittish as mice.

The man was filthy. He wore ragged jeans, caked socks, no shoes, and a torn, filthy jacket that said CATS . . . THE MUSICAL.

Leon touched his leg. The man jerked awake and sat up.

"Hey, man, you okay?" They backed away a few feet.

Cats shivered, clutching his abdomen. He coughed long.

"He's scary. Le's go." Bear Man wanted to get back to his toys.

"I need help," Cats muttered. "I hurt, man."

"There's a clinic over on—"

"Can't go to no clinic," Cats muttered as if they'd insulted him. So he had a record. Yeah, this mutt was trouble.

"I need medicine. You got some? I pay you. I got money."

Which they wouldn't've believed except that Cats was a can picker. And good at it, they could see. Beside him was a huge bag of soda and beer cans he'd culled from the trash.

"We don't got no pills. You wanna bottle? Some nice T-bird."

Cats struggled to his feet. "I don't want no bottle. Some kids beat me up. I need medicine." He groaned and held his side.

Leon said, "There's this guy, okay? Was trying to sell us some pills yesterday. Didn't care who saw him, selling everything."

"I got money." Cats fumbled in his filthy pocket and pulled out three crumpled twenties. "See? So where he be?"

"Over near City Hall. Old subway station."

"I'm sick, man. Why somebody beat me up? I's pickin' some cans's all." Cats wiped his forehead. "I'ma see him. What his name?"

"I don't know," Leon said. "Joe or something. Maybe Jodie."

"Jodie. Man, I need somethin'. I'm sick, man. I'm sick." He staggered off, moaning and dragging his bag of cans behind him.

Sitting next to Jodie on the mattress, Stephen was listening through the tap box to the Hudson Air phone line. Ron Talbot was arguing with a distributor who handled turbine parts. Because it was Sunday, they were having trouble getting items for the repairs. There were no other calls.

He clicked the phone off, frustrated. Were the Wife and Friend still in the safe house? Had they been moved? What was Lincoln, king of the worms, thinking now? How clever was he?

And *who* was he? Stephen tried to picture him as a target through the Redfield telescope. All he saw was a mass of worms and a face looking at him calmly through a greasy window.

He realized that Jodie'd said something to him. "What?"

"What did your stepfather do?"

"Lou? Well, just odd jobs, mostly. Hunted and fished a lot. He was a hero in Vietnam. He went behind enemy lines and killed fifty-four people. Politicians and people like that."

"He taught you all this, about what you do?"

"He started me." As a boy, Stephen would walk behind Lou while they trooped through the hills, hot drops of sweat falling down their noses and into the crooks of their index fingers curled around the triggers of their Winchesters. They'd lie still in the grass for hours.

Don't you squint that left eye, soldier.

Sir, never, sir.

Squirrels, wild turkeys, deer in season or out, bears when they could find them, dogs on slow days.

"Make 'em dead, soldier. Watch me." *Ka-rack.* The thud against the shoulder, the bewildered eyes of an animal dying.

And at night, sitting in front of a fire in the backyard as the sparks flew toward the sky and the open window where his mother stood cleaning the supper dishes with a toothbrush, the taut little man—Stephen at fifteen was as tall as Lou—would sip from the bottle of Jack Daniel's and talk and talk and talk, whether Stephen was listening or not.

"Tomorrow I want you to bring down a deer with just a knife. Can you do that, soldier?"

"Yes, sir, I can."

"Now, what you do is you find a family—doe and calves. You come up close. That's the hard part. To kill the doe, you endanger the calf. You move for her baby. She'll come after you. Then *swick!* Cut through her neck." Another sip. "Hey, boy, aren't we having a high old time!"

Then Lou would go inside to inspect the plates, and sometimes when there was still a dot of grease on one, Stephen would listen to the slaps and whimpers from inside the house as he lay on his back beside the fire and watched the sparks fly toward the dead moon.

Jodie now asked, "How come you couldn't be in the marines?"

"Well, it was stupid," Stephen said, then paused. "I got into some trouble when I was a kid. There was this man in our town, you know, a bully. I saw him twisting this woman's arm. She was sick, and what was he doing hurting her? So I said if he didn't stop, I'd kill him. Well, it got out of hand. I grabbed a rock and hit him. I wasn't thinking. I did a couple years for manslaughter. The criminal record kept me out of the marines."

Jodie's hand pressed Stephen's shoulder. "That's not one bit fair. I'm real sorry," he said. Jodie's green eyes were bright.

Stephen, who never had any trouble looking any man in the eye, glanced at Jodie once, then down. And from somewhere totally weird this image came to mind. Jodie and Stephen together in the cabin, hunting and fishing. Cooking over a campfire.

He stood quickly and looked out the window. The street was deserted except for a clutch of homeless men—four whites and one Negro.

Stephen squinted. The Negro, lugging a big garbage bag full of soda and beer cans, was arguing, looking around, gesturing, offering the bag to one of the white guys, who kept shaking his head. Stephen watched them argue for a few minutes, then returned to the mattress, sat down next to Jodie. "Let's talk about what we're going to do. There's somebody looking for me."

Jodie laughed. "Seems to me after what happened back at that building, there's a buncha people looking for you."

"There's one person in particular. His name's Lincoln."

Jodie nodded. "That's his first name?"

"I don't know. I've never met anyone like him."

"Who is he?"

A worm. . . .

"Maybe a cop. FBI. A consultant. I don't know exactly." Stephen remembered the Wife describing him to Ron—the way somebody'd talk about a guru. He felt cringey again. He put his hand on Jodie's shoulder, and the bad feeling went away. "This is the second time he's stopped me. I'm trying to figure him out, and I can't."

"What do you have to figure out?"

"If he's going to move them out of their safe house."

"Move who? The people you're trying to kill?"

"Yeah. He's going to try to outguess me. He's thinking."

The thin man whispered, "You seem shook up or something."

"I can't see him. I can't see what he's going to do. Everybody else's ever been after me I can see."

"What do you want me to do?" Jodie asked.

Stephen rummaged in his book bag, found a black cell phone, and handed it to Jodie.

"Whatsis?" the man asked.

"A phone. For you to use."

"A cell phone. Cool." Jodie examined it as if he'd never seen one. Stephen said, "Snipers always have a spotter. He locates the target and figures out how far away it is, things like that."

"You want me to do that for you?"

"Yep. See, I think Lincoln's going to move them. I just have this feeling." He looked at his watch. "Okay, here's the thing. At twelve thirty this afternoon, what I want you to do is walk down the street like a homeless person and watch the safe house. Maybe you could look through trash cans or something."

"For bottles. I do that all the time."

"You find out what kind of car they get into, then call me and tell me. I'll be on the street around the corner in a car, waiting. But you'll have to watch out for decoys."

"Okay. I can do that. You'll shoot them in the street?"

"It depends. I'll be ready to improvise."

Jodie studied the phone. "I don't know how it works."

Stephen showed him. "Call when you're in position."

Jodie looked up. "You know, after this's over and I go through the rehab thing, why don't we get together sometime? We could have some juice or coffee or something. Huh? You wanna do that?"

"Sure," Stephen said. "We could—"

But suddenly a huge pounding shook the door. Spinning around like a dervish, whipping his gun from his pocket, Stephen dropped into a two-handed shooting position.

"Open the door," a voice from outside shouted. "Now! You in there, Jo-die? Where are you?"

Stephen stepped to the boarded-over window and looked out again. The Negro guy from across the street. He wore a tattered jacket that read CATS . . . THE MUSICAL.

"Where'sa little man?" the Negro said. "Jodie Joe."

Stephen said, "You know him?"

Jodie looked out, shrugged, and whispered, "I don't know."

The homeless man called, "I know you here, man. Jo-die. Jo-die!"

"He'll just go away," Jodie said.

Stephen said, "Wait. Maybe we can use him. Remember what I told you? Delegate. This is good. He looks scary. If you take him along with you, they'll focus on him, not you."

"I need some *stuff,* man," the Negro moaned. "Come on. Please, man. I got the wobblies!" He kicked the door hard.

"Go on out," Stephen said. "Tell him you'll give him something if he goes with you. Just have him go through the trash while you're watching the traffic. It'll be perfect."

"Well, okay." Jodie took a deep breath, then stepped outside. "Hey, keep it down," he said to the man. "What you want?"

Stephen watched the Negro look over Jodie with his crazed eyes. "Word up you selling pills, man. I got money. Where my money?" He slapped his pockets several times before realizing he was clutching the precious twenties in his left hand.

"Okay," Jodie said, "but you gotta do something for me first. Help me go through some trash, pick some cans."

"Cans?" the man roared. "What you need a nickel for?"

"I give you the pills free, only you gotta help me."

"Free?" The Negro looked around as if he was trying to find somebody to explain this. "Where I gotta look for bottles?"

"Wait." Jodie stepped inside and said to Stephen, "He'll do it."

"Good job." Stephen smiled.

Jodie grinned back. He started to turn back to the door, but Stephen said, "Hey."

The little man paused.

Stephen blurted suddenly, "It's good I met you."

"I'm glad I met you too"—Jodie hesitated for a minute—"partner." He stuck his hand out.

"Partner," Stephen echoed. He had a fierce urge to take his glove off so he could feel Jodie's skin on his. But he didn't.

Craftsmanship had to come first.

Chapter Eight

. . . Hour 25 of 45

THE debate was feverish.

"I think you're wrong, Lincoln," Lon Sellitto said. "We gotta move 'em. He'll hit the safe house again."

Rhyme wished Dellray were here—and Sachs too, though she was with the joint city-federal tactical force searching abandoned subway locations. So far they hadn't found any trace of the Dancer or his compatriot.

"No," Rhyme said adamantly. "He'll come after them wherever they are. We know the turf there; we know something about his approach. We've got good ambush coverage."

"That's a good point," Sellitto conceded.

"It'll also throw him off stride. He's debating right now too. If we move them—which I think is what he's guessing we'll do—he'll try for a transport hit. And security on the road is always worse than fixed premises. No, we have to keep them where they are and anticipate the next attempt. Be ready to move in."

But am I right? Rhyme wondered. What is the Dancer thinking? Do I really know?

A figure appeared in the doorway, one of the officers from the front door. He handed Thom an envelope and returned to his post.

"What's that?" Rhyme said.

Thom opened it and read. "The FBI tracked down a sand expert." It was the other case. Rhyme glanced at the report: "Substance submitted for analysis is not technically sand. It is oolite, coral rubble from reef formations, and contains cross sections of marine worm tubes and gastropod shells. Most likely source is the northern Caribbean: Cuba, the Bahamas."

Caribbean. Interesting. Well, after the Dancer was bagged and tagged, he and Sachs would get back to the missing-agent case.

SILENTLY the ESU troops surrounded the subway station. Several locals had reported a druggie selling pills out of the place. He was a slightly built man—in line with a small shoe.

The station was, almost literally, a hole in the wall, supplanted years before by the fancier City Hall stop a few blocks away. The 32-E teams went into position, while S&S set up their microphones and infrareds and other officers cleared the street of traffic. The commander moved Sachs away from the main entrance, out of the line of fire. They gave her the job of guarding an exit that had been barred and padlocked. She actually wondered if Rhyme had cut a deal with Haumann to keep her safe.

Rain fell around her, a chill rain from a dirty gray sky, tapping loudly on the refuse banked in front of the bars. Was the Dancer inside? She couldn't imagine he would give up without a violent struggle. And it infuriated her that she wouldn't be part of it.

She stepped down the stairs, then flattened against the wall. She examined the iron bars and the chain and rusty padlock. She peered inside the dim tunnel and could see nothing, hear nothing.

Where is he? And what's the delay?

She heard the answer a moment later in her earphone: They were waiting for backup. Haumann had called in more officers.

No, no, no, she thought. That was all wrong. All the Dancer has to do is take one peek outside and see that not a single car or taxi or pedestrian is going by and he'll know instantly there's a tactical operation under way. There'll be a bloodbath. Don't they get it?

Sachs climbed back to street level. A few doors away was a drugstore. She bought two cans of butane and borrowed the storekeeper's awning rod, a five-foot-long piece of steel.

Back at the exit, Sachs slipped the awning rod through one of the chain links and twisted until the chain was taut. She pulled on a Nomex glove and emptied the butane on the metal, watching it grow frosty from the freezing gas—Amelia hadn't walked a beat in Times Square for nothing; she knew enough about breaking and entering to take up a second line of work.

She gripped the rod in both hands and began to twist. With a soft snap the link cracked in half. She caught the chain, set it quietly in a pile of leaves, and pushed inside, sweeping her Glock from its holster, thinking, I missed you at three hundred yards; I won't at thirty. She thought momentarily of Rhyme. He wouldn't approve of this, of course. But he didn't know.

She disappeared into the dim corridor, leaped over the ancient wooden turnstile, and started along the platform toward the station. She heard voices before she got twenty feet.

"I have to leave. Understand? I'm saying, go away."

White male. Was it the Dancer?

Heart slamming in her chest. Breathe slow. Shooting is breathing.

"Yo, what you sayin'?" Another voice. Black male. Something about it scared her. "I can get money. I got sixty, I tell you that?"

"I changed my mind, okay? I'll give you some pills."

"You ain' tole me where we goin'. Where? Tell me."

Sachs started up the stairs slowly.

"You're not going anywhere. I want you to go away. Here. Here's a dozen demmies. Take 'em and go."

"A dozen. And I ain't gotta pay you?" He brayed a laugh.

Approaching the top of the stairs. She could almost peer into the station itself. She was ready to shoot. He moves more than six inches, girl, take him out. Forget the rules. Forget—

Suddenly the stairs vanished.

"Ugh." A grunt from deep in her throat as she fell.

She'd placed her foot on a trap. The top step rested only on two shoe boxes. They collapsed under her weight, sending her backward down the stairs. The Glock flew from her hand, and as she started to shout, "Ten thirteen!" she realized that the cord linking her to her radio had been yanked out.

Sachs fell with a thud onto the concrete landing, her head slamming into the handrail. She rolled onto her stomach, stunned.

"Oh, great." The white guy's voice from the top of the stairs.

"Who the devil's that?" the black voice asked.

She lifted her head. The white guy snagged a baseball bat and started down the stairs.

I'm dead, she thought. I'm dead.

The switchblade rested in her pocket. It took every ounce of energy to roll onto her back to fish for her knife. But it was too late. He stepped on her arm, pinning it to the ground, and he gazed down at her.

Oh, man, Rhyme, blew it bad. Wish we'd had a better farewell night. I'm sorry. . . . I'm sorry.

With a tendony hand tough as a bird claw, the small man pulled the knife from her pocket. He tossed it away. "Now you're gonna tell me what you're doing here," he muttered, swinging the bat absently. "Who are you?"

"Her name's Mizz Amelia Sachs," said the homeless guy, suddenly sounding a lot less homeless. He moved up quickly and took the bat away. "And unless I'm most mistaken, she's come here to bust your little butt. Just like me." Sachs squinted to see him straighten up and turn into Fred Dellray, pointing a very large automatic pistol at the astonished man.

"You're a cop?" he sputtered. "This is just my stinkin' luck!"

"Nup," Dellray said. "Luck didn't have a bitsy thing to do with it. Now I'm gonna cuff you, an' you're gonna let me or you gonna hurt for months and months. We all together on that?"

"AND what do we have here?" Rhyme asked, giving a soft puff into the Storm Arrow control straw to scoot forward.

"An itsy piece of garbage," offered Fred Dellray, cleaned up and back in his green suit. He turned his alarming stare on Jodie. "Uh, uh, uh. Don't say a word. Not till we ask fo' it."

"You fooled me." The poor man was completely bewildered.

"Quiet, you little skel."

Rhyme wasn't pleased Dellray had gone out on his own, but he couldn't argue. The agent got results. And he'd saved Amelia's hide.

She'd be here soon. The medics had taken her for a rib X ray. He'd been dismayed to learn that his talk the other night had had no effect; she'd gone into the subway after the Dancer alone.

She's as pigheaded as me, he thought.

"I wasn't going to hurt anybody," Jodie protested.

"Hard o' hearing? I said don't say a word."

"I didn't know who she was."

"No, that pretty silver badge of hers didn't give nothin' away."

Sellitto walked up close. "Tell us more about your friend."

"I'm not his friend. He kidnapped me. I was—"

"You were boosting pills. We know. Keep going."

"He said he was there to kill some people. I thought he was going to kill me too. He told me to stand still, and this cop came. I didn't know he was going to kill him." He paused.

Sellitto looked up from the evidence bags. "Keep going."

"Well, he said he'd pay me to get him out of there, and I led him through this tunnel to the subway."

"Who hired him?" Sellitto asked. "He mention a name?"

"He didn't say." Jodie's voice quavered. "Look"—he turned to Dellray—"he wanted you to help. But soon as he left, I was going to the police. I was. He's a scary guy. I'm afraid of him."

"What were you supposed to do?" Rhyme asked.

"I was supposed to go through the trash bins in front of some town house and watch for cars leaving. Then call on that phone there. I was going to come to you."

"Man, you're useless when you lie," Dellray said.

"Look, I was *going* to," he said. "I figured there was a reward."

Rhyme glanced at the greedy eyes and tended to believe him. He looked at Sellitto, who nodded in agreement.

"You cooperate now," Sellitto grumbled, "and we might just keep you out of jail. I don't know about money. Maybe. When were you supposed to be there?"

"At twelve thirty."

They had fifty minutes left. "What's he look like?"

"In his early, mid-thirties, I guess. Not tall. But he was strong. Man, he had muscles. Crew-cut black hair. Round face."

"Did he give you a name? Anything? Where he's from?"

"I don't know. He has kind of a southern accent. Oh, and one thing—he said he killed a guy in his town when he was a kid."

"When he was a kid?" Rhyme spat out in dismay. "They seal juvenile records."

"What else?" Dellray barked.

"Look," Jodie said, "I've done some bad stuff, but I've never hurt anybody. This guy kidnaps me, and he's got all these guns and is one crazy messed-up guy, and I was scared to death. You woulda done the same thing I did. So you want to arrest me, do it, but I'm not gonna say anything else. Okay?"

Amelia Sachs appeared in the doorway.

"Tell them," Jodie said to her. "I didn't hurt you. Tell 'em."

She glanced at him the way you'd look at a wad of used chewing gum. "He was going to brain me with a Louisville Slugger."

"Not so, not so!"

"You okay, Sachs?" Rhyme asked.

"A bruise is all. On my back."

Sellitto, Sachs, and Dellray huddled with Rhyme, who told Sachs what Jodie had reported. Sellitto and Dellray said they believed the little skel but they should keep him on a tight leash.

Rhyme reluctantly agreed. It seemed impossible to get ahead of the Dancer without this man's help.

Sellitto called him over. "All right, here's the deal. You help us, you make the call like he wanted *and* we get him, then we'll drop all charges and get you some reward money."

"How much?" Jodie asked. "I need money for a rehab program. I need another ten thousand."

Sellitto looked at Dellray. "What's your snitch fund like?"

"We could go there," the agent said, "if you do halfsies."

"Really?" Jodie smiled. "Then I'll do whatever you want."

STEPHEN was moving through alleys, riding on buses, dodging the cops he saw and the Worm he couldn't see. The Worm, watching him through every window. The Worm, getting closer.

He thought about Jodie. About what he'd said. Heck, maybe they *could* get coffee after the job was over. Real coffee, double strong, like the kind Stephen's mother made for his stepfather— water at a rolling boil, exactly two and three-quarter level table-spoons per cup, not a single black ground spilled *anywhere.* And was fishing or hunting totally out of the question?

It wasn't too late to change the plans. There were still alternatives. He could tell Jodie to abort the mission. He could take the Wife and the Friend on his own.

Abort, soldier? What are you talking about?

Sir, nothing, sir. I am considering all eventualities, sir.

Stephen climbed off the bus and slipped into the alley behind a fire station on Lexington. He rested the book bag behind a Dumpster, slipped his knife from the sheath under his jacket.

Jodie. Joe D. The way the man had looked at him. *I'm glad I met you too, partner.*

Stephen shivered suddenly. He closed his eyes and pressed up against the brick wall, smelled the wet stone. Jodie was—

Soldier, what is going on there?

Sir, I . . .

What? Spit it out. Now, soldier!

Sir, I have ascertained that the enemy was trying psychological warfare. It was unsuccessful. I am ready to proceed as planned.

And Stephen realized, as he opened the back door to the firehouse, that there'd be no changing plans now. This was a perfect setup, and he couldn't waste it, particularly when there was a chance not only of killing the Wife and the Friend but of killing Lincoln the Worm and the redheaded woman cop too.

Jodie would call on Stephen's phone in fifteen minutes. Stephen would hear the high-pitched voice one last time.

Infiltrate, evaluate, delegate, isolate, eliminate. He really had no choice. Besides, he thought, what would we ever have to talk about after we'd finished our coffee?

WAITING.

Rhyme was now alone in his bed upstairs, listening in on the special ops frequency. He was dead tired. It was noon on Sunday. He'd had very little sleep, and he was exhausted, mostly from trying to outthink the Dancer. It was taking its toll on his body.

Cooper was in the lab. Everyone else was at the safe house, Amelia Sachs too. Once Rhyme, Sellitto, and Dellray had decided how to counter what they believed would be the Dancer's next effort to kill Percey Clay and Brit Hale, Thom checked Rhyme's blood pressure, asserted his virtual parental authority, and ordered his boss into bed. They'd ridden up in the elevator, Rhyme oddly silent, wondering if he'd guessed right again.

Rhyme was now leaning his head back into his luxurious down pillow. Thom had slipped the voice-recognition headset over his head, and despite his fatigue, Rhyme himself had gone through the steps of talking to the computer and having it patch into the special ops frequency. This system *was* amazing. It made him feel different about himself. He'd been resigned to never leading a life that approached normal. Yet with this machine he *did* feel normal.

He rolled his head in a circle and let it ease back into the pillow, trying not to think of the debacle with Sachs last night.

Motion nearby. The male falcon strutted into view. Rhyme saw a flash of white breast; then the bird turned his blue-gray back and looked out over Central Park.

The radio clattered. It was Amelia Sachs calling in. She sounded tense. "We're all on the top floor with Jodie," she said. "Wait. Here's the truck."

An armored 4 × 4 with mirrored windows, filled with four officers from the tactical team, was being used as the bait. It would be followed by a plumbing-supply van containing six 32-E troopers. Two officers were standing by as decoys.

"The decoys're downstairs," Sachs said. "Here they go. On the run." A click as the radio went dead.

Another click. Sellitto. "They made it. Looks good. Starting to drive. The tail cars're ready."

"All right," Rhyme said. "Tell Jodie to make the call."

"Okay, Linc. Here we go." The radio clicked off.

Waiting. To see if this time he'd outthought the Dancer.

STEPHEN'S cell phone brayed. He flipped it open. " 'Lo."

"Hi. It's me. It's—"

"I know," Stephen said. "Don't use names."

"Right, sure." Jodie sounded nervous as a cornered raccoon. A pause; then the little man said, "Well, I'm here."

"Good. You got that Negro to help you?"

"Um, yeah. He's here."

"And where are you exactly?"

"Across the street from that town house. There's a van just pulled up. A big blue Yukon. It has mirrored windows."

"That means they're bulletproof."

"Oh, really? It's neat how you know all this stuff."

You're going to die, Stephen said to him silently.

"This man and a woman just ran out of the alley with, like, ten cops. I'm sure it's them. Are you in a car?"

"Of course," Stephen said. "Some cheap Japanese thing. I'm going to follow them till they get to some deserted area."

"You see 'em?" Jodie asked, sounding uncomfortable.

"I see them," Stephen said. "I'm pulling into traffic now."

"A Japanese car," Jodie said. "Like a Toyota or something?"

Why, you scummy little traitor, Stephen thought bitterly.

Stephen was, in fact, watching the Yukon and backup vans speed past him. He wasn't, however, in any Japanese car, cheap or otherwise. He wasn't in any car at all. Wearing the fireman's uniform he'd just stolen, he was standing on the street corner exactly one hundred feet from the safe house, watching the real version of the events Jodie was fictionalizing. There was no Jodie, no Negro.

Stephen picked up his gray remote-detonation transmitter. He set the frequency to the bomb in Jodie's phone and armed the device. "Stand by," he said.

"Heh." Jodie laughed. "Will do, sir."

Stephen pushed the TRANSMIT button.

The explosion was astonishingly loud. It rattled panes and sent a million pigeons reeling into the sky. Stephen saw the glass and wood from the top floor of the safe house go spraying into the alley. He'd expected Jodie to be nearby. Maybe in a police van in front. But he couldn't believe his good fortune that Jodie'd actually been inside. It was perfect.

He wondered who else had died in the blast. Lincoln the Worm, he prayed. The redheaded cop?

Smoke curled from the top window. Now just a few more minutes until the rest of his team joined him.

RHYME ordered the computer to shut off the radio and answer the ringing phone. "Yes," he said.

"Lincoln." It was Lon Sellitto. "He blew the bomb."

"I know." Rhyme had heard it; the safe house was a mile or so from his bedroom, but his windows had rattled and the peregrines had taken off, angry at the disturbance.

What had tipped Rhyme to the cell phone bomb had been tiny fingernails of polystyrene that Sachs had found in the trace at the subway station. That and residue of plastic explosive. Rhyme had simply matched the polystyrene to the phone the Dancer'd given to Jodie and called the bomb squad down at the Sixth Precinct. Two detectives had rendered the phone safe, then mounted a much smaller wad of explosive and the same firing circuit in an oil drum near one of the safe-house windows, pointed into the alley like a mortar.

Rhyme had guessed that the Dancer's tactic was to use the bomb to divert attention away from the van and give him a better chance to assault it. The killer had also probably guessed that Jodie would turn. Rhyme secretly admired the man's brilliance.

Sellitto explained, "We've got two tail cars behind a Nissan. That might be it." A long pause. "Stupid," he muttered.

"What?"

"Oh, nothing. It's just nobody called Central to tell 'em to ignore the reports of the blast. We've got fire trucks coming in. The decoy van's turning east, Linc. Nissan's following."

"Okay, Lon. Is Amelia there? I want to talk to her."

"What the . . ." Sellitto said. "We got fire trucks all over the place. Didn't somebody—"

No, somebody didn't, Rhyme thought. You can't think of—

"Have to call you back, Lincoln. We gotta do something. There are fire trucks up on the sidewalk."

THE room darkened, curtains drawn.

Percey Clay was afraid. She detested it here. Closed in. Another sip from the flask. Rhyme had told her about the trap. That the Dancer would be following the van he believed Percey and Hale were in. They'd stop his car and arrest or kill him. In ten minutes they'd have him, the man who had changed her life forever.

Roland Bell had ordered her to stay locked in her room, lights out. Everyone was upstairs on the top floor. She'd heard the bang of the explosion, but she hadn't been expecting the fear it brought. Unbearable.

She walked to the door, unlocked it, stepped into the dark, deserted corridor. There was slight motion at the end of the hall. A shadow from the stairwell. She looked at it. It wasn't repeated.

Brit Hale's room was only ten feet away. She wanted badly to go talk to him. But she didn't want him to see her this way—pale, hands shaking. She stepped back into her room, closed the door, returned to the bed.

Did she hear footsteps?

"COMMAND mode." The box dutifully came up on-screen.

Lincoln Rhyme heard a faint siren in the distance.

And it was then that he realized his mistake. Fire trucks. "Oh, no," he muttered. The Dancer would have stolen a fireman's or medic's uniform and was strolling into the safe house at this moment. "No! How could I be so far off?"

The computer heard the last word of Rhyme's sentence and dutifully shut off his communications program.

"No!" Rhyme cried. "No!"

But the system couldn't understand his loud, frantic voice, and with a silent flash a message came up: "Do you really want to shut off your computer?"

"No," he whispered desperately.

Another message: "What would you like to do now?"

"Thom!" he shouted. "Somebody, please!"

But the door was closed; there was no response.

Rhyme's left ring finger—his one working finger—twitched dramatically. "Command mode," he said, fighting to stay calm.

"I did not understand what you just said. Please try again."

Where was the Dancer now? Was he inside already? Was he just about to shoot Percey Clay or Brit Hale? Or Amelia Sachs?

"Thom! Mel!"

"I did not understand . . ."

Why wasn't I thinking better? "Command mode," he said breathlessly, trying to master the panic.

The command mode message box popped up.

"Cursor down," he gasped. "Cursor stop. Double-click."

Dutifully an icon of a walkie-talkie popped up on the screen. He pictured the fearless Dancer moving up behind Percey Clay with a knife or garrote.

A NIGHTMARE.

Stephen Kall, in ski mask and bulky fireman's coat, lay pinned down in the corridor of the safe house, behind the body of one of two U.S. marshals he'd just killed.

Another shot, closer, digging a piece out of the floor near his head. Fired by the detective with the thinning brown hair—the one he'd seen in the window before. He crouched in a doorway, but Stephen couldn't get a clean shot at him. The detective held automatic pistols in both his hands and was an excellent shot.

Stephen crawled forward another yard, toward an open door. Panicked, cringey, coated with worms.

Stephen had blown open the alley door with a cutting charge and run inside, expecting to find the interior a fiery shambles and the Wife and Friend blown to pieces. But the Worm had fooled him again. He'd figured out that the phone was booby-trapped. The only thing they hadn't expected was that he'd hit the safe house again. Still, when he burst inside, he was met by frantic fire from two marshals. But he'd managed to kill them.

He had no more than a minute at the most. He felt so wormy he wanted to cry. Lincoln the Worm. Was this him? The balding detective with the two guns?

Another volley from Stephen's gun, and—damn—the detective dived right into it and kept coming. Any other cop in the world would've run for cover. Stephen reloaded, fired again. Another yard, almost to the doorway.

"This's Bell!" the cop shouted into his microphone. "We need backup."

Bell. Stephen noted the name. So he's not Lincoln the Worm.

The cop reloaded and continued to fire. A dozen shots, two dozen. Stephen admired his technique. The cop parked a slug in the wall an inch from Stephen's face, and Stephen sent back a shot that landed just as close.

Bell moved forward, firing both guns. Stephen lowered his head and tossed a one-second-delay flash bang. The grenade detonated, and the cop stumbled to his knees, hands over his face.

Stephen had guessed that because of the guards and Bell's furious efforts to stop him, either the Wife or the Friend was in this room. Stephen had also guessed that whoever it was would be hiding in the closet or under the bed. He was wrong.

As he glanced into the doorway, he saw a figure come charging at him with a lamp, uttering a wail of fear and anger. Five fast shots, well grouped. The body flew backward to the floor.

Good job, soldier.

Footsteps coming. No time to finish. Evacuate.

He ran to the back door and stuck his head out, shouting for more firemen. A half-dozen of them ran up cautiously. He nodded them inside. "Gas line just blew. Get everybody out. Now!"

And he disappeared into the alley, then stepped into the street, dodging the fire trucks, the ambulances, the police cars. Shaken, yes. But satisfied. His job was now two-thirds finished.

AMELIA Sachs didn't know how the Dancer'd done it, and she didn't care. She wanted only a fair glimpse of the target and two seconds to sink half a clip of 9-mm hollow-points into him.

The light Glock in her hand, she pushed into the second-floor corridor. Behind her were Sellitto, Dellray, and a young uniform. Jodie cowered on the floor behind them.

Down the dark corridor, fast glance into each of the rooms, crouching below chest height, where a muzzle would be pointed.

Sachs came to the room just as two of Haumann's troops entered from the destroyed back doorway.

"Cover," she called, and before anyone had a chance to stop her, she leaped through the door fast, Glock up. She froze at the sight of the gun muzzle aimed at her chest.

"Lord," Roland Bell muttered, and lowered his weapon. His hair was mussed, and his face was sooty. Two bullets had torn his shirt and streaked over his body armor.

Then her eyes took in the terrible sight on the floor.

There were stories the crime scene would tell, and for that reason she knew she should help Percey Clay to her feet and lead her away from her slain friend. But all Sachs could do was watch the small woman with the squat, unpretty face cradle Brit Hale's bloody head, muttering, "Oh, no, oh, no."

Sachs's face was a mask, unmoving, untouched by tears.

TWO hundred and thirty yards from the safe house.

Red and blue lights from the dozens of emergency vehicles flashed and tried to blind him, but he was sighting through the telescope and was oblivious to anything but the reticles. Stephen scanned back and forth over the kill zone. He had recovered the Model 40 from under the water tower, where he'd hidden it that morning. The weapon was loaded and locked, and he was ready to murder.

At the moment it wasn't the Wife he was after.

The front door of the safe house swung open, and Jodie stepped out uneasily. He looked around, squinted.

You . . .

Stephen easily moved the reticles onto his chest.

Go ahead, soldier, fire your weapon. He can identify you.

Sir, I am adjusting for tracking and windage.

He betrayed you, soldier. Take him out.

Sir, yes, sir. He is ice-cold. He is dead meat.

He squeezed. Slowly, slowly.

But the gun wasn't firing. As he lifted the sights to Jodie's head, Jodie's eyes, which had been scanning the rooftops, saw him.

Stephen had waited too long. He jerked the trigger like a boy on the .22-rifle range at summer camp.

Jodie leaped out of the way, pushing the cops with him aside.

He got off two more rounds, but Jodie was under cover.

And then the return fire began. A dozen guns, then a dozen more.

Why did I wait? Why? I could have shot him and been gone.

The sound of a helicopter. More sirens.

Evacuate, soldier, evacuate.

Stephen threw the Model 40 into the case, slung the book bag over his shoulder, and slid down the fire escape into the alley.

Chapter Nine

"It's not pleasant," Thom told Amelia Sachs.

From behind Rhyme's bedroom door she heard, "I want that bottle, and I want it now!" followed by a howl of rage. Sachs knew the only reason he wasn't throwing things was because he couldn't.

"You might want to wait a little," Thom warned.

She opened the door. "We can't wait."

Rhyme snarled, "I want that bottle." He was a sight. His hair was disheveled, and his eyes were red. The Macallan bottle was on the floor. He must have tried to grab it with his teeth and knocked it over.

He noticed Sachs, but all he said was a brisk "Pick it up."

"We've got work to do, Rhyme."

"Pick up that bottle."

She did, and placed it on the shelf. "You've had enough."

"Pour some whisky in my glass. Thom, get in here."

"Rhyme," she snapped, "we've got evidence to look at."

"Evidence! The Dancer got inside, didn't he? Fox in the henhouse. Fox in the henhouse."

"I've got a vacuum filter full of trace, I've got a slug. You oughta be like a kid on his birthday, all the evidence I've got. Quit feeling sorry for yourself, and let's get to work."

He didn't respond. She saw his bleary eyes focused past her on the doorway. She turned. There was Percey Clay.

Immediately Rhyme's eyes dropped to the floor. He fell silent.

Sure, Sachs thought. Can't misbehave in front of his new love.

Percey walked into the room, looked at the mess that was Rhyme.

"Lincoln, what's going on?" Sellitto had accompanied Percey.

"Three dead, Lon. He got three more. Fox in the henhouse."

"Lincoln," Sachs blurted, "you're embarrassing yourself."

Wrong thing to say. Rhyme slapped a bewildered gaze on his face. "I'm not embarrassed. Do I look embarrassed? Anyone? *Am I embarrassed?*" He finally looked at Percey. "What are you doing here? You're supposed to be on Long Island."

"I want to talk to you."

He said nothing at first, then, "Give me a drink at least."

Percey poured herself and Rhyme glasses. Sachs glared at her.

"Here's a classy lady," Rhyme said. "I kill her partner, and she still shares a drink with me. *You* didn't do that, Sachs."

"Rhyme, you can be such a jerk," Sachs spat out. "Where's Mel?"

"Sent him home. Nothing more to do. We're shipping her off to Long Island, where she'll be safe. Hit me again."

Percey began to, but Sachs said, "He's had enough."

"Don't listen to her," Rhyme blurted. "She's mad at me. I don't do what she wants, and so she gets mad."

Oh, thank you, Rhyme. Let's air linen in public, why don't we? She turned her beautiful cold eyes on him. He didn't even notice; he was gazing at Percey Clay.

Who said, "You made a deal with me. The next thing I know, there're two agents about to take me off to Long Island. I thought I could trust you."

"But if you trust me, you'll die."

"It was a risk," Percey said. "You told us there was a chance he'd get into the safe house."

"Sure. But you didn't know that I figured it out. I figured out he was in a fireman's uniform. I knew it five minutes before he got in. It's just that I couldn't call anyone. I couldn't pick up the phone. Hale died because of me."

Sachs felt pity for him, and it was sour. She was torn apart by his pain, yet she didn't have a clue how to comfort him.

He nodded toward the computer. "Oh, I got cocky. I got to thinking I was pretty normal. Driving around like a racecar driver in the Storm Arrow, flipping on lights, changing CDs. What bull." He closed his eyes.

A sharp laugh, surprising everyone, filled the room. Percey Clay, pouring more Scotch into her glass, then Rhyme's, said, "There's bull here, for sure. But it's only what I'm hearing from you."

"Don't," Rhyme warned ambiguously, glaring.

"Oh, please," she muttered dismissively. "Don't what? You're saying that somebody's dead because of technical failure. That gives you the right to have a tantrum? To renege on your promises?" She tossed back her liquor and gave an exasperated sigh. "Do you have any idea what I do for a living?"

Rhyme started to speak, but Percey cut him off. "Think about this. I sit in a little aluminum tube going four hundred knots, six miles above the ground. It's sixty below zero outside, and the winds are a hundred miles an hour. I'm only alive *because* of machines." Another laugh. "How's that different from you?"

"You don't understand," he said snippily. "You can walk around."

"Walk around? I'm at fifty thousand feet, I open that door and my blood boils in seconds."

Rhyme's met his match. He's speechless, Sachs thought.

Percey continued. "I'm sorry, Detective, but I don't see a lick of difference between us. We're both products of twentieth-century science. We rely."

Come on, Rhyme, Sachs thought. Let her have it.

The criminalist said, "But if *I* screw up, people die."

"Oh? And what happens if my deicer fails? What if a pigeon flies into my pitot tube on an approach? I am dead. In your case, they might get a chance to recover from their gunshots."

Rhyme seemed completely sober now. His eyes were swiveling around the room as if looking for evidence to refute her argument.

"Now," Percey said evenly, "my suggestion is you stop this Dancer once and for all, because I am on my way to the airport right now to finish repairing my aircraft, and then I'm flying that job tonight, like we agreed. Or do I have to call my lawyer?"

He was still speechless. A moment passed.

Sachs jumped when Rhyme called in his booming baritone, "Thom! *Thom!* Get in here."

The aide peered around the doorway suspiciously.

"I've made a mess here. Look, I knocked my glass over. And my hair's mussed. Would you mind straightening up? Please?"

"Are you fooling with us, Lincoln?" Thom asked.

"And Lon? Call Mel Cooper. He must have taken me seriously. Scientists! No sense of humor. We'll need him back here."

Sachs wanted to flee. To get in her car and tear up the roads in Nassau County at 120 miles an hour. She couldn't stand to be in the same room with this woman a moment longer.

"All right, Percey," Rhyme said, "take Detective Bell with you, and we'll make sure plenty of troopers are with you too. Get up to your airport. Do what you have to do."

"Thank you, Lincoln." She nodded, and offered a smile. Just enough of one to make clear who the undisputed winner in this contest was. Well, some sports Amelia Sachs believed she was doomed to lose. Champion shooter, decorated cop, a demon of a driver, and pretty good criminalist, Sachs nonetheless possessed an unjacketed heart. Her father had sensed this; he'd been a romantic too. "They oughta make body armor for the soul, Amie," he'd said to her. "They oughta do that."

Good-bye, Rhyme, she thought. Good-bye.

And his response to this tacit farewell? A minuscule glance and a gruff, "Let's look at that evidence, Sachs. Time's a-wasting."

"WHAT did you find?" Rhyme asked Sachs.

She'd found all the casings from the Dancer's 7.62-mm Beretta. But they'd been dipped in cleansers to eliminate even the prints of the employees of the ammunition company so no one could trace the purchase back to a certain plant and shipment. And he'd apparently loaded them with his knuckles to avoid prints. An old trick.

"Keep going," Rhyme said.

"Pistol slugs." Three flattened, and one in pretty good shape.

"Scan them for prints," Rhyme ordered.

"I did," she said, her voice clipped. "Nothing."

Cooper looked at a piece of cotton in a plastic bag. He asked, "What's that?"

Sachs said, "Oh, I got one of his rifle slugs too."

"What?" Rhyme blinked.

"He got off a few shots from the roof as Jodie stepped out. Two of them hit the front door. This one hit dirt and didn't go off."

"Wait," Cooper said. "That's one of the explosive rounds?" He gingerly set the bag on the table and stepped back, pulling Sachs along with him.

"What's the matter?" Sachs asked.

"Explosive bullets're very unstable. Could go off any minute."

Sachs asked, "Why didn't it go off?"

"The dirt'd be soft impact. And he makes them himself. Maybe his quality control wasn't so good for that one."

"He makes them himself?" Rhyme asked, looking at Sachs, and for a moment the rift between them vanished. They smiled and said simultaneously, "Fingerprints!"

Cooper said, "Maybe. But how're you going to find out?"

"I'll take it apart," Sachs said.

"No, Sachs," Rhyme said. "We'll wait for the bomb squad."

"We don't have time." She bent over the bullet. "I'll put my vest on top of it, work from behind it." She stripped her blouse off, ripped the Velcro straps of her body armor, and set up a tent. "What do I do?"

No, Sachs, no, Rhyme thought.

"If you don't tell me, I'll just cut it apart." She picked up a forensic razor saw. The blade hovered over the bag.

Rhyme sighed, nodded to Cooper. "Tell her what to do."

"All right. Unwrap it carefully. Here, put it on this towel."

She exposed a surprisingly tiny bullet with an off-white tip.

"That cone'll go right through body armor and two walls."

"Okay." She turned it aside, toward the wall.

"Sachs," Rhyme said soothingly, "use forceps. Please."

She hesitated and took a hemostat from Cooper to grip the base of the slug. "How do I open it up?"

"You'll have to work the cone off," Cooper said.

Sweat was rolling down her face. "Okay. With pliers?"

Cooper put a pair of needle-nosed pliers in her right hand. "You'll have to twist hard. But don't fracture it."

"Hard, but not too hard," she muttered.

"Think of all those cars you worked on, Sachs," Rhyme said. "Those old ceramic spark plugs."

She nodded absently and lowered her head behind the tepee of her body armor, her eyes squinting shut.

Oh, Sachs, Rhyme thought. He heard a very faint snap.

She froze for a moment, then looked over the armor. "It came off. It's open."

Cooper said, "Do you see the explosive?"

She looked inside. "Yes."

He handed her a can of light machine oil. "Drip some of this inside the shell casing, then tilt it. The plastic should fall out."

She added the oil, then tilted the slug. Nothing happened.

"Damn," she muttered. She shook it. Hard.

"Sachs!" Rhyme gasped.

A tiny white thread fell out, followed by grains of powder.

"Okay," Cooper said, exhaling. "It's safe." Using a needle probe, he rolled the plastic onto a glass slide. He walked in the smooth gait of criminalists around the world—back straight, hand buoyed—to the microscope. He mounted the explosive.

"Use gentian violet," Rhyme said. "Just a little contrast."

Cooper sprayed it, then mounted the slide in the scope. The image popped onto Rhyme's screen simultaneously.

"Yes!" he shouted. "There it is." The whorls and bifurcations were very visible. "You nailed it, Sachs. Good job."

But when Cooper examined Rhyme's printout, he sighed. "No AFIS in the world could pick up anything from this."

"All that effort," Rhyme spat out, "wasted."

A sudden laugh from Amelia Sachs, staring at the evidence charts, CS-1, CS-2. "Put them together. We've got another partial."

Cooper looked at Rhyme. "I've never heard of doing that."

Neither had Rhyme. A defense lawyer'd go to town if cops started assembling perps' fingerprints.

"Sure," Rhyme said. "Do it."

Cooper grabbed the other image from the wall, and they started to work. He made photocopies of the prints so they were the same size. Then he and Sachs began fitting them together like a jigsaw puzzle. They were like children, trying variations, arguing playfully. Sachs went so far as to take out a pen and connect several lines. Finally they had about three quarters of a right index fingerprint.

Cooper held it up. "I have my doubts about this, Lincoln."

But Rhyme said, "It's art, Mel. It's beautiful. Put it through AFIS. Authorize a priority search, all states."

Five minutes later the screen fluttered and a new image came up: "Your request has found 1 match. 14 points of comparison. Statistical probability of identity, 97%."

"I don't believe it," Sachs muttered. "We've got him."

"Who is he, Mel?" Rhyme asked softly.

"He's not the Dancer anymore," Cooper said. "He's Stephen Robert Kall. Thirty-six. Last known address, fifteen years ago, an R.F.D. number in Cumberland, West Virginia. He did twenty months for manslaughter when he was fifteen." A faint laugh. "He didn't bother to tell Jodie that the victim was Lou Kall, his stepfather."

"Stepfather, hm?"

"Tough reading." Cooper pored over the police reports on the screen. "Seems like there'd been a history of domestic disputes. The boy's mother was dying of cancer, and her husband hit her for something or other. She broke her arm, died a few months later, and Kall got it into his head her death was the stepfather's fault. Want to hear what happened?"

"Go ahead."

"After she died, Stephen and his stepfather were out hunting. The kid knocked him out, stripped him naked, tied him to a tree in the woods. Left him there for a few days. Just to scare him, his lawyer said. But he forgot where he was. By the time the police got to him . . . well, let's just say the infestation was pretty bad. Maggots, mostly. Lived for two days after that. Delirious."

"Man," Sachs whispered.

"When they found him, the boy was there, just sitting next to him, watching." Cooper read, " 'The suspect surrendered without resistance. Appeared in disoriented state. Kept repeating, "Anything can kill, anything can kill." ' "

And Lincoln Rhyme could only agree.

PROFESSIONAL flying is only partly about flying. Flying is also about paperwork. Littering the back of the van transporting Percey Clay to Mamaroneck Airport was a huge stack of charts and documents, information she studied as she filled out the preflight navigation log and the flight plan. She submerged herself in the work.

Roland Bell was beside her, haggard and sullen. The good ole boy was long gone. She grieved for him as much as for herself; it seemed that Brit Hale was the first witness he'd lost.

Just as she finished the last flight-plan card, the van turned the corner and entered the airport. The armed guards examined their IDs and waved them through. Percey noticed that the lights were still on in the office. She told the driver to stop, and she climbed out. Bell and her other bodyguards walked in with her, vigilant and tense.

Ron Talbot, grease-stained and exhausted, sat in the office, wiping his sweating forehead. His face was an alarming red.

"Ron"—she gave him a hug—"are you all right?"

"Brit," he said, shaking his head, gasping. "He got Brit too. Percey, you shouldn't be here. Go someplace safe."

She stepped back. "What's wrong? You sick?"

"Just tired."

She took the cigarette out of his hand and stubbed it out. "You did the work yourself? On Foxtrot Bravo?"

"Most of it. The guy delivered the new parts an hour ago. I started to mount it. Got a little tired."

"Chest pains?"

"No, not really."

"Ron," she said, "go home. I can finish up." Talbot looked like he couldn't lift a wrench, much less a heavy combustor. She kissed his sweaty forehead.

Talbot struggled to his feet, stood for a moment looking out the window at Foxtrot Bravo. His face revealed an acrid bitterness. It was the same look she'd remembered in his milky eyes when he'd told her that he'd flunked his physical and could no longer fly for a living. He headed out the door.

THEY had a mystery on their hands. Cooper and Sachs had returned to examining the trace found in the treads of the fire trucks and police cars at the scene of the Ed Carney crash. There was the useless dirt, grass, oil, and garbage that Rhyme had expected, but they made one discovery he felt was important. He just didn't have a clue what it meant.

The only indications of bomb residue were tiny fragments of a pliable beige substance. The gas chromatograph–mass spectrometer reported it was C_5H_8.

"Isoprene," Cooper reflected. "Soft rubber, like latex." He peered at a sample in the microscope. "Rubber cement too, and . . . bingo!"

"Don't tease, Mel," Rhyme grumbled.

"Bits of soldering and tiny pieces of plastic embedded in the rubber. Circuit boards."

"Part of the timer?" Sachs wondered aloud.

"No. That was intact," Rhyme reminded. "We have to know whether this's from the bomb or the plane. Sachs, I want you to go up to the airport. Find Percey and have her give you samples of anything with latex, rubber, or circuit boards that would be in the belly of a plane like the one he was flying. And Mel, send the info off to the Bureau's Explosives Reference Collection."

"You want me to go talk to her?" Sachs said. "To Percey?"

"Yes. And don't give her any grief like you've been doing. We need her."

Rhyme didn't have a clue why she pulled on her vest so angrily and stalked out the door without saying good-bye.

AT THE airport Sachs pushed into the huge hangar. She walked up to the scaffolding where Percey was working. Sachs watched as

Percey mounted a large red cylinder—a fire extinguisher, Sachs guessed—into the Lear's engine compartment in ten seconds flat. But another part—it looked like a big metal inner tube—wouldn't fit correctly. Percey's chest heaved as she struggled with it.

Neither woman said anything for a long moment.

Finally Sachs said, "Try a jack. The tolerance is close. All you need is more muscle. The old coercion technique."

Percey looked carefully at the mounting brackets on the metal. "I don't know. You ever mount a combustor in a Lear?"

"Nope. Spark plugs in a V-eight Chevy Monza. You jack up the engine to reach them."

Percey studied the fitting. "I don't have a small enough jack."

"I do. I'll get it."

Sachs stepped outside to the RRV and returned with the accordion jack. She climbed up on the scaffolding.

"Try right there, the engine base. That's I-beam steel."

As Percey positioned the jack, Sachs admired the intricacies of the engine. "How much horsepower?"

Percey laughed. "We rate in pounds of thrust, not horsepower. These Garrett TFE 731s give up about thirty-five hundred pounds each."

"Incredible." Sachs laughed and hooked the handle into the jack. Soon she was breathing hard, struggling to turn the crank.

Percey put her shoulder against the ring and shoved. "You know cars, huh?" she said. "Ever driven an aircraft?"

"No. But maybe I'll think about it." Sachs cranked some more.

"Almost there," Percey said.

With a loud metallic clang the ring popped onto the mounts perfectly. Percey's squat face broke into a faint smile. She tightened the bolts down with a ratcheting socket, then started reconnecting wires and electronic components. "Thanks," she said. A few moments later, "What're you doing here?"

"We found some other materials we think might be from the bomb. But Lincoln didn't know if it was part of the plane or not. Bits of beige latex, circuit board. Sound familiar?"

Percey shrugged. "There're thousands of gaskets in a Lear. They could be latex. And circuit boards? Probably another thousand of them." She nodded to a workbench. "The boards are special orders, but there should be a good stock of gaskets there. Take samples of whatever you need."

Sachs walked over to the bench, began slipping all beige-colored bits of rubber into an evidence bag.

Without glancing at Sachs, Percey said, "I thought you were here to arrest me. Haul me back to jail."

I ought to, Sachs thought, but said, "Just collecting exemplars."

Percey asked, "So what is it?"

Sachs asked, "What do you mean?"

"This, um, tension. Between us. You and me."

"You nearly got a friend of mine killed."

Percey shook her head. She said reasonably, "It's something else. I felt it before Jerry got shot. When I first saw you, in Lincoln Rhyme's room."

Sachs said nothing.

"It's about him, isn't it?"

"Who?"

"You know who I mean. Lincoln Rhyme."

"You think I'm jealous?" Sachs laughed.

"Yes, I do. It's more than just work between you. I think you're in love with him."

"Of course I'm not. That's crazy."

Percey offered a telling glance and carefully twined up excess wire. "Whatever you saw is just respect for his talent. That's all." She lifted a grease-stained hand toward herself. "Come on, Amelia, look at me. I'm short, I'm bossy, I'm not good-looking. Besides, I just lost my husband. I'm not interested in anyone else."

"I'm sorry," Sachs began slowly, "but I've gotta say . . . well, you don't really seem to be in mourning."

"Why? Because I'm trying to keep my company going?"

"No, there's more than that," Sachs replied cautiously. "Isn't there?"

Percey examined Sachs's face. "Ed and I were incredibly close. We were husband and wife and friends and business partners. And yes, he was seeing someone else. It tore me apart. Hell, it tore Ed apart too. He loved me, but he needed his beautiful lovers. But you know, he always came home to me." She paused for a moment and fought the tears.

"And you?"

"Was I faithful?" Percey gave one of her wry laughs. "I'm hardly the kind of girl gets picked up walking down the street. But after I found out about Ed and his girlfriends, I was mad. I saw some other men. Ron and I—Ron Talbot—spent some time together, a few months. He even proposed to me. But Ed was the man I had to be with. That never changed." Her eyes grew distant. "We met in the navy, Ed and I. Both fighter pilots. When he proposed, he wanted to get me a ring, but we were saving every penny to open our own charter company. One night we borrowed this old Norseman they had on the field, and I got us up to six thousand feet. Suddenly he kissed me, took over, and said, 'I got you a diamond after all, Perce.' "

"He did?" Sachs asked.

Percey smiled. "He throttled up, all the way to the fire wall, and pulled the yoke back. The nose went straight up in the air. For a moment, before we started out of the stall, we were looking straight into the night sky. He leaned over and said, 'Take your pick. All the stars of evening. You can have any one you want.' " Percey lowered her head, wiped her eyes with her sleeve, then turned back to the engine. "Believe me, you don't have anything to worry about. Ed was all I ever wanted."

"There's more to it than you know." Sachs sighed. "You remind Rhyme of someone. Someone he was in love with. You show up, and all of a sudden it's like he's with her again."

Percey shrugged. "He and I understand each other. But so what? That doesn't mean anything. Take a look, Amelia. Rhyme loves you."

Sachs laughed. "Oh, I don't think so."

Percey turned and glanced down at Sachs. "Looking at Rhyme and looking at you, I wouldn't give it much more than fifty-fifty. But you know, I had this flight instructor a long time ago. When we'd fly multiengine, he had this game. Lot of instructors'll cut power for a few minutes just to see how you can handle it. But he'd make us land on one engine. Students'd always be asking him, 'Isn't that risky?' His answer was, 'God don't give out certain. Sometimes you just gotta play the odds.' "

Chapter Ten
. . . Hour 32 of 45

AT FIVE p.m. Sunday they summoned Jodie from the downstairs bedroom in the town house, where he'd been under lock and key. He trotted up the stairs reluctantly, clutching his silly book, *Dependent No More.* Rhyme remembered the title. It had been on the *Times* best-seller list for months. In a black mood at the time, he'd thought cynically about himself, Dependent forever.

A team of federal agents were flying from Quantico to Cumberland, West Virginia, Stephen Kall's old town, to pick up what leads they could. "You told us some things about him," Rhyme said to Jodie. "I want to know more. Think hard."

Jodie squinted. Rhyme supposed he was considering what he could say to mollify them. But he was surprised when Jodie said, "Well, for one thing, he's afraid of you."

"Me?" Rhyme asked, astonished. "He knows about me?"

"He knows your name's Lincoln and you're out to get him."

"How?"

"I don't know," the man said, then added, "You know, he made a couple of calls on that cell phone. He listened for a long time."

"Oh, hellfire," Dellray sang out. "He's tapping a line."

"Of course," Rhyme cried. "Probably the Hudson Air office. That's how he found out about the safe house."

To Jodie, Rhyme said, "What else does he know about me?"

"He knows you're a detective. I don't think he knows where

you live or your last name. But you scare the wits out of him."

If Rhyme's belly had been able to register the lub-dub of excitement and pride, he'd have felt it now. Let's see, Stephen Kall, if we can't give you a little more to be afraid of.

"You helped us once, Jodie. I need you to help us again."

"Are you crazy?"

"Shut up and listen," Dellray barked. "Hokay? *Hokay?*"

"I'm not doing any more." The whine really was too much.

"It's in your interest," Sellitto said reasonably, "to help us."

"Gettin' shot's in my interest? Uh-huh. You wanna explain that?"

"Sure, I'll explain it," Sellitto grumbled. "The Dancer knows you dimed him. Back at the safe house it woulda been smart for him just to take off. But he went to the trouble to try to cap you. Now, that tells us that he ain't gonna rest till he clips you."

Dellray said, "And I don't think you wanna have him knocking on yo' door—this week or next year. We all together on that?"

"So," Sellitto resumed, "it's in your interest to help us."

"But you'll give me, like, witness protection?"

Sellitto shrugged. "If you help us, yes."

Jodie's eyes were red and watery. He seemed so afraid. Rhyme wondered what it must be like to live so timidly. A mouse's life.

Too many ways to die.

Sellitto said, "You were there when he killed that agent. That man could be alive now. You can help us stop him."

Jodie absently riffled the pages in his book with a filthy thumb. Finally he looked up and—with surprising sobriety—said, "When I was taking him to my place, I thought I'd maybe push him into a sewer interceptor pipe. Or I know where they have these piles of tie spikes in the subway. I could grab one and hit him over the head. I really, really thought about doing that. But I got scared." He held up the book. " 'Chapter Three. Confronting Your Demons.' I've never stood up to anything."

"Hey, now's your chance," Sellitto said.

Flipping the tattered pages. Sighing. "Whatta I gotta do?"

"We'll get to that," Rhyme said. "Thom! Thom! Come here."

The exasperated face poked around the corner. "Yessss?"

"I'm feeling vain," Rhyme announced. "I need a mirror."

"What? A mirror?"

"A big one. And would you please comb my hair."

THE U.S. Medical and Healthcare van pulled onto the tarmac. If the two white-jacketed employees carting a quarter-million dollars' worth of human organs were concerned about the machine gun–armed cops ringing the field, they gave no indication of it. The only time they flinched was when King, the bomb squad German shepherd, searched the cargo cases. "Um, I'd watch that dog there," one of them said. "I imagine liver's liver and heart's heart." But King behaved like a thorough professional.

Percey and her freelance copilot Brad Torgeson had already done the walk-around, accompanied by Roland Bell, three troopers, and King. This was the most meticulous preflight visual in the history of aviation.

King continued his examination inside the plane. Rhyme and Sachs had found no match for the latex discovered at the crash site, and got the idea that the rubber might have been used to seal explosives so that dogs couldn't smell it. So Percey and Brad stood down while Tech Services went through the plane inside and out with hypersensitive microphones, listening for a timer.

Clean. Meanwhile, Agent Dellray had arranged with the FAA that the flight plan be sealed. The taxiway here and at each of their arrival cities would be guarded by uniformed patrolmen.

Now, engines started, Brad in the right-hand seat and Roland Bell shifting uneasily in his seat behind them, Percey Clay spoke to the tower. "Lear Niner Five Foxtrot Bravo ready for taxi."

"Roger, Niner Five Foxtrot Bravo. Cleared onto taxiway."

A touch to the smooth throttles, and the sprightly plane turned onto the taxiway. Percey wobbled the throttles a little closer to the fire wall, and the Learjet sped forward to the hold position where the killer had placed the bomb on Ed's plane. She looked out the window and saw two cops standing guard.

"Lear Niner Five Foxtrot Bravo," ground control called. "Proceed to and hold short of runway five left."

When cleared for takeoff, she turned the Lear onto the runway, straightened the nosewheel, and pushed the throttles forward. They began racing down the concrete strip. Fifty knots, sixty, seventy . . .

"Eighty knots," Brad called out. "Cross-check."

"Check," she called after a glance at the airspeed indicator.

"V One," Brad sang out. "Rotate."

Removing her right hand from the throttles and taking the yoke, Percey eased back, rotating the Lear upward, hearing the sweet grind of the turbofans behind her. In this sleek silver needle she felt herself flying into the heart of the sky, leaving behind the cumbersome, the heavy, the painful.

As they banked upward, she heard a gasp from Roland Bell.

"You having fun, Officer?" she called back.

"I'm just tickled," he said, looking nervously out the large round window. "You know, you can see straight down. Why'd they make it that way?"

Percey laughed. "On airliners they try to keep you from realizing you're flying. Where's the fun? What's the point?"

"I can see a point or two," he said, chewing his Wrigley's with energetic teeth. He closed the curtain.

At six thousand feet they broke through the cloud cover into a sky that was as spectacular as any sunset Percey had ever seen. She and Brad began the mundane tasks of setting the autopilot that would guide them to Chicago as straight as a samurai's arrow.

Bell gave a soft laugh. "You wanna know something?"

"What?" said Percey.

"This is the first time I've seen you looking halfway comfortable since I met you."

"Only place I really feel at home."

"Two hundred miles an hour, a mile up in the air, and you feel safe."

"No. Four hundred miles an hour, four miles up."

"Uh, thanks for sharing that."

WORMS. . . .

Stephen Kall, sweating, stood in a filthy bathroom in a Cuban Chinese restaurant. Scrubbing to save his soul. Until his cuticles were bleeding.

Soldier, that blood is evidence. You can't leave it there—

Sir, I'm busy, sir. Go away!

Scrub, scrub, scrub, scrub. Lincoln the Worm is looking for me. Everywhere Lincoln the Worm looks, worms appear.

Soldier, you can't—

Go away!

Stephen dried his hands, then grabbed the Fender guitar case and the book bag, pushed into the restaurant. The alarmed patrons stared at his bloody hands, his crazed expression.

"Worms," he muttered in explanation. "Cringey worms." Then burst outside onto the street and hurried down the sidewalk. Thinking about what he had to do. He had to kill Jodie, of course. Have to kill him, have to kill him, have to . . .

Why, soldier?

And he had to kill Lincoln the Worm because the worms would get him if he didn't. Have to kill, have to, have to . . .

Are you listening to me, soldier? Are you?

That was all there was left to do. Lincoln, dead. Jodie, dead.

Have to kill, have to . . . Then nothing more to keep him here.

As for the Wife—he looked at his watch. Just after seven p.m. Well, she was probably dead already.

DELLRAY cinched up Jodie tight in a bulletproof vest and tossed him a windbreaker. The vest was thick Kevlar on top of a steel sheet. It weighed forty-two pounds, and Rhyme didn't know a cop in the city who wore a vest like this. It actually gave little Jodie a muscular physique.

"But what if he shoots my head?" Jodie asked.

"He wants me a lot more than you," Rhyme said.

"And how's he gonna know I'm staying here?"

"How d'ya think, mutt?" Dellray snapped. "I'ma tell him."

"Okay," Sellitto said. "Take him downtown."

Two undercover officers ushered Jodie out the door.

After he'd left, Dellray sighed. Flicking open his cell phone, he placed a scripted call to the Dancer's tapped line at Hudson Air.

SITTING in a stolen car not far from Jodie's subway station home, Stephen Kall watched a government-issue sedan pull up. Jodie and two cops climbed out, scanning the rooftops. Jodie ran inside and, five minutes later, escaped back to the car with two bundles under his arm. According to what Stephen had heard on the tap, Lincoln had agreed that Jodie could get some stuff from his place in exchange for some information about the killer.

Stephen could see no tail cars. What he'd heard on the tap was accurate. They pulled into traffic, and he started after them, thinking there was no place in the world like Manhattan for following and not being seen. The unmarked car drove fast, but he stayed with it. The sedan slowed when they got to Central Park West and drove past a town house in the Seventies. There were two men in front, wearing street clothes, but they were obviously cops. A signal passed between them and the driver.

So that's it. That's Lincoln the Worm's house.

The car continued north. Stephen did too for a little ways, then parked suddenly and climbed out, hurrying into the trees with the guitar case. He moved quietly.

Like a deer, soldier.

Yes, sir.

He vanished into a stand of brush and found a good nest under a lilac tree. He opened the case. The car containing Jodie had made a U-turn and now screeched up to the town house. Two cops climbed out and escorted a very scared Jodie along the sidewalk. Stephen flipped the covers off the telescope and took careful aim.

Suddenly a black car drove past, and Jodie spooked and pulled away, running into the alley. His escorts spun around, hands on their weapons, staring at the car. They looked at the quartet of Latino girls inside and laughed. One of them called to Jodie.

But Stephen wasn't interested in the little man right now. He couldn't get both the Worm and Jodie, and Lincoln was the one he had to kill now. He could taste it. It was a hunger, a need.

To shoot the face in the window, to kill the worm.

Have to, have to, have to, have to . . .

He was looking through the telescope, scanning the building's windows. And there he was. Lincoln the Worm.

For some reason Stephen wasn't the least surprised to see that the Worm was crippled. In fact, this was how he knew the handsome man in a fancy motorized wheelchair *was* Lincoln. Because Stephen believed it would take an extraordinary man to catch him. Someone whose essence was his mind. Worms could crawl over Lincoln all day long and he'd never even feel them.

The explosive rounds were in the clip. He chambered one. Lincoln was speaking to someone he couldn't see. The room seemed to be a laboratory. He saw lab equipment and a computer screen.

Stephen wrapped the sling around himself, spot-welded the rifle butt to his cheek. He centered on Lincoln the Worm's ear as he stared at the computer screen. The pressure on the trigger began to build. Harder. Harder . . .

Then Stephen saw it. Very faint—a slight unevenness on Lincoln the Worm's sleeve. Not a wrinkle. A distortion.

He clicked to a higher resolution on the scope and looked at the type on the computer screen. The letters were backward.

A mirror!

He was sighting on a mirror. It was another trap.

Stephen closed his eyes. Cringey now. Smothering in worms. He looked around. He knew there must be a dozen search-and-surveillance troopers with Big Ears microphones just waiting to pinpoint the gunshot and nail him in a cross fire.

In absolute silence he replaced the gun into the guitar case.

Soldier . . .

Sir, go away, sir.

Soldier, what are you—

Sir, damn you, sir! Go to hell.

Stephen slipped through the trees and walked casually around the meadow. He turned suddenly off the path, paused in the bushes, looking around him. They'd been so worried he'd notice if the park was deserted, they hadn't closed the entrances.

That was their mistake.

Stephen saw a group of men about his age dressed in sweats, carrying racquetball cases, talking loudly as they walked. Their hair glistened from showers. He fell in behind them, offered one of them a big smile. Swinging the guitar case jauntily, he followed them toward the tunnel that led to the Upper East Side.

DUSK surrounded them. In front of her, Percey Clay saw the cusp of light that was Chicago.

Chicago Center cleared them down to twelve thousand feet.

"Starting descent," she announced. "ATIS."

Brad clicked his radio to the automated airport information system and set the altimeter. Percey said into her microphone, "Chicago Approach, this is Lear Niner Five Foxtrot Bravo. With you inbound at twelve thousand. Heading two eight zero."

"Evening, Foxtrot Bravo. Descend and maintain one zero thousand. Expect vectors runway twenty-seven right."

Percey refused to look down. Somewhere below and ahead of them was the grave of her husband and his aircraft.

Maybe he'd started to call her right about here.

"HE'S gone," Dellray said. "But he was there, they're pretty sure."

Rhyme closed his eyes in disgust. "I don't believe it." He glanced up at the big mirror he'd ordered them to prop up across the room and scowled, bitterly disappointed that this trick too hadn't worked. "Where's Jodie?" he asked.

Dellray snickered. "Hiding in the alley. Saw some car go by and spooked. He'll come back when he gets cold."

"Or to get his money." Sachs started toward the window.

"No," Rhyme said to her. "We still don't know for certain he's gone."

Sellitto stood away from the glass as he drew the drapes shut. It was then that Cooper's phone rang. He took the call.

"Lincoln, it's the Bureau's bomb people. They've checked the Explosives Reference Collection. No leads on the specific type of rubber, but it's not inconsistent with a material used in altimeter detonators. A latex balloon filled with air expands when the plane goes up, because of the low pressure at higher altitudes, and presses into a switch on the bomb wall. The bomb goes off."

"But this bomb was detonated by a timer."

"They're just telling me about the latex."

Rhyme looked at the plastic bag containing the timer, and he thought, Why's it in such perfect shape? Mounting it behind the steel had seemed careless at first. Now he wondered.

"Tell him the plane exploded as it *descended*," Sachs said.

Cooper relayed the comment, then listened. "He says it could be a construction variation. As the plane climbs, the expanding balloon trips a switch that arms the bomb. When the plane descends, the balloon shrinks and closes the circuit. That detonates it."

Rhyme whispered, "The timer's a fake. He mounted it so it wouldn't be destroyed. So we'd think it was a time bomb. How high was Carney's plane when it exploded?"

Sellitto raced through the NTSB report. "Five thousand feet."

"So it armed when they climbed through five thousand and detonated when he went below it near Chicago," Rhyme said.

"But," Cooper asked, "why go to all the trouble to fool us into thinking it was one kind of bomb and not another?"

Sachs figured it out as fast as Rhyme did. "Oh, no!" she cried. "The squad was looking for a *time* bomb tonight. Listening for the timer. Percey and Bell've got an altitude bomb on board."

"SINK rate twelve hundred feet per minute," Brad sang out.

Percey gentled the yoke of the Lear back slightly, slowing the descent. They passed through fifty-five hundred feet.

She heard a chirping sound. Roland Bell's cell phone.

"Five three hundred feet," Brad called.

An instant later a voice shouted, "Pull up!" Bell crouched beside Percey, brandishing his cell phone.

"What?"

"There's a bomb on! Altitude bomb. It goes off when we hit five thousand feet. Pull up! Up! Go higher! Now!"

Percey shouted, "Set power, ninety-eight percent."

Brad shoved the throttles forward. Percey pulled the Lear into a ten-degree rotation. Bell landed with a crash on the floor. Brad said, "Five thousand two, five four . . . Six thousand feet."

Percey Clay had never declared an emergency in all her years flying. But now she said, "Mayday, Mayday, Lear Niner Five Foxtrot Bravo."

"Go ahead, Foxtrot Bravo."

"Be advised, Chicago Approach. We have reports of a bomb on board. Need immediate clearance to one zero thousand feet and a heading for holding pattern over unpopulated area."

"Roger, Niner Five Foxtrot Bravo," the air-traffic controller said calmly. "Um, maintain present heading of two four zero. Cleared to ten thousand feet. We are vectoring all aircraft around you." Brad glanced uneasily at Percey as he sent out the automatic radar warning signal that Foxtrot Bravo was in trouble.

Bell's phone chirped again. He listened, sighed, then asked Percey, "Did Northeast Aircraft Distributors deliver a fire extinguisher cartridge?"

"He put it in there?" she asked bitterly.

"Looks like it. The truck had a flat tire just after it left the warehouse. Driver was busy for about twenty minutes."

Percey glanced involuntarily toward the engine. "And I installed it myself."

A moment later, through the radio, Percey heard the patch of a unicom call. It was Lincoln Rhyme. "Percey, can you hear me?"

"Loud and clear. That jerk pulled a fast one, hm?"

"Looks like it. How much flying time do you have?"

"Hour forty-five minutes. About."

"All right. Can you unbolt the engine somehow? Let it drop off?"

"Not from the inside."

"Is there any way you could refuel in midair?"

"Refuel? Not with this plane."

"Could you fly high enough to freeze the bomb mechanism?"

She was amazed at how fast his mind worked. "Maybe. But even at nosedive I don't think any bomb parts'd stay frozen. And the Mach buffet would probably tear us apart."

Rhyme was silent. Brad swallowed and wiped his hands on his razor-creased slacks. Roland Bell rocked back and forth. Hopeless, Percey thought, staring down at the murky blue dusk.

"Lincoln," she asked, "are you there?"

She heard his voice. He was calling someone. In a testy tone he was demanding, "Not *that* map. You know which one."

Silence. Oh, Ed, Percey thought. Our lives have always followed parallel paths. Maybe our deaths will too.

Then she heard Rhyme asking, "On the fuel you've got left, how far can you fly?"

She looked at Brad, who was punching in the figures. He said, "If we got some altitude, say, eight hundred miles."

"Got an idea," Rhyme said. "Can you make it to Denver?"

"AIRPORT elevation's at fifty-one eighty feet," Brad said, reviewing the *Airman's Guide of Denver International.* "We were that outside of Chicago, and the thing didn't blow."

"How far?" Percey asked.

"From present location, nine oh two miles."

Percey debated for no more than a few seconds. "We go for it." Then, into the radio, "The gas'll be real close, Lincoln. We've got a lot to do. I'll get back to you."

Brad eyeballed the map. "Turn left, heading two six six."

"Two six six," she repeated. Then called ATC. "Chicago Center, Niner Five Foxtrot Bravo. We may have an altitude-sensitive bomb. Request VORs for Denver."

"Roger, Foxtrot Bravo. We'll have those in a minute."

Brad asked, "Please advise the weather en route, Chicago."

"High-pressure front moving through Denver. Head winds from fifteen at ten thousand to seventy knots at twenty-five."

"Ouch." Brad returned to his calculations. After a moment he said, "Fuel depletion fifty-five miles short of Denver."

ATC asked, "Foxtrot Bravo, ready to copy VOR frequencies?"

While Brad took down the information, Percey thought about her little speech to Lincoln Rhyme. She hadn't realized how true her words were, how dependent she and Rhyme were on fragile bits of metal and plastic. Maybe about to die because of them.

Fifty-five miles short. What could they do?

Why wasn't her mind as far-ranging as Rhyme's? How could she conserve fuel? Flying higher was more fuel-efficient. Flying lighter was too. Throwing out the U.S. Medical shipment would buy them some miles. But she knew she'd never do it.

"Brad," she asked abruptly, "what's our glide ratio?"

"A Lear 35A? No idea."

The Lear was fourteen thousand pounds. Still, any aircraft will glide. "Well, let's think. What'd the sink rate be at idle?"

"We could keep it at twenty-three hundred, I think."

A vertical drop of about thirty miles per hour. "Now calculate if we burned fuel to take us up to fifty-five thousand feet, when would we deplete?"

"Fifty-five?" Brad asked with surprise. He punched in numbers. "We'd burn a lot down here, but after thirty-five thousand the efficiency goes way up. Go to one engine, we'd deplete about eighty-three miles short. But of course, then we'd have altitude."

Percey Clay, who could dead reckon without a calculator, saw the numbers stream past in her head. Flameout at fifty-five thousand, sink rate of twenty-three—they could cover a little over eighty miles before touching down. Maybe more if the head winds were kind.

Brad came up with the same conclusion. "Be close."

God don't give out certain.

She said, "Chicago Center. Lear Foxtrot Bravo requests clearance to five five thousand feet." *Sometimes you just gotta play the odds.*

The air-traffic controller said, "Uh, Foxtrot Bravo, you're a

Lear 35. Maximum operating ceiling is forty-five thousand feet."

"That's affirmative, but we need to go higher."

"Your seals've been checked lately?"

Pressure seals. Doors and windows. What kept the aircraft from exploding. "They're fine." She neglected to mention that it had been shot full of holes and jury-rigged back together that afternoon.

"Roger, cleared to five five thousand, Foxtrot Bravo."

And Percey said something that few, if any, Lear pilots had ever said: "Roger, out of ten for fifty-five thousand." Then she rotated the plane, and it began to rise. They sailed upward.

All the stars of evening.

Ten minutes later Percey cut number two engine and felt the slight swerve as their left-side thrust vanished. She adjusted the rudder to compensate for the yaw, then climbed out of her seat. "I'm having a cup of coffee. Hey, Roland, how d'you like yours again?"

FOR a torturous forty minutes there was silence in Rhyme's room. No one's phone rang with leads. No faxes came in. No computer voices reported, "You've got mail."

Then, at last, Sellitto's phone brayed. He unfolded it. "Yeah?"

Rhyme watched the cop's doughy, stoic face. Sellitto flipped the phone closed. "That was Roland Bell," he said. "He just wanted us to know they're outta gas."

THREE different warning buzzers went off simultaneously.

Low fuel, low oil pressure, low engine temperature.

With a faint clatter number one engine quit coughing and went silent. The cockpit went black as a closet.

"I forgot. No electricity. Drop the RAT," Percey ordered.

Brad groped for the lever, and the ram air turbine dropped beneath the aircraft. The slipstream turned the prop, which powered a generator, providing controls and lights. But not flaps, gear, speed brakes.

A moment later some lights returned. Percey was staring at the vertical speed indicator. It showed a descent rate of thirty-five hundred feet per minute. They were dropping at close to fifty miles an hour.

Why? she wondered. Why was the calculation so far off?

Because of the rarefied air here! She was calculating sink rate based on denser atmosphere. She pulled back on the yoke to arrest the descent. It dropped to twenty-one hundred feet per minute. But the airspeed dropped too. The controls went mushy. There'd be no recovery from a powerless stall in an aircraft like this.

Forward with the yoke. They dropped faster, but the airspeed picked up. For nearly fifty miles she played this game. Air-traffic control told them where the head winds were strongest, and she tried to find the perfect combination of altitude and route. Finally, her muscles aching, Percey said, "Give 'em a call, Brad."

"Denver Center, this is Lear Six Niner Five Foxtrot Bravo, with you out of one six thousand feet, nineteen miles from touchdown."

"We have you, Foxtrot Bravo. Come right, heading two five zero. Understand you are power-free, is that correct?"

"We're the biggest damn glider you ever saw, Denver."

"Roger. You want trucks?"

"Everything. We think we've got a bomb on board."

"Denver Approach," Percey asked, "what's the altimeter?"

"Um, we have three oh point nine six, Foxtrot Bravo."

"It's rising?"

"Affirmative, Foxtrot Bravo. High-pressure front moving in."

No! That would increase the ambient pressure, which would shrink the balloon, as if they were lower than they actually were.

Brad punched in numbers, then stared at her. "The bomb may blow fifty feet above the ground."

"Okay." Percey took a deep breath. How accurate had the Coffin Dancer been when he'd made the detonator? She looked over at Bell. "Roland, one thing. When we stop, get out as fast as you can."

"Ten miles to runway," Brad called. "Speed two hundred knots. Altitude nine thousand feet. We need to slow descent."

She pulled up on the yoke slightly, and the speed dropped dramatically. The shaker stick began to vibrate. Stall now, and they'd die. Forward again. Nine miles, eight . . . Blisters between her thumbs and index fingers. Seven, six . . .

"Five miles from touchdown. Airspeed two hundred ten knots."

"Gear down," Percey commanded.

Brad spun the wheel that manually lowered the heavy gear. It was a major effort. "Gear down," he called, panting.

Airspeed dropped to one hundred eighty knots. Way too fast. Without reverse thrusters they'd burn up even the longest runway in a streak.

Back on the stick. Stall warning. Forward on the stick.

"Two and a half miles, altitude nineteen hundred feet."

Hands sweating, straining forward, she looked out over the silver nose. There were the strobes of the approach lights, the blue dots of the taxiway, the orange-red of the runway. They'd touch down in thirty seconds, but the airspeed was still way too high. Without flaps even a two-mile-long runway vanishes in an instant.

So Percey sideslipped.

This is a simple maneuver in a private plane. You bank to the left and hit the right rudder pedal. Percey didn't know if anyone had ever used it in a seven-ton jet. "Need your help here," she called to Brad, gasping at the pain shooting through her raw hands. He gripped the yoke and shoved on the pedal too. This slowed the aircraft, though the left wing dropped precipitously.

"Airspeed?" she called.

"One fifty knots. Sink rate twenty-six hundred."

Too fast. There were the approach strobes right in front of her—guiding them down, down, down. Just as they hurtled toward the scaffolding of the lights, she shouted, "My aircraft!"

Brad released the yoke. Percey straightened from the sideslip and brought the nose up. The plane flared beautifully and grabbed air, halting the steep descent right before the end of the runway.

Percey eased the stick forward. The plane dipped dramatically, and Percey yanked all the way back on the yoke. The silver bird shuddered, then settled gently on the concrete.

"Full brakes." She and Brad jammed their feet down on the rudder pedals. Instantly smoke filled the cabin. They were still speeding at a hundred miles an hour.

Grass, she thought. I'll veer if I have to. Wreck the undercarriage, but I'll save the cargo. Seventy miles per hour, sixty . . .

"Fire light, right wheel," Brad called. "Fire light, nosewheel."

Forget it, she thought, and pressed down with all her weight.

The Lear began to skid and shudder. She compensated with the nosewheel. More smoke. Sixty miles per hour, fifty, forty.

"The door," she called to Bell.

In an instant the detective pushed it outward, and it became a staircase. Fire trucks converged on the aircraft. With a wild groan Lear N695FB skidded to a stop ten feet from the end of the runway.

The first voice to fill the cabin was Bell's. "Okay, Percey, out!"

Bell hustled her and Brad out the door, then leaped to the concrete himself and led them away from the aircraft. One of his guns was in his hand. At one time Percey would have thought he was being paranoid. No longer.

They paused about a hundred feet from the plane. As Percey looked at Foxtrot Bravo—her beautiful silver skin glistening under the spotlights—there was a deafening bang. Everyone except Bell and Percey hit the ground as the aircraft disintegrated in a huge flash of orange flame, strewing bits of metal into the air.

"Oh," Percey gasped, her hand rising to her mouth.

There was no fuel left in the tanks, of course, but the precious cargo burned furiously as the fire trucks streamed forward, pointlessly shooting snowy foam on the ruined metallic corpse.

Chapter Eleven
. . . Hour 42 of 45

IT WAS after three a.m., Rhyme noted. Percey Clay was flying back to the East Coast on an FBI jet, and in just a few hours she'd be on her way to the courthouse to get ready for her grand jury appearance. And Rhyme still had no idea where the Coffin Dancer was, what he was planning, what identity he was now assuming.

Sellitto's phone brayed. He listened; then his face screwed up. "The Dancer just got somebody else. They found a body—ID-proofed—in a tunnel in Central Park. Near Fifth Avenue."

"Completely ID-proofed?" Amelia Sachs asked.

"Did it up right, sounds like. Removed the hands, teeth, jaw, and clothes. White male, early thirties. Clean, athletic. Haumann thinks he's some yuppie from the East Side."

"Okay," Rhyme said. "Bring it here."

"The body? Well, okay."

"So the Dancer's got a new identity," Rhyme mused angrily. "How's he going to come at us next?" He sighed, looked at Dellray. "What safe house're you going to put Percey in?"

"Ours," a new voice said.

They looked at the heavyset man in the doorway. "*Our* safe house," Reggie Eliopolos said. "We're taking custody." The prosecutor waved a protective-custody order.

"That's not a good idea," Rhyme said.

"It's better than your idea of getting our last witness killed."

"Believe me," Rhyme said, "the Dancer'll figure it out."

"He'd have to be a mind reader," Eliopolos said. He looked around, spotted Jodie. "Joseph D'Oforio? You're coming too."

The little man stared back. "Hey, hold on a minute—"

"We're just going to make sure you're safe until the grand jury."

"Grand jury! Nobody said anything about testifying."

"Well," Eliopolos said, "you're a material witness."

"I'm not going to testify."

"Then you're going to do time for contempt. In general population. And I'll bet you know how safe you'll be there." Jodie's face shriveled. "Oh, and Rhyme?" Eliopolos turned. "I'm charging you with interference with a criminal investigation."

"The hell you are," Sellitto said.

"The hell I am. He could've ruined the case, letting her make that flight. I'm having the warrant served Monday. And I'm going to supervise the prosecution myself."

Rhyme said softly, "He's been here, you know."

Eliopolos stopped speaking. After a moment he asked, "Who?"

"He was right outside that window not an hour ago, pointing a sniper rifle, loaded with explosive shells, into this room."

Eliopolos's eyes flickered. "Why didn't he shoot?"

"Ah," Rhyme said. "That's the million-dollar question. All we know is he's killed some young man in Central Park and ID-proofed the body. I don't doubt for one minute that he knows the bomb didn't kill Percey and he's on his way to finish the job."

Sachs said, "You've never been up against anybody like him."

Rhyme glanced at Amelia and saw the hollowness in her eyes, the despair. Eliopolos was stealing away her chance to get the Dancer. The killer had come to be the dark focus of her life, all because of a single misstep at the airport. Sachs's life had been snapped in that single moment of what she saw as cowardice. But unlike Rhyme's case, there was—he believed—a chance for her to mend.

Oh, Sachs, how it hurts to do this, but I have no choice. He said to Eliopolos, "All right. But you have to do one thing in exchange, or I won't tell you where Percey is."

Eliopolos's gaze was icy. "What do you want?"

"The Dancer's shown an interest in targeting the people looking for him. If you're going to protect Percey, I want you to protect the chief forensic investigator in the case too."

"You?" the lawyer asked.

"No, Amelia Sachs," Rhyme replied.

"Rhyme, no," she said, frowning.

Reckless Amelia Sachs . . . And I'm putting her square in the kill zone. He motioned her over to him.

"I want to stay here," she said. "I want to find him."

He whispered. "Don't worry, Sachs, he'll find *you*. I want you with Percey. You're the only one who understands him. There's a chance this is the first fish of his that's going to get away, and he doesn't like that one bit. He's desperate. I know it."

She debated for a moment, then nodded.

"Okay," Eliopolos said. "Come on. We've got a van waiting."

Rhyme said, "Sachs?"

She paused, and Eliopolos said, "Time pressure here, Officer."

"I'll be down in a minute." She handily won the staring contest, and Eliopolos and his trooper escort led Jodie downstairs.

"Sachs." Rhyme thought of saying something about avoiding heroics, about Jerry Banks, about being too hard on herself, about giving up the dead, but he settled for, "Shoot first."

She placed her right hand on his left. He closed his eyes and tried so very hard to feel the pressure of her skin on his. He believed he did, if just in his ring finger.

He looked up at her. She said, "And you keep a minder handy, okay?" Nodding at Sellitto and Dellray.

An EMS medic appeared in the door, looking around the room— at Rhyme, at the equipment, at the beautiful lady cop. "Somebody wanted a body?" he asked uncertainly.

"In here!" Rhyme shouted. "Now! We need it now!"

THEY drove through a gate and then down a one-lane driveway. It extended for what seemed like miles.

"If this's the driveway," Roland Bell said, "can't wait to see the house." He and Amelia Sachs flanked Jodie, who irritated everybody no end as he fidgeted nervously, his bulletproof vest banging into them as he examined shadows and dark doorways and passing cars on the Long Island Expressway. In the back were two 32-E officers armed with machine guns. Percey Clay was in the front passenger seat. When they'd picked up her and Bell at La Guardia, Sachs had been shocked at the sight of the woman. Her complete resignation.

Percey was on the phone with Ron Talbot. Sachs deduced that U.S. Medical hadn't even waited for the cinders of her airplane to cool before canceling the contract. Percey hung up and said absently, "The insurance company isn't even going to pay for the cargo. They say I assumed a known risk. So that's it." She added briskly, "We're bankrupt."

Pine trees swept past. As they came to the house, Jodie played with the seat belt, knocking into Sachs again.

"Sorry," he muttered. She wanted to slug him.

THE NIGHT WAS OVERCAST, FILLED with swatches of mist, but Sachs could see enough to note that the house was a rambling combination of logs and clapboard. The forest around it had been cleared for two hundred yards. There was a large, still lake behind the house.

Reggie Eliopolos climbed out of the lead van and motioned everyone out. He led them into the building, handing them off to a round man who seemed cheerful, though he never once smiled.

"Welcome," he said. "I'm U.S. Marshal David Franks. Want to tell you a little about your home away from home here. The most secure witness-protection enclave in the country. We have weight and motion sensors built into the entire perimeter of the place. Can't be broken through without setting off all sorts of other alarms. Anything happens, you'll hear a siren. Just stay where you are. Don't go outside. We've got four marshals inside. Two outside at the front guard station, two in the back by the lake. And hit that panic button there and there'll be a Huey full of SWAT boys here in twenty minutes."

Jodie's face said twenty minutes seemed like a very long time. Sachs had to agree with him.

Eliopolos said, "We're going to have an armored van here at six to take you to the grand jury. Sorry you won't get much sleep. But if I'd had my way, you'd've been here all night."

No one said a word of farewell as he walked out the door.

Franks continued. "Don't go outside without an escort. That phone there"—he pointed to a beige phone in the corner of the living room—"is secure. So that's it. Any questions?"

Percey said, "Yeah. You got any booze?"

Franks bent to a cabinet and pulled out a bottle of vodka and one of bourbon. "We like to keep our guests happy." He set the bottles on the table. "I'm headed home. 'Night, Tom," he said to the marshal at the door, and nodded to the foursome, standing incongruously in the middle of the varnished-wood hunting lodge, two bottles of liquor between them.

The phone rang, startling them. One of the marshals got it on the third ring. "Hello?" He glanced at the two women. "Amelia Sachs?"

She nodded and took the receiver.

It was Rhyme. "Sachs, how safe is it?"

"Pretty good," she said. "High tech. Any luck with the body?"

"Four missing males reported in Manhattan in the last four hours. We're thinking a lawyer. Ask Jodie if the Dancer ever mentioned getting into the courthouse for the grand jury."

Jodie didn't think so. Sachs told Rhyme this.

"Okay. Thanks. I'll check in later, Sachs."

After they hung up, Percey asked, "You want a nightcap?"

Sachs and Roland Bell didn't. But Jodie opted for a fast shot of whiskey, then headed off to bed toting his self-help book.

OUTSIDE in the thick spring air, cicadas chirped and bullfrogs belched their peculiar, unsettling calls.

As he looked out the window into the darkness, Jodie could see the starbursts of searchlights radiating through fog. He walked to the door of his room, looked out. Two marshals sat in a small security room twenty feet away. They seemed bored. He listened and heard nothing other than the snaps and ticks of an old house late in the evening.

Jodie returned to his bed and sat on the sagging mattress. He picked up his battered, stained copy of *Dependent No More*. Let's get to work, he thought. He opened the book wide and tore a small patch of tape off the bottom of the spine. A long knife slid onto the bed. Made of ceramic-impregnated polymer, it wouldn't register on a metal detector. It was sharp as a razor on one edge, serrated like a surgical saw on the other. He'd made it himself. Like most serious weapons, it did only one thing: It killed. And it did this very very well.

He had no qualms about picking it up. He was the owner of new fingerprints. The skin on the pads of fingers and thumbs had been burned away chemically last month by a surgeon in Switzerland, and a new set of prints had been etched in by laser.

Sitting on the edge of the bed, eyes closed, he took a mental stroll through the common room, remembering the location of every door, every window, every piece of furniture, the potential weapons. He steered his imaginary self to the telephone in the corner and spent a moment considering the safe house's communications system. He was completely familiar with how it worked, and he knew that if he cut the line, the drop in voltage would send a signal to the marshals' panel and a field office. Leave it intact. *Not a problem, just a factor.*

On to examining the common-room video cameras the marshal had "forgotten" to tell them about. They harbored a serious design flaw—tap the middle of the lens hard and this misaligned the optics. The image in the security monitor would go black, but there'd be no alarm.

Thinking about the lighting. He could shut out five of eight lights until all the marshals were dead. Thinking of distances, angles of view from outside. Noting the location of each of his victims.

He slipped the knife into his pocket and stepped to the door.

Silently he eased into the kitchen, stole a slotted spoon from a rack, walked to the refrigerator, and poured himself a glass of milk. Into the common room, meandering to the bookshelves for something to read. As he passed each video camera, he reached up with the spoon and slapped the lenses. Then he set the milk and spoon on a table and headed into the security room.

"Hey, check out the monitors," one marshal was muttering.

"Yeah?" the other asked, not really interested.

Jodie walked past the first marshal, who started to ask, "Hey, sir, how you doing?" when—*swish, swish*—Jodie tidily opened the man's throat. His partner reached for his gun. Jodie stabbed him once, and he dropped to the floor. It was a noisy death, but Jodie couldn't do more knife work on the man. He needed the uniform and had to kill him with a minimum of blood.

As Jodie stripped, the dying marshal's eyes flickered to his biceps. They focused on the tattoo.

As Jodie bent down to undress the marshal, he said, "It's called Danse Macabre. See? Death's dancing with his next victim. That's her coffin behind them. Do you like it?"

He asked this with genuine curiosity, though he expected no answer. And received none.

MEL COOPER, CLAD IN LATEX gloves, stood over the body.

"I could try the plantars," he suggested, discouraged.

The friction ridge prints on the soles of the feet were as unique as fingerprints, but they weren't catalogued in AFIS databases. "Don't bother," Rhyme muttered.

Who *is* this? he wondered, looking at the savaged body in front of him. Oh, this was the worst feeling in the world—to have a piece of evidence, yet to be unable to decipher it. His eyes strayed to the evidence chart on the wall. The body was like the green fibers they'd found at the hangar—significant, but its meaning unknown. And without anything else to go on, blood work wouldn't help.

Fingerprint . . . I'd give anything for a nice friction ridge print, Rhyme thought. Maybe— He laughed out loud.

"What?" Sellitto asked. Dellray lifted an arching brow.

"He doesn't have any hands, but what's the one part of his anatomy he'd be sure to touch?" Everyone looked at each other.

"If he peed in the last couple of hours," Cooper said.

Donning a double layer of latex gloves, he went to work with Kromekote skin-printing cards. He lifted two excellent prints and fed them through the AFIS system.

The message came up on the screen: "Please wait."

Be on file, Rhyme thought desperately. Please be on file.

He was. But when the results came back, Sellitto, closest to Cooper's computer, stared at the screen in disbelief.

"What in the world?" the detective said.

"What?" Rhyme cried. "Who is it?"

"It's Kall."

"What?"

"It's Stephen Kall," he repeated. "There's no doubt."

How? Rhyme was wondering. How on earth?

POETRY was not lost on him. The Coffin Dancer—I like that, he thought. Much better than silly Jodie.

Names were important, he knew. He read philosophy—the act of designating is unique to humans. The Dancer now spoke silently to the late Stephen Kall. It was me you heard about. I'm the one who calls my victims corpses. You call them wives, husbands, whatever you like. But once I'm hired, they're corpses.

Wearing a U.S. marshal's uniform, he started down the dim hallway. On his way to find Corpse Three.

The Wife, if you will, Stephen Kall. What a mixed-up, nervous creature you were. With your scrubbed hands and your "infiltrate, evaluate, delegate, isolate, eliminate." There's only one rule in this business: You stay one step ahead of every living soul.

He now had two pistols but wouldn't use them prematurely. If he stumbled now, he'd never have another chance to kill Percey Clay before the grand jury met. Moving silently into a parlor where two more U.S. marshals sat. One saw the uniform and returned to his paper, then looked up again. "Wait," he said.

But the Dancer's knife didn't wait. The man slid forward to die on page 6 of the *Daily News* so quietly that his partner never turned from the TV. "Wait for what?" he asked, eyes on the screen.

He died slightly more noisily, but no one in the compound seemed to notice. The Dancer stowed the bodies under a table.

At the back door he made certain there were no sensors on the door frame and then slipped outside. The two marshals in the front were vigilant, but their eyes were turned away from the house. They both died almost silently. As for the two in the back overlooking the lake, the first marshal gave a plaintive scream, but no one seemed to notice. The sound, the Dancer decided, was very much like the call of a loon, waking to the beautiful pink-and-gray dawn.

"SOMEBODY killed *him?*" Sellitto muttered. "Why?"

But why was not a criminalist's question.

Evidence was. Rhyme glanced at the crime scene charts on his wall, scanning all the clues of the case. The fibers, the bullets, the broken glass.

Analyze. Think. You know the procedure. You've done it a million times. You identify the facts. You state your assumptions.

Assumptions, Rhyme thought. There was one glaring assumption in this case from the beginning: the belief that Kall was the Coffin Dancer. But what if the Dancer'd been using him as a weapon? If so, there'd be some evidence that didn't fit.

He pored over the charts carefully. But there was nothing unaccounted for except the green fiber from the airport hangar.

"We don't have any of Kall's clothes," Rhyme said. "Do we have anything he came in contact with?"

Sellitto shrugged. "Well, Jodie."

"He changed clothes here, didn't he? I want to look at them."

"Uck," Dellray said. "They're excessively unpleasant."

Cooper found them. He brushed them out over sheets of clean newsprint, then mounted samples of the trace under the scope.

"What do we have?" Rhyme looked over the computer screen.

"What's that white stuff?" Cooper asked. "Those grains. There's a lot of it. It was in the seams of his pants."

Rhyme felt his face flush. "I know what it is," he whispered. "It's oolite. A wind-borne sand in the Bahamas."

"Bahamas?" Cooper asked, frowning. "What else did we just hear about the Bahamas?" He looked around the lab.

But Rhyme's eyes were seated on the bulletin board, where was pinned the FBI's report on the sand Amelia Sachs had found last week in Tony Panelli's car. "Substance submitted for analysis is not technically sand. It is coral rubble from reef formations. . . . Most likely source is the northern Caribbean: Cuba, the Bahamas."

Dellray's missing agent—a man who would know where the most secure federal safe house in Manhattan was. Who would tell whoever was torturing him the address. So that the Dancer could wait there, wait for Stephen Kall to show up, befriend him, and then arrange to get captured and get close to the victims.

"Jodie's the Dancer," Rhyme cried. "Call the safe house now!"

Sellitto picked up the phone and dialed.

Was it too late? Oh, Amelia, what've I done?

The sky was a metallic rosy color. A siren sounded far away. The male peregrine falcon was awake, about to go hunting.

Sellitto looked up desperately. "There's no answer," he said.

PERCEY LAY BACK ON HER BED, closed her eyes. Sachs lifted the bourbon glass from her hand and shut out the lights. Pausing in the corridor to look out at the dawn, she realized the secure phone had been ringing a long time.

Why wasn't anybody answering it?

She couldn't see the two guards. The enclave seemed darker than before. Spooky, she thought. And smelling of what?

The phone continued to chirp, then went quiet, cut off in the middle of a ring. Silence. Then a tap, a faint scrape.

She stepped into her room and groped for the switch. She pulled her blouse off and removed the bulky body armor. Not as bulky as Jodie's, of course. What a kick he was. The little . . . What was Dellray's word? Skel, short for skeleton. Scrawny little loser. She pulled on her blouse again and lay down on the comforter. Closed her eyes.

The Coffin Dancer, she mused. How would he come at them? What would his weapon be? *His deadliest weapon is deception.*

She had a sudden urge to talk to Rhyme, to see if he'd found anything. She could hear him saying, "If I'd found something, I would've called, wouldn't I? I said I'd check in." Still, she doubted he was asleep. She pulled her cell phone out of her pocket and clicked it on. It immediately chirped.

She hesitantly answered it. " 'Lo?"

"Thank God." The panicked tone chilled her.

"Hey, Rhyme. What's—"

"Listen very carefully. Are you alone?"

"Yeah. What's going on?"

"Jodie's the Dancer. Stephen Kall was the diversion. Jodie killed him. It was his body in the park."

"But how—"

"No time. He's going for the kill right now. If the marshals're dead, find Percey and Bell and get out. Dellray's scrambled SWAT, but it'll be twenty or thirty minutes."

"But there're eight guards. He can't take them all out—"

"Sachs, remember who he is. Call me when you're safe."

She raced to her door, threw it open, drew her gun. The black living room and corridor gaped. She listened. A shuffle. A clink of metal. Where were the sounds coming from?

Sachs trotted as quietly as she could to Bell's room. He was dozing in an armchair but woke as she came in.

"Hey now," he said, "what's going on?"

"Jodie's the Dancer. Rhyme just called."

"What? How?"

"I don't know." She stepped through the doorway, shivering in panic. "Where're the guards?" The hall was empty. Then she recognized the smell she'd wondered about. It was blood. Like hot copper. And she knew then that all the guards were dead. She took out her Glock, then frowned. "No! My clip. It's gone." She slapped her utility belt. The clips in the keepers were gone too.

Bell drew his Glock and Browning. They too were clipless.

"In the car!" she stammered. "He was sitting between us. Fidgeting all the time."

Bell said, "I saw a gun case in the living room. A couple of hunting rifles." They could just make it out in the dim light of dawn. Bell hurried to it. Sachs ran to Percey's room and looked in. The woman was asleep on the bed. Sachs closed the door and stepped back into the corridor.

Bell ran up. "It's been broken into. All the rifles're gone."

"Let's get Percey and get out of here."

A footstep not far away. A click of a bolt-action rifle's safety. Sachs grabbed Bell's collar and pulled him to the floor. The gunshot was deafening as the bullet broke the sound barrier directly over them. She smelled her own burning hair.

They sprinted for Percey's door. It opened just as they got there, and she stepped out. Bell's full-body tackle shoved her back. Sachs tumbled in, slammed the door shut, locked it, and ran to open the window. "Go, go, go, go."

Bell lifted a stunned Percey Clay off the floor as several high-powered rifle slugs tore through the lock.

They rolled through the window into the dawn and ran and ran and ran through the grass.

Chapter Twelve

 SACHS stopped beside the lake. Mist, tinted red and pink, wafted in ghostly tatters over the still gray water. "Go on," she shouted to Bell and Percey. "Those trees." She pointed to the end of a field on the other side of the lake.

Sachs glanced back at the lodge. There was no sign of Jodie. She dropped into a crouch over the body of one of the marshals. His holsters were empty, of course—clip cases too.

But he *is* human, Rhyme.

And frisking the cool body, she found what she was looking for. She pulled his backup weapon out of his ankle holster. A silly gun. A tiny five-shot Colt revolver with a two-inch barrel.

She glanced at the lodge just as Jodie's face appeared in the window. He lifted the rifle. Sachs squeezed off a round, then sprinted around the lake after Bell and Percey. They ran fast, weaving sideways through the dewy grass.

A hundred yards from the house they heard the first shot. It kicked up dirt near Percey's leg. "Down," Sachs cried, pointing to a dip in the earth. They rolled to the ground just as he fired again.

They were still fifty feet from the trees, but to try for them now would be suicide. Sachs lifted her head. An instant later the slug snapped through the air beside her. She felt the same draining terror as at the airport. She pressed her face into the grass.

Bell looked up fast and then down again. Another shot inches from his face. "I think I saw him," the detective drawled. "Bushes to the right of the house. On that hill."

Sachs rolled five feet to the right, poked her head up fast, ducked again. Bell was right: The killer was on the side of a hill; she'd seen the faint glint from the rifle's scope. If he moved up to the crest of the hill, the pit they were hiding in would become a perfect kill zone.

Five minutes passed without a shot. He'd be working his way up cautiously. When would the SWAT chopper get here?

Sachs squeezed her eyes closed, smelled the dirt, the grass.

You know him better than anybody, Sachs.

But Rhyme, she thought, this isn't Stephen Kall. It wasn't *Jodie's* mind I peered into.

Get into his mind, Sachs. *His deadliest—* My *deadliest weapon is deception.*

"Both of you," Sachs called suddenly, looking around. "There." She pointed toward a slight ravine. Bell nodded solemnly and pulled Percey after him into the shallow notch.

Sachs checked the pistol. Four rounds left. Plenty if I'm right.

"Whatever happens, stay down." Sachs rose to her knees, preparing herself.

"That's a hundred-yard shot, Amelia," Bell whispered.

She ignored him and stood up. She didn't crouch, didn't turn sideways. She just slipped into the familiar two-hand target pistol stance. Facing the house, facing the prone figure halfway up the hill who pointed the telescopic sight directly at her. The stubby pistol felt as light as a Scotch glass in her hand.

She aimed at the glare of the scope, a football field away. Sweat and mist forming on her face. She forced the panic away.

Take your time. Wait. . . . Listen, listen.

Now!

She spun around and dropped to her knees as the rifle jutting from the grove of trees behind her, fifty feet away, fired. The bullet split the air just over her head.

Sachs found herself staring at Jodie's astonished face, the hunting rifle still at his cheek. He realized she'd figured out his tactic. How he'd propped one of the guards on the hill with a rifle while he jogged up the road and circled behind.

For a moment neither of them moved. A faint smile crossed Sachs's face as she lifted the pistol in both hands.

Frantic, he ejected the shell and chambered another round. As he lifted the gun to his cheek, Sachs fired. Two shots. Both clean hits. Saw him fly backward, the rifle sailing through the air.

"Stay with Percey, Detective," Sachs called to Bell.

She found Jodie in the grass, lying on his back. One of her bullets had shattered his left shoulder. The other had hit the telescopic sight and blown metal and glass into his right eye.

She cocked her tiny gun and pressed the muzzle against his temple. She frisked him. A single Glock and a long carbide knife.

"Clear," she called. She cuffed him.

The Dancer coughed and spit, wiped blood out of his good eye. Then he lifted his head. He spotted Percey Clay as she slowly rose from the grass, staring at her attacker.

The Coffin Dancer gave a horrifying moan and lay still.

The trio stood around him, watching his blood soak the grass and the innocent crocuses. Soon they heard the whup-whup-whup of a helicopter skimming the trees.

"AIN'T kosher, Lincoln. Can't do it." Lon Sellitto was insistent.

But so was Lincoln Rhyme. "Give me a half hour with him."

"They hit the roof when I suggested it. You're civilian."

It was nearly ten on Monday morning. Percey's appearance before the grand jury had been postponed until the next afternoon. The navy divers had found the duffel bags that Phillip Hansen had sunk deep in Long Island Sound. They were being raced to an FBI PERT team downtown for analysis.

"What're they worried about?" Rhyme asked petulantly. "It's not as if I can beat him up. *I* caught him. I deserve a chance to talk to him."

"Aw, give him a little time," Dellray said to Sellitto.

Sellitto said, "Oh, all right. I'll make the call."

"WHAT'S your real name? Is it really Joe or Jodie?"

"How 'bout what *you* call me? The Dancer. I like that."

The small man examined Rhyme carefully with his good eye. His left arm was in a shoulder cast, but he still wore thick cuffs attached to a waist shackle. His feet were chained too.

"Whatever you like." Rhyme continued to study the man as if he were an unusual pollen spore picked up at a crime scene.

The Dancer smiled. Because of the damaged facial nerves and the bandages, his expression was grotesque. Tremors occasionally shook his body, and his fingers twitched; his broken shoulder rose and fell involuntarily. Rhyme had a curious feeling—that he himself was healthy and it was the prisoner who was the cripple.

In the valley of the blind the one-eyed man is king.

The Dancer smiled. "You're just dying to know how I did it, aren't you?"

Rhyme clucked his tongue. "Oh, I know how you did it. I just asked you here to talk to you—the man who almost outthought me."

" 'Almost.' " The Dancer laughed. Another twisted smile. It was really quite eerie. "Okay, then tell me."

Rhyme sipped from his straw. It was fruit juice. He'd astonished Thom by asking him for Hawaiian Punch instead of Scotch. "All right. You were hired to kill Ed Carney, Brit Hale, and Percey Clay. You were paid a lot, I'd guess. Six figures."

"Seven," the Dancer said proudly.

Rhyme lifted an eyebrow. "You deposited the money in the Bahamas. You'd gotten Stephen Kall's name from somewhere— probably a mercenary network—and you hired him as a subcontractor. Anonymously, maybe by E-mail. You'd never meet him face to face, of course. And I assume you tried him out?"

"Of course. A hit outside Washington. I watched him every step of the way. I think he saw me and came after me to take care of witnesses. Very professional."

Rhyme continued. "You knew he was good, but you weren't sure he was good enough to kill all three of them. You probably thought he could get one at the most but would provide enough diversion for you to get close to the other two."

The Dancer nodded, reluctantly impressed. "Him killing Hale surprised me. Oh, yes. And it surprised me even more that he got away and got the second bomb onto Percey Clay's plane."

"You guessed that you'd have to kill at least one victim yourself, so last week you became Jodie, hawking your drugs so that people on the street'd know about you. You kidnapped the agent in front of the Federal Building, found out which safe house they'd be in. You let Stephen kidnap you. You left plenty of clues to your subway hideout. We all trusted you. Sure, we did—Stephen didn't have a clue *you'd* hired him. All he knew was that you betrayed him. Perfect cover for you. But risky."

"What's life without risk?" the Dancer asked playfully.

"When Kall was in the park, you slipped out of the alley, found him, and killed him. And then we invited you out to Long Island. Fox in the henhouse. That's the bare bones."

The man's good eye closed momentarily, then opened again. Red and wet, it stared at Rhyme. "What was it?" he finally asked. "What tipped you?"

"Sand," Rhyme answered. "From the Bahamas."

"I turned my pockets out. I vacuumed."

"In the folds of the seams."

"Yes. Sure." After a moment the Dancer added, "He was right to be scared of you. Stephen, I mean."

"But you weren't scared."

"No," the Dancer said. "I don't get scared." Suddenly he nodded, as if he'd finally noticed something that had been nagging him. "Ah, trying to peg the accent, are you?"

Rhyme had been.

"But see, it changes. By the way, why're you interrogating me? You're crime scene. I'm caught. Time for beddy-bye. End of story. Say, Lincoln, I like chess. I love chess. You ever play?"

He'd used to like it. He and Claire Trilling had played quite a bit. Thom had been after him to play it on the computer. "I haven't played for a long time."

"You and I'll have to play a game of chess sometime. You want to know a mistake some players make? They get curious about their opponents. That confuses them. It can be dangerous. See, the game is all on the board, Lincoln." A lopsided smile. "I'm surprised at you. You're a criminalist—the best I've ever seen. And here you are on some pathetic sentimental journey. Who am I? The headless horseman. Beelzebub. Queen Mab. I'm 'them,' as in 'Look out for them; they're after you.' You won't get my name, rank, or serial number. I don't play according to the Geneva convention."

Rhyme could say nothing.

There was a knock on the door. The transport had arrived.

The guards gripped the Dancer by his good arm and lifted him to his feet. He was dwarfed by the two tall men.

"Lincoln?"

"Yes?"

"You're going to miss me. You'll be bored." His single eye burned into Rhyme's. "Without me you're going to die."

AN HOUR later heavy footsteps announced the arrival of Lon Sellitto. He was accompanied by Sachs and Dellray. Trouble.

Sachs sighed. Dellray grimaced.

"Okay, tell me," Rhyme snapped.

"The duffel bags. Guess what was inside?" Sellitto said.

Rhyme sighed, exhausted and not in the mood for games. "Detonators, plutonium, and Jimmy Hoffa's body."

Sachs said, "A bunch of Westchester County yellow pages and five pounds of rocks."

"What? You're sure they were phone books, not encrypted business records?"

"Bureau cryptology looked 'em over good," Dellray said.

"They're gonna release Hansen's miserable carcass," Sellitto muttered darkly. "They're not even presenting it to the grand jury. All those people died for nothing."

Rhyme was lost in thought, staring at the evidence chart on the wall. What was nagging? he wondered. Something seemed wrong here. Very wrong.

Green fiber, phone books, and rocks.

Rhyme remembered something the Dancer had told him—seven figures.

He was vaguely aware of people talking to him. Of Sachs stepping forward, trying to figure out what he was looking at. "Wait," he said.

The green fiber. He stared at it on the chart.

And suddenly he was shouting, "Thom! Thom! I need to make a phone call. I don't know where he gets to sometimes. Lon, will you call for me?"

PERCEY Clay had just returned from burying her husband when Sellitto tracked her down. Wearing black, she now sat in the crinkly wicker chair beside Rhyme's bed. Roland Bell was standing nearby.

Percey eyed Rhyme with impatient curiosity, and he realized that no one had delivered the news. Cowards, he thought.

"Percey, they won't be presenting the case against Hansen to the grand jury. Those duffel bags? There was nothing in them."

"No!" Her face grew pallid. "So they're letting him go?"

"They can't find a connection between him and the Dancer."

Her hands rose to her face. "It was all a waste, Ed and Brit."

Rhyme asked her, "What's happening to your company now?"

Percey wasn't expecting the question. "I'm sorry?"

"Your company? What's going to happen to Hudson Air?"

"We'll sell it. We've had an offer from another company."

"What other company?"

"I frankly don't remember. Ron's been talking to them."

"That's your partner Ron Talbot, right? Would he know about the financial condition of the company?"

"Sure. As much as the accountants and more than me."

"Could you call him, ask him to come down here?"

"I suppose so. He's probably home from the service by now."

"And Sachs?" he said, turning to her. "We've got another crime scene. I need you to search it. As fast as possible."

RHYME looked over the big man coming through the doorway, wearing a shiny dark blue suit. It had the cut of a uniform about it. Rhyme supposed it was what he'd worn when he flew.

Percey introduced them. "So you got that bastard," Talbot grumbled. "Think he'll get the chair?"

"I only collect the trash," Rhyme said, pleased as always when he could think up a melodramatic line. "What the D.A. does with it is up to him. Did Percey tell you about Hansen?"

"Yeah. She said the evidence was fake. Why'd he do that?"

"I think I can answer that, but I need some more information. Percey tells me the company hasn't been doing well."

Talbot shrugged. "Been a tough couple years. Deregulation, lots of small carriers. Margins've shrunk."

"What if the Dancer was hired to murder Percey and Ed so that the killer could buy the company at a discount."

"What company? Ours?" Percey asked, frowning.

"Why would Hansen do that?" Talbot said, wheezing.

"I didn't actually say Hansen. What if it was somebody else?"

"Who?" Percey asked.

"I'm not sure. It's just . . . that green fiber."

"Green fiber?" Talbot followed Rhyme's eyes to the chart.

"Everyone seems to've forgotten about it. Except me. That fiber. Sachs, my partner," he said, nodding to her. "She found it in the empty hangar Hansen leased. The hangar—one of many things designed to implicate Hansen."

"But the hijacking," Talbot said, "when he stole the guns and killed those soldiers. Everybody knows he's a murderer."

"Oh, he probably is," Rhyme agreed. "But he didn't play bombardier with those phone books. Somebody else did. Somebody who never thought we'd find the duffel bags." Percey stirred uneasily.

"Who?" Talbot demanded.

Amelia Sachs pulled three large evidence envelopes out of a canvas bag and rested them on the table. Inside two of them were accounting books. The third contained white envelopes.

"Those came from your office, Talbot," said Rhyme.

He laughed weakly. "You can't take those without a warrant."

Percey Clay frowned. "I gave them permission, Ron."

Rhyme glanced at Mel Cooper, who said, "The green fiber came from a ledger sheet. The white ones from an envelope. There's no doubt they match."

Rhyme said to Talbot, "Everybody at the airport knew Hansen was under investigation. You thought you'd use that fact. So you waited until one night when Percey and Ed and Brit Hale were working late. You stole Hansen's plane; you dumped the fake duffel bags. You hired the Dancer. He told me he was paid seven figures for the hit." Rhyme shook his head. "That should have tipped me right there. Hansen could have had all three witnesses killed for a couple hundred thousand. Professional killing's a buyer's market nowadays. The man ordering the hit was an amateur."

The scream rose from Percey Clay's mouth, and she leaped for Talbot. "How could you? Why?" Talbot backed up.

Rhyme continued. "Hudson Air's a lot more successful than you were thinking, Percey. Only most of it was going into Talbot's pocket. He knew he was going to get caught someday, and he needed to get you and Ed out of the way."

"The stock-purchase option," she said. "As a partner, you had a right to buy our interest at a discount if we die. How could you?" she repeated in a hollow voice.

Talbot raged, "Because I loved you!"

"What?" Percey gasped.

"You laughed when I said I wanted to marry you, and you went back to him." He sneered. "Ed Carney, the handsome fighter pilot." His face was purple with fury. "Then I lost the last thing I had—I was grounded. I couldn't fly anymore. I watched the two of you logging hundreds of hours a month while all I could do was sit at a desk and push papers. You had each other—you had flying. You don't have a clue what it's like to lose everything you love!"

Sachs and Sellitto saw Talbot tense. They anticipated his trying something, but they hadn't guessed his strength. As Sachs stepped forward, unholstering her weapon, Talbot scooped the tall woman completely off her feet and flung her into the evidence table, knocking Mel Cooper back into the wall. Talbot pulled the Glock from her hand and swung it toward the others.

"All right, throw your guns on the floor. Do it now. Now!"

"Come on, man," Dellray said, rolling his eyes. "What're you gonna do? Climb out the window? You ain't going nowhere."

Talbot shoved the gun toward Dellray's face, his eyes desperate. He reminded Rhyme of a cornered bear. The agent and the cops tossed their guns onto the ground. Bell dropped both of his.

"Where does that door lead?" Talbot nodded to the wall.

"That's a closet," Rhyme said quickly.

Talbot opened it, eyed the tiny elevator, pointed the gun at Rhyme.

"No," Sachs shouted. She was back on her feet.

"Ron," Percey cried, "think about it. Please."

Sachs looked at the pistols on the floor, ten feet away.

No, Sachs, Rhyme thought. Don't.

Talbot's eyes were now flicking back and forth from Dellray and Sellitto to the elevator, trying to figure out the switch pad.

Sellitto said, "Come on, Talbot. Put the gun down."

Please, Sachs, don't do it. He'll see you. He'll go for a head shot—amateurs always do—and you'll die.

She tensed, eyes on Dellray's Sig-Sauer. The instant Talbot looked back at the elevator, Sachs leaped for the floor and snagged Dellray's weapon as she rolled. Before she could lift it, Talbot shoved the Glock at her face.

"No!" Rhyme shouted.

The gunshot was deafening. Windows rattled, and the falcons took off into the sky. Ron Talbot, a tiny red hole in his temple, stood perfectly still, then dropped in a spiral to the ground.

"Oh, brother," said Mel Cooper, staring down at his skinny little .38 Smith & Wesson, held in Roland Bell's steady hand. The detective had eased up behind Cooper and slipped the weapon off the narrow belt holster on the back of the tech's belt.

The wailing filled the room as Percey Clay dropped to her knees over the body and, sobbing, pounded her fist into Talbot's dense shoulder again and again. Finally Roland Bell put his arm around the petite woman and led her from the body of her friend and enemy.

A LITTLE thunder, a sprinkling of spring rain late at night. The window was open wide, and the room was filled with cool evening air.

Amelia Sachs popped the cork and poured Cakebread chardonnay into Rhyme's tumbler and her glass. She looked down and gave a faint laugh. "I don't believe it."

On the computer beside the Clinitron was a chess program.

"I've never seen you play games," she said.

In a clear voice Rhyme said, "Rook to queen's bishop four. Checkmate."

A pause. The computer said, "Congratulations," followed by a digitized version of Sousa's "Washington Post" march.

"It's not for entertainment," he said. "Keeps the mind sharp. It's my Nautilus machine. You want to play sometime, Sachs?"

"I don't play chess," she said after a swallow of the fine wine. "Some lousy knight goes for my king, I'd rather blow him away. By the way, how much did they find?"

"The money Talbot had hidden? Over five million."

"Where's the Dancer?"

"In SD." Special Detention, a little-known facility in the Criminal Courts Building. Rhyme had never seen it—few cops had—but in thirty-five years no one had ever broken out.

Amelia Sachs took a fortifying sip of wine, and whatever was coming was coming now. She inhaled deeply, then blurted, "Rhyme, you should go for it." Another sip. "I wasn't sure I was going to say that."

"Beg pardon?"

"She's right for you. It could be real good."

They rarely had trouble looking at each other's eyes, but Sachs looked down at the floor. "I know how you feel about her. And she doesn't admit it, but I know how she feels about you."

"Who?"

"You know who. Percey Clay. You're thinking she's a widow, she's not going to want someone in her life right now. But you heard what Talbot said—Carney had a girlfriend. They stayed together because they were friends. And because of the company."

"I never—"

"Go for it, Rhyme. Come on. I really mean that. You think it'd never work. But she doesn't care about your situation. Hey, she's right—you're both real similar."

There are times when you just need to lift your hands and let them flop into your lap in frustration. "Sachs, where on earth did you get this idea?"

"Oh, please. It's so obvious. I've seen how you've been since she showed up. How you look at her. How obsessed you've been to save her. I know what's going on."

"What *is* going on?"

"She's like Claire Trilling, the woman who left you a few years ago. That's who you want."

Oh. He nodded. So that's it.

He smiled, said, "Sure, Sachs, I have been thinking about Claire a lot the past few days. I lied when I said I hadn't been."

"Whenever you mentioned her, I could tell you were still in love with her. Percey reminded you of Claire, and you realized you could be with someone again. With her, I mean. Not with me. Hey, that's life."

"Sachs, it's not Percey you should've been jealous of. She's not the one that booted you out of bed the other night. It was the Dancer."

Another splash of wine in her glass. She swirled it and looked down at the pale liquid. "I don't understand."

"The other night?" He sighed. "I had to draw the line between us, Sachs. Don't you see? I can't be close to you like that, not *that* close, and still send you in harm's way. I can't let it happen again."

"Again?" she asked. Then her face flooded with understanding.

Ah, that's my Amelia, he thought. A fine criminalist. A good shot. And she's as quick as a fox.

"Oh, no, Lincoln, Claire was . . ."

He was nodding. "She was one of the techs I assigned to search the crime scene in Wall Street. She set off the Dancer's bomb."

Which is why he'd been so obsessed with the man. Why he'd wanted, so uncharacteristically, to debrief the killer. He wanted to catch the man who'd killed his lover. Wanted to know all about him. It was revenge, undiluted revenge. Lincoln Rhyme, for all the overwhelming stasis of his life, was as much a hunter as the falcons on his window ledge.

"So that's it, Sachs. It has nothing to do with Percey. And as much as I wanted you to spend the night—to spend every night—I can't risk loving you any more than I do."

It was so astonishing—bewildering—to Lincoln Rhyme to be having this conversation. After the accident he'd come to believe that the oak beam that had snapped his spine actually did its worst damage to his heart. But the other night, Sachs close to him, he'd realized how wrong he was.

"You understand, don't you, Amelia?" Rhyme whispered.

"Last names only," she said, smiling, walking to the bed.

She bent down and kissed him on the mouth. He pressed back into his pillow for a moment, then returned the kiss.

"No, no," he persisted. But he kissed her hard once again.

Her purse dropped to the floor. Her jacket and watch went on the bedside table, followed by her Glock.

They kissed again, but he pulled away. "Sachs, it's too risky."

"God don't give out certain," she said, their eyes locked on each other's. Then she stood and walked to the light switch.

"Wait," he said. Into the microphone hanging on the bedframe he commanded, "Lights out."

The room went dark.

JEFFERY DEAVER

"I wrote my first book when I was eleven," Jeffery Deaver recently told an Internet chat room full of fans. "Of course, I spent two days on the book and four weeks on the cover art. So I postponed my career for a while." Diverted briefly by a stint in law school and the legal profession, he has since written fourteen suspense novels, including the international best sellers *A Maiden's Grave* and *The Bone Collector*. Deaver says he adheres to the "theory of combat writing—I write whenever I can," which turns out to be ten to twelve hours a day. When one fan wrote, "I do have to say that you have kept me up late," Deaver replied, "Good—I love to keep people up late at night."

The volumes in this series are issued
every two to three months. A typical volume
contains four outstanding books in condensed
form. None of the selections in any volume has
appeared in *Reader's Digest* magazine. Any reader
may receive this service by writing to
The Reader's Digest Association (Canada) Ltd.,
1125 Stanley Street, Montreal, Quebec H3B 5H5.

ACKNOWLEDGMENTS

Pages 6–7: illustration by Robert Hunt.
Pages 166–167: photo by David Leach.
Pages 280–281: photo by SuperStock.
Pages 426–427: illustration by Dan Gonzalez.

The original editions of the books in this volume are published and copyrighted as follows:
No Safe Place, published by Alfred A. Knopf, Inc.
distributed by Random House of Canada Limited at $35.00
© 1998 by Richard North Patterson
Somebody's Baby, published by William Morrow and Company, Inc.
distributed by The Hearst Book Group of Canada at $30.50
© 1998 by Elaine Kagan
Riptide, published by Warner Books, Inc.
distributed by Fenn Publishing Company Ltd. at $29.95
© 1998 by Douglas Preston and Lincoln Child
The Coffin Dancer, published by Simon & Schuster
distributed by Distican Inc. at $35.00
© 1998 by Jeffery Deaver